RANDOM
HOUSE

LARGE
PRINT

ALSO BY JO NESBØ
AVAILABLE FROM
RANDOM HOUSE LARGE PRINT

The Snowman

The Leopard

The Leopard

JO NESBØ

Translated from the Norwegian by Don Bartlett

R A N D O M   H O U S E
L A R G E   P R I N T

Translation copyright © 2011 by Don Bartlett

All rights reserved.
Published in the United States of America by
Random House Large Print in association with
Alfred A. Knopf, New York.
Distributed by Random House, Inc., New York.

Originally published in Norway as **Panserhjerte**
by H. Aschehoug & Co. (W. Nygaard), Oslo, in 2009.
Copyright © 2009 by Jo Nesbø.
This translation was originally published in Great Britain
by Harvill Secker, an imprint of the Random House
Group Ltd., London, in 2011.

Cover design by Peter Mendelsund

The Library of Congress has established a Cataloging-in-
Publication record for this title.

ISBN: 978-0-307-99066-2

www.randomhouse.com/largeprint

FIRST LARGE PRINT EDITION

Printed in the United States of America

10 9 8 7 6 5 4 3 2 1

This Large Print edition published in accord with
the standards of the N.A.V.H.

Part One

1

The Drowning

She awoke. Blinked in the pitch darkness. Yawned,
and breathed through her nose. She blinked again.
Felt a tear run down her face, felt it dissolve the salt of
other tears. But saliva was no longer entering her
throat; her mouth was dry and hard. Her cheeks were
forced out by the pressure from inside. The foreign
body in her mouth felt as though it would explode
her head. But what was it? What was it? The first
thing she thought when she awoke was that she
wanted to go back. Back into the dark, warm depths
that had enveloped her. The injection he had given
her had not worn off yet, but she knew pain was on
the way, felt it coming in the slow, dull beat of her
pulse and the jerky flow of blood through her brain.
Where was he? Was he standing right behind her?
She held her breath, listened. She couldn't hear anything, but she could sense a presence. Like a leopard.
Someone had told her leopards made so little noise
they could sneak right up to their prey in the dark.
They could regulate their breathing so that it was in
tune with yours. Could hold their breath when you
held yours. She was certain she could feel his body
heat. What was he waiting for? She exhaled again.

And at that same moment was sure she had felt breath on her neck. She whirled around, hit out, but was met by air. She hunched up, tried to make herself small, to hide. Pointless.

How long had she been unconscious?

The drug was wearing off. The sensation lasted only for a fraction of a second. But it was enough to give her the foretaste, the promise. The promise of what was to come.

The foreign body placed on the table in front of her had been the size of a billiard ball, made of shiny metal with punched-out small holes and figures and symbols. From one of the holes protruded a red wire with a looped end, which instantly made her think of the Christmas tree that would need decorating at her parents' house on December 23, in seven days. With shiny balls, Christmas pixies, hearts, candles and Norwegian flags. In eight days they would be singing a traditional Christmas carol, and she would see the twinkling eyes of her nephews and nieces as they opened their presents. All the things she should have done differently. All the days she should have lived to the full, avoiding escapism, should have filled with happiness, breath and love. The places she had merely traveled through, the places she was planning to visit. The men she had met, the man she had still not met. The fetus she had gotten rid of when she was seventeen, the children she had not yet had. The days she had wasted for the days she thought she would have.

Then she had stopped thinking about anything except the knife that had been brandished before her. And the gentle voice that had told her to put the ball in her mouth. She had done so; of course she had. With her heart thumping she had opened her mouth as wide as she could and pushed the ball in, with the wire left hanging outside. The metal tasted bitter and salty, like tears. Then her head had been forced back, and the steel burned against her skin as the knife was laid flat against her throat. The ceiling and the room were illuminated by a standard lamp, leaning against the wall in one of the corners. Bare, gray concrete. Apart from the lamp, the room contained a white plastic picnic table, two chairs, two empty beer bottles and two people. Him and her. She smelled a leather glove as a finger tugged lightly at the red loop hanging from her mouth. And the next moment her head seemed to explode.

The ball had expanded and forced itself against the inside of her mouth. But however wide she opened her jaws, the pressure was constant. He had examined her with a concentrated, engaged expression, like an orthodontist checking to see whether the braces were fitting as they should. A little smile intimated satisfaction.

With her tongue she could feel circular ridges around the holes in the ball, and that was what was pressing against her palate, against the soft flesh of her tongue, against her teeth, against the uvula. She had tried to say something. He had listened patiently to the inarticulate sounds emerging from her mouth.

Had nodded when she gave up, and had taken out a syringe. The drop on the tip had glinted in the flash-light's beam. He had whispered something in her ear: "Don't touch the wire."

Then he had injected her in the neck. She was out in seconds.

She listened to her own terrified breathing as she blinked in the darkness.

She had to do something.

She placed her palms on the chair seat, which was clammy from her perspiration, and pushed herself up. No one stopped her.

She advanced with tiny steps until she hit a wall. Groped her way along to a smooth, cold surface. The metal door. She pulled at the bolt. It didn't budge. Locked. Of course it was locked. What had she been thinking? Was that laughter she could hear, or was the sound coming from inside her head? Where was he? Why was he playing with her like this?

Do something. Think. But to think, she would first have to get rid of this metal ball before the pain drove her insane. She put her thumb and first finger in the corners of her mouth. Felt the ridges. Tried in vain to get her fingers under one of them. Had a coughing fit and a panic attack when she couldn't breathe. She realized that the ridges had made the flesh around her windpipe swell, that soon she would be in danger of suffocating. She kicked the metal door, tried to scream, but the ball stifled the sound.

She gave up again. Leaned against the wall. Listened. Was that his wary tread she could hear? Was he moving around the room? Was he playing blindman's buff with her? Or was it her blood throbbing past her ears? She steeled herself against the pain and forced her mouth shut. The ridges were hardly down before they sprang back and forced her mouth open again. The ball seemed to be pulsating now, as though it had become an iron heart, a part of her.

Do something. Think.

Springs. The ridges were spring-loaded.

They had jumped up when he pulled the wire.

"Don't touch the wire," he had said.

Why not? What would happen?

She slid down the wall until she was sitting. Cold damp rose from the concrete floor. She wanted to scream again, but she couldn't. Quiet. Silence.

All the things she should have said to those she loved, instead of the words that had served to fill the silence with those to whom she was indifferent.

There was no way out. There was just her and this unbelievable pain, her head exploding.

"Don't touch the wire."

If she pulled it, the ridges might retract into the ball, and she would be spared the pain.

Her thoughts ran in the same circles. How long had she been here? Two hours? Eight hours? Twenty minutes?

If all she had to do was pull the wire, why hadn't she already done it? Because the warning had been given by an obvious sicko? Or was this part of the game? Being tricked into resisting the temptation to stop this quite unnecessary pain? Or was the game about defying the warning and pulling the wire, causing . . . causing something dreadful to happen? What would happen? What was this ball?

Yes, it was a game, a brutal game. And she had to play. The pain was intolerable, her throat was swelling; soon she would suffocate.

She tried to scream again, but it subsided into a sob, and she blinked and blinked, without producing any further tears.

Her fingers found the string hanging from her lips. She pulled tentatively until it was taut.

There was so much she regretted not having done, naturally. But if a life of self-denial would have placed her anywhere else besides here, right now, she would have chosen that. She just wanted to live. Any sort of life. As simple as that.

She pulled the wire.

The needles shot out of the circular ridges. They were two and a half inches long. Four burst through her cheeks on each side, three into the sinuses, two up the nasal passages and two out through the chin. Two needles pierced the windpipe and one the right eye, one the left. Several needles penetrated the rear part of the palate and reached the brain. But that was not the direct cause of her death. Because the metal ball impeded movement, she was unable to spit out the blood pouring from the wounds into her mouth.

Instead it ran down her windpipe and into her lungs, not allowing oxygen to be absorbed into her bloodstream, which in turn led to cardiac arrest and what the pathologist would call in his report cerebral hypoxia—that is, lack of oxygen to her brain. In other words, Borgny Stem-Myhre drowned.

2

The Illuminating Darkness

DECEMBER 18

The days are short. It's still light outside, but here, in my clipping room, there is eternal darkness. In the light from my work lamp the people in the pictures on the wall look so irritatingly happy and unsuspecting. So full of expectations, as though they take it for granted that all life lies before them, a perfectly calm ocean of time, smooth and unruffled. I have taken clippings from the newspaper, snipped off all the lachrymose stories about the shocked family, edited out the gory details about the finding of the body. Contented myself with the inevitable photo a relative or a friend has given a persistent journalist, the picture of when she was in her prime, smiling as though immortal.

The police don't know a lot. Not yet. But soon they will have more to work with.

What is it, where is it, whatever it is that makes a murderer? Is it innate, is it in a gene, inherited potential that some have and others do not? Or is it shaped by need, developed in a confrontation with the world, a survival strategy, a lifesaving sickness, rational insanity? For just as sickness is a fevered bombardment of the body, insanity is a vital retreat to a place where one can entrench oneself anew.

For my part, I believe that the ability to kill is fundamental to any healthy person. Our existence is a fight for gain, and whoever cannot kill his neighbor has no right to an existence. Killing is, after all, only hastening the inevitable. Death allows no exceptions, which is good, because life is pain and suffering. In that sense, every murder is an act of charity. It just doesn't seem like that when the sun warms your skin or water wets your lips and you recognize your idiotic lust for life in every heartbeat and are ready to buy mere crumbs of time with everything you have accrued through life: dignity, status, principles. That is when you have to dig deep, to give a wide berth to the confusing, blinding light. Into the cold, illuminating darkness. And perceive the hard kernel. The truth. For that is what I had to find. That is what I found. Whatever it is that makes a person into a murderer.

What about my life? Do I also believe it is a calm, unruffled ocean of time?

Not at all. Before long I, too, will be lying on

death's refuse heap, together with all the other role players in this little drama. But whatever stage of decay my body may attain, even if all that remains is the skeleton, it will have a smile on its lips. This is what I live for now: my right to exist, my chance to be cleansed, to be cleared of all dishonor.

But this is only the beginning. Now I am going to switch off the lamp and go out into the light of day. The little that is left.

3

Hong Kong

The rain did not stop first thing. Nor second thing. In fact, it didn't stop at all. It was mild and wet, week upon week. The ground was saturated, European highways caved in, migratory birds did not migrate and there were reports of insects hitherto unseen in northern climes. The calendar showed that it was winter, but Oslo's parkland was not just snowless, it was not even brown. It was as green and inviting as the artificial turf in Sogn, where despairing keep-fit fans had resorted to jogging in their Bjørn Dæhlie tights as they waited in vain for conditions around Lake Sognsvann to allow skiing. On New Year's Eve the fog was so thick that the sound of fireworks carried from the center of Oslo right out to suburban

Asker, but you couldn't see a thing, even if you set them off in your backyard. Nevertheless, that night Norwegians lit six hundred kroners' worth of fireworks per household, according to a consumer survey, which also revealed that the number of Norwegians who realized their dream of a white Christmas on Thailand's white beaches had doubled in just three years. However, it seemed as if the weather had run amok also in Southeast Asia: Ominous clouds usually seen only on weather charts in the typhoon season were now lined up across the China Sea. In Hong Kong, where February tends to be one of the driest months of the year, rain was bucketing down, and poor visibility meant that Cathay Pacific Flight 731 from London had to circle again before coming in to land at Chek Lap Kok Airport.

"You should be happy we don't have to land at the old airport," said the Chinese-looking passenger next to Kaja Solness, who was squeezing the armrests so hard her knuckles were white. "It was in the center of town. We would have flown straight into one of the skyscrapers."

Those were the first words the man had uttered since they had taken off twelve hours earlier. Kaja eagerly grabbed the chance to focus on something other than the fact that they were temporarily caught in turbulence.

"Thank you, sir—that was reassuring. Are you English?"

He recoiled as if someone had slapped him, and she realized she had mortally offended him by suggesting that he belonged to the previous colonialists: "Erm . . . Chinese, perhaps?"

He shook his head firmly. "Hong Kong Chinese. And you, miss?"

Kaja Solness wondered for a moment if she should reply, "Hokksund Norwegian," but confined herself to "Norwegian," which the Hong Kong Chinese man mused on for a while, then delivered a triumphant "Aha!" before amending it to "Scandinavian" and asked her what her business was in Hong Kong.

"To find a man," she said, staring down at the bluish gray clouds in the hope that terra firma would soon reveal itself.

"Aha!" repeated the Hong Kong Chinese. "You are very beautiful, miss. And don't believe all you hear about the Chinese only marrying other Chinese."

She managed a weary smile. "Hong Kong Chinese, do you mean?"

"Particularly Hong Kong Chinese." He nodded with enthusiasm, holding up a ringless hand. "I deal in microchips. The family has factories in China and South Korea. What are you doing tonight?"

"Sleeping, I hope." Kaja yawned.

"What about tomorrow evening?"

"I hope by then I'll have found him and I'll be on my way back home."

The man frowned. "Are you in such a hurry, miss?"

Kaja refused the man's offer of a lift and caught a bus, a double-decker, to downtown. One hour later she was standing alone in a corridor at the Empire Kowloon Hotel, taking deep breaths. She had put the key card into the door of the room she had been allocated and now all that remained was to open it. She forced her hand to press down the handle. Then she jerked the door open and stared into the room.

No one there.

Of course there wasn't.

She entered, wheeled her bag to the side of the bed, stood by the window and looked out. First down at the swarm of people in the street seventeen floors below, then at the skyscrapers that in no way resembled their graceful, or at any rate pompous, sisters in Manhattan, Kuala Lumpur or Tokyo. These looked like anthills, terrifying and impressive at the same time, like a grotesque testimony to how humankind is capable of adapting when seven million inhabitants have to find room in not much more than four hundred square miles. Kaja felt exhaustion creeping up on her, kicked off her shoes and fell back on the bed. Even though it was a double room and the hotel sported four stars, the four-foot-wide bed occupied all the floor space. And it hit home that from among all these anthills she now had to find one particular person, a man who, all the evidence suggested, had no particular wish to be found.

For a moment or two she weighed the options: closing her eyes or springing into action. Then she pulled herself together and got to her feet. Took off her clothes and went into the shower. Afterward she stood in front of the mirror and confirmed without a hint of self-satisfaction that the Hong Kong Chinese man was right: She was beautiful. This was not her opinion; it was as close to being a fact as beauty can be. The face with the high cheekbones, the pronounced but finely formed raven-black eyebrows, the almost-childlike wide eyes, the green irises that shone with the intensity of a mature young woman. The honey-brown hair, the full lips that seemed to be kissing each other in her somewhat broad mouth. The long, slim neck, the equally slim body, with the small breasts that were no more than mounds, swells on a sea of perfect, though winter-pale, skin. The gentle curve of her hips. The long legs that persuaded two Oslo modeling agencies to make the trip to her school in Hokksund, only to have to accept her refusal with a rueful shake of the head. And what had pleased her most was when one of them said as he left: "OK, but remember, my dear: You are not a perfect beauty. Your teeth are small and pointed. You shouldn't smile so much."

After that she had smiled with a lighter heart.

Kaja put on a pair of khaki trousers and a thin waterproof jacket and floated weightlessly and soundlessly down to the lobby.

"Chungking Mansions?" the receptionist asked, unable to refrain from cocking an eyebrow, and pointed. "Kimberley Road, up to Nathan Road, then left."

All hostels and hotels in Interpol member countries are legally obliged to register foreign guests, but when Kaja had called the Norwegian ambassador's secretary to check where the man she was looking for had last registered, the secretary had explained that Chungking Mansions was neither a hotel nor a mansion, in the sense of a wealthy residence. It was a collection of stores, takeout shops, restaurants and probably more than a hundred classified and non-classified hostels, with everything from two to twenty rooms spread over four large apartment towers. The rooms for rent could be characterized as everything from simple, clean and cozy to rat holes and one-star prison cells. And most important of all: At Chungking Mansions a man with modest demands of life could sleep, eat, live, work and propagate without ever leaving the anthill.

Kaja found the entrance to Chungking on Nathan Road, a busy shopping street with brand-name goods, polished shop fronts and tall display windows. She entered the complex amid cooking fumes from fast-food outlets, hammering from cobblers, radio broadcasts of Muslim prayer meetings and tired looks in used-clothes shops. She flashed a quick smile at a bewildered backpacker with a **Lonely Planet** guidebook in his hand and frozen white legs sticking out of overoptimistic camouflage shorts.

A uniformed guard looked at the note Kaja showed him, said, "Elevator C," and pointed down a corridor.

The line in front of the elevator was so long that she didn't get in until the third attempt, when the passengers were squeezed up tight in a creaky, vibrating iron chest that made Kaja think of the Gypsies who buried their dead vertically.

The hostel was owned by a turban-clad Muslim who immediately, and with great enthusiasm, showed her a tiny box of a room, where by some miracle they had found space for a wall-mounted TV at the foot of the bed and a gurgling air-conditioning unit above the headboard. The owner's enthusiasm waned when she interrupted his sales spiel to produce a photo of a man with his name spelled as it would have been in his passport, and asked where he was now.

On seeing the reaction, she hastened to inform him that she was the man's wife. The embassy secretary had explained to her that waving an official ID card around in Chungking would be "counterproductive." And when Kaja added, for safety's sake, that she and the man in the photo had five children together, the hostel owner's attitude underwent a dramatic change. A young Western heathen who had already brought so many children into the world earned his respect. He expelled a heavy sigh, shook his head and said in mournful, staccato English, "Sad, sad, lady. They come and take his passport."

"Who did?"

"Who? The triad, lady. It's always the triad."

Naturally enough, she was aware of the organization, but she had some vague notion that the Chinese mafia primarily belonged to the world of cartoons and kung-fu films.

"Sit yourself down, lady." He quickly found a chair, onto which she slumped. "They were after him, he was out, so they took his passport."

"Passport? Why?"

He hesitated.

"Please, I have to know."

"Your husband bet on horses, I am sorry to say."

"Horses?"

"Happy Valley. Racecourse. It is an abomination."

"Does he owe money? To the triad?"

He nodded and shook his head several times to confirm and regret, alternately, this fact of life.

"And they took his passport?"

"He will have to pay back the debt if he wants to leave Hong Kong."

"He can only get a new passport from the Norwegian embassy."

The turban waggled from side to side. "Ah, you can get a false passport here in Chungking for eighty American dollars. But this is not the problem. The problem is Hong Kong is an island, lady. How did you get here?"

"Plane."

"And how will you leave?"

"Plane."

"One airport. Tickets. All names on computer. Many control points. Many at airport who get money from the triad to recognize faces. Understand?"

She nodded slowly. "It's difficult to escape."

The hostel owner shook his head with a guffaw. "No, lady. It's impossible to escape. But you can hide in Hong Kong. Seven million people. Easy to go underground."

Lack of sleep was catching up on Kaja, and she closed her eyes. The owner must have misunderstood, because he laid a consoling hand on her shoulder and mumbled, "There, there."

He wavered, then leaned forward and whispered, "I think he still here, lady."

"Yes, I know he is."

"No, I mean here in Chungking. I see him."

She raised her head.

"Twice," he said. "At Li Yuan's. He eat there. Cheap rice. Don't tell anyone I said. Your husband is good man. But trouble." He rolled his eyes so that they almost disappeared into his turban. "Lots of trouble."

Li Yuan's comprised a counter, four plastic tables and a Chinese man who sent her an encouraging smile when, after six hours, two portions of fried rice, three coffees and two quarts of water, she awoke with a jolt, lifted her head from the greasy table and looked at him.

"Tired?" He laughed, revealing an incomplete set of front teeth.

Kaja yawned, ordered her fourth cup of coffee and continued to wait. Two Chinese men came and sat at the counter without speaking or ordering. They didn't even spare her a glance, for which she was glad. Her body was so stiff from sitting on the plane that pain shot through her whatever sedentary position she adopted. She rolled her head from side to side to try to stimulate circulation. Then backward. Her neck cracked. She stared at the bluish-white fluorescent tubes in the ceiling before lowering her head. And stared straight into a pale, hunted face. He had stopped in front of the closed steel shutters in the corridor and scanned Li Yuan's tiny establishment. His gaze rested on the two Chinese men by the counter. Then he hurried on.

Kaja got to her feet, but one leg had gone to sleep and gave way under her weight. She grabbed her bag and limped after the man as fast as she could.

"Come back soon," she heard Li Yuan shout after her.

He had looked so thin. In the photographs he had been a broad, tall figure, and on the TV talk show he had made the chair he was sitting on look like it had been manufactured for Pygmies. But she had not the slightest doubt it was him: the dented, shaven skull, the prominent nose, the eyes with the spider's web of blood vessels and the alcoholic's washed-out, pale-blue irises. The determined chin with the surprisingly gentle, almost beautiful mouth.

She stumbled onto Nathan Road. In the gleam of the neon light she caught sight of a leather jacket towering above the crowd. He didn't appear to be walking fast, yet she had to quicken her pace to keep up. He turned off the busy shopping street and she let the distance between them increase as they moved onto narrower, less populated streets. She registered a sign saying MELDEN ROW. It was tempting to go and introduce herself, get it all over with. But she had decided to stick to the plan: to find out where he lived. It had stopped raining, and all of a sudden a scrap of cloud was drawn aside and the sky behind was high and velvet black, with glittering, pinhole stars.

After walking for twenty minutes, he came to a sudden halt at a corner, and Kaja was afraid she had been discovered. However, he didn't turn around, just took something from his jacket pocket. She stared in amazement. A baby's bottle?

He disappeared around the corner.

Kaja followed and came into a large, open square packed with people, most of them young. At the far end of the square, above wide glass doors, shone a sign written in English and Chinese. Kaja recognized the titles of some of the new films she would never see. Her eyes found his leather jacket, and she saw him put the bottle down on the low plinth of a bronze sculpture representing a gallows with an empty noose. He continued past two fully occupied benches and took a seat on the third, where he picked up a newspaper. After about twenty seconds he got up again, walked back to the sculpture, grabbed the bottle as he passed, put it into his pocket and returned the same way he had come.

It had started to rain when she saw him enter Chungking Mansions. She slowly began to prepare her speech. There was no longer a line by the elevators; nevertheless he ascended a staircase, turned right and went through a swinging door. She hurried after him and suddenly found herself in a deserted, run-down stairwell with an all-permeating smell of cat piss and wet concrete. She held her breath, but all she could hear were dripping sounds. As she made the decision to go on up, she heard a bang beneath her. She sprinted down the stairs and found the only thing that could have made such a bang: a dented metal door. She held the handle, felt the trembling come, closed her eyes and cursed to herself. Then she ripped open the door and stepped into the darkness. That is to say: out.

Something ran across her feet, but she neither screamed nor moved.

At first she thought she had entered an elevator shaft. But when she looked up, she glimpsed blackened brick walls covered with a tangled mass of water pipes, cables, distorted chunks of metal and collapsed, rusty iron scaffolding. It was a courtyard, a few square yards of space between towers. The only light came from a small patch of stars high above.

Although there wasn't a cloud in the sky, water was splashing down onto the pavement and her face, and she realized it was condensation from the small, rusty air-conditioning units protruding from the building. She retreated and leaned back against the iron door.

Waited.

And, eventually, from the dark, she heard: "What do you want?"

She had never heard his voice before. Well, she had heard it on the talk show when they were discussing serial killers, but hearing it in reality was quite different. There was a worn, hoarse quality that made him sound older than his forty years. But at the same time there was a secure, self-assured calm that belied the hunted face she had seen outside Li Yuan's. Deep, warm.

"I'm Norwegian," she said.

There was no response. She swallowed. She knew that her first words would be the most important.

"My name is Kaja Solness. I have been tasked with finding you. By Gunnar Hagen."

No reaction to the name of his Crime Squad boss. Had he gone?

"I work as a detective on murder investigations for Hagen," she said into the blackness.

"Congratulations."

"No congratulations necessary. Not if you've been reading Norwegian papers for the last months." She could have bitten her tongue. Was she trying to be funny? Had to be the lack of sleep. Or nerves.

"I mean congratulations on a well-accomplished mission," said the voice. "I have been found. Now you can go back."

"Wait," she said. "Don't you want to hear what I have to say?"

"I'd prefer not to."

But the words she had jotted down and practiced rolled out. "Two women have been killed. Forensic evidence suggests it's the same perp. Beyond that we don't have any leads. Even though the press has been given minimal info, they've been screaming that another serial killer is on the loose. Some commentators have written that he may have been inspired by the Snowman. We've called in experts from Interpol, but they haven't made any headway. The pressure from the media and authorities—"

"By which I mean no," the voice said.

A door slammed.

"Hello? Hello? Are you there?"

She fumbled her way forward and found a door. Opened it before terror managed to gain a foothold, and she was in another darkened stairwell. She glimpsed light farther up and climbed three steps at a time. The light was coming through the glass of a swinging door, and she pushed it open. Entered a plain, bare corridor in which attempts to patch the peeling plaster had been given up, and damp steamed off the walls like bad breath. Leaning against the wall were two men with cigarettes hanging from the corners of their mouths, and a sweet stench drifted toward her. They appraised her through sluggish eyes. Too sluggish to move, she hoped. The smaller of the two was black, of African origin, she assumed. The big one was white and had a pyramid-shaped scar on his forehead, like a warning triangle. She had read in **The Police** magazine that Hong Kong had almost thirty thousand officers on the street and was reckoned to be the world's safest metropolis. But then that was on the street.

"Looking for hashish, lady?"

She shook her head, tried to flash a confident smile, tried to act as she had advised young girls to do when she had visited schools: to look like someone who knew where she was going, not like someone who had lost the flock, like prey.

They returned her smile. The only other doorway

in the corridor had been bricked up. They took their hands out of their pockets, the cigarettes from their mouths.

"Looking for fun, then?"

"Wrong door, that's all," she said, turning to go back out. A hand closed around her wrist. Her terror tasted like tinfoil in her mouth. In theory, she knew how to get out of this. Had practiced it on a rubber mat in an illuminated gym with an instructor and colleagues gathered around her.

"Right door, lady. Right door. Fun is this way." The breath in her face stank of fish, onions and marijuana. In the gym there had been only one adversary.

"No, thanks," she said, struggling to keep her voice steady.

The black man sidled up, grabbed her other wrist and said in a voice that slipped in and out of falsetto: "We'll show you the way."

"Only there's not much to see, is there."

All three turned toward the swinging door.

She knew according to his passport he was six foot four, but standing there in the doorway that had been built to Hong Kong measurements, he looked at least seven feet tall. And twice as wide as only an hour ago. His arms hung down by his sides, slightly away from his body, but he didn't move, didn't stare, didn't snarl, just looked calmly at the white man and repeated: "Is there, **jau-ye?**"

She felt the white man's fingers tense and relax around her wrist, noticed the black man shift weight from foot to foot.

"**Ng-goy**," said the man in the doorway.

She felt their hands hesitantly let go.

"Come on," he said, lightly taking her arm.

She felt the heat in her flushed cheeks as they walked out. Heat produced by tension and shame. Shame at how relieved she was, how tardily her brain had functioned in the situation, how willing she had been to let him take on two harmless drug dealers who only wanted to ruffle her a little.

He accompanied her up two floors and in through the swinging door, where he positioned her in front of an elevator, pressed the arrow for down, stood beside her and focused his gaze on the illuminated "11" above the elevator door. "Guest workers," he said. "They're alone and bored."

"I know," she said defiantly.

"Press **G** for ground floor, turn right and go straight ahead until you're on Nathan Road."

"Please listen to me. You are the only person in Crime Squad with the appropriate expertise to catch serial killers. After all, it was you who caught the Snowman."

"True," he said. She registered a movement in his eyes, and he ran a finger along his jaw under his right ear. "And then I resigned."

"Resigned? Went on leave, you mean."

"Resigned. As in **finished**."

It was only now that she noticed the unnatural protrusion of his right jawbone.

"Gunnar Hagen says that when you left Oslo he agreed to give you leave until further notice."

The man smiled, and Kaja saw how it changed his face completely. "That's because Hagen can't get it into his head . . ." He paused, and the smile vanished. His eyes were directed toward the light above the elevator that now read "5." "Nonetheless, I don't work for the police any longer."

"We need you . . ." She inhaled. Knew that she was skating on thin ice, but that she had to act before she lost sight of him again. "And you need us."

His eyes shifted back to her. "What on earth makes you think that?"

"You owe the triad money. You buy dope off the street in a baby's bottle. You live"—she grimaced—"here. And you don't have a passport."

"I'm enjoying myself here. What do I need a passport for?"

The elevator pinged, the door creaked open and hot, stinking air rose off the bodies inside.

"I'm not going!" Kaja said, louder than she had anticipated, and noticed the faces looking at her with a mixture of impatience and obvious curiosity.

"Yes, you are," he said, placing a hand in the middle of her back and pushing her gently but firmly inside. She was immediately surrounded by human bodies closing in on her and making it impossible for her to move or even turn. She twisted her head in time to see the doors gliding shut.

"Harry!" she shouted.

But he had already gone.

4

Sex Pistols

The old hostel owner placed a thoughtful finger on his forehead under the turban and looked at her long and hard. Then he picked up the telephone and dialed a number. He said a few words in Arabic and rang off. "Wait," he said. "Maybe, maybe not."

Kaja smiled and nodded.

They sat observing each other from either side of the narrow table that served as a reception desk.

Then the phone rang. He picked it up, listened and put it down without a word.

"One hundred and fifty thousand dollars," he said.

"One hundred and fifty?" she repeated in utter disbelief.

"Hong Kong dollars, lady."

Kaja did some mental arithmetic. That would be about 130,000 Norwegian kroner. Roughly double what she had been authorized to pay.

It was past midnight, and almost forty hours since she had slept, when she found him. She had trawled the H-Block for three hours. Had sketched out a map of the interior as she moved through hostels, cafés, snack bars, massage clubs and prayer rooms until she arrived at the cheapest rooms and dormitories, where the imported labor force from Africa and Pakistan stayed, those who had no rooms, just cubicles without doors, without TVs, without air-conditioning and without a private life. The black night porter who admitted Kaja looked at the photo for a long time and at the hundred-dollar bill she was holding for even longer before he took it and pointed to one of the cubicles.

Harry Hole, she thought. Gotcha.

He was lying supine on a mattress, breathing almost without sound. He had a deep frown on his forehead, and the prominent jawbone under his right ear was even more defined now that he was asleep. From the other cubicles she heard men coughing and snoring. Water dripped from the ceiling, hitting the brick floor with deep, disgruntled sighs. The opening to the cubicle let in a cold blue stripe of light from the fluorescent tubes in reception. She saw a clothes cupboard in front of the window, a chair and a plastic bottle of water beside the mattress. There was a bittersweet smell, like burned rubber. Smoke rose from a cigarette end in an ashtray beside the baby's bottle on the floor. She sat down on the chair and discovered that he was holding something in his hand. A greasy yellowish-brown clump. Kaja had seen enough hash the year she worked in a patrol car to know this was not hash.

It was almost two o'clock when he awoke.

She heard a tiny change in the rhythm of his breathing, and then the whites of his eyes shone in the dark.

"Rakel?" He whispered it. And went back to sleep.

Half an hour later he opened his eyes wide, gave a start, cast around and made a grab for something under the mattress.

"It's me," Kaja whispered. "Kaja Solness."

The body at her feet stopped in midmovement. Then it collapsed and fell back on the mattress.

"What the hell are you doing here?" he groaned, his voice still thick with sleep.

"Fetching you," she said.

He chuckled, his eyes closed. "Fetching me? Still?"

She took out an envelope, leaned forward and held it up in front of him. He opened one eye.

"Plane ticket," she said. "To Oslo."

The eye closed again. "Thanks, but I'm staying here."

"If I can find you, it's only a matter of time before they do, too."

He didn't answer. She waited while listening to his breathing and the water that dripped and sighed. Then he opened his eyes again, rubbed under his right ear and hoisted himself up onto his elbows.

"Got a smoke?"

She shook her head. He threw off the sheet, stood up and went over to the cupboard. He was surprisingly pale, considering he had been living in a subtropical climate, and so lean that his ribs showed, even on his back. His build suggested that at one time he had been athletic, but now the wasted muscles appeared as sharp shadows under the white skin. He opened the cupboard. She was amazed to see that his clothes lay folded in neat piles. He put on a T-shirt and a pair of jeans, the ones he had been wearing the day before, and with some difficulty tugged a creased packet of cigarettes out from his pocket.

He slipped into a pair of flip-flops and edged past her with a click of his lighter.

"Come on," he said softly as he passed. "Supper."

It was nearly three in the morning. Gray iron shutters had been pulled down over shops and restaurants in Chungking. Apart from at Li Yuan's.

"So how did you wind up in Hong Kong?" Kaja asked, looking at Harry, who, in an inelegant but effective way, was shoveling shiny glass noodles into his mouth from the white soup bowl.

"I flew. Are you cold?"

Kaja automatically removed her hands from under her thighs. "But why here?"

"I was on my way to Manila. Hong Kong was only supposed to be a stopover."

"The Philippines. What were you going to do there?"

"Throw myself into a volcano."

"Which one?"

"Well, which ones can you name?"

"None. I've just read that there are loads of them. Aren't some of them in . . . er, Luzon?"

"Not bad. There are eighteen active volcanoes in all, and three of them are in Luzon. I wanted to go up Mount Mayon. Eight thousand feet. A stratovolcano."

"Volcano with steep sides formed by layer upon layer of lava after an eruption."

Harry stopped chewing and looked at her. "Any eruptions in modern times?"

"Loads. Thirty?"

"Records say forty-eight since 1616. Last one in 2006. Can be held to account for at least three thousand murders."

"What happened?"

"The pressure built up."

"I mean to you."

"I'm talking about me." She fancied she saw a hint of a smile. "I exploded and started drinking on the plane. I was ordered off in Hong Kong."

"There are several flights to Manila."

"I realized that apart from volcanoes Manila has nothing that Hong Kong doesn't have."

"Such as?"

"Such as distance from Norway."

Kaja nodded. She had read the reports on the Snowman case.

"And most important," he said, pointing with a chopstick, "Hong Kong's got Li Yuan's glass noodles. Try them. That's reason enough to apply for citizenship."

"That and opium?"

It was not her style to be so direct, but she knew she would have to swallow her natural shyness. This was her one shot at achieving what she had come to do.

He shrugged and concentrated on the noodles.

"Do you smoke opium regularly?"

"Irregularly."

"And why do you do that?"

He answered with food in his mouth. "So that I don't drink. I'm a drunk. There, for example, is another advantage of Hong Kong compared with Manila. Lower sentences for dope. And cleaner prisons."

"I knew about your alcoholism, but are you a drug addict?"

"Define drug addict."

"Do you have to take drugs?"

"No, but I want to."

"Why?"

"To numb the senses. This sounds like a job interview for a job I don't want, Solness. Have you ever smoked opium?"

Kaja shook her head. She had tried marijuana a few times while backpacking around South America but had not been particularly fond of it.

"But the Chinese have. Three hundred years ago the British imported opium from India to improve the trade balance. They turned half of China into junkies just like that." He flicked the fingers of his free hand. "And when, sensibly enough, the Chinese authorities banned opium, the British went to war for their right to drug China into submission. Imagine Colombia bombing New York because the Americans confiscated a bit of cocaine on the border."

"What's your point?"

"I see it as my duty as a European to smoke some of the shit we have imported into this country."

Kaja could hear herself laughing. She really needed to get some sleep.

"I was tailing you when you did the deal," she said. "I saw how you do it. There was money in the bottle when you put it down. And opium afterward. Isn't that right?"

"Mm," Harry said with a mouth full of noodles. "Have you worked at the Narc Unit?"

She shook her head. "Why the baby's bottle?"

Harry stretched his arms above his head. The soup bowl in front of him was empty. "Opium stinks something awful. If you've got a ball of it in your pocket or in foil, the narcotics dogs can sniff you out even in a huge crowd. There is no money back on baby's bottles, so no chance of some kid or some drunk stealing it during a handover. That has happened."

Kaja nodded slowly. He had started to relax; it was just a question of persisting. Anyone who hasn't spoken his mother tongue for a while gets chatty when he meets a compatriot. It's natural. Keep going.

"You like horses?"

He was chewing on a toothpick. "Not really. They're so damned moody."

"But you like betting on them?"

"I like it, but compulsive gambling is not one of my vices."

He smiled, and again it struck her how his smile transformed him, made him human, accessible, boyish. And she was reminded of the glimpse of open sky she had caught over Melden Row.

"Gambling is a poor winning strategy long-term. But if you have nothing left to lose, it's the only strategy. I bet everything I had, plus a fair amount I didn't have, on one single race."

"You put everything you had on one horse?"

"Two. A quiniela. You pick out the two horses to come in first and second, regardless of which of the two is the winner."

"And you borrowed money from the triad?"

For the first time she saw astonishment in Harry's eyes.

"What makes a serious Chinese gangster cartel lend money to an opium-smoking foreigner who has nothing to lose?"

"Well," Harry said, producing a cigarette, "as a foreigner, you have access to the VIP box at the Happy Valley Racecourse for the first three weeks after your passport has been stamped." He lit his cigarette and blew smoke at the ceiling fan, which was turning so slowly that the flies were taking rides on it. "There is a dress code, so I had a suit made. The first two weeks were enough to give me a taste for it. I met Herman Kluit, a South African who earned himself a fortune in minerals in Africa. He taught me how to lose quite a lot of money in style. I simply loved the concept. The evening before race day in the third week Kluit invited me to dinner, at which he entertained the guests by exhibiting his collection of African torture instruments from Goma. And that was where I got insider info from Kluit's chauffeur. The favorite for one of the races was injured, but this tidbit was being kept secret because it was going to run anyway. The point was that it was such a clear favorite that a minus pool came into question—that is, it would be impossible to earn any money by betting on it. However, there was money to be earned by hedging your bets with several of the others. For example, with quinielas. But, of course, that would require quite a bit of capital if you were going to earn anything. I was given a loan by Kluit on the basis of my honest face. And a made-to-measure suit." Harry studied the glow of his cigarette and seemed to be smiling at the thought.

"And?" Kaja asked.

"And the favorite won by six lengths." Harry shrugged. "When I explained to Kluit that I didn't own a bean he seemed genuinely sorry and explained politely that, as a businessman, he was obliged to stick to his business principles. He assured me that these did not include the use of Congolese torture weapons, but quite simply selling debts to the triad at a discount. Which, he conceded, was not a lot better. But in my case he would wait thirty-six hours before he sold so that I could get out of Hong Kong."

"But you didn't go?"

"Sometimes I'm a little slow on the uptake."

"And afterward?"

Harry opened his hands. "This. Chungking."

"Future plans?"

Harry shrugged and went to stub out his cigarette. And Kaja was reminded of the record cover Even had shown her with the picture of Sid Vicious from the

Sex Pistols. And the music playing in the background, "No future, no future."

"You've heard what you need, Kaja Solness."

"Need?" She frowned. "I don't understand."

"Don't you?" He stood up. "Do you think I babble on about opium and debts because I'm one lonely Norwegian meeting another?"

She didn't answer.

"It's because I want you to appreciate that I am not the man you guys need. So that you can go back without feeling you haven't done your job. So that you don't get into trouble in stairwells, and I can sleep in peace without wondering whether you will lead my creditors straight to me."

She looked at him. There was something severe, ascetic, about him, yet this was contradicted by the amusement dancing in his eyes, saying that you didn't need to take everything so seriously. Or to be more exact: that he didn't give a flying fuck.

"Wait." Kaja opened her bag and took out a small red booklet, passed it to him and observed the reaction. Saw incredulity spread across his face as he flicked through it.

"Shit, looks just like my passport."

"It is."

"I doubt Crime Squad had the budget for this."

"Your debts have sunk in value," she lied. "I got a discount."

"I hope for your sake you did, because I have no intention of returning to Oslo."

Kaja subjected him to a long stare. Dreading it.

There was no way out now. She was being forced to play her final card, the one Gunnar Hagen had said she should leave to last if the old bastard proved obdurate.

"There is one more thing," Kaja said, bracing herself.

One of Harry's eyebrows shot into the air; perhaps he detected something in her intonation.

"It's about your father, Harry." She could hear that she had instinctively used his first name. Convinced herself it was meant sincerely, not just for effect.

"My father?" He said this as if it came as something of a surprise that he had one.

"Yes. We contacted him to find out if he knew where you were living. The long and short of it is he's ill."

She looked down at the table.

Heard him exhale. The drowsiness was back in his voice. "Seriously ill?"

"Yes. And I'm sorry to be the one to have to tell you this."

She still did not dare to raise her gaze. Ashamed. Waited. Listened to the machine-gun sounds of Cantonese on the TV behind Li Yuan's counter. Swallowed and waited. She would have to sleep soon.

"When does the plane leave?"

"At eight," she said. "I'll pick you up in three hours outside here."

"I'll get there under my own steam. There are a couple of things I have to fix first."

He held out his palm. She questioned him with her eyes.

"For that I need the passport. And then you should eat. Get a bit of meat on your bones."

She wavered. Then she handed him the passport and the ticket.

"I trust you," she said.

He sent her a blank look.

Then he was gone.

The clock above Gate C4 in Chek Lap Kok Airport showed a quarter to eight, and Kaja had given up. Of course he wasn't coming. It was a natural reflex for animals and humans to hide when hurt. And Harry Hole was definitely hurt. Reports on the Snowman case had described in detail the murders of all the women. But Gunnar Hagen had added what had not been included. How Harry Hole's ex-girlfriend, Rakel, and her son, Oleg, had ended up in the clutches of the deranged killer. How she and her son had fled the country as soon as the case was over. And how Harry had handed in his resignation and left town. He had been more hurt than she had realized.

Kaja had already handed in her boarding pass, was on her way up to the ramp and beginning to consider the formulation of her report on the failed mission, when she saw him jogging through the slanted sunbeams that penetrated the terminal building. He was carrying a plain carry-on bag over his shoulder and a bag from a duty-free shop and was puffing away furiously at a cigarette. He stopped at the gate. But instead of giving the waiting personnel his boarding pass, he put down his bag and sent Kaja a despairing look.

She went back to the gate.

"Problems?" she asked.

"Sorry," he said. "Can't come."

"Why not?"

He pointed to the duty-free bag. "Just remembered that in Norway the allowance per person is one carton of cigarettes. I've got two. So unless . . ." He didn't bat an eye.

She rolled her eyes heavenward, trying not to look relieved. "Give it to me."

"Thank you very much," he said, opening the bag, which she happened to notice did not contain any bottles, and passing her an opened carton of Camels with one pack already gone.

She walked in front of him to the plane so that he would not be able to see her smile.

Kaja stayed awake long enough to catch take-off, Hong Kong disappearing beneath them, and Harry's eyes watching the cart as it approached fitfully with its joyful clink of bottles. And him closing his eyes and answering the stewardess with a barely audible, "No, thank you."

She wondered whether Gunnar Hagen was right, whether the man beside her was really what they needed.

Then she was gone, unconscious, dreaming that

she was standing in front of a closed door. She heard a lone, frozen birdcall from the forest and it sounded so strange because the sun was shining high in the sky. She opened the door . . .

She woke with her head lolling on his shoulder and dried saliva at the corners of her mouth. The captain's voice announced that they were approaching the runway at London Heathrow.

5

The Park

Marit Olsen liked to ski in the mountains. But she hated jogging. She hated her wheezing gasps after only a hundred yards, the tremorlike vibrations in the ground as she planted each foot, the slightly bemused looks from walkers and the images that appeared when she saw herself through their eyes: the quivering chins, the flab that bounced around in the stretched tracksuit and the helpless, open-mouthed, fish-out-of-water expression she herself had seen on very overweight people who were exercising. That was one of the reasons she scheduled her three runs per week in Frogner Park for ten o'clock at night: The place was as good as deserted. The people who were there saw as little as possible of her as she puffed her way between the few lamps that illuminated the paths crisscrossing Oslo's largest park. And of those few who saw her there were fewer still who recognized the Socialist MP for Finnmark. Forget "recognized." There were few people who had ever seen Marit Olsen. When she spoke—usually on behalf of her home region—she did not attract the attention that others, her more photogenic colleagues, did. In addition, she had not said or done anything wrong in the course of the two sessions she had been sitting as a Stortinget representative. At least that was how she explained it to herself. The **Finnmark Dagblad** editor's explanation, that she was a political lightweight, was no more than malicious wordplay on her physical appearance. The editor had not, however, ruled out the possibility that one day she might be seen in a Socialist government, since she met the most telling requirements: She was not educated, not male and not from Oslo.

Well, he might have been right that her strengths did not lie in large, complicated castles in the air. But she had a common touch, she was folksy enough to know the opinions of ordinary men and women and she could be their voice here among all the self-centered, self-satisfied voters in the capital. For Marit Olsen shot from the hip. That was her real qualification; that was what had taken her to where she was, after all. With her verbal intelligence and wit—which southerners liked to call "northern Norwegian" and "gritty"—she was a sure winner in the few debates in which she had been allowed to participate. It was just a question of time before they would have to take note of her. So long as she could get rid of these extra pounds. Surveys proved that people had less confidence in overweight public figures, who were subconsciously perceived to be lacking in self-control.

She came to an incline, clenched her teeth and slowed her pace, went into what seemed very much like a walk, if she was honest. Power walk. Yes, that's what it was. The march toward power. Her weight was decreasing, her eligibility for office increasing.

She heard the crunch of gravel behind her and automatically her back went rigid, her pulse rising a few further notches. It was the same sound she had heard while out jogging three days ago. And two days before that. Both times someone had been running behind her for close to two minutes before the sound had gone. Marit had turned around on the previous occasion and seen a black tracksuit and a black hood, as though it were a commando training behind her. Except that no one, and especially not a commando, could find any purpose in jogging as slowly as Marit.

Of course, she could not be sure that this was the same person, but something about the sound of the footsteps told her it was. There was just a bit of a slope up to the Monolith, then it was an easy downhill run home, to Skøyen, her husband and a reassuringly unprepossessing, overfed Rottweiler. The steps came closer. And now it was not so wonderful that it was ten at night and the park was dark and deserted. Marit Olsen was frightened of several things, but primarily she was frightened of foreigners. Yes, indeed, she knew it was xenophobia and ran counter to party policy, but fearing whatever is alien nevertheless constitutes a sensible survival strategy. Right now she wished she had voted against all the immigrant-friendly bills her party had pushed, and that she had shot from her notorious hip a bit more.

Her body was moving all too slowly, her thigh muscles ached, her lungs were screaming for air and she knew that soon she would not be able to move at all. Her brain tried to combat the fear, tried to tell her she was not exactly an obvious target for rape.

Fear had borne her aloft; she could see over the hill now, down to Madserud Allé. A car was reversing out of a driveway. She could make it—there was little more than a hundred yards left. Marit Olsen ran onto the slippery grass and down the slope, only just managing to stay on her feet. She could no longer hear the steps behind her; everything was drowned out by her panting. The car had backed onto the road now; there was a grinding of gears as the driver went from reverse to first. Marit was nearing the bottom, only a few yards before the road, the blessed cones of light emitted by the headlights. Her considerable body weight had a slight start on her in the descent, and now it was relentlessly pulling her forward, to the point that her legs could no longer keep up. She fell headlong into the road, into the light. Her stomach, encased in sweaty polyester, hit the pavement, and she half-slid, half-rolled forward. Then Marit lay still, the bitter taste of road dust in her mouth and her grazed palms stinging from contact with gravel.

Someone was standing over her. Grabbed her shoulders. With a groan she rolled onto her side and held her arms over her face in defense. Not a commando, just an elderly man wearing a hat. The car door behind him was open.

"Are you all right, **frøken**?" he inquired.

"What do you think?" said Marit Olsen, feeling the anger boil inside her.

"Wait! I've seen you somewhere before."

"Well, that's a shock," she said, waving away his helping hand and struggling noisily to her feet.

"Aren't you on that comedy show?"

"You . . ." she said, staring into the dark, silent void of the park and massaging her notorious hip. "Mind your own fucking business, grandpa."

6

Homecoming

A Volvo Amazon, the last to roll out of the Volvo factory in 1970, had stopped in front of the pedestrian crossing by the arrivals terminal at Gardermoen Airport in Oslo.

A line of nursery-school children paraded past the car in chafing rain gear. Some of them glanced with curiosity at the strange old car with rally stripes along the hood, and at the two men behind the windshield wipers that swished away the morning rain.

The man in the passenger seat, Politioverbetjent (shortened to POB) Gunnar Hagen, knew that the sight of children walking in hand in hand ought to make him smile and think of solidarity, consideration for others and a society where everyone looked after everyone else. But Hagen's first association was a search party hunting for a person they expected to find dead. That was what working as the head of Crime Squad did to you. Or, as some wit had written in English on Harry Hole's office door: I SEE DEAD PEOPLE.

"What the heck's a nursery-school class doing at an airport?" asked the man in the driver's seat. His name was Bjørn Holm, and the Amazon was his dearest possession. The mere smell of the noisy but uncannily efficient heater, the sweat-ingrained imitation leather and the dusty rear shelf gave him inner peace. Especially if it was accompanied by the engine at the right speed, that is, about fifty miles an hour on flat road, and Hank Williams on the cassette player. Bjørn Holm from Krimteknisk, the Forensics Unit in Bryn, was a hillbilly from Skreia with snakeskin cowboy boots, a moon face and bulging eyes, which lent him a constantly surprised expression. This face had caused more than one leader of an investigation to misjudge Bjørn Holm. The truth was that he was the greatest crime-scene talent since the glory days of Weber. Holm was wearing a soft suede jacket with fringes and a knitted Rastafarian hat, under which grew the most vigorous, intensely red sideburns Hagen had seen this side of the North Sea, and they as good as covered his cheeks.

Holm swung the Amazon into the short-term parking lot, where it stopped with a gasp, and the two men got out. Hagen turned up his coat collar, which of course did nothing to prevent the rain from bombarding his shiny pate. It was wreathed by black hair so thick and so fertile that some suspected Gunnar Hagen of having perfectly normal hair growth but an eccentric hairdresser.

"Tell me—is that jacket really waterproof?" Hagen asked as they strode toward the entrance.

"Nope," said Holm.

Kaja Solness had called them while they were in the car and informed them that the Scandinavian Airlines plane had landed ten minutes early. And that she had lost Harry Hole.

After entering through the swinging doors, Gunnar Hagen looked around, saw Kaja sitting on her suitcase by the taxi counter, signaled her with a brief nod and headed for the door to the customs area. He and Holm slipped in as it opened for passengers leaving. A guard moved to stop them, but nodded, indeed almost bowed, when Hagen held up his ID card and barked a curt "Police."

Hagen turned right and walked straight past the customs officials and their dogs, past the metal counters that reminded him of the carts at the Pathology Institute, and into the cubicle behind.

There he came to such a sudden halt that Holm walked into him from behind. A familiar voice wheezed between clenched teeth. "Hi, boss. Regretfully, I'm unable to stand to attention right now."

Bjørn Holm peered over Hagen's shoulder.

It was a sight that would haunt him for years.

Bent over the back of a chair was the man who was a living legend not just at Oslo Police HQ but in every police station across Norway, for good or ill. A man with whom Holm himself had worked closely. But not as closely as the male customs official standing behind the legend with a latex-clad hand, partially obscured by the legend's pale white buttocks.

"He's mine," Hagen said to the official, waving his ID card. "Let him go."

The official stared at Hagen and seemed reluctant to release him, but when an older officer with gold stripes on his epaulets came in and nodded briefly with closed eyes, the customs official twisted his hand around one last time and removed it. The victim gave a loud groan.

"Get your pants on, Harry," Hagen said, and turned away.

Harry pulled up his trousers and said to the official peeling off the latex glove, "Was it good for you, too?"

Kaja Solness rose from the suitcase when her three colleagues came back through the door. Bjørn Holm went to drive the car around while Gunnar Hagen went to get something to drink from the kiosk.

"Are you often checked?" Kaja asked.

"Every time," Harry said.

"Don't think I've ever been stopped at customs."

"I know."

"How do you know?"

"Because there are a thousand small telltale signs they look for, and you have none of them. Whereas I have at least half."

"Do you think customs officers are so prejudiced?"

"Well, have you ever smuggled anything?"

"No." She laughed. "OK, then, I have. But if they're so good, they should have seen that you're also a policeman. And let you through."

"They did see."

"Come on. That only happens in films."

"They saw, all right. They saw a fallen policeman."

"Oh, yes?" said Kaja.

Harry rummaged for his pack of cigarettes. "Let your eyes drift over to the taxi counter. There's a man with narrow eyes, a bit slanted. See him?"

She nodded.

"He's tugged at his belt twice since we came out. As if there were something heavy hanging from it. A pair of handcuffs or a baton. An automatic reaction if you've been in patrol cars or in lockup for a few years."

"I've worked in patrol cars, and I've never—"

"He's working for Narc now and keeps an eye open for people who look a bit too relieved after passing through customs. Or go straight to the bathroom because they can't stand having the goods up their rectum any longer. Or suitcases that change hands between a naïve, helpful passenger and the smuggler who got the idiot to carry the luggage containing all the dope through customs."

She tilted her head and squinted at Harry with a little smile playing on her lips. "Or he might be a normal guy whose pants keep slipping down, and he's waiting for his mother. And you're mistaken."

"Certainly," said Harry, looking at his watch and the clock on the wall. "I'm always making mistakes. Is that really the time?"

The Volvo Amazon glided onto the highway as the streetlights came on.

In the front seats Holm and Solness were deep in conversation as Townes Van Zandt sang in controlled sobs on the cassette player. In the backseat, Gunnar Hagen was stroking the smooth pig-leather briefcase he was holding on his lap.

"I wish I could say you looked good," he said in a low voice.

"Jet lag, boss," said Harry, who was lying more than sitting.

"What happened to your jaw?"

"It's a long, boring story."

"Anyway, welcome back. Sorry about the circumstances."

"I thought I had handed in my resignation."

"You've done that before."

"So how many times do you want it?"

Gunnar Hagen looked at his former inspector and lowered his eyebrows and voice even further. "As I said, I'm sorry about the circumstances. And I appreciate that the last case took a lot out of you. That you and your loved ones were involved in a way that . . . well, could make anyone wish for a different life. But this is your job, Harry, this is what you're good at."

Harry sniffed as though he had already contracted the typical homecoming cold.

"Two murders, Harry. We're not even sure how they've been carried out, only that they're identical. But thanks to recent costly experiences, we know what we're facing." The POB paused.

"Doesn't hurt to say the words, boss."

"I'm not so sure about that."

Harry looked out at the snowless brown countryside. "People have cried wolf a number of times, but events have shown that a serial killer is a rare beast."

"I know." Hagen nodded. "The Snowman is the only one we've seen in this country during my period in office. But we're pretty certain this time. The victims have nothing to do with each other, and the sedative found in their blood is identical."

"That's something. Good luck."

"Harry . . ."

"Find someone qualified for the job, boss."

"**You're** qualified."

"I've gone to pieces."

Hagen took a deep breath. "Then we'll put you together again."

"Beyond repair," Harry said.

"You're the only person in this country with the skills and the experience to deal with a serial killer."

"Fly in an American."

"You know very well things don't work like that."

"Then I'm sorry."

"Are you? Two people dead so far, Harry. Young women . . ."

Harry waved a dismissive hand when Hagen opened his briefcase and pulled out a brown file.

"I mean it, boss. Thank you for buying my passport and all that, but I'm finished with photos and reports full of blood and gore."

Hagen gave Harry a wounded expression, but still kept the file on his lap.

"Peruse this—that's all I'm asking. And don't tell anyone we're working on this case."

"Oh? Why's that?"

"It's complicated. Just don't mention it to anyone, OK?"

The conversation in the front of the car had died, and Harry focused on the back of Kaja's head. Since Bjørn Holm's Amazon had been made long before anyone used the term **whiplash,** there was no headrest, and, with her hair pinned up, Harry could see her slim neck, see the white down on her skin, and he mused about how vulnerable she was, how quickly things changed, how much could be destroyed in a matter of seconds. That was what life was: a process of destruction, a disintegration from what at the outset was perfect. The only suspense involved was whether we would be destroyed in one sudden act or slowly. It was a sad thought, yet he clung to it. Until they were through the Ibsen Tunnel, a gray, anonymous component of the capital's traffic machinery that could have been in any city in the world. Nevertheless it was at that particular moment that he felt it. A huge, unalloyed pleasure at being here. In Oslo. Home. The feeling was so overwhelming that for a few seconds he was oblivious to why he had returned.

Harry gazed at 5 Sofies Gate as the Amazon sailed out of view behind him. There was more graffiti on the front of the building than when he had left, but the blue paint beneath was the same.

So he had refused to take the case. He had a father lying in the hospital. That was the only reason he was here. What he didn't tell them was that if he'd had the choice of knowing about his father's illness or not, he would have chosen not to know. Because he hadn't returned out of love. He had returned out of shame.

Harry peered up at the two black windows on the second floor that were his.

Then he opened the door and walked into the back-yard. The garbage can was standing where it always had. Harry pushed open the lid. He had promised Hagen he would take a look at the case file. Mostly so that his boss would not lose face—after all, the pass-port had cost Crime Squad quite a few kroner. Harry dropped the file onto the burst plastic bags leaking cof-fee grounds, diapers, rotten fruit and potato peels. He inhaled and wondered at how surprisingly interna-tional the smell of garbage was.

Nothing had been touched in his two-room flat, yet something was different. A powder-gray hue, as though someone had just left but his frosty breath was still there. He went into the bedroom, put down his bag and fished out the unopened carton of cigarettes. Everything was the same there, gray as the skin of a two-day-old corpse. He fell back onto the bed. Closed his eyes. Greeted the familiar sounds. Such as the drip from the hole in the gutter onto the lead flashing around the window frame. It wasn't the slow, comforting **drip-drip** from the ceiling in Hong Kong, but a feverish drumming, somewhere in the transition between dripping and running water, like a reminder that time was passing, the seconds were racing, the end of a number line was approaching. It had made him think of the main character in **La Linea,** the Italian cartoon, who, after four minutes, always ended up falling off the edge of the cartoonist's line into oblivion.

Harry knew that there was a half-full bottle of Jim Beam in the cupboard under the sink. Knew that he could start where he had left off in this flat. Shit, he had been wrecked even before he got into the taxi to the airport that day several months ago. No wonder he had not managed to drag himself to Manila.

He could go straight into the kitchen now and pour the contents down the sink.

Harry groaned.

Wondering who she resembled was so much nonsense. He knew who she resembled. She resembled Rakel. They all resembled Rakel.

Gallows

"But I'm scared, Rasmus," said Marit Olsen. "That's what I am!"

"I know," said Rasmus Olsen, in that muted, congenial voice that had accompanied and comforted his wife for more than twenty-five years, through political decisions, driving tests, bouts of fury and the odd panic attack. "It's just natural," he said, putting his arm around her. "You work hard, you have a lot on your mind. Your brain doesn't have any spare capacity to shut out that kind of thought."

"That kind of thought?" she said, turning to face him on the sofa. She had lost interest in the DVD they were watching—**Love Actually**—a long time before. "That kind of thought, that kind of nonsense—is that what you mean?"

"The important thing is not what I think," he said, his fingertips poised to touch. "The important—"

"Thing is what **you** think," she said, mimicking his voice. "For Christ's sake, Rasmus, you've gotta stop watching that Dr. Phil show."

He released a silky-smooth chuckle. "I'm just saying that you, as a member of Stortinget, can obviously ask for a bodyguard to accompany you if you feel threatened. But is that what you want?"

"Mm," she purred as his fingers began to massage the exact spot where she knew he knew she loved it. "What do you mean by **what you want?**"

"Give it some thought. What do you imagine is going to happen?"

Marit Olsen gave it some thought. Closed her eyes and felt his fingers massaging calm and harmony into her body. She had met Rasmus when she had been working at the Norwegian employment service in Alta, Finnmark. She had been elected as an official for NTL, a union for state employees, and they had sent her south to a training workshop at the Sørmarka Conference Center. There a thin man with vivid blue eyes beneath a fast-receding hairline had approached her the first evening. He had talked in a way that was reminiscent of redemption-happy Christians at the youth club in Alta. Except that he was talking politics. He worked in the secretariat for the Socialist party, helping MPs with practical office jobs, travel and the press and even, on the odd occasion, writing a speech for them.

Rasmus had bought her a beer, asked if she wanted to dance and, after four increasingly slow popular numbers, with increasingly close physical contact, had asked if she wanted to join him. Not in his room, but in the party.

After returning home she had started going to party meetings in Alta, and in the evenings she and Rasmus had long telephone conversations about what they had done and thought that day. Of course, Marit had never said it aloud: that sometimes she thought the best time they had spent together was when they were twelve hundred miles apart. Then the Appointments Committee had called, put her on a list and, presto, she was elected to the Alta Town Council. Two years later she was the vice chairperson of the Alta Socialist party, the next year she was sitting on the County Council, and then there was another telephone call, and this time it was the Appointments Committee for Stortinget.

And now she had a tiny office in Stortinget, a partner who helped her with her speeches, and prospects of climbing the ladder as long as everything went according to plan—and she avoided blunders.

"They'll detail a policeman to keep an eye on me," she said. "And the press will want to know why a woman MP no one has ever heard of should be walking around with a fucking bodyguard at the taxpayers' expense. And when they find out why—she **suspected** someone had been following her in the park—they will write that with **that** kind of reasoning every woman in Oslo will be asking for state-subsidized police protection. I don't want any protection. Drop it."

Rasmus laughed silently and used his fingers to massage his approval.

The wind howled through the leafless trees in Frogner Park. A duck with its head drawn deep into its plumage drifted across the pitch-black surface of the lake. Rotting leaves stuck to the tiles of the empty pools at Frogner Park. The place seemed abandoned for all eternity, a lost world. The wind blew up a storm in the deep pool and sang its monotonous lament beneath the thirty-two-foot-high diving tower, which stood out against the night sky like a gallows.

8

Snow Patrøl

It was three o'clock in the afternoon when Harry awoke. He opened his bag, put on a set of clean clothes, found a woolen coat in the closet and went out. The drizzle roused Harry enough for him to look moderately sober as he entered the brown smoky rooms of Schrøder's. His table was taken, so he went into the corner, under the TV.

He looked around. He spotted a couple of people he hadn't seen before, hunched over beer glasses; otherwise time had stood still. Rita came and placed a white mug and a steel carafe of coffee in front of him.

"Harry," she said. Not as a form of welcome, but to confirm that it was indeed he.

Harry nodded. "Hi, Rita. Old newspapers?"

Rita scuttled off to the back room and returned with a pile of yellowing papers. Harry had never been given a clear explanation as to why they kept newspapers at Schrøder's, but he had benefited from this arrangement on more than one occasion.

"Been a long time," said Rita, and was gone. And Harry remembered what he liked about Schrøder's, apart from its being the closest bar to his flat. The short sentences. And respect for your private life. Your return was noted; no elucidation was required.

Harry downed two mugs of the surprisingly unpleasant coffee while flicking through the newspapers in a fast-forward kind of way, to furnish himself with a general perspective of what had happened in the kingdom over the last months. Not much, as usual. Which was what he liked best about Norway.

Someone had won **Norwegian Idol,** a celeb had been eliminated from a dance competition, a soccer player in the third division had been caught taking cocaine and Lene Galtung, daughter of the shipping magnate Anders Galtung, had preinherited some of the millions and gotten engaged to a better-looking but presumably less affluent man, an investor named Tony. The editor of **Liberal,** Arve Støp, wrote that it was beginning to be embarrassing that Norway, which wanted to stand out as a social-democratic model, was still a monarchy. Nothing had changed.

In the December newspapers Harry saw the first articles about the murders. He recognized Kaja's description of the crime scene, a basement in an office complex under construction in Nydalen. The cause of death was unclear, but the police suspected foul play.

Harry thumbed through, preferring to read about a politician who boasted that he was resigning to spend more time with his family.

Schrøder's newspaper archives were by no means

complete, but the second murder appeared in a paper dated a couple of weeks later.

The woman had been found behind a wrecked Datsun dumped at the edge of some woods by Lake Dausjøen in Maridalen. The police did not rule out a "criminal act," but nor did they reveal any details about the cause of death.

Harry's eyes scanned the article and established that the reason for police silence was the usual: They had no leads, **nada;** the radar was sweeping across an open sea of nothingness.

Only two murders. Yet Hagen had seemed so certain of his facts when he said this was a serial killer. So what was the connection? What was it that the press didn't say? Harry could feel his brain beginning to pursue the old, familiar paths; he cursed himself for his inability to refrain and continued to leaf through.

When the coffee carafe was empty, he left a crumpled banknote on the table and went into the street. He tightened his coat around him and squinted up at the gray sky.

He hailed a taxi, which pulled over to the curb. The driver leaned across and the rear door swung open. A trick you rarely saw nowadays, and one Harry decided to reward with a tip. Not just because he could step right in, but because the window in the door had reflected a face at the wheel of a car parked behind the cab.

"Rikshospital," Harry said, wriggling to the middle of the backseat.

"Right away," said the driver.

Harry studied the rearview mirror as they drove off. "Oh, could you go to Five Sofies Gate first, please?"

At Sofies Gate the taxi waited, its diesel engine clattering away, while Harry mounted the staircase with long, quick strides and his brain assessed the range of possibilities. The triad? Herman Kluit? Or good old paranoia? The gear lay where he had left it before taking off, in the toolbox in the food cupboard. The old, expired ID card. Two sets of Hiatt handcuffs with a spring-loaded arm for speed-cuffing. And the service revolver, a .38-caliber Smith & Wesson.

Returning to the street, he looked neither left nor right, just jumped straight into the taxi.

"Rikshospital?" asked the driver.

"Drive in that direction, at any rate," Harry answered, studying the mirror as they turned up Stensberggata and then Ullevålsveien. He saw nothing. Which meant one of two things. It was good old paranoia. Or the guy was a pro.

Harry hesitated, then said finally, "Rikshospital."

He continued to keep an eye on the mirror as they passed Vestre Aker Church and Ullevål University Hospital. Whatever he did, he mustn't lead them straight to where he was most vulnerable. Where they would always try to strike. The family.

The country's biggest hospital was situated high above the town.

Harry paid the driver, who thanked him for the tip and repeated the trick with the rear door.

The façades of the buildings rose in front of Harry and the low cloud cover seemed to sweep away the roofs.

He took a deep breath.

Olav Hole's smile from the hospital pillow was so gentle and frail that Harry had to swallow.

"I was in Hong Kong," Harry replied. "I had to do some thinking."

"Did you get it done?"

Harry shrugged. "What do the doctors say?"

"As little as possible. Hardly a good sign, but I've noticed that I prefer it like that. Tackling life's realities has, as you know, never been our family's strong suit."

Harry wondered whether they would talk about Mom. He hoped not.

"Do you have a job?"

Harry shook his head. His father's hair hung over his forehead, so tidy and white that Harry felt as if it weren't his hair but an accessory that had been handed out with the pajamas and slippers.

"Nothing?" his father said.

"I've had an offer to lecture at a police college."

It was almost the truth. Hagen had offered him that after the Snowman case, as a kind of leave of absence.

"Teacher?" His father chuckled cautiously, as if any further effort would be the end of him. "I thought one of your principles was never to do anything I had done."

"It was never like that."

"That's all right. You've always done things your way. This police stuff . . . Well, I suppose I should just be grateful you haven't done what I did. I'm no model for anyone to follow. You know, after your mother died . . ."

Harry had been sitting in the white hospital room for twenty minutes and already felt a desperate urge to flee.

"After your mother died, I struggled to make sense of anything. I retreated into my shell, found no joy in anyone's company. It was as though loneliness brought me closer to her, or so I thought. But it's a mistake, Harry." His father's smile was as gentle as an angel's. "I know losing Rakel hit you hard, but you mustn't do what I did. You mustn't hide, Harry. You mustn't lock the door and throw away the key."

Harry looked down at his hands, nodded and felt ants crawling all over his body. He had to have something, anything.

A nurse came in, introduced himself as Altman, held up a syringe and said, with a slight lisp, that he was going to give "Olav" something to help him sleep. Harry felt like asking if he had something for him, too.

His father lay on his side, the skin on his face sagging; he looked older than he had on his back. He gazed at Harry with heavy, blank eyes.

Harry stood up so abruptly that the chair legs scraped loudly on the floor.

"Where are you going?" Olav asked.

"Out for a smoke," Harry said. "I won't be long."

Harry sat on a low brick wall with a view of the parking lot and lit up a Camel. On the other side of the highway he could see Blindern and the university buildings where his father had studied. There were those who asserted that sons always became, to some degree or other, disguised variants of their fathers, that the experience of breaking out was never more than an illusion; you returned; the gravity of blood was not only stronger than your willpower, it was your willpower. To Harry it had always seemed he was evidence of the contrary. So why had seeing his father's naked, ravaged face on the pillow been like looking into a mirror? Listening to him speak like hearing himself? Hearing him think, the words . . . like a dentist's drill that found Harry's nerves with unerring accuracy. Because he was a copy. Shit! Harry's searching gaze had found a white Corolla in the parking lot.

Always white—that was the most anonymous color. The color of the Corolla outside Schrøder's, the one with the face behind the wheel, the same face that had stared at him with its narrow, slanting eyes less than twenty-four hours before.

Harry tossed away his cigarette and hurried inside. Slackened his pace when he entered the corridor leading to his father's room. He turned where the corridor widened to an open waiting area and pretended to search through a pile of magazines on the table while scanning the people sitting there from the corner of his eye.

The man had hidden himself behind a copy of **Liberal**.

Harry picked up a **Se og Hør** gossip rag with a picture of Lene Galtung and her fiancé and left the waiting area.

Olav Hole was lying with his eyes closed. Harry bent down and put his ear to Olav's mouth. He was breathing so lightly it was barely audible, but Harry felt a current of air on his cheek.

He sat for a while on the chair beside the bed, watching his father as his mind played back poorly edited childhood memories in arbitrary order and with no other central theme than that they were things he remembered clearly.

Then he placed the chair by the door, which he opened a crack, and waited.

It was half an hour before he saw the man come from the waiting area and walk down the corridor. Harry noticed that the squat, robust-looking man was unusually bowlegged; he seemed to be walking with a beach ball stuck between his knees. Before entering a door marked with the international sign for the men's room, he plucked at his belt. As if something heavy were hanging from it.

Harry got up and followed.

Stopped outside the restroom and breathed in. It had been a long time. Then he pushed open the door and slipped in.

The restroom was like the whole hospital: clean, nice, new and too big. Along the main wall there were six cubicle doors, none with an OCCUPIED sign above the lock. On the shorter wall four sinks, and on the other long wall four porcelain urinals at hip height. The man was standing at a urinal, with his back to Harry. On the wall above him ran a horizontal pipe. It looked solid. Solid enough. Harry took out his revolver and handcuffs. International etiquette in men's rooms is not to look at each other. Eye contact, even unintentional, is cause for murder. Accordingly, the man didn't turn to look at Harry. Not when Harry locked the outside door with infinite care, not when he walked over slowly and not when he placed the gun barrel against the roll of fat between the man's neck and head and whispered what a colleague used to claim all police officers should be allowed to say at least once in their careers: "Freeze."

The man did exactly that. Harry could see the gooseflesh appear on the roll of fat as the man stiffened.

"Hands up."

The man lifted a couple of short, powerful arms above his head. Harry leaned forward. And realized at that moment it had been a blunder. The man's speed was breathtaking. Harry knew from the hours spent studying up on hand-to-hand combat techniques that knowing how to take a beating was as important as giving one. The art was to let your muscles relax, to appreciate that punishment cannot be avoided, only reduced. So, when the man spun around with his knee raised, Harry reacted as supplely as a dancer, following the movement. He moved his body in the same direction as the kick. The foot hit him above the hip. Harry lost balance, fell and slid along the tiled floor until he was out of range. He remained there, sighed and looked at the ceiling as he took out his pack of cigarettes. He poked one in his mouth.

"Speed-cuffing," Harry said. "Learned it the year I took an FBI course in Chicago. Cabrini-Green. The digs were the pits. For a white man, there was nothing to do in the evenings unless you wanted to go out and get yourself robbed. So I sat indoors practicing two things: loading and unloading my service pistol as fast as I could in the dark, and speed-cuffing on a table leg."

Harry levered himself up onto his elbows.

The man still had his short arms stretched up above his head. His wrists were shackled to the handcuffs on either side of the pipe. He stared blankly at Harry.

"Mr. Kluit send you?" Harry asked in English.

The man held Harry's gaze without blinking.

"The triad? I've paid my debts—haven't you heard?" Harry studied the man's expressionless face. The features could have been Asian, but he didn't have a Chinese face or complexion. Mongolian, maybe? "So what do you want from me?"

No answer. Which was bad news, as the man had most probably not come to ask for anything, but to do something.

Harry stood up and walked in a semicircle so that he could approach him from the side. He held the revolver to the man's temple while slipping his left hand inside the man's suit jacket. His hand ran over the cold steel of a weapon, then found a wallet and plucked it out.

Harry stepped back three paces.

"Let's see . . . Mr. Jussi Kolkka." Harry held an American Express card up to the light. "Finnish? I suppose you know some Norwegian, then?"

No answer.

"You've been a policeman, haven't you? When I saw you in arrivals at Gardermoen, I thought you were an undercover narcotics cop. How did you know I was catching that particular flight, Jussi? It's all right if I call you Jussi, isn't it? It feels sort of natural to address a guy with his schlong hanging out by his first name."

There was a brief throaty noise before a gobbet of spit came whirling through the air, rotating on its axis, and landed on Harry's chest.

Harry looked down at his T-shirt. The black snuff spit had drawn a diagonal line through the second **o** and it now read SNOW PATRØL.

"So you do understand Norwegian," Harry said. "Who do you work for then, Jussi? And what do you want?"

Not a muscle stirred in Jussi's face. Someone shook the door handle outside, swore and went away.

Harry sighed. Then he raised his revolver until it was level with the Finn's forehead and cocked it.

"You might suppose, Jussi, that I'm a normal, sane person. Well, this is how sane I am. My father is lying helpless in his sickbed in there. You've found out, and that presents me with a problem. There's only one way to solve it. Fortunately, you're armed so I can tell the police it was self-defense."

Harry pressed the hammer back still farther. And felt the familiar nausea.

"Kripos."

Harry stopped the hammer. "Repeat."

"I'm in Kripos," he hissed in Swedish, with the Finnish accent witty speech makers at Norwegian wedding receptions are so fond of.

Harry stared at the man. He didn't have a second's doubt that he was telling the truth. Yet it was totally incomprehensible.

"In my wallet," the Finn snarled, not letting the fury in his voice reach his eyes.

Harry opened the wallet again and checked inside. Removed a laminated ID card. There wasn't much information, but it was adequate. The man in front of Harry was employed by Kriminalpolitisentralen, Kripos for short, the central crime unit in Oslo that assisted in—and usually led—the investigations into murder cases affecting the whole of the country.

"What the hell does Kripos want with me?"

"Ask Bellman."

"Who's Bellman?"

The Finn uttered a brief sound; it was difficult to determine whether it was a cough or laughter. "POB Bellman, you stupid fuck. My chief. Let me go now, handsome."

"Fuck," Harry said, inspecting the card again. "Fuck, fuck, fuck." He dropped the wallet on the floor and made for the door.

"Hey! Hey!"

The Finn's shouts faded as the door slid shut behind Harry, and he walked down the corridor to the exit. The nurse who had been with his father was coming from the opposite direction and nodded with a smile when they were close enough. Harry tossed the tiny key for the handcuffs up in the air.

"There's a flasher in the boys' room, Altman."

By instinct, the nurse caught the key with both hands. Harry could feel the open-mouthed stare on his back until he was out the door.

9

The Dive

It was a quarter to eleven at night. Forty-eight degrees Fahrenheit, and Marit Olsen remembered that the weather forecaster had said it would be even milder tomorrow. In Frogner Park there wasn't a soul to be seen. Something about the pools made her think of laid-up ships, of abandoned fishing villages with the wind whispering through house walls, and fairgrounds out of season. Fragmented memories of her childhood. Like the drowned fishermen who haunted Tronholmen, who emerged from the sea at night, with seaweed in their hair and fish in their mouths and nostrils. Ghosts without breath, but who were wont to scream cold, hoarse seagull cries. The dead with their swollen limbs, which snagged on branches and were wrenched off with a ripping sound—not that this halted their advance toward the isolated house in Tronholmen. Tronholmen, where Grandma and Grandpa lived. Where she herself lay trembling in the children's room. Marit Olsen breathed out. Kept breathing out.

Down there the wind was still, but up here at the top of the thirty-two-foot-high diving platform you could feel the air moving. Marit felt her pulse throbbing in her temples, in her throat, in her groin, blood streaming through every limb, fresh and life-giving. Living was wonderful. Being alive. She had hardly been out of breath after scaling all the steps of the tower, had just felt her heart, that loyal muscle, racing wildly. She stared down at the empty pool beneath her, to which the moonlight lent an almost unnatural bluish sheen. Farther away, at the end of the pool, she could see the large clock. The hand had stopped at ten past five. Time stood still. She could hear the city, see car lights on Kirkeveien. So close. And yet too far. Too far away for anyone to hear her.

She was breathing. And was dead, nonetheless. She had a rope as thick as a hawser around her neck and could hear the gulls screaming, ghosts she would soon be joining. But she was not thinking about death. She was thinking about life, how much she would have liked to live. All the small things, and the big things, she would like to have done. She would have traveled to countries she hadn't seen, watched her nephews and nieces grow, seen the world come to its senses.

It had been a knife; the blade had glistened in the light from the street lamp, and it had been held to her throat. Fear is said to release energy. Not in her case—it had stolen all her energy, deprived her of the power to act. The thought of steel cutting into her flesh had turned her into a quivering bundle of helplessness. So when she had been told to climb over the fence, she had not been able to, and had fallen to the ground and lain there like a beanbag, tears streaming down her cheeks. Because she knew what was going to happen. She would do everything she could not to be cut and knew she would not be able to prevent it. Because she wanted so much to live. A few more years, a few more minutes—it was the same crazy, blind rationality that drove everyone.

She had started to explain that she couldn't climb over; she had forgotten that he had told her to keep her mouth shut. The knife had writhed like a snake, sliced her mouth, twisted around, crunched against her teeth and then been pulled out. The blood had gushed at once. The voice had whispered something behind the mask and nudged her forward along the fence. To a place in the bushes where she was pushed through a gap in it.

Marit Olsen swallowed the blood that continued to fill her mouth and looked down at the spectator stands beneath her; they, too, were bathed in the blue moonlight. They were so empty; it was a courtroom without spectators or jury, just a judge. An execution without a mob, just the executioner. A final public appearance that no one had considered worth attending. It struck Marit that she lacked as much appeal in death as in life. And now she couldn't speak, either.

"Jump."

She saw how beautiful the park was, even now in winter. She wished the clock at the end of the pool were working so that she could see the seconds of life she was stealing.

"Jump," the voice repeated. He must have removed his mask, for his voice had changed; she recognized it now. She turned her head and stared in shock. Then she felt a foot on her back. She screamed. She no longer had ground beneath her feet; for one astonishing moment she was weightless. But the ground was pulling her down, her body accelerated and she registered that the bluish-white porcelain of the pool was racing toward her, to smash her into pieces.

Nine feet above the bottom of the pool the rope tightened around Marit Olsen's neck and throat. It was an old-fashioned type, made of linden and elm, and had no elasticity. Marit Olsen's stout body was not checked to any appreciable degree; it detached itself from the head and hit the base of the pool with a dull thud. The head and the neck were left on the rope. There wasn't much blood. Then the head tipped forward, slipped out of the noose, fell onto Marit Olsen's blue tracksuit top and rolled across the tiles with a rumble.

Then the pool was still again.

Part Two

Reminders

At three o'clock in the morning Harry abandoned his attempts to sleep and got up. He turned on the tap in the kitchen and put a glass underneath, held it there until the water overflowed and trickled down his wrist, cold. His jaw ached. His attention was held by two photographs pinned up over the kitchen counter.

One, with a couple of disfiguring creases, showed Rakel in a light-blue summer dress. But it wasn't summer; the leaves behind her were autumnal. Her dark-brown hair cascaded down onto her bare shoulders. Her eyes seemed to be searching for something behind the lens, perhaps the photographer. Had he taken the photo himself? Strange that he couldn't remember.

The other was of Oleg. Taken with Harry's cellphone camera at Valle Hovin skating rink during a training session last winter. At that time, a delicate young boy, but if he had continued his training he would have soon filled out that red skinsuit of his. What was he doing now? Where was he? Had Rakel managed to create a home for them wherever they were, a home that felt safer than the one they had in Oslo? Were there new people in her life? When Oleg became tired, or lost concentration, did he still refer to Harry as "Dad"?

Harry turned off the tap. He was conscious of the cupboard door against his knees. Jim Beam was whispering his name from inside.

Harry pulled on a pair of trousers and a T-shirt, went into the sitting room and put on Miles Davis's **Kind of Blue.** It was the original, the one where they didn't compensate for the reel tape in the studio running a tiny bit slow, so the whole record was an almost imperceptible displacement of reality.

He listened for a while before increasing the volume to drown the whispering from the kitchen. Closed his eyes.

Kripos. Bellman.

He had never heard the name. He could, of course, have called Hagen and inquired, but he couldn't be bothered. Because he had a feeling he knew what this might be about. Best to let sleeping dogs lie.

Harry had come to the last track, "Flamenco Sketches," then he gave up. He got to his feet and left the sitting room for the kitchen. In the hall he turned left, emerged wearing Doc Martens boots and went out.

He found it under a split plastic bag. Something akin to dried pea soup coated the front of the file.

Back in his sitting room he sat down in the green wing chair and began to read with a shiver.

The first woman was Borgny Stem-Myhre, thirty-three years old, originally from Levanger, in the north.

Single, no children, resident of Sagene in Oslo. Worked as a hairstylist, had a large circle of acquaintances, particularly among hairdressers, photographers and people in the fashion press. She frequented several of Oslo's restaurants, and not just the coolest. Besides that, she liked the outdoors and liked hiking or skiing from mountain cabin to mountain cabin.

"You can take the woman out of Levanger, but you can't take Levanger out of the woman," was the general summary of interviews with her colleagues. Harry assumed the remark came from colleagues who had succeeded in erasing their own small-town upbringings.

"We all liked her. In this line of business she was one of the few who was genuine."

"It's incomprehensible. We can't understand how anyone could take her life."

"She was too nice. And sooner or later all the men she fell for exploited her. She became a toy for them. She aimed too high—that was basically the problem."

Harry studied a photograph of her. One in the file from when she was still alive. Blond, maybe not natural. Run-of-the-mill looks, no obvious beauty, but she was smartly dressed in a military jacket and a Rastafarian hat. Smartly dressed and too nice—did they go together?

She had been to Mono restaurant for the monthly launch and preview of the fashion magazine **Sheness.** That had been between seven and eight, and Borgny had told a colleague/friend that she would be at home preparing for a photo shoot the day after, at which the photographer had wanted a "jungle meets punk meets eighties look."

They assumed she would go to the nearest taxi stand, but none of the taxi drivers in the vicinity at the time in question (computerized lists from Norgestaxi and Oslo Taxi attached) had recognized the photograph of Borgny Stem-Myhre or had driven to Sagene. In short, no one had seen her after she left Mono. Until two Polish bricklayers had shown up for work, noticed that the padlock on the iron bomb-shelter door had been snapped, and gone in. Borgny had been lying in the middle of the floor, in a contorted position, with all of her clothes on.

Harry examined the photo. The same military jacket. The face looked as if it had been made up with white foundation. The flash cast sharp shadows against the cellar wall. Photo shoot. Smart.

The pathologist had determined that Borgny Stem-Myhre died somewhere between ten and eleven o'clock at night. In her blood were traces of the drug ketanome, a strong anesthetic that worked fast even when injected intramuscularly. But the direct cause of death was drowning, triggered by blood from wounds in the mouth. And this was where the most disturbing elements came in. The pathologist found twenty-four stab wounds in the mouth, symmetrically distributed and at the same depth, two and a half inches—those that did not pierce the face, that is. But the police were at a loss as to what kind of weapon or instrument had been used. They had simply never seen anything like it. There were absolutely no forensic clues: no fingerprints, no DNA, not even shoe or boot prints, as the concrete floor had been cleaned the day before in preparation for heating cables and floor covering. In the report filed by Kim Erik Lokker, a forensics officer who must have been appointed after Harry's time, there was a photograph of two gray-black pebbles found on the floor that did not originate from the gravel around the crime scene. Lokker pointed out that small stones often got stuck in boots with a heavy-duty tread, and came loose when worn on firmer ground, such as this concrete floor. Furthermore, these stones were so unusual that if they turned up later in the investigation, for example in a gravel path, they might well find a match. There was one addition to the report after it had been signed and dated: Small traces of iron and coltan had been found on two molars.

Harry could already guess the conclusion. He flicked through.

The other woman's name was Charlotte Lolles. French father, Norwegian mother. Resident of Lambertseter, in Oslo. Twenty-nine years old. Qualified lawyer. Lived alone, but had a boyfriend: one Erik Fokkestad, who had been quickly eliminated from suspicion. He had been at a geology seminar in Yellowstone National Park in Wyoming. Charlotte should have joined him, but had let a serious property dispute on which she had been working take priority.

Colleagues had last seen her at the office on Monday evening at around nine. She had probably never returned home. Her briefcase of papers had been found next to her body behind the abandoned car in Maridalen. In addition, both parties in the property dispute had solid alibis. The postmortem report highlighted bits of paint and rust found under Charlotte Lolles's nails, which fit with the crime scene report's mention of scrape marks around the car's trunk lock, as though she had been trying to get it open. Closer examination of the lock revealed that it had been picked at least once. But hardly by Charlotte Lolles. Harry formed a mental image of her chained to something locked inside the trunk and speculated that that was why she had been trying to escape. Something the killer had taken with him afterward. But what? And how? And why?

Records of the interview with a female colleague from the law firm included a quote: "Charlotte was an ambitious person and always worked late. Although how efficient she was, I don't know. Always gentle, but not as outgoing as her smiles and Mediterranean appearance would have suggested. Quite private, basically. She never talked about her boyfriend, for example. But my bosses liked her very much."

Harry could imagine the female colleague serving up one intimate revelation after another about her boyfriend, without getting more than a smile from Charlotte in return. His investigative brain was on autopilot now: Perhaps Charlotte had held back from embracing a clingy sisterhood, perhaps she had had something to hide. Perhaps . . .

Harry studied the photographs. Hardish but attractive features. Dark eyes, she looked like . . . Shit! He closed his eyes. Opened them again. Flicked through to the pathologist's report. Skimmed through the document.

He had to check Charlotte's name at the top to make sure he wasn't reading the report on Borgny for a second time. Anesthetic. Twenty-four wounds to the mouth. Drowning. No external violence, no signs of sexual violence. The only difference was that the time of death was between eleven and midnight. However, this report also had an additional note about traces of iron and coltan found on the victim's teeth. Presumably because Krimteknisk had later realized that it might be relevant, since it was found on both victims. Coltan. Wasn't Schwarzenegger's Terminator made of that?

Harry realized he was wide awake now and found himself perching on the edge of the chair. He felt the stirrings, the excitement. And the nausea. Like when he took his first drink, the one that made his stomach turn, the one his body desperately rejected. And soon he would be begging for more. More and more. Until it destroyed him and everyone around him. As this was doing. Harry jumped up so quickly he went dizzy, grabbed the file, knew it was too thick, but still managed to tear it in two.

He picked up the bits of paper and took them back to the trash container. Let them fall down the side and lifted the plastic bags so that the documents slipped right down, to the very bottom. The garbage truck would be around tomorrow or the day after, he hoped.

Harry went back and sat down in the green chair.

As night softened into a grayish hue, he heard the first sounds of a waking town. But over the regular drone of the first rush-hour traffic on Pilestredet, he could also hear a distant, reedy police siren gyrating through the frequencies. Could be anything. He heard another siren winding up. Anything. And then another. No, not anything.

The landline rang.

Harry lifted the receiver.

"Hagen speaking. We've just received a mess—"

Harry put down the phone.

It rang again. Harry looked out of the window. He hadn't called Sis. Why not? Because he didn't want to show himself to his little sister—his most enthusiastic, most unconditional admirer. The woman who had what she called "a touch of Down syndrome" and still coped with her life immeasurably better than he did his own. She was the only person he could not allow himself to disappoint.

The telephone stopped ringing. And started again.

Harry snatched at the phone. "No, boss. The answer is no, I don't want the job."

The other end of the line was quiet for a second. Then an unfamiliar voice said, "Oslo Energy here. Herr Hole?"

Harry cursed to himself. "Yes?"

"You haven't paid the bills we sent you, and you haven't responded to our final notices. I'm calling to say we are cutting off the electricity supply to Five Sofies Gate at midnight tonight."

Harry didn't answer.

"We will reconnect only when we've received the outstanding amount."

"And that is?"

"With fees for reminders and disconnection, plus interest, it's fourteen thousand, four hundred and sixty-three kroner."

Silence.

"Hello?"

"I'm here. I'm sort of broke right now."

"The outstanding amount will be recovered by our collection agency. In the meantime we'll have to hope the temperature doesn't fall below freezing. Won't we?"

"We will," Harry confirmed, and hung up.

The sirens outside rose and fell.

Harry went for a nap. He lay there for a quarter of an hour with his eyes closed before giving up, getting dressed again and leaving the flat to catch a tram to Rikshospital.

II

Print

When I woke up this morning, I knew I had been there again. In the dream it is always like that: We are lying on the ground, blood is flowing, and when I glance to the side, she's there looking at us. She looks at me with sorrow in her eyes, as if it is only now that she has discovered who I am, only now that she has unmasked me, seen that I am not the man she wants.

Breakfast was excellent. It's on teletext. "Woman MP found dead in pool at Frogner Park." The news sites are full of it. Print out, snip, snip.

Before very long the first websites will publish the name. Thus far the so-called police investigation has been such a ridiculous farce that it has been irritating rather than exciting. But this time they will invest all their resources; they won't play at investigation the way they did with Borgny and Charlotte. After all, Marit Olsen was an MP. It's time this was stopped. Because I have appointed the next victim.

Crime Scene

Harry was smoking a cigarette outside the hospital entrance. Above him the sky was pale blue, but beneath him, the town, lying in a dip between low green mountain ridges, was wreathed in mist. The sight reminded him of his childhood in Oppsal, when he and Øystein had skipped the first lesson at school and gone to the German bunkers in Nordstrand. From there they had looked down on the pea-souper enveloping downtown Oslo. But with the years the morning fog had gradually drifted away from Oslo, along with industry and wood-burning.

Harry crushed the cigarette with his heel.

Olav Hole looked better. Or perhaps it was merely the light. He asked why Harry was smiling. And what had actually happened to his jaw.

Harry said something about being clumsy, wondering at what age the change took place, when children started protecting parents from reality. Around the age of ten, he concluded.

"Your little sister was here," Olav said.

"How is she?"

"Fine. When she heard you were back, she said that now she would look after you. Because she's big now, and you're small."

"Mm. Smart girl. How are you today?"

"Well. Very well, actually. Think it's about time I got out of here."

He smiled, and Harry smiled back.

"What do the doctors say?"

Olav Hole was still smiling. "Far too much. Shall we talk about something else?"

"Of course. What would you like to talk about?"

Olav Hole reflected. "I'd like to talk about her."

Harry nodded. And sat silently listening to his father tell him about how he and Harry's mother had met. Gotten married. About her illness when Harry was a boy.

"Ingrid helped me all the time. All the time. But she needed me so rarely. Until she fell ill. Sometimes I thought the illness was a blessing."

Harry flinched.

"It gave me the chance to repay her, you understand. And I did. Everything she asked me, I did." Olav Hole fixed his eyes on his son. "Everything, Harry. Almost."

Harry nodded.

His father kept talking. About Sis and Harry, how wonderfully gentle Sis had been. And what willpower Harry had possessed. How frightened he had been but kept it to himself. When he and Ingrid had listened at the door, they had heard Harry crying and cursing invisible monsters in turn. However, they knew they shouldn't go in to console and reassure him. He would become furious, shout that they were ruining everything and tell them to get out.

"You always wanted to fight the monsters on your own, Harry."

Olav Hole told the ancient story about Harry not speaking until he was nearly five. And then—one day—whole sentences just flowed out of him. Slow, earnest sentences with adult words; they had no idea where he had learned them.

"But your sister is right." Olav smiled. "You're a small boy again. You don't speak."

"Mm. Do you want me to speak?"

Olav shook his head. "You have to listen. But that's enough for now. You'll have to come back another day."

Harry squeezed his father's left hand with his right and stood up. "Is it OK if I stay in Oppsal for a few days?"

"Thanks for the offer. I didn't want to hassle you, but the house does need to be looked after."

Harry dropped his plan to tell him that the power was going to be cut off in his flat.

Olav rang a bell and a young smiling nurse came in and used his father's first name in an innocent, flirty way. And Harry noted how his father deepened his voice as he explained that Harry needed the suitcase containing the keys. He saw the way the sick man in the bed tried to fluff his plumage for her. And for some reason it didn't seem pathetic; it was the way it should be.

In parting, his father repeated: "Everything she asked me." And whispered: "Except one thing."

Leading him to the storage room, the nurse told Harry the doctor wanted to have a couple of words with him. After locating the keys in the suitcase, Harry knocked on the door the nurse had indicated.

The doctor nodded toward a seat, leaned back in his swivel chair and pressed his fingertips together. "Good thing you came home. We had been trying to get hold of you."

"I know."

"The cancer has spread."

Harry nodded. Someone had once told him that that was a cancer cell's function: to spread.

The doctor studied him, as though considering his next move.

"OK," Harry said.

"OK?"

"OK, I'm ready to hear the rest."

"We don't usually say how much time a person has left. The errors of judgment and the psychological strain that ensue are too great for that. However, in this case, I think it is appropriate to tell you he is already living on borrowed time."

Harry nodded. Gazed out the window. Fog was still as thick down below.

"Do you have a cell number we can contact you on should anything happen?"

Harry shook his head. Was that a siren he heard down in the fog?

"Anyone you know who can pass on a message?"

Harry shook his head again. "Not a problem. I'll call in and visit him every day. OK?"

The doctor nodded and watched Harry get up and stride out.

It was nine by the time Harry got to the Frogner pool. The whole of Frogner Park measured about 120 acres, but since the public pool constituted a small fraction of this and, furthermore, was fenced in, the police had an easy job cordoning off the crime scene; they had simply run a tape around the entire fence and put a guard in the ticket office. The kettle of crime-correspondent vultures was in flight and they swooped in, then stood cackling outside the gate wondering when they would gain access to the cadaver. For Christ's sake, this was a bona-fide MP—didn't the public have a right to photos of such a prominent corpse?

Harry bought an americano at Kaffepikene. They had chairs and tables on the pavement throughout February, and Harry took a seat, lit a cigarette and watched the flock in front of the ticket booth.

A man sat down on the chair next to him.

"Harry Hole himself. Where have you been?"

Harry looked up. Roger Gjendem, the **Aftenposten** crime correspondent, lit a cigarette and gestured toward Frogner Park. "At last Marit Olsen gets what she wants. By eight this evening she'll be a celebrity. Hanging herself from the diving tower? Good career move." He turned to Harry and grimaced. "What happened to your jaw? You look dreadful."

Harry didn't answer. Just sipped his coffee and said nothing to alleviate the embarrassing silence, in the futile hope that the journalist would get that he was not desirable company. From the bank of fog above them came the noise of whirring rotors. Roger Gjendem peered up.

"Gotta be **Verdens Gang.** Typical of that tabloid to hire a helicopter. Hope the fog doesn't lift."

"Mm. Better that no one gets photos than **VG** does?"

"Right. What do you know?"

"I'm sure less than you," said Harry. "The body was found by one of the nightwatchmen at dawn, and he called the police right away. And you?"

"Head torn off. Woman jumped from the top of the tower with a rope around her neck, it seems. And she was pretty hefty, as you know. Over two hundred pounds.

"They've found threads that may match her tracksuit on the part of the fence where they figure she entered. They didn't find any other clues, so they think she was alone."

Harry inhaled the cigarette smoke. **Head torn off.** They spoke the way they wrote, these journalists, the inverted pyramid, as they called it: the most important information first.

"Happened in the early hours, I suppose?" Harry fished.

"Or in the evening. According to Marit Olsen's husband, she left home at a quarter to ten to go jogging."

"Late for a jog."

"Must have been when she usually jogged. Liked having the park to herself."

"Mm."

"By the way, I tried to track down the nightwatch-man who found her."

"Why?"

Gjendem gave Harry a surprised look. "To get a firsthand account, of course."

"Of course," Harry said, sucking on his cigarette.

"But he seems to have gone into hiding. He's not here or at home. Must be in shock, poor fella."

"Well, it's not the first time he's found bodies in the pool. I assume the detective leading the investigation has seen to it that you can't lay your hands on him."

"What do you mean, it's not the first time?"

Harry shrugged. "I've been called here two or three times before. Kids sneaking in during the night. One time it was suicide, another an accident. Four drunken friends on their way home from a party wanted to play, see who dared to stand closest to the edge of the diving board. The boy who won the dare was nineteen. The oldest was his brother."

"Damn," Gjendem said dutifully.

Harry checked his watch as if he had to hurry off.

"Must have been some strength in that rope," Gjendem said. "Head torn off. Ever heard the like?"

"Tom Ketchum," said Harry, draining the rest of his coffee in one swig and getting up.

"Ketchup?"

"Ketchum. Hole-in-the-Wall Gang. Hanged in New Mexico Territory in 1901. Standard gallows—they just used too much rope."

"Oh. How much?"

"Just over six feet."

"Not more? He must have been a fat lump."

"Nope. Tells you how easy it is to lose your head, doesn't it."

Gjendem shouted something after him, but Harry didn't catch it. He crossed the parking lot north of the pool, continued across the grass and took a left over the bridge to the main gate. The fence was more than eight feet high all the way around. **Over two hundred pounds.** Marit Olsen might have tried, but she did not get over the pool fence unaided.

On the other side of the bridge, Harry turned left so that he could approach the pool area from the opposite angle. He stepped over the orange police tape and stopped at the top of the slope by a shrub. Harry had forgotten an alarming amount over recent years. But the cases stuck. He could still remember the names of the four boys on the diving tower. The older brother's distant eyes as he answered Harry's questions in a monotone. And the hand pointing to the place where they had gotten in.

Harry chose his steps carefully, not wishing to destroy possible clues, and bent the shrub to one side. Oslo's park-maintenance people planned well in advance. If they planned at all. The tear in the fence was still there.

Harry crouched down and studied the jagged edges of the tear. He could see dark threads. Someone who had not sneaked in, but had forced her way through here. Or was pushed. He looked for other evidence. From the top of the tear hung a long black piece of wool. The tear was so high that the person must have been standing upright to touch the fence at that point. The head. Wool made sense, a woolen hat. Had Marit Olsen been wearing a woolen hat? According to Roger Gjendem, Marit Olsen had left home at a quarter to ten to jog in the park. As usual, he had surmised.

Harry tried to visualize it. He imagined an abnormally mild evening in the park. He saw a large, sweaty woman jogging. He didn't see a woolen hat. He couldn't see anyone else wearing a woolen hat, either. Not because it was cold, at any rate. But perhaps so as not to be seen or recognized. Black wool. A face mask, maybe.

He stepped out of the bushes with care.

He hadn't heard them coming.

One man held a pistol—probably a Steyr—Austrian, semiautomatic. It was pointed at Harry. The man behind it had blond hair and an open mouth with a powerful underbite; now, when he emitted a grunt of a laugh, Harry remembered the nickname belonging to Truls Berntsen from Kripos: Beavis. As in **Beavis and Butt-Head.**

The second man was short and unusually bowlegged and had his hands in the pockets of a coat that Harry knew concealed a gun and an ID card bearing a Finnish-sounding name. But it was the third man, the one in an elegant gray trench coat, who attracted Harry's attention. He stood to the side of the other two, but there was something about the gunman and the Finn's body language, the way they partly addressed Harry, partly this man. As though they were an extension of him, as though this man were **actually** holding the gun. What struck Harry about the man was not his almost-feminine good looks. Nor that his eyelashes were so clearly visible above and below his eyes, incurring suspicions he used makeup. Nor the nose, the chin, the fine shape of his cheeks. Nor that his hair was thick, dark, gray, elegantly cut and a great deal longer than was standard for the force. Nor the many tiny colorless blemishes in the suntanned skin that made him look as if he had been exposed to acid rain. No, what struck Harry was the hatred. The hatred in the eyes that bored into him, a hatred so fierce that Harry seemed to sense it physically, as something white and hard.

The man was cleaning his teeth with a toothpick. His voice was higher and softer than Harry would have imagined. "You've trespassed into territory that has been cordoned off for an investigation, Hole."

"An incontrovertible fact," Harry said, looking around him.

"Why?"

Harry eyed the man, quietly rejecting one potential answer after the other until he realized he simply didn't have one.

"Since you appear to know me," Harry said, "who do I have the pleasure of meeting?"

"I doubt it will be much of a pleasure for either of us, Hole. So I suggest you leave the area now and never show your face near a Kripos crime scene again. Is that understood?"

"Well, received but not completely understood. What about if I can help the police in the form of a tip about how Marit Olsen—"

"The only help you've given the police," the gentle voice interrupted, "has been to besmirch its reputation. In my book, you're a drunk, a lawbreaker and vermin, Hole. So my advice to you is this: Crawl back under the stone you came from before someone crushes you with his heel."

Harry looked at the man, and his gut instinct and his brain concurred: Take it. Withdraw. You have no ammunition to counter with. Be smart.

And he really wished he were smart; he would really have appreciated that quality. Harry took out his pack of cigarettes.

"And that someone would be you, would it, Bellman? You are Bellman, aren't you? The genius who sent the sauna ape after me?" Harry nodded toward the Finn. "Judging from that attempt, I doubt you would be able to crush . . . er . . . er . . ." Harry struggled feverishly to remember the analogy, but it wouldn't come. Fucking jet lag.

Bellman interceded. "Get lost now, Hole." The POB jerked his thumb behind him. "Come on. Scram."

"I—" Harry began.

"That's it," Bellman said with a broad smile. "You're under arrest, Hole."

"What?"

"You've been told three times to vacate the crime scene and you haven't complied. Hands behind your back."

"Now listen here!" Harry snarled with a niggling feeling that he was a very predictable rat caught in a laboratory maze. "I just want—"

Berntsen, alias Beavis, jogged his arm, knocking the cigarette out of his mouth and onto the wet ground. Harry bent down to pick it up, but got Jussi's boot in his backside and toppled forward. He banged his head on the ground and tasted earth and bile. And heard Bellman's soft voice in his ear.

"Resisting arrest, Hole? I told you to put your hands behind your back, didn't I? Told you to put them here . . ."

Bellman placed his hand lightly on Harry's bottom. Harry breathed hard through his nose without moving. He knew exactly what Bellman was after. Assault on a police officer. Two witnesses. Paragraph 127. Sentence: five years. Game over. And even though this was already as clear as day to Harry, he knew that Bellman would get what he wanted before long. So he concentrated on something else, excluded Beavis's grunted laugh and Bellman's cologne from his mind. He thought about her. About Rakel. He put his hands behind his back on top of Bellman's hand and turned his head. Now the wind had blown away the fog hanging over them and he could see the slim white diving tower outlined against the gray sky. Something was dangling aloft from the platform, a rope, perhaps.

The handcuffs clicked gently into place.

Bellman stood in the parking lot by Middelthunsgate as they drove away. The wind was tugging gently at his coat.

The lockup officer was reading the newspaper when he noticed the three men in front of the counter.

"Hi, Tore," Harry said. "Got a nonsmoker with a view?"

"Hi, Harry. Long time no see." The officer picked up a key from the cupboard behind him and passed it to Harry. "Honeymoon suite."

Harry saw the confusion on Tore's face when Beavis leaned forward, grabbed the key and snarled, "He's the prisoner, you idiot."

Harry grimaced an apology to Tore as Jussi frisked him and turned up some keys and a wallet.

"Would you mind calling Gunnar Hagen, Tore? He—"

Jussi snatched at the handcuffs, cutting into Harry's skin, and Harry tumbled backward after the two men, heading for lockup.

Once they had locked him in the eight-by-five-foot cell, Jussi went back to Tore to sign the papers while Beavis stood outside the barred door, peering in at Harry. Harry could see he had something on his chest and waited. And at last it came, in a voice shaking with suppressed fury.

"How does it feel, eh? You being such a fucking hotshot, catching two serial killers, being on TV and all that? And here you are now, looking at bars from the inside, eh?"

"What are you so angry about, Beavis?" Harry asked softly, and he closed his eyes. He could feel the swell in his body as if he had just come ashore after a long voyage.

"I'm not angry. But as far as punks shooting good policemen are concerned, I'm furious with them."

"Three mistakes in one sentence," Harry said, lying down on the cell bed. "First of all, it's 'is,' not 'are'; second, Inspector Waaler was not a good policeman and third, I didn't shoot him. I pulled off his arm. Here, up by the shoulder." Harry demonstrated.

Beavis's mouth opened and shut, but nothing emerged.

Harry closed his eyes again.

13

Office

The next time Harry opened his eyes, he had been lying in the cell for two hours, and Gunnar Hagen was standing outside struggling to open the door with the key.

"Sorry, Harry—I was in a meeting."

"Suited me fine, boss," Harry said, stretching on the bed with a yawn. "Am I being released?"

"I spoke to the police lawyer, who said it was OK. Custody is detention, not a punishment. I heard two Kripos men brought you in. What happened?"

"I'm hoping you can tell me."

"I can tell you?"

"Ever since I landed in Oslo I've been followed by Kripos."

"Kripos?"

Harry sat up and ran a hand through the brushlike bristles on his head. "They tracked me to Rikshospital. They arrested me on a formality. What's going on, boss?"

Hagen raised his chin and stroked the skin over his larynx. "Hell, I should have anticipated this."

"Anticipated what?"

"That it would leak out that we were trying to run you to earth. That Bellman would try to stop us."

"A few main clauses would be nice."

"It's pretty complicated, as I told you. It's all about budget cuts and redundancies in the force. About jurisdiction. The old fight, Crime Squad versus Kripos. Whether there are enough resources for two specialist branches with parallel expertise in a small country. The discussion flared up when Kripos got a new second in command, one Mikael Bellman."

"Tell me about him."

"Bellman? Police college, brief period of service in Norway before washing up in Europol in The Hague. Came back to Kripos a wonder boy, ready to move onward and upward. Nothing but grief from day one, when he wanted to employ an ex-colleague from Interpol, a foreigner."

"Not Finnish, by any chance?"

Hagen nodded. "Jussi Kolkka. Police training in Finland, but has none of the formal qualifications required for police status in Norway. The trade union went ballistic. The solution was, of course, that Kolkka would be temporarily employed on an exchange. Bellman's next initiative was to make it clear that the rules should be interpreted in such a way that on bigger murder investigations, Kripos would decide whether it was their case or the police district's, not vice versa."

"And?"

"And that is quite unacceptable, goes without saying. We have the country's largest murder unit here at Police HQ, we decide which cases we take within the Oslo district, what we need help with and where we request Kripos to take control. Kripos was established to offer their know-how to police districts handling murder cases, but Bellman has, at the drop of a hat, endowed the department with his emperor status. The Ministry of Justice was drawn into the matter. And they soon saw their chance to do what we have managed to keep a lid on for so long: to centralize murder investigations so that there is one headquarters. They don't give two hoots about our arguments concerning the dangers of standardization and inbreeding, the importance of local knowledge and the spread of skills, recruitment and—"

"Thank you—you're preaching to the converted."

Hagen held up a hand. "Fine, but the Ministry of Justice is working now on an appointment . . ."

"And . . . ?"

"They say they're going to be pragmatic. It's all about

exploiting scarce resources in the most cost-effective way. If Kripos can show that they achieve their best results by being unencumbered by police districts—"

"Then all the power goes to Kripos HQ in Bryn," Harry said. "Big office for Bellman and bye-bye, Crime Squad."

Hagen hunched his shoulders. "Something of that nature. When Charlotte Lolles was found dead behind the Datsun and we saw the similarities with the woman murdered in the cellar of the new building, there was a head-on collision. Kripos said that even though the bodies were found in Oslo, a double murder is a matter for Kripos, not the Oslo Police District, and started their own independent investigation. They've realized that the battle for the ministry's support will stand or fall on this case."

"So it's just a question of solving the case before Kripos?"

"As I said, it's complicated. Kripos refuses to share info with us even though they've made no headway. Instead they went to the ministry. The chief constable here received a call to say that the ministry **would like to see** Kripos allowed to manage this case until they've made up their mind about how to allocate areas of responsibility in the future."

Harry shook his head slowly. "It's beginning to sink in. You got desperate . . ."

"I wouldn't use that word."

"Desperate enough to dig up the old serial-killer hunter Hole. An outsider no longer on the payroll, who could investigate the matter on the q.t. That was why I couldn't say anything to anyone."

Hagen sighed. "Bellman found out anyway, obviously. And stuck a tail on you."

"To see whether you were complying with the ministry's request. To catch me in flagrante delicto, reading old reports or questioning old witnesses."

"Or even more effective: to disqualify you from the game. Bellman knows one single mistake would be enough to have you suspended, one single beer while on duty, one single breach of service rules."

"Mm. Or resisting arrest. He's thinking of taking the case further, the prick."

"I'll talk to him. He'll drop it when I tell him you don't want the case anyway. We don't dump police officers in the shit when there's no point." Hagen glanced at his watch. "I've got work waiting for me. Let's get you out."

They walked out of lockup and across the parking lot and stopped at the entrance to Police HQ, a tower of concrete and steel presiding over the area. Beside them, attached to Police HQ by an underground culvert, stood the old gray walls of Botsen, Oslo District Prison. Beneath them, Grønland stretched down to the fjord and harbor. The building façades were winter-pale and filthy, as though ash had rained down on them. The cranes by the harbor stood like gallows outlined against the sky.

"Not a pretty sight, eh?"

"No," Harry said, breathing in.

"But there's something about this town, nonetheless."

Harry nodded. "There is that."

They stood there for a while, rocking back on their heels, hands in pockets.

"Chilly," Harry said.

"Not really."

"S'pose not, but my thermostat is still set to Hong Kong temperatures."

"I see."

"You've got a cup of coffee waiting for you upstairs?" Harry motioned to the sixth floor. "Or was it work? The Marit Olsen case?"

Hagen didn't answer.

"Mm," Harry said. "So Bellman and Kripos have that, too."

Harry received the odd measured nod on his way through the corridors of the red zone on the sixth floor. He might have been a legend in the building, but he had never been a popular man.

They passed the office door where someone had glued the piece of paper saying I SEE DEAD PEOPLE.

Hagen cleared his throat. "I had to let Magnus Skarre take over your office. Everywhere else is bursting at the seams."

"No problem," Harry said.

They each took a paper cup of the infamous percolated coffee from the kitchenette.

Inside Hagen's office Harry settled into the chair facing the POB's desk, where he had sat so many times.

"You've still got it, I see," Harry said, pointing with his head to the memento on the desk that, at first sight, resembled a white exclamation mark. It was a stuffed little finger. Harry knew it had once belonged to a Japanese Second World War commander. In retreat, the commander had cut off his finger in front of his men to apologize for not being able to return and pick up their dead. Hagen loved to use the story when he was teaching middle management about leadership.

"And you still haven't." Hagen nodded toward the hand, minus middle finger, Harry was using to hold the paper cup.

Harry conceded the point and drank. The coffee hadn't changed, either. Liquefied asphalt.

Harry grimaced. "I need a team of three."

Hagen drank slowly and put down the cup. "Not more?"

"You always ask that. You know I don't work with large teams of detectives."

"In that case I won't complain. Fewer people means less chance of Kripos and the Ministry of Justice catching wind of our investigations into the double murder."

"Triple murder," Harry said with a yawn.

"Hold on. We don't know if Marit Olsen—"

"Woman alone at night, abducted, murdered in an unconventional manner. The third time in little old

Oslo. Triple. Believe me. But however many there are of us, you can take it from me that we will take damn good care that our paths don't cross those of Kripos."

"Yes," Hagen said. "I do know that. That's why it's a condition that if the investigation were to be brought to light, it has nothing to do with Crime Squad."

Harry closed his eyes.

Hagen went on. "Of course we will regret that some of our employees have been involved, but make it clear that this is something the notorious maverick Harry Hole initiated on his own, without the knowledge of the unit head. And you will confirm that version of events."

Harry opened his eyes again and stared at Hagen.

Hagen met his stare. "Any questions?"

"Yes."

"Shoot."

"Where's the leak?"

"Pardon?"

"Who's informing Bellman?"

Hagen rolled his shoulders. "I don't have the impression that he has any systematic access to what we're doing. He could have caught a sniff of your return in lots of places."

"I know Magnus Skarre has a habit of talking anywhere and anyhow."

"Don't ask me any more questions, Harry."

"OK. Where should we set up shop?"

"Right. Right." Gunnar Hagen nodded several times as if that were something they had already discussed. "As far as an office is concerned . . ."

"Yes?"

"As I said, the place is full to bursting, so we'll have to find somewhere outside, but not too far away."

"Fine. Where, then?"

Hagen looked out of the window. At the gray walls of Botsen.

"You're kidding," Harry said.

14

Recruitment

Bjørn Holm entered the conference room at Krimteknisk in the Bryn district of Oslo. Outside the windows, the sun was relinquishing its grip on the house fronts and casting the town into afternoon gloom. The parking lot was packed, and in front of the entrance to Kripos, across the road, there was a white minivan with a satellite dish on the roof and the Norwegian Broadcasting Corporation logo on its side.

The only person in the room was his boss, Beate Lønn, an unusually pale, petite and quiet-mannered woman. Had one not known any better, one might have thought a person like this would have problems leading a group of experienced, professional, self-aware, always quirky and seldom conflict-shy forensics officers. Had one known better, one would have realized she was the only person who could deal with them. Not primarily because they respected the fact that she stood erect and proud despite losing two policemen to the eternity shift, first her father and later the father of her child. But because, in their group, she was the best, and radiated such unimpeachability, integrity and gravity that when Beate Lønn whispered an order with downcast gaze and flushed cheeks, it was carried out on the spot. So Bjørn Holm had come as soon as he was informed.

She was sitting in a chair drawn up close to the TV monitor.

"They're recording live from the press conference," she said without turning. "Take a seat."

Holm immediately recognized the people on the screen. How strange it was, it struck him, to be watching signals that had traveled thousands of miles out into space and back, just to show him what was happening right now on the opposite side of the street.

Beate Lønn turned up the volume.

"You have understood correctly," said Mikael Bellman, leaning toward the microphone on the table in front of him. "For the present we have neither leads nor suspects. And to repeat myself once again: We have not ruled out the possibility of suicide."

"But you said—" began a voice from the body of journalists present.

Bellman cut her off. "I said we regard the death as **suspicious.** I am sure you're familiar with the terminology. If not, you should . . ." He left the end of the sentence hanging in the air and pointed to a person behind the camera.

"**Stavanger Aftenblad**," came the slow bleat of the Rogaland dialect. "Do the police see a connection between this death and the two in—"

"No! If you'd been following, you would have heard me say that we **do not rule out** a connection."

"I caught that," continued the slow, imperturbable dialect. "But those of us here are more interested in what you think rather than what you **don't rule out**."

Bjørn Holm could see Bellman giving the man the evil eye as impatience strained at the corners of his mouth. A uniformed woman officer at Bellman's side placed her hand over the microphone, leaned in to him and whispered something. The POB's face darkened.

"Mikael Bellman is getting a crash course in how to deal with the media," said Bjørn Holm. "Lesson one, stroke the ones with hair, especially the provincial newspapers."

"He's new to the job," Beate Lønn said. "He'll learn."

"Think so?"

"Yes. Bellman's the type to learn."

"Humility's hard to learn, I've heard."

"Genuine humility, that's true. But to grovel when it suits you is basic to modern communication. That's what Ninni's telling him. And Bellman's smart enough to appreciate that."

On-screen, Bellman coughed, forced an almost boyish smile and leaned in to the microphone. "I apologize if I sounded a bit brusque, but it's been a long day for all of us, and I hope you understand that we are simply impatient to get back to the investigation of this tragic case. We have to finish here, but if any of you have any further questions, please direct them to Ninni, and I promise I will try to return to you later this evening. Before the deadline. Is that OK?"

"What did I say?" Beate laughed triumphantly.

"A star is born," Bjørn said.

The picture dissolved and Beate Lønn turned. "Harry called. He wants me to hand you over."

"Me?" said Bjørn Holm. "To do what?"

"You know very well what. I heard you were with Gunnar Hagen at the airport when Harry arrived."

"Whoops." Holm smiled, revealing both top and bottom sets of teeth.

"I assume Hagen wanted to use you in Operation Persuasion since he knew you were one of the few people Harry liked working with."

"We never got that far, and Harry turned down the job."

"But now it seems he has changed his mind."

"Really? What made him do that?"

"He didn't say. He just said he thought it was right to go through me."

"Sure. You're the boss here."

"You can take nothing for granted where Harry is concerned. I know him pretty well, as you're aware."

Holm nodded. He was aware. Knew Jack Halvorsen, Beate's partner and the soon-to-be father of their child, had been killed while working for Harry. One freezing cold winter's day, in broad daylight, in Grünerløkka, stabbed in the chest. Holm had arrived right afterward. Hot blood soaking down into the blue ice. A policeman's death. No one had blamed Harry. Apart from Harry, that is.

He scratched his sideburns. "So what did you say?"

Beate took a deep breath and watched the journalists and photographers hurrying out of the Kripos building. "The same as I'm going to tell you now. The Ministry of Justice has let it be known that Kripos has priority, and accordingly there is no chance that I can pass on forensics officers to anyone other than Bellman for this case."

"But?"

Beate Lønn drummed a Bic pen on the table, hard. "But there are other cases besides this double murder."

"Triple murder," Holm said, and after a sharp look from Beate, he added, "believe me."

"I don't know exactly what Inspector Hole is investigating, but it is definitely not any of these murder cases. He and I are totally agreed on that," Beate said. "And you are thereby transferred to that case or those cases—of which I know nothing. For two weeks. Copy of first report on whatever you do to be on my desk five working days from now. Understood?"

Inwardly, Kaja Solness was beaming like a sun and felt an almost irresistible desire to do a couple of spins in her swivel chair.

"If Hagen says OK, of course I'll join you," she said, trying to contain herself, but she could hear the exultation in her voice.

"Hagen says OK," said the man leaning against the door frame with his arm over his head, forming a diagonal in her doorway. "So it's just Holm, you and me. And the case we're working on is confidential. We start tomorrow. Meet at seven in my office."

"Er . . . seven?"

"**Sieben.** Seven. Oh-seven-hundred hours."

"I see. Which office?"

The man grinned and explained.

She looked at him in disbelief. "We've got an office in the prison?"

The diagonal in the doorway relaxed. "Meet up, all systems go. Questions?"

Kaja had several, but Harry had already left.

The dream has begun to appear in the daytime, too, now. A long way off I can still hear the band playing "Love Hurts." I notice a few boys standing around us, but they don't move in. Good. As for me, I'm looking at her. See what you've done, I try to say. Look at him now. Do you still want him? My God, how I hate her, how I want to tear the knife out of my mouth and stick it in her, stab holes in her, see it gush out: blood, guts, the lie, the stupidity, her idiotic self-righteousness. Someone should show her how ugly she is on the inside.

I saw the press conference on TV. Incompetent oafs! No clues. No suspects! The golden first forty-eight hours, the sands are running out, hurry, hurry. What do you want me to do? Write it on the wall in blood?

It's you who are allowing this killing to go on.

The letter is finished.

Hurry.

15

Strobe Lights

Stine eyed the boy who had just spoken to her. He had a beard, blond hair and a woolen hat. Indoors. And this was no indoor hat, but a thick hat to keep your ears warm. A snowboarder? Anyway, when she took a closer look, this was no boy, but a man. Over thirty. At any rate, there were white wrinkles in the brown skin.

"So?" she shouted over the music booming out through the stereo system at Krabbe. The recently opened restaurant had proclaimed it was the new hangout for Stavanger's young avant-garde musicians, filmmakers and writers, of whom there were quite a few in this otherwise business-oriented, dollar-counting oil town. It would turn out that the in-crowd had not yet decided whether Krabbe deserved their favor or not. As indeed Stine had not yet decided whether this boy-man deserved hers.

"It's just I think you should let me tell you about it," he said with a confident smile, looking at her with a pair of eyes that seemed much too pale blue to her. But perhaps that was the lighting in here? Strobe lights? Was that cool? Time would tell. He turned the beer glass in his hand and leaned back against the bar so that she had to lean forward if she wanted to hear what he was saying, but she didn't fall for that one. He was wearing a thick down jacket, yet there was not a drop of sweat to be seen on his face under that ridiculous hat. Or was that cool?

"There are very few people who've biked through the delta district of Burma and returned sufficiently alive to tell the tale," he said.

Sufficiently alive. A talker, then. She liked that up to a point. He looked like someone. Some American action hero from an old film or a TV show from the eighties.

"I promised myself that if I got back to Stavanger I would go out, buy myself a beer and accost the most attractive girl I could see and say what I am saying now." He thrust out his arms and wore a big white smile. "I think you're the girl by the pagoda."

"What?"

"Rudyard Kipling, missy. You're the girl waiting for the English soldier by the old Moulmein pagoda. So what do you say? Will you join me and walk barefoot on the marble in Shwedagon? Eat cobra meat in Bago? Sleep till the Muslims' call to prayers in Rangoon and wake to the Buddhists' in Mandalay?"

He breathed in. She bent forward. "So I'm the most attractive girl in here, am I?"

He looked around. "No, but you've got the biggest boobs. You're good-looking, but the competition is too fierce for you to be the best-looking one. Shall we go?"

She laughed and shook her head. Didn't know whether he was fun or just crazy.

"I'm with some girls. You can try that trick on someone else."

"Elias."

"What?"

"You were wondering what my name was. In case we meet again. And my name's Elias. Skog. You'll forget that, but you'll remember Elias. And we'll meet again. Before you imagine, actually."

She slanted her head. "Oh, yes?"

Then he drained his glass, put it on the bar, smiled at her and left.

"Who was he?"

It was Mathilde.

"Don't know," Stine said. "He was nice. But weird. Talked like he came from eastern Norway."

"Weird?"

"There was something odd about his eyes. And teeth. Are there strobe lights in here?"

"Strobe lights?"

Stine laughed. "No, it's that toothpaste-colored solarium light. Makes your face look like a zombie's."

Mathilde shook her head. "You need a drink. Come on."

Stine turned toward the exit as she followed. She thought she had seen a face against a pane, but no one was there.

16

Speed King

It was nine o'clock at night, and Harry was walking through downtown Oslo. He had spent the morning lugging chairs and tables into the new office. In the afternoon he had gone up to Rikshospital, but his father was undergoing some tests. So he had doubled back, copied reports, made a few calls, booked a ticket to Bergen, popped down to the shops and bought a SIM card the size of a cigarette end.

Harry strode out. He had always enjoyed moving from east to west in this compact town, seeing the gradual but obvious changes in people, fashion, ethnicity, architecture, shops, cafés and bars. He stopped into a McDonald's, had a hamburger, stuffed three straws in his coat pocket and continued his journey.

Half an hour after standing in the ghettolike

Pakistani Grønland, he found himself in the neat, slightly sterile and very white West End land. Kaja Solness's address was on Lyder Sagens Gate and turned out to be one of those large old timber houses that attracted a long line of Oslo-ites on the rare occasions one of them was for sale. Not to buy—very few could afford that—but to see, dream about and receive confirmation that Fagerborg really was what it purported to be: a neighborhood where the rich were not too rich, the money was not too new and no one had a swimming pool, electric garage doors or any other vulgar modern invention. For the Fagerborger, quite literally the "fine burghers," did as they always had done here. In the summer they sat under apple trees in their large shaded gardens on the garden furniture that was as old, impractically large and stained black as the houses from which it had been carried. And when it was transported back and the days became shorter, candles were lit behind the leaded windows. On Lyder Sagens Gate there was a Yuletide atmosphere from October through March.

The front gate gave a screech so loud that Harry hoped it made any need for a dog superfluous. The gravel crunched beneath his boots. He had been as happy as a child to be reunited with his boots when he found them in the closet, but now they were drenched right through.

He went up the porch steps and pressed the bell. There was no nameplate beside it.

In front of the door was a pair of pretty ladies'

shoes and a pair of men's shoes. Size twelve, Harry estimated. Kaja's husband was big, they seemed to suggest. For, naturally, she had a husband; he didn't know why he had thought any differently. Because he had, hadn't he? It was of no consequence. The door opened.

"Harry?" She was wearing an open and much too large woolen jacket, faded jeans and felt slippers that were so old Harry could swear they had liver spots. No makeup. Just a surprised smile. Nevertheless she seemed to have been expecting him. Expected that he would like to see her this way. Of course, he had already seen it in her eyes in Hong Kong, the fascination so many women have for any man with a reputation, good or bad. Though he had not made a comprehensive analysis of every single thought that had led him to this door. Just as well he had saved himself the effort. Size twelve shoes. Or twelve and a half.

"I got your address from Hagen," Harry said. "You live within walking distance of my flat so I thought I would drop by instead of calling."

She smirked. "You don't have a cell?"

"Wrong." Harry produced a red phone from his pocket. "I was given this by Hagen, but I've already forgotten the PIN. Am I disturbing you?"

"No, no." She opened the door wide and Harry stepped in.

It was pathetic, but his heart had been beating a bit faster while he waited for her. Fifteen years ago that would have annoyed him, but he had resigned himself and accepted the banal fact that a woman's beauty would always have this modicum of power over him.

"I'm making coffee. Would you like some?"

They had moved into the living room. The walls were covered with pictures and the shelves had so many books he doubted she could have read them all herself. The room had a distinctly masculine character. Large, angular furniture, a globe, a hookah, vinyl records on more shelves, maps and photographs of high, snow-covered mountains on the walls. Harry concluded that he was a great deal older than she was. A TV was on, but without the volume.

"Marit Olsen is the main item on all the news broadcasts," Kaja said, lifting the remote and switching off the TV. "Two of the opposition leaders stood up and demanded quick results. They said the government had been systematically dismantling the police force. Kripos won't get much peace for the next few days."

"Yes please to the coffee," Harry said, and Kaja scurried into the kitchen.

He sat on the sofa. A John Fante book lay facedown on the coffee table, beside a pair of ladies' reading glasses. Next to it were photos of the Frogner pool. Not of the crime scene itself, but of the people who had gathered outside the tape to rubberneck. Harry gave a grunt of satisfaction. Not only because she had taken work home, but because crime scene officers continued to take these photos. It had been Harry who insisted they always photograph the crowd. It was something he had learned at the FBI course about serial killings; the killer returning to the scene of a crime was no myth. The King brothers in San Antonio and the Kmart man had been arrested precisely because they couldn't restrain themselves from returning to admire their handiwork, to see all the commotion they had caused, to feel how invulnerable they were. The photographers at Krimteknisk called it Hole's Sixth Commandment. And, yes, there were nine other commandments. Harry riffled through the photos.

"You don't take milk, do you?" Kaja shouted from the kitchen.

"Yes."

"Do you? At Heathrow—"

"I mean yes, as in yes, you're right, I don't take milk."

"Aha. You've gone over to the Cantonese system."

"What?"

"You've stopped using double negatives. Cantonese is more logical. You like logical."

"Is that right? About Cantonese?"

"I don't know." She laughed from the kitchen. "I'm just trying to sound clever."

Harry could see that the photographer had been discreet; he'd shot from hip height, no flash. The spectators' attention was directed toward the diving tower. Dull eyes, half-open mouths, as if they were bored of waiting for a glimpse of something dreadful, something for their albums, something with which they could scare the neighbors out of their wits. A man holding a cell phone up in the air; he was definitely taking photos. Harry took the magnifying glass from the pile of reports and scrutinized their faces one by one. He didn't know what he was looking for. His brain was empty; it was the best way, so as not to miss whatever might be there.

"Can you see anything?" She had taken up a position behind his chair and bent down to see. He caught a mild fragrance of lavender soap, the same he had smelled on the plane when she had fallen asleep on his shoulder.

"Mm. Do you think there's anything to see here?" he asked, taking the coffee mug.

"No."

"So why did you bring the photos home?"

"Because ninety-five percent of all police work is searching in the wrong place."

She had just quoted Harry's Third Commandment.

"And you have to learn to enjoy the ninety-five percent, too. Otherwise you'll go mad."

Fourth Commandment.

"And the reports?" Harry asked.

"All we have are the reports on the murders of Borgny and Charlotte, and there's nothing in them. No forensic leads, no accounts of unusual activities. No tip-offs about bitter enemies, jealous lovers, greedy heirs, deranged stalkers, impatient drug dealers or other creditors. In short—"

"No leads, no apparent motives, no murder weapons. I would have liked to start interviewing people in the Marit Olsen case, but, as you know, we're not working on it."

Kaja smiled. "Of course not. By the way, I spoke to a political journalist from **VG** today. He said none of the journalists at Stortinget knew anything about Marit Olsen being depressed or having personal crises or suicidal thoughts. Or enemies, in her professional or her private life."

"Mm."

Harry skimmed the row of spectators' faces. A woman with sleepwalker eyes and a child on her arm.

"What do these people want?" Behind them: the back of a man leaving. Down jacket, woolen hat. "To be shocked. Shaken. Entertained. Purified . . ."

"Incredible."

"Mm. And so you're reading John Fante. You like older things, do you?" He nodded toward the room, the house. And he meant the room, the house. But reckoned she would drop in a comment about the husband if he was a lot older than her, as Harry guessed he was.

She looked at him with enthusiasm. "Have you read Fante?"

"When I was young and was going through my Bukowski period I read one whose title eludes me. I bought them mostly because Charles Bukowski was an ardent fan." He made a show of checking his watch. "Whoops, time to go home."

Kaja looked at him in amazement and then at the untouched cup of coffee.

"Jet lag." Harry smiled, getting to his feet. "We can talk tomorrow at the meeting."

"Of course."

Harry patted his trouser pocket. "By the way, I've run out of cigarettes. The tax-free Camel cigarettes you took through customs for me . . ."

"Just a minute." She smiled.

When she came back with the carton, Harry was standing in the hall, with his jacket and boots already on.

"Thank you," he said, taking out one of the packs and opening it.

When he was outside on the steps, she leaned against the door frame. "Perhaps I shouldn't say this, but I have a feeling that this was some kind of test."

"Test?" Harry said, lighting a cigarette.

"I won't ask what the test was for, but did I pass?"

Harry chuckled. "It was just this." He walked down the steps waving the carton. "Oh-seven-hundred hours."

Harry let himself into his flat. Pressed the light switch and established that the electricity had not been disconnected. Took off his coat, went into the sitting room, put on Deep Purple, his favorite band in the category of can't-help-being-funny-but-brilliant-anyway. "Speed King." Ian Paice on drums. He sat down on the sofa and pressed his fingertips against his forehead. The dogs were yanking at the chains. Howling, snarling, barking, their teeth tearing at his innards. If he let them loose, there would be no way back. Not this time. Before, there had always been good enough reasons to stop drinking again. Rakel, Oleg, the job, perhaps even

Dad. He didn't have any of them anymore. It couldn't happen. Not with alcohol. So he had to have an alternative intoxicant. He could control intoxication. Thank you, Kaja. Was he ashamed? Of course he was. But pride was a luxury he couldn't always afford.

He took the bottom pack out of the carton. You could hardly see that the seal on the pack had been broken. It was a fact that women like Kaja were never checked at customs. He opened the pack and pulled out the tinfoil. Unfolded it and looked at the brown ball. Inhaled the sweet smell.

Then he set about his preparations.

Harry had seen all possible ways of smoking opium, everything from the complicated, ritual procedures of opium dens, which were nothing less than Chinese tea ceremonies, through all sorts of pipe arrangements to the simplest: lighting the ball, placing a straw over it and inhaling for all you were worth as the goods literally went up in smoke. Whatever method you chose, the principle was the same: to get the substances—morphine, thebaine, codeine and a whole bouquet of other chemical friends—into your bloodstream. Harry's method was straightforward. He taped a steel spoon to the end of the table, placed a tiny particle of the lump, no bigger than the head of a matchstick, in the spoon and heated it with a lighter. When the opium began to burn he held an ordinary glass over it to collect the smoke. Then he put a drinking straw, one with a flexible joint, in the glass and inhaled. Harry noted that his fingers worked without a hint of a tremble. In Hong Kong he had regularly kept a check on his dependency level; seen in that light, he was the most disciplined drug abuser he knew. He could predetermine his dose of alcohol and stop there, however plastered he was. In Hong Kong he had cut out opium for a week or two and taken only a couple of analgesic tablets, which would not have prevented withdrawal symptoms anyway, but which perhaps had a psychological effect since he knew they contained a tiny amount of morphine. He was not hooked. On drugs in general he was, but on opium in particular: no. Though it was a sliding scale, of course. Because while he was taping the spoon into position he could already feel the dogs calming down. For they knew now, knew they would soon be fed.

And could be at peace. Until the next time.

The burning hot lighter was already scorching Harry's fingers. On the table were the straws from McDonald's.

A minute later he had taken the first drag.

The effect was immediate. The pains, even those he didn't know he had, vanished. The associations, the images, appeared. He would be able to sleep tonight.

Bjørn Holm couldn't sleep.

He had tried reading Escott's **Hank Williams: The Biography,** about the country legend's short life and long death, listening to a bootleg Lucinda Williams CD of a concert in Austin, and counting Texas longhorns, but to no avail.

A dilemma. That's exactly what it was. A problem without a proper solution. Forensics Officer Holm hated that type of problem.

He huddled up on the slightly too short sofa bed that had been among the goods he'd brought from Skreia, along with his vinyl collection of Elvis, the Sex Pistols, Jason & the Scorchers, three hand-sewn suits from Nashville, an American Bible and a dining-room suite that had survived three generations of Holms. But he couldn't concentrate.

The dilemma was that he had made an interesting discovery while examining the rope with which Marit Olsen had been hanged—or to be more precise, beheaded. It wasn't a clue that would necessarily produce anything, but nonetheless the dilemma remained the same: Would it be right to pass the information on to Kripos or to Harry? Bjørn Holm had identified the tiny shells on the rope during the time he was still working for Kripos, when he was talking to a freshwater biologist at the Biological Institute, University of Oslo. But then Beate Lønn had transferred him to Harry's unit before the report had been written, and, sitting down at the computer tomorrow to write it, he would in fact be reporting to Harry.

OK, technically perhaps it wasn't a dilemma; the information belonged to Kripos. Giving it to anyone else would be regarded as a dereliction of duty. And what did he owe Harry Hole, actually? Hole had never given him anything but aggravation. He was quirky and inconsiderate at work. Positively dangerous when drinking. But on the level when sober. You could rely on him turning up, and there would be no bullshit and no "You owe me." An irksome enemy, but a good friend. A good man. A damn good man. A bit like Hank, in fact.

Bjørn Holm groaned and rolled over to face the wall.

Stine woke with a start.

In the dark she heard a grinding sound. She rolled onto her side. The ceiling was dimly lit; the light came from the floor beside the bed. What was the time? Three o'clock in the morning? She stretched and grabbed her cell phone.

"Yes?" she said with a voice that made her seem more sleepy than she was.

"After the delta I was sick of snakes and mosquitoes, and me and the motorbike headed north along the Burmese coast to Arakan."

She recognized the voice right away.

"To the island of Sai Chung," he said. "There's an active mud volcano I heard was about to explode. And on the third night I was there, it erupted. I thought there would just be mud, but, you know, it spewed good old-fashioned lava as well. Thick lava that flowed so slowly through the town that we could blithely walk away from it."

"It's the middle of the night." She yawned.

"Yet still it wouldn't stop. Apparently they call it cold lava when it's so sticky, but it consumed everything in its path. Trees with fresh green leaves were like Christmas trees for four seconds until they were turned to ashes and were gone. The Burmese tried to escape in cars loaded with their stuff, but they had spent too much time packing. The lava was moving that fast, after all! When they'd emerge from their house with the TV set, the lava would already be up to their walls. They threw themselves inside their cars, but the heat punctured the tires. Then the gasoline caught fire and they clambered out like human torches. Do you remember my name?"

"Listen, Elias—"

"I said you would remember."

"I have to sleep. I've got classes tomorrow."

"I am such an eruption, Stine. I'm cold lava. I move slowly, but I'm unstoppable. I'm coming to where you are."

She tried to remember if she had told him her name. And automatically directed her gaze to the window. It was open. Outside, the wind soughed, peaceful, reassuring.

His voice was low, a whisper. "I saw a dog entangled in barbed wire, trying to flee. It was in the path of the lava. But then the stream veered left, passed right by. A merciful God, I supposed. But the lava brushed against it. Half the dog simply vanished, evaporated. Before the rest burned up. So it was ashes, too. Everything turns to ashes."

"Yuck—I'm hanging up."

"Look outside. Look, I'm already up against the house."

"Stop it!"

"Relax—I'm only teasing." His loud laughter pealed in her ears.

Stine shuddered. He must be drunk. Or crazy. Or both.

"Sleep tight, Stine. See you soon."

He broke the connection. Stine stared at the phone. Then she switched it off and threw it to the foot of her bed. Cursed because she already knew. She would get no more sleep that night.

17

Fibers

It was 6:58. Harry Hole, Kaja Solness and Bjørn Holm were walking through the culvert, a three-hundred-yard-long subterranean corridor connecting Police HQ and Oslo District Prison. Now and then it was used to transport prisoners to Police HQ for questioning, sometimes for sports training sessions in the winter and in the bad old days for extremely unofficial beatings of particularly intractable prisoners.

Water from the ceiling dripped onto the concrete with wet kisses that echoed down the dimly lit corridor.

"Here," Harry said as they reached the end.

"**Here?**" asked Bjørn Holm.

They had to bend their heads to pass under the stairs leading to the prison cells. Harry turned the key in the lock and opened the iron door. The musty smell of heated, dank air hit him.

He pressed the light switch. Cold blue light from fluorescent tubes enveloped a square concrete room with gray-blue linoleum on the floor and nothing on the walls.

The room had no windows, no radiators, none of the facilities you expect in a space supposed to function as an office for three people, apart from desks with chairs and a computer each. On the floor there was a coffee machine stained brown and a water cooler.

"The boilers heating the whole prison are in the adjacent room," Harry said. "That's why it's so hot in here."

"Basically not very homey," Kaja said, sitting at one of the desks.

"Right—sort of reminiscent of hell," Holm said, pulling off his suede jacket and undoing one shirt button. "Is there cell coverage here?"

"Just about," Harry said. "And an Internet connection. We have everything we need."

"Apart from coffee cups," Holm said.

Harry shook his head. From his jacket pocket he produced three white cups, and he placed one on each of the three desks. Then he pulled a bag of coffee from his inside pocket and went over to the machine.

"You've taken them from the cafeteria," Bjørn said, raising the cup Harry had put down in front of him. " 'Hank Williams'?"

"Written with a felt pen, so be careful," Harry said, tearing open the coffee pouch with his teeth.

" 'John Fante'?" Kaja read on her cup. "What do you have?"

"For the time being, nothing," Harry said.

"And why not?"

"Because it will be the name of our main suspect of the moment."

Neither of the other two said anything. The coffee machine slurped up the water.

"I want three names on the table by the time this is ready," Harry said.

They were done with their second cup of coffee and into the sixth theory when Harry interrupted the session.

"OK, that was the warm-up, just to get the gray matter working."

Kaja had just launched the idea that the murders were sexually motivated and that the killer was an ex-con with a record for similar crimes who knew that the police had his DNA and therefore did not spill his seed on the ground, but masturbated into a bag or some such receptacle before leaving the scene. Accordingly, she said, they should start going through criminal records and talking to staff in the Sexual Offenses Unit.

"But don't you believe we're onto something?" she said.

"I don't believe anything," Harry answered. "I'm trying to keep my brain clear and receptive."

"But you must believe something?"

"Yes, I do. I believe the three murders have been carried out by the same person or persons. And I believe it's possible to find a connection that in turn might lead us to a motive that in turn—if we're very, very lucky—will lead us to the guilty party or parties."

" 'Very, very lucky.' You make it sound as if the odds are not good."

"Well." Harry leaned back on his chair with his hands behind his head. "Several yards of books have been written about what characterizes serial killers. In films, the police call in a psychologist who, after reading a couple of reports, gives them a profile that invariably fits. People believe that **Henry: Portrait of a Serial Killer** is an accurate depiction. But in reality serial killers are, sad to say, as different from one another as everyone else. There is only one thing that distinguishes them from other criminals."

"And that is . . . ?"

"They don't get caught."

Bjørn Holm laughed, realized it was inappropriate and shut up.

"That's not true, is it?" Kaja said. "What about . . . ?"

"You're thinking of the cases where a pattern emerged and they caught the person. But don't forget all the unsolved murders we still think are one-offs, where a connection was never found. Thousands."

Kaja glanced at Bjørn, who was nodding meaning-fully.

"You believe in connections?" she said.

"Yep," Harry said. "And we have to find one with-out going down the path of interviewing people, which might give us away."

"So?"

"When we predicted potential threats in the Secu-rity Service we did nothing but look for possible con-nections, without talking to a living soul. We had a NATO-built search engine long before anyone had heard of Yahoo or Google. With it we could sneak in anywhere and scan practically everything with any connection to the Net. That's what we have to do here as well." He glanced at his watch. "And that's why in one and a half hours I'll be sitting on a plane to Bergen. And in three hours I'll be talking to an unemployed colleague who I hope can help us. So let's finish up here, shall we? Kaja and I have talked quite a bit, Bjørn. What do you have?"

Bjørn Holm jerked in his chair, as if roused from sleep.

"Me? Er . . . not much, I'm afraid."

Harry rubbed his jaw carefully. "You've got some-thing."

"Nope. Neither Forensics nor the detectives on the case have got so much as a lump of fly shit. Not in the Marit Olsen case, nor in either of the other two."

"Two months," Harry said. "Come on."

"I can give you a summary," said Bjørn Holm. "For two months we have analyzed, x-rayed and stared ourselves stupid at photos, blood samples, strands of hair, nails, all sorts. We've gone through twenty-four theories of how and why he's stabbed twenty-four holes in the mouths of the first two victims in such a way that all the wounds point inward to the same central point. With no result. Marit Olsen also had wounds to the mouth, but they were inflicted with a knife and were sloppy, brutal. In short: **nada**."

"What about those small stones in the cellar where Borgny was found?"

"Analyzed. Lots of iron and magnesium, some aluminum and silica. So-called basalt rock. Porous and black. Any the wiser?"

"Both Borgny and Charlotte had iron and coltan on the insides of their molars. What does that tell us?"

"That they were killed with the same goddamn instrument, but that doesn't get us any closer to what it was."

Silence.

Harry coughed. "OK, Bjørn, out with it."

"Out with what?"

"What you've been brooding about ever since we got here."

The forensics officer scratched his sideburns while eyeballing Harry. Coughed once. Twice. Glanced at Kaja, as if to solicit help there. Opened his mouth, closed it.

"Fine," Harry said. "Let's move on to—"

"The rope."

The other two stared at Bjørn.

"I found shells on it."

"Oh, yes?" Harry said.

"But no salt."

They were still staring at him.

"That's pretty unusual," Bjørn went on. "Shells. In freshwater."

"So?"

"So I checked it out with a freshwater biologist. This particular mollusc is called a Jutland blue shell mussel—it's the smallest of the pool mussels and has been observed in only two lakes in Norway."

"And the nominations are?"

"Øyeren and Lyseren."

"Østfold," Kaja said. "Neighboring lakes. Big ones."

"In a densely populated region," Harry said.

"Sorry," Holm said.

"Mm. Any marks on the rope that tell us where it might have been bought?"

"No, that's the point," Holm said. "There are no marks. And it doesn't look like any rope I've seen before. The fiber is one hundred percent organic; there's no nylon or any other synthetic materials."

"Hemp," Harry said.

"What?" Holm said.

"Hemp. Rope and hash are made from the same material. If you want a joint, you can just stroll down to the harbor and light up the mooring ropes of the Danish ferry."

"It's not hemp," Bjørn Holm said over Kaja's laughter. "The fiber's made from the elm and the linden tree. Mostly elm."

"Homemade Norwegian rope," Kaja said. "They used to make rope on farms long ago."

"On farms?" Harry queried.

Kaja nodded. "As a rule every village had at least one ropemaker. You just soaked the wood in water for a month, peeled off the outer bark and used the bast fiber inside. Twined it into rope."

Harry and Bjørn swiveled around to face Kaja.

"What's the matter?" she asked hesitantly.

"Well," Harry said, "is this general knowledge everyone ought to possess?"

"Oh, I see," Kaja said. "My grandfather made rope."

"Aha. And for rope-making you need elm and linden?"

"In principle you can use bast fibers from any kind of tree."

"And the composition?"

Kaja shrugged. "I'm no expert, but I think it's unusual to use bast from several different trees for the same rope. I remember that Even, my big brother, said that Granddad used only linden because it absorbs very little water. So he didn't need to tar his."

"Mm. What do you think, Bjørn?"

"If the compositon is unusual, it will be easier to trace where it was made, of course."

Harry stood up and began to pace back and forth. There was a heavy sigh every time his rubber soles relinquished the linoleum. "Then we can assume production was limited and sales were local. Do you think that sounds reasonable, Kaja?"

"Guess so, yes."

"And we can also assume that the centers of production and consumption were in close proximity. These homemade ropes would hardly have traveled far."

"Still sounds reasonable, but . . ."

"So let's take that as our starting point. You two begin mapping out local ropemakers near Øyeren and Lyseren."

"But no one makes ropes like that anymore," Kaja protested.

"Do the best you can." Harry looked at his watch, grabbed his coat from the back of the chair and walked to the door. "Find out where the rope was made. I presume Bellman knows nothing about these Jutland blue shell mussels. That right, Bjørn?"

Bjørn Holm forced a smile by way of answer.

"Is it OK if I follow up the theory of a sexually motivated murder?" Kaja asked. "I can talk to someone I know at Sexual Offenses."

"Negative," Harry said. "The general order to keep your trap shut about what we're doing applies in particular to our dear colleagues at Police HQ. There seems to be some seepage between HQ and Kripos, so the only person we speak to is Gunnar Hagen."

Kaja had opened her mouth, but a glance from Bjørn was enough to make her close it again.

"But what you can do," Harry said, "is get hold of a volcano expert. And send him the test results of the small stones."

Bjørn's fair eyebrows rose a substantial way up his forehead.

"Porous black stone, basalt rock," Harry said. "I would reckon lava. I'll be back from Bergen at four-ish."

"Say hello to Baa-baargen Police HQ," Bjørn bleated and raised his coffee cup.

"I won't be going to the police station," Harry said.

"Oh? Where then?"

"Sandviken Hospital."

"Sand—"

The door slammed behind Harry. Kaja watched Bjørn Holm, who was staring at the closed door with a stunned expression on his face.

"What's he going to do there?" she asked. "See a pathologist?"

Bjørn shook his head. "Sandviken Hospital is a mental hospital."

"Really? So he's going to meet a psychologist who's a serial-killer specialist?"

"I knew I should have said no," Bjørn whispered, still staring at the door. "He's clean out of his mind."

"Who's out of his mind?"

"We're working in a prison," Bjørn said. "We're risking our jobs if the boss finds out what we're up to, and the colleague in Bergen . . ."

"Yes?"

"She is seriously out of her mind."

"You mean she's . . . ?"

"Certifiably out of her mind."

18

The Patient

For every step the tall policeman took, Kjersti Rødsmoen had to take two. Even so, she was left behind as they walked along the corridor of Sandviken Hospital. The rain was pouring down outside the high, narrow windows facing the fjord, where the trees were so green you would have thought spring had arrived before winter.

The day before, Kjersti Rødsmoen had recognized the policeman's voice at once. As though she had been waiting for him to call. And to make the very request he did: to talk to the Patient. The Patient had come to be called that to give her maximum anonymity after the strain of the detective work on her most recent murder case had sent her right back to square one: the psychiatric ward. In fact, she had recovered with remarkable speed, had moved back home, but the press—which was still hysterically pursuing the Snowman case long after it had been cleared up—had not left her in peace. And one evening, a few months ago, the Patient had called Rødsmoen and asked if she could return.

"So she's in serviceable shape?" the police officer asked. "On medication?"

"Yes to the first," Kjersti Rødsmoen said. "The second is confidential." The truth was the Patient was so well that neither medicine nor hospitalization was required any longer. Nevertheless Rødsmoen had wondered whether she should let him visit her; he had been on the Snowman case and could cause old issues to emerge. Kjersti Rødsmoen had, in her time as a psychiatrist, come to believe more and more in repression, in shutting things off, in oblivion. It was an unfashionable view within the profession. On the other hand, meeting a person who had been on that particular case might be a good test of how robust the Patient had become.

"You've got half an hour," Rødsmoen said before opening the door to the common room. "And don't forget that the mind is tender."

The last time Harry had seen Katrine Bratt she had been unrecognizable. The attractive young woman with the dark hair and the glowing skin and eyes had gone, to be replaced by someone who reminded him of a dried flower: lifeless, frail, delicate, wan. He had had a feeling he might crush her hand if he squeezed too hard.

So it was a relief to see her now. She looked older, or perhaps she was just tired. But the gleam in her eyes returned as she smiled and got up.

"Harry H.," she said, giving him a hug. "How's it going?"

"Fair to middling," Harry said. "And you?"

"Dreadful," she said. "But a lot better."

She laughed, and Harry knew she was back. Or that enough of her was back.

"What happened to your jaw? Does it hurt?"

"Only when I speak and eat," Harry said. "And when I'm awake."

"Sounds familiar. You're uglier than I remember, but I'm glad to see you anyway."

"Same to you."

"You mean same to me, except for the ugly bit?"

Harry smiled. "Naturally." He looked around. The other patients in the room stared out of the window, at their laps or straight at the wall. But no one seemed interested in him or Katrine.

Harry told her what had happened since the last time they'd seen each other. About Rakel and Oleg, who had moved to an unnamed destination abroad. About Hong Kong. About his father's illness. About the case he had taken on. She even laughed when he said she mustn't tell anyone.

"What about you?" Harry asked.

"They want me out of here, really; they think I'm well and I'm taking up someone else's place. But I like it here. The room service stinks, but it's safe. I've got TV and can come and go as I want. In a month or two I'll move back home, maybe—who knows."

"Who knows?"

"No one. The madness is intermittent. What do you want?"

"What do you want me to want?"

She gave him a long, hard look before answering.

"Apart from wanting you to have a burning desire to fuck me, I want you to have some use for me."

"And that's exactly what I have."

"A desire to fuck me?"

"Some use for you."

"Shit. Well, OK. What's it about?"

"Do you have a computer with Internet access here?"

"We have a communal computer in the recreation room, but it isn't connected to the Net. They wouldn't risk that. The only thing it's used for is playing solitaire. But I've got my own computer in my room."

"Use the communal one." Harry put his hand in his pocket and tossed a dongle across the table. "This is a mobile office, as they called it in the shop. You just plug it into—"

"One of the USB ports," Katrine said, taking the device and pocketing it. "Who pays the subscription?"

"I do. That is, Hagen does."

"Yippee—there's gonna be some surfing tonight. Any hot new porno sites I should know about?"

"Probably." Harry pushed a file across the table. "Here are the reports. Three murders, three names. I want you to do the same as you did on the Snowman case. Find connections we've missed. Have you heard any media reports on the case?"

"Yes," Katrine Bratt said without looking at the file. "They were women. That's the connection."

"You read newspapers . . ."

"Barely. Why do you believe they're any more than random victims?"

"I don't believe anything. I'm looking."

"But you don't know what you're looking for?"

"Correct."

"But you're sure Marit Olsen's killer is the same person who killed the other two? The method was completely different, I understand."

Harry smiled. Amused by Katrine's attempt to hide the fact that she had scrutinized every detail in the papers. "No, Katrine, I'm not sure. But I can hear you've drawn the same conclusion as I have."

"'Course. We were soul mates, remember?"

She laughed, and at a stroke she was Katrine again, and not the skeleton of the brilliant, eccentric detective he had only just gotten to know before everything crumbled. Harry felt, to his surprise, a lump in his throat. Fucking jet lag.

"Can you help me, do you think?"

"To find something Kripos has spent two months not finding? With an outdated computer in the recreation room of a mental institution? I don't even know why you're asking me. There are folks at Police HQ who are a lot more computer-savvy than me."

"I know, but I have something they don't. And cannot give them: the password to the underground."

She fixed him with an uncomprehending stare. Harry checked that no one was within earshot.

"When I was working for the Security Service, POT, on the Redbreast case, I gained access to the search engine they were using to trace terrorists. They use secret back doors on the Net like MILNET, the American military network, made before they released the Net for commercial purposes through ARPANET in the eighties. ARPANET became, as you know, the Internet, but the back doors are still there. The search engines use Trojan horses that update the passwords, codes and upgrades at the first entry point. Plane ticket bookings, hotel reservations, road tolls, Internet banking: These engines can see everything."

"I'd heard rumors of the search engines, but I honestly thought they were nonexistent," Katrine said.

"They do exist. They were set up in 1984. The Orwellian nightmare come true. And best of all, my password is still valid. I checked it."

"So what do you need me for? You can do this yourself, can't you?"

"Only POT is allowed to use the system, and only in emergency situations. As with Google, your searches can be traced back to the user. If it's discovered that I or anyone else at Police HQ have been using the search engines, we risk a prison sentence. But if the search were traced and led back to a communal computer in a psychiatric hospital . . ."

Katrine Bratt laughed. Her other laugh, the evil-witch variety. "I'm beginning to see. Katrine Bratt, the brilliant detective, is not my strongest qualification here, but"—she threw up her hands—"Katrine Bratt the patient is. Because she, being of unsound mind, cannot be prosecuted."

"Correct." Harry smiled. "And you're one of the

few people I can trust to keep your mouth shut. And if you're not a genius, you're definitely smarter than the average detective."

"Three smashed nicotine-stained fingers up your tiny little asshole."

"No one can find out what we're up to. But I promise you we're the Blues Brothers here."

" 'On a mission from God'?" she quoted.

"I've written the password on the back of the SIM card inside the dongle."

"What makes you think I know how to use the search engines?"

"It's like Googling. Even I worked that out when I was at POT." He gave a wry smile. "After all, the engines were created for the police."

She released a deep sigh.

"Thank you," Harry said.

"I didn't say anything."

"When can you have something for me, do you think?"

"Fuck you!" She banged the table with her hand. Harry noticed a nurse glance in their direction. Harry held Katrine's wild stare. Waited.

"I don't know," she whispered. "I don't think I should be sitting in the recreation room using illegal search engines in broad daylight, if I can put it like that."

Harry got up. "OK. I'll contact you in three days."

"Haven't you forgotten something?"

"What?"

"To tell me what's in it for me?"

"Well," Harry said, buttoning up his coat, "now I know what you want."

"What I want . . ." The surprise on her face gave way to amazement as the meaning dawned on her, and she shouted after Harry, who was already on his way to the door: "You cheeky bastard! And presumptuous, too!"

Harry got into the taxi, said, "Airport," removed his cell phone and saw three missed calls from one of the only two numbers he had in his contacts. Good—that meant they had something.

He called back.

"Lake Lyseren," Kaja said. "Rope-making business there. Closed down fifteen years ago. The county officer responsible for Ytre Ene-bakk can show us the place this afternoon. He had a couple of persistent criminals in the area, but small potatoes: break-ins and car theft. Plus one who had done time for beating up his wife. He's sent us a list of men, though, and I'm going to run a check with Criminal Records right now."

"Good. Pick me up from Gardermoen on the way to Lyseren."

"It's not on the way."

"You're right. Pick me up anyway."

19

The White Bride

Despite the slow speed, Bjørn Holm's Volvo Amazon was rolling and pitching on the narrow road that snaked between Østfold's meadows and fields.

Harry was asleep in the backseat.

"So no sex offenders around Lake Lyseren," Bjørn said.

"None that have been caught," Kaja corrected. "Didn't you see the survey in **VG**? One in twenty say they have committed what might be termed sexual abuse."

"Do people really answer that sort of questionnaire honestly? If I'd pushed a girl too far I think my brain would've goddamn rationalized it away afterward."

"Is that what you did?"

"Me?" Bjørn swung out and overtook a tractor. "Nope. I'm one of the nineteen. Ytre Enebakk. Christ, what's the name of that comic who hails from these parts? The bumpkin with the cracked glasses and moped. What's-his-face from Ytre Enebakk. Hilarious parody."

Kaja shrugged. Bjørn looked into the mirror, but found himself looking down Harry's open mouth.

As arranged, the county officer for Ytre Enebakk was waiting for them by the treatment plant on the

Vøyentangen peninisula. They parked, he introduced himself as Skai—the Norwegian name for the
synthetic leather that Bjørn Holm seemed to hold in
such high regard—and they accompanied him to a
jetty, where a dozen boats bobbed up and down in
the calm waters.

"Early to have boats in the lake, isn't it?" Kaja said.

"There hasn't been any ice this year—won't be,
either," the officer said. "First time since I was born."

They stepped into a broad, flat-bottomed boat,
Bjørn with greater caution than the others.

"It's green here," Kaja said as the officer pushed off
from the jetty with a pole.

"Yes," he said, peering down into the water and
pulling the cord to start the engine. "The ropery is
over there, on the deep side. There's a path, but the
terrain is so steep that it's best to go by boat." He
flicked forward the handle on the side of the engine.
A bird of indeterminate species took off from a tree
inside the bare forest and shrieked a warning.

"I hate the sea," Bjørn said to Harry, who could just
hear his colleague above the hacking sound of the
two-stroke outboard motor. They slipped through the
gray afternoon light in a channel between the six-
foot-high rushes. Crept past a pile of twigs that Harry
assumed must have been a beaver's den and out
through an avenue of man-grovelike trees.

"This is a lake," Harry said. "Not the sea."

"Same shit," Bjørn said, shifting closer to the middle of his seat. "Give me inland, cow muck and rocky
mountains."

The channel widened, and there it lay in front of them: Lake Lyseren. They chugged past islands and islets from which winter-abandoned cabins with black windows seemed to be staring at them through wary eyes.

"Basic cabins," the officer said. "Here you're free from the stress down on the gold coast, where you have to compete with your neighbor for the biggest boat or the most attractive cabin renovation." He spat into the water.

"What's the name of that TV comic from Ytre Enebakk?" Bjørn shouted over the drone of the motor. "Cracked glasses and moped."

The officer sent Holm a blank look and shook his head slowly.

"The ropery," he said.

In front of the bow, right down by the lake, Harry saw an old wooden building, oblong in shape, standing alone at the foot of a steep slope, dense forest on both sides. Beside the building, steel rails ran down the mountainside and disappeared into the black water. The red paint was peeling off the walls, with gaping spaces for windows and doors. Harry squinted. In the fading light it looked as if there were a person in white standing at a window staring at them.

"Jeez, the ultimate haunted house." Bjørn laughed.

"That's what they say," said County Officer Skai, cutting the engine.

In the sudden silence they could hear the echo of Bjørn's laughter from the other side and a lone sheep bell reaching them from far across the lake.

Kaja took the rope, jumped onto the shore and,

being of a nautical bent herself, tied a half-hitch around a rotten green pole protruding from among the water lilies.

The others got out of the boat and onto the huge rocks serving as a wharf. Then they entered through the doorway and found themselves in a deserted, narrow rectangular room smelling of tar and urine. It hadn't been so easy to discern from the outside because the extremities of the building merged into the dense forest, but while the room was barely seven feet across, it must have been more than two hundred feet from end to end.

"They stood at opposite ends of the building and twined the rope," Kaja explained before Harry could ask.

In one corner lay three empty bottles and signs of attempts to light a fire. On the facing wall, a net hung in front of a couple of loose boards.

"No one wanted to take over after Simonsen," Skai said, looking around. "It's been empty ever since."

"What are the rails at the side of the building for?" Harry asked.

"Two things. To raise and lower the boat he used to collect timber. And to hold the sticks underwater while they soaked. He tied the sticks to the iron carriage, which must be up in the boathouse. Then he cranked the carriage down under the water and wound it back up after a few weeks, when the wood was ready. Practical fellow, Simonsen."

They all gave a start at a sudden noise from the forest outside.

"Sheep," the officer said. "Or deer."

They followed him up a narrow wooden staircase to the first floor. An enormously long table stood in the center of the room. The corners of the room were enshrouded in darkness. The wind blew in through the windows—with borders of jagged glass set in the frames—making a low whistling sound, and it caused the woman's bridal veil to flap. She stood looking out over the lake. Beneath the head and torso was the skeleton: a black iron stand on wheels.

"Simonsen used her as a scarecrow," Skai said, nodding toward the shop dummy.

"Pretty creepy," Kaja said, taking up a position beside Skai and shivering inside her coat.

He cast a sideways glance at her, then gave a crooked smile. "The kids around here were terrified of her. The adults said that at full moon she walked around the district chasing the man who had jilted her on her wedding day. And you could hear the rusty wheels as she approached. I grew up right behind here, in Haga, you see."

"Did you?" asked Kaja, and Harry smothered a grin.

"Yes," said Skai. "By the way, this was the only woman known to be in Simonsen's life. He was a bit of a recluse. But he could certainly make rope."

Behind them Bjørn Holm took down a coil of rope hanging from a nail.

"Did I say you could touch anything?" the officer said without turning.

Bjørn hurriedly put back the rope.

"OK, boss," Harry said, sending Skai a closed smile. "Can we touch anything?"

The officer examined Harry. "You still haven't told me what kind of case this is."

"It's confidential," Harry said. "Sorry. Fraud Squad. You know."

"That right? If you're the Harry Hole I think you are, you used to work on murders."

"Well," Harry said, "now it's insider trading, tax evasion and fraud. One moves upward in life."

Officer Skai pinched an eye shut. A bird shrieked.

"Of course, you're right, Skai," Kaja said with a sigh. "But I'm the person who has to deal with the red tape for the search warrant from the prosecutor. As you know, we're understaffed and it would save me a lot of time if we could just . . ." She smiled with her tiny, pointed teeth and gestured toward the coil of rope.

Skai looked at her. Rocked to and fro on his rubber heels a couple of times. Then he nodded.

"I'll wait in the boat," he said.

Bjørn set to work immediately. He placed the coil on the long table, opened the little knapsack he had with him, switched on a flashlight attached to a cord with a fishhook on the end and secured it between two boards in the ceiling. He took out his laptop and a portable microscope shaped like a hammer, plugged the microscope into the USB port on the laptop, checked it was transmitting pictures to the screen and clicked on an image he had transferred to the laptop before they'd departed.

Harry stood beside the bride and gazed down at the lake. In the boat he could see the glow of a cigarette. He eyed the rails that went down into the water. The deep end. Harry had never liked swimming in freshwater, especially after the time he and Øystein had skipped school, gone to Lake Hauktjern in Østmarka and jumped off the Devil's Tip, which people said was forty feet high. And Harry—seconds before he hit the water—had seen a snake gliding through the depths beneath him. Then he was enveloped by the freezing cold bottle-green water, and in his panic he swallowed half the lake and was sure he would never see daylight or breathe air again.

Harry smelled the fragrance that told him Kaja was standing behind him.

"Bingo," he heard Bjørn Holm whisper.

Harry turned. "Same type of rope?"

"No doubt about it," Bjørn said, holding the microscope against the rope end and pressing a key for high-resolution images. "Linden and elm. Same thickness and length of fiber. But the **bingo** is reserved for the recently sliced rope end."

"What?"

Bjørn Holm pointed to the screen. "The photo on the left is the one I brought with me. It shows the rope from the Frogner pool, magnified twenty-five times. And on this rope I have a perfect . . ."

Harry closed his eyes so as to relish to the full the word he knew was coming.

". . . match."

He kept his eyes closed. The rope Marit Olsen was

hanged with not only had been made here, but had been cut from the rope they had before them. And it was a recent cut. Not so long ago, he had been standing where they were standing. Harry sniffed the air.

An all-embracing darkness had fallen. Harry could hardly make out anything white in the window as they left.

Kaja sat in the front of the boat with him. She had to lean close so that he could hear her over the drone of the motor.

"The person who collected the rope must have known his way around this area. And there can't be many links in the chain between that person and the killer . . ."

"I don't think there are any links at all," Harry said. "The cut was recent. And there are not many reasons for rope to change hands."

"Local knowledge—lives nearby or has a cabin here," Kaja mused aloud. "Or he grew up here."

"But why come all the way to a disused ropery to get a few yards of rope?" Harry asked. "How much does a long rope cost in a shop? A couple of hundred kroner?"

"Perhaps he happened to be in the vicinity and knew the rope was there."

"OK, but **in the vicinity** would mean he must have been staying in one of the nearby cabins. For everyone else it's a fair-size boat trip. Are you making . . . ?"

"Yes, I'm making a list of the closest neighbors. By the way, I tracked down the volcano expert you asked for. A nerd up at the Geological Institute. Felix Røst. He seems to do a bit of volcano-spotting. Traveling all over the world to look at volcanoes and eruptions and that sort of thing."

"Did you talk to him?"

"Just his sister, who lives with him. She asked me to email or text. He doesn't communicate in any other way, she said. Anyway, he was out playing chess. I sent him the stones and the information."

They advanced at a snail's pace through the shallow channel to the pontoon. Bjørn held up the flashlight like a lantern to light their way through the hazy mist drifting across the water. The officer cut the motor.

"Look!" whispered Kaja, leaning even closer to Harry. He could smell her scent as he followed her index finger. From the rushes behind the jetty emerged a large, lone white swan, cutting through the veil of mist into the flashlight's beam.

"Isn't it just . . . beautiful," she whispered, entranced, then laughed and fleetingly squeezed his hand.

Skai accompanied them to the treatment plant. Then they got into the Volvo Amazon and were about to set off when Bjørn feverishly wound down the window and shouted to the officer: **"Fritjof!"**

Skai stopped and turned slowly. The light from a street lamp fell onto his heavy, expressionless face.

"The funny guy on TV," Bjørn shouted. "Fritjof from Ytre Enebakk."

"Fritjof?" Skai said and spat. "Never heard of him."

Twenty-five minutes later, as the Amazon turned onto the highway by the incinerator in Grønmo, Harry made a decision.

"We must leak this information to Kripos," he said.

"What?" Bjørn and Kaja said in unison.

"I'll talk to Beate, then she'll pass the message on so that it looks like her people at Krimteknisk have discovered the business with the rope and not us."

"Why?" Kaja asked.

"If the killer lives in the Lyseren area, there'll have to be a door-to-door search. We don't have the means or the manpower for that."

Bjørn Holm smacked the steering wheel.

"I know," Harry said. "But the most important thing is that he's caught, not who catches him."

They drove on in silence, with the false ring of the words hanging in the air.

20

Øystein

No electricity. Harry stood in the dark hall flipping the light switch on and off. Did the same in the sitting room.

Then he sat down in the wing chair, staring into the black void.

After he had sat there for a while, his cell rang.

"Hole."

"Felix Røst."

"Mm?" Harry said. The voice sounded as if it belonged to a slender, petite woman.

"Frida Larsen, his sister. He asked me to call and say that the stones you found are mafic, basalt lava. All right?"

"Just a minute. What does that mean? Mafic?"

"It's hot lava, over eighteen hundred degrees Fahrenheit, low viscosity, which thins it and allows it to spread over a wide distance on eruption."

"Could it have come from Oslo?"

"No."

"Why not? Oslo is built on lava."

"Old lava. This lava is recent."

"How recent?"

He heard her put her hand over the phone and speak. But he couldn't hear any other voices. She must have received an answer, though, because soon afterward she was back.

"He says anything from five to fifty years. But if you were thinking of establishing which volcano it comes from, you've got quite a job on your hands. There are more than fifteen hundred active volcanoes in the world. And those are just the ones we know about. If there are any other queries, Felix can be contacted by email. Your assistant has the address."

"But . . ."

She had already hung up.

He considered calling back, but changed his mind and punched in another number.

"Oslo Taxi."

"Hi, Øystein, this is Harry H."

"You're kidding. Harry H. is dead."

"Not quite."

"OK, then I must be dead."

"Feel like driving me from Sofies Gate to my childhood home?"

"No, but I'll do it anyway. Just have to do this trip." Øystein's laugh morphed into a cough. "Harry H.! Damn . . . Call you when I'm there."

Harry hung up, went into the bedroom, packed a bag in the light from the street lamp outside the window and chose a couple of CDs from the sitting room in the light from his cell. Carton of smokes, handcuffs, service pistol.

He sat in the wing chair, making use of the dark to repeat the revolver exercise. Started the stopwatch on his wrist, flicked out the cylinder of his Smith & Wesson, emptied and loaded. Four cartridges out, four in, without a speed-loader, just nimble fingers. Flicked the cylinder back in so that the first cartridge was first in line. Stop. Nine sixty-six. Almost three seconds over the record. He opened the cylinder. He had messed up. The first chamber ready to fire was one of the two empty ones. He was dead. He repeated the exercise. Nine fifty. And dead again. When Øystein called, after twenty minutes, he was down to eight seconds and had died six times.

"Coming," Harry said.

He walked into the kitchen. Looked at the cupboard under the sink. Hesitated. Then he took down the photos of Rakel and Oleg and put them in his inside pocket.

"Hong Kong?" sniffed Øystein Eikeland. He turned his bloated alcoholic face, with its huge hooter and sad, drooping mustache, to Harry in the seat next to him. "What the hell d'you do there?"

"You know me," Harry said as Øystein stopped on red outside the Radisson SAS Hotel.

"I fucking do not," Øystein said, sprinkling tobacco into his rolling paper. "How would I?"

"Well, we grew up together. Do you remember?"

"So? You were already a fucking enigma then, Harry."

The rear door was torn open and a man wearing a coat got in. "Airport express, main station. Quick."

"Taxi's taken," Øystein said without turning.

"Nonsense—the sign on the roof's lit."

"Hong Kong sounds groovy. Why d'you come home, actually?"

"I beg your pardon," said the man in the backseat.

Øystein poked the cigarette between his lips and lit up. "Tresko called to invite me to a get-together tonight."

"Tresko doesn't have any friends," Harry said.

"He doesn't, does he. So I asked him, 'Who are your friends?' '**You**,' he said, and asked me, 'And yours, Øystein?' '**You**,' I answered. 'So it's just the two of us.' We'd forgotten all about you, Harry. That's what happens when you go to . . ." He funneled his lips and, in a staccato voice, said, "Hong Kong!"

"Hey!" came a shout from the backseat. "If you're done, perhaps we might . . ."

The light changed to green, and Øystein accelerated away.

"Are you coming, then? It's at Tresko's place."

"Stinks of toe-fart there, Øystein."

"He's got a full fridge."

"Sorry—I'm not in a party mood."

"Party mood?" Øystein snorted, smacking the wheel with his hand. "You don't know what a party mood is, Harry. You always backed off parties. Do you remember? We'd bought some beers, intending to go to some fancy address in Nordstrand with loads of women. And you suggested you, me and Tresko go to the bunkers instead and drink on our own."

"Hey, this isn't the way to the airport express!" came a whine from the backseat.

Øystein braked for red again, tossed his wispy shoulder-length hair to the side and addressed the backseat. "And that was where we ended up. Got drunk and that fella started singing 'No Surrender' until Tresko chucked empty bottles at him."

"Honest to God!" the man cried, tapping his forefinger on the glass of a TAG Heuer watch. "I **have** to catch the last plane to Stockholm."

"The bunkers are great," Harry said. "Best view in Oslo."

"Yep," Øystein said. "If the Allies had attacked there, the Germans would've shot them to bits."

"Right." Harry grinned.

"You know, we had a standing agreement, him and me and Tresko," Øystein said, but the suit was now desperately scanning the rain for vacant taxis. "If the fucking Allies come, we'll fucking shoot the meat off their carcasses. Like this." Øystein pointed an imaginary machine gun at the suit and fired a salvo. The suit stared in horror at the crazy taxi driver, whose chattering noises were causing small foam-white drops of spit to land on his dark, freshly ironed suit trousers. With a little gasp he managed to open the car door and stumble out into the rain.

Øystein burst into coarse, hearty laughter.

"You were missing home," Øystein said. "You wanted to dance with the Killer Queen at Ekeberg Restaurant again."

Harry chuckled and shook his head. In the side mirror he saw the man charging madly toward the National Theater Station. "It's my father. He's ill. He doesn't have much time left."

"Oh, shit." Øystein pressed the accelerator again. "Good man, too."

"Thank you. Thought you would want to know."

"'Course I fucking do. Have to tell my folks."

"So, here we are," Øystein said, parking outside the garage and the tiny yellow timber house in Oppsal.

"Yup," Harry said.

Øystein inhaled so hard the cigarette seemed to be catching fire, held the smoke down in his lungs and let it out again with a long, gurgling wheeze. Then he tilted his head slightly and flicked the ash into the ashtray. Harry experienced a sweet pain in his heart. How many times had he seen Øystein do exactly that, seen him lean to the side as though the cigarette were so heavy that he would lose balance. Head tilted. The ash on the ground in a smokers' shed at school, in an empty beer bottle at a party they had gate-crashed, on cold, damp concrete in a bunker.

"Life's fucking unfair," Øystein said. "Your father was sober, went walking on Sundays and worked as a teacher. While my father drank, worked at the Kadok factory, where everyone got asthma and weird rashes, and didn't move an inch once he was ensconced on the sofa at home. And the guy's as fit as a fuckin' fiddle."

Harry remembered the Kadok factory. **Kodak** backward. The owner, from Sunnmøre, had read that Eastman had called his camera factory Kodak because it was a name that could be remembered and pronounced all over the world. But Kadok was forgotten, and it shut down several years ago.

"All things pass," Harry said.

Øystein nodded as though he had been following his train of thought.

"Call if you need anything, Harry."

"Yep."

Harry waited until he heard the wheels crunching on the gravel behind him and the car was gone before he unlocked the door and entered. He switched on the light and stood still as the door clicked shut. The smell, the silence, the light falling on the coat closet: Everything spoke to him; it was like sinking into a pool of memories. They embraced him, warmed him, made his throat constrict. He removed his coat and kicked off his shoes. Then he started to walk. From room to room. From year to year. From Mom and Dad to Sis, and then to himself. The boy's room. The Clash poster, the one where the guitar is about to be smashed on the floor. He lay on his bed and breathed in the smell of the mattress. And then came the tears.

21

Snow White

It was two minutes to eight in the evening when Mikael Bellman was walking up Karl Johans Gate, one of the world's more modest streets. He was in the middle of the kingdom of Norway, at the midpoint of the axis. To the left, the university and knowledge; to the right, the National Theater and culture. Behind him, in the Palace Gardens, the Royal Palace, situated on high. And right in front of him: power. Three hundred paces later, at exactly eight o'clock, he mounted the stone steps to the main entrance of Stortinget. The parliament building, like most of Oslo, was not particularly big or impressive. And security was minimal. There were only two lions carved from Grorud granite standing on either side of the slope that led to the entrance.

Bellman went up to the door, which opened noiselessly before he had a chance to push. He arrived at reception and stood looking around. A security guard appeared in front of him with a friendly but firm nod toward a Gilardoni X-ray machine. Ten seconds later it had revealed that Mikael Bellman was unarmed; there was metal in his belt, but that was all.

Rasmus Olsen was waiting for him, leaning against the reception desk. Marit Olsen's thin widower shook hands with Bellman and walked ahead as he automatically switched on his guide voice.

"Stortinget, three hundred and eighty employees, a hundred and sixty-nine MPs. Built in 1866, designed by Emil Victor Langlet. A Swede, by the way. This is the hall known as Trappehallen. The stone mosaics are called Society, Else Hagen, 1950. The king's portrait was painted . . ."

They emerged into Vandrehallen, which Bellman recognized from the TV. A couple of faces, neither familiar, flitted past. Rasmus explained to him that there had just been a committee meeting, but Bellman was not listening. He was thinking that these were the corridors of power. He was disappointed. Fine to have all the gold and red, but where was the magnificence, the stateliness, that was supposed to instill awe at the feet of those who ruled? This damned humble sobriety; it was like a weakness, of which this tiny and, not so long ago, poor democracy in Northern Europe could not rid itself. Yet he had returned. If he had not been able to reach the top among the wolves of Europol, he would certainly succeed here, in competition with midgets and second-rate cops.

"This entire room was Reichskommissar Terboven's office during the war. No one has such a large office nowadays."

"What was your marriage like?"

"I beg your pardon?"

"You and Marit. Did you fight?"

"Er . . . no." Rasmus Olsen looked shaken, and he started walking faster. As if to leave the policeman behind, or at least to move beyond the hearing range of others. It was only when they were sitting behind the closed office door in the group secretariat that he released his trembling breath. "Of course we had our ups and downs. Are you married, Bellman?"

Mikael Bellman nodded.

"Then you know what I mean."

"Was she unfaithful?"

"No. I think I can count that one out."

Since she was so fat? Bellman felt like asking, but he dropped it. He had what he was after. The hesitation, the twitch at the corner of his eye, the almost imperceptible contraction of the pupil.

"And you, Olsen, have you been unfaithful?"

Same reaction. Plus a certain flush to the forehead under the receding hairline. The answer was brief and resolute. "No, in fact I haven't."

Bellman angled his head. He didn't suspect Rasmus Olsen. So why torment the man with this type of question? The answer was as simple as it was exasperating. Because he had no one else to question, no other leads to follow. He was merely taking out his frustration on this poor man.

"What about you?"

"What about me?" Bellman said, stifling a yawn.

"Have you been unfaithful?"

Bellman smiled. "My wife is too beautiful. Furthermore, we have two children. You and your wife were childless, and that encourages a little more . . . fun. I was talking to a source who said that you and your wife were having problems a while ago."

"I assume that's the next-door neighbor. Marit talked quite a bit with her, yes. There was a jealous patch some months ago. I had recruited a young girl to the party at a union conference. That was how I met Marit, so she . . ."

Rasmus Olsen's voice disintegrated, and Bellman saw that tears were welling up in his eyes.

"It was nothing. But Marit went to the mountains for a couple of days to think things over. Afterward everything was fine again."

Bellman's phone rang. He took it out, saw the name on the display and answered with a curt "Yes." And felt his pulse and fury increase as he listened to the voice.

"Rope?" he repeated. "Lyseren? That's . . . Ytre Enebakk? Thanks."

He stuffed the phone in his coat pocket. "I have to go, Olsen. Thank you for your time."

On his way out Bellman briefly stopped and looked around the room Terboven, the German Nazi, had occupied.

It was one o'clock in the morning and Harry was sitting in the living room listening to Martha Wainwright singing "Far Away": "Whatever remains is yet to be found."

He was exhausted. In front of him on the coffee table was his cell phone, the lighter and the silver foil containing the brown clump. He hadn't touched it. But he had to sleep soon, find a rhythm, have a break. In his hand he was holding a photo of Rakel. Blue dress. He closed his eyes. Smelled her scent. Heard her voice. "Look!" Her hand exerted a light squeeze. The water around them was black and deep, and she floated, white, soundless, weightless on the surface. The wind raised her veil and showed the white feathers beneath. Her long, slim neck formed a question mark. Where? She stepped ashore, a black iron skeleton with chafing, wailing wheels. She entered the house and vanished from sight. And reappeared on the first floor. She had a noose around her neck and there was a man by her side wearing a black suit with a white flower in his lapel. In front, with his back to them, stood a priest in a white cloak. He was reading slowly. Then he turned. His face and hands were white. Made of snow.

Harry awoke with a start.

Blinked in the dark. Sound. But not Martha Wainwright. Harry grabbed the luminous, vibrating phone on the coffee table.

"Yes," he said with a voice like sludge.

"I've got it."

He sat up. "You've got what?"

"The link. And there aren't three dead. There are four."

22

Search Engine

"First of all, I tried the three names you gave me," said Katrine Bratt. "Borgny Stem-Myhre, Charlotte Lolles and Marit Olsen. But the search didn't produce anything sensible. So I put in all the missing persons in Norway over the last twelve months as well. And then I had something to work with."

"Wait," Harry said. He was wide awake now. "Where the hell did you get the missing persons from?"

"Intranet at Missing Persons Unit, Oslo Police District. What did you think?"

Harry groaned, and Katrine went on.

"There was one name that in fact linked the other three. Are you ready?"

"Well . . . ?"

"The missing woman is named Adele Vetlesen,

twenty-three years old, living in Drammen. She was reported missing by her partner in November. A connection appeared on the Norwegian State Railway ticketing system. On the seventh of November Adele Vetlesen booked a train ticket online from Drammen to Ustaoset. The same day Borgny Stem-Myhre bought a train ticket from Kongsberg to the same place."

"Ustaoset's not exactly the center of the universe," Harry said.

"It's not a place—it's a chunk of mountain. Where Bergen families have built their mountain cabins with old money and the Tourist Association has built cabins on the peaks, so that Norwegians can preserve Amundsen and Nansen's heritage and trudge from cabin to cabin with skis on their feet, fifty pounds on their backs and a taste of mortal fear in the hinterland of the mind. Adds spice to life, you know."

"Sounds like you've been there."

"My ex-husband's family has a cabin in the mountains. They're so rich and revered that they have neither electricity nor running water. Only social climbers have a sauna and a Jacuzzi."

"The other connections?"

"There wasn't a train ticket in the name of Marit Olsen. However, a payment was registered on the cash dispenser in the restaurant car on the corresponding train the day before. At two-thirteen p.m. According to the railway timetable that would be somewhere between Ål and Geilo, in other words before Ustaoset."

"Less convincing," Harry said. "The train goes right through to Bergen. Perhaps she was going there."

"Do you think . . . ?" Katrine Bratt started, then faltered, waited and went on in hushed tones. "You think I'm stupid? The hotel at Ustaoset booked an overnight stay in a double room for one Rasmus Olsen, who, according to the Civil Registration System, resides at the same address as Marit Olsen. So I assumed that—"

"Yes, that's her husband. Why are you whispering?"

"Because the night porter just walked past, OK? Listen, we've placed two murder victims and one missing person in Ustaoset on the same day. What do you think?"

"Well, it's a significant coincidence, but we can't exclude the possibility that it's pure chance."

"Agreed. So here's the rest. I searched for Charlotte Lolles plus Ustaoset, but didn't get a hit. So I concentrated on the date to see where Charlotte Lolles might have been when the other three were in Ustaoset. Two days before, Charlotte had paid for diesel at a gas station outside Hønefoss."

"That's a long way from Ustaoset."

"But it's in the right direction from Oslo. I tried to find a car registered in her name or a possible partner's. If they have an AutoPASS and have driven through several toll booths you can follow their movements."

"Mm."

"The problem is that she had neither a car nor a live-in partner, not officially, anyway."

"She had a boyfriend."

"It's possible. But the search engine found a car in a EuroPark garage in Geilo, paid for by an Iska Peller."

"That's just a mile or so away from Ustaoset. But who's . . . er, Iska Peller?"

"According to the credit card info she's a resident of Bristol, Sydney, Australia. The point is that she scores high on a relational search with Charlotte Lolles."

"Relational search?"

"It works like this, OK. Based on the last few years, names come up for people paying with a card at the same restaurant at the same time, which suggests that they have eaten together and split the bill. Or for people who are members of the same gym with matching enrollment dates or have plane seats next to each other more than once. You get the picture."

"I get the picture," Harry repeated, copying her Bergensian intonation. "And I'm sure you've checked out the make of car and whether it uses—"

"Yes, I have, and it uses diesel," Katrine answered sharply. "Do you want to hear the rest or not?"

"By all means."

"You can't prebook beds in these self-service Tourist Association cabins. If all the beds are taken when you arrive, you just have to bed down on the floor, on a mattress or in a sleeping bag with your own mat. It costs only a hundred and seventy a night, and you can either put cash into a box at the cabin or leave an envelope with authorization to charge your account."

"In other words, you can't see who has been in which cabins and when?"

"Not if they pay cash. But if they've left an authorization, afterward there would be a transaction on their account between them and the Tourist Association, mentioning the cabin used and the date the payment was for."

"I seem to remember it's a pain searching through bank transactions."

"Not if the engine is given the right criteria by a sharp human brain."

"Which is the case, I take it?"

"That's the general idea. Iska Peller's account was charged for two beds at four of the Tourist Association cabins, each a day's hike from the next."

"A four-day skiing trip."

"Yes. And they stayed at the last one, the Håvass cabin, on the seventh of November. It's only half a day's walk from Ustaoset."

"Interesting."

"What's really interesting is that there are two other accounts that were charged for overnight stays at the Håvass cabin on the seventh of November. Guess whose?"

"Well, it'll hardly be Marit Olsen's or Borgny Stem-Myhre's since I assume Kripos would have found out that two of the murder victims had recently stayed at the same place the same night. So it must be the missing girl's. What was her name?"

"Adele Vetlesen. And you're right. She paid for two

people, but there's no way of knowing who the other person was."

"Who's the other person who paid with an authorization slip?"

"Not so interesting. From Stavanger."

Nevertheless Harry picked up a pen and noted the name and address of the individual concerned and also of Iska Peller in Sydney. "Sounds like you're good at search engines," he said.

"Yep," she said. "It's like flying an old bomber. A little rusty and slow to get going, but when you're in the air . . . my goodness. What do you think of the results?"

Harry pondered.

"What you've done," he said, "is to locate one missing woman and a woman who presumably has nothing to do with the case at the same place at the same time. In itself, nothing to shout about. But you've made it more likely that one of the murder victims—Charlotte Lolles—was with her. And you've located two of the murder victims—Borgny Stem-Myhre and Marit Olsen—in the immediate vicinity of Ustaoset. So . . ."

"So?"

"So, my congratulations. You've kept your part of the bargain. Now, as for mine . . ."

"Save your breath and wipe that grin off your face. I didn't mean it. I'm of unsound mind—didn't you realize?"

She smacked down the receiver.

23

Passenger

She was alone on the bus. Stine rested her forehead against the window so that she wouldn't see her reflection. Stared out into the deserted, pitch-black bus station. Hoping someone would come. Hoping no one would come.

He had been sitting by a window in Krabbe with a beer in front of him, staring at her, motionless. Woolen hat, blond hair and those wild blue eyes. His eyes laughed, penetrated, implored, called her name. In the end she had told Mathilde that she wanted to go home. But Mathilde had just started a conversation with an American oil guy and wanted to stay a little longer. So Stine had grabbed her coat, run from Krabbe to the bus station and gotten on a bus to Våland.

She looked at the red numbers on the digital clock above the driver. Hoping the doors would shut and the bus would start moving. One minute left.

She didn't raise her eyes, not even when she heard the running footsteps, heard the breathless voice request a ticket from the driver at the front, nor when he sat down on the seat beside her.

"Hey, Stine," he said. "I think you're avoiding me."

"Oh, hi, Elias," she said, without shifting her gaze from the rain-wet pavement. Why had she sat so far back in the bus, so far from the driver?

"You shouldn't be out alone on a night like this, you know."

"Shouldn't I?" she mumbled, hoping someone would come, anyone.

"Don't you read the newspapers? Those two women in Oslo. And now, the other day, that MP. What was her name again?"

"No idea," Stine lied, feeling her heart rate gallop.

"Marit Olsen," Elias said. "Socialist party. The other two were Borgny and Charlotte. Sure you don't recognize the names, Stine?"

"I don't read newspapers," Stine said. Someone had to come soon.

"Great women, all three of them," he said.

"'Course, you knew them, didn't you?" Stine regretted the sarcastic tone immediately. It was fear.

"Not well though," Elias said. "But the first impression was good. I'm—as you know—the kind who attaches a lot of importance to first impressions."

She stared at the hand he cautiously placed on her knee.

"You . . ." she said, and even in that one syllable she could hear herself begging.

"Yes, Stine?"

She looked up at him. His face was as open as a child's, his eyes genuinely curious. She wanted to scream, jump up, when she heard the steps and voice up by the driver. A passenger. A man. He came to the back of the bus. Stine tried to catch his eye, to make him understand, but the brim of his hat covered the upper half of his face, and he was busy checking his change and putting the ticket in his wallet. Her breathing was lighter when he took a seat right behind them.

"It's incredible that the police haven't discovered the connection between them," Elias said. "It shouldn't be so difficult. They must know that all three women liked to go cross-country skiing in the mountains. They stayed at the cabin in Håvass on the same night. Do you think I should tell them?"

"Maybe," Stine whispered. If she was quick, perhaps she could squeeze past Elias and jump off the bus. But she had hardly articulated the thought in her mind before the hydraulics hissed, the doors slid shut and the bus set off. She closed her eyes.

"I just don't want to be involved. I hope you can understand that, Stine."

She nodded slowly, her eyes still closed.

"Good. Then I can tell you about someone else who was there. Someone I'm sure you know."

Part Three

24

Stavanger

"It smells of . . ." Kaja said.

"Shit," Harry said. "Cow variety. Welcome to the district of Jæren."

The dawn light leaked from the clouds sweeping across the spring-green fields. From behind stone walls cows stared mutely at their taxi. They were on their way downtown from Stavanger Sola Airport.

Harry leaned forward between the front seats. "Could you speed it up, driver?" He held up his ID card. The driver beamed and gave it some gas, and they accelerated onto the highway.

"Are you afraid we're too late?" Kaja asked as Harry fell back.

"Didn't answer the phone, didn't turn up for work," Harry said, not needing to complete his reasoning.

After he had spoken to Katrine Bratt the night before, Harry had skimmed over what he had noted down. He had the names, telephone numbers and addresses of two living persons who had probably stayed in a cabin in November with the three murder victims. He had checked his watch, worked out it was early morning in Sydney and called Iska Peller's number. She had answered and sounded very surprised when Harry broached the topic of the Håvass cabin.

She hadn't been able to tell Harry much about the overnight stay because she had been stuck in a bedroom with a high fever. Perhaps because she had been wearing wet, sweaty clothes for too long, perhaps because skiing from cabin to cabin had been a baptism of fire for an inexperienced langlaufer like herself. Or perhaps simply because flu strikes at random. At any rate, she had only just managed to drag herself to Håvass, where she had been ordered straight to bed by her companion, Charlotte Lolles. There, Iska Peller had drifted in and out of dream-filled sleep as her body ached, sweated and froze in turn. Whatever had gone on among the others in the cabin, whoever they were, well, she hadn't picked up anything, as she and Charlotte had been the first to arrive. The next day she had stayed in bed until the others had left, and she and Charlotte were collected on a snowmobile by a local policeman Charlotte had managed to contact. He had driven them to his place, where he had invited them to stay overnight since he said the only hotel was full. They had accepted, but that night they changed their minds and caught a late train to Geilo to stay at a hotel there. Charlotte hadn't told Iska anything in particular about the night in the Håvass cabin. An uneventful night, apparently.

Five days after the ski trip Iska had left Oslo for Sydney, still with a temperature, and had kept in regular email contact with Charlotte but hadn't noticed anything out of the ordinary. That is, until she received the shocking news that her friend had been found dead behind a wrecked car on the edge of some woods by Lake Dausjøen, just outside the urban sprawl of Oslo.

Harry had explained to Iska Peller with some care, but without beating around the bush, that they were worried about the people who had been in the cabin on the night of November 7 and that, after hanging up, he would call the head of the crime division in Sydney South Police District, Neil McCormack, whom Harry had worked for on one occasion. McCormack, he said, would require further details from her and—even though Australia was a long way from Oslo—provide police protection until further notice. Iska Peller seemed to accept this with equanimity.

Then Harry had called the second number he had been given, the number in Stavanger. He had tried four times, but no one had answered. He knew, of course, that this did not mean anything in itself. Not everyone slept with his cell switched on beside him. But Kaja Solness clearly did. She answered on the second ring, and when Harry said they were going to Stavanger on the first flight and that she should be on the airport express by five past six, she had uttered one word: "OK."

They had arrived at Oslo's Gardermoen Airport at half past six and Harry had tried the number again, without success. An hour later they had landed at Stavanger Sola Airport, and Harry called with the same result. On their way to the taxi line, Kaja managed to contact the employer, who said that the person they were looking for had not turned up for work at the usual time. She had informed Harry, and he had gently placed his hand on the small of her back and led her firmly past the taxi line and into a taxi in the face of loud protests, which he met with: "Thank you, and may you have a wonderful day, folks."

It was exactly 8:16 when they arrived at the address, a white timber house in Våland. Harry let Kaja pay, got out and left the door open. Studied the house front, which revealed nothing. Inhaled the damp, fresh, though still mild Vestland air. Braced himself. Because he already knew. He might be mistaken, of course, but he knew with the same certainty that he knew Kaja would say, "Thank you," after being given the receipt.

"Thank you." The car door closed.

The name was next to the middle of the three bells, by the front door.

Harry pressed the button and heard the bell ring somewhere in the house's innards.

One minute and three attempts later he pressed the bottom bell.

The old lady who opened the door smiled at them.

Harry noted that Kaja instinctively knew who should speak. "Hello, I'm Kaja Solness. We're from the police. The floor above you isn't answering. Do you know if anyone is at home?"

"Probably. Even though it's been quiet there this morning," the lady said. And, on seeing Harry's elevated eyebrows, hastened to add: "You can hear everything here, and I heard people last night. Since I rent out the flat I think I ought to keep an ear open."

"Keep an ear open?" Harry queried.

"Yes, but I don't stick . . ." The lady's cheeks flushed pink. "There's nothing wrong, is there? I mean, I've never had any problems at all with—"

"We don't know," Harry said.

"The best thing to do would be to check," Kaja said. "So if you have a key . . ." Harry knew a variety of set phrases would be whirring around Kaja's brain now, and waited for the continuation with interest. "Then we would like to assist you in ensuring that everything is in order."

Kaja Solness was a bright woman. If the house owner agreed to the proposal and they found something, the report would say they were summoned. There was no question of their having forced their way in or having ransacked the place without a warrant.

The woman hesitated.

"But you can also let yourself in after we've gone." Kaja smiled. "And then call the police. Or the ambulance. Or . . ."

"I think it's best if you come with me," the woman said after a deep furrow of concern entrenched itself in her brow. "Wait here and I'll fetch the keys."

The flat they entered one minute later was clean, tidy and almost completely unfurnished. At once Harry recognized the silence that is so present, so oppressive, in bare flats in the morning, when the hustle and bustle of the working day is a scarcely audible noise on the outside. But there was also a smell he recognized. Glue. He spotted a pair of shoes, though no outdoor clothing.

In the kitchenette there was a large teacup in the sink, and on the shelf above cans proclaiming they contained teas of unknown origin to Harry: oolong, Anji Bai Cha. They advanced through the flat. On the sitting-room wall was a picture Harry thought was K2, the popular killing machine of a mountain in the Himalayas.

"Check that one, will you?" Harry asked, nodding to the door with a heart on it, and walked to what he assumed must be the bedroom door. He took a deep breath, pressed down the handle and pushed open the door.

The bed was made, the room tidy. A window was ajar, no smell of glue, air as fresh as a child's breath. Harry heard the landlady take up a position in the doorway behind him.

"So odd," she said. "I heard them last night, I did. But there was only one person's steps."

"Them?" Harry said. "You're sure there was more than one person?"

"Yes, I heard voices."

"How many?"

"Three, I would say."

Harry peered into the closet. "Men? Women?"

"You can't hear absolutely everything, I'm afraid."

Clothes. A sleeping bag and a knapsack. More clothes.

"Why would you say there were three?"

"After one left, I heard noises from up here."

"What sort of noises?"

The landlady's cheeks flushed again. "Banging. As if . . . well, you know."

"But no voices?"

The landlady considered the question. "No, no voices."

Harry walked out of the room. And to his surprise saw that Kaja was still standing in the hall by the bathroom door. There was something about the way she was standing—as though facing a strong headwind.

"Something up?"

"Not at all," Kaja said quickly, lightly. Too lightly.

Harry went over and stood beside her.

"What is it?" he asked in a whisper.

"I . . . just have a tiny problem with closed doors."

"OK," Harry said.

"That's . . . that's just how I am."

Harry nodded. And that was when he heard the sound. The sound of allotted time, of a line running out, of seconds disappearing, a quick, hectic drumming of water that doesn't quite flow and doesn't quite drip. A tap on the other side of the door. And he knew he had not been mistaken.

"Wait here," Harry said. He pushed open the door.

The first thing he noticed was that the smell of glue was even stronger inside.

The second was that a jacket, a pair of jeans, pants, a T-shirt, two black socks, a hat and a thin wool sweater were lying on the floor.

The third was that water was dripping in an almost continuous line from the tap into a bathtub so full that water was escaping down the overflow at the side.

The fourth was that the water in the bath was red—blood, from what he could tell.

The fifth was that the glazed eyes above the taped mouth of the naked, corpse-white person lying at the bottom of the bath faced the side. As if trying to glimpse something in the blind spot, something he hadn't seen coming.

The sixth was that he couldn't see any indications of violence, no external injuries that would explain all the blood.

Harry cleared his throat and wondered how he could ask the landlady in the most considerate way possible to come in and identify her lodger.

But he didn't have to; she was already at the door.

"Omigod!" she groaned. And then, stressing every single syllable: "Oh my God!" And, finally, in a wailing tone invoking even greater emphasis: "Oh my Lord God Almighty . . ."

"Is it . . . ?" Harry began.

"Yes," the woman said with a tear-filled voice. "That's him. That's Elias. Elias Skog."

25

Territory

The woman had clasped her hands in front of her mouth, and mumbled through her fingers. "But what have you done, dear Elias? A vein?"

"I'm not sure he did anything," Harry said, leading her from the bathroom to the front door of the flat. "Could I ask you to call the police station in Stavanger and tell them to send forensics officers? Tell them we have a crime scene here."

"Crime scene?" Her eyes were large and black with shock.

"Yes, say that. Use the emergency number, one-one-two, if you like. OK?"

"Y-yes."

They heard the woman stomping down the stairs to her flat.

"We've got about a quarter of an hour before they get here," Harry said. They removed their shoes, put them in the hall and walked into the bathroom in stockinged feet. Harry looked around. The sink was full of long blond hair, and on the bench a tube was squeezed flat.

"That looks like toothpaste," Harry said, bending over the tube, trying not to touch it.

Kaja went closer. "Super Glue," she stated. "Strongest there is."

"That's the stuff you shouldn't get on your fingers, isn't it?"

"Works in no time. If your fingers are pressed together for too long, they'll be stuck. Then you'll either have to cut them apart or tug until the skin comes off."

Harry stared first at Kaja. Then at the body in the bath.

"Fucking hell," he said slowly. "This can't be true . . ."

POB Gunnar Hagen had had his doubts. Perhaps it was the stupidest thing he had done since he came to Police HQ. Forming a group to run an investigation, against the ministry's orders, could get him into trouble. Making Harry Hole the leader was asking for trouble. And trouble had just knocked on the door and walked in. Now it was standing in front of him in the shape of Mikael Bellman. And as Hagen listened, he noticed the strange marks on the Kripos POB's face, which were shining whiter than usual, as if they were illuminated by something red hot inside, cooled fission in a nuclear reactor, a potential explosion that was under control for the moment.

"Beate Lønn from Krimteknisk asked us to carry out a cabin-to-cabin search in the Lake Lyseren area around an old ropery. One of her officers was said to have found out that the rope used to hang Marit Olsen originates from there. So far, so good . . .″

Mikael Bellman rocked back on his heels. He hadn't even taken off his floor-length trench coat. Gunnar Hagen steeled himself for what was to follow. Which came in painfully protracted form, with somewhat perplexed intonation.

"But when we spoke to the officer in Ytre Enebakk, he told me that the herostratic Harry Hole was one of three officers involved in the investigation. Hence, one of your men, Hagen."

Hagen didn't answer.

"I assume you are aware of the consequences of placing yourself above Ministry of Justice orders, Hagen."

Hagen still didn't answer, but he met Bellman's glare.

"Listen," Bellman said, loosening a button on his coat and sitting down after all. "I like you, Hagen. I think you're a good policeman, and I will need good men."

"When Kripos has total power, you mean?"

"Exactly. I could benefit from having someone like you in a prominent position. You have a military academy background, you know the importance of thinking tactically, of avoiding battles you can't win, of realizing when retreat is the best way to win . . ."

Hagen nodded slowly.

"Good," Bellman said, rising to his feet. "Let's say Harry Hole inadvertently found himself by Lake

Lyseren; it was a coincidence, had nothing to do with Marit Olsen. And such coincidences are hardly likely to recur. Can we agree on that . . . Gunnar?"

Hagen flinched involuntarily when he heard his first name in the other man's mouth, like an echo of a first name he himself had once spoken, his predecessor's, in an attempt to create a joviality for which there was no basis. But he let it go. For he knew that this was the kind of battle Bellman had been talking about. And that, furthermore, he was about to lose the war. And that the conditions of surrender that Bellman had offered him could have been worse. A lot worse.

"I'll have a word with Harry," he said and took Bellman's outstretched hand. It was like squeezing marble: hard, cold and lifeless.

Harry took a swig and unhooked the final joint of his forefinger from the handle of the landlady's translucent coffee cup.

"So you're Inspector Harry Hole from Oslo Police District," said the man sitting on the opposite side of the landlady's coffee table. He had introduced himself as Inspector Colbjørnsen, "with a **C**," and now he repeated Harry's title, name and affiliation with the stress on **Oslo**. "And what brings the Oslo Police to Stavanger, Herr Hole?"

"The usual," Harry said. "Fresh air, beautiful mountains."

"Oh, yes?"

"The fjord. Cliff jumping from Pulpit Rock, if we have time."

"So Oslo has sent us a comedian? You're participating in an extreme sport—I can tell you that much. Any good reason why we were not informed of this visit?"

Inspector Colbjørnsen's smile was as thin as his mustache. He was sporting one of those funny little hats only very old men and super-self-aware hipsters have. Harry was reminded of "Popeye" Doyle in **The French Connection.** And guessed that Colbjørnsen would not shy away from sucking a lollipop or stopping on his way out of the door with an "Oh, just one more thing."

"I would guess there must be a fax at the bottom of the in-tray," Harry said, looking up at the man in the white outfit as he entered. The forensics officer's overalls rustled as he took off his white hood and plumped down into a chair. He looked straight at Colbjørnsen and muttered a local profanity.

"Well?" asked Colbjørnsen.

"He's right," the crime scene officer said and nodded in Harry's direction, without glancing at him. "The kid up there has been stuck to the bottom of the bathtub with Super Glue."

" 'Has been'?" said Colbjørnsen, looking at his subordinate with a quizzical eyebrow. "Passive form. Aren't you a bit premature in ruling out the possibility that Elias Skog did it himself?"

"And managed to turn on the tap so he would drown in the slowest, most painful manner conceivable?" Harry suggested. "After taping up his mouth so that he couldn't scream?"

Colbjørnsen sent Harry another razor-thin smile. "I'll tell you when you can interrupt, **Oslo.**"

"Stuck fast from top to toe," the officer continued. "The back of his head was shaved and smeared with glue. The same with his shoulders and back. Buttocks. Arms. Both legs. In other words—"

"In other words," Harry said, "when the killer was finished with the gluing job, Elias had been lying there for a while and the adhesive had been hardening. He turned the tap a little way and left Elias Skog to a slow death by drowning. And Elias began his fight against time and death. The water rose slowly but his strength was ebbing away. Until mortal fear had him in its grip and gave him the energy for a last desperate attempt to pull himself free. And he did. He freed the strongest of his limbs from the bottom of the bathtub. His right leg. He simply tore it off, and you can see the skin left on the bath surface. Blood spurted into the water as Elias banged his foot to rouse the landlady downstairs. And she heard the banging."

Harry nodded toward the kitchen, where Kaja was trying to calm and console the elderly lady. They could hear her bitter sobs.

"But she misunderstood. She thought her lodger was bonking a girl who had accompanied him home."

He looked at Colbjørnsen, who had turned pale and no longer exhibited any signs of wanting to interrupt.

"And all the time Elias was losing blood. A lot of blood. All the skin from his leg was gone. He became weaker, more tired. In the end, his determination began to fade. He gave up. Perhaps he was already unconscious from loss of blood as the water rose into his nostrils." Harry fixed his eyes on Colbjørnsen. "Or perhaps not."

Colbjørnsen's Adam's apple was running a shuttle service.

Harry looked down at the dregs in the coffee cup. "And now I think Detective Solness and I should thank you for your hospitality and return to Oslo. Should you have any more questions, you can reach me here." Harry jotted down a number in the margin of a newspaper, tore it off and passed it over the table. Then he got to his feet.

"But . . ." said Colbjørnsen, getting to his feet as well. Harry towered eight inches above him. "What was it you wanted with Elias Skog?"

"To save him," Harry said, buttoning up his coat.

"Save? Was he mixed up in something? Wait, Hole—we have to get to the bottom of this." But there was no longer the same authority in Colbjørnsen's voice.

"I'm sure you officers in the Stavanger force are perfectly capable of working this out for yourselves," Harry said, walking to the kitchen door and motioning to Kaja that they were leaving. "If not, I can recommend Kripos. Say hello to Mikael Bellman from me, if you have to."

"Save him from what?"

"From what we were unable to save him from," Harry said.

In the taxi on the way to Sola, Harry stared out of the window at the rain hammering down on the unnaturally green fields. Kaja didn't say a word. For which he was grateful.

26

The Needle

Gunnar Hagen was in Harry's chair waiting for them when Harry and Kaja stepped into the hot, damp office.

Bjørn Holm, who was sitting behind Hagen, shrugged and gestured that he didn't know what the POB wanted.

"Stavanger, I hear," Hagen said, getting up.

"Yes," Harry said. "Don't get up, boss."

"It's your chair. I'll be going soon."

"Oh?"

Harry inferred that it was bad news. Bad news of a certain significance. Bosses don't hasten down the culvert to Botsen Prison to tell you your travel invoice has been completed incorrectly.

Hagen remained standing, so Holm was the only person in the room to be seated.

"I'm afraid I have to inform you that Kripos has

already discovered that you are working on the murders. And I have no choice but to close the investigation."

In the ensuing silence Harry could hear the boiler rumbling in the adjacent room. Hagen ran his eyes over them, meeting each gaze in turn and stopping at Harry. "I can't say this is an honorable discharge, either. I gave you clear instructions that this was to be a discreet operation."

"Well," Harry said, "I asked Beate Lønn to leak information about a certain ropery to Kripos, but she promised she would do it in a way that made Krimteknisk appear to be the source."

"And I'm sure she did," Hagen said. "It was the county officer in Ytre Enebakk who gave you away, Harry."

Harry rolled his eyes and uttered a low curse.

Hagen clapped his hands together and a dry bang resounded between the brick walls. "So that's why, sadly, I have to command you to drop all investigative work immediately. And to clear this office within forty-eight hours. **Gomen nasai.**"

Harry, Kaja and Bjørn looked at one another as the iron door closed and Hagen's hurried footsteps faded down the culvert.

"Forty-eight hours," Bjørn said at length. "Anyone want fresh coffee?"

Harry kicked the garbage can beside the desk. It hit the wall with a crash, spilling its modest contents and rolling back toward him.

"I'll be at Rikshospital," he said and strode toward the door.

Harry had positioned the hard wooden chair by the window and listened to his father's regular breathing as he flicked through the newspaper. A wedding and a funeral side by side. On the left, pictures of Marit Olsen's funeral, showing the Norwegian prime minister's serious, compassionate face, party colleagues' black suits and the husband, Rasmus Olsen, behind a pair of large, unbecoming sunglasses. On the right, an article announcing that the shipping magnate's daughter Lene would get her Tony in the spring, with photos of the (A-list) wedding guests who would all be flown into St. Tropez. On the back page, it said that the sun would go down today at precisely 5:15 in Oslo. Harry looked at his watch and established that it was in fact doing that now, behind the low clouds that would not release either rain or snow. He watched the lights coming on in all the homes on the side of the ridge around what had once been a volcano. In a way, it was a liberating thought that the volcano would open beneath them one day, swallow them up and remove all traces of what had once been a contented, well-organized and slightly sad town.

Forty-eight hours. Why? It wouldn't take them more than two hours to clear out their so-called office.

Harry closed his eyes and considered the case. Wrote a last mental report for his personal archive.

Two women killed in the same way, drowning in their own blood, with ketanome in the bloodstream. One woman hanged from a diving tower, with a rope taken from an old ropery. One man drowned in his own bathtub. All the victims had probably been in the same cabin at the same time. They didn't know yet who else had been there, what the motive behind the murders could be or what had gone on in the Håvass cabin that day or night. There was just effect, no cause. Case closed.

"Harry . . ."

He hadn't heard his father wake, and he turned.

Olav Hole looked renewed, but perhaps that was because of the color in his cheeks and the feverish glow in his eyes. Harry got up and moved his chair over to his father's bedside.

"Have you been here long?"

"Ten minutes," Harry lied.

"I've slept so well," Olav said. "And had such wonderful dreams."

"I can see. You look like you're ready to get up and leave."

Harry plumped his pillow, and his father let him do it even though they both knew that it wasn't necessary.

"How's the house?"

"Fine," Harry said. "It will stand forever."

"Good. There's something I want to talk to you about, Harry."

"Mm?"

"You're a grown man now. You'll lose me in a natural way. That's how it should be. Not how you lost your mother. You were on the verge of going insane."

"Was I?" Harry said, straightening the pillowcase.

"You demolished your room. You wanted to kill the doctors, those who had infected her, and even me. Because I had . . . well, because I hadn't discovered it earlier, I suppose. You were so full of love."

"Of hatred, you mean?"

"No, of love. It's the same currency. Everything starts with love. Hatred is just the other side of the coin. I've always thought that your mother's death was what drove you to drink. Or rather the love for your mother."

"Love is a killer," Harry mumbled.

"What?"

"Just something someone once said to me."

"I did everything your mother asked me to do. Apart from one thing. She asked me to help her when the time came."

It felt as if someone had injected ice-cold water into Harry's chest.

"But I couldn't. And do you know what, Harry? It has given me nightmares. Not a day has passed when I haven't thought about not being able to fulfill that wish for her, for the woman I loved above all else on this earth."

The thin wooden chair creaked as Harry jumped up. He walked over to the window. He heard his father draw breath a couple of times behind him, deep, trembling. Then it came.

"I know that this is a heavy burden to impose on you, son. But I also know that you're like me—it will haunt you if you don't. So let me explain what you do . . ."

"Dad," Harry said.

"Can you see this hypodermic needle?"

"Dad! Stop!"

Everything went quiet behind him. Except for the rasp of his breathing. Outside, Harry saw the black-and-white film of a town with facelike clouds pressing their blurred, leaden-gray features against the rooftops.

"I want to be buried in Åndalsnes," his father said.

Buried. The word sounded like an echo from Easter with Mom and Dad in Lesja, when Olav Hole, with great earnestness, explained to Harry and Sis what they should do if they were buried in an avalanche and they had constrictive pericarditis, a hardened sac around the heart that prevented it from expanding. An armored heart. Around them were flat fields and gently sloping ridges; it was a bit like when stewardesses on domestic flights over Inner Mongolia explain how to use life jackets. Absurd, but nevertheless it gave them a feeling of security, the sense that they would all survive if they just did the right things. And now Dad was saying that wasn't true, after all.

Harry coughed. "Åndalsnes . . . to be with Mom . . . ?"

Harry fell quiet.

"And I want to lie alongside my fellow villagers."

"You don't know them."

"Well, who do we know? At least they and I are from the same place. Perhaps ultimately that's what it's about. The tribe. We want to be with our tribe."

"Do we?"

"Yes, we do. Whether we are aware of it or not, that's what we want."

The nurse named Altman came in, flashed a quick smile at Harry and tapped his watch.

Harry went downstairs and met two uniformed policemen on their way up. He nodded automatically; it was a convention. They stared at him in silence, as though he were a stranger.

Usually Harry longed for solitude and all the benefits that came with it: peace, calm, freedom. But, standing at the tram stop, suddenly he didn't know where to go. Or what to do. He just knew that being alone in the house in Oppsal would be unbearable right now.

He dialed Øystein's number.

Øystein was on a long trip to Fagernes, but suggested a beer at Lompa at around midnight to celebrate the relatively satisfactory completion of another day in Øystein Eikeland's life. Harry reminded Øystein that Harry was an alcoholic, and received the response that even an alcoholic had to go on a bender once in a while, didn't he?

Harry wished Øystein a safe journey and hung up. Glanced at his watch. And the question arose again. Forty-eight hours. Why?

A tram stopped in front of him and the doors banged open. Harry peered into the invitingly warm, lit carriage. Then he turned and began to walk down toward town.

27

Kind, Light-Fingered and Tight-Fisted

"I was in the vicinity," Harry said. "But I suppose you're on your way out."

"Not at all." Kaja, who was standing in the doorway with a thick down jacket on, smiled. "I was sitting on the veranda. Come in. Take the slippers over there."

Harry removed his shoes and followed her through the living room. They each sat down on an enormous wooden chair on the covered veranda. It was quiet and deserted on Lyder Sagens Gate, only one parked car. But on the first floor of the house across the road Harry could see the outline of a man in an illuminated window.

"That's Greger," Kaja said. "He's eighty now. He's sat like that and followed everything that's happened on the street since the war, I think. I like to believe he looks after me."

"Yes, we need that," Harry said, taking out a pack of cigarettes. "To believe someone is looking after us."

"Do you have a Greger as well?"

"No," Harry said.

"Can I have one?"

"A cigarette?"

She laughed. "I smoke occasionally. It makes me . . . calmer, I think."

"Mm. Thought about what you're going to do? After these forty-eight hours, I mean."

She shook her head. "Back to Crime Squad. Feet on the table. Wait for a murder that is trivial enough for Kripos not to whisk it away from under our noses."

Harry tapped out two cigarettes, put them between his lips, lit both and passed her one.

"**Now, Voyager,**" she said. "Hen . . . Hen . . . What was the name of the man who did that?"

"Henreid," Harry said. "Paul Henreid."

"And the woman whose cigarette he lit?"

"Bette Davis."

"Killer film. Would you like to borrow a thicker jacket?"

"No, thanks. Why are you sitting on the veranda, by the way? It's not exactly a tropical night."

She held up a book. "My brain is sharper in cold air."

Harry read the front cover. "**Materialistic Monism.** Hm. Long-forgotten fragments from philosophy studies spring to mind."

"Right. Materialism holds that everything is matter and energy. Everything that happens is a part of a larger calculation, a chain reaction, consequences of something that has already happened."

"And free will is illusory?"

"Yep. Our actions are determined by our brain's

chemical composition, which is determined by who chose to have children with whom, which in turn is determined by their brain chemistry. And so on. Everything can be taken back to the big bang, for example, and even farther back. Including the fact that this book came to be written, and what you're thinking right now."

"I remember that part." Harry nodded and blew smoke into the winter night. "Made me think of the meteorologist who said that if only he had all the relevant variables he could forecast all future weather."

"And we could prevent murders before they took place."

"And predict that cigarette-cadging policewomen would sit on cold verandas with expensive philosophy books."

She laughed. "I didn't buy the book myself; I found it on the shelf here." She pouted and sucked at the cigarette, and got smoke in her eyes. "I never buy books—I only borrow them. Or steal them."

"I don't exactly see you as a thief."

"No one does—that's why I'm never caught," she said, resting the cigarette on the ashtray.

Harry coughed. "And why do you pilfer?"

"I only steal from people I know and who can afford it. Not because I'm greedy, but because I'm a little cheap. When I was in college, I stole toilet-paper rolls from the school restrooms. By the way, have you thought of the title of the Fante book that was so good?"

"No."

"Text me when you remember it."

Harry chuckled. "Sorry, I don't text."

"Why not?"

Harry shrugged. "I don't know. I don't like the concept. Like native people who don't want their photo taken because they think they'll lose a bit of their souls, maybe."

"I know!" she said with enthusiasm. "You don't want to leave traces. Tracks. Irrefutable evidence of who you are. You want to know that you are going to disappear, utterly and totally."

"You've hit the nail on the head," Harry said drily, and inhaled. "Do you want to go back in?" He nodded toward her hands, which she had put between her thighs and the chair.

"No, it's just my hands that are cold." She smiled. "Warm heart, though. What about you?"

Harry gazed across the yard's fence, toward the road. At the car standing there. "What about me?"

"Are you like me? Kind, light-fingered and tight-fisted?"

"No, I'm evil, honest and tight-fisted. What about your husband?"

It came out harder than Harry had intended, as though he wanted to put her in her place because she . . . because she what? Because she was sitting here and was beautiful and liked the same things as he did and lent him slippers belonging to a man she pretended didn't exist.

"What about him?" she asked with a tiny smile.

"Well, he's got big feet," Harry heard himself say,

feeling an urgent desire to bang his head on the table.

She laughed out loud. The laughter trilled into the dark Fagerborg silence that lay over the houses, lawns and garages. The garages. Everyone had a garage. There was only one car parked in the street.

Of course there could be a thousand reasons for it being there.

"I don't have a husband," she said.

"So . . ."

"So it's a pair of my brother's slippers you're wearing on your feet."

"And the shoes on the steps . . . ?"

"Are also my brother's, and are there because I suspect that men's size twelve-and-a-half shoes have a deterrent effect on evil men with sinister plans."

She sent Harry a meaningful look. He chose to believe the ambiguity was not intended.

"So your brother lives here?"

She shook her head. "He died. Ten years ago. It's Daddy's house. In the last years, when Even was studying at Blindern, he and Daddy lived here."

"And your father?"

"He died soon after Even. And since I was already living here, I took over the house."

Kaja drew her legs up onto the chair and rested her head on her knees. Harry gazed at the slim neck, the hollow where her pinned-up hair was taut and a few loose strands fell back onto her skin.

"Do you often think about them?" Harry asked.

She raised her head from her knees.

"Mostly about Even," she said. "Daddy moved out when we were small, and Mommy lived in her own bubble, so Even became sort of both parents in one for me. He looked after me, encouraged me, brought me up; he was my role model. He could do no wrong in my eyes. When you've been as close to someone as Even and I were to each other, that closeness never wears off. Never."

Harry nodded.

With a tentative cough, Kaja said: "How's your father?"

Harry studied the cigarette glow.

"Don't you think it's odd?" he said. "Hagen giving us forty-eight hours. We could have cleared the office in two with ease."

"I suppose—now that you say so."

"Maybe he thought we could spend our final two days doing something useful."

Kaja looked at him.

"Not investigating the present murder case, of course. We'll have to leave that to Kripos. But the Missing Persons Unit needs help, I hear."

"What do you mean?"

"Adele Vetlesen is a young woman who, to my knowledge, is not connected with any murder case."

"You think we should . . . ?"

"I think we should meet for work at seven tomorrow morning," Harry said. "And see if we can do something useful."

Kaja Solness sucked on the cigarette again. Harry stubbed his out.

"Time to go," he said. "Your teeth are chattering."

On his way out he tried to see if there was anyone in the parked car, but it was impossible without going closer. And he chose not to go any closer.

In Oppsal the house was waiting for him. Big, empty and full of echoes.

He went to bed in the boy's room and closed his eyes.

And dreamed the dream he so often had. He is standing by a marina in Sydney, a chain is hauled up, a poisonous jellyfish rises to the surface. It is not a jellyfish but red hair floating around a white face. Then came the second dream. The new one. It had first appeared in Hong Kong, just before Christmas. He is on his back staring up at a nail protruding from the wall—a face is impaled on it, a face, a sensitive-looking face with a neatly trimmed mustache. In the dream Harry has something in his mouth, something that feels as if it would blow his head to pieces. What was it, what was it? It was a promise. Harry twitched. Three times. Then he fell asleep.

28

Drammen

"So it was you who reported Adele Vetlesen missing," Kaja confirmed.

"Yes," said the young man sitting in front of her at People & Coffee. "We lived together. She didn't come home. I felt I had to do something."

"Of course," Kaja said with a glance at Harry. It was half past eight. It had taken them thirty minutes to drive from Oslo to Drammen after the trio's morning meeting, which had ended in Harry discharging Bjørn Holm. Holm hadn't said much, had expelled a deep sigh, washed his coffee cup and then driven back to Krimteknisk in Bryn to resume his work there.

"Have you heard anything from Adele?" the man asked, looking from Kaja to Harry.

"No," Harry said. "Have you?"

The man peered over his shoulder at the counter, to make sure there weren't any customers waiting. They were perched on high bar stools in front of the window, facing one of Drammen's many squares—that is, an open area that was used as a parking lot. People & Coffee sold coffee and cakes at airport prices and tried to give the impression they belonged to an American chain, and indeed perhaps they did. The man Adele Vetlesen lived with, Geir Bruun, appeared to be around thirty, was unusually white, with a shiny, perspiring crown and constantly wandering blue eyes. He worked at the place as a "barista," a title that had attracted awe-inspiring respect in the nineties when coffee bars had first invaded Oslo. And it also involved making coffee, an art form that—the way Harry saw it—was primarily about avoiding obvious pitfalls. As a policeman, Harry used people's intonation, diction, vocabulary and grammatical solecisms to place them. Geir Bruun neither dressed nor combed his hair nor behaved like a homosexual, but as soon as he opened his mouth, it was impossible to think of anything else. There was something about the rounding of the vowels, the tiny, redundant lexical embellishments, the lisping that almost seemed feigned. Harry knew that the guy could be a diehard heterosexual, but he had already decided that Katrine had jumped to a premature conclusion when she described Adele Vetlesen and Geir Bruun as living together. They were just two people who had shared a downtown flat for financial reasons.

Geir Bruun said, "I remember she went to some kind of mountain cabin in the autumn." He uttered this as though it were a concept he found fairly alien. "But that wasn't where she disappeared."

"We know that," Kaja said. "Did she go there with anyone, and if so, do you know who?"

"No idea. We didn't talk about that sort of thing—it was enough to share a bathroom, if you know what I mean. She had her private life, I had mine. But I doubt she would have gone into the wilds on her own, if I may put it like that."

"Oh?"

"Adele did very little on her own. I don't see her in a cabin without a guy. But impossible to say who. She was—if I may be frank—a bit promiscuous. She had no female friends, though she compensated with male friends. Whom she kept apart. Adele didn't live a double life so much as a quadruple life. Or thereabouts."

"So she was dishonest?"

"Not necessarily. I remember she gave me advice on honest ways to break up with someone. She said that once while she was being banged from behind she took a photo over her shoulder with her cell, wrote the name of the guy, sent the photo and then deleted the addressee. All in one swift operation." Geir Bruun's face was expressionless.

"Impressive," Harry said. "We know she paid for two people in the mountains. Could you give us the name of a male friend, so we could start our inquiries there?"

"'Fraid I can't," Geir Bruun said, "but when I reported her missing, you guys checked who she'd been talking to on the phone over the previous few weeks."

"Which officers, precisely?"

"I don't remember any names. Local police."

"Fine—we have a meeting at the police station now," Harry said, looking at his watch and getting up.

"Why," asked Kaja, who hadn't moved, "did the police stop investigating the case? I don't even recall reading about it in the newspapers."

"Don't you know?" the man said, signaling to two women with a stroller that he would attend to them immediately. "She sent a postcard."

"Postcard?" Harry said.

"Yes. From Rwanda. Down in Africa."

"What did she write?"

"It was very brief. She'd met her dream guy, and I

would have to pay the rent on my own until she was back in March. The bitch."

It was walking distance to the police station. An inspector with a squat pumpkin head and a name Harry forgot as soon as he heard it received them in a smoke-filled office, served them coffee in plastic cups that burned their fingers, and cast long looks at Kaja every time he considered himself unobserved.

He began by delivering a lecture about there being somewhere between five hundred and a thousand missing Norwegians at any one time. Sooner or later they would all turn up. If the police were to investigate every missing-person case whenever there was suspicion of a criminal act or an accident, they wouldn't have time for anything else. Harry stifled a yawn.

In Adele Vetlesen's case they had even received a sign of life; they had it somewhere. The inspector got up and stuck his pumpkin head into a drawer of hanging files and reappeared with a postcard, which he laid before them. There was a photo of a conical mountain with a cloud around the peak, but no text to explain what the mountain was called or where in the world it was. The handwriting was scratchy, dreadful. Harry could just decipher the signature. Adele. There was a stamp bearing the name Rwanda and the envelope was postmarked Kigali, which Harry seemed to recall was the capital.

"Her mother confirmed it was her daughter's handwriting," the inspector said and explained that at the mother's insistence they had checked and found Adele Vetlesen's name on the passenger list of a Brussels Airlines flight to Kigali via Entebbe, Uganda, on November 25. Furthermore, they had carried out a hotel search through Interpol, and a hotel in Kigali—the inspector read out his notes: Hotel Gorilla!—had indeed had an Adele Vetlesen down as a guest the same night she arrived by plane. The only reason Adele Vetlesen was still on the missing-persons list was that they didn't know precisely where she was now, and that a postcard from abroad did not technically change her status.

"Besides, we're not exactly talking about the civilized part of the world here," the inspector said, throwing up his arms. "Huti, Tutsu, or whatever they're called. Machetes. Two million dead. Get me?"

Harry saw Kaja close her eyes as the inspector with the schoolmaster's voice and a string of interpolated dependent clauses explained how little life was worth in Africa, where human trafficking was hardly an unknown phenomenon, and how in theory Adele could have been abducted and forced to write a postcard, since blacks would pay a year's salary to sink their teeth into a blond Norwegian girl, wouldn't they?

Harry examined the postcard and tried to block out the pumpkin man's voice. A conical mountain with a cloud around the peak. He glanced up when the inspector with the forgettable name cleared his throat.

"Yes, now and then you can understand them, can't you?" he said with a conspiratorial smile directed at Harry.

Harry got up and said work was waiting in Oslo. Would Drammen be so kind as to scan the postcard and email it on for them?

"To a handwriting expert?" the inspector asked, clearly displeased, and studied the address Kaja had noted down for him.

"Volcano expert," Harry said. "I'd like you to send him the picture and ask if he can identify the mountain."

"Identify the mountain?"

"He's a specialist. He travels around examining them."

The inspector shrugged, but nodded. Then he accompanied them to the main door. Harry asked if they had checked whether there had been any calls on Adele's cell phone since she left.

"We know our job, Hole," the inspector said. "No outgoing calls. But you can imagine the cellular network in a country like Rwanda . . ."

"Actually, I can't," Harry said. "But then I've never been there."

"A postcard!" Kaja groaned when they were standing on the square by the unmarked police car they had requisitioned from Police HQ. "Plane ticket and hotel record in Rwanda! Why couldn't your computer freak in Bergen have found that, so we wouldn't have had to waste half a day in fucking Drammen?"

"Thought that would put you in a great mood," Harry said, unlocking the door. "Got yourself a new friend, and perhaps Adele isn't dead after all."

"Are **you** in a great mood?" Kaja asked.

Harry looked at the car keys. "Feel like driving?"

"Yes!"

Strangely enough, none of the speed boxes flashed, and they were back in Oslo in twenty minutes flat.

They agreed they would take the light things, the office equipment and the desk drawers, to Police HQ first, and wait with the heavy things until the day after. They put them on the same cart Harry had used when they were setting up their office.

"Have you been given an office yet?" Kaja asked when they were halfway down the culvert. Her voice cast long echoes.

Harry shook his head. "We'll put the things in yours."

"Have you applied for an office?" she asked, and stopped.

Harry kept going.

"Harry!"

He stopped.

"You asked about my father," he said.

"I didn't mean to . . ."

"No, of course not. But he doesn't have much time left. OK? After that I'll be off again. I just wanted to . . ."

"Wanted to what?"

"Have you heard of the Dead Policemen's Society?"

"What is it?"

"People who worked at Crime Squad. People I cared about. I don't know if I owe them something, but that's the tribe."

"What?"

"It's not much, but it's all I have, Kaja. They're the only ones I have any reason to feel loyalty toward."

"A police unit?"

Harry started walking. "I know, and it'll probably pass. The world will go on. It's just restructuring, isn't it? The stories are in the walls, and now the walls are coming down. You and yours will have to make new stories, Kaja."

"Are you drunk?"

Harry laughed. "I'm just beaten. Finished. And it's fine. Absolutely fine."

His phone rang. It was Bjørn.

"I left my Hank biography on my desk," he said.

"I've got it here," Harry said.

"What a sound. Are you in a church?"

"The culvert."

"Jeez, you've got coverage there?"

"Seems we've got a better phone network than Rwanda. I'll leave the book in reception."

"That's the second time I've heard Rwanda and cell phones mentioned in the same breath today. Tell them I'll pick it up tomorrow, OK?"

"What did you hear about Rwanda?"

"It was something Beate said. About coltan—you

know the bits of metal we found on the teeth of the two with the stab wounds in their mouths."

"The Terminator."

"Eh?"

"Nothing. What's that got to do with Rwanda?"

"Coltan's used in cell phones. It's a rare metal and the Democratic Republic of the Congo has almost the entire world supply. Snag is that the deposits are in the war zone, where no one keeps an eye on it, so in all the chaos smart operators are stealing it and shipping it over to Rwanda."

"Mm."

"See you."

Harry was about to pocket his phone when he noticed he had an unread text message. He opened it.

MOUNT NYIRAGONGO. LAST ERUPTION 2002. ONE OF FEW VOLCANOES WITH LAVA LAKE IN CRATER. IN DR CONGO BY GOMA. FELIX.

Goma. Harry stood watching the drips from a pipe in the ceiling. That was where Kluit's instruments of torture originated.

"What's up?" Kaja asked.

"Ustaoset," Harry said. "And the Congo."

"And what's that supposed to mean?"

"I don't know," Harry said. "But I'm a nonbeliever as far as coincidences are concerned." He grabbed the cart and swung it around.

"What are you doing?" Kaja asked.

"U-turn," Harry said. "We've still got more than twenty-four hours left."

29

Kluit

It was an unusually mild evening in Hong Kong. The skyscrapers cast long shadows on the Peak, some almost as far as the house where Herman Kluit was sitting on the terrace, a bloodred Singapore sling in one hand and the telephone in the other. He was listening while watching the lines of traffic twisting and turning like fireworms way below.

He liked Harry Hole, had liked him from the first moment he had clapped eyes on the tall, athletic but obviously alcoholic Norwegian stepping into Happy Valley to put his last money on the wrong horse. There was something about the aggressive expression, the arrogant bearing, the alert body language that reminded him of himself as a young mercenary soldier in Africa. Herman Kluit had fought everywhere, on all sides, serving the paymasters. In Angola, Zambia, Zimbabwe, Sierra Leone, Liberia. All countries with dark pasts and even darker futures.

But nowhere had been darker than the country about which Harry had asked. The Congo. That was where they had eventually found the vein of gold. In the form of diamonds. And cobalt. And coltan. The village chief belonged to the Mai Mai, who thought water made them invulnerable. But otherwise he was a sensible man. There was nothing you couldn't fix in Africa with a bundle of notes or—in a pinch—a supply of Kalashnikovs.

In the course of one year Herman Kluit became a rich man. In the course of three he was wealthy beyond anyone's wildest dreams. Once a month they had traveled to the closest town, Goma, and slept in beds instead of on the jungle floor, where a carpet of mysterious bloodsucking flies emerged from holes every night and you woke up like a half-eaten corpse. Goma. Black lava, black money, black beauties, black sins. Half of the men in the jungle had contracted malaria, the rest sicknesses with which no white doctor was conversant and which were subsumed under the generic term **jungle fever.** That was the affliction Herman Kluit suffered from, and even though it left him in peace for long periods, he was never completely free.

The only remedy Herman Kluit knew of was the Singapore sling. He had been introduced to the drink in Goma by a Belgian who owned a fantastic house that had reportedly been built by King Leopold back when the country was known as the Congo Free State. It was the monarch's private playpen and treasure chest, situated down by the banks of Lake Kivu, with women and sunsets so beautiful that for a while you could forget the jungle, the Mai Mai and those flies.

It was the Belgian who had shown Herman Kluit

the king's little treasury in the cellar. There he had collected everything, from the world's most advanced clocks, rare weapons and imaginative instruments of torture to gold nuggets, unpolished diamonds and preserved human heads.

That was where Herman Kluit had first come face-to-face with what they called a Leopold's apple. By all accounts it had been developed by one of the king's Belgian engineers to use on recalcitrant tribal chiefs who would not say where they found their diamonds. The earlier method had been to use buffaloes. They covered the chief in honey, tied him to a tree and brought along a captured forest buffalo, which began to lick off the honey. The point of this was that the buffalo's tongue was so coarse that it licked off skin and flesh with it. But it took time to catch a buffalo, and they could be hard to stop once they had started. Hence Leopold's apple. Not that it was particularly effective from a torturer's angle—after all, the apple prevented the prisoner from speaking. But the effect on the natives who witnessed what happened when the interrogator pulled the string for the second time was impressive. The next man asked to open wide couldn't speak fast enough.

Herman Kluit nodded to his Filipina housemaid for her to take away the empty glass.

"You remember rightly, Harry," Herman Kluit said. "It's still on my mantelpiece. Fortunately I do not know if it has ever been used. A souvenir. It reminds me of what there is in the heart of darkness. That's always useful, Harry . . . No, I've neither seen it nor heard of it being used anywhere else. It's a complicated piece of technology, you know, with all these springs and needles. Requires a special alloy . . . Coltan is correct . . . Yes, indeed. Very rare. The person from whom I purchased my apple, Eddie Van Boorst, claimed only twenty-four had been made, and that he had twenty-two of them, one of which was twenty-four-carat gold . . . That's right—there are twenty-four needles as well. How did you know? Apparently the number twenty-four had something to do with the engineer's sister—I don't recall what. But that may also have been something Van Boorst said to push up the price. He's Belgian, after all."

Kluit's laughter transmuted into coughing. Damned fever.

"However, he ought to have some idea of where the apples are. He lived in a splendid house in Goma, in north Kivu, by the border to Rwanda . . . The address?" Kluit coughed again. "Goma gets a new street every day, and now and then half the town is buried under lava, so addresses don't exist, Harry. But the post office has a list of all the whites . . . No, I have no idea if he still lives in Goma. Or whether he is still alive, for that matter. Life expectancy in the Congo is thirty-something, Harry. For whites also. Besides, the town is as good as under siege . . . Exactly . . . No, of course you haven't heard of the war. No one has."

Dumbfounded, Gunnar Hagen stared at Harry and leaned across his desk.

"You want to go to Rwanda?" he said.

"Just a flying visit," Harry said. "Two days, including the flights."

"To investigate what?"

"What I said. A missing-persons case. Adele Vetlesen. Kaja will go to Ustaoset to see if she can find out who Adele was traveling with before she disappeared."

"Why can't you just call up and ask them to check the guest book?"

"Because the cabin in Håvass is self-service," said Kaja, who had settled in the chair next to Harry's. "But anyone who stays in a Tourist Association cabin has to sign the guest book and state his or her destination. It's compulsory because if anyone's reported missing in the mountains, the search party will know where to concentrate their efforts. I'm hoping Adele and her companion gave a full name and address."

Gunnar Hagen scratched his wreath of hair with both hands. "And none of this has anything to do with the other murders?"

Harry stuck out his bottom lip. "Not as far as I can see, boss. Can you?"

"Hm. And why should I decimate the travel budget for such an extravagant trip?"

"Because human trafficking is a priority," Kaja said. "As per the minister of justice's statement to the press earlier this week."

"Anyway," Harry said, stretching upward and entwining his fingers behind his head, "it may well be that other things come to light in the process, things that might lead to us cracking other cases."

Gunnar Hagen scrutinized his inspector thoughtfully.

"Boss," Harry added.

30

Guest Book

A sign on an unassuming yellow station building announced that the train was in Ustaoset. Kaja checked that they had arrived on schedule, 10:44. She looked out. The sun was shining on the snow-covered plains and porcelain-white mountains. Apart from a clump of houses and a two-story hotel, Ustaoset was bare rock. To be fair, there were small cabins dotted around and the odd confused shrub, but it was still a wilderness. Beside the station building, almost on the platform itself, stood a lonely SUV with the engine idling. From the train it had seemed as if there weren't a breath of wind. But when Kaja alighted, the wind seemed to pierce right through her clothing: special thermal underwear, anorak, ski boots.

A figure jumped out of the SUV and came toward her. He had the low winter sun behind him. Kaja squinted. Light, confident walk, a brilliant smile and an outstretched hand. She stiffened. It was Even.

"Aslak Krongli," the man said, giving her hand a firm squeeze. "County officer."

"Kaja Solness."

"It's cold, isn't it? Not like in the lowlands, eh?"

"Exactly," Kaja said, returning the smile.

"I can't join you at the cabin today. There's been an avalanche. A tunnel's closed, and we have to redirect traffic." Without asking, he took her skis, swung them over his shoulder and began to walk toward the SUV. "But I've got the man who keeps an eye on the mountain cabins to drive you there. Odd Utmo. Is that all right?"

"Fine," said Kaja, who was only too pleased. It meant perhaps she could escape all the questions about why the Oslo Police were suddenly interested in a missing-persons case from Drammen.

Krongli drove her the quarter-mile or so to the hotel. There was a man sitting on a yellow snowmobile in the icy square in front of the entrance. He was wearing a red snowsuit, a leather hat with ear flaps, a scarf around his mouth and large goggles.

When he pushed up the goggles and mumbled his name, Kaja saw that one eye was a white, transparent membrane, as though there had been a milk spillage. The other eye studied her from top to toe without embarrassment. The man's erect posture could have belonged to a youngster, but his face was old.

"Kaja. Thanks for turning up at such short notice," she said.

"I'm paid," Odd Utmo said, then looked at his watch, pulled down the scarf and spat. Kaja saw the glint of an orthodontic brace between the snuff-stained teeth. The gobbet of tobacco made a black star on the ice.

"Hope you've had a bite to eat and a piss."

Kaja laughed, but Utmo had already straddled the snowmobile and turned his back on her.

She looked at Krongli, who in the meantime had firmly stowed the skis and poles under the straps so they now spanned the length of the snowmobile, together with Utmo's skis and a bundle of what looked like red sticks of dynamite, plus a rifle with telescopic sights.

Krongli shrugged and flashed his boyish smile again. "Good luck, hope you find . . ."

The rest was drowned out by the roar of the engine. Kaja quickly mounted. To her relief she saw handles she could hold on to, so that she wouldn't have to cling to the white-eyed old man. The exhaust fumes surrounded them; then they started with a jerk.

Utmo stood with his knees like shock absorbers and used his body weight to balance the snowmobile, which he guided past the hotel, over a snowdrift into the soft snow and diagonally up the first gentle slope. On reaching the top, which offered a view to the north, Kaja saw a boundless expanse of white spread out before them. Utmo turned with an inquiring expression. Kaja nodded back that everything was OK. Then he accelerated. Kaja watched the buildings disappear through the fountain of snow spraying off the drive belts.

Kaja had often heard people say that snowy plains made them think of deserts. It made her think of the days and nights with Even on his ocean racer.

The snowmobile sliced through the vast, empty landscape. The combination of snow and wind had erased, smoothed over, leveled the contours until they were one huge ocean in which the tall mountain, Hallingskarvet, towered like a menacing monster wave. There were no sudden movements; the weight of the snowmobile and the softness of the snow made the ride gentle, cushioned. Kaja rubbed her nose and cheeks carefully to ensure enough blood was circulating. She had seen what even relatively minor frostbite could do to faces. The engine's monotonous roar and the terrain's reassuring uniformity had lulled her into a drowsy state until the engine died and they came to a standstill. She woke up and looked at her watch. Her first thought was that the engine had cut out and they were at least a forty-five-minute drive from civilization. How far was it on skis? Three hours? Five? She had no idea. Utmo had already jumped off and was loosening the skis from the scooter.

"Is there something wrong . . . ?" she began, but stopped when Utmo stood up and pointed to the little valley in front of them.

"Håvass cabin," he said.

Kaja squinted through her sunglasses. And, indeed, at the foot of the mountain face she saw a small black cabin.

"Why don't we drive—"

"Because people are stupid, and that's why we have to creep up on the cabin."

"Creep?" Kaja said, hurriedly clipping on her skis, as Utmo had.

He pointed the pole to the side of the mountain. "If you drive the scooter into such a narrow valley, sound ricochets to and fro. Loosens new snow . . ."

"Avalanche," Kaja said. She remembered something her father had told her after one of his trips to the Alps. More than sixty thousand troops had died in avalanches there during the Second World War, and most of them had been caused by sound waves from artillery fire.

Utmo stopped for a moment and faced her. "These nature freaks from town think they're being clever when they build cabins in sheltered areas. But it's just a question of time before they're covered in snow, too."

"Too?"

"The Håvass cabin has been here only three years. This year is the first winter with decent avalanche snow. And soon there's going to be more."

He pointed westward. Kaja shielded her eyes. On the snowy horizon she could see what he meant. Heavy, gray-white cumulus clouds were building giant mushroom formations against the blue background.

"Going to snow all week," said Utmo, unhitching the rifle from the snowmobile and hanging it over his shoulder. "If I were you, I'd hurry. And don't shout."

They entered the valley in silence, and Kaja felt the

temperature fall as they reached the shade and the cold filled the depressions in the ground.

They undid their skis by the black timber cabin and rested them against the wall, and Utmo took a key from his pocket and inserted it into the lock.

"How do overnight guests get in?" Kaja asked.

"They buy a skeleton key. Fits all four hundred and fifty Tourist Association cabins nationwide." He twisted the key, pressed down the handle and pushed the door. Nothing happened. He cursed under his breath, placed his shoulder against the door and shoved. It came away from the frame with a shrill scream.

"Cabins shrink in the cold," he muttered.

Inside it was pitch black and smelled of paraffin and a wood-burning stove. Kaja inspected the cabin. She knew the lodging arrangements were very simple. You came, entered details in the guest book, took a bed, or a mattress if it was crowded, lit the fire, cooked your own food in the kitchen, where there was a stove and cooking utensils, or if you used the food provided in the cupboards, you put some money in a can. You paid for your stay in the same can or you filled in a bank authorization slip. All payments were on the honor system.

The cabin had four north-facing bedrooms with four bunk beds in each. The sitting room faced south and had traditional decor, solid pine furniture. There was a large open fireplace for a homey effect and the wood-burning stove for more efficient heating. Kaja calculated that there was seating space for twelve to fifteen people around the table, and sleeping space for double that if people squeezed together and used the floor and mattresses. She visualized the light from candles and the fire flickering over familiar and unfamiliar faces as conversation covered the day's skiing and the next day's plans over a beer or a glass of wine. Even's ruddy complexion smiled at her, and he toasted her from one of the darkened corners.

"The guest book's in the kitchen," Utmo said, pointing to one of the doors. Still standing by the front door with hat and gloves on, he seemed impatient. Kaja was holding the door handle and about to press it when an image flashed into her mind. County Officer Krongli. He had looked similar. She had known the thought would reappear—she just hadn't known when.

"Can you open the door for me?" she said.

"Eh?"

"It's stuck," Kaja said. "The cold."

She closed her eyes as she listened to him approach, heard the door open with barely a sound, felt his astonished gaze on her. Then she opened her eyes and went in.

There was a smell of slightly rancid fat in the kitchen. Her pulse raced as her eyes skimmed over the surfaces, cupboards. She spotted the black leather-bound register on the countertop under the window. It was attached to the wall by a blue nylon cord.

Kaja breathed in. She walked over to the book. Flicked through.

Page after page of handwritten names, scribbled by the guests. Most had observed the rule and noted down their next destination.

"In fact, I'd been planning to come here over the weekend to check the book for you," she heard Utmo say behind her. "But obviously the police couldn't wait, could they?"

"No," said Kaja, thumbing through the dates. November. November 6. November 8. She flicked back. And forward again. It wasn't there.

November 7 was gone. She laid the book flat. The jagged edges of the torn sheet stood upright. Someone had taken it.

31

Kigali

The airport at Kigali, Rwanda, was small, modern and surprisingly well organized. However, it was Harry's experience that international airports told you little or nothing about the country in which they were situated. In Mumbai, India, there was total calm and efficiency; at JFK in New York paranoia and chaos. The passport line took a tiny lurch forward, and Harry followed. Despite the pleasant temperature, he could feel sweat trickling down between his shoulder blades under the thin cotton shirt. He thought again about the figures he had seen at Schiphol Airport in Amsterdam, where the delayed Oslo plane had finally landed. Harry had worked up a sweat running through the corridors, the alphabet and the ever larger numbers of the gates to catch the flight to Kampala, Uganda. As corridors crossed he had seen something out of the corner of his eye. A figure that had seemed vaguely familiar. He had been looking into the light and the figure was too far away for him to make out the face. Once onboard the plane, the last passenger, Harry had concluded the patently obvious: It had not been her. What were the chances of it happening? There was no chance the boy next to her had been Oleg. He couldn't have grown that much.

"Next."

Harry stepped forward to the window and presented his passport, landing card, a copy of the visa application he had printed off the Net and the crisp sixty dollars the visa had cost.

"Business?" the passport official asked, and Harry met his eyes. The man was tall and thin and his skin was so dark that it reflected light. Probably Tutsi, Harry thought. They controlled the national borders now.

"Yes."

"Where?"

"The Congo," Harry said, then used the local name to distinguish the two Congo countries.

"Congo Kinshasa," the passport official corrected.

He pointed to the landing card Harry had filled in

on the plane. "Says here you're staying at Hotel Gorilla in Kigali."

"Just tonight," Harry said. "Then I'm going to the Congo tomorrow, one night in Goma and then back here and home. It's a shorter drive than from Kinshasa."

"Have a pleasant stay in the Congo, busy man," the uniformed official said with a hearty laugh. He smacked the stamp down on the passport and returned it.

Half an hour later Harry filled in the hotel registration card at Gorilla, signed it and was given a key attached to a wooden gorilla. When Harry went to bed it was eighteen hours since he had left his home in Oppsal. He stared at the fan howling at the foot of the bed. It provided hardly a puff of air even though the blades were rotating at a hysterical speed. He wasn't going to be able to sleep.

The driver asked Harry to call him Joe. Joe was Congolese and spoke fluent French and rather more halting English. He had been hired by contacts at a Norwegian aid organization based in Goma.

"Eight hundred thousand," Joe said, guiding the Land Rover along a potholed but perfectly navigable paved road winding between green meadows and mountain slopes that were cultivated from top to bottom. Occasionally, he was charitable and braked so as not to run down people walking, cycling, wheeling and carrying goods at the edge of the road, but as a rule they made lifesaving leaps at the very last second.

"They kill eight hundred thousand in just few months in 1994. The Hutus invade their kind, old neighbors and cut them down with machetes because they Tutsis. The propaganda on the radio say that if your husband is Tutsi it is your duty as Hutu to kill him. Cut down the tall trees. Many flee along this road . . ." Joe pointed out of the window. "Bodies pile up. Some places it is impossible to pass. Good times for vultures."

They drove on in silence.

They passed two men carrying a big cat bound to a pole by its legs. Children were dancing and cheering beside it and sticking pins into the dead animal. The coat was sun-colored with patches of shade.

"Hunters?" Harry asked.

Joe shook his head, glanced in the mirror and answered in a mixture of English and French: "Hit by car, **je crois.** That one is almost impossible to hunt. It is rare, has large territory, only hunts at night. Hides and blends into environs during the day. I think it is very lonely animal, Harry."

Harry watched men and women working in the fields. At several points there was heavy machinery and men repairing the road. Down in a valley he saw a highway under construction. In a field children in blue school uniforms were kicking a soccer ball around and shouting.

"Rwanda is good," Joe said.

Two and a half hours later Joe pointed through the windshield. "Lake Kivu. Very nice, very deep."

The surface of the huge expanse of water seemed to reflect a thousand suns. The country on the other side was the Democratic Republic of the Congo. Mountains rose on all sides. A single white cloud encircled the peak of one of them.

"Not much cloud," Joe said as if intuiting what Harry was thinking. "The killer mountain. Nyiragongo."

Harry nodded.

An hour later they had passed the border and were driving into Goma. On the roadside an emaciated man in a torn jacket was sitting and staring ahead through desperate, crazed eyes. Joe steered the vehicle carefully between the craters in the muddy path. A military jeep was in front of them. The swaying soldier manning the machine gun looked at them with cold, weary eyes. Above them roared airplane engines.

"UN," Joe said. "More guns and grenades. Nkunda come closer to the city. Very strong. Many people escape now. Refugees. Maybe Monsieur Van Boorst, too, eh? I not see him long time."

"You know him?"

"Everybody know Mr. Van. But he has **Ba-Maguje** in him."

"Ba-what?"

"**Un mauvais ésprit.** A demon. He makes you thirsty for alcohol. And takes away your emotions."

The air-conditioning unit was blowing cold air.

The sweat was running down between Harry's shoulder blades.

They had stopped midway between two rows of shacks, in what Harry realized was a kind of downtown in Goma. People hastened to and fro on the almost impassable path between the shops. Black boulders were piled up alongside the houses and served as foundations. The ground looked like stiffened black icing, and gray dust whirled up in air that stank of rotten fish.

"Là," Joe said, pointing to the door of the only brick house in the row. "I wait in the car."

Harry noticed a couple of men stop in the street as he exited the car. They gave him the neutral, dangerous gaze that relayed no warning. Men who knew that acts of aggression were more effective without a warning. Harry headed straight for the door without looking to either side, showing that he knew what he was doing there, where he should go. He knocked. Once. Twice. Three times. **Shit! Fucking long way to come just to—**

The door opened a fraction.

A wrinkled white face with questioning eyes stared at him.

"Eddie Van Boorst?" Harry asked.

"**Il est mort,**" said the man in a voice so hoarse it sounded itself like a death rattle.

Harry remembered enough school French to understand that the man was claiming Van Boorst was dead. He tried in English. "My name is Harry Hole. I was given Van Boorst's name by Herman Kluit in Hong Kong. I'm interested in a Leopold's apple."

The man blinked twice. Stuck his head out of the door and looked left and right. Then he opened the door a little more. **"Entrez,"** he said, motioning Harry in.

Harry ducked beneath the low door frame and just managed to bend his knees in time; the floor inside was seven inches lower.

There was a smell of incense. As well as something else familiar—the sweet stench of an old man who had been drinking for several days.

Harry's eyes became used to the dark, and he discovered that the small, frail old man was wearing an elegant burgundy silk dressing gown.

"Scandinavian accent," said Van Boorst in Hercule Poirot English and placed a cigarette in a yellowing holder between his thin lips. "Let me guess. Definitely not Danish. Could be Swedish. But I think Norwegian. Yes?"

A cockroach showed its antennae through a crack in the wall behind him.

"Mm. An expert on accents?"

"A mere pastime," said Van Boorst, flattered, pleased. "In small nations like Belgium you have to learn to look outward, not inward. And how is Herman?"

"Fine," Harry said, turning to his right and seeing two pairs of bored eyes looking at him. One from a photo above the bed in the corner. A framed portrait of a person with a long gray beard, powerful nose, short hair, epaulets, chain and sword. King Leopold, unless Harry was much mistaken. The other pair of eyes belonged to the woman lying on her side in the bed with only a blanket draped over her hips. The light from the window above her fell on her small, supple young girl's breasts. She responded to Harry's nod with a fleeting smile that revealed a large gold tooth among all the white ones. She couldn't have been more than twenty. On the wall behind the slim waist Harry glimpsed a nail hammered into the cracked plaster. From the nail dangled a pair of pink handcuffs.

"My wife," said the little Belgian. "Well, one of them."

"Mistress Van Boorst?"

"Something of that kind. You want to buy? You have money?"

"First I want to see what you've got," Harry said.

Eddie Van Boorst went to the door, opened it a crack and peered outside. Shut it and locked up. "Only got your driver with you?"

"Yes."

Van Boorst puffed on his cigarette while studying Harry through the folds of skin that gathered when he squinted.

Then he went to a corner of the room, kicked away the carpet, bent down and pulled at an iron ring. A trapdoor opened. The Belgian waved Harry down into the cellar first. Harry assumed it was a precaution based on experience, and did as he was told. A ladder led into pitch darkness. Harry reached solid ground after only the seventh rung. Then a light was switched on.

Harry looked around the room; the ceiling was full height and there was a level cement floor. Shelves and cupboards covered three of the walls. On the shelves were the day-to-day products: well-used Glock pistols, a Smith & Wesson .38, boxes of ammunition, a Kalashnikov. Harry had never held the famous Russian automatic rifle known officially as the AK-47. He stroked the wooden stock.

"An original from the first year of production, 1947," Van Boorst said.

"Seems like everyone down here has one," Harry said. "The most popular cause of death in Africa, I've heard."

Van Boorst nodded. "For two simple reasons. First, when the Communist countries started exporting the Kalashnikov here after the Cold War, the gun cost as much as a fat chicken in peacetime. And no more than a hundred dollars in wartime. Second, it works, no matter what you do with it, and that's important in Africa. In Mozambique they like their Kalashnikovs so much it's on their national flag."

Harry's eyes stopped at the letters discreetly stamped on a black case.

"Is that what I think it is?" Harry asked.

"Märklin," said Van Boorst. "A rare rifle. It was manufactured in very limited numbers, as it was a fiasco. Much too heavy and large a caliber. Used to hunt elephants."

"And humans," Harry said softly.

"Do you know the weapon?"

"World's best telescopic sights. Not exactly something you need to hit an elephant at a hundred yards. Perfect for an assassination." Harry ran his fingers along the case as the memories streamed back. "Yes, I know it."

"You can have it cheap. Thirty thousand euros."

"I'm not after a rifle this time." Harry turned to the shelving unit in the middle of the room. Grotesque white wooden masks grimaced at him from the shelves.

"The Mai Mai tribe's spiritual masks," said Van Boorst. "They think that if they dip themselves in holy water, the enemy's bullets cannot hurt them. Because the bullets will also turn to H_2O. The Mai Mai guerrillas went to war against the government army with bows and arrows, shower hats on their heads and bath plugs as amulets. I am not kidding you, **monsieur.** Naturally, they were mown down. But they like water, the Mai Mai do. And white masks. And their enemies' hearts and kidneys. Lightly grilled with mashed corn."

"Mm," Harry said. "I hadn't expected that such a basic house would have such a full cellar."

Van Boorst chuckled. "Cellar? This is the ground floor. Or was. Before the eruption six years ago."

Everything fell into place for Harry. Black boulders, black icing. The floor upstairs that was lower than the street.

"Lava," Harry said.

Van Boorst nodded. "It flowed straight through the center of town and took my house by Lake Kivu. All the wooden houses around here burned to the ground; this brick house was the only one left standing, but was half buried in lava." He pointed to the wall. "There you can see the front door to what was street level six years ago. I bought the house and just put in a new door where you entered."

Harry nodded. "Lucky the lava didn't burn down the door and fill this floor, too."

"As you can see, the windows and doors are in the wall facing away from Nyiragongo. It's not the first time. The fucking volcano spews lava on this town every ten or twenty years."

Harry cocked an eyebrow. "And still people move back?"

Van Boorst shrugged. "Welcome to Africa. But the volcano is damn useful. If you want to get rid of a troublesome corpse—which is a fairly normal problem in Goma—you can of course sink it in Lake Kivu. But it is **still** down there. Whereas if you use Nyiragongo . . . People think that volcanoes have these red-hot, bubbling lava lakes at the bottom, but most do not. None of them, in fact—apart from Nyiragongo. Eighteen hundred degrees Fahrenheit. Drop something down there and, **poof,** it is gone. It returns as a gas. It is the only chance anyone in Goma has to reach heaven." He broke into a hacking laugh. "I witnessed an overenthusiastic coltan-hunter drop a tribal chief's daughter on a chain into the crater up there once. The chief wouldn't sign the papers giving the hunters the right to mine on their territory. Her hair caught fire at sixty feet above the lava. At thirty feet above, the girl was burning like a candle. And fifteen feet farther down she was dripping. I am not exaggerating. Skin, flesh, it flowed off her bones . . . Is this what you were interested in?" Van Boorst had opened a cupboard and taken out a metal ball. It was shiny, perforated with tiny apertures and smaller than a tennis ball. From a slightly larger opening there hung a wire loop. It was the same instrument Harry had seen at Herman Kluit's house.

"Does it work?" Harry asked.

Van Boorst sighed. He stuck his little finger in the loop and pulled. There was a loud bang and the ball jumped in the Belgian's hand. Harry stared. Protruding from the holes in the ball were what looked like antennae.

"May I?" he asked, and put out his hand. Van Boorst passed him the ball and watched with great vigilance as Harry counted the antennae.

Harry nodded. "Twenty-four," he said.

"Same as the number of apples made," said Van Boorst. "The number had some symbolic value for the engineer who designed and made it. It was the age of his sister when she took her own life."

"And how many of them do you have in your cupboard?"

"Only eight. Including this pièce de résistance in gold." He took out a ball that gleamed in the light from the electric bulb, then returned it to the cupboard. "But it is not for sale. You would have to kill me to get your paws on that one."

"So you've sold thirteen since Kluit bought his?"

"And for ever-increasing sums. It is a guaranteed investment, Monsieur Hole. Old instruments of torture have a loyal body of followers who are keen to pay, **croyez-moi.**"

"I believe you," Harry said, trying to press down one of the antennae.

"Spring-loaded," Van Boorst said. "Once the wire has been pulled, the victim will not be able to remove the apple from his mouth. Nor will anyone else, for that matter. Do not take step two if you want to retract the circular ridges. Don't pull the wire, please."

"Step two?"

"Give it to me."

Harry passed Van Boorst the ball. The Belgian carefully threaded a pen through the loop, held it horizontally and at the same height as the ball and then let go of the ball. As the wire became taut there was another bang. The Leopold's apple jiggled six inches below the pen and the sharp needles sticking out of each of the antennae glistened.

"Å faen," Harry swore in Norwegian.

The Belgian smiled. "The Mai Mai called the device 'Blood of the Sun.' This sweet child has several names." He placed the apple on the table, put the pen in the opening where the wire came from, pushed hard, and the needles and antennae retracted with a bang, and the royal apple regained its smooth, round shape.

"Impressive," Harry said. "How much?"

"Six thousand dollars," Van Boorst said. "Usually I

add a bit each time, but you can have it for the same price I sold the last one."

"Why's that?" Harry asked, running his forefinger over the sleek metal.

"Because you have come a long way," Van Boorst said, blowing cigarette smoke into the room. "And because I like your accent."

"Mm. And who was the last buyer?"

Van Boorst chuckled. "Just as no one will ever find out that you have been here, I will not tell you about my other customers. Does that not sound reassuring, Monsieur . . . ? See, I have already forgotten your name."

Harry nodded. "Six hundred," he said.

"I beg your pardon?"

"Six hundred dollars."

Van Boorst emitted the same brief chuckle. "Ridiculous. But the price you mention happens to be the price of a three-hour guided tour of the nature preserve where there are mountain gorillas. Would you prefer that, Monsieur Hole?"

"You can keep the royal apple," Harry said, taking out a slim wad of twenty-dollar bills from his back pocket. "I'm offering you six hundred for information about who bought apples from you."

He placed the wad on the table in front of Van Boorst. And on the top an ID card.

"Norwegian police," Harry said. "At least two women have been killed by the product over which you have a monopoly."

Van Boorst bent over the money and studied the ID card without touching either.

"If that is the case I am truly sorry," he said, and it sounded as if his voice had become even more gravelly. "Believe me. But my personal security is probably worth more than six hundred dollars. If I were to talk openly about all the people who have shopped here, my life expectancy would be—"

"You should worry more about your life expectancy in a Congolese prison," Harry said.

Van Boorst laughed again. "Nice try, Hole. But the chief of police in Goma happens to be a personal acquaintance of mine, and anyway"—he threw his arms in the air—"what have I done, after all?"

"What you have done is less interesting," Harry said, taking a photo out of his breast pocket. "The Norwegian state is one of the most important providers of aid to the Congo. If the Norwegian authorities call Kinshasa, name you as a noncooperative source of the murder weapon in a Norwegian double murder, what do you think will happen?"

Van Boorst was no longer smiling.

"You won't be falsely convicted of anything—gracious, no," Harry said. "You'll just be on remand, which should not be confused with punishment. It's the judicious confinement of a person while a case is being investigated and perhaps there are fears that evidence may have been tampered with. But it is prison nevertheless. And this investigation could take a long time. Have you ever seen the inside of a Congolese prison, Van Boorst? No, I suppose there are not many white men who have."

Van Boorst pulled the dressing gown around him more tightly. Eyed Harry while gnawing at the cigarette holder. "OK," he said, "a thousand dollars."

"Five hundred," Harry said.

"Five? But you—"

"Four," Harry said.

"Done!" Van Boorst shouted, raising his arms into the air. "What do you want to know?"

"Everything," Harry said, leaning against the wall and producing a pack of cigarettes.

When, half an hour later, Harry stepped out of Van Boorst's house and into Joe's Land Rover, darkness had fallen.

"The hotel," Harry said.

The hotel turned out to be right down by the lake. Joe warned Harry against swimming. Not because of the Guinea parasite he would be unlikely to discover until one day a thin worm began to wriggle under his skin, but because of the methane gas that rose from the bottom in the form of large bubbles that could render him unconscious and precipitate drowning.

Harry sat on the balcony, looking down on two long-legged creatures walking stiltlike over the illuminated lawn. They looked like flamingos in peacock costume. On the floodlit tennis court two young black boys were playing with just two balls, both so ragged that they looked like rolled-up socks sailing to and fro across the semi-torn net. Every now and then airplanes thundered across the sky.

Harry heard the clink of bottles at the bar. It was exactly sixty-eight paces from where he was sitting. He had counted when he entered. He took out his phone and called Kaja's number.

She sounded happy to hear his voice. Happy, anyway.

"I'm snowbound in Ustaoset," she said. "It's coming down horses and cows here, not cats and dogs. But at least I've been invited to dinner. And the guest book was interesting."

"Oh, yes?"

"The page for the day we're interested in was missing."

"There you go. Did you check if—"

"Yes, I checked if there were any fingerprints or if the writing had gone through to the next page." She giggled, and Harry guessed that she had had a couple of glasses of wine.

"Mm. I was thinking more of—"

"Yes, I checked what had been written the day before and after. But almost no one stays more than one night in such basic accommodations. Unless they're snowed in. And the weather was clear on the seventh of November. But the officer up here has promised me that he'll check the guest books at the surrounding cabins on the days before and after to see which guests might have stayed over at Håvass on their trek."

"Good. Sounds like we're getting warmer."

"Maybe. How about you?"

"A little cooler here, I'm afraid. I've found Van Boorst, but none of the fourteen customers he dealt with were Scandinavian. He was fairly sure. I have six names and addresses, but they're all known collectors. Otherwise there were a few names he half-remembered, a few descriptions, that's all. There are two more apples, but Van Boorst happened to know they were still in the hands of a collector in Caracas. Did you check out Adele and her visa?"

"I called the Rwandan consulate in Sweden. I have to confess I expected chaos but everything was very organized."

"The Congo's small, straightforward big brother."

"They had a copy of Adele's visa application, and the dates matched. The period covered by the visa is well out of date now, but of course they had no idea where she was. They told me to contact the immigration authorities in Kigali. I was given a number, tried it and was bounced around between offices like a pinball, until I was put through to an English-speaking know-it-all who pointed out that there was no cooperation agreement with Rwanda in that area, regretted politely that he would have to decline my request and wished me and my family a long and happy life. You haven't gotten a sniff of anything, either?"

"No. I showed Van Boorst the photo of Adele. He said the only woman who had bought anything off him was a woman with big rust-red curls and an East German accent."

"East German accent? Does such a thing exist?"

"I don't know, Kaja. This man walks around in a dressing gown, has a cigarette holder and is an alcoholic and a specialist in accents. I'm trying to keep my mind on the case and then get out."

She laughed. White wine, Harry wagered. Red-wine drinkers don't laugh as much.

"But I have an idea," he said. "Landing cards."

"Yes?"

"You have to give the address of where you plan to stay on your first night. If they hold on to the cards in Kigali and there is further info, such as a forwarding address, perhaps I can find out where Adele went. That might be a lead. For all we know she may be the only person alive who knows who was at the Håvass cabin that night."

"Good luck, Harry."

"Good luck to you, too."

He hung up. Of course he could have asked her who she was having dinner with, but if that had been relevant to the investigation she would probably have told him.

Harry sat on the balcony until the bar closed and the clinking of bottles stopped, to be replaced by the sounds of lovemaking from an open window above. Throaty, monotonous cries. They reminded him of the gulls at Åndalsnes when he and his grandfather used to get up at the crack of dawn to go fishing. His father never went with him. Why not? And why had Harry never thought about it, why hadn't he instinctively known that Olav didn't feel at home in a fishing boat? Had he already understood, as a five-year-old, that his father had opted for an education and left the farm precisely so that he wouldn't have to sit in a boat? Nevertheless, his father wanted to return and spend eternity there. Life was strange. Death, at any rate.

Harry lit up a cigarette. The sky was starless and black apart from above the Nyiragongo crater, where a red glow smoldered. Harry felt a smarting pain as an insect stung him. Malaria. Methane gas. Lake Kivu glittered in the distance. Very nice, very deep.

A boom resounded from the mountains, and the sound rolled across the lake. Volcanic eruption or just thunder? Harry looked up. Another clap; the echo rang between the mountains. And another echo, distant, reached Harry at the same time.

Very deep.

He stared, wide-eyed, into the darkness, hardly noticing that the heavens were opening and the rain was hammering down and drowning the gull cries.

32

Police

"I'm glad you got away from the Håvass cabin before this swept in," Officer Krongli said. "You could have been stranded there for several days." He nodded toward the hotel restaurant's large panoramic window. "But it's wonderful to see, don't you think?"

Kaja looked out at the heavy snowfall. Even had been like that, too; he was excited by the power of nature, regardless of whether it was working for him or against him.

"I hope my train will finally get through," she said.

"Yes, of course," Krongli said, fingering his wineglass in a way that suggested to Kaja that wining and dining was not something he did that often. "We'll make sure it does. And check out the guest books from the other cabins."

"Thank you," Kaja said.

Krongli ran a hand through his unruly locks and put on a wry smile. Chris de Burgh with "The Lady in Red" oozed like syrup through the loudspeakers.

There were only two other guests in the restaurant, two men in their thirties, each sitting at a table with a white cloth, each with a beer in front of him, staring at the snow, waiting for something that wasn't going to happen.

"Doesn't it get lonely here sometimes?" Kaja asked.

"Depends," the rural policeman said, following her glance. "If you don't have a wife or family, it means you tend to gather at places like this."

"To be lonely together," Kaja said.

"Yep," Krongli said, pouring more wine into their glasses. "But I suppose it's the same in Oslo, too?"

"Yes," Kaja said. "It is. Do you have any family?"

Krongli shrugged. "I did live with someone. But she found life too empty here, so she moved down to where you live. I can understand her. You have to have an interesting job in a place like this."

"And you do?"

"I think so. I know everyone here, and they know me. We help one another. I need them and they . . . well . . ." He twirled the glass.

"They need you," Kaja said.

"I believe so, yes."

"And that's important."

"Yes, it is," Krongli said firmly, looking up at her. Even's eyes. Which had the embers of laughter in them; something amusing or something to be happy about always seemed to have just happened. Even if it hadn't. Especially when it hadn't.

"What about Odd Utmo?" Kaja said.

"What about him?"

"He left as soon as he had dropped me off. What does he do on an evening like tonight?"

"How do you know he isn't sitting at home with his wife and children?"

"If I've ever met a recluse, Officer—"

"Call me Aslak," he said, laughing and tipping back his glass. "And I can see that you're a real detective. But Utmo hasn't always been like that."

"He hasn't?"

"Before his son disappeared he was apparently pretty approachable. Yes, now and then he was nothing less than affable. But I suppose he's always had a dangerous temper."

"I would have thought a man like Utmo would be single."

"His wife was good-looking, too. When you consider how ugly he is. Did you see his teeth?"

"I saw he was wearing braces, yes."

"He says it's so that his teeth don't go crooked." Aslak Krongli shook his head, with laughter in his eyes, though not in his voice. "But it's the only way to make sure they don't fall out."

"Tell me, was that really dynamite he was carrying on his snowmobile?"

"You saw it," Krongli said. "Not me."

"What do you mean?"

"There are lots of residents up here who can't quite see the romanticism of sitting for hours with a fishing rod by the mountain lakes, but who would like to have the fish they regard as their own on the dinner table."

"They throw dynamite into the lakes?"

"As soon as the ice has gone."

"Isn't that somewhat illegal?"

Krongli held up his hands in defense. "As I said, I didn't see anything."

"No, that's true—you only live here. Do you have dynamite, too, by any chance?"

"Just for the garage. Which I'm planning to build."

"Right. What about Utmo's gun? Looked modern, with the telescopic sights and so on."

"Certainly is. Utmo was good at hunting bears. Until he went half blind."

"I saw his eye. What happened?"

"Apparently his boy spilled a glass of acid on him."

"Apparently?"

Krongli rolled his shoulders. "Utmo is the only person left who knows what happened. His son disappeared when he was fifteen. Soon afterward his wife disappeared as well. But that was eighteen years ago, before I moved up here. Since then Utmo has lived alone in the mountains, no TV, no radio, doesn't even read the papers."

"How did they disappear?"

"You tell me. There are lots of sheer drops around Utmo's farm where you might fall. And the snow. The son's shoe was found after an avalanche, but there was no sign of him after the snow melted that year, and it was strange to lose a shoe like that up in the snow. Some thought it was a bear. Though, as far as I know, there weren't any bears up here eighteen years ago. And then there were those who reckoned it was Utmo."

"Oh? Why's that?"

"Well . . . ," Aslak said, dragging it out, "the boy had a bad scar on his chest. People figured he'd gotten that from his father. It was something to do with the mother, Karen."

"How so?"

"They were competing for her."

Aslak shook his head at the question in Kaja's eyes. "This was before my time. And Roy Stille, who has been an officer here since the dawn of time, went to the house, but only Odd and Karen were there. And they both said the same thing: The boy had gone out hunting and hadn't returned. But this was in April."

"Not hunting season?"

Aslak shook his head. "And since then no one has seen him. The following year, Karen disappeared.

Folk here believe it was the grief that broke her and she took a one-way ticket off a cliff."

Kaja thought she detected a little quiver in the officer's voice, but concluded it must have been the wine.

"What do you believe?" she asked.

"I believe it's true. The boy was caught by an avalanche. He suffocated under the snow. The snow melted and he was carried into a lake and that's where he is. With his mother, let's hope."

"Sounds nicer than the bear story, anyway."

"Well, it isn't."

Kaja looked up at Aslak. There was no laughter in his eyes now.

"Buried alive in an avalanche," he said, and his gaze wandered out of the window, to the drifting snow. "The darkness. The loneliness. You can't move, it holds you in its iron grip, laughs at your attempts to free yourself. The certainty that you're going to die. The panic, the mortal fear when you can't breathe. There's no worse way to go."

Kaja took a gulp of wine. She put down the glass. "How long were you lying there?" she asked.

"I thought it was three, maybe four hours," Aslak said. "When they dug me out, they said I had been trapped for fifteen minutes. Another five and I would have been dead."

The waiter came and asked if they wanted anything else; he would take last orders in ten minutes. Kaja said no, and the waiter responded by putting the bill in front of Aslak.

"Why does Utmo carry a gun?" Kaja asked. "As far as I'm aware, it isn't the hunting season now."

"He says it's because of beasts of prey. Self-defense."

"Are there any here? Wolves?"

"He never tells me exactly what kind of animal he means. By the way, there's a rumor going around that at night the boy's ghost walks the plains. And that if you see him, you have to be careful, because it means there's a sheer drop or an avalanche nearby."

Kaja finished her drink.

"I can have drinking hours extended for a bit if you like."

"Thanks, Aslak, but I have to be up early tomorrow."

"Ooh," he said, laughing with his eyes and scratching his locks. "Now that sounds like I . . ." He paused.

"What?" Kaja said.

"Nothing. I suppose you have a husband or boyfriend down south."

Kaja smiled, but didn't answer.

Aslak stared at the table, and said quietly, "Well, there you go: Provincial policeman couldn't take his drink and started babbling."

"That's all right," she said. "I don't have a boyfriend. And I like you. You remind me of my brother."

"But?"

"But what?"

"Don't forget I'm a real detective, too. I can see you're no hermit. There is someone, isn't there?"

Kaja laughed. Normally she would have left it at that. Maybe it was the wine. Maybe it was because she liked Aslak Krongli. Maybe it was because she didn't have anyone to talk to about that sort of thing, not since Even died, and Aslak was a stranger, a long way from Oslo, someone who didn't talk to her circle of acquaintances.

"I'm in love," she heard herself say. "With a police officer." She put the glass of water to her mouth to hide a flurry of confusion. The strange thing was that it hadn't struck her as true until she heard the words said aloud.

Aslak raised his glass to hers. "**Skål** to the lucky guy. And the lucky girl, I hope."

Kaja shook her head. "There's nothing to **skål** about. Not yet. Maybe ever. My God, listen to me . . ."

"We don't have anything else to do, do we? Tell me more."

"It's complicated. **He's** complicated. And I don't know if he wants me. In fact, that part is fairly straightforward."

"Let me guess. He's got someone, and he can't let go."

Kaja sighed. "Perhaps. I honestly don't know. Aslak, thank you for all your help, but I—"

"Have to go to bed now." The police officer rose. "I hope it all goes sour with your friend, you want to escape from your broken heart and the city and that you could envisage giving this a chance." He passed her a piece of paper with a Hol Police Station letterhead.

Kaja read it and laughed out loud. "A post in the sticks?"

"Roy Stille is retiring in the autumn and good officers are hard to find," Aslak said. "It's our advertisement for the job. We put it out last week. Our office is in Geilo. Time off every alternate weekend and free dentistry."

As Kaja went to bed she could hear the distant rumbles. Thunder and snow rarely came as a joint package.

She called Harry and got his voice mail. Left a little ghost story about the local guide Odd Utmo with the rotten teeth and braces, and about his son who had to be even uglier since he had been haunting the district for eighteen years. She laughed. Realized she was drunk. Said good night.

She dreamed about avalanches.

It was eleven o'clock in the morning. Harry and Joe had left Goma at seven and crossed the border to Rwanda without any problems, and Harry was standing in an office on the first floor of the terminal building at Kigali Airport. Two uniformed officers were giving him the once-over. Not in an unfriendly way, but to check that he really was who he claimed to be: a Norwegian policeman. Harry put his ID card back in his jacket pocket and felt the smooth paper of the coffee-brown envelope he had there. The problem was that there were two of them. How do you bribe two public servants at once? Ask them to share the contents of the envelope and politely request that they not snitch on each other?

One officer, the same one who had inspected Harry's passport two days before, pulled his beret back on his head. "So you want a copy of whose landing card? Could you repeat the date and the name?"

"Adele Vetlesen. We know she arrived at this airport on the twenty-fifth of November. And I'll pay a finder's fee."

The two officers exchanged glances, and one left the room on the other's cue. The remaining officer walked over to the window and surveyed the runway and the little DH8 that had landed and would, in fifty-five minutes, be transporting Harry on the first phase of his journey home.

"Finder's fee," the officer repeated quietly. "I assume you know it is illegal to try to bribe a public servant, Mr. Hole. But you probably thought, shit, this is Africa."

Harry felt his shirt sticking to his back. The same shirt. Perhaps they sold shirts at the Nairobi airport. If he got that far.

"That's right," Harry said.

The officer laughed and turned. "Tough guy, eh! Are you a hard man, Hole? I saw you were a policeman when you arrived."

"Oh?"

"You examined me with the same circumspection that I examined you."

Harry shrugged.

The door opened. The other officer was back,

accompanied by a woman dressed like a secretary with clickety-clack heels and glasses on the tip of her nose.

"I'm sorry," she said in impeccable English, looking at Harry. "I've checked the date. There was no Adele Vetlesen on that flight."

"Mm. Could there be a mistake?"

"Unlikely. Landing cards are filed by date. The flight you're talking about is a thirty-seven-seater DH8 from Entebbe. It didn't take long to check."

"Mm. If that's the case, may I ask you to check something else for me?"

"You may ask, of course. What is it?"

"Could you see if any other foreign women arrived on that flight?"

"And why should I do that?"

"Because Adele Vetlesen was booked onto that flight. So either she used a false passport here—"

"I doubt that very much," the passport officer said. "We check all the passport photos very carefully before they are scanned by a machine that matches the passport number against the International Civil Aviation Organization register."

"Or someone else was traveling in Adele Vetlesen's name and then used their own, genuine passport to pass through here. Which is more than possible, as passport numbers are not checked before passengers board the aircraft."

"True," the chief passport official said, pulling at his beret. "Airline staff only make sure the name and photo match more or less. For that purpose you can have a false passport made for fifty dollars anywhere in the world. It's only when you get off the plane at your final destination and have to go through checks that your passport number is matched and false passports are revealed. But the question is the same: Why should we help you, Mr. Hole? Are you on an official mission here and do you have the papers to support that?"

"My official mission was in the Congo," Harry lied. "But I found nothing there. Adele Vetlesen is missing, and we fear she may have been murdered by a serial killer who has already murdered at least three other women, among them a government MP. Her name is Marit Olsen—you can verify that on the Net. I'm conscious that the procedure now is for me to return home and go through formal channels, as a result of which we will lose several days and give the killer a further head start. And time to kill again."

Harry saw that his words had made some impression on them. The woman and the chief official conferred, and the woman marched off again.

They waited in silence.

Harry looked at his watch. He hadn't checked in for his flight yet.

Six minutes had passed when they heard the click-clack heels coming closer.

"Eva Rosenberg, Juliana Verni, Veronica Raúl Gueño and Claire Hobbes." She spat out the names, straightened her glasses and put four landing cards on the table in front of Harry before the door had even closed again. "Not many European women come here," she said.

Harry's eyes ran down the cards. All of them had given Kigali hotels as their address, but not the Hotel Gorilla. He looked at their home addresses. Eva Rosenberg's was in Stockholm.

"Thank you," Harry said, noting down the names, addresses and passport numbers on the back of a taxi receipt he found in his jacket pocket.

"I regret that we can't be of any more assistance," the woman said, pushing her glasses up again.

"Not at all," Harry said. "You've been a great help. Really."

"And now, Mr. Policeman," said the tall, thin officer, with a smile that lit up his black-as-night face.

"Yes?" Harry said in anticipation, ready to take out the coffee-brown envelope.

"Now it's time we got you checked in on the flight to Nairobi."

"Mm," Harry said, looking at his watch. "I may have to catch the next one."

"Next one?"

"I have to go back to the Hotel Gorilla."

Kaja was sitting in the Norwegian railway's so-called comfort coach, which—apart from offering free newspapers, two cups of free coffee and an outlet for your laptop—meant that you sat like sardines in a can instead of in the almost-empty economy areas. So when her phone rang and she saw it was Harry, that was where she hurried.

"Where are you?" Harry asked.

"On the train. Passing Kongsberg right this minute. And you?"

"Hotel Gorilla in Kigali. I've gotten a look at Adele Vetlesen's hotel registration card. I won't get away now before the afternoon flight, but I'll be home early tomorrow. Could you call your friend the pumpkin head at the Drammen Police, and see if we can borrow the postcard Adele wrote? You can ask him to come to the train station with it. The train stops at Drammen, doesn't it?"

"You're pushing your luck. I'll try, anyway. What are we going to do with it?"

"Compare the handwriting. There's a handwriting expert named Jean Hue who worked at Kripos before he retired. Get him to the office at seven tomorrow."

"So early? D'you think he'll—"

"You're right. I'll scan Adele's registration card and email it to you so you can go to Jean's place with both this evening."

"This evening?"

"He'll be happy to see you. If you had any other plans, they are hereby canceled."

"Great. By the way, sorry about the late call last night."

"No problem. Entertaining story."

"I was a little tipsy."

"Thought so."

Harry hung up.

"Thanks for all your help," he said.

The receptionist responded with a smile.

The coffee-brown envelope had finally found a new owner.

Kjersti Rødsmoen went into the common room and over to the woman looking out of the window at the rain falling on Sandviken's timber houses. In front of her was an untouched slice of cake with a little candle on it.

"This phone was found in your room, Katrine," she said softly. "The ward sister brought it to me. You know they're forbidden, don't you?"

Katrine nodded.

"Anyway," Rødsmoen said, passing it over, "it's ringing."

Katrine Bratt took the vibrating cell phone and pressed "answer."

"It's me," said the voice at the other end. "I've got four women's names here. I'd like to know which of them was not booked on BA flight one-oh-one to Kigali on the twenty-fifth of November. And to receive confirmation that this person was not in any reservation system for a Rwandan hotel that same night."

"I'm fine, thanks, Auntie."

Silence for a second.

"I see. Call when you can."

Katrine passed the phone back to Rødsmoen. "My aunt wishing me many happy returns."

Kjersti Rødsmoen shook her head. "Rules say the

use of phones is forbidden. So there's no reason why you shouldn't have a phone, so long as you don't use it. Just make sure the ward sister doesn't see it, OK?"

Katrine nodded, and Rødsmoen left.

Katrine sat looking out of the window for a while longer, then got up and went toward the recreation room. The ward sister's voice reached her as she was about to cross the threshold.

"What are you going to do, Katrine?"

Katrine answered without turning. "Play solitaire."

33

Leipzig

Gunnar Hagen took the elevator down to the basement.

Down. Downer. Downtrodden. Downsized.

He got out and set off through the culvert.

But Bellman had kept his promise; he hadn't blabbed. And he had thrown him a line, a top-management post in the new, expanded Kripos. Harry's report had been short and to the point. No results. Any idiot would have realized it was time to start swimming toward the lifebuoy.

Hagen opened the door at the end of the culvert without knocking.

Kaja Solness smiled sweetly while Harry Hole—

sitting in front of the computer screen with a telephone to his ear—didn't even turn around, just sang out, "Siddown-boss-want-some-crap-coffee?" as though the unit head's doppelgänger had announced his forthcoming arrival.

Hagen stood in the doorway. "I received the message that you were unable to find Adele Vetlesen. Time to pack up. Time was up ages ago, and you're needed for other cases. At least you are, Kaja Solness."

"**Dankeschön,** Günther," Harry said on the telephone, put it down and swiveled around.

"**Dankeschön?**" Hagen repeated.

"Leipzig Police," Harry said. "By the way, Katrine Bratt sends her regards, boss. Remember her?"

Hagen eyed his inspector with suspicion. "I thought Bratt was in a mental institution."

"No doubt about that," Harry said, getting up and making for the coffee machine. "But the woman's a genius at searching the Net. Speaking of searches, boss . . ."

"Searches?"

"Could you see your way to giving us unlimited funds to mount a search?"

Hagen's eyes almost popped out. Then he burst out laughing. "You're fucking incredible, Harry. You've just wasted half the travel budget on a fiasco in the Congo and now you want a police search operation? This investigation comes to a halt right now. Do you understand?"

"I understand . . ." Harry said, pouring coffee into

two cups and passing one to Hagen, ". . . so much more. And soon you will, too, boss. Grab my chair and listen to this."

Hagen looked from Harry to Kaja. Stared skeptically at the coffee. Then he sat down. "You've got two minutes."

"It's quite simple." Harry said. "Based on Brussels Airlines passenger lists, Adele Vetlesen traveled to Kigali on the twenty-fifth of November. But according to passport control, no one of that name entered the country. What happened is that a woman with a false passport made out in Adele's name traveled from Oslo. The false passport would have worked without a hitch until she reached her final destination in Kigali, because that's where it's computer-checked and the number's matched. So this mysterious woman must have used her own passport, which was genuine. Passport control officials don't ask to see the name on your ticket, so any mismatch between passport and ticket is not discovered. So long as no one looks, of course."

"But you did?"

"Yep."

"Couldn't it just be an administrative oversight? They forgot to register Adele's arrival?"

"Indeed. But then there's the postcard . . ."

Harry nodded to Kaja, who held up a card. Hagen saw a picture of something akin to a smoking volcano.

"This was mailed from Kigali the same day she was supposed to have arrived," Harry said. "But first of all, this is a picture of Nyiragongo, a volcano situated in the Congo, not Rwanda. Second, we got Jean Hue to compare the handwriting on this card with the check-in card the alleged Adele Vetlesen filled in at the Hotel Gorilla."

"He established beyond a doubt what even I can see," Kaja said. "It's not the same person."

"All right, all right," Hagen said. "But where are you going with all of this?"

"Someone has gone to great effort to make it seem as if Adele Vetlesen went to Africa," Harry said. "My guess is that Adele was in Norway and was forced to write the card. Then it was taken to Africa by a second person, who sent it back. All to give the impression that Adele had traveled there and written home about her dream guy and that she wouldn't be back before March."

"Any idea who the impersonator might be?"

"Yes."

"Yes?"

"The immigration authorities at Kigali Airport found a card made out in the name of Juliana Verni. But our friendly fruitcake in Bergen says this name was not registered on any airline passenger lists to Rwanda or at any hotels with modern, electronic booking equipment on the date in question. But she is on the Rwandan passenger list from Kigali three days later."

"Would I like to know how you acquired this information?"

"No, boss. But you would like to know who and where Juliana Verni is."

"And that is?"

Harry looked at his watch. "According to the information on the landing card, she lives in Leipzig, Germany. Ever been to Leipzig, boss?"

"No."

"Nor me. But I know it's famous for being the home of Goethe, Bach and one of the waltz kings. What's his name again?"

"What has this got to do with . . . ?"

"Well, you see, Leipzig is also famous for holding the main archives of the Stasi, the security police. The town was in the old East Germany. Did you know that over the forty years East Germany existed, the German spoken there developed in such a way that a sensitive ear can hear the difference between East and West Germans?"

"Harry—"

"Sorry, boss. The point is that in late November a woman with an East German accent was in the town of Goma in the Congo, which is just a three-hour drive from Kigali. And I'm positive that, while there, she bought the murder weapon that took the lives of Borgny Stem-Myhre and Charlotte Lolles."

"We've been sent a copy of the form the police keep when passports are issued," Kaja said, passing Hagen a sheet of paper.

"Matches Van Boorst's description of the buyer," Harry said. "Juliana Verni had big rust-red curls."

"Brick-red," Kaja said.

"I beg your pardon?" Hagen said.

Kaja pointed to the sheet. "She's got one of the old-fashioned passports with hair color listed. They called it "brick-red." German thoroughness, you know."

"I've also asked the police in Leipzig to confiscate her passport and check that it has a stamp from Kigali on the date in question."

Gunnar Hagen stared blankly at the printout. He appeared to be trying to absorb what Harry and Kaja had said. At length he looked up with one raised bushy eyebrow. "Are you telling me . . . are you telling me that you may have the person who . . ." The POB swallowed, struggled to find an indirect way of saying it, terrified that this miracle, this mirage, might vanish if he said it aloud. But he gave up the attempt. "Is our serial killer?"

"I'm not saying any more than what I'm saying," Harry said. "For the moment. My colleague in Leipzig is going through her personal data and criminal records now, so we'll soon know a bit more about Fräulein Verni."

"But this is fantastic news," Hagen said, sending a smile from Harry to Kaja, who gave him a nod of encouragement.

"Not," Harry said, with a swig from his cup of coffee, "for Adele Vetlesen's family."

Hagen's smile faded. "True. Do you think there's any hope for . . . ?"

Harry shook his head. "She's dead, boss."

"But . . ."

At that moment the telephone rang.

Harry took it. "**Ja, Günther!**" And repeated with a strained smile: "**Ja, Dirty Harry. Genau.**"

Gunnar Hagen and Kaja observed Harry as he listened in silence. Harry rounded off the conversation with a "**Danke**" and cradled the receiver. Cleared his throat.

"She's dead."

"Yes, you said that," Hagen said.

"No, Juliana Verni is. She was found in the Elster River on the second of December."

Hagen cursed under his breath.

"Cause of death?" Kaja asked.

Harry stared into the distance. "Drowning."

"Might have been an accident."

Harry shook his head slowly. "She didn't drown in water."

In the ensuing silence they heard the rumble of the boiler in the adjacent room.

"Wounds in the mouth?" Kaja asked.

Harry nodded. "Twenty-four, to be precise. She was sent to Africa to bring back the instrument that would kill her."

34

Medium

"So Juliana Verni was found dead in Leipzig three days after she flew home from Kigali," Kaja said. "Where she'd traveled as Adele Vetlesen, checked in at the

Hotel Gorilla as Adele Vetlesen and sent a postcard written by the real Adele Vetlesen, probably dictated."

"That's about the size of it," said Harry, who was in the process of brewing some more coffee.

"And you think that Verni must have done that in collusion with someone," Hagen said. "And this second person killed her to cover the traces."

"Yes," Harry said.

"So it's just a question of finding the link between her and this second person. That shouldn't be too difficult. They must have been very close if they committed this kind of crime together."

"Well in that case I'd have thought it would be pretty difficult."

"Why's that?"

"Because," Harry said, smacking down the lid of the machine and flicking the switch, "Juliana Verni had a record. Drugs. Prostitution. Vagrancy. In short, she was the type it would have been easy to hire for a job like this, if the money was right. And everything so far suggests that the person behind it won't have left any clues for us, that he has considered most angles. Katrine discovered that Verni traveled from Leipzig to Oslo. From there she continued to Kigali using Adele's name. Nevertheless, Katrine did not find so much as a phone conversation between Verni's cell and Norway. This person has been scrupulous."

Hagen shook his head dejectedly. "So close . . ."

Harry sat on the desk. "There is another dilemma we have to resolve. The overnight guests at Håvass cabin that night."

"What about them?"

"We cannot exclude the possibility that the page torn out of the guest book is a hit list. They have to be warned."

"How? We don't know who they are."

"Through the media. Even if it means we would be letting the killer know we've picked up his trail."

Hagen slowly shook his head. "Hit list. And you've only reached this conclusion now?"

"I know, boss." Harry met Hagen's eyes. "If I'd gone to the media with a warning as soon as we stumbled on the Håvass cabin, it might have saved Elias Skog's life."

The room went quiet.

"We can't go to the media," Hagen said.

"Why not?"

"If someone responds to the media alert, perhaps we can find out who else was in the cabin and what really happened," Kaja said.

"We can't go to the media," Hagen said, getting to his feet. "We've been investigating a missing-persons case and uncovered links with a murder case, which is in Kripos's hands. We have to pass the information on and let them take it further. I'll call Bellman."

"Wait!" Harry said. "Should he take all the credit for what we've done?"

"I'm not sure there will be any credit to share," Hagen said, heading for the door. "And you can start moving out now."

"Isn't that a little hasty?" Kaja said.

The other two looked at her.

"I mean, we've still got a missing person here. Shouldn't we try to locate her before we clear out?"

"And how were you going to go about that?" Hagen asked.

"As Harry said before. A search."

"You don't even know where you should fucking search."

"Harry knows."

They looked at the man who had just grabbed the jug from the coffee machine with one hand and was holding his cup under the mud-brown stream with the other.

"Do you?" Hagen said at length.

"Yes, I do," Harry said.

"Where?"

"You'll get into hot water," Harry said.

"Shut up, and out with it," Hagen said, without noticing the contradiction. Because he was thinking, here I am, doing it again. What was it about this tall, fair-haired policeman who always managed to drag others along when he took headlong plunges?

Olav Hole looked up at Harry and the woman beside him.

She had curtsied when she introduced herself, and Harry had noticed that his father had liked that; he was always complaining that women had stopped curtsying.

"So you're Harry's colleague," Olav said. "Does he behave himself?"

"We're off to organize an operation," Harry said. "Just dropped by to see how you were."

His father smiled wanly, shrugged and beckoned Harry to come closer. Harry leaned forward, listened. And flinched.

"You'll be all right," Harry said in a sudden hoarse voice and stood up. "I'll be back this evening, OK?"

In the corridor Harry stopped Altman and motioned for Kaja to go on ahead.

"Listen, I was wondering if you could do me a big favor," he said when Kaja was out of range. "My father's just told me that he's in pain. He would never admit that to you because he's afraid you'll give him more painkillers, and, well, he has a pathological fear of becoming dependent on . . . drugs. There's a bit of family history here, you see."

"You thee," the nurse lisped and there was a moment of confusion until Harry realized that Altman had repeated "You see." "The problem is that I'm being shifted between wards at the moment."

"I'm asking this as a personal favor."

Altman screwed up one eye behind his glasses, staring thoughtfully at a point between himself and Harry. "I'll see what I can do."

"Thank you."

Kaja drove while Harry was on the phone to the chief of operations at Briskeby Fire Station.

"Your father seems like a nice man," Kaja said as Harry hung up.

Harry took that in. "Mom made him good," he said. "When she was alive he was good. She brought out the best in him."

"Sounds like something you've been through yourself," she said.

"What?"

"Someone made you good."

Harry looked out of the window. Nodded.

"Rakel?"

"Rakel and Oleg," Harry said.

"Sorry, I didn't mean to—"

"It's all right."

"It's just that when I came to Crime Squad everyone was talking about the Snowman case. About him trying to kill them. And you. But it was already over before the case began, wasn't it?"

"In a way," Harry said.

"Have you had any contact with them?"

Harry shook his head. "We had to try to put it behind us. Help Oleg to forget. When they're that young they still can."

"Not always," Kaja said with a rueful smile.

Harry glanced at her. "And who made you good?"

"Even," she answered without any hesitation.

"No great romantic passions?"

She shook her head. "No extra-larges. Just a few smalls. And one medium."

"Got your cap set at someone?"

She chuckled. " 'Cap set at someone'?"

Harry smiled. "My vocabulary is somewhat old-fashioned in that area."

She hesitated. "I suppose I'm a bit hung up on a guy."

"And the prospects are . . . ?"

"Poor."

"Let me guess," Harry said, winding down the window and lighting a cigarette. "He's married and says he'll leave his wife and kids for you, but never does?"

She laughed. "Let me guess. You're the type who thinks he's so damned good at reading other people's minds because he only remembers the times he got it right?"

"He says you've just got to give him some time?"

"Wrong again," she said. "He doesn't say anything."

Harry nodded. He was about to ask more questions when it struck him: He didn't want to know.

35

The Dive

The mist drifted across the shiny black surface of Lake Lyseren. Along the banks the trees stood with bowed shoulders like somber, silent witnesses. The tranquillity was broken by shouted commands, radio communication and splashes as divers toppled backward off rubber dinghies. They had started on the shore closest to the ropery. The heads of the search-and-recovery teams had sent their divers out in a fan formation, and now they were standing on land, crossing off the squares on the defined search grid they had covered, and signaling with a pull on the lifelines when they wanted the divers to stop or come back. The professional divers, such as Jarle Andreassen, also had wires in the lines that went up to full-face masks, allowing them to stay in verbal contact.

It was only six months since Jarle had taken his rescue course, and his pulse was still up during these dives. And a high pulse meant higher oxygen consumption. The more experienced men at Briskeby Fire Station called him "The Float," as he had to rise to the surface and exchange oxygen cylinders so often.

Jarle knew that there was still good daylight at the top, but down here it was as black as night. He tried to swim at the regulation five feet above the lake bed, yet he still stirred up mud, which reflected the glare from his flashlight and partially blinded him. Even though he knew there were other divers a few yards away on either side, he felt alone. Alone and frozen to the marrow. And there were probably still hours of diving ahead of them. He knew he had less air left than the others, and cursed to himself. Being the first fire station diver to change cylinders was fine by him, but he feared he would have to surface before the voluntary club divers as well. He refocused in front of him and then stopped breathing. Not as a conscious action to reduce consumption, but because in the middle of his flashlight beam, inside the swaying forest of stalks that grew in the muddy bed closer to land, he could see a form floating free. A form that did not belong down here, that would be unable to live here. An alien feature. That was what made it so fascinating and at the same time so frightening. Or perhaps it was the beam from his flashlight shining on the dark eyes that made it look as if it were alive.

"Everything OK, Jarle?"

It was the team head. One of his tasks was to listen to his divers' breathing. Not just to be sure they were breathing, but to hear if there were signs of anxiety. Or excessive calm. At seventy feet the brain began to store so much nitrogen that the so-called rapture of the deep could emerge, the nitrogen narcosis that meant you began to forget things, that simple jobs became more difficult and could, at greater depths, produce dizziness, tunnel vision and downright irrational behavior. Jarle didn't know if they were just yarns that did the rounds, but he had heard of divers who had pulled off their masks with a smile at 150 feet below. So far the only narcosis he had experienced was the cozy red wine–induced serenity that he enjoyed with his partner late on Saturday nights.

"Everything's fine," Jarle Andreassen said and started breathing again. He sucked in the mixture of oxygen and nitrogen and heard it rumble past his ears as he released clusters of bubbles that fought their way desperately to the surface.

It was a large red stag. It was hanging upside down, its huge antlers apparently caught on the rock face. It must have been feeding on the bank and fallen. Or perhaps something or someone had chased it into the water. What else would it have been doing there? It had probably gotten tangled up in the rushes and the long stems of the water lilies, tried to struggle free, with the result that it had only gotten even more enmeshed in the tough green tentacles. And then it must have gone under and wrestled on until it drowned. Sunk to the bottom and lain there until the bacteria and the body's chemistry had filled it with gas and it had risen toward the top again, but the antlers had snagged on the lattice of green plants growing down here. In a few days the gas would have drained from the cadaver and it would have sunk again. Just like a drowned human body. The same thing was as likely to have happened to the person they were looking for, and that was why the body had not been found: It had never floated to the surface. If so, it would be lying down here somewhere, probably covered with a layer of mud. Mud that inevitably swirled upward as they approached, which meant that even small, defined search areas such as this could keep their secrets concealed for all eternity.

Jarle Andreassen took out his large diver's knife, swam over to the stag and cut the stems obstructing the antlers. He had an inkling his boss would not appreciate that, but he couldn't bear the thought of this handsome beast being held underwater. The cadaver rose a couple of feet, but then there were more stems holding it back. Jarle was careful not to let his lifeline get snarled in the reeds and made some hurried slashes. Then he felt a pull on the line. Hard enough for him to feel irritation. Hard enough for him to lose concentration for a moment. The knife slipped out of his hand. He shone his flashlight downward and caught a glimpse of the blade before it was lost from view in the mud. Cautiously he swam after it. Thrust his hand into the mud drifting up toward him like ash. Groped along the bottom. Felt stones, branches, slippery, rotten and green. And something hard. Chain. Probably from a boat. More chain. Something else. Solid. The contours of something. A hole, an opening. He heard the sudden hiss of bubbles before his brain could formulate the thought: that he was afraid.

"Everything OK, Jarle? Jarle?"

No, everything was not OK. For even through thick gloves, even with a brain that seemed unable to absorb enough air, he had no doubts about where his hand had strayed. Into the open mouth of a human body.

Part Four

36

Helicopter

Mikael Bellman arrived at the lake in a helicopter. The rotor blades whisked the mist into cotton candy as he bent double and dashed from the passenger seat across the field to the ropery. Kolkka and Beavis followed at a half-run. From the opposite direction came four men carrying a stretcher. Bellman stopped them and lifted the blanket. The stretcher bearers averted their faces as Bellman leaned over and studiously examined the naked white bloated body.

"Thank you," he said and let them continue toward the helicopter.

Bellman stopped at the top of the slope and looked down on the people standing between the building and the water. Among the divers divesting themselves of their equipment and dry suits he could see Beate Lønn and Kaja Solness. Farther away was Harry Hole, talking to a man Bellman guessed was Skai, the local county officer.

The POB signaled to Beavis and Kolkka that they should wait, and with lithe, nimble steps, he glided down the slope.

"Hello, Skai," Bellman said, brushing twigs off his long coat. "Mikael Bellman, Kripos. We've spoken on the phone."

"Correct," Skai said. "The night his people found some rope here." He jerked his thumb back toward Harry.

"And now it seems he's here again," Bellman said. "The question is, of course, what he's doing at my crime scene."

"Well," Harry said, clearing his throat, "first, this is hardly a crime scene. Second, I'm looking for a missing person. And it does seem as if we've found what we were looking for. How's the triple murder going? Found anything? You got our information about the Håvass cabin?"

The county officer acknowledged a glance from Bellman and absented himself in discreet haste.

Bellman surveyed the lake while running a forefinger along his lower lip as if to rub in some ointment. "All right, Hole, you are aware that you have just ensured that both you and your superior officer, Gunnar Hagen, have not only lost your jobs but will also be charged with dereliction of duty?"

"Mm, because we do the job we've been entrusted with?"

"I think the minister of justice will be demanding a pretty detailed explanation as to why you initiated a search for a missing person right outside the ropery that supplied the rope used to kill Marit Olsen. I gave you Crime Squad people a chance. You won't get another. Game over, Hole."

"Then we'll have to give the minister of justice a pretty detailed explanation, Bellman. Naturally, it will include information about how we found out where the rope came from, how we got on to the trail of Elias Skog and the Håvass cabin, how we found out that there was a fourth victim named Adele Vetlesen and how we found her here today. A job Kripos, with all its manpower and resources, failed to carry out over two months. Eh, Bellman?"

Bellman didn't answer.

"Frightened it might affect the minister of justice's decision on who is best suited to investigate murders in this country?"

"Don't overplay your hand, Hole. I'll crush you just like that." Bellman snapped his fingers.

"OK," Harry said. "Neither of us has a winning hand, so what if I pass over the kitty?"

"What the hell do you mean?"

"You get everything. Everything we have. We don't take credit for anything."

Bellman looked askance at Harry. "And why should you help us?"

"Simple," Harry said, plucking the last smoke from the pack. "I get paid for helping to catch the killer. That's my job."

Bellman grimaced and his head and shoulders moved as if he were laughing, but not a sound issued forth. "Come on, Hole, what do you want?"

Harry lit his cigarette. "I don't want Gunnar Hagen, Kaja Solness or Bjørn Holm to take the rap for this. Your prospects in the force won't be affected."

Bellman squeezed his full lower lip between thumb and first finger. "I'll see what I can do."

"And I want to be part of this. I want access to all

the material you have and to resources for the investigation."

"That's enough!" Bellman said, raising a hand. "Are you hard of hearing, Hole? I told you to stay away from this case."

"We can catch this killer, Bellman. Right now that should be more fucking important than who's in charge afterward, shouldn't it?"

"Don't you . . . !" Bellman shouted, but held back when he saw a couple of heads turn in their direction. He took a step closer to Harry and lowered his voice. "Don't you talk to me as if I were an idiot, Hole."

The wind blew the smoke from Harry's cigarette into Bellman's face, but he didn't blink. Harry shrugged.

"Do you know what, Bellman? I don't think this has much to do with power or politics. You're a little boy who wants to be the hero who saves the day. Simple as that. And you're scared I'll ruin the epic. But there's an easy way of resolving this. What about unzipping and seeing who can piss as far as the divers' dinghy?"

When Mikael Bellman laughed this time, it was for real, with volume and everything. "You should read the warning signs, Harry."

His right hand shot out, so quickly that Harry didn't manage to react, struck the cigarette between his lips and knocked it away. It hit the water with a hiss.

"Smoking kills. Have a good day."

Harry heard the helicopter take off as he watched

his last cigarette floating in the water. The gray wet paper, the black dead tip.

Night had started to fall as the diving team's boat dropped Harry, Kaja and Beate ashore by the parking lot. There was sudden movement amid the trees, followed by camera flashes. Harry instinctively held up an arm, and he heard Roger Gjendem's voice from out of the darkness.

"Harry Hole, there are rumors flying around that you've found a young woman's body. What's her name and how sure are you that this is connected with the other murders?"

"No comment," Harry said, plowing his way through, half blinded. "For the moment this is a missing-persons case, and the only thing we can say is that a woman has been found who might be the missing person. As far as the murder cases I assume you're referring to are concerned, talk to Kripos."

"Woman's name?"

"She has to be identified first and relatives informed."

"But you're not ruling out—"

"As usual, I'm not ruling out anything, Gjendem. Press conference to follow."

Harry got into the car; Kaja had already started the engine and Beate Lønn was sitting in the backseat. They trundled onto the main road to the flashes of cameras behind them.

"Now," Beate Lønn said, leaning forward between the seats, "I still haven't been given an explanation as to how your search for Adele Vetlesen led here."

"Deductive logic, pure and simple," Harry said.

"Goes without saying," Beate said, sighing.

"In fact, I'm embarrassed I didn't figure it out before," Harry said. "I went around wondering why the killer had made the effort to go all the way out to a disused ropery just for a piece of rope. Especially since that rope—unlike what he could have bought in a shop—could be traced back here. The answer was, of course, obvious. Nevertheless, it was only when I sat looking into a deep African lake that I realized. He didn't come here for the rope. He must have used the rope for something here—because it happened to be lying around—and then taken it home, where he later used it to kill Marit Olsen. The reason he came here was that he already had a body he needed to dispose of. Adele Vetlesen. The local man, Skai, spelled it out for us the first time we came here. This is the deep end of the lake. The killer filled her trousers with rocks, tied up the waist and legs with rope, then dropped her overboard."

"How do you know she was dead before she came here? He might have drowned her."

"There was a large cut around her neck. It's my bet the postmortem will show that there wasn't any water in her lungs."

"And that ketanome is in her bloodstream, the same as with Charlotte and Borgny," Beate said.

"I'm told ketanome is a fast-working anesthetic," Harry said. "Strange I'd never heard of it before."

"Not so strange," Beate said. "It's an old cheapo version of Ketalar, which is used to anesthetize patients with the advantage that they can still breathe by themselves," Beate said. "Ketanome was banned in the EU and Norway in the nineties because of side effects, so now you generally see it in underdeveloped countries. Kripos considered it a major clue for a while, but got nowhere with it."

As they dropped Beate off at Krimteknisk in Bryn forty minutes later, Harry asked Kaja to wait and he got out of the car.

"There was one thing I wanted to ask you," Harry said.

"Oh, yes?" Beate said, shivering and rubbing her hands together.

"What were you doing at a potential crime scene? Why wasn't Bjørn there?"

"Because Bellman assigned Bjørn to special duties."

"And what does that mean? Cleaning the latrines?"

"No. Coordination of Krimteknisk and strategic planning."

"What?" Harry raised his eyebrows. "That's a fucking promotion."

Beate shrugged. "Bjørn's good. It wasn't premature. Anything else?"

"No."

"Bye."

"Bye. Oh, by the way, just a moment. I asked you

to tell Bellman where we'd found the rope. When did you pass the message on?"

"You called me at night, remember, so I waited until the following morning. Why's that?"

"No reason," Harry said. "No reason."

When he got back into the car, Kaja quickly slipped her phone into her pocket.

"News of the body's already on the **Aftenposten** website," she said.

"Oh, yes?"

"They say there's a big picture of you with your full name and that you're referred to as 'heading the investigation.' And of course they're linking this case with the other murders."

"So, that's what they're doing. Mm. Are you hungry?"

"Very."

"Do you have any plans? If not, I'll treat you to a meal."

"Great. Where?"

"Ekeberg Restaurant."

"Ooh. Fancy. Any particular reason you chose that one?"

"Well, it came to mind when a pal of mine was recounting an old story."

"Tell me."

"There's nothing to tell, it's just the usual adolescent thi—"

"Adolescent! Come on!"

Harry chuckled. And as they approached down-town and it started snowing at the top of Ekeberg

Ridge, Harry told her about the Killer Queen, the darling of Ekeberg Restaurant, once the most attractive functionalist building in Oslo. Which today—post-renovation—it was again.

"But in the eighties it was so run-down that people had actually given up on the place. It had become a boozy dance restaurant where you went around to tables and asked for a partner, trying not to knock over the glasses. And then shuffled around the floor propping each other up."

"I see."

"Øystein, Tresko and I used to go to the top of the German bunkers on Nordstrand beach, drink beer and wait for puberty to pass. When we were seventeen we ventured over to the restaurant, lied about our ages and went in. You didn't have to lie much—the place needed all the cash it could get. The dance band stank, but at least they played 'Nights in White Satin.' And they had a star attraction who guested almost every night. We called her the Killer Queen. A female man-o'-war, she was."

"A **man-o'-war**?" Kaja laughed. "Set your cap at?"

"Yup," Harry said. "Bore down on you like a galleon in full rig, mean, sexy and dead scary. Equipped like a fairground. Curves on her like a roller coaster."

Kaja laughed even louder. "The local amusement park, no less?"

"In a way," Harry said. "But she went to Ekeberg Restaurant primarily to be seen and adored, I think. And for the free drinks from faded dance-floor kings, of course. No one ever saw the Killer Queen go home with any of them. Perhaps that was what fascinated us. A woman who'd had to go down a league or two for admirers, but in a way still had style."

"And then what?"

"Øystein and Tresko said they would each buy me a whiskey if I dared ask her to dance."

They crossed the tram lines and drove up the steep hill to the restaurant.

"And?" Kaja said.

"I dared."

"And then?"

"We danced. Until she said she was sick of having her feet trodden on and it would be better if we went for a walk. She left first. It was August, hot, and, as you can see, there's only forest around here. Thick foliage and loads of paths to hidden places. I was drunk, but still so excited that I knew she would be able to hear the tremor in my voice if I said anything. So I kept my trap shut. And that was fine; she did all the talking. And the rest, too. Afterward she asked me if I wanted to go home with her."

Kaja sniggered. "Ooh. And what happened there?"

"We can talk about that during the meal. We're here."

They came to a halt in the parking lot, got out and walked up the steps to the restaurant. The head waiter welcomed them at the entrance to the dining area and asked for the name. Harry answered that they hadn't reserved a table.

The waiter could barely restrain himself from rolling his eyes.

"Full for the next two months," Harry snorted as they left, after buying cigarettes at the bar. "I think I liked the place better when water was leaking into the restaurant and rats squealed at you from behind the toilets. At least we could get in."

"Let's have a smoke," Kaja suggested.

They walked over to the low brick wall from where the forest sloped downward into Oslo. The clouds in the west were tinged with orange and red, and the lines of traffic on the highway glittered like phosphorescence against the blackness of the town. It seemed to be lying there in wait, keeping watch, Harry thought. A camouflaged beast of prey. He tapped out two cigarettes, lit them and passed one to Kaja.

"The rest of the story," Kaja said, inhaling.

"Where were we?"

"The Killer Queen took you home."

"No, she asked if I wanted to go. And I politely declined."

"Declined? You're lying. Why?"

"Øystein and Tresko asked me that when I got back. I told them I couldn't just leave when I had two pals and free whiskey waiting for me."

Kaja laughed and blew smoke over the view.

"But of course that was a lie," Harry said. "Loyalty had nothing to do with it. Friendship means nothing to a man if he has a tempting enough offer. Nothing. The truth is that I didn't dare. The Killer Queen was simply in the scariest league of all for me."

They sat silently for a while, listening to the hum of the town and watching the smoke curl upward.

"You're thinking," Kaja said.

"Mm. I'm thinking about Bellman. How well informed he is. He not only knew I was coming to Norway, he even knew which flight I was on."

"Perhaps he has contacts at Police HQ."

"Mm. And at Lake Lyseren today Skai said that Bellman had called him about the rope the same evening that we'd been at the ropery."

"Really?"

"But Beate says she didn't tell Bellman about the rope until the morning after we'd been there." Harry followed the glow of tobacco on its flight over the slope. "And Bjørn has been promoted to coordinator for forensics and strategic planning."

Kaja stared at him in surprise. "That's not possible, Harry."

He didn't answer.

"Bjørn Holm! Would he have kept Bellman informed about what we were doing? You two have worked together for so long; you're . . . friends!"

Harry shrugged. "As I said, I think"—he dropped his cigarette onto the ground and crushed it with a swivel of his heel—"friendship means nothing to a man if he has a tempting enough offer. Do you dare join me for today's special at Schrøder's?"

I dream all the time now. It was summer, and I loved her. I was so young and thought that if you wanted something enough it was yours to have.

Adele, you had her smile, her hair and her faithless heart. And now Aftenposten says they have found you. I hope you were as foul on the outside as you were on the inside.

It also says they've put Inspector Harry Hole on the case. He was the one who caught the Snowman. Perhaps there's hope; perhaps the police can save lives, after all?

I've printed out a photo of Adele from the **Verdens Gang** website and pinned it on the wall, next to the torn page from the Håvass cabin guest book. Including mine, there are only three more names now.

37

Profile

The special at Schrøder's was bubble and squeak served with fried eggs and raw onions.

"Nice," said Kaja.

"The cook must be sober today," Harry agreed. Then he pointed. "Look."

Kaja turned and looked up at the TV Harry was indicating.

"Well, hello!" she said.

Mikael Bellman's face filled the screen, and Harry signaled to Rita that they wanted the volume up. Harry studied the movements of Bellman's mouth. The soft, quasi-feminine features. The gleam in the intense brown eyes beneath the elegantly formed eyebrows. The white patches, like sleet on his skin, didn't disfigure him; actually, they made him more interesting to look at, like an exotic animal. If his number were not unlisted, as was the case with most detectives, his voice mail would be full of lusting and lovelorn messages afterward. Then the sound came on.

". . . at Håvass cabin on the night of the seventh of November. So we are appealing to those of you who were there to come forward to the police as quickly as possible."

Then the newsreader returned, and there was a new item.

Harry pushed his plate away and waved for coffee. "Let me hear your thoughts about this killer now that we've found Adele. Give me a profile."

"Why?" Kaja asked, sipping water from her glass. "Starting tomorrow we'll be working on other cases."

"Just for fun."

"Does the profiling of serial killers come under your definition of fun?"

Harry sucked on a toothpick. "I know there's a good answer to that, but I can't think of it."

"You're sick."

"So who is he?"

"It's still a he, first of all. And still a serial killer. I don't necessarily think Adele was number one."

"Why not?"

"Because it was so flawless that he must have kept a clear head. The first time you kill you're not so clear-headed. Besides, he hid her so well that we definitely were not intended to find her. That suggests he may be behind many of the present missing-persons statistics."

"Good. More."

"Erm . . ."

"Come on. You just said that he did a good job of hiding Adele Vetlesen. The first of the murder victims we know anything about. How do the other murders develop?"

"He becomes bolder, more self-assured. He stops hiding them. Charlotte is found behind a car in the forest and Borgny in a cellar beneath a downtown office building."

"And Marit Olsen?"

Kaja mulled this over. "It's too overblown. He's lost control, his grip is going."

"Or," Harry said, "he's gone up to the next level. He wants to show everyone how clever he is, so he starts exhibiting his victims. The murder of Marit Olsen in the Frogner pool is a huge scream for attention, but there are few indications of failing control in the execution. The rope he used was at worst careless, but otherwise he left no clues. Disagree?"

She deliberated and shook her head.

"Then there's Elias Skog," Harry said. "Anything different there?"

"He tortures the victim with a slow death," Kaja said. "The sadist in him reveals itself."

"A Leopold's apple is also an instrument of torture," Harry said. "But I agree with you that this is the first time we've seen sadism. At the same time, it's a conscious choice. He reveals himself; he doesn't let others do it. He is still directing the show, he's in charge."

The coffeepot and cups were plunked down in front of them.

"But . . ." Kaja said.

"Yes?"

"Doesn't it seem a bit odd that a sadistic killer would leave the crime scene before he can witness the victim's suffering and final death? According to the landlady, she could hear banging noises from the bathroom after the guest had gone. He ran off—funny, eh?"

"Good point. So what have we got? A fake sadist. And why does he fake it?"

"Because he knows we'll try to profile him, the way we're doing now," Kaja said eagerly. "And then we'll go looking for him in the wrong places."

"Mm. Maybe. A sophisticated killer, if so."

"What do you think, O venerable wise one?"

Harry poured the coffee. "If this is really a serial killer, I think the murders are well spread out."

Kaja leaned across the table, and her pointed teeth glistened as she whispered, "You think it might **not** be a serial killer?"

"Well, there's a signature missing. Usually, there are special aspects of the murder that mark a serial killer, and thus certain things that recur throughout. Here we have no indications that the killer did anything sexual during the killing. And there's no similarity in the methods used, apart from Borgny, Charlotte and Juliana all being murdered with a Leopold's apple. The crime scenes are quite different, and so are the victims. Both sexes, different ages, different backgrounds, different physiques."

"But they have not been selected at random; they spent the same night in the same cabin."

"Precisely. And that's why I'm not absolutely convinced we're up against a classic serial killer. Or, rather, not one with a classic motive to kill. For serial killers, the killing itself is generally enough of a motive. If, for example, the victims are prostitutes. It doesn't really matter whether they are sinners, just that they are easy prey. I know of only one serial killer who had criteria for the selection of individual victims."

"The Snowman."

"I don't think a serial killer chooses his victims from a random page of a cabin guest book. And if anything happened at Håvass to give the killer a motive, we're not talking about classic serial murders. Besides, the move to show himself was too quick for the usual serial killer."

"What do you mean?"

"He sent a woman to Rwanda and the Congo to cover up a murder and at the same time to buy the murder weapon for the next. Afterward he killed her. In other words, he went to extremes to hide one murder, yet for the next one, a few weeks later, he did absolutely nothing. And for the next murder again, he's like a matador shoving his balls in our faces with a flourish of his cloak. This is a personality change at fast-forward speed. It doesn't make sense."

"Do you think there could be several killers? Each with a different method?"

Harry shook his head. "There is one similarity. The killer doesn't leave any clues. If serial killers are rare, one who kills without leaving any clues is a white whale. There is only one of them in this case."

"Right, so what are we saying here?" Kaja threw up her arms. "A serial killer with multiple-personality disorder?"

"A white whale with wings," Harry said. "No, I don't know. And anyway, it doesn't matter. We're only doing this for fun. It's a Kripos case now." He drained his coffee. "I'm going to take a taxi to the hospital."

"I can drive you."

"Thank you but no. Go home and prepare for new and interesting cases."

Kaja heaved a weary sigh. "The business with Bjørn . . ."

"Must not be mentioned to a soul," Harry said. "Have a good sleep."

Altman was leaving Harry's father's room at Rikshospital when he arrived.

"He's asleep," the nurse said. "I gave him ten milligrams of morphine. You can sit here, no problem, but he's unlikely to stir for several hours."

"Thank you," Harry said.

"That's OK. I had a mother who . . . well, who had to put up with more pain than was necessary."

"Mm. Do you smoke, Altman?"

Harry saw from the guilt-ridden reaction that Altman did, and invited him to join him outside. The two men smoked while Altman, first name Sigurd, explained that it had been because of his mother that he had specialized in anesthesia.

"So when you gave my father an injection just now . . ."

"Let's say it was a favor from one son to another." Altman smiled. "But I cleared it with the doctor, naturally. I would like to keep my job."

"Wise," Harry said. "Wish I were as wise."

They finished their cigarettes, and Altman was about to go when Harry asked, "Since you're an anesthesia expert, could you tell me how a person might get hold of ketanome?"

"Oh, dear," Altman said. "I probably shouldn't answer that."

"It's OK," Harry said with a wry smile. "It's about the murder case I'm working on."

"Aha. Well, unless you work in anesthesia, ketanome is very hard to get hold of in Norway. It works like a bullet, almost literally—the patient is knocked flat. But the side effects—ulcers—are nasty. In addition, the risk of cardiac arrest with an overdose is high. It's been used for suicide. But not anymore. Ketanome was banned in the EU and Norway some years ago."

"I know that, but where would you go to get it now?"

"Well, ex-Soviet states. Or Africa."

"The Congo, for example?"

"Definitely. The producer sells it at bargain-basement prices since the European ban, so it ends up in poor countries. It's always like that."

Harry sat by his father's bedside watching his frail pajama-clad chest rise and fall. After an hour he got up and left.

Harry decided he would postpone making a call until he had unlocked the house, put on "Don't Get Around Much Anymore"—one of his father's Duke Ellington records—and taken out the brown clump. He saw that Gunnar Hagen had left a message, but he had no intention of listening to it, as he knew roughly what it was about. Bellman would have been nagging him again: From now on they were not allowed to touch the murder case, however compelling their excuses. And Harry was to report for normal duties if he still wanted a job with the police. Well, perhaps not the last part. It was time to head off on his travels. And the travels should start here, now, tonight. He took out the lighter with one hand while the other brought up the two texts he had received. The first was from Øystein. He suggested "a gentlemen's night out" in the not-too-distant future, with an invitation to Tresko, who was probably the most well-to-do of the three. The second was a number Harry didn't recognize. He opened the message.

**I SEE FROM THE AFTENPOSTEN WEBSITE
THAT YOU'RE IN CHARGE OF THE CASE. I
CAN HELP. ELIAS SKOG TALKED BEFORE
HE WAS GLUED TO THE BATH. C.**

Harry dropped the lighter, which hit the glass table with a loud bang, and he felt his heart race. During murder cases they always got loads of people ringing in with tip-offs, advice and hypotheses. People who were willing to swear they had seen, heard or been told all sorts of things, and couldn't the police spare them a moment to listen? Often it was the same old voices again and again, but there were always some new, mixed-up windbags. Harry was quite certain that this was not one of them. The press had written a lot about the case; readers possessed a considerable amount of information. The general public had not been told that Elias Skog had been glued to the bath, however. Or been given Harry's cell number.

38

Permanent Scarring

Harry had turned down Duke Ellington and sat with the phone in his hand. This person knew about the Super Glue. And had his number. Should he check the name and address of the caller, perhaps even have the person arrested because there was a chance he might frighten him off? On the other hand, whoever it was expected an answer.

Harry pressed "return call."

It buzzed twice, then he heard a deep voice. "Yes?"

"This is Harry Hole."

"Nice to talk to you again, Hole."

"Mm. When have we spoken before?"

"Don't you remember? Elias Skog's flat. Super Glue."

Harry felt the carotid artery in his neck throb, cramp the space in his throat.

"I was there. Who am I speaking to, and what were you doing there?"

The other end went quiet for a second and Harry immediately concluded the person had hung up. But then the voice was back with a drawn-out "Oh, sorry, I may have signed the message with just **C**. Did I?"

"Yes, you did."

"I generally do. This is Inspector Colbjørnsen. From Stavanger. You gave me your number, remember?"

Harry cursed himself, realized he was still holding his breath and let it out in a long hiss.

"Are you there?"

"Uh-huh," Harry said, grabbing the teaspoon on the table and scraping off a bit of the opium. "You said you had something for me?"

"Yes, I do. But on one condition."

"Which is?"

"It stays between us."

"Why's that?"

"Because I don't want that prick Bellman coming over here thinking he's God's gift to criminal investigations. He and fucking Kripos are trying to get a monopoly over the whole country. Far as I'm concerned he can go to hell. The problem is my bosses. I'm not allowed to touch the fucking Skog case."

"So why come to me?"

"I'm a simple lad from the provinces, Hole. But when I see in **Aftenposten** that you've been given the case I know what's going to happen. I know you're like me—you won't just lie down and die."

"Well . . ." Harry said, looking at the opium in front of him.

"So if you can use this to outsmart the smart-ass and it leads to Bellman's plans for the evil empire being shelved, accept it with my blessing. I'll wait until the day after tomorrow before sending Bellman my report. That gives you a day."

"What've you got?"

"I've spoken to people in Skog's circle, which was small, as he was an oddball, unusually intense and traveled around the world on his own. Two persons in all. The landlady. And a girl we traced via the phone numbers he had called in the days leading up to his death. Her name is Stine Ølberg, and she said she spoke to Elias the night he was killed. They were on the bus leaving town, and he said he'd been to the Håvass cabin at the same time as the murdered women in the newspapers. He thought it was strange no one had discovered they'd all been to the same cabin and he'd been wondering about whether to go to the police. But he was reluctant because he had no desire to get involved. And I can understand that. Skog had been in trouble with the police before. He'd been reported for stalking on two occasions. He hadn't done anything illegal, to be fair to him. He was, as I said, just the intense type. Stine said she had been frightened of him, but that evening it was the opposite: He was the one who had seemed frightened."

"Interesting."

"Stine had pretended not to know who the three murder victims were, and then Elias had said that he would tell her about someone else who had been there, someone he was sure she did know. And this is the really interesting part. The man is well known. At least a B-list celebrity."

"Oh, yes?"

"According to Elias Skog, Tony Leike was there."

"Tony Leike. Should I know who that is?"

"He lives with the daughter of Anders Galtung, the shipping magnate."

A couple of newspaper headlines flashed in Harry's mind.

"Tony Leike is a so-called investor, which means he has become rich and no one quite understands how, just that it certainly wasn't by dint of hard work. Not only that—he's a real pretty boy. Hardly Mr. Nice Guy, though. And this is the critical part. The guy's got a sheet."

" 'Sheet'?" Harry asked, affecting incomprehension to imply what he thought of Colbjørnsen's Americanisms.

"A record. Tony Leike has a conviction for violent assault."

"Mm. Checked the charge?"

"Years ago Tony Leike beat up and maimed one Ole S. Hansen on the seventh of August between eleven-twenty and eleven forty-five p.m. It happened outside a dance hall in the town where Tony was living with his grandfather. Tony was eighteen, Ole seventeen, and of course it was over a skirt."

"Mm. Jealous kids fighting after they've been drinking is not exactly unusual. Did you say violent assault?"

"Yes; in fact, there was more. After Leike had knocked down the other boy, he sat on him and carved up the poor lad's face with a knife. He was permanently scarred, though the report said it could have been much worse if people hadn't dragged Leike off."

"But no more than the one conviction?"

"Tony Leike was known for his temper and was regularly involved in brawls. At the trial a witness said that at school Leike had tried to strangle him with a belt because he had said something less than flattering about Tony's father."

"Sounds like someone should have a long chat with Leike. Do you know where he lives?"

"On your turf. Holmenveien . . . wait . . . number one seventy-two."

"West End. Hm. Thanks, Colbjørnsen."

"Not at all. Erm, there was one other thing. A man

got on the bus after Elias. He got off at the same stop as Elias, and Stine says she saw the man following him. But she couldn't give a description because his face was hidden by a hat. Might be of some significance, or not."

"Right."

"So I'm counting on you, Hole."

"Counting on what?"

"You doing the right thing."

"Mm."

"Good night."

Harry sat listening to the Duke. Then he grabbed the phone and looked up Kaja's number. He was about to press the "call" button but hesitated. He was doing it again. Dragging people down with him. Harry tossed the phone aside. There were two options. The smart one, which was to call Bellman. Or the stupid one, which was to go it alone.

Harry sighed. Who was he kidding? He had no choice. So he stuffed the lighter in his pocket, wrapped up the ball in silver foil, put it in the liquor cabinet, undressed, set the alarm for six and went to bed. No choice. A prisoner of his own behavior patterns, whereby every action was compulsive. In that sense, he was neither better nor worse than those he pursued.

And with this thought he fell asleep, a smile on his lips.

The night is so blessedly still, it heals your sight, clears your mind. The new, old policeman. Hole.

I'll have to tell him that. I won't show him everything, just enough for him to understand. Then he
can stop it. So that I don't have to do what I do. I
spit and spit, but blood fills my mouth, over and
over again.

39

Relational Search

Harry arrived at Police HQ at a quarter to seven in
the morning. Apart from the security guard at the
reception desk there was no one around in the large
atrium inside the heavy front doors.

He nodded to the guard, swiped his card in the
reader by the gate and took the elevator down to the
cellar. From there he loped through the culvert and
unlocked the room. He lit the day's first cigarette and
called the cell number while the computer booted
up. Katrine Bratt sounded sleepy.

"I want you to run those relational searches of
yours," Harry said. "Between a Tony Leike and each
of the murder victims. Including Juliana Verni from
Leipzig."

"The recreation room's free until half past eight,"
she said. "I'll get going this minute. Anything else?"

Harry hesitated. "Could you check on a Jussi
Kolkka for me? Policeman."

"What's the story with him?"

"That's the point," Harry said. "I don't know what the story is."

Harry put down the phone and set to work on the computer.

Tony Leike had one conviction—that was correct. And according to the register he had been in trouble with the police on two other occasions as well. As Colbjørnsen had indicated, both were for physical violence. In the first instance the charge had been withdrawn and in the second the case had been dropped.

Harry Googled Tony Leike's name and got a number of hits: minor newspaper mentions—most of which were connected with his fiancée, Lene Galtung—but also some in the financial press, where he was referred to alternately as an investor, a speculator and an ignorant sheep. This last, in **Kapital,** was a reference to Leike belonging to the flock that mimicked a lead sheep, the psychologist Einar Kringlen, in everything he did: from buying stocks, mountain cabins and cars to choosing the right restaurant, drink, woman, office, house and vacation destination.

Harry searched through the links until he stopped at an article in a financial newspaper.

"Bingo," he mumbled.

Tony Leike was clearly able to stand on his own two feet. Or in his own two mining boots. At any rate the **Finansavisen** wrote about a mining project with Leike as the entrepreneur and enthusiast. He was photographed alongside his colleagues, two young men with side parts. They were not wearing the standard designer suits, but overalls and work clothes, and were sitting on a pile of wood in front of a helicopter and smiling. Tony Leike wore the biggest smile of them all. He was broad-shouldered, long-limbed, dark, both his skin and his hair, and he had an impressive aquiline nose that in conjunction with his coloring made Harry think that he must have at least a dash of Arab blood in his veins. But the reason for Harry's restrained outburst was the headline: KING OF THE CONGO?

Harry continued to follow the links.

The yellow press was more interested in the imminent wedding to Lene Galtung and the guest list.

Harry glanced at his watch. Five past seven. He called the duty officer.

"I need assistance for an arrest on Holmenveien."

"Detention?"

Harry knew very well that he didn't have enough to ask the prosecutor for an arrest warrant.

"To be brought in for questioning," Harry said.

"I thought you said arrest. And why do you need assistance if it's only—"

"Could you have two men and a car ready outside the garage in five minutes?"

Harry received a snort by way of response, which he interpreted as a yes. He took two puffs of his cigarette, stubbed it out, got up, locked the door and left. He was thirty-five feet down the culvert when he heard a faint noise behind him, which he knew was the landline ringing.

He had come out of the elevator and was on his way to the door when he heard someone shout his name. He turned and saw the security guard waving to him. By the counter Harry saw the back of a mustard-yellow woolen coat.

"This man was asking for you," the receptionist said.

The woolen coat turned. It was the type that is supposed to look as if it is cashmere, and on occasion it is. In this case, Harry assumed it was. Because it was filled out by a broad-shouldered, long-limbed man with dark eyes, dark hair and possibly a dash of Arab blood in his veins.

"You're taller than you appear in the photos," said Tony Leike, exhibiting a row of porcelain dental high-rises and an outstretched hand.

"Good coffee," said Tony Leike, looking as if he meant it. Harry studied Leike's long, distorted fingers, which were wrapped around the coffee cup. It wasn't contagious, Leike had explained as he had proffered his hand to Harry, just good old-fashioned arthritis, an inherited affliction that—if nothing else—made him a reliable meteorologist. "But, to be frank, I thought they gave inspectors slightly better offices. A little warm?"

"The prison boiler," Harry said, sipping his coffee.

"So you read about the case in **Aftenposten** this morning?"

"Yes, I was having breakfast. Almost choked on it, to be honest."

"Why's that?"

Leike rocked in his chair, like a Formula 1 driver in a bucket seat before the start. "I trust what I say can remain between us."

"Who is **us**?"

"The police and me. Preferably you and me."

Harry hoped his voice was neutral and did not reveal his excitement. "The reason being?"

Leike took a deep breath. "I don't want it to come out that I was in the Håvass cabin at the same time as the MP Marit Olsen. For the moment I have a very high media profile because of my impending wedding. It would be unfortunate if I were to be linked with a murder investigation right now. The press would be on it and that might . . . things would emerge from my past that I would prefer remain dead and buried."

"I see," Harry said innocently. "Of course, I will have to weigh a number of factors, and for that reason cannot promise anything. But this is not an interview, just a conversation, and I don't usually leak this kind of thing to the press."

"Nor to my . . . er, nearest and dearest?"

"Not unless there is a reason for it. If you're afraid it will be made public that you were here, why did you come?"

"You asked people who were at the cabin to come forward, so it's my civic duty, isn't it?" He sent Harry a questioning look. And then made a face. "Christ, I was frightened. I knew that those who were there that night were next in line. Jumped in my car and drove straight here."

"Has anything happened recently to make you concerned?"

"No." Tony Leike sniffed the air thoughtfully. "Apart from a break-in through the cellar door a few days ago. Christ, I should get an alarm, shouldn't I?"

"Did you report it to the police?"

"No, they only took a bike."

"And you think serial killers steal bicycles on the side?"

Leike shook his head with a smile. Not the sheepish smile of someone who is ashamed of having said something stupid, Harry thought. But the disarming, winning smile that says, "You got me there, pal," the gallant congratulation from someone used to his own victories.

"Why did you ask for me?"

"The papers said you were in charge, so I thought it only natural. Anyway, as I said, I was hoping it would be possible to keep this between as few people as possible, so I came straight to the top."

"I'm not the top, Leike."

"Aren't you? **Aftenposten** gave the impression you were."

Harry stroked his jutting jaw. He hadn't made up

his mind about Tony Leike. He was a man with a groomed exterior and bad-boy charm that reminded Harry of an ice-hockey player he had seen in an underwear ad. He seemed to want to present an air of unruffled, worldly-wise smoothness but also to come across as a sincere human being with feelings that could not be hidden. Or perhaps it was the other way around; perhaps the smoothness was sincere and the feelings were pretense.

"What were you doing at Håvass, Leike?"

"Skiing, of course."

"On your own?"

"Yes. I'd had a few stressful days at work and needed some time off. I go to Ustaoset and Hallingskarvet a lot. Sleep in cabins. That's my terrain, you could say."

"So why don't you have your own cabin there?"

"Where I would like to have a cabin you can't get permission to anymore. National park regulations."

"Why wasn't your fiancée with you? Doesn't she ski?"

"Lene? She . . ." Leike took a sip of coffee. The kind of sip you take in midsentence when you need a bit of thinking time, it struck Harry. "She was at home. I . . . we . . ." He looked at Harry with an expression of mild desperation, as though pleading for help. Harry gave him none.

"Shit. No pressure, eh?"

Harry didn't answer.

"OK," Leike said as though Harry had given a response in the affirmative. "I needed a breather, to get away. To think. Engagement, marriage . . . these are grown-up issues. And I think best on my own. Especially up there on the snowy plains."

"And thinking helped?"

Leike flashed the enamel wall again. "Yes."

"Do you remember any of the others in the cabin?"

"I remember Marit Olsen, as I said. She and I had a glass of red wine together. I didn't know she was an MP until she said."

"Anyone else?"

"There were a few others sitting around I barely greeted. But I arrived quite late, so some must have gone to bed."

"Oh?"

"There were six pairs of skis in the snow outside. I remember that clearly because I put them in the hall in case of an avalanche. I remember thinking the others were perhaps not very experienced mountain skiers. If the cabin is buried under ten feet of snow you're in a bit of a fix without any skis. I was first up in the morning—I usually am—and was off before the others had stirred."

"You say you arrived late. You were skiing alone in the dark?"

"Head flashlight, map and compass. The trip was a spontaneous decision, so I didn't catch the train to Ustaoset until the evening. But, as I said, they are familiar surroundings—I'm used to finding my way across the frozen wastes in the dark. And the weather was good, moonlight reflecting off the snow. I didn't need a map or a light."

"Can you tell me anything about what happened in the cabin while you were there?"

"Nothing happened. Marit Olsen and I talked about red wine and then about the problems of keeping a modern relationship going. That is, I think her relationship was more modern than mine."

"And she didn't say anything had happened in the cabin?"

"No."

"What about the others?"

"They sat by the fire talking about ski trips, and drinking. Beer, perhaps. Or some kind of sports drink. Two women and a man, between twenty and thirty-five, I would guess."

"Names?"

"We just nodded and said hello. As I said, I had gone up there to be alone, not to make new friends."

"Appearance?"

"It's quite dark in these cabins at night, and if I say one was blond, the other dark, that might be way off the mark. As I said, I don't even remember how many people were there."

"Dialects?"

"One of the women had a kind of west coast dialect, I think."

"Stavanger? Bergen? Sunnmøre?"

"Sorry, I'm not good at this sort of thing. It might have been west coast, could have been south."

"OK. You wanted to be alone, but you talked to Marit Olsen about relationships."

"It just happened. She came over and sat down next to me. Not exactly a wallflower. Talkative. Fat and cheery." He said that as if the two words were a natural collocation. And it struck Harry that the photo of Lene Galtung he had seen was of an extremely thin woman—to judge by the latest average weight for Norwegians.

"So, aside from Marit Olsen, you can't tell us anything about any of the others? Not even if I showed you photos of those we know to have been there?"

"Oh," Leike said with a smile, "I think I can do that."

"Yes?"

"When I was in one room looking for a bunk to crash on, I had to switch on the light to see which was free. And I saw two people asleep. A man and a woman."

"And you think you can describe them?"

"Not in great detail, but I'm pretty sure I would recognize them."

"Oh?"

"You sort of remember faces when you see them again."

Harry knew that what Leike said was right. Witnesses' descriptions were all over the place as a rule, but give them a lineup and they rarely made a mistake.

Harry walked over to the filing cabinet they had dragged back to the office, opened the respective victims' files and removed the photographs. He gave the five photos to Leike, who flipped through them.

"This is Marit Olsen, of course," he said, passing it back to Harry. "And these are the two women who were sitting by the fire, I think, but I'm not sure." He passed Harry the pictures of Borgny and Charlotte. "This may have been the boy." Elias Skog. "But none of these were asleep in the bedroom. I'm sure about that. And I don't recognize this one, either," he said, passing back the photo of Adele.

"So you're unsure about the ones you were in the same room with for a good while, but you're sure about those you saw for a couple of seconds?"

Leike nodded. "They were asleep."

"Is it easier to recognize people when they're asleep?"

"No, but they don't look back at you. So you can stare unobserved."

"Mm. For a couple of seconds."

"Maybe a bit longer."

Harry put the photos back in the files.

"Do you have any names?" Leike asked.

"Names?"

"Yes. As I said, I was the first up and I had a couple of slices of bread in the kitchen. The guest book was in there and I hadn't signed in. While I was eating I opened it and studied the names that had been entered the night before."

"Why?"

"Why?" Tony rolled his shoulders. "It's often the same people on these mountain skiing trips. I wanted to see if there was anyone I knew."

"Was there?"

"No. But if you give me the names of people you

know or think were there, maybe I can remember if I saw them in the guest book."

"Sounds reasonable, but I'm afraid we don't have any names. Or addresses."

"Well, then," Leike said, buttoning up his woolen coat. "I'm afraid I can't be of much help. Except that you can cross my name off."

"Mm," Harry said. "Since you're here, I've got a couple more questions. So long as you have time?"

"I'm my own boss," Leike said. "For the time being, anyway."

"OK. You say you have a troubled past. Could you give me a rough idea of what you mean?"

"I tried to kill a guy," Leike said without embellishment.

"I see," Harry said, leaning back in his chair. "Why was that?"

"Because he attacked me. He maintained I'd stolen his girl. The truth was that she neither was his girl nor wanted to be, and I don't steal girls. I don't have to."

"Mm. He caught you two in the act and hit her, right?"

"What do you mean?"

"I'm trying to understand what sort of situation may have led to you trying to kill him. If you mean it literally, that is."

"He hit me. And that was why I did my best to kill him. With a knife. And I was well on the way to succeeding when a couple of my pals dragged me off him. I was convicted for aggravated assault. Which is pretty cheap for attempted murder."

"You realize that what you're saying now could make you a prime suspect?"

"In this case?" Leike looked askance at Harry. "Are you kidding me? You have a bit more common sense than that, don't you?"

"If you've wanted to kill once . . ."

"I've wanted to kill several times. I assume I've done it, too."

"Assume?"

"It's not so easy to see black men in the jungle at night. For the most part you shoot indiscriminately."

"And you did that?"

"In my depraved youth, yes. After paying for my crime, I went into the army and from there straight to South Africa and got a job as a mercenary."

"Mm. So you were a mercenary in South Africa?"

"Three years. And South Africa is just the place where I enlisted; the fighting took place in the surrounding countries. There was always war, always a market for pros, especially for whites. The blacks still think we're smarter, you know. They trust white officers more than their own."

"Perhaps you've been to the Congo, too?"

Tony Leike's right eyebrow formed a black chevron. "How so?"

"You went there a while back, so I wondered."

"It was called Zaire then. But most of the time we weren't sure which fucking country we were in. It was just green, green, green and then black, black, black until the sun rose again. I worked for a so-called security firm at some diamond mines. That was where I learned to read a map and compass from a head flashlight. The compass is a waste of time there—too much metal in the mountains."

Tony Leika leaned back in his chair. Relaxed and unafraid, Harry noted.

"Speaking of metal," Harry said, "I think I read somewhere that you've got a mining business down there."

"That's right."

"What sort of metal?"

"Heard of coltan?"

Harry nodded slowly. "Used in cell phones."

"Exactly. And in game consoles. When world cellphone production took off in the nineties my troops and I were on a mission in the northeast of the Congo. Some Frenchmen and some natives ran a mine there, employing kids with pickaxes and spades to dig out the coltan. It looks like any old stone but you use it to produce tantalum, which is the element that's really valuable. And I knew that if I could just get someone to finance me I could run a proper, modern mining business and make my partners and myself wealthy men."

"And that was what happened?"

Tony Leike laughed. "Not quite. I managed to borrow money, was screwed by slippery partners and lost everything. Borrowed more money, was screwed again, borrowed even more and earned a bit."

"A bit?"

"A few million to pay off debts. But I had a network of contacts and some headlines, as of course I was counting chickens before they hatched, which was enough to be adopted into the circle where the big money was. To become a member, it's the number of digits in your fortune that counts, not whether there's a plus or minus in front." Leike laughed again, a hearty ringing laugh, and it was all Harry could do to restrain a smile.

"And now?"

"Now we're waiting for the big payoff because it's time for coltan to be harvested. Yes, indeed, I've said it for long enough, but this time it's true. I've had to sell my shares in the project in exchange for call options so that I could pay my debts. Now things are set, and all I have to do is get hold of money to redeem my shares so that I can become a full partner again."

"Mm. And the money?"

"Someone will see the sense in lending me the money against a small share. The return is enormous, the risk minimal. And all the big investments have been made, including local bribes. We have even cleared a runway into the jungle so that we can load directly onto freight planes and get the stuff out via Uganda. Are you wealthy, Harry? I can see if there's any chance for you to have a slice of the action."

Harry shook his head. "Been to Stavanger recently, Leike?"

"Hm. In the summer."

"Not since then?"

Leike gave the question some thought, then shook his head.

"You're not absolutely sure?" Harry asked.

"I'm presenting my project to potential investors, and that means a lot of traveling. Must have been to Stavanger three or four times this year, but not since the summer, I don't think."

"What about Leipzig?"

"Is this the point where I have to ask whether I need a lawyer, Harry?"

"I just want you eliminated from the case as soon as possible, so that we can concentrate on more relevant issues." Harry ran his forefinger across the bridge of his nose. "If you don't want the media to catch wind of this, I assume you won't want to involve a lawyer, or to be summoned to formal interviews, and so forth?"

Leike nodded slowly. "You're right, of course. Thank you for your advice, Harry."

"Leipzig?"

"Sorry," Leike said, with genuine regret in his voice and face. "Never been there. Should I have been?"

"Mm. I also have to ask you where you were on certain days and what you were doing."

"Go on."

Harry dictated the four dates in question while Leike wrote them into a Moleskine notebook.

"I'll check as soon as I'm in my office," he said. "Here's my number, by the way." He passed Harry a business card with the inscription TONY C. LEIKE, ENTREPRENEUR.

"What does the C stand for?"

"You tell me," Leike said, getting to his feet. "Tony's only short for Anthony, of course, so I thought I needed an initial. Gives a bit more gravitas, don't you think? Think foreigners like it."

Instead of taking the culvert, Harry accompanied Leike up the stairs to the prison and knocked on the glass window. A guard came and let them in.

"Feels like I'm taking part in an episode with the Olsen Gang," Leike said when they were standing on the gravel path outside old Botsen Prison's fairly imposing walls.

"It's a little more discreet like this," Harry said. "You're beginning to become a recognizable face, and people are arriving for work now at Police HQ."

"Speaking of faces, I see someone has broken your jaw."

"Must have fallen and hit myself."

Leike shook his head and smiled. "I know something about broken jaws. That one's from a fight. You've just let it grow together again, I can see. You should have it looked at—it's not a big job."

"Thanks for the tip."

"Did you owe them a lot of money?"

"Do you know something about that, too?"

"Yes!" Leike exclaimed, his eyes widening. "Unfortunately."

"Mm. One last thing, Leike—"

"Tony. Or Tony C." Leike flashed his shiny masticatory apparatus. Like someone without a care in the world, Harry thought.

"Tony. Have you ever been to Lake Lyseren? The one in Øst—?"

"Yes, of course. Are you crazy!" Tony laughed. "The Leike farm is in Rustad. I went to my grandfather's there every summer. Lived there for a couple of years, too. Fantastic place, isn't it? Why d'you want to know?" His smile vanished at once. "Oh, shit, that's where you found the woman! A coincidence, eh?"

"Well," Harry said, "it's not so unlikely. Lyseren is a big lake."

"True enough. Thanks again, Harry." Leike proffered his hand. "And if any names crop up to do with the Håvass cabin, or someone comes forward, just call me and I'll see if I can remember them. Full cooperation, Harry."

Harry watched himself shake hands with the man he had just decided had killed six people in the last three months.

Fifteen minutes after Leike left Katrine Bratt called.

"Yes?"

"Negative on four of them," she said.

"And the fifth?"

"One hit. Deep in digital information's innermost intestinal tract."

"Poetic."

"You'll like it. On the sixteenth of February Elias Skog was called by a number that is not registered in anyone's name. A secret number, in other words. And that could be the reason that the Oslo—"

"Stavanger."

"Police didn't see the link before. But inside the innermost intestines—"

"By which you mean on Telenor's internal, highly protected register?"

"Something like that. The name of one Tony Leike, one seventy-two Holmenveien, turned up as the invoiced subscriber for this secret number."

"Yes!" Harry shouted. "You're an angel."

"Poorly chosen metaphor, I believe. Since you sound as if I've just sentenced a man to life imprisonment."

"Talk to you later."

"Wait! Don't you want to hear about Jussi Kolkka?"

"I'd almost forgotten about that. Shoot."

She shot.

40

The Offer

Harry found Kaja in Crime Squad, in the red zone on the sixth floor. She perked up when she noticed him standing in the doorway.

"Always got an open door?" he asked.

"Always. And you?"

"Closed. Always. But I can see you've thrown out the guest's chair. Smart move. People like to chew the fat."

She laughed. "Doing anything exciting?"

"In a way," he said, entering and leaning against the wall.

She placed both hands against the edge of her desk and pushed, and she and the chair sailed across the floor to the filing cabinet. There, she opened a drawer, pulled out a letter and presented it to Harry. "Thought you'd like to see this."

"What is it?"

"The Snowman. His lawyer has applied for him to be transferred from Ullersmo to a normal hospital, for health reasons."

He perched on the edge of the desk and read. "Mm. Scleroderma. It's progressing fast. Not too fast, I hope. He doesn't deserve that."

He looked up and saw that she was shocked.

"My great-aunt died of scleroderma," she said. "A terrible disease."

"And a terrible man," Harry said. "Incidentally, I really agree with those who say that the capacity to forgive says something about the essential quality of a person. I'm the lowest grade."

"I didn't mean to criticize you."

"I promise to be better in my next life," Harry said, looking down and rubbing his neck. "Which, if the Hindus are right, will probably be as a bark beetle. But I'll be a **nice** bark beetle."

He looked up and saw that what Rakel called his "damned boyish charm" was having an effect. "Listen, Kaja, I've come here to make you an offer."

"Oh?"

"Yes." Harry heard the solemnity in his voice. The voice of a man with no capacity to forgive, no consideration, no thoughts for anything except his own objectives. And plied the inverted persuasion technique that had worked for him far too often. "Which I would recommend you decline. I have, you see, a tendency to destroy the lives of those I become involved with."

To his astonishment, he saw that her face had flushed scarlet.

"But I don't think it would be right to do this without you," he continued. "Not now that we're so close."

"Close . . . to what?" The blush had gone.

"Close to apprehending the guilty party. I'm on my way to the prosecutor now to request a warrant for his arrest."

"Oh . . . of course."

"Of course?"

"I mean, arrest whom?" She heaved herself back to the desk. "For what?"

"Our killer, Kaja."

"Really?" He watched her pupils grow slowly, pulsating. And knew what was going on inside her. The blood rush before bringing down, felling the wild animal. The arrest. Which would be on her CV. How could she resist?

Harry nodded. "His name is Tony Leike."

The color returned to her cheeks. "Sounds familiar."

"He's about to marry the daughter of—"

"Oh, yes, he's engaged to the Galtung girl." She frowned. "Do you mean to say you have evidence?"

"Circumstantial. And coincidences."

He saw her pupils contract again.

"I'm sure this is our man, Kaja."

"Convince me," she said, and he could hear the hunger. The desire to swallow everything raw, to have a pretext for making the craziest decision of her life so far. And he had no intention of protecting her against herself. For he needed her. She was media-perfect: young, intelligent, a woman, ambitious. With an appealing face and record. In short, she had everything he did not have. She was a Joan of Arc the Ministry of Justice would not want to burn at the stake.

Harry breathed in. Then he repeated the conversation he had had with Tony Leike. In detail. Without wondering at how he was able to reproduce what had been said word for word. His colleagues had always considered this ability remarkable.

"Håvass cabin, Congo and Lake Lyseren," Kaja said after he had finished. "He's been to all the places."

"Yes, and he's been convicted for violence. And he admits his intention was to kill."

"Great. But—"

"The really great part comes now. He called Elias Skog. Two days before Skog was found murdered."

Her pupils were black suns.

"We've got him," she said softly.

"Does the **we** mean what I think it does?"

"Yes."

Harry sighed. "You realize the risks of joining me in this? Even if I'm right about Leike, there's no guarantee that this arrest and a successful prosecution of the case are enough to tip the balance of power in Hagen's favor. And then you'll be in the doghouse."

"What about you?" She leaned across the desk. Her tiny piranha teeth glistened. "Why do **you** think it's worth the risk?"

"I'm a washed-up cop with little to lose, Kaja. For me, it's this or nothing. I can't do Narc or Sexual Offenses, and Kripos will never make me an offer. But for you personally this is probably a poor decision."

"My decisions usually are," she said, serious now.

"Good," Harry said, standing up. "I'll go and get the prosecutor. Don't run away."

"I'll be here, Harry."

Harry pivoted straight into the face of a man who had clearly been standing in the doorway for some time.

"Sorry," the man said with a broad smile. "I'd just like to borrow the lady for a while."

He nodded toward Kaja, laughter dancing in his eyes.

"Be my guest," Harry said, giving the man his abbreviated form of a smile, and strode off down the corridor.

"Aslak Krongli," Kaja said. "What brings a country boy to the big bad city?"

"The usual, I suppose," said the officer from Ustaoset.

"Excitement, neon lights and the buzz of the crowd?"

Aslak smiled. "Work. And a woman. Can I take you out for a cup of coffee?"

"Not right now," Kaja said. "Things are happening, so I have to hold the fort. But I'd be happy to buy you a cup in the cafeteria. It's on the top floor. If you go ahead, that'll give me time to make a phone call."

He gave her a thumbs-up and was gone.

Kaja closed her eyes and drew in a long, quivering breath.

The prosecutor's office was on the sixth floor, so Harry didn't have far to walk. The lawyer on duty, a young woman who had obviously been taken on since Harry last visited the office, peered over her glasses as he stepped in.

"Need a blue chit," Harry said.

"And you would be?"

"Harry Hole, Inspector."

He presented his ID card even though he could see from her somewhat frenetic reaction that she had heard of him. He could just imagine what, and decided not to go there. For her part, she noted down his name on the search-and-arrest warrant and scrutinized his card with an exaggerated squint, as though the spelling were extremely complicated.

"Two check marks?" she asked.

"Fine," Harry said.

She put a check next to "arrest" and "search" and leaned back in her chair in a way that Harry bet was a copy of the you've-got-thirty-seconds-to-persuade-me pose she had seen more seasoned lawyers adopt.

Harry knew from experience that the first argument was the weighty one—that was when prosecutors made up their minds—so he started with the call Leike had made to Elias Skog two days before the murder. This despite Leike's assertions when talking to Harry that he didn't know Skog and hadn't spoken to him at the cabin. Argument number two was the assault conviction that Leike admitted was attempted murder, and Harry could already see that the blue chit was in the bag. So he spiced things up with the coincidences of the Congo and Lake Lyseren, without entering into too much detail.

She removed her glasses.

"Basically, I'm sympathetic," she said. "However, I need to give the matter a little more thought."

Harry cursed inwardly. A more experienced lawyer would have given him the warrant there and then, but she was so green she didn't dare without consulting one of the others. There should have been an "in training" sign on her door, so that he could have gone to one of the others. Now it was too late.

"It's urgent," Harry said.

"Why's that?"

She had him there. Harry made an airy gesture with his hand, the kind that is supposed to say everything, but says nothing.

"I'll make a decision right after lunch"—she pointedly peered down at the form—"Hole. I'll put the blue chit in your mailbox, if it gets clearance."

Harry clenched his teeth to make sure he didn't say anything hasty. Because he knew she was behaving in a proper manner. Naturally, she was overcompensating for the fact that she was young, inexperienced and a woman in a male-dominated world. But she showed a determination to be respected; from the outset she demonstrated that the steamroller technique would not work on her. Well done. He felt like grabbing her glasses and smashing them.

"Could you call my inside line when you've made up your mind?" he said. "For the moment my office is quite a distance from the mailboxes."

"Fine," she said graciously.

Harry was in the culvert, about fifty yards from the office, when he heard the door open. A figure came out, hastily locked up after himself, turned and began to hurry toward Harry. And stiffened when he caught sight of him.

"Did I startle you, Bjørn?" Harry asked gently.

The distance between them was still over twenty yards, but the walls cast the sound toward Bjørn Holm.

"A little," said the man from Toten, straightening the multicolored Rasta hat covering his red hair. "You sneak up on people."

"Mm. And you?"

"What about me?"

"What are you doing here? I thought you had enough to do in Kripos. You've been given a wonderful new job, I hear." Harry stopped two yards from Holm, who was obviously taken aback.

"Not sure about wonderful," Holm said. "I'm not allowed to work on what I like best."

"Which is?"

"Forensics. You know me."

"Do I?"

"Eh?" Holm frowned. "Coordination of forensics and strategic planning—what's that s'posed to be when it's at home? Passing on messages, calling meetings, sending out reports."

"It's a promotion," Harry said. "The start of something good, don't you think?"

Holm snorted. "Know what I think? I think Bellman's put me there to keep me out of the loop, to make sure I don't get any firsthand info. Because he suspects that if I do, he's not sure he'll get it before you."

"But he's mistaken there," Harry said, standing face-to-face with the forensics officer.

Bjørn Holm blinked twice. "What the fuck is this, Harry?"

"Yes, what the fuck is it?" Harry heard the anger making his voice tight, metallic. "What the fuck were you doing in the office, Bjørn? All your crap is gone now."

"Doing?" Bjørn said. "Fetching this." He held up his right hand. It was clutching a book. "You said you'd leave it in reception, remember?"

Hank Williams: The Biography.

Harry felt shame flood into his cheeks.

"Mm."

"Mm," Bjørn mimicked.

"I had it with me when we moved out," Harry said. "But we did a U-turn halfway down the culvert and came back. Then I forgot all about it."

"OK. Can I go now?"

Harry stepped aside, and listened to Bjørn stomping down the culvert between curses.

He unlocked the office.

Flopped into the chair.

Looked around.

The notebook. He flicked through. He hadn't taken any notes from the conversation, nothing that would pinpoint Tony Leike as a suspect. Harry opened the drawers in the desk to see if there were any signs of someone having rifled them. It all looked untouched. Could Harry have been wrong after all? Could he hope that Holm was not leaking information to Mikael Bellman?

Harry glanced at his watch. Praying the new prosecutor ate quickly. He struck an arbitrary key on the computer and the screen came to life. It was still showing the page with his last Google search. In the search box the name shone out at him: Tony Leike.

41

The Blue Chit

"So," said Aslak Krongli, twirling his coffee cup.

Kaja thought it looked like an egg cup in his large hand. She had taken a seat opposite him at the table closest to the window. The police cafeteria was situated on the top floor and was of standard Norwegian design—that is, light and clean, but not so cozy that people would be tempted to sit for longer than necessary. The great advantage of the room was its view of the town, but that didn't seem to interest Krongli much.

"I checked the guest books at the other self-service cabins in the area," he went on. "The only people who had written in the book that they were planning to spend the next night at Håvass cabin were Charlotte Lolles and Iska Peller, who were in Tunvegg the night before."

"And we already know about them," Kaja said.

"Yes. So in fact I have only two things that might be of interest to you."

"And they are?"

"I was speaking on the phone to an elderly couple who were at the Tunvegg cabin the same night as Lolles and Peller. They said that a man had turned up in the evening, had a bite to eat, changed his shirt, then went on his way heading southwest. Even though it was dark. And the only cabin in that direction is Håvass."

"And this person . . ."

"They barely saw him. Seemed as if he didn't want to be seen, either; he didn't take off his balaclava or his old-fashioned slalom goggles, not even when changing his shirt. The wife said she thought he might have had a serious injury at one time."

"Why was that?"

"She could only remember thinking this, couldn't say why. Nevertheless, he might have changed direction when he was out of sight, and skied to another cabin."

"Suppose so," Kaja said, checking her watch.

"Anyone come forward in response to your crime alert, by the way?"

"No," Kaja said.

"You look as though you mean yes."

Kaja's eyes shot up at Aslak Krongli, who reacted by holding up his palms. "Country clod in town! Sorry—I didn't mean anything by that."

"All right," Kaja said.

They both inspected their coffee cups.

"You said there were two things I might be interested in," Kaja said. "What's the second?"

"I know I'm going to regret saying this," Krongli said. The quiet laughter was back in his eyes.

Kaja guessed immediately which direction the conversation was going to take and knew he was right: He would regret it.

"I'm staying at the Plaza and wondered if you would like to have dinner with me there tonight."

She could see by his expression that her own was not difficult to read.

"I don't know anyone else in town," he said, contorting his mouth into a grimace that might have been intended as a disarming smile. "Apart from my ex, that is, and I don't dare call her."

"Would've been nice . . ." Kaja began, and paused. Past Conditional. She saw that Aslak Krongli was already regretting his approach. "But I'm afraid I'm otherwise engaged."

"Fine—this was short notice." Krongli smiled, threaded his fingers through his unruly, curly hair. "What about tomorrow?"

"I . . . er, I'm pretty busy these days, Aslak."

Krongli nodded, apparently to himself. "Of course. Of course you're busy. The man who was in your room when I arrived is perhaps the reason?"

"No, I've got new bosses now."

"It wasn't bosses I had in mind."

"Oh?"

"You said you were in love with a policeman. And it seemed to me he didn't have much difficulty persuading you. Less than me, anyway."

"No, no, that wasn't him! Are you out of your mind? I . . . erm, must have had too much to drink that night." Kaja could hear her own inane laughter and felt the blood rising up her neck.

"Oh, well," Krongli said, finishing his coffee. "I'll

have to go out into the big, cold city. I suppose there are museums to visit and bars to patronize."

"Yes, you have to make the most of the opportunity."

He arched an eyebrow and his eyes danced. The way Even's had at the end.

Kaja accompanied him out. As he shook her hand, she couldn't help herself. "Call me if it gets too lonely and I'll see if I can slip away."

She interpreted his smile as gratitude for allowing him the chance to decline an offer or at least to decide not to take her up on it.

Standing in the elevator to the sixth floor, Kaja was reminded of what he had said, ". . . **didn't have much difficulty persuading you**." How long had he actually been standing there by the door, eavesdropping?

At one o'clock the telephone in front of Kaja rang.

It was Harry. "I've finally got the blue chit. Ready?"

She could feel her heart beating faster. "Yes."

"Vest?"

"Vest and a weapon."

"Delta will take care of weapons. They're ready in a vehicle outside the garage, just have to go down. And bring the blue chit from my mailbox, OK?"

"OK."

Ten minutes later they were in one of Delta's blue twelve-seaters heading west through downtown. Kaja listened to Harry explaining that he had called Leike half an hour earlier at the building where he rented an office and they had said he was working off-site

today. Harry had called his home number on Holmenveien, Tony Leike had answered and Harry had
hung up. To lead the operation, Harry had specifi-
cally requested Milano, a dark, squat man with massive eyebrows, who did not have a drop of Italian
blood in his veins, despite his surname.

They passed through the Ibsen Tunnel, and rectan-
gles of reflected light slid over the helmets and visors
of the eight elite officers, who appeared to be in deep
meditation.

Kaja and Harry sat in the rear seat. Harry was
wearing a black jacket with POLITI written in large
yellow letters at the front and back, and had taken
out his service revolver to check that there were bullets in all the chambers.

"Eight men from Delta and a blender," Kaja said,
referring to the blue light rotating on the roof of the
minivan. "Sure this isn't a bit over the top?"

"It **has** to be over the top," Harry said. "If we want
to attract attention to the person who initiated this
arrest, then we need a bigger party factor than usual."

"Did you leak it to the press?"

Harry eyed her.

"If you want attention, I mean," she said. "Imagine it—Leike, the celebrity, being arrested for the
murder of Marit Olsen. They would pass up on the
birth of a princess for that."

"And what about if his fiancée is there?" Harry
said. "Or the mother? Are they going to be in the
papers and on live TV, too?" He jerked the revolver
and the cylinder clicked into place.

"What are we going to do with the big party factor, then?"

"The press come later," Harry said. "They question the neighbors, passersby, us. They find out what a magnificent show it was. That'll do me. No innocents involved, and we get our front page."

She sent him a sideways glance as the shadows of the next tunnel passed over them. They crossed Majorstuen and went up Slemdalsveien, past Vinderen, and she saw him staring out of the window, at the tram stop, a naked expression of torment on his face. She felt an urge to place a hand over his, to say something, anything, that could remove that expression. She looked at his hand. It was holding the revolver, squeezing it, as though it were all he had. This could not go on; something was going to burst. Had already burst.

They climbed higher and higher; the town lay beneath them. They crossed the tram lines and then the lights began to flash behind them and the barrier was lowered.

They were on Holmenveien.

"Who's coming with me to the door, Milano?" Harry shouted to the passenger seat in the front.

"Delta Three and Delta Four," Milano shouted back, turning and pointing to a man with a large figure 3 chalked onto the chest and back of his combat suit.

"OK," Harry said. "And the rest?"

"Two men on each side of the house. Procedure Dyke one-four-five."

Kaja knew this was code for the formation. It had been borrowed from American football, and the aim was to communicate quickly without anyone else understanding, in case they had managed to tune in to the radio frequencies that Delta used. They came to a halt a couple of houses down from Leike's. Six of the men checked their MP5's and jumped out. Kaja saw them move up through the neighbors' large yards of brown, withered grass, bare apple trees and the tall hedges they had a proclivity for in west Oslo. Kaja checked her watch. Forty seconds had passed when Milano's radio crackled. "Everyone in position."

The driver released the clutch, and they drove slowly toward the house. Tony Leike's recently acquired home was yellow, a single-story building, impressively large, but the address was more resplendent than the architecture, which lay somewhere between functionalist and a wooden box, as far as Kaja could judge.

They stopped outside two garage doors at the end of a gravel drive leading to the front door. Several years back, during a hostage crisis in Vestfold, where Delta had surrounded a house, the hostage takers had escaped by strolling down a path from the house into the garage, starting up the homeowner's car and simply driving off, to the open-mouthed amazement of the heavily armed police bystanders.

"Stay back and follow me," Harry said to Kaja. "Next time it's your turn."

They got out and Harry immediately made for the house, with the two other policemen one step behind and to the side, in a triangular formation. Kaja could

hear from Harry's voice that his pulse was accelerated. Now she could see it in his body language, too,
from the tenseness of his neck, from the exaggeratedly supple way he was moving.

They went up the steps. Harry rang the bell. The
other two had positioned themselves at each side of
the door, backs against the wall.

Kaja counted. Harry had told her in the car that in
the FBI manual it said you had to ring or knock,
shout, "Police!" and "Please open up!" repeat and
then wait ten seconds before you entered. The Norwegian police had no such precise instructions, but
that didn't mean there weren't guidelines.

On this afternoon on Holmenveien, however,
none of them was in evidence.

The door burst open. Kaja automatically recoiled a
step when she saw the Rasta hat in the doorway, then
saw Harry's shoulders swivel and heard the sound of
fist on flesh.

42

Beavis

The reaction had been instinctive; Harry had simply
not been able to prevent it.

When Forensics Officer Bjørn Holm's moonlike
face had appeared in Tony Leike's doorway and

Harry had seen the other officers in full swing behind him, he realized in a flash what had happened and everything went black.

He just felt the punch register along his arm into his shoulder and then the pain in his knuckles. Opening his eyes again, he saw Bjørn Holm on his knees in the hall with blood streaming from his nose into his mouth and dripping from his chin.

The two Delta officers had leapt forward and pointed their weapons at Holm, but were obviously in a state of bewilderment. They had probably seen his familiar Rasta hat before and were aware the other men in white were crime scene officers.

"Report back that the situation is under control," Harry said to the man with the figure 3 on his chest. "And that the suspect has been arrested. By Mikael Bellman."

Harry slumped in the chair with his legs stretched out as far as Gunnar Hagen's desk.

"It's very simple, boss. Bellman found out we were about to arrest Tony Leike. For Christ's sake, they've got the public prosecutor's office right across the street, in the same building as Krimteknisk. All he had to do was amble over and pick up a blue chit from one of the lawyers there. He was probably done in two minutes, while I waited for two fucking hours!"

"You don't need to shout," Hagen said.

"**You** don't need to, but **I** do!" Harry shouted, banging the armrest. "Shit, shit, shit!"

"You should be happy Holm's not going to report you. Why did you hit **him**, anyway? Is he the leak?"

"Anything else you wanted, boss?"

Hagen looked at his inspector. Then he shook his head. "Take a couple of days off, Harry."

Truls Berntsen had been called a lot of things in his childhood. Most of the nicknames were forgotten now. But he had been given a name soon after he finished school in the early nineties that had stuck: Beavis. The cartoon idiot on MTV. Blond hair, underbite and grunted laugh. OK, maybe he did laugh like that. Had ever since primary school, especially when someone was given a beating. Especially when he himself was given a beating. He had read in a comic that the guy who made **Beavis and Butt-Head** was named Judge; he couldn't recall the first name. But at any rate, this Judge guy said he imagined that Beavis's father was a drunkard who beat his son. Truls Berntsen remembered he had just thrown the comic on the floor and left the shop, laughing this grunt laughter.

He had two uncles who were in the police force, and he had managed to satisfy the entrance requirements by the skin of his ass and with two letters of recommendation. And scraped through the exam with at least one helping hand from the guy at the next desk. It was the least he could do; they had been pals since they were small. Sort of pals. To be honest, Mikael Bellman had been his boss since they were twelve years old, when they met on a large building site that was being dynamited in Manglerud. Bellman had caught him trying to set fire to a dead rat. And had shown him how much more fun it was to stuff a stick of dynamite down the rat's throat. Truls had even been allowed to light it. And since that day he had followed Mikael Bellman wherever he went—when he was given permission. Mikael knew how to navigate the things Truls did not: school, gym class. And how to talk so that no one would give you any shit. He even had girls; one of them was older and had tits Mikael was allowed to stroke as much as he liked. There was only one thing Truls was better at: taking a beating. Mikael always backed down when any of the bigger boys found it hard to accept that the show-off had outdone them in the art of bad-mouthing and went for him with clenched fists. Then Mikael shoved Truls in front of him. For Truls could take a beating. He had plenty of training from home. They could knock him around until blood was drawn, but he still stood there with his grunted laugh, which just made them even angrier. But he couldn't stop himself; he simply had to laugh. He knew that afterward he would receive a pat on the shoulder from Mikael, and if it was a Sunday, Mikael might say that Julle and TV were having another race, and they would go stand on the bridge below the Ryen intersection, smell the sun-baked pavement and listen to the Kawasaki 1000cc engines revving up as the cheerleaders screamed and shouted. And then Julle's and TV's bikes would tear down Sunday's traffic-free highways and pass beneath them and on to the tunnel and Bryn, and they might—if Mikael was in a good mood and Truls's mother was working a shift at Aker University Hospital—go and eat Sunday lunch with Fru Bellman.

Once Mikael had rung the bell at Truls's house and his father had shouted that Jesus had come to collect his disciple.

They had never argued. That is, Truls had not retaliated if Mikael was in a stinking mood and took it out on him. Not even at the party when Mikael had called him Beavis and everyone had laughed, and Truls had instinctively known that the name would stick. He had retaliated only once. The time Mikael had called his father one of the drunks from the Kadok factory. Then Truls had gone for Mikael with a raised fist. Mikael had curled up with an arm over his head, told him to take it easy, laughed and said he was just joking, he was sorry. But afterward it was Truls who had been sorry and apologized.

One day Mikael and Truls had gone into one of the gas stations where they knew Julle and TV stole fuel. Julle and TV would fill the Kawasaki tanks from the self-service pumps while their girls sat on the back with their denim jackets casually tied around their waists, covering the license plates. Then the boys would jump on their bikes and ride off full-throttle.

Mikael gave the owner of the gas station the full names and addresses of Julle and TV, but of just one of the girls, TV's girlfriend. The owner had looked skeptical, wondering whether he hadn't seen Truls's face before on a CCTV camera; at any rate he resembled the lad who had stolen a jerrican of gasoline not long before the empty workmen's shed at Manglerud had gone up in flames. Mikael had said he didn't want any reward for the information; he just wanted the guilty parties held responsible for their actions. He assumed the owner was aware of his social duty. The owner had nodded, somewhat surprised. Mikael had that effect on people. As they left, Mikael said he was going to apply to police college after school and Beavis should consider doing the same—there were even policemen in his family.

Later, Mikael had gotten together with Ulla, and Truls and he hadn't seen so much of each other. But after school and police college they had been employed by the same police station in Stovner, a real east Oslo suburb, with gang crimes, burglaries and even the odd murder. After a year Mikael had married Ulla and been promoted. Truls, or Beavis, as he had been called from day three, roughly, reported to him, and the future had looked good for Truls and radiant for Mikael. Until some knucklehead, a civilian temp in the payroll office, had accused Bellman of smashing his jaw after the Christmas party. He had no proof, and Truls knew for certain that Mikael had not done it. But in all the hubbub Mikael had applied for a move anyway, been accepted at Europol and moved to the head office in The Hague, where he soon became a star, too.

When Mikael returned to Norway and Kripos, the

second thing he did was to ring Truls and ask: "Beavis, are you ready to blow up rats again?"

The first was to employ Jussi.

Jussi Kolkka was an expert in half a dozen martial arts whose names you forget before they have been fully articulated. He had worked at Europol for four years, and before that he had been a policeman in Helsinki. Jussi Kolkka had been forced to resign from Europol because he had crossed the line during an investigation into a series of rapes targeting teenage girls in southern Europe. Kolkka had, it was said, beaten up a sex offender so badly that even his lawyer had had trouble recognizing him. But he had no trouble threatening Europol with a lawsuit. Truls had tried to get Jussi to tell him the gory details, but he had just stared into the distance without speaking. Fair enough—Truls wasn't the talkative type, either. And he had noticed that the less you spoke, the greater the chance people underestimated you. Which was not always a bad thing. Nevertheless, tonight they had reason to celebrate. Mikael, he, Jussi and Kripos had won. And in Mikael's absence they would have to call the shots themselves.

"Shut up!" shouted Truls, pointing to the TV attached to the wall above the bar at Kafé Justisen. And heard his own nervous, grunting laugh when his colleagues actually did what he said. There was silence around the tables and the bar. Everyone was staring at the newsreader, who looked straight into the camera and announced what they had been waiting for.

"Today Kripos arrested a man suspected of killing six people, including Marit Olsen."

Cheers broke out and mugs of beer were swung, silencing the newsreader until a deep voice with a Finnish-Swedish accent boomed, "Shut up!"

The Kripos officers obeyed again and focused their attention on Mikael Bellman, who was standing outside their building in Bryn with a furry microphone thrust into his face.

"This person is a suspect, will be interviewed by Kripos and thereafter appear in court for a preliminary hearing," Mikael Bellman said.

"Does that mean you believe the police have solved this case?"

"Finding the perpetrator and getting him convicted are two different things," Bellman said with a tiny smile at the corners of his mouth. "However, our investigation at Kripos has uncovered so much circumstantial evidence and so many coincidences that we considered it appropriate to make an immediate arrest, as there was a risk of further crimes and of tampering with evidence."

"The man you have arrested is in his thirties. Can you tell us any more about him?"

"He has a previous conviction for violence; that is all I can say."

"On the Internet there are rumors circulating about the man's identity. Suggesting he's a well-known investor who, among other things, is engaged to the daughter of a famous shipowner. Can you confirm these rumors, Bellman?"

"I don't think I have to confirm or deny anything except that we at Kripos are fairly confident that we will soon have this case solved."

The reporter turned to the camera for a wrap-up, but was drowned out by the round of applause at Justisen.

Truls ordered another beer as one of the detectives got up onto a chair and proclaimed that Crime Squad could suck his dick, at least the tip, if they said "Pretty please." Laughter resounded around the packed, sweaty, fetid room.

At that moment the door opened and in the mirror Truls saw a figure fill the entrance.

He felt a strange excitement at the sight, a tremulous certainty that something was going to happen, that someone would be hurt.

It was Harry Hole.

Tall, broad-shouldered, lean-faced, with deep-set bloodshot eyes, he just stood there. And although no one shouted for the crowd to shut up, the silence spread from the front to the back of Justisen, until a last **shh** was heard to quiet two garrulous forensics officers. When the silence was complete, Hole spoke.

"So you're celebrating the job you succeeded in stealing from us, are you?"

The words were low, almost a whisper, and yet every syllable reverberated around the room.

"You're celebrating having a boss who's prepared to step over dead bodies—those that have piled up outside and those that will soon be carried from the sixth floor at Police HQ—just so that he can be the Sun King of fucking Bryn. Well, here's a hundred-krone note."

Truls could see Hole waving a bill.

"You don't have to steal this. Here, buy yourselves beer, forgiveness, a dildo for Bellman's three-some . . ." He crumpled up the bill and tossed it onto the floor. From the corner of his eye he could see Jussi was already moving. "Or another snitch."

Hole lurched to the side to gain balance, and it was then that Truls realized that the guy—despite enunci-ating with the diction of a priest—was as stewed as a prune.

The next moment Hole performed a half-pirouette as Jussi Kolkka's right hook hit him on the chin, and then a deep, almost gallant bow, as the Finn's left buried itself in his solar plexus. Truls guessed that in a few seconds Hole—when he had gotten some air back in his lungs—was going to vomit. In here. And Jussi was obviously thinking the same—that he would be better outside. It was a won-der to see how the tubby, almost log-shaped Finn lifted his foot high with the suppleness of a ballerina, placed it against Harry's shoulder and gently pushed so that the crumpled detective rocked backward and through the door from which he'd come.

The drunkest and youngest of them howled with laughter, but Truls grunted. A couple of the older ones yelled, and one screamed that Kolkka should damn well behave himself. But no one did anything. Truls knew why. Everyone here remembered the story. Harry had dragged the uniform through the dirt, shat in the nest, taken the life of one of their best men.

Jussi marched solemnly toward the bar, as if he had carried out the garbage. Truls whinnied and grunted. He would never understand Finns or Samis or Eskimos or whatever the hell they were.

From farther back in the room a man had stood up and made his way to the door. Truls hadn't seen him at Kripos before, but he had the circumspect eye of a policeman under all that dark, curly hair.

"Tell me if you need any help with him, Sheriff," someone shouted from his table.

Three minutes later, when Celine Dion had been turned back up and the conversation had resumed its previous levels, Truls ventured forth, put his foot on the hundred-krone note and took it to the bar.

Harry had his breath back. And he vomited. Once, twice. Then he collapsed again. The pavement was so cold it stung his ribs through his shirt and so heavy he seemed to be supporting it and not vice versa. Bloodred spots and wriggling black worms danced in front of his eyes.

"Hole?"

Harry heard the voice, but knew that if he showed he was conscious it would be open season for a kicking. So he kept his eyes closed.

"Hole?" The voice had come closer and he felt a hand on his shoulder.

Harry also knew that the alcohol would have reduced his speed, accuracy and ability to judge distances, but he did it anyway. He opened his eyes, twisted over and aimed for the larynx. Then he collapsed again.

He had missed by a foot and a half.

"I'll get you a taxi," the voice said.

"Fuck off, you fucking bastard," Harry groaned.

"I'm not Kripos," the voice said. "My name's Krongli. The county officer from Ustaoset."

Harry turned and squinted up at him.

"I'm just a little drunk," Harry said hoarsely and tried to breathe calmly so that the pain wouldn't force the contents of his stomach up again. "No big deal."

"I'm a little drunk, too." Krongli smiled, putting an arm around Harry's shoulders. "And, to be frank, I have no idea where to get a taxi. Can you stand upright?"

Harry got one and then two legs beneath him, blinked a couple of times and established that at least he was vertical again. Semi-embracing an officer from Ustaoset.

"Where are you sleeping tonight?" Krongli asked.

Harry looked askance at the officer. "At home. And preferably on my own, if that's all right with you."

At that moment a police car pulled up in front of them, and the window slid down. Harry heard the tail end of some laughter and then a composed voice.

"Harry Hole, Crime Squad?"

"'S me." Harry sighed.

"We've just received a phone call from one of the

Kripos detectives requesting that we drive you home safe and sound."

"Open the door, then!"

Harry got into the backseat, lolled against the headrest, closed his eyes, started to feel everything rotating, but preferred that to watching the two in the front ogling him. Krongli asked them to call him at a number when "Harry" was safely home. What the hell gave him the idea he was his pal? Harry heard the hum of the window and then the pleasant voice from the front seat again.

"Where do you live, Hole?"

"Keep going straight ahead," Harry said. "We're going to pay someone a visit."

When Harry felt the car set off, he opened his eyes, turned and saw Aslak Krongli still standing on Møllergata.

43

House Call

Kaja lay on her side staring into the darkness of her bedroom. She had heard the gate open and now there were footsteps on the gravel outside. She held her breath and waited. Then the doorbell rang. She slipped into her dressing gown and went over to the window.

Another ring. She opened the curtains a fraction. And sighed.

"Drunken police officer," she said out loud in the room.

She put her feet into slippers and shuffled into the hall toward the door. Opened it and stood in the doorway with crossed arms.

"Hello there, schweedie," the policeman slurred. Kaja wondered if he was putting on an act. Or if it was his pitiful actual state.

"What brings you here so late?" Kaja asked.

"You. Can I come in?"

"No."

"But you said I could get in touch if I was too lonely. And I **was.**"

"Aslak Krongli," she said. "I'm in bed. Go to your hotel now. We can have a coffee tomorrow morning."

"I need coffee now, I think. Ten minutes and we'll call for a taxi, eh? We can talk about murders and serial killers to pass the time. What do you say?"

"Sorry," she said. "I'm not alone."

Krongli straightened up at once, with a movement that made Kaja suspect he was not as drunk as he had seemed at first. "Really? Is he here, that policeman you said you were so hung up on?"

"Maybe."

"Are they his?" the officer drawled, kicking the enormous shoes beside the doormat.

Kaja didn't answer. There was something in Krongli's voice—no, behind it—something she hadn't heard there before. Like a low-frequency, barely audible growl.

"Or have you just put the shoes there to frighten off unwanted visitors?" Laughter in his eyes. "There's no one here, is there, Kaja?"

"Listen, Aslak—"

"The policeman you're talking about, Harry Hole, screwed up earlier this evening. Turned up at Justisen as drunk as a skunk, picked a fight and got one. A patrol car passed by to give him a lift home. So you must be free tonight after all, eh?"

Her heart beat faster; she was no longer cold under the dressing gown.

"Perhaps they drove him here instead," she said and could hear her voice was different now.

"No, they called me and said they had driven him way up the hill to visit someone. When they found out he wanted to go to Rikshospital and they strongly advised against it, he just jumped out at the traffic light. I like my coffee strong, OK?"

An intense gleam had come into his eyes, the same Even used to get when he wasn't well.

"Aslak, go now. There are taxis on Kirkeveien."

His hand shot out, and before she could react he had grabbed her arm and pushed her inside. She tried to free herself, but he put an arm around her and held her tight.

"Do you want to be just like her?" his voice hissed in her ear. "To cut and run, to scram? To be like all you fucking . . ."

She groaned and twisted, but he was strong.

"Kaja!"

The voice came from the bedroom, where the door stood open. A firm, imperious man's voice that, under different circumstances, Krongli might have recognized, as he had heard it only an hour earlier, at Justisen.

"What's going on, Kaja?"

Krongli had already let go and was staring at her, with eyes wide and jaw agape.

"Nothing," Kaja said, not letting Krongli out of her sight. "Just a drunken bumpkin from Ustaoset who's on his way home."

Krongli backed toward the front entrance without a word. Slipped out and slammed the door. Kaja went over, locked it and rested her forehead against the cold wood. She felt like crying. Not out of fear or shock. But despair. Everything around her was collapsing. Everything she had thought was clean and right had finally begun to appear in its real light. It had been happening for some time, but she hadn't **wanted** to see. Because what Even had said was true: No one is as they seem, and most of life, apart from honest betrayal, is lies and deceit. And the day we discover we are no different is the day we no longer want to live.

"Are you coming, Kaja?"

"Yes."

Kaja pushed off from the door through which she would so much have liked to flee. Went into the bedroom. The moonlight fell between the curtains and onto the bed, onto the bottle of Champagne he had brought with him to celebrate, onto his naked, athletic torso, onto the face she had once thought the most handsome on this earth. The white patches on his face shimmered like luminous paint. As if he were aglow inside.

44

The Anchor

Kaja stood in the doorway looking at him. Mikael Bellman. To outsiders: a competent, ambitious POB, a happily married father of three and soon-to-be head of the new Kripos leviathan that would lead all murder investigations in Norway. To her, Kaja Solness: a man she had fallen in love with from the moment they'd met, who had seduced her with all the arts at his disposal, plus a few others. She had been easy game, but that wasn't his fault; it was hers. By and large. What was it Harry had said? "He's married and says he'll leave his wife and kids for you, but never does?"

He had hit the nail on the head. Of course. That's how banal we are. We believe because we want to believe. In gods, because that dulls the fear of death. In love, because it enhances the notion of life. In what married men say, because that is what married men say.

She knew what Mikael would say. And then he said it.

"I have to be going. She'll start wondering."

"I know." Kaja sighed and, as usual, did not ask the questions that always popped up when he said that: Why not stop her wondering? Why not do what you've said for so long? And now a new question emerged: **Why am I no longer sure I want him to do this?**

Harry clung to the banisters on his way up to the Hematology Department at Rikshospital. He was soaked in sweat and frozen, and his teeth were chattering like a two-stroke engine. And he was drunk. Drunk on Jim Beam, drunk and full of devilry, full of himself, full of shit. He staggered along the corridor; he could already make out the door to his father's room at the end.

A nurse's head poked out from a duty room, looked at him and was gone again. Harry had fifty yards to go to the door when the nurse, plus a male nurse with a shaved head, skidded into the corridor and cut him off.

"We don't keep medicines on this ward," the bald-headed nurse said.

"What you are saying is not only a gross lie," Harry said, trying to control his balance and the chattering of his teeth, "but a gross insult. I'm not a junkie, but a son here to visit his father. So please, move out of my way."

"I apologize," said the female nurse, who seemed quite reassured by Harry's immaculate pronunciation. "But you smell like a brewery, and we cannot allow—"

"A brewery is beer," Harry said. "Jim Beam is bourbon. Which would require you to say I smell like a distillery, **frøken.** It's—"

"Nevertheless," the male nurse said, grabbing Harry by the elbow. And let it go just as quickly when his own hand was twisted around. He groaned and grimaced with pain before Harry released him. Harry rose to his full height and eyeballed him.

"Call the police, Gerd," the nurse said softly, without letting Harry out of his sight.

"If you don't mind, I'll deal with this," said a voice with a suggestion of a lisp. It was Sigurd Altman. He walked up with a file under his arm and a friendly smile on his face. "Do you have time to come with me to where we keep drugs, Harry?"

Harry swayed back and forth twice. Focused on the small, thin man with the round glasses. Then he nodded.

"This way," said Altman, who had already continued walking.

Altman's office was, strictly speaking, a storeroom. There were no windows, there was no noticeable ventilation, but there was a desk and a computer, and a cot, which he explained was for night shifts, so that he could sleep or be roused whenever needed. And a lockable cabinet Harry assumed contained a range of chemical uppers and downers.

"Altman," Harry said, sitting on the edge of the bed, smacking his lips loudly as though they were coated with glue. "Unusual name. Only know one person called that."

"Robert," said Sigurd, sitting on the only chair in the room. "I didn't like who I was in the little village where I grew up. As soon as I got away I applied to change my surname from a much too common **-sen**. I justified my application by saying, as was the truth, that Robert Altman was my favorite director. And the case officer must have had a hangover that day because it was approved. We can all do with being reborn once in a while."

"**The Player**," Harry said.

"**Gosford Park**," Altman said.

"**Short Cuts**."

"Ah, a masterpiece."

"Good, but overrated. Too many themes. The direction and editing make the plot unnecessarily complicated."

"Life is complicated. People are complicated. Watch it again, Harry."

"Mm."

"How's it going? Any progress on the Marit Olsen case?"

"Progress," Harry said. "The guy who did it was arrested today."

"Jeez, well, I can understand you celebrating." Altman pressed his chin to his chest and peered over his glasses. "I have to confess I'm hoping I can tell my grandchildren that it was my information about ketanome that cracked the case."

"By all means, but it was a phone call to one of the victims that gave him away."

"Poor things."

"Poor who?"

"Poor all of them, I assume. So why the haste to see your father right now, tonight?"

Harry put his hand in front of his mouth and produced a noiseless belch.

"There is a reason," Altman said. "However drunk you are, there's always a reason. On the other hand, that reason is none of my business, so perhaps I should keep my mou—"

"Have you ever been asked to carry out euthanasia?"

Altman shrugged. "A few times, yes. As an anesthesia nurse, I'm an obvious choice. Why?"

"My father asked me."

Altman nodded slowly. "It's a heavy burden to place on someone. Is that why you came here now? To get it over with?"

Harry's gaze had already wandered around the room to see if there was anything alcoholic to drink. Now it did another round. "I came to ask for forgiveness. For not being able to do it for him."

"You hardly need forgiveness for that. Taking a life is not something you can demand of anyone, let alone of your own son."

Harry rested his head in his hands. It felt hard and heavy, like a bowling ball.

"I've done it once before," he said.

Altman's voice sounded more surprised than actually shocked. "Carried out euthanasia?"

"No," Harry said. "Refused to carry it out. For my worst enemy. He has an incurable, fatal and very painful disease. He is slowly being suffocated by his own shrinking skin."

"Scleroderma," Altman said.

"When I arrested him, he tried to make me shoot him. We were alone at the top of a tower, just him and me. He had killed an unknown number of people and hurt me and people I love. Permanent damage. My gun was pointing at him. Just us. Self-defense. I didn't risk a thing by shooting him."

"But you preferred him to suffer," Altman said. "Death was too easy for him."

"Yes."

"And now you feel you're doing the same with your father—you're making him suffer rather than allowing him release."

Harry rubbed his neck. "It's not because I hold with the principles of the sanctity of life or any of that bullshit. It's weakness, pure and simple. It's cowardice. Christ, you don't have anything to drink here, do you, Altman?"

Sigurd Altman shook his head. Harry wasn't sure if it was in answer to his last question or the other things he had said. Perhaps both.

"You can't just disregard your own feelings like that, Harry. You, like everyone else, are trying to leapfrog the fact that we are governed by notions of what's right and wrong. Your intellect may not have all the arguments for these notions, but nonetheless they are rooted deep, deep inside you. Right and wrong. Perhaps it's things you were told by your parents when you were a child, a fairy tale with a moral your grandmother read, or something unfair you experienced at school and you spent time thinking through. The sum of all these half-forgotten things." Altman leaned forward. " 'Anchored deep within' is in fact a pretty apposite expression. Because it tells you that you may not be able to see the anchor in the depths, but you damn well can't move from the spot—that's what you float around and that's where your home is. Try to accept that, Harry. Accept the anchor."

Harry stared down at his folded hands. "The pain he has—"

"Physical pain is not the worst thing a human has to deal with," Altman said. "Believe me, I see it every day. Not death, either. Nor even fear of death."

"What is the worst, then?"

"Humiliation. To be deprived of honor and dignity. To be disrobed, to be cast out by the flock. That's the worst punishment; it's akin to being buried alive. And the only consolation is that the person will perish fairly quickly."

"Mm." Harry kept eye contact with Altman. "You don't have anything in that cupboard to lighten the atmosphere, do you?"

45

Questioning

Mikael Bellman had been dreaming about free fall again. Climbing solo on El Chorro, the fingerhold that isn't, the mountain wall racing past your eyes, the ground accelerating toward you. The alarm clock ringing at the last moment. He wiped the egg yolk from his mouth and looked up at Ulla, who was standing right behind him and filling his cup with coffee from the carafe. She had learned to recognize the precise moment when he was ready to eat, and it was then and not a second before that he wanted his coffee, boiling hot, poured into the blue cup. And that was only one of the reasons he appreciated her. Another was that she kept herself in such good shape that she still attracted admiring glances at the parties they were invited to more and more often. Ulla had, after all, been Manglerud's undisputed beauty queen when they got together; he had been eighteen, she nineteen. A third reason was that Ulla, without making any great fuss about it, had set aside her dreams of further education so that he could make his job their priority. But the three most important reasons sat around the table arguing about who should have the plastic figure in the cornflakes box and who should sit in front today when she drove them to school.

Two girls, one boy. Three perfect reasons to appreciate the woman and her genes' compatibility with his.

"Will you be late again tonight?" she asked, furtively stroking his hair. He knew she loved his hair.

"It might be a long session," he said. "We're starting with the suspect today." He knew that over the course of the day the papers would publish what they already knew: that the arrestee was Tony Leike. But he had made it a principle never to reveal confidentialities even at home. That also enabled him to explain overtime regularly with "I can't talk about that, darling."

"Why didn't you question him yesterday?" she asked while buttering the children's bread for their packed lunches.

"We had to gather more facts. And finish searching his house."

"Did you find anything?"

"Afraid I can't be that specific, darling," he said and gave her the regretful confidentiality look so as not to reveal the fact that she had actually put her finger on a sensitive point. Bjørn Holm and the crime scene officers hadn't found anything during the search that linked Leike to any of the murders. Fortunately, for the moment, however, that was of minor importance.

"Softening him up in a cell overnight won't hurt," Bellman said. "It'll just make him more receptive when we start. And the first part of the questioning is always the crunch."

"Is it?" she asked, and he could tell she was trying to sound interested.

"I have to be going." He got up and kissed her on the cheek. Yes, he certainly did appreciate her. The thought of forgoing her and the children, the framework and infrastructure that had enabled him to rise through the ranks, through the classes, was of course absurd. To follow the impulses of his heart, to throw up everything for love, or whatever it was, was utopian, a dream he could think and talk about, with Kaja as a listener. But if he was going to dream, Mikael Bellman preferred dreams that were grander than that.

He inspected his front teeth in the hall mirror and checked that his silk tie was straight. The press were bound to be out in force.

How long would he be able to keep Kaja? He thought he had detected some doubts in her last night. And a lack of enthusiasm in their lovemaking. But he also knew that as long as he was heading for the top, as he had been doing so far, he would be able to control her. It wasn't that Kaja was a gold digger, with clear objectives of what he, as overall boss, could do for her own career. It wasn't about intellect; it was pure biology. Women could be as modern as they liked, but when it came to submitting to the alpha male, they were still at primate level. However, if she was beginning to entertain doubts because she thought that he would never renounce his wife for her sake, perhaps it was time to give her some encouragement. After all, he needed her to feed him with inside info about Crime Squad for a while yet, until all the loose ends were tied up, until this battle was over. And the war won.

He went over to the window while buttoning up his coat. The house they had taken over from his parents was in Manglerud, not the best area of town, if you asked the West Enders. But those who had grown up here had a tendency to stay; it was a quarter with soul. And it was his quarter. With a view over the rest of Oslo. Which would also soon be his.

"They're coming now," the uniformed officer said. He stood in the doorway of one of the new interview rooms at Kripos.

"OK," Mikael Bellman said.

Some interrogators liked to have the interviewee led to the room first, to keep him or her waiting, to make it clear who was in charge. So that they could enjoy the great entrance and go in hard right away while they had the perp at his or her most defensive and vulnerable. Bellman preferred to be seated and ready when the suspect was ushered in. To mark his territory, to announce who owned the room. He was still able to keep the suspect waiting while he skimmed through his papers, able to feel the nervousness mounting in the room and then—when the time was ripe—raise his eyes and shoot. But these were the fine details of interview techniques. Which, naturally, he was happy to discuss with other competent chief interrogators. Again, he checked that the red recording light was switched on. Fiddling with technical equipment after the suspect had arrived could spoil the preliminary establishment of status.

Through the window he saw Beavis and Kolkka enter the adjacent office. Between them walked Tony Leike, whom they had brought from the lockup at Police HQ.

Bellman took a deep breath. Yes, his pulse was a little faster now. A mixture of aggression and nerves. Tony Leike had declined the opportunity to have a lawyer present. In essence, of course, that was an advantage for Kripos; it gave them greater latitude. But at the same time it was a signal that Leike thought he had little to fear. Poor sucker. He can't have known that Bellman had proof that Leike had called Elias Skog just before he was murdered. Skog, whose name Leike had claimed he didn't even know.

Bellman looked down at the papers and heard Leike entering the room. Beavis closed the door behind him, as he had been instructed.

"Take a seat," Bellman said without looking up.

He heard Leike do what he was told.

Bellman stopped at an arbitrary piece of paper and stroked his lower lip with a forefinger while slowly counting to himself, from one upward. The silence quivered in the small, enclosed room. One, two, three. He and his colleagues had been sent to a workshop on the new interrogation methods they were being instructed to use—so-called investigative viewing—the point of which, according to these ungrounded academic types, was openness, dialogue and trust. Four, five, six. Bellman had listened quietly—after all, the program had been chosen at the highest level—but what sort of characters did these people actually think Kripos interviewed? Sensitive but obliging souls who tell you everything you want to know in exchange for a shoulder to cry on? They insisted that the methods the police had employed until now, those used in the traditional nine-step American FBI model, were inhuman and manipulative and made innocent people confess to crimes they hadn't committed, and therefore were counterproductive. Seven, eight, nine. OK, so say it put the odd suggestible chicken in the coop, but what was that compared with the grinning scum who strolled away, doubled over in laughter at "openness, dialogue and trust"?

Ten.

Bellman pressed his fingertips together and raised his eyes.

"We know you called Elias Skog from Oslo, and that two days later you were in Stavanger. And that you killed him. These are the facts we have, but what I am wondering is why. Or didn't you have a motive, Leike?"

That was step one of the nine-step model drawn up by the FBI agents Inbau, Reid and Buckley: the confrontation, the attempt to use the shock effect to land a knockout punch right away, the declaration that the interrogators knew everything already, so there was no point denying guilt. This had one sole aim: confession. Here Bellman combined step one with another interviewing technique: linking one fact with one or several nonfacts. In this case he linked the incontestable date of the phone call with the contention that Leike had been to Stavanger and he was a killer. Hearing the proof for the first claim, Leike would automatically conclude that they also had concrete proof for the others. And that these facts were so simple and irrefutable that they could jump straight to the only thing left to answer: Why?

Bellman saw Leike swallow, saw him bare his white milestone-size teeth in an attempted smile, saw the confusion in his eyes and knew that they had already won.

"I didn't call any Elias Skog," Leike said.

Bellman sighed. "Do you want me to show you the listed calls from Telenor?"

Leike shrugged. "I didn't call. I lost my cell phone a while back. Maybe someone called him using that?"

"Don't try to be smart, Leike. We're talking about your landline."

"I didn't call him—I'm telling you."

"I heard. According to official records, you live alone."

"Yes, I do. That is—"

"Your fiancée sleeps over now and then. And sometimes you get up earlier than she does and go to work while she's still in your house?"

"That happens. But I'm at hers more often than not."

"Well, now. Does Galtung's heiress daughter have a more luxurious pad than you, Leike?"

"Maybe. Cozier, at any rate."

Bellman crossed his arms and smiled. "Nonetheless, if you didn't call Skog from your house, she must have. I'm giving you five seconds to start talking sense to us, Leike. In five seconds, a patrol car on the streets of Oslo will receive orders to drive with sirens blaring to that cozy little pad of hers, handcuff her, bring her here and allow her to phone her father to tell him you're accusing her of calling Skog. So that Anders Galtung can gather the meanest pack of hard-bitten lawyers in Norway for his daughter, and you gain a real adversary. Four seconds . . . three seconds."

Leike shrugged again. "If you think that's enough to issue an arrest warrant for a young woman with a perfect, unblemished record, go ahead. But I somehow doubt it would be me who gained an adversary."

Bellman observed Leike. Had he underrated him, after all? He was more difficult to read now. Anyway, that was step one over. Without a confession. Fine, there were eight left. Step two in the nine-step model was to sympathize with the suspect by making his actions seem normal. But that presupposed he knew the motive or he was working with something he could make seem normal. A motive for killing all the guests who had happened to stay over at a ski cabin was not self-evident, over and above the obvious truism that most serial killers' motives are hidden in the psyche where the majority of us never go. In his preparations Bellman had therefore decided to tread lightly on the sympathy step before jumping straight into the motivation step: giving the suspect a reason to confess.

"My point, Leike, is that I'm not your adversary. I'm just someone who wants to understand why you do what you do. What makes you tick. You're clearly an able, intelligent person; you only have to look at what you've achieved in business. I'm fascinated by people who set objectives and pursue them, regardless of what others think. People who set themselves apart from the madding crowd of mediocrity. I may even say that I can recognize myself in that bracket. Maybe I understand you better than you think, Tony."

Bellman had asked a detective to call one of Leike's stock exchange buddies to find out whether Leike preferred his first name pronounced as "Toeny" or "Tonny." The answer was "Toeny." Bellman hit the right pronunciation, caught his eye and attempted to hold it.

"Now I'm going to say something perhaps I shouldn't, Tony. Because of a number of internal issues, we can't devote a lot of time to this case, and that is why I would like a confession. Normally we wouldn't offer a deal to a suspect with such overwhelming evidence against him, but it would expedite procedures. And for a confession—which, in fact, we do not even need to obtain a conviction—I will offer you a reduced sentence, which will be considerable. I am afraid I'm restricted by legal guidelines with regards to offering a specific figure, but let's just say between you and me that it will be **consider-**

able. All right, Tony? It's a promise. And now it's on tape." He pointed to the red light on the table between them.

Leike subjected Bellman to a long, reflective look. Then he opened his mouth. "The two who brought me in told me your name was Bellman."

"Call me Mikael, Tony."

"They also said you were a very intelligent man. Tough, but trustworthy."

"I think you will discover that to be borne out, yes."

"You said considerable, didn't you?"

"You have my word." Bellman felt his pulse rising.

"All right," Leike said.

"Good," said Mikael Bellman lightly, touching his lower lip with thumb and forefinger. "Shall we start at the beginning?"

"Fine," Leike said, taking from his back pocket a piece of paper that Truls and Jussi must have let him keep. "I was given the dates and times by Harry Hole so this should be quick. Borgny Stem-Myhre died somewhere between ten and eleven p.m. on the sixteenth of December in Oslo."

"Correct," Bellman said, sensing an incipient exultation in his heart.

"I checked the calendar. At that time I was in Skien, in the Peer Gynt Room, Ibsen House, where I was talking about my coltan project. This can be confirmed by the person who arranged for the room and roughly one hundred and twenty potential investors who were present. I assume you know it takes about two hours to drive there. The next was Charlotte Lolles between . . . let's see . . . it says between eleven o'clock and midnight on the third of January. At that time I was having dinner with a few minor investors in Hamar. Two hours by car from Oslo. By the way, I took the train, and I tried to find the ticket, but sadly without any luck."

He smiled in apology to Bellman, who had stopped breathing. And for a second Leike's milestone teeth appeared between his lips as he concluded: "But I hope that at least **some** of the twelve witnesses present during the dinner may be regarded as reliable."

"Then he said there was a possibility he could be charged with the murder of Marit Olsen, because even though he had been at home with his fiancée, he had, in fact, also been alone for two hours skiing on the floodlit course in Sørkedalen that evening."

Mikael Bellman shook his head and stuffed his hands even deeper into his coat pockets as he examined **The Sick Child.**

"At the time when Marit Olsen died?" Kaja asked, inclining her head and looking at the mouth of the pale, presumably dying girl. She generally concentrated on one thing whenever they met at the Munch Museum. Sometimes it could be the eyes, another time the landscape in the background, the sun or simply Edvard Munch's signature.

"He said that neither he nor the Galtung woman—"

"Lene," Kaja corrected.

"Could remember exactly when, but it could have been quite late; it usually was, because he liked to have the course to himself."

"So Tony Leike could have been in Frogner Park instead. If he was in Sørkedalen he would have passed through the toll booths twice, on the way out and back in. If he has an AutoPASS on his windshield the time is automatically recorded. And then—"

She had turned and stopped abruptly when she met his frigid eyes.

"But of course you've already checked that," she said.

"We didn't need to," Mikael said. "He doesn't have an AutoPASS—he stops and pays cash. And so there is no record of the journey."

She nodded. They strolled on to the next picture, stood behind a few Japanese tourists who were noisily pointing and gesticulating. The advantage of meeting at the Munch Museum during the week—apart from the fact that it lay between Kripos in Bryn and Police HQ in Grønland—was that it was one of those tourist destinations where you were guaranteed never to meet colleagues, neighbors or acquaintances.

"What did Leike say about Elias Skog and Stavanger?" Kaja asked.

Mikael shook his head again. "He said he could probably be charged with that one, too. Since he had slept alone that night, and thus had no alibi. So I asked him if he had gone to work the next day and he answered that he couldn't remember, but he assumed he had turned up at seven, as usual. And that I could check with the receptionist at his office if I considered it important. I did, and it transpired that Leike had booked one of the meeting rooms for a quarter past nine. And, talking with a few of the investor types in the office, I found out that two of them had been at the meeting with Leike. If he had left Elias Skog's place at three in the morning he would have needed a plane to make it. And his name is not on any passenger lists."

"That doesn't mean much. He may have been traveling under a false name and ID. And anyway, we still have his phone call to Skog. How did he explain that away?"

"He didn't even try—he just denied it." Bellman snorted. "What is it that people think is so good about **The Dance of Life**? They don't even have proper faces. Look like zombies, if you ask me."

Kaja studied the dancers in the painting. "Perhaps they are," she said.

"Zombies?" Bellman chuckled. "Do you mean that?"

"People who go around like dancers, but feel dead inside, buried, decomposing. No question."

"Interesting theory, Solness."

She hated it when he used her surname, which he did as a rule when he was angry or simply found it appropriate to remind her of his intellectual superiority. Which she let him do because it was obviously important to him. And perhaps he was intellectually superior. Wasn't it part of what had made her fall for him, his conspicuous intelligence? She didn't have a clear recollection anymore.

"I have to go back to work," she said.

"And do what?" Mikael asked, yawning and looking at the security guard behind the rope at the back of the room. "Count files and wait for Crime Squad to be wound up? You know you've given me a massive problem with this Leike, don't you?"

"I have?" she burst out, incredulous.

"Keep it down, dear. You were the one who tipped me off about what Harry had dug up on Leike. Told me he was going to arrest him. I trusted you. I trusted you so much that I arrested Leike on the basis of your tip-off and subsequently as good as told the press the case was in the bag. And now this shit has exploded in our fucking faces. The guy has a watertight alibi for at least two of the murders. We're going to have to let him go at some point today. Daddy-in-law Galtung is no doubt already amassing the lawyers from hell to sue us, and the minister of justice will want to know how the fuck we could have committed such a blunder. And now the head on the block won't be yours, Hole's or Hagen's, but mine, Solness. Do you understand? Mine alone. And we're going to have to do something about that. **You're** going to have to do something about it."

"And what would that be?"

"Not much, a trifle, and we'll sort out the rest. I want you to take Harry out. Tonight."

"Out? Me?"

"He likes you."

"What makes you think that?"

"Didn't I tell you I saw you two sitting and smoking on the veranda?"

Kaja went pale. "You arrived late, but you didn't say anything about having seen us."

"You were so preoccupied with each other you didn't hear the car, so I parked and watched. He likes you, my love. Now I want you to take him somewhere. For a couple of hours, no more."

"Why?"

Mikael Bellman smiled. "He's spending too much time sitting at home. Or lying. Hagen should never have given him time off; people like Hole can't deal with it. And we don't want him to drink himself to death up in Oppsal, do we now? Take him to eat somewhere. The movies. A beer. Just make sure he isn't at home between eight and ten. And be careful. I don't know if he's sharp or just paranoid, but he examined my car very closely the night he left your place. All right?"

Kaja didn't answer. Mikael's smile was the one she could dream about in the long periods when he wasn't there, when job and family obligations prevented him from meeting her. So how come the same smile now made her feel as if her stomach were being turned inside out?

"You . . . you weren't thinking of . . ."

"I'm thinking of doing whatever I have to," Mikael said, looking at his watch.

"Which is?"

He shrugged. "What do you think? Swapping the head on the block, I guess."

"Don't ask me to do this, Mikael."

"But I'm not asking you, dear. I'm ordering you."

Her voice was barely audible. "And if . . . if I were to refuse?"

"Then I'll not only crush Hole, I'll crush you, too."

The light from the ceiling fell on the tiny white patches on his face. So handsome, she thought. Someone should paint him.

The marionettes are dancing as they should now. Harry Hole found out I called Elias Skog. I like him. I think perhaps we could have been friends if we had met when we were children or in our teens. We have a couple of things in common. Like intelligence. He is the only detective who seems to have the ability to see behind the veil. That also means, of course, I will have to be careful with him. I am looking forward to seeing how this develops. With childlike glee.

Part Five

46

Red Beetle

Harry opened his eyes and stared up at a large, square red beetle crawling toward him between the two empty bottles. It purred like a cat. It stopped, then purred again, tapped its way two more inches toward him along the glass coffee table, leaving a tiny trail in the ash. He stretched out his hand, grabbed it and put it to his ear. Heard his own voice sound like a rock being crushed. "Stop calling me, Øystein."

"Harry—"

"Who the hell is this?"

"It's Kaja. What are you doing?"

He looked at the display to make sure the voice was telling the truth. "Resting." He felt his stomach preparing to evacuate its contents. Again.

"Where?"

"On the sofa. I'll hang up now unless it's important."

"Does that mean you're at home in Oppsal?"

"Well, let me see. The wallpaper's right, anyway. Kaja, I have to go."

Harry threw the phone to the end of the sofa, lurched to his feet, stooped to find his center of gravity and staggered forward, using his head as a navigation aid and battering ram. It led him into the kitchen without any major collisions, and he placed his hands on both sides of the sink before the fountain of vomit gushed from his mouth.

Opening his eyes again, he saw that the dish rack was still over the sink. The thin yellowish-green vomit was running down a single upright plate. Harry turned on the tap. One of the advantages of being an alcoholic back off the wagon was that by day two your sick stops blocking the drain.

Harry drank a little water from the tap. Not much. Another advantage the experienced alcoholic possesses is a knowledge of what his stomach can tolerate.

He went back to the living room, legs akimbo, as if he had just filled his pants. Which, as a matter of fact, he had not yet checked. He lay down on the sofa and heard a low croak coming from the far end. A small voice from a miniature person was calling his name. He groped between his feet and put the red cell to his ear again.

"What's up?"

He wondered what he should do with the gall that was burning his throat like lava—cough it up or swallow it? Or let it burn, as he deserved.

He listened as she explained she wanted to see him. Would he meet her at Ekeberg Restaurant? Like now. Or in an hour's time.

Harry looked at the two empty bottles of Jim Beam on the coffee table and then at his watch. Seven. The liquor stores were closed. Restaurant bar.

"Now," he said.

He clicked off, and the phone rang again. He looked at the display and pressed answer. "Hi, Øystein."

"**Now** you're answering! Shit, Harry, I was beginning to wonder if you'd done a Hendrix."

"Can you drive me to Ekeberg Restaurant?"

"What the hell d'you think I am? A fucking cab-driver?"

Eighteen minutes later Øystein's car stood outside the steps to Olav Hole's house and he called through the opened window with a grin. "Need any help locking the fucking door, you drunken asshole?"

"Dinner?" Øystein exclaimed as they drove by Nordstrand. "To fuck her or because you have fucked already?"

"Calm down. We work together."

"Exactly. As my ex-wife used to say: 'You want what you see every day.' She must have read it in a glossy magazine. Only she didn't mean me, but that bastard at the office."

"You haven't been married, Øystein."

"Could have been. The guy wore a Norwegian sweater and a tie and spoke Nynorsk. Not dialect, but fucking national-romantic Nynorsk, Ivar Aasen–style, I kid you not. Can you imagine what it's like to sleep alone thinking that right now your could-have-been-wife is busy fucking someone on a desk? You visualize a colored sweater and a bare white ass going hammer and tongs, until it stops and seems to suck in its cheeks and the clod howls: '**Eg kjem!**' 'I'm coming!' In Nynorsk."

Øystein glanced at Harry, but there was no reaction.

"Christ, Harry, this is great humor. Are you **that** drunk?"

Kaja sat by the window, deep in thought, taking stock of the town, when a low cough made her turn. It was the head waiter; he had that apologetic it's-on-the-menu-but-the-kitchen-says-we-don't-have-it look, and had stooped very low over her, but spoke in such muffled tones that she could still hardly hear him.

"I regret to say that your company has arrived." Then he amended his statement with a blush. "I mean, I regret to say we could not admit him. He's a bit . . . animated, I'm afraid. And our policy in such—"

"Fine," Kaja said, getting up. "Where is he?"

"He's outside waiting. I'm afraid he bought a drink from the bar on the way in, and he has got it with him. Perhaps you might be so kind as to bring the glass back in. We could lose our license for that sort of thing, you know."

"Of course—just get me my coat, would you, please?" said Kaja, hurrying through the restaurant with the waiter nervously tripping along after her.

On emerging, she saw Harry. He was swaying next to the low wall by the slope, where they had stood last time.

She joined him. There was an empty glass on the wall.

"Doesn't look like we're meant to eat at this restaurant," she said. "Any suggestions?"

He shrugged and took a sip from his hip flask. "Bar at the Savoy. If you're not too hungry."

She pulled her coat around her more tightly. "I'm not that hungry, actually. What about showing me around a bit? This is your stomping ground, and I've got a car. You could show me the bunkers where you used to spend your time."

"Cold and ugly," Harry said. "Stink of piss and wet ash."

"We could smoke," she said. "And admire the view. Have you got anything better to do?"

A cruise ship, lit up like a Christmas tree, glided slowly and soundlessly through the dark to the town on the fjord beneath them. They were sitting on wet concrete on top of a bunker, but neither Harry nor Kaja felt the cold creeping into their bodies. Kaja sipped at the hip flask Harry had passed her.

"Red wine in a hip flask?" she said.

"That was all that was left in Dad's cabinet. Just emergency supplies anyway. Favorite male actor?"

"Your turn to start," she said, taking a longer swig.

"Robert De Niro."

She made a face. "**Analyze This? Meet the Fockers?**"

"I swore eternal allegiance after **Taxi Driver** and **The Deer Hunter.** But, yes, it has been at some cost. What about you?"

"John Malkovich."

"Mm. Good. Why?"

She deliberated. "I think it's the cultivated evil. Not something I like as a human quality, but I love the way he reveals it."

"And then he has a feminine mouth."

"Is that good?"

"Yep. All the best actors have feminine mouths. And/or a high-pitched feminine voice. Kevin Spacey, Philip Seymour Hoffman." Harry took a cigarette from the pack and offered her one.

"Only if you light it for me," she said. "Those boys are not exactly overmasculine."

"Mickey Rourke. Woman's voice. Woman's mouth. James Woods. Kissable mouth, like an obscene rose."

"But not a high-pitched voice."

"Bleating voice. Sheep. Ewe."

Kaja laughed and took the lit cigarette. "Come on. Macho men in films have deep, hoarse voices. Take Bruce Willis, for example."

"Yes, take Bruce Willis. Hoarse fits. But deep? Hardly." Harry scrunched up his eyes and whispered in falsetto, facing the town: " 'From up here it doesn't look like you're in charge of jack shit.' "

Kaja burst out laughing; the cigarette shot from her mouth and bounced down the wall and into the thick shrubs, sending off sparks.

"Bad?"

"Sensationally bad," she gasped. "Damn, now you've made me forget the macho actor with the feminine voice I was going to say."

Harry rolled his shoulders. "You'll think of it."

"Even and I also used to have a place like this,"

Kaja said, taking another cigarette and holding it between thumb and forefinger as if it were a nail she was going to hammer in. "Somewhere for ourselves we thought no one else knew, where we could hide and tell each other secrets."

"Feel like telling me about it?"

"About what?"

"Your brother. What happened?"

"He died."

"I know. I thought you would tell me the rest."

"And what is the rest?"

"Well, why have you canonized him, for example."

"Have I?"

"Haven't you?"

Her searching gaze lingered on him. "Wine," she said.

Harry passed her the hip flask and she took a greedy swig.

"He left a note," she said. "Even was so sensitive and vulnerable. At times he could be all smiles and laughter; it was like he brought the sunshine when he arrived. If you had any problems, they seemed to evaporate when he appeared, like . . . erm, like dew in the sun. And in the black periods it was the opposite. Everything went quiet around him; a brooding tragedy seemed to hang in the air and you could hear it in his silence. Music in a minor key. Beautiful and terrible at once—do you understand? And yet, some of the sunshine seemed to have been stored in his eyes, because they continued to laugh. It was eerie."

She shivered.

"It was during summer vacation, a sunny day, the kind only Even could make. We were at our summer house in Tjøme, and I had gotten up and gone straight to the shop to buy strawberries. When I returned breakfast was ready, and Mommy called up to the first floor for Even to come down. But he didn't answer. We assumed he was sleeping—now and then he slept really late. I went up to fetch something from my room and tapped on his door and called out, 'Strawberries,' as I passed. I was still listening for a response when I opened the door to my room. When you go into your own room, you don't look around—you just look for whatever it is you want, the bedside table where you know your book is, the windowsill or the box of fishing lures. I didn't see him right away, only noticed that something about the light was not as it should have been. Then I glanced to the side and at first saw only his bare feet. I knew every inch of his feet—he used to pay me a krone to tickle them; he loved that. My first thought was that he was flying, at last he had learned to fly. My gaze continued upward; he was wearing the pale-blue sweater I had knitted for him. He had hanged himself from the lamp with an extension cord. He must have waited until I'd gone out, and then come into my room. I wanted to run, but I couldn't move—my legs were rooted to the floor. So I stood there staring at him, and he was so close, and I called my mother—I did all the things that should have produced a shout, but not a sound would come out of my mouth."

Kaja bent her head and flicked her cigarette. Took a tremulous breath.

"I can remember only fragments of the rest. They gave me medicine to calm me down. When I recovered, three days later, they had already buried him. They said it was just as well I wasn't there, that the strain might have been too great. I fell ill right afterward and was in bed with a fever for long periods over the summer. I've always thought it was a little too hurried, the funeral, as if there were something shameful about the way he had died. You know what I mean?"

"Mm. You said he had written a note?"

Kaja gazed across the fjord. "It was on my bedside table. He wrote that he had fallen in love with a girl he could never have, he didn't want to live anymore and asked for forgiveness for all the pain he was inflicting on us, and that he knew we loved him."

"Mm."

"That came as quite a surprise. Even had never told me there was a girl, and he used to tell me most things. Had it not been for Roar—"

"Roar?"

"Yes. I had my first boyfriend that summer. He was so nice and patient, visited me almost every day when I was ill and listened to me talking about Even."

"About what an immeasurably wonderful person he had been."

"You've got it."

Harry shrugged. "I did the same when my mother died. Øystein wasn't as patient as Roar. He asked me straight out if I was founding a new religion."

Kaja giggled and sucked on her cigarette. "I think Roar eventually felt that the memory of Even was smothering all life as he knew it, including himself. It was a brief relationship."

"Mm. But Even was still there."

She nodded. "Behind every single door I opened."

"That's why, isn't it?"

She nodded again. "When I came home from the hospital that summer and had to go to my bedroom, I couldn't open the door. I simply couldn't. Because I knew that if I did, he would be hanging there again. And it would be my fault."

"It's always our fault, isn't it?"

"Always."

"And no one can persuade us that it isn't—not even **we** can do that." Harry stubbed out his cigarette in the dark. Lit another.

The cruise ship beneath them had slid into the quay.

A gust of wind whistled through the gun slits, making a hollow, gloomy sound.

"Why are you crying?" he asked softly.

"Because it **is** my fault," she whispered with tears rolling down her cheeks. "Everything is my fault. You've known all along, haven't you?"

Harry inhaled. Took out the cigarette and blew on the glow. "Not all along."

"Since when?"

"Since I saw Bjørn Holm's face in the doorway on Holmenveien. Bjørn Holm is a good forensics officer, but no De Niro. And he was genuinely surprised."

"Was that all?"

"It was enough. I knew from his expression that he had no idea I was on to Leike. Therefore he had not seen anything on my computer, and he had not passed it on to Bellman. And if Holm wasn't the mole, there was only one other person it could have been."

She nodded and dried her tears. "Why didn't you say anything? Why didn't you do anything? Why didn't you behead me?"

"What would have been the point? I assumed you had a good reason."

She shook her head and let the tears flow.

"I don't know what he promised you," Harry said. "I would guess a leading position in the new, all-powerful Kripos. And I was right when I said that the guy you were hung up on was married and told you he would leave his wife and kids for your sake, but he never would."

She sobbed quietly, her neck bent as though it had become too heavy. Like a rain-burdened flower, Harry thought.

"What I don't understand is why you wanted to meet me this evening," he said, giving his cigarette a disapproving look. Perhaps he should change brands. "I thought at first it was because you wanted to tell me you were the mole, but I soon realized it wasn't. Are we waiting for someone? Is something going to happen? I mean, I've been sidelined—what harm can I do to them now?"

She looked at her watch. Sniffled. "Can we go back to your place, Harry?"

"Why? Is someone waiting for us there?"

She nodded.

Harry drained his hip flask.

The door had been broken down. The splinters of wood on the floor suggested it had been levered open with a crowbar. Nothing refined, no attempt to be discreet. Police break-in.

Harry turned on the steps and looked at Kaja, who had gotten out of the car and stood with crossed arms. Then he went inside.

The living room was dark; the only light came from the liquor cabinet, which was open. But it was enough for him to recognize the person sitting in shadow by the window.

"Bellman," Harry said. "You're sitting in my father's armchair."

"I took the liberty," Bellman said. "Since the sofa had a particular smell. Even the dog shied away."

"May I offer you something?" Harry nodded toward the cabinet and sat down on the sofa. "Or did you find something for yourself?"

Harry could discern Bellman shaking his head. "Not me. But the dog did."

"Mm. I take it that you have a search warrant, but I am curious about the grounds given."

"An anonymous tip-off about you having smuggled drugs into the country via an innocent third party and the possibility that it was here."

"And it was?"

"The sniffer dogs found something, a ball of some yellowish-brown substance wrapped in silver foil. Doesn't look like the usual sort of thing we confiscate in this country, so for the moment it's not clear what we're dealing with. But we're considering having it analyzed."

"Considering?"

"It **might** be opium, or it **might** be a lump of plasticine or clay. It depends."

"Depends on what?"

"On you, Harry. And me."

"Really?"

"If you agree to do us a favor, I might tend to the view that it is plasticine and overlook any tests. A boss has to prioritize his resources, isn't that so?"

"You're the boss. What sort of favor?"

"You're a man who doesn't like beating around the bush, Hole, so let me give it to you straight. I want you to take on the role of scapegoat."

Harry saw a brown ring of Jim Beam at the bottom of the bottle on the table but resisted the temptation to put it to his lips.

"We've just had to release Tony Leike, as he has watertight alibis for at least two of the murders. All we have on him is a phone call to one of the victims. We've been a bit forceful with the press. Together with Leike and his future father-in-law, they could make things uncomfortable for us. We'll have to issue a press release tonight. And it will say that the arrest was undertaken on the basis of the blue chit you, the controversial Harry Hole, wheedled out of the poor sylphlike prosecutor at Police HQ. And that this was a solo operation that you, and you alone, organized, and you shoulder all of the responsibility. Kripos smelled a rat after the arrest, intervened and, in conversation with Leike, clarified the facts. And immediately released him. You will have to join us and sign the press release, and you will never make a statement about the investigation again, not a word. Understood?"

Harry contemplated the dregs in the bottle a second time. "Mm. A tough order. Do you think the press will swallow the story after you were standing with your hands raised, taking the credit for the arrest?"

"I assumed responsibility, the press release will say. I saw fronting the arrest as a management responsibility, even though we had misgivings that a policeman might have committed a blunder. But when Harry Hole later insisted on being allowed to take his place at the front, I didn't stand in his way because he was an experienced inspector and didn't even work for Kripos."

"And my motivation is that if I don't sign I will be charged with drug smuggling and possession?"

Bellman pressed his fingertips together and rocked back in the chair.

"Correct. But more important for your motivation is perhaps the fact that I can see to it that you're held on remand, effective immediately. Shame, since I know you would have liked to be at the hospital with your father, who, I understand, has little time left. Very sad business."

Harry leaned back against the sofa. He knew he ought to have been angry. The old—the younger—Harry would have been. But what this Harry wanted most was to bury himself in the sweat-and-vomit-stained sofa, close his eyes and hope they would get lost, Bellman, Kaja, the shadows by the window. But his brain continued its automatic acquired reasoning.

"Quite apart from me," he heard himself say, "why would Leike bear out this version? He knows it was Kripos who arrested him, who questioned him."

Harry knew the answer before Bellman spelled it out.

"Because Leike knows that there will always be an unpleasant shadow hanging over someone who has been arrested. Especially unpleasant for someone such as Leike, who at this moment is trying to win the trust of investors, of course. The best way to rid himself of this shadow is to endorse a version that maintains the arrest was due to a loose cannon, an isolated unprofessional element in the police force who ran amok. Agreed?"

Harry nodded.

"Anyway, as far as the force is concerned—"

"I am protecting the name of the entire force by assuming all the guilt," Harry said.

Bellman smiled. "I've always held you to be a relatively intelligent man, Hole. Does that mean we have reached an understanding?"

Harry considered. If Bellman went now he could see whether there really were a few drops of whiskey left in the bottle. He nodded.

"Here's the press release. I want your name there." Bellman pushed pen and paper across the coffee table. It was too dark to read. That didn't matter. Harry signed.

"Good," said Bellman, taking the piece of paper and getting up. The light from a street lamp outside fell onto his face, causing the war paint to shine. "This is best for all of us. Think about it, Harry. And get some rest."

The victor's merciful attentions, Harry thought, closing his eyes and feeling Morpheus welcome him into his arms. Then he opened his eyes again, struggled to his feet and followed Bellman down the steps. Kaja was still standing, with arms crossed, beside her car.

Harry saw Bellman send a nod of acknowledgment to Kaja, who responded with a shrug of the shoulders. Watched him cross the street, get into a car, the same one he had seen on Lyder Sagens Gate that evening, watched him start the engine and drive off. Kaja had come to the foot of the steps. Her voice was still thick with tears.

"Why did you hit Bjørn Holm?"

Harry turned to go in, but she was faster, taking two steps at a time. She came between him and the door and blocked the way. Her breathing was accelerated and hot against his face.

"You hit him when you knew he was innocent. Why?"

"Go now, Kaja."

"I'm not going!"

Harry looked at her. Knowing it was something he could not explain. How much it had hurt and surprised him when he realized the ramifications. Hurt him enough to make him lash out, punch the astonished, innocent moon-shaped face, the very reflection of his own gullible naïveté.

"What do you want to know?" he asked and heard the metallic tone, the fury creeping into his voice. "I really believed in you, Kaja. So I should congratulate you. Congratulate you on a job well done. Can you go away now?"

He saw the tears well up in her eyes again. Then she stepped aside, and he staggered in and slammed the door behind him. Remained in the hall in the soundless vacuum after the bang, in the good silence, the void, the wonderful nothingness.

47

Fear of the Dark

Olav Hole blinked into the darkness.

"Is that you, Harry?"

"Yes, it's me."

"It's night, isn't it?"

"Yes, it's night."

"How are you?"

"I'm alive."

"Let me put on the light."

"No need. I'm going to tell you something."

"I recognize the tone. I'm not sure I want to hear."

"You'll read about it in the papers tomorrow anyway."

"And you have a different version you want to tell me?"

"No, I just want to be first."

"Have you been drinking, Harry?"

"Do you want to hear?"

"Your grandfather drank. I loved him. Drunk or sober. There are not many people who can say that about a drunken father. No, I don't want to hear."

"Mm."

"And I can say that to you, too. I have loved you. Always. Drunk or sober. You weren't even difficult. Although you were always argumentative. You were at war with most people, not least with yourself. But loving you, Harry, is the easiest thing I have done."

"Dad—"

"There's no time to talk about trivia, Harry. I don't know if I've ever told you this, Harry; I feel as if I have, but sometimes we think things so often that we simply believe they have been said aloud. I've always been proud of you, Harry. Have I told you that often enough?"

"I—"

"Yes?" Olav Hole listened in the dark. "Are you crying, son? That's fine. Do you know what made me proudest? I've never told you this, but when you were in your teens one of your teachers called us. He said you'd been fighting in the playground again. With two of the boys from the grade above, but this time it hadn't turned out so well—they'd had to send you to the hospital to have your lip sewn and a tooth taken out. I stopped your allowance, remember? Anyway, Øystein told me about the fight later. You flew at them because they'd filled Tresko's knapsack with water from the school fountain. If I remember correctly, you didn't even like Tresko much. Øystein said the reason you'd been hurt so badly was that you didn't give in. You got up time after time and in the end you were bleeding so much that the big boys became alarmed and went on their way."

Olav Hole laughed quietly. "I didn't think I could tell you at the time—it would only have been asking for more fights—but I was so proud I could have wept. You were brave, Harry. You were scared of the dark, but that didn't stop you going there. And I was the world's proudest dad. Did I ever say that, Harry? Harry? Are you there?"

Free. The Champagne bottle smashes against the wall, and the bubbles run down the wallpaper like boiling cerebral matter, over the pictures, the newspaper clippings, the printout off the Net showing Harry Hole accepting the blame. Free. Free of blame, free to send the world into hell again. I tread on the broken glass, tread it into the floor, hear it crunch. And I'm barefoot. I skid on my own blood. Laughing until I howl. Free. Free!

Hypothesis

Neil McCormack, the head of the crime division, Sydney South, ran a hand through his thinning mop of hair while studying the bespectacled woman across the table in the interview room. She had come straight from the publishing house where she worked. Her suit was plain and creased, but there was nevertheless something about Iska Peller that made him presume it was expensive, wasn't just meant to impress simple souls like himself. However, her address suggested that she was not particularly well off. Bristol was not the most fashionable area of Sydney. She seemed adult and sensible. Definitely not the type to dramatize, exaggerate, attract attention for attention's sake. Besides, they were the ones who had called her in; she hadn't come to the Sydney Police of her own accord. He looked at his watch. McCormack had arranged to go sailing with his son this afternoon; they were due to meet in Watsons Bay, where the boat was moored. That's why he hoped this wouldn't take long. And everything had been fine until the last snippet of information.

"Miss Peller," McCormack said, leaning back and folding his hands over his impressive potbelly, "why didn't you tell anyone about this before?"

She hunched her shoulders. "Why should I? No one asked, and I can't see that it has any relevance to Charlotte's murder. I'm telling you now because you've asked me in such detail. I thought what happened in the cabin was what you were interested in, not the kind of . . . incident that took place afterward. And that was what it was. A tiny incident, soon over, soon forgotten. You find idiots like him everywhere. As an individual you can't take on the task of reporting every single creep."

McCormack growled. Of course she was right. And he didn't feel like following up on the matter, either. There was always so much more trouble, unpleasantness and, not least, work when the person in question had a professional handle that either started or finished with the word **police.** He gazed out of the window. The sun was glittering on the sea by Port Jackson and on the Manly side, where smoke was still rising despite the fact that it had been a week since the season's last bush fire had been extinguished. The smoke was drifting south. A fine, warm northerly. Perfect for sailing. McCormack had liked Hole. Or "Holy," as he called the Norwegian. He had done a brilliant job when he'd helped them with the clown murder. But the lofty, fair-haired Norwegian had sounded weary on the phone. McCormack genuinely hoped that Holy wasn't going to keel over again.

"Let's take it from the start, shall we, Miss Peller?"

. . .

Mikael Bellman entered the Odin conference room and heard the conversations stop at once. He strode over to the speaker's chair, put down his notes, connected his laptop to the USB port and stood in the middle of the floor with his legs anchored. The investigation unit numbered thirty-six officers, three times what was normal for murder cases. They had been working for so long without results that he had had to boost morale a couple of times, but, generally speaking, they had stuck to it like heroes. That was why Bellman had allowed not only himself but his staff to enjoy what had seemed like their great triumph: the arrest of Tony Leike.

"You will have read the papers today," he opened, surveying the assembly.

He had saved their hides. The front pages of two of the three biggest newspapers bore the same photograph: Tony Leike getting into a car outside Police HQ. The third had a picture of Harry Hole, an archive photo from a talk show where he had been discussing the Snowman.

"As you can see, Inspector Hole has assumed responsibility. Which is only right and proper."

His words bounced back to him off the walls, and he met the silent officers' morning-weary gazes. Or was it a different kind of tiredness? In which case, it would have to be confronted. Because things were coming to a head now. The Kripos boss had dropped by to say that the Ministry of Justice had called and was asking questions. The sands of time were running out.

"We don't have a prime suspect anymore," he said. "But the good news is we have fresh leads. And they all take us from the Håvass cabin to Ustaoset."

He went to the laptop and tapped a key, and the first page of a PowerPoint presentation he had prepared came to life.

Half an hour later he had been through all the facts they possessed, with names, times and assumed routes.

"The question," he said, switching off the computer, "is what kind of murders we are dealing with here. I think we can exclude the typical serial killer. The victims have not been chosen at random inside a demographic group; they are tied to a specific place and a specific time. Accordingly, there is reason to believe that we are also talking about a specific motive that may even be perceived as rational. If so, that makes the task considerably easier for us: find the motive and we have the killer."

Bellman saw several detectives nod.

"The problem is that there are no witnesses to tell us anything. The only one we know to be alive, Iska Peller, was ill in bed, alone. The others either are dead or have not come forward. We know, for example, that Adele Vetlesen was with a man she had met recently, but no one in her circle of acquaintances seems to know anything about him, so we have to assume it was a short-lived relationship. We're looking at the men she contacted by phone or on the Net, but it will take time to work our way through them. And in the absence of witnesses we will have to find our own starting point. We need hypotheses for the motive. What is the motive for killing at least four people?"

"Jealousy or hearing voices," someone from the back replied.

"All our experience tells us that."

"Agreed. Who might hear voices commanding them to kill?"

"Anyone with a psychiatric record," came a singsong response from Finnmark.

"And anyone without one," said someone else.

"Good. Who might be jealous?"

"Partner or spouse of someone there."

"And who might that be?"

"But we've checked the victims' partners' alibis and potential motives," another said. "That's the first thing we do. And either they didn't have partners or we eliminated them from our inquiries."

Mikael Bellman knew all too well they were just putting their foot on the accelerator while the wheels spun around in the same rut they had been in for a while, but the important point now was that they were ready to do exactly that: accelerate. For he was in no doubt that the Håvass cabin was a plank that could be levered under the wheel to get them out of the rut.

"We didn't eliminate **all** the partners and spouses," Bellman said, rocking on his heels. "We just didn't think every one was a suspect. Who didn't have an alibi for the time his wife was killed?"

"Rasmus Olsen!"

"Correct. And when I went to Stortinget and spoke to Rasmus Olsen he admitted that there had been what he called a little 'jealous patch' some months ago. A woman Rasmus had been flirting with. And Marit Olsen went to the Håvass cabin for a couple of days to think things over. The days may match. Perhaps she did more than think. Perhaps she paid him back in kind. And here's a thought. On the night in question, when the victims were at the Håvass cabin, Rasmus Olsen was not in Oslo; he was booked into a hotel in Ustaoset. What was Rasmus doing in the area if his wife was in Håvass? And did he spend the night in the hotel or did he go for a longish ski trip?"

The eyes in front of him were no longer heavy-lidded or tired—quite the opposite; he was igniting a spark in them. He waited for an answer. Working in such a large investigative group was not normally the most efficient way to do this kind of improvised brainstorming, but they had worked on the case for so long that all the participants had had their opinions, their surefire hunches and fanciful hypotheses rejected and their egos flattened.

A young detective attempted a punt. "He may have arrived at the cabin in the evening unannounced and caught her in the act. The guy saw and sneaked off again. Then planned the whole thing at his leisure."

"Maybe," Bellman said, going over to the speaker's chair and holding up a note. "Argument one in favor of such a theory: I've just been given this by Telenor. It shows that Rasmus Olsen spoke to his wife on the phone sometime that morning. So let's assume he knew which cabin she was going to. Argument two in favor of this hypothesis is the weather report, which shows there was a moon and clear visibility all evening and night, so he could easily have skied there, as Tony Leike did. Argument one against the hypothesis: Why kill anyone apart from his wife and her alleged partner?"

"Maybe she had more than one," shouted one of the female detectives, a short, buxom number Bellman had figured was sufficiently lesbian for him to have toyed with the idea of inviting her to Kaja's one night. No more than a passing thought, of course. "Perhaps there was a whole fucking orgy going on up there."

Laughter all around. Good—that lightened the atmosphere.

"He may not have seen who she was having sex with, didn't even know if it was a woman or a man, just that someone was under the covers with her," another voice said. "And so he hedged his bets."

More laughter.

"Come on—we can't waste time on this garbage," said Eskildsen, a veteran, though no one knew exactly how long he had been a detective. The room fell silent. "Any of you young 'uns remember the case they solved at Crime Squad a few years back, when everyone thought there was a serial killer on the loose?" Eskildsen continued. "When they got the killer it turned out he only had a motive for murdering number three. But because he knew he would come under suspicion if she was the only victim, he killed the others to camouflage it as an insane rampage."

"Jesus Christ," shouted a young officer. "Did the Crime Squad actually manage to solve a case? Must have been a fluke."

The young man looked around with a grin, and his face slowly colored as no response was forthcoming. Everyone with any investigative experience at all remembered the case. It was on the syllabus of all police colleges throughout Scandinavia. It was a legend. As indeed was the man who'd cracked it.

"Harry Hole."

"G'day, Holy, mate. Neil McCormack here. How are you? And where are you?"

McCormack thought he heard Harry answer, "In a coma," but assumed he must have been saying the name of some Norwegian town.

"I talked to Iska Peller. She didn't have a lot to say about the night at the cabin. However, the following evening—"

"Yes?"

"She and her friend Charlotte were picked up from the cabin by a cop from the outback and taken to his place. Turned out that while Miss Peller was trying to sleep off her flu, the policeman and her friend were having a glass of grog in the sitting room, and he tried to seduce Charlotte. Got pretty physical, so physical that she shouted for help, Miss Peller woke up, and she rushed into the room, where the policeman had already pulled her friend's ski pants down to her knees. He stopped, and Miss Peller and her friend decided to go to the train station and stay at a hotel somewhere . . . I'm afraid I can't—"

"Geilo."

"Thank you."

"You say 'tried to seduce,' Neil, but you mean **rape,** I suppose?"

"No, I had to do the rounds with Miss Peller before we landed on a precise formulation. She said her friend's description was that the policeman had pulled down her trousers against her will, but he hadn't touched her intimate parts."

"But—"

"We can perhaps assume it was his intention, but we don't know. The point is that nothing punishable by law had happened yet. Miss Peller accepted that. After all, they hadn't bothered to report the matter— they just skedaddled. The cop had even found a village wacko to run all three of them to the station and he had helped them board the train. According to Miss Peller, the man seemed relatively unfazed by the whole business; he was more interested in getting Charlotte's phone number than apologizing. As if it were just perfectly normal bloke-meets-Sheila stuff."

"Mm. Anything else?"

"No, Harry. Except that we've given her police protection, as you suggested. Twenty-four-hour service, tucker and necessities brought to the door. She can just enjoy the sun. If the sun shines in Bristol, that is."

"Thanks, Neil. If anything—"

"Should crop up, I'll ring. And vice versa."

"Of course. Take care."

Says you, McCormack thought, hanging up and peering out at the blue afternoon sky. The days were a bit longer now in the summer—he could still get in an hour and a half's sailing before it was dark.

Harry got out of bed and went for a shower. Stood motionless, letting the boiling-hot water run down his body for twenty minutes. Then he came out, dried his sensitive, red-flecked skin and dressed. Saw from his cell phone that he had received eighteen calls while he had been asleep. So they had managed to get hold of his number. He recognized the first numbers as those of Norway's three biggest newspapers and the two most important TV channels, since they all had switchboard numbers beginning with the same prefixes. The remainder were more arbitrary and probably belonged to comment-hungry journalists. But his gaze paused at one of the numbers, although he couldn't say why. Because there were some bytes up in his brain that had fun memorizing numbers, perhaps. Or because the dialing code told him it was Stavanger. He flicked back through his call log and found the number from three days earlier. Colbjørnsen.

Harry called back and squeezed the phone between cheek and shoulder as he tied his boots and noted that it was time he bought some new ones. The iron plate in the sole, so that you could tread on nails without worrying, was hanging off.

"Fucking shit, Harry. They really hung you out to dry in the papers today. They butchered you. What does your boss say?"

Colbjørnsen sounded ill from overindulgence. Or just ill.

"I don't know," Harry said. "I haven't spoken to him."

"Crime Squad comes out OK. It's you personally carrying the entire can. Did your boss make you take one for the team?"

"No."

The question came after a long silence. "It wasn't . . . it wasn't Bellman, was it?"

"What do you want, Colbjørnsen?"

"Shit, Harry. I've been running a somewhat illegal solo investigation, just like you. So first of all I have to know whether we're still on the same team or not."

"I haven't got a team, Colbjørnsen."

"Great—I can hear you're still on our team. The losers."

"I'm on my way out."

"Right. I had another chat with Stine Ølberg, the girl Elias Skog was so taken by."

"Yes?"

"It transpires that Skog told her more about what went on in the cabin that night than I had understood at the first interview."

"I've started to believe in second interviews," Harry said.

"Eh?"

"Nothing. Come on—out with it."

49

Bombay Garden

Bombay Garden was the kind of restaurant that did not appear to have the right to keep going, but, unlike its trendier competitors, it had managed to survive year after year. Its location in the center of east Oslo was dire, down a side street between a timber warehouse and a disused factory that was now a theater. The liquor license had come and gone after countless breaches of the rules; the same was also true for its license to serve food. The health inspectors had on one occasion found a species of rodent in the kitchen they had not been able to identify, beyond declaring it had a certain similarity to **Rattus norvegicus.** In the comments box of the report the inspector had let rip and described the kitchen as a "crime scene" where "murders of the foulest kind had unquestionably taken place." The slot machines along the walls brought in quite a bit of money, but were regularly vandalized and robbed. The Vietnamese owners did not use the place to launder drug money, as some suspected, though. The reason Bombay Garden could keep its head above water was to be found at the back, behind two closed doors. Concealed there was a so-called private club, and to be allowed in you had to apply for membership. In practice, that meant you filled out an application at the bar of the restaurant, membership was granted on the spot and you paid a hundred kroner as an annual fee. Afterward you were escorted in and the door was locked behind you.

Then you stood in a smoke-filled room—since smoking laws do not pertain to private clubs—and in front of you there was a miniature oval racecourse, thirteen by six and a half feet. The course itself was covered with green felt and had seven tracks. Seven flat metal horses, each attached to a pin, moved forward in spasmodic jerks. The speed of each horse was determined by a computer that hummed and buzzed under the table, and was—as far as anyone had ascertained—completely arbitrary and legitimate. That is, the computer program gave some of the horses a greater chance of a higher speed, which was reflected in the odds and thus any eventual payout. Around the racecourse sat the club members—some were regulars, others were new faces—in comfortable leather swivel chairs, smoking, drinking the restaurant's beer at membership prices, cheering on their horse or the combination they had backed.

Since the club operated in a legal gray area with respect to gambling laws, the rules were that if twelve or more members were present, the stake was restricted to a hundred kroner per member, per race. If there were fewer than twelve, the club's regulations stipulated it was regarded as a limited gathering, and at small private gatherings you could not prevent adults from making private wagers. How much they chose to bet was up to the participants. For this reason, it was conspicuous how often precisely eleven people could be counted in the back room of the Bombay Garden. And where the garden came into the picture, no one knew.

At ten past two in the afternoon a man with the club's most recent membership, forty seconds old, to be precise, was admitted into the room, where he soon established that the only people there, apart from himself, were one member sitting in a swivel chair with his back to him and a man of presumably Vietnamese origin who was clearly administering the races and stakes; at any rate, he was wearing the kind of waistcoat croupiers do.

The back in the swivel chair was broad and filled out the flannel shirt. Black curls hung down onto the collar.

"Are you winning, Krongli?" Harry asked, sitting in the chair beside him.

The man's head of curls twisted around. "Harry!" he shouted, with genuine pleasure in his voice and on his face. "How did you find me?"

"Why do you think I'm looking for you? Perhaps I'm a regular here."

Krongli laughed as he watched the horses jerking down the long stretch, each with a tin jockey on its back. "No, you aren't. I come here whenever I'm in Oslo, and I've never seen you."

"OK. Someone told me I'd probably find you here."

"Hell, have I got a reputation? Perhaps it's not quite appropriate for a policeman to come here, even though it's on the right side of the law."

"Regarding right side of the law," Harry said, shaking his head to the croupier, who had pointed to the beer tap with a raised eyebrow. "There was something I wanted to talk to you about."

"Fire away," Krongli said, concentrating on the racecourse, where the blue horse on the far track was in the lead, but heading toward a wide outside bend.

"Iska Peller, the Australian woman you gave a lift to from the Håvass cabin, says you groped her friend, Charlotte Lolles."

Harry didn't detect any change in Krongli's concentrated expression. He waited. At length, Krongli looked up.

"Do you want me to react?"

"Only if you want to," Harry said.

"I interpret that as **you** would like me to. **Groped** is the wrong word. We flirted a bit. Kissed. I wanted to go further. She thought it was enough. I attempted a little constructive persuasion, what women often expect of a man—after all, that's part of the role play between the sexes. But nothing more than that."

"That doesn't match what Iska Peller says Charlotte told her. Do you think Peller's lying?"

"No."

"No?"

"But I do think Charlotte wanted to give a slightly different version to her friend. Catholic girls like to appear more virtuous than they are, don't they?"

"They decided to spend the night in Geilo rather than at your house. Even though Peller was ill."

"She was the one who insisted on leaving. I don't know what was going on between those two—friendship between girls is often a complicated business. And it's my bet the Peller girl doesn't have a boyfriend." He lifted the half-empty glass in front of him. "Where are you going with this, Harry?"

"It's a little strange you didn't say anything to Kaja Solness about meeting Charlotte Lolles when Kaja was in Ustaoset."

"And it's a little strange you're still working on this case. Thought it was a Kripos matter, especially after the newspaper headlines today." Krongli's attention was back on the horses. Out of the bend came the yellow horse on the third track, leading by a tin horse's length.

"Yes," Harry said. "But rape cases are still a Crime Squad matter."

"Rape? Haven't you sobered up yet, Harry?"

"Well." Harry pulled a pack of cigarettes from his trouser pocket. "I'm more sober than I hope you were, Krongli." He stuffed a crumpled cigarette between his lips. "All the times you beat up and raped your ex up there in Ustaoset."

Krongli turned slowly to Harry, knocking over his beer glass with his elbow. The beer was soaked up by the green felt; the stain advanced like the Wehrmacht over a map of Europe.

"I've just come from the school where she works," Harry continued, lighting the cigarette. "She was the one who told me I'd probably find you here. She also told me that when she left you and Ustaoset, she was escaping rather than moving out. You—"

Harry got no further. Krongli was fast, spun his chair around with his foot and was on Harry before he could react. Harry felt the grip around his hand, knew what was coming, knew because this was what they practiced from the first year at police college: the police power half nelson. And yet he was a second too late, two days' drinking too sluggish, forty years too stupid. Krongli twisted his wrist and arm behind his back and pushed his temple forward into the felt. The side of his damaged jaw; Harry screamed with pain and blacked out for a second. Then he was back in the pain and made a frenetic attempt to free himself. Harry was strong, always had been, but immediately knew he had no hope against Krongli. The powerfully built officer's breath was hot and moist against his face.

"You shouldn't have done that, Harry. You shouldn't have spoken to the whore. She says whatever comes into her head. Does whatever comes into her head. Did she show you her cunt? Did she, Harry?"

There was a crunch inside Harry's head as Krongli increased the pressure. A yellow and then a green horse banged against Harry's forehead and nose respectively as he brought up his right foot and stamped. Hard. Krongli screamed, then Harry twisted out of the half nelson, turned and struck. Not with his fist—he had destroyed enough bones with that nonsense—but with his elbow. It hit Krongli where Harry had learned the effect was greatest—not on the point of the chin, but slightly to the side. Krongli staggered backward, fell over a low swivel chair and landed on the floor with his feet pointing north. Harry noticed that the material of the Converse shoe on Krongli's right foot was torn and bloodstained after its meeting with an iron plate under a boot that definitely should have been thrown away. He also noticed that his cigarette was still hanging from his lips. And—out of the corner of his eye—that the red horse in the first track rode in as the clear winner.

Harry bent down, grabbed Krongli's collar, pulled him up and dumped him in the chair. Took a deep drag, felt it burn and warm his lungs.

"I agree this rape case of mine doesn't have a lot going for it," he said. "At least since neither Charlotte Lolles nor your wife reported you. That's why, as a detective, I have to try to dig a little deeper. And that's why I come back to the Håvass cabin."

"What the hell are you talking about?" Krongli sounded as if he had caught a bad chill.

"There's this girl in Stavanger who Elias Skog confided in the same evening he was murdered. They were on a bus and Elias told her about the night at Håvass when he'd witnessed what he subsequently thought might have been a rape."

"Elias?"

"Elias, yes. I suppose he must have been a light sleeper. He was woken in the night by sounds outside the bedroom window and looked out. The moon was up and he saw two people in the shadow under the ridge of the outhouse roof. The woman was facing him, with the man behind her, hiding his face. Elias's impression was that they were screwing, the woman seeming to perform a belly dance and the man with his hand over her mouth, obviously so that they wouldn't disturb anyone. And when the man had dragged her into the outhouse, Elias—disappointed not to see a full live show—had gone back to bed. It was only when he read about the murders that he'd started to wonder. Perhaps the woman had been wriggling to get away. The hand over her mouth might have been to suffocate calls for help." Harry took another drag. "Was it you, Krongli? Were you there?"

Krongli rubbed his chin.

"Alibi?" Harry asked airily.

"I was at home, in bed, alone. Did Elias Skog say who the woman was?"

"No. Nor the man, as I said."

"It wasn't me. And you're living dangerously, Hole."

"Shall I take that as a threat or a compliment?"

Krongli didn't answer. But there was a gleam in his eyes, yellow and cold.

Harry stubbed out his cigarette and got up. "By the way, your ex didn't show me anything. We were in the staff room. Something tells me she's afraid of being alone with a man in a room. So you achieved something, didn't you, Krongli."

"Don't forget to look over your shoulder, Hole."

Harry turned. The croupier appeared completely

unruffled by the scene and had already set up the horses for another race.

"Wan' a bet?" he asked in pidgin Norwegian, smiling.

Harry shook his head. "Sorry—got nothing to bet with."

"All the more to win," the croupier said.

Harry allowed that to sink in and concluded that either it was a linguistic error or his logic didn't carry that far. Or it was just another terrible Oriental proverb.

50

Corruption

Mikael Bellman waited.

This was the best. The seconds waiting for her to open up. Wondering with excitement whether—and yet at the same time sure—she would again exceed his expectations. For every time he saw her he realized that he had forgotten how beautiful she was. Every time the door opened, it was as if he needed a moment to assimilate all her beauty. To let the confirmation sink in. Confirmation that from the selection of men who wanted her—in practice, any heterosexual man with good eyesight—she had chosen him. Confirmation that he was the leader of the pack, the alpha male, the male with the first claim to mate with the females. Yes, it could be articulated in such banal and vulgar terms. Being an alpha male was not something you aspired to; you were born to it. Not necessarily the easiest or the most comfortable life for a man, but if you were called, you could not resist.

The door opened.

She was wearing the white high-necked sweater and had put her hair up. She looked tired; her eyes had less sparkle than usual. And still she had the elegance, the class, of which even his wife could only dream. She said, "Hi," told him she was sitting on the veranda, turned her back on him and walked through the house. He followed, collecting a beer from the fridge, and sat down in one of the ridiculously large, heavy chairs on the veranda.

"Why do you sit outside?" he said. "You'll catch pneumonia."

"Or lung cancer," she said, hoisting the half-smoked cigarette from the edge of the ashtray and picking up the book she was reading. He skimmed the cover. **Ham on Rye.** Charles . . . he squinted . . . Bukowski? As in the Swedish auction rooms?

"I've got good news," he said. "We've not only averted a minor catastrophe, we've turned the whole Leike incident to our advantage. The Ministry of Justice phoned today." Bellman put his feet on the table and studied the label on the beer bottle. "They wanted to thank me for intervening with such resolution and ensuring Leike was released. They were very worried about what Galtung and his pack of lawyers might have done if Kripos hadn't acted so quickly. And they wanted a personal assurance that I would have my hands on the wheel and no one outside Kripos would have the opportunity to foul things up."

He put the bottle to his mouth and drank. Banged it down hard on the table. "What do you think, Bukowski?"

She lowered her book and met his eyes.

"You should show a little interest," he said. "This concerns you as well, you know. What do you think about the case, my love? Come on. You're a murder investigator."

"Mikael—"

"Tony Leike is a violent criminal, and we allowed ourselves to be duped by that. Because we know you can't rehabilitate violent criminals. The ability and the desire to kill are not granted to all; it's innate or acquired. But when the killer is in you, it's damned difficult to get it out again. Perhaps the killer in this case knows we know that? Knows that if he served us up Tony Leike, we would go into a frenzy and all cheer in unison, 'Hey, the case is cracked—it's the guy with the violent streak!' And that was why he broke into Tony Leike's house and called Elias Skog. To stop us searching for any of the others who were in Håvass."

"The call from Leike's house was before anyone outside the police knew that we had found the link with the Håvass cabin."

"So what? He must have figured that it was only a matter of time before we stumbled on it. Damn, we should have found it long before!" Bellman grabbed the bottle again.

"So who is the killer?"

"The eighth guest in the cabin," Mikael Bellman said. "The boyfriend Adele Vetlesen took along, but whom no one knows."

"No one?"

"I've had more than thirty officers on the job. We've combed Adele's flat. Nothing in writing. No diaries, no cards, no letters, barely any emails or texts. Those male acquaintances whom we have identified have been questioned and eliminated. Also the female ones. And none of them thinks it strange that she changed partners as frequently as panties and did it without telling anyone. The only thing we have found out is that Adele was supposed to have said to a girlfriend that this cabin escort had a couple of what she termed 'turn-ons' and 'turn-offs.' The turn-on was that he had asked her to go to a nighttime rendezvous at an empty factory dressed as a nurse."

"If that was the turn-on, I dread to think what the turn-off was."

"The turn-off was apparently that when he spoke he reminded Adele of her flat mate. The girlfriend didn't have a clue what Adele meant by that."

"The flat mate isn't a mate in the biological sense." Kaja yawned. "Geir Bruun is gay. If this eighth guest tried to shift the murders onto Tony Leike he must have known Leike had a criminal record."

"The assault conviction is information that's open to the public. Also the location—in Ytre Enebakk municipality. Leike was on the way to becoming a murderer while living with his grandfather by Lake Lyseren. If you wanted to direct police suspicions toward Leike, where would you dump Adele Vetlesen's body? In a place where the police could find a link to him and a conviction on his record, of course. That was why he chose Lake Lyseren." Mikael Bellman paused. "Tell me—am I boring you?"

"No."

"You look so bored."

"I . . . I have a lot to think about."

"When did you start smoking? So, I have a plan for how to find the eighth guest."

Kaja stared at him.

Bellman sighed. "Aren't you going to ask me how, darling?"

"How?"

"By using the same strategy as he does."

"Which is?"

"Focusing on an innocent person."

"Isn't that the strategy you always use?"

Mikael Bellman looked up sharply. Something was beginning to dawn on him. Something about being an alpha male.

He explained the plan to her. Told her how he would entice the man out.

Afterward, he was shaking from cold and anger. He didn't know what made him angrier: the fact that she didn't respond with either a negative or a positive comment, or that she sat there smoking, to all outward signs completely untouched by the case. Didn't she understand that his career, his moves, in these very critical days would be decisive for her future as well? If she couldn't count on being the next Fru Bellman, she could at least rise through the ranks under his auspices, provided that she was loyal and continued to deliver. Or perhaps his anger was a result of the question she had asked. It had been about him. The other one. The old, doddery alpha male.

She had asked about opium. Asked if he really would have used it, had Hole not ceded to his demand that he accept the responsibility for Leike's arrest.

"Of course," Bellman said, trying to see her face, but it was too dark. "Why shouldn't I have? He smuggled drugs."

"I'm not thinking of him. I'm thinking of whether you would have brought discredit on the police force."

He shook his head. "We can't let ourselves be corrupted by that sort of consideration."

Her laughter sounded dry as it met the dense night cold. "You indisputably corrupted him."

"He's corruptible," Bellman said, draining the bottle in one swig. "That's the difference between him and me. Now, Kaja, are you trying to tell me something?"

She opened her mouth. Wanted to say it. Should have said it. But at that moment his cell rang. She saw him clutch his pocket as he did what he usually did, formed his lips into a pout. Which did not signify a kiss, but that she should shut up. In case it was his wife, his boss or anyone else he didn't want to know that he came here to fuck a Crime Squad officer who gave him all the information he needed to outmaneuver the unit competing with him over murder investigations. To hell with Mikael Bellman. To hell with Kaja Solness. And above all to hell with . . .

"He's gone," Mikael Bellman said, putting the phone back in his pocket.

"Who?"

"Tony Leike."

51

Letter

Hi Tony,

You've been wondering who I could be for a long time now. So long that I think it may be time I revealed my hand. I was at the cabin in Håvass that night, but you didn't see me. No one saw me—I was as invisible as a ghost. But you know me. Know me all too well. And now I'm coming to get you. The only person who can stop me now is you. Everyone else is dead. There's just you and me left, Tony. Is your heart beating a little faster now? Does your hand grope for a knife? Do you slash blindly through the dark, dizzy with terror that your life will be taken from you?

52

Visit

Something had woken him. A sound. There were hardly any sounds out here, none he didn't know anyway, and those didn't wake him. He got up, placed the soles of his feet on the cold floor and peered through the window. His terrain. Some called it a deserted wasteland, whatever that meant. Because it was never deserted here; there was always something. Like now. An animal? Or could it be him? The ghost? There was something outside—that was for certain. He looked at the door. It was locked and bolted on the inside. The rifle was in the storehouse. He shivered in the thick red flannel shirt he wore both day and night up here. The sitting room was so empty. It was so empty out there. So empty in the world. But it wasn't deserted. There were the two of them, the two of them who were left.

Harry was dreaming. About an elevator with teeth, about a woman with a cocktail stick between

cochineal-red lips, a clown with his smiling head
under his arm, a bride dressed in white at the altar
with a snowman, a star drawn in the dust of a TV
screen, a one-armed girl on a diving board in
Bangkok, the sweet smell of urinal blocks, the outline
of a human body on the inside of a blue plastic water
bed, a compressor drill and blood spurting into his
face, hot and deathly. Alcohol had acted as a cross,
garlic and holy water against ghosts, but tonight
there had been a full moon and a virgin's blood, and
now they came swarming from the darkest corners
and deepest graves and tossed him between them in
their dance, fiercer and wilder than ever, to the cardiac rhythms of mortal fear and the incessant shrill
fire alarm here in hell. Then there was sudden silence.
Complete silence. It was here again. It filled his
mouth. He couldn't breathe. It was cold and pitch
black and he was unable to move, he . . .

Harry twitched and blinked in the darkness,
dazed. An echo reverberated between the walls. An
echo of what? He grabbed his revolver from the bedside table, placed the soles of his feet on the cold floor
and went downstairs, into the living room. Empty.
The empty liquor cabinet was still lit. There had been
a solitary bottle of Martell Cognac. His dad had
always been careful with alcohol—he knew what
genes he was carrying—and the Cognac was for
guests. There had not been many guests. The dusty,
half-full bottle had disappeared in the tidal wave with
Captain Jim Beam and Able Seaman Harry Hole.
Harry sat down in the armchair, stuck his finger

through the tear on the armrest. He closed his eyes and visualized himself filling a glass halfway. The deep gurgles from the bottle, the sparkling golden-brown liquid. The smell, the quiver as he put the glass to his mouth and he felt his body fighting it, panic-stricken. Then he emptied the contents down his throat.

It was like a blow to the temple.

Harry opened his eyes wide. It had gone all quiet again.

And just as suddenly it was there again.

It bored its way along his auditory canals. The fire alarm in hell. The same one that had woken him. The doorbell. Harry looked at his watch. Half past twelve.

He went into the hall, switched on the outside light, saw an outline through the wavy glass, held the revolver in his right hand while grabbing the lock with his left thumb and forefinger and tore the door wide open.

In the moonlight he could see ski tracks crossing the drive. They were not his. And ghosts didn't leave trails, did they?

They went around the house, to the back.

At that moment it struck him that the bedroom window was open. He should have . . . He held his breath. Someone seemed to be breathing with him. Not someone, something. An animal.

He turned. Opened his mouth. His heart had stopped beating. How could it have moved so quickly, without making a sound, how could it have gotten so . . . close?

Kaja stared at him.

"May I come in?" she asked.

She was wearing an oversize raincoat, her hair was sticking up in all directions, her face was pale and drawn. He blinked hard a couple of times to check he wasn't still dreaming. She had never been more beautiful.

Harry tried to vomit as quietly as he could. He hadn't tasted booze for more than a day, and his stomach was a sensitive creature of habits that rebelled against sudden bouts of drinking and sudden abstinence. He flushed, carefully drank a glass of water and returned to the kitchen. The kettle was making rumbling sounds on the stove and Kaja was sitting on one of the kitchen chairs, looking up at him.

"So Tony Leike's gone," he said.

She nodded. "Mikael had given instructions that he was to be contacted. But no one could find him; he wasn't at home or in his office, and he hadn't left any messages. No Leike on any airline or ferry passenger lists for the last twenty-four hours. Eventually a detective managed to contact Lene Galtung. She believes he may have gone into the mountains. To think. Apparently he does that. If so, he must have caught the train, because the car's still in the garage."

"Ustaoset," Harry said. "He said that was his terrain."

"Anyway, he definitely hasn't gone to a hotel."

"Mm."

"They think he's in danger."

"They?"

"Bellman. Kripos."

"I thought that was 'we.' And why would Bellman want to contact Tony Leike, anyway?"

She closed her eyes. "Mikael has concocted a plan. To lure the killer out."

"Oh?"

"The killer's trying to remove everyone who was at the Håvass cabin that night. So Michael wanted to try to persuade Leike to be the decoy in a setup. Get Leike to go for an interview with a newspaper, talk about the tough time he's been through and how he was going to relax on his own at a particular place to be revealed in the paper."

"Where Kripos would set a trap."

"Yes."

"But now the plan's up the creek, and that's why you're here?"

She gazed at him without blinking. "We have one person left we can use as a decoy."

"Iska Peller? She's in Australia."

"And Bellman knows she's under police protection, and you've been in contact with her and someone named McCormack. Bellman wants you to persuade her to come here."

"Why should I agree?"

She looked down at her hands. "You know. Same coercion tactics as last time."

"Mm. When did you discover there was opium in the cigarette carton?"

"When I was putting the carton on the shelf in my bedroom. You're right—it has a strong smell. And I remembered the smell from your hostel. I opened the carton and saw the seal on the bottom packet had been broken. And found the clump inside. I told Mikael. He told me to hand over the carton whenever you asked."

"Perhaps that made it easier for you to betray me. Knowing I had used you."

She slowly shook her head. "No, Harry. It didn't make it easier. Perhaps it should have, but—"

"But?"

She shrugged. "Passing on this message is the last favor I do for Mikael."

"Oh?"

"Then I'm going to tell him I won't see him anymore."

The kettle's rumbling noises stopped.

"I should have done this a long time ago," she said. "I have no intention of asking you to forgive me for what I've done, Harry—that's too much to ask. But I thought I would tell you face to face so that you can understand. That's actually why I've come to see you now. To tell you that I did it out of stupid, stupid love. Love corrupted me. And I didn't think I was corruptible." She put her head in her hands. "I deceived you, Harry. I don't know what to say. Except that deceiving myself feels even worse."

"We're all corruptible," Harry said. "We just demand different prices. And different currencies. Yours is love. Mine is self-medicating. And do you know what?"

The kettle sang again, this time an octave higher.

"I think it makes you a better person than me. Coffee?"

He spun right around and stared at the figure. It was standing straight in front of him, unmoving, as if it had been there a long time, as if it were his shadow. It was so quiet; all he could hear was his own breathing. Then he sensed a movement, something being lifted in the dark, heard a low whistle through the air, and at that moment a strange thought struck him. The figure was just that, his very own shadow. He . . .

The thought appeared to falter, time was dislocated, the visual connection was broken for a second.

He stared before him in amazement and felt a hot bead of sweat run down his forehead. He spoke, but the words were meaningless; there was a fault in the connection between brain and mouth. Again he heard a low whistle. Then the sound was gone. All sound—he couldn't even hear his own breathing. And he discovered that he was kneeling and that the telephone was on the floor beside him. Ahead, a white stripe of moonlight ran across the coarse floorboards, but it vanished when the sweat reached the bridge of his nose, ran into his eyes and blinded him. And he understood it was not sweat.

The third blow felt like an icicle being driven through his head and throat and into his body. Everything froze.

I don't want to die, he thought, and tried to raise a protective arm over his head, but he was unable to move a single limb, and realized he was paralyzed.

He didn't register the fourth blow, but from the wood smell he concluded he was lying facedown on the floor. He blinked several times and sight returned to one eye. Directly in front of him he saw a pair of ski boots. And slowly sounds returned: his heaving gasps, the other's calm breathing, the blood dripping from his nose onto the floorboards. The other's voice was a mere whisper, but the words seemed to be screamed into his ear: "Now there's only one of us."

As the clock struck two they were still sitting in the kitchen talking.

"The eighth guest," Harry said, pouring more coffee. "Close your eyes. How does he appear to you? Quick, don't think."

"He's full of hatred," Kaja said. "Angry. Out of balance, nasty. The kind of guy women like Adele run into, check out and reject. He's got piles of pornographic magazines and films at home."

"What makes you think that?"

"I don't know. His asking Adele to go to an empty factory dressed in a nurse's uniform."

"Go on."

"He's effeminate."

"In what way?"

"Well, high-pitched voice. Adele said he reminded her of her gay flat mate when he spoke." She drew her cup to her mouth and smiled. "Or perhaps he's a film actor. With a squeaky voice and a pout. I still can't remember the name of the macho actor with the feminine voice."

Harry held up his cup in a toast. "And the things I told you about Elias Skog and the late-night incident outside the cabin. Who were they? Had he witnessed a rape?"

"It wasn't Marit Olsen, anyway," Kaja said.

"Mm. Why not?"

"Because she was the only fat woman there, so Elias Skog would have recognized her and used her name when describing the scene."

"Same conclusion I came to. But was it rape, you think?"

"Sounds like it. He put his hand over her mouth, stifled her cries, pulled her inside the outhouse—what else could it have been?"

"But why didn't Elias Skog automatically think it was rape?"

"I don't know. Because there was something about the way . . . the way they were standing, their body language."

"Exactly. The subconscious understands much more than the conscious mind. He was so sure it was consensual sex that he simply went back to bed. It wasn't until long after, reading about the murders and being reminded of a half-forgotten scene, that he had formed the idea it might have been rape."

"A game," Kaja said. "That might smack of rape. Who does that? Not a man and a woman who have just met at a cabin and sneak out to become a little better acquainted. You have to be a bit more comfortable with each other."

"So it's two people who've been together before," Harry said. "Which to our knowledge can only be . . ."

"Adele and the mystery man. The eighth guest."

"Either that or someone else turned up that night." Harry flicked ash off the cigarette.

"Where's the bathroom?" Kaja asked.

"Through the hall to the left."

He watched the cigarette smoke curl upward into the lamp shade over the table. Waited. He hadn't heard the door open. He got up and went after her.

She was standing in the hall staring at the door. In the dim light he could see her taking gulps of air, could see a moist pointed tooth glistening. He placed a hand on her back and even there, through her clothes, he could feel her heart beating. "Do you mind if I open it?"

"You must think I'm mental," she said.

"We all are. I'm opening it now, OK?"

She nodded, and he opened the door.

Harry was sitting at the kitchen table when she returned. She had put on her raincoat.

"Think I'll have to go home now."

Harry nodded and accompanied her to the front door. Watched as she stooped to pull on her boots.

"It only happens when I'm tired," she said. "The door stuff."

"I know," Harry said. "I'm the same with elevators."

"Oh?"

"Yes."

"Tell me more."

"Another time, maybe. Who knows—perhaps we'll see each other again."

She fell quiet. Took a long time to zip up her boots. Then, all of a sudden, she stood up, so close to him that he was aware of her scent following her, like an echo.

"Tell me now," she said with a wild expression in her eyes he was unable to interpret.

"Well," he said, his fingertips tingling, as if he had been cold and was warming up again. "When we were young my little sister had very long hair. We had been visiting my mother in the hospital and were about to get into the elevator. Dad was waiting downstairs—he couldn't stand hospitals. Sis stood too near to the gap and her hair got caught between the elevator and the wall. And I was so horror-stricken that I couldn't move. I watched Sis being dragged up by her hair."

"What happened?" she asked.

They were standing a bit too close, he thought. They were standing at the limits of their personal space. And they knew. He took a breath.

"She lost a lot of hair. It grew back. I . . . lost something else. Which didn't grow back."

"You think you failed her."

"It's a fact that I failed her."

"How old were you?"

"Old enough to fail her." He smiled. "Think that's almost enough self-pity for one night, don't you? My father liked you curtsying."

Kaja chuckled. "Good night." She curtsied.

He opened the front door for her. "Good night."

She moved onto the steps and turned.

"Harry?"

"Yes?"

"Weren't you lonely in Hong Kong?"

"Lonely?"

"I watched you while you were asleep. You looked so . . . alone."

"Yes," he said. "I was lonely. Good night."

They stood there half a second too long. Five tenths of a second before and she would have been down the steps and he would have been on his way back to the kitchen.

Her fingers closed around his neck and pulled his head down as she hoisted herself up on tiptoes. Her eyes lost focus, became a glittering sea and then she shut them. Her lips were half open as they met his. She held him and he didn't move, just felt the sweet dagger in his stomach, like a rush of morphine.

She let go of him.

"Sleep well, Harry."

He nodded.

She turned and walked away. He closed the door quietly behind him.

He cleared away the cups, rinsed the kettle and had just put it away when the doorbell rang.

He went to answer it.

"I forgot something," she said.

"What was that?" he asked.

She lifted her hand and stroked his brow. "What you look like."

He pulled her close. Her skin. The scent. He fell, a wonderful dizzying spiral downward.

"I want you," she whispered. "I want to make love to you."

"And I want you, too."

They let go. Looked at each other. A sudden formality seemed to come between them, and for a moment it appeared to him that she had regrets. That he also had regrets. It was too much, too quickly. There were too many other things, there was too much baggage, too many good reasons. Nonetheless she took his hand, timid almost, whispered, "Come on," and led him up the stairs.

The bedroom was cold and smelled of parents. He switched on the light.

The spacious double bed was made with two duvets and pillows.

Harry helped her to change the bed linens.

"Which side is his?" she asked.

"This one." Harry pointed.

"And he continued to sleep there after she was gone," she said, as if to herself. "Just in case."

They undressed without peeking. Crept under the duvets and met there.

At first they lay close to each other, kissing, exploring, careful not to ruin anything before they knew how it would be. Listened to each other's breathing and the odd isolated car rushing by. Then their kisses became greedier, their touching bolder, and he heard the excited hiss of her breath against his ear.

"Are you frightened?" he asked.

"No," she groaned, grabbing hold of his erection, adjusting her hips and guiding him in, but he moved her hand and did it himself.

There was barely a sound, only a gasp as he penetrated her. He closed his eyes, lay still, enjoying the sensations. Then he began to move slowly, carefully. Opened his eyes, met hers. She seemed on the verge of tears.

"Kiss me," she whispered.

Her tongue coiled around his, smooth underneath, rough on top. Faster and deeper, slower and deeper. She rolled him over without letting go of his tongue and sat astride him. She pressed against his stomach every time she came down on him. Then her tongue released his, and she leaned back and let out a moan. Twice, a deep animal noise that rose, and became high-pitched as she gasped for air and went quiet again. Her throat was thick with the scream that didn't come. He raised his hand, placed his fingers against the quivering blue artery under the skin on her neck.

And then she screamed, as if in pain, in anger, in

liberation. Harry felt his scrotum tighten and came. It was perfect, so unbearably perfect that he threw his hand in the air and banged the wall behind him with his fist. And, as though she had been given a lethal injection, she collapsed on top of him.

They lay like this, limbs strewn randomly, like the dead. Harry felt the blood rush in his ears and well-being surge through his body. That and something he could have sworn was happiness.

He slept and was woken by her getting back into bed and snuggling up close to him. She was wearing one of Olav's undershirts. She kissed him, mumbled something and was gone, her breathing light and serene. Harry stared at the ceiling. Letting his thoughts churn, knowing there was no point resisting.

It had been so good. It hadn't been so good since . . . since . . .

The blind wasn't pulled down and at half past five cones of light from passing cars began to travel across the ceiling as Oslo woke and dragged itself off to work. He looked at her again. And then he was gone, too.

53

Heel Hook

When Harry woke it was nine o'clock, the room was bathed in daylight and there was no one lying beside him. There were four messages on his phone.

The first was from Kaja, saying she was on her way home to get changed for work. And thanking him for . . . he couldn't hear what, just a shriek of laughter before she hung up.

The second was from Gunnar Hagen, who was wondering why Harry had not answered any of his calls and saying the press were on his back because of Tony Leike's unjustified arrest.

The third was from Günther, who repeated the **Dirty Harry** witticism and said the Leipzig police had not found Juliana Verni's passport and therefore could not confirm whether it had been stamped in Kigali or not.

The fourth was from Mikael Bellman, who simply told Harry to be at Kripos by two. He assumed Solness had passed on his instructions.

Harry got up. He felt good. Better than good. Fantastic, maybe. He listened to his body. OK—fantastic was an exaggeration.

Harry went downstairs, took out a packet of crispbreads and made the important phone call first.

"You're talking to Søs Hole." It was Søs, or Sis, as Harry called her. Her voice sounded so formal he had to smile.

"And you're talking to Harry Hole," he said.

"Harry!" She screamed his name two more times.

"Hi, Sis."

"Dad said you were home! Why haven't you called before?"

"I wasn't ready, Sis. Now I am. Are you?"

"I'm always ready, Harry. You know that."

"Yes, I do. Lunch in town before visiting Dad sometime soon? My treat."

"Yes! You sound happy, Harry. Is it Rakel? Have you been speaking to her? I spoke to her yesterday. What was that sound? Harry?"

"Just the crispbreads falling out of the packet onto the floor. What did she want?"

"To ask about Dad. She'd heard he's ill."

"Was that all?"

"Yes. No. She said Oleg was fine."

Harry swallowed. "Good. Let's talk soon, then."

"Don't forget. I'm so happy you're home, Harry! I have so much to tell you!"

Harry put the phone on the countertop and was bending down to pick up the crispbreads when the phone hummed again. Sis was like that, remembering things she should have said after they had hung up. He straightened up.

"What is it?"

Sonorous clearing of throat. Then a voice introduced itself as Abel. The name was familiar, and

Harry instantly ransacked his memory. There were the files of old murder cases, neatly organized with data that never seemed to be deleted: names, faces, house numbers, dates, sound of a voice, color and year of a car. But he could suddenly forget the name of neighbors who had lived in his building for three years or when Oleg's birthday was. They called that the detective memory.

Harry listened without interrupting.

"I see," he said at length. "Thank you for calling."

He hung up and tapped in a new number.

"Kripos," answered a weary receptionist. "You are trying to get through to Mikael Bellman."

"Yes. Hole from Crime Squad. Where's Bellman?"

The receptionist informed him of the POB's whereabouts.

"Logical," Harry said.

"I beg your pardon." She yawned audibly.

"That's what he's doing, isn't it?"

Harry slipped the phone into his pocket. Stared out of the kitchen window. Crispbread crunched under his feet as he walked.

SKØYEN CLIMBING CLUB it said on the glass door facing the parking lot. Harry pushed the door and entered. On his way in, he had to wait for a class of excited schoolchildren on their way out. He flipped off his boots by a shoe rack at the bottom of the stairs. In the large hall, there were half a dozen people climbing up the thirty-foot walls, although they looked more like the artificial papier-mâché mountainsides of Tarzan films Harry and Øystein had seen at the Symra Cinema when they were kids. Except that these were peppered with multicolored holds and pegs with loops and carabiner hooks. A discreet smell of soap and sweaty feet emanated from the blue mats on the floor that Harry walked across. He stopped beside a bow-legged, squat man staring intently up at the overhang above them. A rope went from his climbing harness to a man who at that moment was swinging like a pendulum from one arm twenty-seven feet above them. At the end of one arc he swung up a foot, threaded the heel under a pink pear-shaped hold, put the other foot on a piece of the structure and clipped the climbing rope into the top anchor in one elegant sweeping movement.

"Gotcha!" he shouted, and leaned back on the rope and placed his legs against the wall.

"Great heel hook," Harry said. "Your boss is a bit of a poseur, isn't he?"

Jussi Kolkka neither answered nor graced Harry with a glance, just pulled the lever on the rope brake.

"Your receptionist told me you'd be here," Harry said to the man being lowered toward them.

"Regular slot every week," Bellman said. "One of the perks of being a policeman is being able to train during working hours. How are you, Harry? Muscles look defined, at any rate. Lots of muscle per pound, I reckon. Ideal for climbing, you know."

"For limited ambitions," Harry said.

Bellman landed with legs shoulder-width apart

and pulled down some rope so that he could slacken the figure-eight knot.

"I didn't understand that."

"I can't see the point of climbing so high. I clamber around a few crags now and then."

"Clambering," Bellman snorted, loosening the harness and stepping out of it. "You know, it hurts more to fall from six feet without a rope than it does from ninety feet with one?"

"Yes," Harry said, a smile tugging at his mouth. "I know."

Bellman sat down on one of the wooden benches, pulled off the ballet-shoe-like climbing slippers and rubbed his feet while Kolkka brought down the rope and started to gather it in a coil. "You got my message?"

"Yes."

"So what's the hurry? I'm seeing you at two."

"That was what I wanted to clarify with you, Bellman."

"Clarify?"

"Before we meet the others. Agreeing on the conditions for me to join the team."

"**The team?**" Bellman laughed. "What are you talking about, Harry?"

"Do you want me to spell it out for you? You don't need me to call Australia and persuade a woman to come here to act as a decoy—you can do that yourself without a problem. What you're asking for is **help**."

"Harry! Really now . . ."

"You look exhausted, Bellman. You've started to

feel it, haven't you? You've felt the pressure escalate since Marit Olsen." Harry sat down on the bench beside him. Even then, he was almost four inches taller. "Feeding frenzy in the press every fucking day. Impossible to walk past a newspaper stand or switch on the TV without being reminded of the Case. The Case you haven't solved. The Case your bosses are nagging you about all the time. The Case that requires a press conference a day, where the vultures scream questions into one another's beaks. And now the man you yourself released has vanished into the blue beyond. The vultures swarm in, some of them cackling in Swedish, Danish and even English. I've been where you are now, Bellman. Soon they'll be talking fucking French. For this is the Case you **have** to solve, Bellman. And the Case has gone stale."

Bellman didn't answer, but his jaw muscles were grinding. Kolkka had packed the rope in the sack and came toward them, but Bellman waved him away. The Finn turned and waddled toward the exit like an obedient terrier.

"What do you want, Harry?"

"I'm offering you the chance to get this sorted out one-on-one, instead of at a meeting."

"You want me to **ask** you for help?"

Harry saw Bellman's complexion redden.

"What sort of bargaining position do you imagine you're in, Harry?"

"Well, I imagine it's better than it has been for a while."

"You're mistaken there."

"Kaja Solness doesn't want to work for you. Bjørn Holm you've already promoted, and if you send him back to being a crime scene officer he'll be only too pleased. The only person you can hurt now is me, Bellman."

"Have you forgotten I can lock you up so that you can't visit your father before he dies?"

Harry shook his head. "There's no one to visit anymore, Bellman."

Mikael Bellman arched an eyebrow in surprise.

"They called from the hospital this morning," Harry said. "My father went into a coma last night. Dr. Abel says he won't come out of it. Whatever was left unsaid between my father and me will remain unsaid."

54

Tulip

Bellman looked at Harry in silence. That is, the brown deerlike eyes were directed toward Harry, but his gaze was inverted. Harry knew that a committee meeting was in progress there, a meeting with a lot of dissenting opinions, it seemed. Bellman slowly loosened the strings of the chalk bag hanging around his waist, as if to gain time. Time to think. Then he angrily stuffed the chalk bag in his knapsack.

"If—and only **if**—I asked you for help without having anything to pressure you with," he said, "why on earth would you do it?"

"I don't know."

Bellman stopped packing and looked up. "You don't know?"

"Well, it definitely wouldn't be out of love for you, Bellman." Harry breathed in. Fidgeted with a pack of cigarettes. "Let's say that even those who believe themselves to be homeless occasionally discover that they have a home. A place where you could imagine being buried one day. And do you know where I want to be buried, Bellman? In the park in front of Police HQ. Not because I love the police or have been a fan of what is known as esprit de corps. Quite the opposite—I spit on the police officer's craven loyalty to the force, that incestuous camaraderie that exists only because people think they may need a favor one rainy day. A colleague who can exact vengeance, testify or, if necessary, turn a blind eye for you—I hate all that."

Harry faced Bellman.

"But the police is all I have. It's my tribe. And my job is to clear up murders. Whether it is for Kripos or Crime Squad. Can you grasp something like that, Bellman?"

Mikael Bellman squeezed his lower lip between thumb and first finger.

Harry motioned to the wall. "What grade was the climb, Bellman? Seven plus?"

"Eight, minimum. On sight."

"That's tough. And I guess you think this is even tougher. But that's how it has to be."

Bellman cleared his throat. "Fine. Fine, Harry." He pulled the strings of his knapsack tight again. "Will you help us?"

Harry put his cigarettes back in his pocket and lowered his head.

"Of course."

"I'll have to check with your boss to see if it's all right first."

"Save yourself the effort," Harry said, getting up. "I've already informed him I'm working with your group from now on. See you at two."

Iska Peller peered out of the window of the two-story brick building, at the row of identical houses on the other side of the street. It could have been any street in any town in England, but it was the tiny district of Bristol in Sydney, Australia. A cool southerly had picked up. The afternoon heat would release its grip as soon as the sun went down.

She heard a dog bark and the heavy traffic on the highway two blocks away.

The man and woman in the car opposite had just been relieved; now there were two men. They drank slowly from their paper cups with lids. In their own good time, because there is no reason in the world to hurry when you have an eight-hour shift ahead of you and nothing at all is going to happen. Ratchet down a gear, slow the metabolism, do what the Aborigines do: go into that torpid, dormant state that is their diapause and where they can be for hours on end, days on end, if need be. She tried to visualize how these slow coffee drinkers could be of any help if anything **really** happened.

"I'm sorry," she said, trying to repress the tremble in her voice caused by suppressed fury. "I would have liked to help you find who killed Charlotte, but what you're suggesting is utterly out of the question." Then her anger gained the upper hand after all. "I can't believe you're even asking! I'm enough of a decoy here. Ten wild horses couldn't drag me back to Norway. You're the police, you get paid to catch that monster—why can't **you** be the bait?"

She hung up and threw down the phone. It hit the cushion on the armchair and one of her cats jumped up and darted into the kitchen. She hid her face in her hands and let the tears flow again. Dear Charlotte. Her dear, dear, beloved Charlotte.

She had never been afraid of the dark before, but now she thought of nothing else; soon the sun would go down and night would come. It was relentless, returning again and again.

The phone played the opening bars of an Antony and the Johnsons song, and the display lit up on the cushion. She walked over and eyed it. Felt the hairs on her neck rising. The caller's number started with 47. From Norway again.

She put the phone to her ear.

"Yeah?"

"Me again."

She sighed with relief. Just the policeman.

"I was wondering: If you don't want to come here in person, could we at least have the use of your name?"

Kaja studied the man held in the red-haired woman's embrace, her head bowed over his bared neck.

"What can you see?" Mikael asked. His voice echoed around the walls of the museum.

"She's kissing him," Kaja said, stepping back from the painting. "Or comforting him."

"She's biting him and sucking his blood," Mikael said.

"Why do you think that?"

"It's one of the reasons Munch called this **The Vampire.** Everything ready?"

"Yes, I'm taking the train to Ustaoset soon."

"Why did you want to meet here now?"

Kaja took a deep breath. "I wanted to tell you that we can't go on meeting."

Mikael Bellman rocked on his heels. "**Love and Pain.**"

"What?"

"That's what Munch originally called this painting. Did Harry go over the details of our plan with you?"

"Yes. Did you hear what I said?"

"Thank you, Solness—my hearing is excellent. Unless my memory is at fault, you've said that a couple of times before. I suggest you give it some thought."

"I've finished giving it some thought, Mikael."

He stroked the knot of his tie. "Have you slept with him?"

She gave a start. "Who?"

Bellman chuckled.

Kaja didn't turn around; she kept her eyes firmly fixed on the woman's face as his steps receded into the distance.

The light seeped through the gray steel blinds, and Harry warmed his hands around a white coffee cup with KRIPOS inscribed on it in blue letters. The conference room was identical to the one in Crime Squad, where he had spent so many hours of his life. Light, expensive and yet spartan in that cool modern way that is not intentionally minimalist, just somewhat soulless. A room that demands efficiency so that you can get the hell out of it.

The eight people there constituted what Bellman declared the inner core of the investigative unit. Harry knew only two of them: Bjørn Holm and a robust, down-to-earth but not very imaginative female detective known as the Pelican who had once worked at Crime Squad. Bellman had introduced Harry to everyone, including Ærdal, a man in horn-rimmed glasses and an off-the-rack brown suit that reminded one of East Germany. He sat at the far end of the table, cleaning his nails with a Swiss Army knife. Harry conjectured that he had a background in the military police. They had given their reports. Which all supported Harry's contention: that the case was in a rut. He noted the defensive attitude, particularly in the report on the search for Tony Leike. The officer responsible went through which passenger lists had been checked with which companies, to no avail, and which authorities in which telephone company had told them that none of their base stations had picked up signals from Leike's phone. He informed them that no hotels in town had anyone on their books under the name of Leike, but naturally the Captain (even Harry knew the self-appointed and overenthusiastic police informant–cum–receptionist at Hotel Bristol) called to say he had seen a person answering Tony Leike's description. The officer gave a report that went into an impressive level of detail, but failed to notice that what emerged was a defense of the result. **Zilch. Nada.**

Bellman sat at the head of the table with crossed legs and trouser creases that were still as sharp as a knife. He thanked the officers for their reports and made a more formal introduction of Harry by reading quickly from a kind of CV: graduation from police college, FBI course on serial killers in Chicago, the clown murder case in Sydney, promotion to inspector and of course the Snowman investigation.

"So Harry is a part of this team, effective today," Bellman said. "He reports to me."

"And is subject to only your orders as well?" the Pelican boomed. Harry recalled that what she was doing now was precisely what had given her the nickname, the way she pushed her chin forward, the long, beaklike nose and the protracted, thin neck as she peered over her glasses, skeptical and voracious at the same time, considering whether she wanted you on the menu or not.

"He is not subject to anyone's orders," Bellman said. "He has a free role in the team. We may consider Inspector Hole a consultant. Isn't that right, Harry?"

"Why not?" Harry said. "An overpaid, overrated guy who thinks he knows something you don't."

Cautious titters around the table. Harry exchanged glances with Bjørn Holm, who sent him a nod of encouragement.

"Except that in this instance he does," Mikael Bellman said. "You've been talking to Iska Peller, Harry."

"Yes," Harry said. "But first I'd like to hear more about your plan to use her as a decoy."

The Pelican cleared her throat. "It hasn't been formulated in detail. For the time being, our plan is to bring her to Norway, make it public that she's staying at a place where it's obvious to the killer that she would be easy prey. And then sit back and hope he swallows the bait."

"Mm," Harry said. "Simple."

"Experience tells us simplicity works," said the Swiss Army knife man in the East German suit, now concentrating on the nail of his right index finger.

"Agreed," Harry said. "But in this instance the decoy won't play ball."

Groans and sighs of despair.

"So I suggest we make it even simpler," Harry said.

"Iska Peller asked why, if we were paid to catch the monster, we couldn't be the bait ourselves."

He looked around the table. At least he had their attention. Convincing them would be harder.

"You see, we have an advantage over the killer. We assume he has the page torn from the Håvass guest book, so he has Iska Peller's name. But he doesn't know what she looks like. We're working on the assumption he was at the cabin that night, but Iska and Charlotte Lolles got there first. And Iska was ill and spent the evening alone in a bedroom she shared solely with Charlotte. She stayed there until all the others had left. In other words, we can set up a little role play with one of our own number acting the part of Iska, without the killer being any the wiser."

Another sweeping scan of the table. The skepticism on their faces was layers thick.

"And how had you envisaged getting someone to come to this performance?" Ærdal asked, snapping the knife shut.

"By Kripos doing what they do best," Harry said.

Silence.

"Which is?" asked the Pelican at length.

"Press conferences," Harry said.

The silence in the room was tangible. Until the laughter shattered it. Mikael Bellman's. They looked at their boss in astonishment. And realized that Harry Hole's plan had already been given the go-ahead.

"So . . ." Harry began.

After the meeting Harry took Bjørn Holm aside.

"Nose still sore?" Harry asked.

"Is that you trying to apologize?"

"No."

"I . . . well, you were lucky my nose didn't break, Harry."

"Could have been an improvement, you know."

"Are you apologizing or not?"

"Sorry, Bjørn."

"Great. And I suppose that means you want a favor?"

"Yes."

"And that is . . . ?"

"I was wondering if you've been to Drammen to check Adele's clothes for DNA. We think she met the guy from the cabin a few times."

"We've been through her wardrobe, but the problem is that the clothes have been washed, worn and probably been in contact with lots of other people afterward."

"Mm. She wasn't a skier, as far as I know. Did you check her skiing gear?"

"She didn't have any."

"What about the nurse's uniform? Perhaps it was only used once and may still have sperm stains on it."

"She didn't have that, either."

"No cheeky miniskirt and hat with a red cross?"

"Nope. There was a pair of light-blue hospital

trousers and top there, but nothing to get you going, exactly."

"Mm. Perhaps she couldn't get hold of the miniskirt variety. Or couldn't be bothered. Could you examine the hospital stuff for me?"

Holm sighed. "As I said, we went through all the clothes there, and whatever could be washed had been washed. Not so much as a stain or a hair."

"Could you take it to the lab? Give it a thorough check?"

"Harry—"

"Thanks, Bjørn. And I was only kidding—you've got a terrific schnoz. Really."

It was four o'clock when Harry fetched Sis in the Kripos car Bellman had placed at his disposal until further notice. They drove to Rikshospital and talked to Dr. Abel. Harry translated the parts Sis didn't understand, and she shed some tears. Then they went to see their father, who had been moved to another room. Sis squeezed Olav's hand and whispered his name again and again as if to rouse him gently from sleep.

Sigurd Altman popped by, put a hand on Harry's shoulder, not too long, and said a few words, not too many.

After dropping off Sis at her little flat by Lake Sognsvann, Harry drove downtown, where he kept going, twisting this way and that through one-way streets, road construction and dead ends. He drove through the red-light district, the shopping area and the drug zone, and it wasn't until he had emerged and the town lay beneath him that he was aware he had been on his way to the German bunkers. He called Øystein, who appeared ten minutes later, parked his taxi beside Harry's car, opened the door, turned up the music and came over and sat on the brick wall next to Harry.

"Coma," Harry said. "Not the worst thing that could happen, I suppose. Got a smoke?"

They sat listening to Joy Division. "Transmission." Ian Curtis. Øystein had always liked singers who died young.

"Shame I never got to talk to him after he fell ill," Øystein said, taking a deep drag.

"You wouldn't have, however long it had taken," Harry said.

"No, that'll have to be my consolation."

Harry laughed. Øystein sent him a sideways glance, smiled, unsure whether you were allowed to laugh when fathers lay on their deathbeds.

"What are you going to do now?" Øystein asked. "Go on a little binge? I can call Tresko and—"

"No," Harry said, stubbing out his cigarette. "I have to work."

"You'd prefer death and depravity to a glass or two?"

"You can drop by and say good-bye while he's still breathing, you know."

Øystein shivered. "Hospitals give me the creeps. Anyway, he can't hear jack shit, can he?"

"It wasn't him I was thinking about, Øystein."

Øystein screwed up his eyes against the smoke. "The little upbringing I had, Harry, I got from your father. D'you know that? My own dad wasn't worth a fucking fly's droppings. I'll go there tomorrow."

"Good for you."

He stared up at the man above him. Saw his mouth move, heard the words issuing forth, but something must have been damaged—he couldn't assemble them into anything sensible. All he understood was that the time had come. The revenge. That he would have to pay. And in a way it was a relief.

He was sitting on the floor with his back to the large, round wood stove. His arms were forced backward around the stove, his hands tied with two ski belts. He threw up from time to time, probably due to the concussion. The bleeding had stopped and sensation had returned to his body, but there was a mist over his vision that came and went. Nonetheless, he was not beset by doubt. The voice. It was a ghost's voice.

"You're going to die quite soon," it whispered. "As she did. But there is still something to gain. You see, you still have to choose how. Unfortunately, there are only two options. Leopold's apple . . ."

The man held up a metal ball perforated with

holes and a small loop of wire hanging from one of them.

"Three of the girls have tasted it. None of them liked it much. But it's pain-free and swift. And you only need to answer this: How? And who else knows? Who have you been working with? Believe me, the apple is preferable to the alternative. Which you, as an intelligent man, have probably worked out is . . ."

The man stood up, flailed his arms in an exaggerated manner, to keep warm, and put on a broad smile. The whisper was all there was to break the silence.

"It's a little cold in here, don't you think?"

Then he heard a scraping sound followed by a low hiss. He stared at the match. At the unwavering yellow tulip-shaped flame.

55

Turquoise

Evening came, a starry sky and bitingly cold.

Harry parked the car on the hill outside the Voksenkollen address he had been given. On a street consisting of large, expensive houses, this one stood out. The building was like something out of a fairy tale, a royal palace with black timbers, immense wooden pillars at the entrance and turf on the roof. In the garden there were two other buildings plus a Disney version of a Norwegian storehouse supported on pillars. Harry thought it unlikely that the shipowner Anders Galtung did not possess a big enough fridge.

Harry rang the doorbell, noticed a camera high up the wall and said his name when requested by a female voice. He walked up a floodlit gravel drive that sounded as if it were eating what was left of his boot soles.

A middle-aged woman with turquoise eyes and wearing an apron received him at the door and led him into an unoccupied living room. She did it with such an elegant mixture of dignity, superiority and professional friendliness that even after she had left Harry with a "Coffee or tea?" he was unsure whether this was Fru Galtung, a servant or both.

When foreign fairy tales came to Norway, kings and nobility did not exist, so in Norwegian versions the king was represented by a well-to-do farmer in ermine. And that was exactly what Harry saw when Anders Galtung came into the living room: a fat, smiling, gentle and somewhat sweaty farmer in a traditional Norwegian sweater. However, after a handshake, the smile was replaced by a concerned expression, more fitting for the occasion. His question—"Anything new?"—was followed by heavy breathing.

"Nothing, I'm afraid."

"Tony has a habit of disappearing, I understand from my daughter."

Harry thought he detected a certain reluctance to articulate the first name of his future son-in-law. The shipowner fell heavily into a rose-colored chair oppo-site Harry.

"Have you . . . any personal theories, Herr Gal-tung?"

"Theories?" Anders Galtung shook his head, mak-ing his jowls quiver. "I don't know him well enough to form theories. Gone to the mountains, gone to Africa—what do I know?"

"Mm. In fact, I came here to speak to your daughter—"

"Lene'll be right here," Galtung interrupted. "I just wanted to inquire first."

"Inquire about what?"

"About what I said, whether there was anything new. And . . . and whether the police are sure the man has a clear conscience."

Harry noticed that "Tony" had been exchanged for "the man" and knew his first instinct had not deceived him: The father-in-law was not enamored of his daughter's choice.

"Do you think he does, Galtung?"

"Me? I would have thought I was showing trust. After all, I am in the process of investing a consider-able sum in this Congo project of his. A very consid-erable sum."

"So a kid in rags knocks on the door and gets a princess plus half a kingdom, like in a fairy tale?"

There was a sudden silence, as Galtung eyed Harry.

"Maybe," he said.

"And maybe your daughter is exerting some pressure on you to invest. The venture is pretty dependent on finance, isn't it?"

Galtung opened his arms. "I'm a shipowner. Risk is what I live off."

"And could die of."

"Two sides of the same coin. In risk markets one man's loss is another man's gain. So far the others have lost, and I hope this trend will continue."

"Other people losing?"

"Shipowning is a family business, and if Leike is going to be family, we have to ensure . . ." He paused as the door opened. She was a tall, blond girl with her father's coarse features and her mother's turquoise eyes, but without her father's bluff farmer-made-good air or her mother's dignified superiority. She walked with a hunched bearing, as if to reduce her height, so as not to stand out, and she observed her shoes rather than Harry when she shook hands and introduced herself as Lene Gabrielle Galtung.

She didn't have a lot to say. And even less to ask. She seemed to cower under her father's gaze every time she answered Harry's questions, and Harry wondered whether his assumption that she had forced her father to invest might be wrong.

Twenty minutes later Harry expressed his gratitude, stood up and, right on invisible cue, there she was again, the woman with the turquoise eyes.

When she opened the front door for him, the cold surged in and Harry stopped to button up his coat. He looked at her.

"Where do you believe Tony Leike is, Fru Galtung?"

"I don't believe anything," she said.

Perhaps she answered too quickly, perhaps there was a twitch at the corner of her eye, perhaps it was just Harry's intense desire to find something, anything, but he was convinced she was telling the truth. The second thing she said did not allow any room for doubt.

"And I am not Fru Galtung. She is upstairs."

Mikael Bellman adjusted the microphone in front of him and surveyed the audience. There was a hushed whisper, but all eyes were directed toward the podium, fearful of missing anything. In the packed room he recognized the journalist from **Stavanger Aftenblad** and Roger Gjendem from **Aftenposten**. He could hear Ninni, who was wearing a freshly ironed uniform, as usual. Someone counted down the seconds to the start, which was normal for live broadcasts of press conferences.

"Welcome, ladies and gentlemen. We have called this press conference to give you an update on what we are doing. Any questions . . ."

Chuckles all around.

". . . will be answered at the end. I will pass the podium over now to the officer leading the investigation, POB Mikael Bellman."

Bellman cleared his throat. Full turnout. The TV channels had been given permission to place their microphones on the podium table.

"Thank you. Let me start by being a party pooper. I can see from the attendance and your faces that we may have ratcheted up your expectations a little too high in calling you here. There will be no announcement of a final breakthrough in the investigation." Bellman saw the disappointment on their faces and heard scattered groans. "We are here in order to fulfill the desire you expressed to be kept informed. I apologize if you had more important things planned for today."

Bellman gave a wry smile, heard a few journalists laugh and knew that he had already been forgiven.

Mikael Bellman gave them the gist of where the investigation stood. That is, he repeated their success stories, such as the rope being traced to a building by Lake Lyseren, finding another victim, Adele Vetlesen, and identifying the murder weapon used in two of the murders: a so-called Leopold's apple. Old news. He saw one of the journalists stifle a yawn. Mikael Bellman looked down at the papers in front of him. At the script. Because that was what it was, a script for a bit of theater, each and every word written down, weighed carefully, gone over. Not too much, not too little; the bait should smell, but it shouldn't stink.

"Finally, something about the witnesses," he began, and the press corps sat up in their chairs. "As you know, we have asked anyone who was at the Håvass cabin on the same night as the murder victims to come forward. And one person by the name of Iska Peller has come forward. She is arriving by plane from Sydney tonight, and she will proceed to the cabin with one of our detectives tomorrow. We will try to reconstruct the crime scene as faithfully as possible."

Normally, they would never have mentioned the name of the witness, but it was important here that the man they were addressing—the murderer—understand that they had indeed found someone from the guest book. Bellman had not laid special emphasis on the word "one" when he mentioned the detective, but that was the message. There would be just two people, the witness and an ordinary detective. In a cabin. Far from civilization.

"We hope, of course, that Miss Peller will be able to give us a description of the other guests present that night."

They had had a long discussion about the wording. They wanted to sow the seed that the witness could bring down the murderer. At the same time Harry thought it important that they not arouse too much suspicion with the witness being accompanied by only one detective, and that the pithy introduction "Finally, something about the witnesses" and the downplayed "We hope, of course" signal that the police did not consider this an important witness who would therefore require high-level protection. They hoped the killer would be of a different opinion.

"What do you think she may have seen? And can you spell the witness's name?"

This was the Rogaland journalist. Ninni leaned forward to remind them that questions would be at the end, but Mikael shook his head.

"We'll have to see what she remembers when she gets to the cabin," Bellman said, stretching toward the microphone labelled NRK. The state channel. Nationwide. "She will be going up there with one of our most experienced detectives and will be there for twenty-four hours."

He looked at Harry Hole standing at the back, saw him give a slow nod. He had driven the point home. Twenty-four hours. The bait was prepared and the trap set. Bellman let his gaze wander farther. It found the Pelican. She had been the only one to protest, to consider it scandalous that they were deliberately setting out to mislead the press. He had asked the group to take five and had talked to her privately. Afterward she had concurred with the majority view. Ninni opened the floor for questions. The assembly came to life, but Mikael Bellman relaxed and made ready to give vague answers, glib formulations and the ever-useful "I'm afraid we can't go into that at this phase of the investigation."

His legs were freezing, so frozen that they were completely numb. How could that be? When the rest of his body was burning? He had screamed so loud he had no voice left; his throat was dry, dried out, riven asunder, an open wound with blood singed to red dust. There was a smell of burned hair and flesh. The stove had seared through his flannel shirt into his back, and as he screamed and screamed they fused. He melted as if he were a tin soldier. Feeling that the pain and the heat had begun to eat into his consciousness and that he was finally slipping into oblivion, he awoke with a start. The man had poured a bucket of cold water over him. The sudden relief had caused him to cry again. Then he heard the hiss of boiling water between his back and the stove and the pain returned with renewed vigor.

"More water?"

He looked up. The man stood over him with another bucket. The mist before his eyes cleared, and for a couple of seconds he saw him with total clarity. The light from the flames through the holes in the stove flickered on his face, making the beads of sweat on his forehead glisten.

"It's very simple. All I need to know is who. Is it someone in the police? Is it one of those who were at Håvass that night?"

"Which night?" he sobbed.

"You know which night. They're almost all dead now. Come on."

"I don't know. I don't have anything to do with this—you have to believe me. Water. Please. Plea—"

"—se? Please as in . . . please?"

The smell. The smell of his body burning. The words he stuttered were no more than a hoarse whisper. "It w-was . . . just m-me."

Gentle laughter. "Smart. You're trying to make it sound like you would do anything to avoid the pain. So that I believe you when you can't cough up the name of your collaborator. But I know you can stand more. You're made of tougher stock."

"Charlotte—"

The man swung the poker. He didn't even feel the blow. Everything went black for one wonderfully long second. Then he was back in hell.

"She's dead!" the man yelled. "Come up with something better."

"I meant the other one," he said, trying to get his brain to work. He remembered now; he had a good memory—why was it failing him? Was he really in such bad shape? "She's Australian—"

"You're lying!"

He felt his eyes wander again. Another shower of water. A moment of clarity.

The voice. "Who? How?"

"Kill me! Mercy! I . . . you know I'm not protecting anyone. Lord Jesus, why should I?"

"I know nothing of the sort."

"So why not kill me? I killed her. Do you hear me? Do it. Revenge is thine."

The man put down the bucket, flopped into a chair, leaned forward with his elbows on the armrests and chin resting on his fists, and answered slowly, as though he hadn't heard what had been said, but was thinking about something else. "You know, I've dreamed about this for so many years. And now, now we're here . . . I had been hoping it would taste sweeter."

The man struck him with the poker one more time. Tilted his head and studied him. With a sour expression, probingly, he stabbed the poker into his ribs.

"Perhaps I lack imagination. Perhaps this justice lacks the appropriate spice?"

Something made the man turn. To the radio. It was on low. The man went over to it, turned up the volume. News. Voices in a large room. Something about the cabin in Håvass. A witness. Reconstruction. He froze; his legs were no longer there. He closed his eyes and again prayed to his god. Not to be liberated from the pain, as he had been doing until now. He prayed for forgiveness, for all his sins to be cleansed by the blood of Jesus, for someone else to bear all that he had done. He had taken a life. Yes, he had. He prayed that he would be bathed in the blood of forgiveness. And then be allowed to die.

Part Six

56

Decoy

A hell of lights. Even with sunglasses Harry's eyes smarted. The sun was shining on the snow, which was shining back at the sun; it was like looking into an ocean of diamonds, of frantically glittering lights. Harry retreated from the window, although he was aware that, seen from the outside, the panes were black, impenetrable mirrors. He checked his watch. They had arrived at Håvass the previous night. Jussi Kolkka had installed himself in the cabin with Harry and Kaja and the others had dug themselves into the snow in two groups of four at opposite ends of the valley, separated by about twenty miles.

There were three reasons for choosing to lay the bait at Håvass. First of all, because their being there made sense. Second, the killer would, they hoped, think he knew the area well enough to feel comfortable about an attack. Third, because it was a perfect trap. The dip where the cabin lay allowed entry from only the northeast and the south. In the east the mountain was too steep and in the west there were so many precipices and crevices that you had to know the terrain very well to make any progress at all.

Harry grabbed the binoculars and tried to spot the others, but all he could see was white. And lights. He had spoken to Mikael Bellman, who was south of him, and Milano, who was in the north. Usually they would have used their cell phones, but up here in the uninhabited mountains the only network that had coverage was Telenor. The former state-owned telephone monopoly had had the capital to build base stations on every wind-blown crag, but since several of the policemen, including Harry, subscribed to other companies, they were using walkie-talkies. So that they could get hold of him in case anything happened at Rikshospital, Harry had left a message on his voice mail before he left, saying that he would have no network coverage, and had given Milano's Telenor number.

Bellman claimed they hadn't been cold during the night, that the combination of sleeping bags, heat-reflecting ground pads and paraffin stoves was so efficient that they'd had to take off clothing. And that now-melted water was dripping from the ceiling of the snow caves they had scraped out from the side of the mountain.

The press conference had been so well covered on TV and radio and in the newspapers that you would have had to be absolutely indifferent to the case not to know that Iska Peller and a police officer had gone to Håvass. Every now and then Kolkka and Kaja went out and pointed to the cabin, the way they had come and the outhouse, Kaja in her role as Iska, Kolkka as the lone detective helping her to reconstruct the events of the fateful night. Harry hid in the sitting room, where he kept his skis and ski poles, so that only the other two had their skis embedded in the snow outside, where they could be seen.

Harry followed a gust of wind blowing a furrow across the bare wastes, swirling up the light, fresh snow that had fallen in the hollow overnight. The snow was driven toward mountain peaks, precipices, slopes, irregularities in the terrain, where it formed frozen waves and great drifts, similar to the one that protruded like a hat brim from the top of the mountain behind the cabin.

Harry knew, of course, that there was no guarantee that the man they were hunting would even show up. For some reason or other Iska Peller might not have been on the hit list; he might not consider this opportunity appropriate; he might have other plans for Iska. Or he might have smelled a rat. And there might be more banal reasons. Ill, on a trip . . .

Nonetheless. If Harry had counted up all the times his intuition had misled him, the number would have told him to give up intuition as a method and guide. But he didn't count them. Instead, he counted all the times intuition had told him something he didn't know he already knew. And now it was telling him the killer was on his way to Håvass.

Harry glanced at his watch again. The killer had twenty hours. In the huge fireplace the spruce crackled and spat behind the fine-mesh screen. Kaja had gone to take a nap in one of the bedrooms while Kolkka sat by the coffee table oiling a disassembled

Weilert P11. Harry recognized the German weapon by the fact that it had no gun sights. The Weilert pistol was made especially for close combat, when you had to remove it from a holster, belt or pocket quickly and with minimal risk of it snagging. In such situations sights were superfluous, anyway; you pointed it at the target and shot—you didn't take aim. The spare pistol, a SIG Sauer, lay next to it, assembled and loaded. Harry felt the shoulder holster of his Smith & Wesson .38 chafe against his ribs.

They had landed by helicopter during the night by Lake Neddalvann, a mile or so away, and had covered the rest of the way on skis. Under different circumstances Harry might have taken in the beauty of a snow-clad expanse bathed in moonlight, of the northern lights playing on the sky, or Kaja's almost euphoric expression as they glided through the white silence as if in a fairy tale, the lack of sound so complete that he had the feeling the scraping noises of their skis would carry for miles across the mountain plateau. But there was too much at stake, too little he could afford to lose, for him to have his eyes on anything except the job, the hunt.

It was Harry who had cast Kolkka in the role of "one detective." Not because Harry had forgotten Kafé Justisen, but if things didn't go according to plan, they could use the Finn's close-combat skills. Ideally, the killer would make a move during the day and be seen by one of the two groups hidden in the snow. But if he came by night, without being noticed before he reached the cabin, the three of them would have to tackle the situation on their own.

Kaja and Kolkka took a bedroom each; Harry slept in the sitting room. The morning had passed without unnecessary chitchat; even Kaja had been quiet. Concentrated.

From the reflection in the window Harry watched Kolkka assemble the gun, aim at the back of Harry's head and pretend to fire a shot. Twenty hours left. Harry hoped the killer would waste no time.

While Bjørn Holm was taking the light blue hospital clothes from Adele's closet, he felt Geir Bruun's eyes on his back from the doorway.

"Why don't you just take everything?" Bruun said. "Then I won't have to bother throwing it out. Where's your colleague Harry, by the way?"

"He's gone skiing in the mountains," Holm said patiently, putting the garments individually in the plastic bags he had brought along.

"Really? Interesting. He didn't strike me as the skiing type. Where?"

"Can't say. Speaking of skis, what was Adele wearing when she went to Håvass? There's no ski gear here."

"She borrowed it from me, of course."

"She borrowed ski stuff from **you**?"

"You sound so surprised."

"You didn't strike me as . . . the skiing type." Holm noticed that his words projected an innuendo that had not been intentional and felt his neck glow.

Bruun chuckled and twirled around in the doorway. "Right, I'm more . . . the clothes type."

Holm cleared his throat and, without knowing why, made his voice go deeper. "May I take a look?"

"Ooh, goodness me," Bruun lisped, seeming to revel in Holm's discomfort. "Come on—let's go and see what I've got."

"Half past four," Kaja said, passing the pot of stew to Harry for the second time. Their hands didn't touch. Nor did their eyes. Nor their words. The night they had shared in Oppsal was as distant as a two-day-old dream. "According to the script, I'm supposed to be standing on the south side now, smoking a cigarette."

Harry nodded and passed the pot to Kolkka, who scraped it out before scarfing down the contents.

"OK," Harry said. "Kolkka, will you take the west-facing window? The sun's low now, so check for the glint of binoculars."

"Not until I've eaten," he answered slowly in Swedish and with emphasis, shoving yet another fully loaded fork into his mouth.

Harry cocked an eyebrow. Glanced at Kaja and motioned for her to go.

When she was outside, Harry sat by the window and combed the plateau and the ridges. "So Bellman employed you when no one else would, eh?" He said it softly, but the silence in the room was so complete he could have whispered it.

A few seconds passed with no response. Harry

assumed Kolkka was processing the fact that Harry had engaged him on a personal matter.

"I know about the rumor that was spread after you were given the boot by Europol. You had beaten up an ex-con during questioning. That's right, isn't it?"

"That's my business," Kolkka said, lifting the fork to his mouth. "But he might not have shown me sufficient respect."

"Mm. The interesting thing was that Europol spread the rumor themselves. So that the rumor would make things easier for them. And for you, I suppose. And of course for the parents and lawyers of the girl you were questioning."

Harry heard the chewing behind him stop.

"So that they got their compensation secretly without having to drag you and Europol into a courtroom. The girl avoided having to sit on the witness stand and say that when you were in her room asking her about the friend who had been raped, you got so excited by the answers that you started to feel her up. Fifteen years old, it says in Europol's internal files."

Harry could hear Kolkka breathing heavily.

"Let's assume that Bellman also read the files," Harry continued. "Was given access via contacts and roundabout methods. Like me. He waited a bit before contacting you. Waited until the anger was out of you, until all the air was gone, until you were on the wheel rim, punctured. And then he picked you up. Gave you a job and gave you back some of the pride you had lost. And knew you would repay him with loyalty. He buys when the market is at the bottom, Kolkka. That's how he gets his bodyguards."

Harry turned to Jussi Kolkka. The Finn's face was white.

"You're bought, but you're hardly paid, Jussi. Slaves like you don't gain respect, not from Massa Bellman and not from me. Christ, you don't even have any self-respect, man."

Kolkka's fork fell to his plate with an almost deafening clatter. He got up, slipped his hand inside his jacket and pulled out a gun. He strode toward Harry and leaned over him. Harry didn't budge, just calmly looked up.

"So how are you going to find your respect again, Jussi? By shooting me?"

The Finn's pupils were quivering with rage.

"Or by working yourself to hell?" Harry looked out at the snowy expanse again.

Heard Kolkka's heavy breathing. Waited. Heard him turn. Heard him move away. Heard him sit down by the west-facing window.

The radio crackled. Harry grabbed the microphone.

"Yes?"

"Soon be dark." It was Bellman's voice. "He's not coming."

"Still keep a lookout."

"What for? It's clouded over and without moonlight we can't see a—"

"If we can't see, neither can he," Harry said. "So keep a lookout for a head flashlight."

The man had switched off the flashlight. He didn't need any light; he knew where the ski trail he was following led. To the Tourist Association cabin. And his eyes would get used to the dark; he would have large, light-sensitive pupils before he arrived. There it was, the log wall with black windows. As though no one were at home. The new snow creaked as the man kicked off and slid down the last few yards. He stopped and listened to the silence for a couple of seconds before soundlessly unclipping his skis. He took out the large, heavy Sami knife with the intimidating boat-shaped blade and the smooth, varnished yellow wooden hilt. It was as good at cutting down branches for a fire as carving up a reindeer. Or slitting throats.

The man opened the door as quietly as he could and entered the hall. Stood listening at the sitting-room door. Silence. Too silent? He pressed the handle and threw open the door while standing back against the wall next to the doorway. Then—to make himself as elusive and small a target as possible—he crouched down and rushed into the darkness with the knife to the fore.

He glimpsed the figure of the dead man sitting on the floor with his head hanging and arms still embracing the stove.

He returned the knife to its sheath and switched on the light by the sofa. It hadn't struck him until now that the sofa was identical to the one at the Håvass cabin. The Tourist Association must have gotten a discount at a job lot. But the sofa cover was old; the cabin had been closed for several years and it was in much too dangerous an area. There had been accidents with people plunging down cliff faces while trying to find the cabin.

Next to the wood stove, the dead man's head rose slowly.

"Sorry to burst in on you like this." He checked that the restraints holding the dead man's hands shackled around the stove were as they should be.

Then he began to unpack his knapsack. He had pulled his hat down and been in and out of the shop in Ustaoset in a flash. Crackers. Bread. Papers. Which had more about the press conference. And this witness at the Håvass cabin.

"Iska Peller," he said aloud. "Australian. She's at the Håvass cabin. What do you think? Could she have seen anything?"

The other man's vocal cords could hardly move enough air for them to make a sound. "Police. Police at cabin."

"I know. It's in the papers. One detective."

"They're there. The police have rented the cabin."

"Oh?" He looked at the other man. Had the police set a trap? And was this bastard in front of him trying to **help** him, to save him from falling into it? The very idea angered him. But this woman must have seen something, anyway; otherwise they wouldn't have brought her all this way from Australia. He grabbed the poker.

"Fuck, you stink. Did you shit in your pants?"

The dead man's head slumped onto his chest. The dead man had obviously moved in here. There were a few personal possessions in the drawers. A letter. Some tools. Some old family photographs. Passport. As if the dead man were planning an escape, thinking he could recover somewhere else. Other than down there, down in the flames, where he would be tortured for his sins. Even though he had begun to think that the dead man might not have been behind all the devilry after all. There are limits to how much pain a man can stand before he talks.

He checked the phone again. No coverage—shit!

And what a stench. The storehouse. He would have to hang him out to dry there. That was what you did with smoked meat.

Kaja had gone to her bedroom, and Harry hoped she would catch some shut-eye before it was her watch.

Kolkka poured the percolated coffee into his own and then Harry's cup.

"Thanks," Harry said, staring into the darkness.

"Wooden skis," Kolkka said, standing by the fireplace and inspecting Harry's skis.

"My father's," Harry said. He had found the ski equipment in the cellar at Oppsal. The poles were new and made of some metal alloy that seemed to weigh less than air. Harry had for a moment wondered whether the hollow pole might have been filled with helium. But the skis were the same old broad mountain ones.

"When I was small we went to my grandfather's cabin in Lesja every Easter. There was this peak my dad always wanted to climb. So he told my sister and me that there was a kiosk at the top where they sold Pepsi, which was my sister's favorite drink. So if we could manage the last slope, then we . . ."

Kolkka nodded and ran a hand over the back of the white skis. Harry took a swig of the fresh coffee.

"Sis always managed to forget from Easter to Easter that it was the same old bluff. And I always wished I could have done the same. But I was lumbered with remembering everything that Dad instilled in me. The mountain code, how to use nature as a compass and how to survive avalanches. Norwegian kings and queens, the Chinese dynasties and American presidents."

"They're good skis," Kolkka said.

"A little too short."

Kolkka sat by the window at the other end of the room. "Yes, you think it will never happen. Your father's skis being too short for you."

Harry waited. Waited. Then it came.

"I thought she was so wonderful," Kolkka said. "And I thought she liked me. Strange. I only touched her breasts. She didn't put up any resistance. I suppose she must have been scared."

Harry succeeded in curbing his urge to leave the room.

"You're right," Kolkka said. "You're loyal to those who lift you out of the garbage heap. Even though you can see they're using you. What else can you do? You have to choose sides."

When Harry realized the conversational tap had been turned off, he got up and went to the kitchen. He went through all the cupboards in a vain attempt to find what he knew was not here, a kind of desperate diversion from the shouting inside his head. "A drink, just one."

He had been given a chance. One. The ghost had undone his chains, lifted him up, sworn because of the stench of the shit and helped him into the bathroom, where he had dropped him on the shower floor and turned on the water. The ghost had stood there for a moment watching him while trying to make a cell-phone call, cursed the lack of coverage and then gone back into the sitting room, where he heard him trying again.

He wanted to cry. He had moved up here, hidden himself away so that no one would be able to find him. Installed himself in the mothballed Tourist Association cabin, taken with him what he needed. Thought he was safe among the precipices. Safe from the ghost. He didn't cry. For as the water seeped through his clothes, soaking the remains of the red flannel shirt stuck to his back, it dawned on him that this was his chance. His mobile phone was in the pocket of his trousers, folded on the chair beside the sink.

He tried to get to his feet, but his legs wouldn't

respond. Didn't matter, it was only a few yards to the chair. He put his scorched black arms on the floor, defied the pain and dragged himself forward, heard the blisters pop, noticed the smell, but in two lunges he was there, searching his pockets, grabbing his phone. He had saved that policeman's number, mostly so that he would recognize it on the display if he called.

He pressed the "call" button. The phone seemed to be drawing breath in the tiny eternity between each ring. One chance. The shower was making too much noise for the man to hear him speak. There! He heard the policeman's voice. He interrupted him with his hoarse whisper, but the voice continued on. And he realized he was talking to voice mail. He waited for the voice to finish, squeezed the phone, felt the skin on his hand tear, but didn't let go. Couldn't let go. Had to leave a message about . . . finish, for Christ's sake, come on, beeps!

He hadn't heard him come in; the shower had drowned out his light steps. The phone was seized from his hand, and he had time to see the ski boot coming.

When he regained consciousness, the man was standing over him and studying his phone with interest.

"So you've got coverage?"

The man left the bathroom dialing a number, then the noise of the shower drowned everything out. But not long after, he was back.

"We're going on a journey. You and I." The man seemed to be in a good mood all of a sudden. The

man was holding a passport in one hand. His passport. In the other hand he was holding the pliers
from the toolbox.

"Open wide."

He swallowed. Lord Jesus, have mercy.

"Open wide, I said!"

"Mercy. I swear I've told you everything I—" He
didn't say any more because a hand had grabbed him
around the throat and stopped the supply of air. He
fought for a while. Then at last came the tears. And
then he opened wide.

57

Thunder

Under the glare of the lamp, Bjørn Holm and Beate
Lønn were standing by the steel table in the laboratory,
staring at the navy-blue ski pants in front of them.

"That is definitely a semen stain," Beate said.

"Or a line of semen," Bjørn Holm said. "Look at
the shape."

"Too little for an ejaculation. Looks like an erect,
wet penis has been shoved up the bottom of the person wearing the ski pants. You said Bruun was homosexual, didn't you?"

"Yes, but he says he hasn't worn them since he lent
them to Adele."

"Then I would say we have semen stains typical of a rape. We'll just have to send them for DNA testing, Bjørn."

"Agreed. What do you think about that?" Holm pointed to the light blue hospital trousers, which had two friction marks under both back pockets.

"What is it?"

"Something that won't go away in the wash, at any rate. It's a nonylphenol-based material called PSG. It's used in car-cleaning products, among other things."

"She's obviously been sitting somewhere."

"Not just sitting—it's deep in the fiber. She's been rubbing. Hard. Like this." He thrust his hips backward and forward.

"I see. Any theories as to why?"

She put on her glasses and looked at Holm as his mouth distorted into a variety of shapes to articulate expressions his brain generated and immediately rejected.

"Dry humping?" Beate asked.

"Yes," Holm said, with relief.

"I see. And where and when does a woman who doesn't work at a hospital wear hospital gear and dry-hump on PSG?"

"Simple," said Bjørn Holm. "At a nighttime rendezvous in a disused PSG factory."

The clouds parted, and again they were bathed in the magic blue light in which everything, even the shadows, became phosphorized, frozen as if for a still-life.

Kolkka had gone to bed, but Harry presumed the Finn was lying in the bedroom with his eyes open and his other senses on maximum alert.

Kaja sat by the window with her chin resting on her hand, looking out. She was wearing her white sweater since they had only electric radiators. They had agreed it might look suspicious if smoke were coming from the chimney all the time when supposedly there were just two people there.

"If you ever miss the starry sky over Hong Kong, look outside now," Kaja said.

"I can't remember any starry sky," Harry said, lighting a cigarette.

"Isn't there anything about Hong Kong you miss?"

"Li Yuan's glass noodles," Harry said. "Every day."

"Are you in love with me?" She had lowered her voice only a fraction and was looking at him attentively while tying an elastic band around her hair.

Harry examined his feelings. "Not right now."

She laughed, her face expressing surprise. "Not right now? What does that mean?"

"That that part of me is tuned out as long as we're here."

She shook her head. "You're damaged goods, Hole."

"About that," Harry said with a crooked smile, "there is little doubt."

"And what about when this job is over in"—she looked at her watch—"ten hours?"

"Then I may be in love with you again," Harry said, placing his hand next to hers on the table. "If not before."

She looked at their hands. Saw how much bigger his were. How much more delicately shaped hers were. How much paler and how gnarled his were, with thick blood vessels twisting and turning all over the backs of his hands.

"So you could be in love before the job is over, after all, eh?" She placed her hand on his.

"I meant the job could be over before—"

She withdrew her hand.

Harry looked at her in surprise. "I just meant—"

"Listen!"

Harry held his breath and listened. But heard nothing.

"What was it?"

"Sounded like a car," Kaja said, peering out. "What do you think?"

"Unlikely, in my opinion," Harry said. "It's more than six miles to the nearest road open in winter. What about a helicopter? Or a snowmobile?"

"Or what about my overactive imagination?" Kaja said with a sigh. "The sound's gone. And, on reflection, perhaps it was never there. Sorry, but you can easily become a little oversensitive when you're afraid and—"

"No," Harry said, getting up. "Suitably afraid. Suitably sensitive. Describe what you heard." Harry took his revolver from his shoulder holster and went to the second window.

"Nothing—I keep telling you!"

Harry opened the window a fraction. "Your hearing's better than mine. Listen for both of us."

They sat listening to the silence. Minutes passed.

"Harry—"

"Shh."

"Come and sit down again, Harry."

"He's here," Harry said half aloud, as though talking to himself. "He's here now."

"Harry, now it's you who's being oversensi—"

There was a muffled boom. The sound was low, deep, sort of slow, no forward thrust, like distant thunder. But Harry knew that thunder seldom occurred with a clear sky at twenty degrees.

He held his breath.

And then he heard it. Another roar, different from the boom, but this, too, was a low frequency, like the sound waves from a bass speaker, sound waves that move air, that are felt in the stomach. Harry had heard this sound only once before, but he knew he would remember it for the rest of his life.

"Avalanche!" Harry yelled and ran toward Kolkka's bedroom, which faced the mountainside. "Avalanche!"

The bedroom door opened and there was Kolkka, wide awake. They could feel the ground shaking. It was a big avalanche. Whether the cabin had a cellar or not, Harry knew they would never be able to make it there. For behind Kolkka fragments of glass from what had once been a window flew past, forced in by the air that avalanches push ahead of them.

"Take my hand!" Harry shouted above the roar and stretched out his hands, one to Kaja and one to Kolkka. He saw them race toward him as the air was sucked out of the cabin, as if the avalanche had breathed out first and then in. He felt Kolkka's hand squeeze his hard and waited for Kaja's. Then the wall of snow hit the cabin.

58

Snow

It was deafeningly quiet and pitch black. Harry tried to move. Impossible. His body seemed to be cast in plaster; he couldn't move one single limb. Indeed, he had actually done what his father had told him: held a hand in front of his face to make room for an air pocket. But he didn't know if there was any air in it. Because Harry couldn't breathe. And he knew the reason why. Constrictive pericarditis. What Olav Hole had explained happened when the chest and diaphragm were packed together so tightly by snow that the lungs were unable to function. Which meant you had only the oxygen that was already in your blood, about a liter, and with normal consumption, at around .25 liters a minute, you would die within four minutes. Panic struck: He had to have air, had to breathe! Harry tensed his body, but the snow was like a boa constrictor that responded by tightening its grip. He knew he had to fight the panic, had to be able to think. And think now. The world outside had ceased to exist; time, gravity, temperature didn't exist. Harry had no idea what was up or down or how long he had been in the snow. Another of his father's wisdoms whirled through his brain. To find your bearings and determine which way you are lying, dribble saliva from your mouth and feel which way it runs down your face. He ran his tongue around his palate. Knew it was fear, the adrenaline, that had dried out his mouth. He opened wide and used the fingers in front of his face to scrabble some snow into his mouth. Chewed, opened again and let the melted ice dribble out. He panicked instantly and jerked as his nostrils filled with water. Closed his mouth and snorted the water out again. Snorted out what was left of the air in his lungs. He was going to die soon.

The water had told him he was upside down and the jerk had told him it was possible to move after all. He tried another jerk, tightened his whole body in a spasm, felt the snow give a little. A little. Enough to escape from the stranglehold of constrictive pericarditis? He breathed in. Got some air. Not enough. The brain must already have been suffering from a lack of oxygen; nevertheless, he clearly recalled his father's words from the Easters up in Lesja. In an avalanche where you can hardly breathe you don't die from a lack of air but from too much CO_2 in your blood. His other hand had met something, something hard, something that felt like wire mesh. Olav Hole: "In snow you're like a shark—you'll die if you don't move. Even though the snow is loose enough for some air to come in, the heat of your breath and body soon forms a layer of ice around you, which means air won't come in and the poisonous carbon dioxide in your breath can't get out. You are simply making your own ice coffin. Do you understand?"

"Yes, Dad, but take it easy, will you? This is Lesja, not the Himalayas."

Mom's laughter from the kitchen.

Harry knew the cabin was filled with snow. And that above him was a roof. And above that probably more snow again. There was no way out. Time was ticking. It would end here.

He had prayed that he wouldn't wake up again. That next time he slipped into unconsciousness would be the last. He was hanging upside down. His head was throbbing as if it would explode. It must have been all the blood filling it.

It was the sound of the snowmobile that had woken him.

He tried not to move. He had done that at first, jerked, tensed his body, tried to free himself. But he had given up his attempts fairly quickly. Not because of the meat hooks in his calves—he had lost feeling in his legs long ago. It was the sound. The sound of tearing flesh and sinews, and muscles that snapped and burst when he jerked and twisted, making the chains attached to the storehouse roof sing.

He stared into the glazed eyes of a stag hanging by its rear legs and looking as if it were in mid-dive, antlers first. He had shot it while poaching. With the same rifle that he had used to kill her.

He heard the plaintive creak of footsteps in the

snow. The door opened and the moonlight plunged inside. Then he was there again. The ghost. And the strange thing was that it was only now, looking at him from upside down, that he was sure.

"It really is you," he whispered. It was so strange speaking without any front teeth. "It really is you. Isn't it?"

The man walked behind him, untied his hands.

"C-can you forgive me, my boy?"

"Are you ready to travel?"

"You killed them all, didn't you."

"Yes," he said. "Let's go."

Harry dug with his right hand. Toward his left hand, the one that was squeezed up against some wire mesh he couldn't identify. Part of his brain told him he was trapped, that it was a hopeless race against time, seconds, that for every breath he took he was one step nearer death. That all he was doing was prolonging his suffering, postponing the inevitable. The other voice said he would rather die in desperation than in apathy.

He had managed to dig his way through to the other hand and put the right hand over the wire mesh. Pressed both hands against it and tried to push, but the mesh wouldn't budge. He sensed that his breathing was already heavier, the snow was becoming smoother and his grave coated with ice. Dizziness came and went, just for a second, but he knew it was the first warning that he was inhaling poisoned air. Soon the drowsiness would come, and the brain would shut down, room by room, like a hotel approaching the low season. And that was when Harry felt it, something he had never experienced before, not even during his worst nights at Chungking Mansions: an overwhelming loneliness. It wasn't the certainty that he would die that suddenly drained him of all will to live, but that he would die here, without anyone, without those he loved, without his father, Sis, Oleg, Rakel . . .

The drowsiness came. Harry stopped digging. Even though he knew this spelled death. A seductive, alluring death, taking him into its arms. Why protest, why fight, why choose pain when he could succumb? Why choose anything other than what he had always done? Harry closed his eyes.

Wait.

The mesh.

It had to be the fireplace screen. The fire. The chimney. Rock. If anything had withstood the avalanche, if there was one place where the mass of snow had not penetrated, it would have to be the chimney.

Harry pushed against the wire again. It wouldn't budge an inch. His fingers clawed the mesh. Powerless, resigned.

It was predestined. This was how it would end. His CO_2-infected brain sensed a logic to it, but was unsure quite what it was. He accepted it, though. He let the sweet, warm sleep envelop him. The sedation. The freedom.

His fingers slid along the wire. Found something

hard, solid. Tips of skis. Dad's skis. He offered no resistance to the thought. It was less lonely like this, with his hand on Dad's skis. Together, in step, they would enter the kingdom of death. Take the last steep slope.

Mikael Bellman stared at what lay before them. Or to be more precise, what **no longer** lay before them. Because it wasn't there anymore. The cabin was gone. From the snow cave it had looked like a little drawing on a large white sheet of paper. That was before the boom and the faraway crash that had woken him. By the time he had finally pulled out his binoculars it was quiet again; there was just a distant, delayed echo reverberating from the Hallingskarvet mountain range. He had stared himself blind through the binoculars, scanned the mountainside beyond. It was as if someone had erased everything from the paper. No drawing, just peaceful and innocently white. It was incomprehensible. A whole cabin buried? They had snapped on their skis and taken eight minutes to arrive at the avalanche scene. Or eight minutes and eighteen seconds. He had noted the time. He was a police officer.

"Christ, the avalanche area is two square miles," he heard a voice shout behind him and watched the frail yellow beams from their flashlights sweep across the snow.

The walkie-talkie crackled. "Rescue Ops says the helicopter will be here in thirty minutes. Over."

Too long, Bellman thought. What was it he had read: After half an hour the chance of surviving

under snow was one in three? And when the helicopter got here, what the hell were they supposed to
do? Stick their sonar probes in the snow to detect the
remains of a cabin? "Thanks, over and out."

Ærdal came alongside. "Some good news! There
are two search-and-rescue dogs in Ål. They're bringing them up to Ustaoset now. The county officer in
Ustaoset, Krongli, isn't at home—at least he's not
answering the phone—but there was a man at the
hotel with a snowmobile, and he can bring them
here." He was flapping his arms to keep warm.

Bellman looked at the snow beneath them. Kaja
was down there somewhere. "How often did they say
there were avalanches here?"

"Every ten years," Ærdal said.

Bellman rocked on his heels. Milano was directing
the others, who were trudging around, prodding the
snow with skis and poles.

"Search-and-rescue dogs?" he said.

"Forty minutes."

Bellman nodded, knowing the dogs would make
no difference one way or the other. By the time they
arrived, almost an hour would have passed since the
avalanche.

The chances of survival would be less than 10 percent even before they started work. After an hour and
a half they would be, to all intents and purposes, zero.

The journey had begun. He was driving a snowmobile. Both light and dark seemed to be coming toward

him, as if the diamond-strewn sky were opening itself and welcoming him. He knew that behind him in the snow stood the man, the ghost, aiming at his burned, charred and blistered back through the sights of a gun. But no bullet could reach him now. He was free, he was going where he intended, taking the path he had always been following. To the place where she had gone, along the same route. He was no longer tied up, and if he had been able to move his arms or legs he would have just stood up on the seat, twisted the accelerator and rushed forward even faster. He was cheering as he took off toward the starry sky.

59

The Burial

Harry sank through layers of dreams, memories and half-chewed thoughts. Everything was fine. Apart from one voice intoning the same sentence, again and again. Dad's voice.

"... and in the end you were bleeding so much that the big boys became alarmed and went on their way."

He tried to hold it at arm's length, to listen to one of the other voices. But even that one belonged to Olav Hole.

"You were scared of the dark, but that didn't stop you going there."

Fuck, fuck, fuck.

Harry opened his eyes to the dark. Wriggled and twisted in the icy snow's iron grip. Tried to kick. Started digging in front of the wire. Made himself a little more room. His fingers found the edge of the fireplace screen. He wasn't going to die. Olav Hole would have to go on ahead; he would have to be that much of a fucking father! His hands were paddling like shovels now that they had some room to move. He got both hands on the inside of the screen and pulled it toward him. There! It shifted. He pulled again. And felt it. Air. Stinking of ash, heavy. But air, nonetheless. For as long as it lasted. He pushed the snow away. Stuffed his hands in; his fingers found something that felt like polystyrene. He realized it was half-burned logs. The screen had stood up to the avalanche; the fireplace was free of snow. He continued to dig.

A few minutes—or perhaps it was seconds—later and he lay curled up in the large fireplace, gulping in air and coughing ash.

And he realized that so far he had been thinking about only one thing: himself.

He moved his arm around the corner of the fireplace, to where Dad's skis had been. Rummaged in the snow until he found what he was searching for. One of the ski poles. He grabbed the basket on the end and pulled. The smooth, light, rigid metal pole slipped through the snow. He brought the pole into the fireplace, placed it between his legs, jammed his boots together and ripped off the basket. Now he had a spear measuring a little more than five feet.

Kaja and Kolkka couldn't be far away from where he had been lying. He conjured up an imaginary grid system, the way they did at crime scenes to examine for clues, and started poking. He worked quickly, poking as hard as he could; it was a calculated risk. The worst-case scenario was he connected with an eye or stabbed a throat, but the best-case scenario was only that they were still breathing. He poked to the left of where he figured he must have been lying and felt the point meet some resistance. He retracted the pole, prodded with care and felt it bounce off again. As he tried to retract it again, he felt the pole jam. He released his grip and saw the pole pulled from him. Someone was holding the point and pulling it to and fro to show signs of life! Harry pulled the pole again, harder this time, but the other person was holding on with amazing strength. Harry needed the pole—it would be in the way when he started digging—so he put his hand in the wrist strap and even then had to use all his might to release the pole.

Harry wondered why he hadn't already put down the pole and started digging. Then he knew why. Hesitated for another second. Then he began to poke the snow again, this time to the right of where he had been. At the fourth prod he made contact. The same springy sensation. Stomach? He held the pole with his fingertips to see if he could detect any rising or falling, breathing, but there was no movement.

The decision ought to have been easy. The shortest way was to the first opening, where there had been signs of life. To save whatever could be saved. Harry was already on his knees and digging like a madman. Toward the second.

His fingers were numb when they reached the body, and he had to use the back of his hand to feel if there was a woolen sweater. The sweater. The white one. He grabbed a shoulder, pushed more snow to the side, freed an arm and pulled the lifeless body through the passage in the snow. Her hair fell across his face; it still had Kaja's aroma. He managed to haul her head and half her upper body onto the hearth and felt for a pulse in her neck, but his fingertips were like cement. He placed his face against hers, but couldn't feel any breath. He opened her mouth, made sure her tongue wasn't in the way, inhaled and breathed into her mouth. Came up for fresh air, suppressed his cough reflex as he inhaled particles of ash and breathed into her mouth again. A third time. He counted: four, five, six, seven. His head was beginning to whirl; he imagined he was back by the fire in the cabin in Lesja, the little boy trying to blow the dying embers into life and his dad laughing as the boy staggered off, dizzy and close to fainting. But he had to go on; he knew the chances of resuscitating her were diminishing by the second.

Leaning over her to blow for the twelfth time, he felt it: a warm current against his face. He held his breath, waited, hardly daring to believe it could be true. The warm current faded. But then it was back.

She was breathing! At that moment her body went into a convulsion and she began to cough. Then he heard her voice, faint.

"Is that you, Harry?"

"Yes."

"Where . . . I can't see."

"It's all right. We're in the fireplace."

Pause.

"What are you doing?"

"Digging for Jussi."

When Harry got Kolkka's head into the fireplace, he had no idea how much time had passed. Only that, as far as Jussi was concerned, there was none left. He lit a match and glimpsed the Finn's large, staring eyes before the flame went out.

"He's dead," Harry said.

"Couldn't you try mouth-to-mouth . . . ?"

"No," Harry said.

"What now?" Kaja asked in a faint, debilitated whisper.

"We have to get out," Harry said, finding her hand. Squeezing it.

"Couldn't we just wait here until they find us?"

"No," he said.

"The match," she said.

Harry didn't answer.

"It went out immediately," Kaja said. "There's no air here, either. The whole cabin is buried under snow. That's why you didn't want to try to revive him. There's not even enough air for us two. Harry . . ."

Harry was on his feet, trying to force his way up the

chimney, but it was too narrow and his shoulders got stuck. He crouched down again, broke both ends off the ski pole to make it into a hollow metal tube, put it up the chimney and got to his feet again, this time with his arms stretched above his head. It just reached. Claustrophobia cut in, but vanished at once, as though the body had decided irrational phobias were a luxury it couldn't afford right now. He pressed his back against one side of the chimney and used his legs to lever himself upward. His thigh muscles ached, he was panting and the dizziness had returned. But he continued, one foot up, press, next foot up . . . The higher he went, the hotter it was, and he knew that meant that the rising hot air couldn't escape. And he realized that if the fire had been lit when the avalanche crashed down on them they would have died long ago of carbon monoxide poisoning. That could have been called good luck in bad. Except that the avalanche was not bad luck. The boom they had heard . . .

The tube hit something above him. He clambered up. Groped with his free hand. It was an iron grille. The kind they put on the tops of chimneys to keep squirrels and other animals out. He ran his finger along the edge. It had been set in concrete. **Fuck!**

Kaja's faint voice reached him. "I'm dizzy, Harry."

"Breathe in deep."

He pushed the tube through the fine-mesh grille.

There was no snow on the other side!

He hardly noticed the lactic acid burning in his thighs, as he excitedly pushed the tube farther up. Only to experience disappointment when it hit something hard: the chimney cowl. He should have remembered that the cabin had such an attractive black metal cowl at the top of the chimney to protect it against snow and rain. He fumbled around until he angled the tube under the edge of the cowl and felt the hard-packed mass of snow, harder than in the cabin. But that could have been because the snow was now being forced down the opening of the hollow pole. He prayed that for every inch of ski pole he pushed into the snow he might feel it, the sudden absence of resistance, which would mean he had broken out of the snow hell. Which meant he could blow the snow out of this suction pipe and suck in air, fresh, life-giving air. Push Kaja up and give her the same injection of anti-death. But the breakthrough never came. He had the tube pressed right through the grille and nothing had happened. He tried anyway, sucked as hard as he could, getting cold, dry snow in his mouth, and it was still blocked. He couldn't stand the pressure on his sides any longer and fell. Shouted, stuck out his arms and legs, felt the skin on his hands being scraped off, but slid farther down. He hit the body beneath with both legs.

"All right?" Harry asked, climbing up into the chimney again.

"Fine," Kaja said with a deep groan. "And you? Bad news?"

"Yes," Harry said, scrambling down beside her.

"What? You aren't in love with me now, either?"

Harry chuckled and drew her to him. "Oh, I am now."

He felt hot tears on her cheeks as she whispered, "Shall we get married, then?"

"Yes, let's," Harry said, aware that it was the poison in his brain talking now.

She laughed. "Till death do us part."

He felt the warmth of her body. And something hard. Her holster with the service revolver. He released her and groped his way to Kolkka. Already he thought he could see how Kolkka's cold face had started to turn to marble. He bored his hand through the snow by the dead man's neck and down to his chest.

"What are you doing?" she mumbled weakly.

"I'm getting Jussi's gun."

He heard her stop breathing for a second. Felt her hand on his back, fumbling, like a small animal that has lost its orientation. "No," she whispered. "Don't do it . . . not like that . . . let's just fall asleep . . . Even."

It was as Harry surmised. Jussi Kolkka had gone to bed wearing his shoulder holster. He undid the button holding the gun in position, gripped the handle and dragged the gun from the snow. Ran a finger down the barrel. No sights—this was a Weilert. He stood up too quickly, felt giddy, looked for support. Then everything went black.

Bellman was looking down at the almost thirteen-foot-deep pit when he heard the intermittent **whump-whump-whump** of the rescue helicopter approaching, like a rug beater on speed. His men were using knapsacks to transport snow, lifting it up with interlocking trouser belts.

"The window!" he heard the man in the pit yell.

"Smash it!" Milano shouted back.

The glass tinkled.

"Oh, my God . . ." he heard. And knew the invocation boded bad news.

"Slide down a ski pole . . ."

Bellman heard dogs barking. And tried to work out how many hours it would take to clear the snow from the cabin. Correction: days.

Harry came to with a terrible pain in his jaw and something warm running down his forehead between his eyes. He guessed he must have hit his head and jaw against the rock when he fell. That was what must have woken him. The strange thing was he was still standing and holding the pistol in his hand. He tried to inhale air that wasn't there. He didn't know if he had enough for a last attempt, but so what? It was simple: There was nothing else he could do. So he stuffed the pistol in his pocket and, between gasps, climbed up the chimney again. Forced his legs against the sides when he was at the top, fumbled with the grille until he found the end of the metal pole that was still stuck in the snow. The pole was vaguely conical, with the larger aperture at Harry's end, where he inserted the gun barrel. It jammed two thirds of the way along its length.

Which also meant that it was perfectly aligned with the ski pole. It was like a silencer but five feet long. A bullet would not penetrate five feet of snow, but what if the pole was only a **short** distance from the end?

He leaned on the pistol so that the recoil wouldn't cause it to come free and fire at an angle. Then he fired. And fired. And fired. It felt as if their eardrums would explode in the hermetically sealed space. After four shots he stopped, put his lips around the pole and sucked.

He sucked in . . . air.

For a second he was so astonished that he almost fell back down. He sucked again, careful not to destroy the tunnel in the snow that the bullet had made. The odd grain of snow fell and settled under his tongue. Air. It tasted like a mild, well-rounded whiskey with ice.

60

Pixies and Dwarfs

Roger Gjendem ran across Karl Johans Gate, where the shops were beginning to open. At Egertorget square he peered up at the red Freia clock and saw that the hands were showing three minutes to ten. He increased his speed.

He had been summoned as a matter of urgency by

Bent Nordbø, their retired and, in all ways, legendary editor in chief, now board member and temple guardian.

He bore right, up Akersgata, where all the newspapers had bunched together in those days when the paper edition was the king of the journalistic heap. He turned left toward the law courts, right up Apotekergata, and stepped, out of breath, into Stopp Pressen. It didn't seem quite to have been able to make up its mind whether it was going to be a sports bar or a traditional English pub. Perhaps both, as the aim was for all types of journalists to feel at home here. On the walls hung press photographs showing what had engaged, shaken, gladdened and hor-rified the nation over the last twenty years. They were mostly of sporting events, celebrities and natural disasters. Plus a number of politicians who fell into the latter two categories.

Since this establishment was within walking distance of the two remaining newspaper offices on Akersgata—**Verdens Gang** and **Dagbladet**—Stopp Pressen was almost considered an extended cafeteria for them, but for the moment there were only two people visible inside: the barman behind the counter, and a man sitting at the table farthest back, beneath a shelf of classic books published by Gyldendal and an old radio, which were obviously meant to give the place a certain cachet.

The man beneath the shelf was Bent Nordbø. He had John Gielgud's superior appearance, John Major's panoramic glasses and Larry King's suspenders. And he was reading a genuine newspaper's newspaper. Roger had heard that Nordbø read only **The New York Times**, the **Financial Times**, **The Guardian**, **China Daily**, **Süddeutsche Zeitung**, **El País** and **Le Monde**, and he read them every day. He might take it into his head to flick through **Pravda** and the Slovenian **Dnevnik**, but he insisted that "East European languages are so heavy on the eye."

Gjendem stopped in front of his table with a cough. Bent Nordbø finished reading the last lines of an article about some Mexican immigrants' revitalization of a former condemned area of the Bronx, and glanced down at the page to make sure there was nothing else of interest. Then he removed his enormous glasses, snatched the handkerchief from the breast pocket of his tweed jacket and looked up at the nervous, and still breathless, man standing by his table.

"Roger Gjendem, I presume."

"Yes."

Nordbø folded the newspaper. Gjendem had also been told that when the man opened it again you could take it that the conversation was over. Nordbø tilted his head and started the not-inconsiderable task of cleaning his glasses.

"You've worked on criminal cases for many years and you know many of the people at Kripos and Crime Squad, don't you?"

"Er . . . yes."

"Mikael Bellman. What do you know about him?"

Harry scrunched up his eyes at the sun flooding into his room. He had just woken up and spent the first seconds shaking off dreams and reconstructing reality.

They had heard his shots.

And uncovered the ski pole at the first thrust of the spade.

Afterward they had told him that what had frightened them most was being shot at while they were digging down to the chimney.

His head ached as if he had been off the booze for a week. Harry swung his legs out of bed and looked around the room he had been given at the Ustaoset hotel.

Kaja and Kolkka had been taken by helicopter to Oslo and Rikshospital. Harry had refused to join them. Only after he had lied and said he'd had loads of air the whole time and was absolutely fine did they let him stay.

Harry put his head under the tap in the bathroom and drank. "Water's never that bad and is sometimes quite nice." Who used to say that? Rakel, when she wanted Oleg to drink up at the table. He switched on his cell phone, which had been off since he left for Håvass. There was coverage here in Ustaoset, the display said. It also showed there was a message waiting. Harry played it, but there was only a second of coughing and laughing before the connection was broken. Harry checked the caller's number. A cell number—could be anyone's. There was something vaguely familiar about it, but it definitely wasn't from Rikshospital. Whoever it was would probably call again if it was important.

In the breakfast room Mikael Bellman sat in solitary majesty with a cup of coffee in front of him. Papers folded and read. Harry didn't need to look at them to know it was more of the same. More about the Case, more about the police's helplessness, more pressure. But today's edition would hardly have been quick enough off the mark to include the death of Jussi Kolkka.

"Kaja's fine," Bellman said.

"Mm. Where are the others?"

"They caught the morning train to Oslo."

"But you didn't?"

"Thought I would wait for you. What do you think?"

"About what?"

"About the avalanche. Just something that can happen?"

"No idea."

"No? Did you hear the boom before it came?"

"Might have been the snowdrift on top falling and hitting the side of the mountain. Which in turn triggered the avalanche."

"Do you think it sounded like that?"

"I don't know what it's supposed to sound like. Noises do definitely trigger avalanches, though."

Bellman shook his head. "Even experienced mountain people believe that myth about sound waves triggering them. I climbed the Alps with an avalanche expert and he told me that people there still believe that the avalanches during the Second World War were caused by cannon fire. The truth is that for a shell to start an avalanche there has to be a direct hit."

"Mm. So?"

"Do you know what this is?" Bellman held up a piece of shiny metal between his thumb and first finger.

"No," Harry said, signaling to the waiter clearing away the breakfast buffet that he wanted a cup of coffee.

Bellman hummed the verse of Wergeland's "Pixies and Dwarfs" about building in the mountains and blowing the rock to pieces.

"Pass."

"You disappoint me, Harry. Well, OK, I may have a head start on you. I grew up in Manglerud in the seventies in an expanding suburban town. They dug plots around us on all sides. The soundtrack of my childhood was dynamite charges going off. After the builders had left I went around finding pieces of red plastic cable and tiny fragments of paper off the dynamite sticks. Kaja told me that they have a special way of fishing up here. Sticks of dynamite are more common than moonshine. Don't say the thought didn't cross your mind."

"OK," Harry said. "That's a part of a blasting cap. When and where did you find it?"

"After you were transported out last night. A couple of the guys and I did a little search around where the avalanche started."

"Any tracks?" Harry took the coffee from the waiter and thanked him.

"No. It's so exposed up there that the wind could have swept away any ski tracks there might have been. But Kaja said she thought she had heard a snowmobile."

"Barely. And there was quite a time between her hearing it and the avalanche. He might have parked the snowmobile well before he got there so that we wouldn't hear it."

"I had the same idea."

"And what now?" Harry took a tentative sip.

"Look for snowmobile tracks."

"The local officer . . ."

"No one knows where he is. But I've got us a snow-mobile, map, climbing rope, ice ax, provisions. So don't get too comfortable with that coffee—there's snow forecast for this afternoon."

To reach the top of the avalanche zone, the Danish hotel manager had explained that they would have to drive in a wide arc west of the Håvass cabin, but not too far northwest, where they would come into the area known as Kjeften. It had been given this name, "Jaws," on account of the fang-shaped rocks scattered around. Sudden crevices and precipices were carved into the plateau, making it an extremely dangerous place to roam in poor weather if you weren't familiar with the surroundings.

It was around noon when Harry and Bellman looked down the mountainside, where they could make out the excavation of the chimney at the bottom of the valley.

Clouds had already moved in from the west. Harry squinted to the northwest. Shadows and contours were erased without the sun.

"It must have come from there," Harry said. "Otherwise we would have heard it."

"Kjeften," Bellman said.

Two hours later, after crossing the snowscape from south to north in a crablike manner without finding any snowmobile tracks, they took a break. Sat next to each other on the seat, drinking from the thermos Bellman had brought with them. A light snow fell around them.

"I once found an unused stick of dynamite on an estate in Manglerud," Bellman said. "I was fifteen years old. In Manglerud there were three things kids could do. Play sports, study the Bible or smoke dope. I wasn't interested in any of them. And certainly not in sitting on the post office window ledge waiting for life to take me from hash and heroin, via glue-sniffing, to the grave. As happened to four boys in my class."

Harry noticed how the old Manglerud patois had crept back into his Norwegian.

"I hated all that," Bellman said. "So my first step

toward policing was to take the stick of dynamite behind the Manglerud church where the dopeheads had their earth bong."

"Earth bong?"

"They had dug a pit in which they placed, upside down, a decapitated beer bottle with a grille inside, where the hash smoked and stank. They had laid plastic tubes under the ground, running from the pit to various points a few feet away. Then they lay on the grass around the bong, each sucking on his tube. I don't know why . . ."

"To cool the smoke." Harry chortled. "You get more of a buzz from less dope. Not bad coming from dope-heads. I've obviously underestimated Manglerud."

"Nevertheless, I pulled out one of the tubes and replaced it with dynamite."

"You blew up the earth bong?"

Bellman nodded, and Harry laughed.

"Soil hailed down for thirty seconds." Bellman smiled.

Silence. The wind rushed, low and rasping.

"Actually, I wanted to say thank you," Bellman said, looking down at his cup. "For getting Kaja out in the nick of time."

Harry shrugged. Kaja. Bellman knew that Harry knew about the two of them. How? And did that mean Bellman knew about Kaja and Harry, as well?

"I had nothing else to do down there," Harry said.

"Yes, you did. I looked at Jussi's body before the helicopter took him away."

Harry didn't answer, just squinted through the thickening snow-flakes.

"The body had a wound in the side of the neck. And there were more on both palms. From the pointed end of a ski pole, perhaps. You found him first, didn't you?"

"Maybe," Harry said.

"The neck wound had fresh blood. His heart must have been beating when he received that wound, Harry. Beating pretty strongly, too. It should have been possible to dig out a living man in time. But you prioritized Kaja, didn't you?"

"Well," Harry said, "I think Kolkka was right." He emptied the rest of his coffee in the snow. "You have to choose sides," he quoted in Swedish.

They found the snowmobile tracks at three o'clock, half a mile from where the avalanche originated, between two large fang-shaped rocks, a refuge from the wind.

"Looks like he paused here," Harry said, pointing along the edge of the track left by the tread of the rubber belt. "The vehicle had time to sink in the snow." He ran his finger along the middle of the left ski runner while Bellman swept away the light, dry, drifting snow.

"Yep," he said, pointing. "He turned here and then drove on northwest."

"We're approaching the cliffs and the snow's getting thicker," Harry said, looking up at the sky and taking out his phone. "We'll have to call the hotel and ask them to send a guide on a snowmobile. Shit!"

"What?"

"No signal. We'll have to make our own way back to the hotel."

Harry studied the display. There was still the missed call from the vaguely familiar number of someone who had left those sounds on his voice mail. The last three digits—where the hell had he seen them? And then it kicked in. The detective memory. The number was in the "Former Suspects" file, and was embossed on a business card.

Along with TONY C. LEIKE, ENTREPRENEUR. Harry slowly raised his gaze and looked at Bellman.

"Leike's alive."

"What?"

"At least his phone is. He tried to call me while we were in Håvass."

Bellman returned Harry's gaze without blinking. Snowflakes settled on his long eyelashes and the white stains seemed to be glowing. His voice was low, almost a whisper. "Visibility's good, don't you think, Harry? And there's no snow in the air."

"Exceptional visibility," Harry said. "Not a fucking flake to be seen."

He quickly jumped back on.

They stuttered through the snowscape, three hundred feet at a time. Located the snowmobile's probable route, swept the tracks with a broom, took bearings, surged forward. The gouge in the left runner, probably caused by an accident, meant they could be sure they were following the right tracks. In a few places, in tiny hollows or on wind-blown hillcrests, the trail was clear and they could make fast progress. But not too fast. Harry had already shouted warnings about precipices twice and they had had some very close shaves. It was getting close to four now. Bellman flicked the headlights on and off, depending on how much snow was drifting in their faces. Harry studied the map. He had no clear idea of where they were, just that they were straying farther and farther from Ustaoset. And that daylight was dwindling. A third of Harry was slowly beginning to worry about the trip back. Which just meant that the two-thirds majority couldn't care less.

At half past four they lost the trail.

The drifting snow was so thick now they could hardly see.

"This is madness," Harry shouted above the roar of the motor. "Why don't we wait until tomorrow?"

Bellman turned to him and answered with a smile.

At five they picked up the trail again.

They stopped and dismounted.

"Leads that way," Bellman said, trudging back to the snowmobile. "Come on!"

"Wait," Harry said.

"Why? Come on—it'll soon be dark."

"When you shouted just now, didn't you hear the echo?"

"Now that you mention it." Bellman stopped. "Rock face?"

"There are no rock faces on the map," Harry said, turning in the direction the tracks indicated.

"Ravine!" he yelled. And received an answer. A very swift answer. He turned back to Bellman.

"I think the snowmobile making these tracks is in serious trouble."

"What do I know about Bellman?" Roger Gjendem repeated to gain some time. "He's reputed to be very competent and extremely professional." What was Nordbø, the legendary editor, really after? "He does all the right things," Gjendem went on. "Learns quickly, can handle us press types now. Sort of a **whiz kid.** Er, that is if you know—"

"I am somewhat conversant with the term, yes," said Bent Nordbø with an acidic smile, his right thumb and forefinger furiously rubbing the handkerchief on his glasses. "However, basically, I am more interested in if there any rumors doing the rounds."

"Rumors?" Gjendem said, failing to notice a relapse into his old habit of leaving his mouth open after speaking.

"I am truly hopeful you understand the concept, Gjendem. Since that is what you and your employer live off. Well?"

Gjendem hesitated. "There are all sorts of rumors."

Nordbø rolled his eyes. "Speculation. Fabrication. Direct lies. I'm not bothered with the niceties here,

Gjendem. Turn the sack of gossip inside out, reveal the malevolence."

"N-negative things, then?"

Nordbø released a ponderous sigh. "Gjendem, do you often hear rumors about people's sobriety, financial generosity, fidelity to partners and nonpsychopathic leadership styles? Could that be because the function of rumors is to please the rest of us by putting us in a better light?" Nordbø was finished with one lens and engaged in cleaning the second.

"It's a very, very idle rumor," Gjendem said and added with alacrity, "and I know for certain of others with the selfsame reputation who categorically are not."

"As an ex-editor I would recommend you delete either 'for certain' or 'categorically'; it's a tautology," Nordbø said. "Categorically are not **what**?"

"Erm. Jealous."

"Aren't we all jealous?"

"Violently jealous."

"Has he beaten up his wife?"

"No, I don't think he's laid a hand on her. Or had reason to. However, those who have given her a second look . . ."

61

The Drop

Harry and Bellman lay on their stomachs at the edge where the snowmobile tracks stopped. They stared down. Steep black rock faces sliced inward to the ground and disappeared in the thickening swirl of snow.

"Can you see anything?" Bellman asked.

"Snow," Harry answered, passing him the binoculars.

"The snowmobile's there." Bellman got up and walked back to their vehicle. "We're climbing down."

"We?"

"You."

"Me? Thought you were the mountaineer here, Bellman."

"Correct," said Bellman, who had already started strapping on the harness. "That's why it's logical for me to operate the ropes and rope brake. The rope's two hundred feet long. I'll lower it as far as it can go. All right?"

Six minutes later Harry stood on the edge with his back to the chasm, binoculars around his neck and a cigarette smoking from his mouth.

"Nervous?" Bellman smiled.

"Nope," Harry said. "Scared shitless."

Bellman checked that the rope ran through the

brake without a hitch, around the narrow tree trunk behind them and to Harry's harness.

Harry closed his eyes, breathed in and concentrated on leaning backward, overriding the body's evolution-conditioned protest, formed from millions of years of experience, that the species cannot survive if it steps off a cliff.

The brain won over the body by the smallest possible margin.

For the first ten feet or so, he could support his legs against the rock face, but as it jutted in, he was left hanging in the air. The rope was released in fits and starts, but its elasticity softened the tightening of the harness against his back and thighs. Then the rope came more evenly, and after a while he had lost sight of the top and was alone, hovering between the white snowflakes and the black cliff faces.

He leaned to the side and peered down. And there, sixty feet below, he glimpsed sharp black rocks protruding from the snow. Steep scree. And in the midst of all the black and white, something yellow.

"I can see the snowmobile!" Harry shouted, and the echo ricocheted between the rock walls. It was upside down, with the skis in the air. Since he and the rope were unaffected by the wind, he could judge that the vehicle lay about ten feet farther along. More than two hundred feet down. Therefore, the snowmobile must have been traveling at an unusually slow speed before it went over.

The rope went taut.

"More!" Harry shouted.

The resonant answer from above sounded as if it had come from a pulpit. "There is no more rope."

Harry stared down at the snowmobile. Something was sticking out from under it to the left. A bare arm. Black, bloated, like a sausage that had been on the grill for too long. A white hand against a black rock. He tried to focus, to force his eyes to see better. Open palm, the right hand. Fingers. Distorted, crooked. Harry's brain rewound. What had Tony Leike said about his illness? Not contagious, just hereditary. Arthritis.

Harry glanced at his watch. Detective's reflex. The dead man was found at 5:54. Darkness covered the walls down in the scree.

"Up!" Harry shouted.

Nothing happened.

"Bellman?"

No answer.

A gust of wind twirled Harry around on the rope. Black rocks. Sixty feet. And all of a sudden, without warning, he felt his heart pound and he automatically grabbed the rope with both hands to make sure it was still there. Kaja. Bellman knew.

Harry breathed in deeply three times, before shouting again.

"It's getting dark, the wind's picking up and I'm freezing my balls off, Bellman. Time to find shelter."

Still no answer. Harry closed his eyes. Was he frightened? Frightened that an apparently rational colleague would kill him on a whim because circumstances happened to be propitious? 'Course he was fucking frightened. For this was no whim. It wasn't chance that he stayed behind to go into the frozen wastes with Harry. Or was it? He took a deep breath. Bellman could easily arrange for this to look like an accident. Climb down afterward and remove the harness and rope, say that Harry had lost his footing in the snow. His throat had gone dry. This was not happening. He hadn't dug his way out of a fucking avalanche just to be dropped down a ravine twelve hours later. By a policeman. This didn't fucking happen, this . . .

The pressure from the harness was gone. He was falling. Free fall. Fast.

"The rumor is that Bellman is supposed to have man-handled a colleague," Gjendem said. "Just because the guy had danced a couple of times too many with her at the police Christmas party. The guy wanted to report a broken jaw and a cracked skull, but had no evidence—the attacker had been wearing a face mask. But everyone knew it was Bellman. Trouble was brewing so he applied for a move to Europol to get away."

"Do you believe there is anything to these rumors, Gjendem?"

Roger shrugged. "It certainly looks as if Bellman has a certain . . . um, predilection for that kind of transgression. We've looked into Jussi Kolkka's background following the avalanche at Håvass. He beat up a rapist under interrogation. And Truls Berntsen, Bellman's sidekick, is not exactly a mama's boy, either."

"Good. I want you to cover this duel between Kripos and Crime Squad. I want you to set off a few bombshells. Preferably about a psychopathic management style. That's all. Then let's see how the minister of justice reacts."

Without any gestures or parting salutations, Bent Nordbø put on his newly polished spectacles, unfolded the newspaper and started to read again.

Harry didn't have time to think. Not one thought. Nor did he see his life passing before him, faces of people he should have said he loved, or feel impelled to walk toward any light. Possibly because you don't get that far when you fall fifteen feet. The harness tightened against his groin and back, but the elasticity in the rope allowed him a gentle slackening of speed.

Then he felt himself being hoisted up again. The wind was blowing snow in his face.

"What the fuck happened?" Harry asked when, fifteen minutes later, he was standing on the edge of the ravine and swaying in the wind as he untied the rope from the harness.

"Scared, were you?" Bellman smiled.

Instead of putting the rope down, Harry wound it around his right hand. Checked that he had enough slack in the rope to have a swing. A short uppercut to the chin. The rope meant he would be able to use his hand again tomorrow, not like when he hit Bjørn Holm and suffered two days of painful knuckles.

He took a step toward Bellman. Saw the POB's surprised expression when he noticed the rope around Harry's fist, saw him retreat, stagger and fall backward in the snow.

"Don't! I . . . I just had to tie a knot at the end of the rope so that it wouldn't slide through the brake . . ."

Harry continued toward him, and Bellman—who was cowering in the snow—automatically raised his arm in front of his face.

"Harry! There . . . there was a gust of wind and I slipped . . ."

Harry stopped, eyed Bellman in surprise. Then he continued past the trembling POB and lumbered through the snow.

The icy wind blew through outer clothing, under-clothes, skin, flesh, muscles and into the bones. Harry grabbed a ski pole strapped to the snowmo-bile, cast around for some other material he could tie to the top, but found nothing, and sacrificing any-thing he was wearing was out of the question. Then he speared the pole into the snow to mark the site. God knows how long it would take them to find it again. He pressed the ignition button. Found the lights, turned them on. And Harry knew at once. Saw it in the snow blowing horizontally into the cones of light and forming an impenetrable white wall: They would never get out of this labyrinth and back to Ustaoset.

62

Transit

Kim Erik Lokker was the youngest forensics officer at Krimteknisk. Accordingly, he was often given jobs of a less forensic nature. Such as driving to Drammen. Bjørn Holm had mentioned that Bruun was a homosexual of the flirtier kind, but that Lokker only had to hand over the clothes and then leave.

When the female GPS voice in the car declared, "You have arrived at your destination," he found himself outside an old apartment building. He parked and wandered through open doors up to the door on the second floor marked with the names GEIR BRUUN/ADELE VETLESEN on a sheet of paper stuck down with two pieces of tape.

Lokker pressed the doorbell once, twice, and at last heard the sounds of someone stomping through the hall.

The door swung open. The man was wearing no more than a towel around his waist. He was unusually pale, and his smooth crown was wet and shiny with sweat.

"Geir Bruun? H-hope I'm not interrupting," said Kim Erik Lokker, holding the plastic bag with outstretched arm.

"Not at all—I'm only screwing," he said in the

affected voice Bjørn Holm had imitated. "What is this?"

"The clothes we borrowed. We have to keep the ski pants until further notice, I'm afraid."

"Really?"

Lokker heard the door behind Geir Bruun open. And an extremely feminine voice chirp: "What is it, darling?"

"Just someone delivering something."

A figure nestled up behind Geir Bruun. She hadn't even bothered with a towel, and Lokker was able to establish that the tiny creature was 100 percent woman.

"Hello there," she twittered over Geir Bruun's shoulder. "If there's nothing else, I'd like him back." She raised a small, graceful foot and kicked. The glass in the door was shaking and rattling long after the door had slammed shut.

Harry had stopped the snowmobile and was staring into the drifting snow.

Something had been there.

Bellman had put his arms around Harry's waist and his head behind his back to shelter from the wind.

Harry waited. Stared.

There it was again.

A cabin. Notched logs. And a storehouse.

Then it was gone again, erased by the snow, as though it had never existed. But Harry had the direction.

So why didn't he just immediately accelerate and head toward it, save their skins? Why did he hesitate? He didn't know. But there was something about the cabin, something he had sensed in the few seconds it became visible. Something about the black windows, the feeling that he was looking at a building that was infinitely abandoned and yet inhabited. Something that was not right. And which made him press the accelerator gently so as not to be heard above the wind.

63

The Storehouse

Harry put a log in the wood stove.

Bellman sat by the table, his teeth chattering. The white stains had taken on a bluish sheen. They had hammered on the door and shouted in the howling wind for a while before smashing a window to an empty bedroom. A bedroom with an unmade bed and a smell that caused Harry to wonder whether someone had slept there very recently. He almost placed a hand on the bed to see if it was still warm. And even though the sitting room would have felt warm anyway—they were so cold—Harry put a hand inside the wood stove to feel if there might be any warm embers under the black ash. But there were not.

Bellman moved closer to the stove. "Did you see anything apart from the snowmobile down in the ravine?"

They were the first words he had uttered since running after Harry, begging not to be left behind and throwing himself on the back of the snowmobile.

"An arm," Harry said.

"Whose arm?"

"How should I know?"

Harry stood up and went to the bathroom. Checked the toiletries. The few there were. Soap and a razor. No toothbrush. One person, one man. Who either didn't brush his teeth or had gone away on a trip. The floor was damp, even along the baseboards, as if someone had hosed it down. Something caught his attention. He crouched down. Half hidden by the baseboard there was something dark. A pebble? Harry picked it up, studied it. It wasn't lava, anyway. He put it in his pocket.

In the kitchen drawers he found coffee and bread. He pressed the bread. Relatively fresh. In the fridge there were two jars of jam, some butter and two beers. Harry was so hungry he imagined he could smell roast pork. He rummaged through the cupboards. Nothing. Shit, did the guy live off bread and jam? He found a packet of crackers on a pile of plates. Same type of plates they had at the Håvass cabin. Same furniture, too. Could this be a Tourist Association cabin? Harry stopped. He wasn't just imagining it; he **could** smell roast—correction: burned—pork.

He went back into the sitting room.

"Can you smell it?"

"What?"

"The smell," Harry said, squatting down by the wood stove. Beside the stove door, on an embossed stag, there were three unidentifiable black bits burned to the cast iron, and they were smoking.

"Did you find any food?" Bellman asked.

"Depends what you mean by food," Harry said pensively.

"There's a storehouse on the other side of the yard. Maybe . . ."

"Instead of 'maybe,' why don't you go and check."

Bellman nodded, got up and went out.

Harry walked over to the desk to see if there was anything he could use to scrape off the burned bits. He pulled out the top drawer. Empty. Harry pulled out the others—all empty. Apart from a sheet of paper in the bottom one. He picked it up. It wasn't paper but a photograph, facedown. The first thing that struck Harry was that it was strange to have a family portrait in a Tourist Association cabin. The photo had been taken in the summer, in front of a farmhouse. A woman and a man sitting on a step with a boy between them. The woman in a blue dress and head scarf, no makeup, a tired smile. The man, with a pinched mouth, stern expression and the serious, closed face you find on embarrassed men who look as though they're hiding a dark secret. But it was the boy in the middle who caught Harry's attention. He resembled the mother; he had her open smile and gentle eyes. But he looked like someone else, too. Those large, white teeth . . .

Harry went back to the wood stove; he was suddenly cold again. The stench of smoking pork . . . He closed his eyes and concentrated on breathing deeply and calmly through his nose a couple of times, but felt the nausea coming nonetheless.

At that moment Bellman stomped in with a broad smile on his face. "Hope you like venison."

Harry woke wondering what had roused him. Was it a sound? Or the absence of sound? For he realized the room was utterly still; the wind had stopped blowing outside. He threw off the blanket and stood up from the sofa.

Walked over to the window and peered outside. It was as if someone had waved a magic wand over the countryside. What, six hours previously, had been hard, merciless wilderness was now gentle, maternal, almost beautiful in the bewitching moonlight. Harry realized he was looking for prints in the snow. He **had** heard a sound. It could have been anything. A bird. An animal. He listened and heard light snoring from behind one bedroom door. So it wasn't that Bellman had gotten up. His gaze followed the footprints leading from the cabin to the storehouse. Or from the storehouse to the cabin? Or both—there were many. Could they be Bellman's from six hours ago? When had it stopped snowing?

Harry pulled on his boots, went out and looked toward the outhouse. No tracks there. He turned his back on the storehouse and pissed against the cabin wall. Why did men do that; why did they have to piss on something? The remnants of a territory-marking instinct? Or . . . Harry became aware that it wasn't what he was pissing on but what he had his back to that was important. The storehouse. He suspected he was being observed from there. He buttoned up, turned and looked at it. Then he moved toward it. Grabbed the spade as he passed the snowmobile. The plan had been to walk straight in, but instead he stood in front of the plain stone steps to the low door. Listened. Nothing. What the hell was he doing? There was no one here. He went up the steps, tried to raise his hand and grasp the handle, but it wouldn't move. What the hell was going on? His heart was beating so hard in his chest that it hurt, as if it wanted to burst out. He was sweating and his body refused to obey orders. And it slowly dawned on Harry that this was exactly how he had heard it described. A panic attack. It was the anger that saved him. He kicked open the door with immense force and crashed into the dark. The door swung shut. There was a strong smell of fat, smoked meat and dried blood. Something moved in the stripe of moonlight and a pair of eyes flashed. Harry swung the spade. And he hit something. Heard the dead sound of meat, felt it give. The door behind him fell open again and the moonlight streamed in. Harry stared at the dead deer hanging in front of him. At the other animal carcasses. He dropped the spade and sank to his knees. Then it came, all at once. The wall cracking, the snow consuming him alive, panicking that he couldn't breathe, the long gasp of pure white fear as he fell toward the black rocks. So lonely. For they had all gone. His father was in a coma, in transit. And Rakel and Oleg were silhouettes against the light at an airport, also in transit. Harry wanted to go back. Back to the dripping room. The solid, damp walls. The sweaty mattress and the sweet smoke that transported him to where they were. Transit. Harry bowed his head and felt hot tears streaming down his face.

I have printed a photo of Jussi Kolkka from Dagbladet's website and pinned it up on the wall next to the others. There wasn't a word in the news about Harry Hole and the other police officers who were there. Or Iska Peller, for that matter. Was it a bluff? They're trying, anyway. And now there is a dead policeman. They're going to try harder. They have to try harder. Do you hear me, Hole? No? You should. I'm so close I could whisper it in your ear.

Part Seven

64

State of Health

Olav Hole's condition was unchanged, Dr. Abel had said.

Harry sat by the hospital bed looking at his unchanged father while a heart monitor played its beep-beep song, interspersed with skipped beats. Sigurd Altman came in, greeted Harry and noted down the screen's figures on a pad.

"Actually, I'm here to visit a Kaja Solness," Harry said, getting up. "But I don't know which ward she's in. Could you . . . ?"

"Your colleague who was brought in by helicopter the other night? She's in intensive care. Only until they have all the test results. She'd been buried in the snow for quite a while. When they said Håvass, I assumed she must have been this witness from Sydney the police were talking about on the radio."

"Don't believe everything you hear, Altman. While Kaja was lying in the snow the Australian lady was safe and warm in Bristol, with her own guards and full room service."

"Hang on." Altman scrutinized Harry. "Were you buried in the snow as well?"

"What makes you say that?"

"The unsteady step you just took. Dizzy?"

Harry shrugged.

"Confused?"

"Constantly," Harry said.

Altman smiled. "You've got a bit too much carbon dioxide in you. The body disposes of it quickly when you breathe in oxygen, but you ought to have a blood test so that we can check your levels."

"No, thank you," Harry said. "How's he getting on?" He nodded toward the bed.

"What did the doctor say?"

"Unchanged. I'm asking you."

"I'm not a doctor, Harry."

"So you don't need to answer like one. Give me an estimate."

"I can't—"

"It'll remain between us."

Sigurd Altman eyed Harry. Was on the point of saying something. Changed his mind. Chewed his lower lip. "Days," he said.

"Not even weeks?"

Altman didn't answer.

"Thanks, Sigurd," Harry said and went to the door.

Kaja's face was pale and beautiful against the pillow-case. Like a flower in an herbarium, Harry thought. Her hand was small and cold in his. On the bedside table was today's **Aftenposten**, with the avalanche-buries-cabin-in-Håvass headline. It described the tragic event and quoted Mikael Bellman, who said it was a great loss that Officer Kolkka had died protecting Iska Peller. He was thankful, however, that the witness had survived and was now safe.

"So the avalanche was started with dynamite?" Kaja said.

"Yes, it's beyond doubt," Harry replied.

"So you and Bellman worked well together up there?"

"Yes, indeed." Harry turned to shield his coughing fit.

"Heard you found a snowmobile at the bottom of a ravine. With a possible body underneath."

"Yes. Bellman stayed in Ustaoset to go back to the site with the local county officer."

"Krongli?"

"No, he couldn't be located. But his deputy, Roy Stille, seemed solid. They've quite a job on their hands, though. We weren't sure where we were, more snow has fallen and it's drifting, and in that terrain . . ." Harry shook his head.

"Any idea who the body might be?"

Harry shrugged. "I would be very surprised if it wasn't Tony Leike."

Kaja's head spun around. "Oh?"

"I haven't told anyone yet, but I saw the corpse's fingers."

"What about them?"

"They were twisted. Tony Leike had arthritis."

"Do you think he started the avalanche? And then drove over the precipice in the dark?"

Harry shook his head. "Tony told me he knew the

area well; it was his terrain. It was a clear day and the snowmobile wasn't going fast—it landed only ten feet from the point where it took off. And he had a burned arm, which was not caused by dynamite. And the snowmobile was not burned."

"Wha—?"

"I think Tony Leike was tortured, killed and then dumped with the snowmobile so that we wouldn't find the body."

Kaja made a face.

Harry rubbed his little finger. He wondered whether it could have frostbite. "What do you think about this Krongli?"

"Krongli?" Kaja chewed on that one. "If it's true he tried to rape Charlotte Lolles, he should never have become a policeman."

"He beat his wife up, too."

"Doesn't surprise me."

"It doesn't?"

"No."

He looked at her. "Is there something you haven't told me?"

Kaja shrugged. "He's a colleague, and I thought he was just drunk, nothing I would spread around, but, yes, I've had a glimpse of that side of him. He came to my place and insisted in a pretty persistent way that we should get intimate."

"But?"

"Mikael was there."

Harry felt himself twitch.

Kaja pushed herself up into a sitting position. "You don't seriously think Krongli might have—"

"I don't know. I only know that whoever started the avalanche must have known the area well. Krongli has a connection with some of those women at Håvass. In addition, Elias Skog said before he was killed that he had seen something that might have been a rape at Håvass. Aslak Krongli sounds like he can be violent.

"And then there's this avalanche. If you wanted to kill a woman you thought was alone with a detective in a remote mountain cabin, how would you do it? Starting an avalanche doesn't exactly give you a guaranteed result. So why not make it simple and effective—take along your favorite murder weapon and go straight to the cabin? Because he knew that Iska Peller and the detective were not on their own. He knew we were waiting for him. So he sneaked in and attacked in the only way that would allow him to escape afterward. We're talking about an insider. Someone who knew about our Håvass theories and understood what was going on when he heard us naming a witness at a press conference. The local county officer at Ustaoset—"

"Geilo," Kaja corrected him.

"Krongli definitely received the urgent call from Kripos requesting permission to land the police helicopter in the national park that night. He must have known the circumstances."

"Then he should also have known that Iska Peller

wasn't there, that we wouldn't have endangered the life of a witness," Kaja said. "So it's odd he didn't keep well away."

Harry nodded. "Good point, Kaja. I agree. I don't think Krongli thought for a second that Peller was in the cabin. I think the avalanche was a continuation of what he's been doing for some time."

"Which is?"

"Playing with us."

"Playing?"

"I received a call from Tony Leike's phone while we were at the cabin. Tony saved my number, and I'm pretty certain it wasn't he who phoned me. The thing is the caller didn't hang up quickly enough—voice mail started recording and I could hear something for a second before the connection was cut. I'm not sure, but to me it sounded like laughter."

"Laughter?"

"The laughter of someone who is amused. Because he'd just heard my message saying that I would have no network coverage for a couple of days. Let's imagine it was Aslak Krongli, who had just had his suspicions confirmed that I was at the cabin in Håvass waiting for the killer."

Harry paused and stared into the air, deep in thought.

"Well?" Kaja said after a while.

"I just wanted to hear how the theory sounded when I said it aloud," Harry said.

"And?"

He got to his feet. "Sounded half-assed, in fact.

But I'll check Krongli's alibis for the dates of the murders. See you."

"Truls Berntsen?"

"Speaking."

"Roger Gjendem, **Aftenposten.** Do you have time to answer a few questions?"

"Depends. If you're going to pester me about Jussi, you'd better talk to—"

"This is not about Jussi Kolkka, but my condolences, by the way."

"OK."

Roger was sitting with his feet up on his office desk in the Post Office Tower, gazing at the low buildings that constituted Oslo Central Station and down to the opera house, which would soon be open. After the conversation with Bent Nordbø at Stopp Pressen he had spent the whole day—and parts of the night—poring over research on Mikael Bellman in greater detail. Apart from the rumor that the temp at Stovner Police Station had been beaten up, there were not a lot of tangible facts. But, as a crime journalist, Roger Gjendem had gathered a number of regular and reliable sources over the years who would gladly inform on their grandmothers for the price of a bottle of booze or a pouch of tobacco. And three of them lived in Manglerud. After a few calls it turned out all three of them had grown up there, too. Perhaps it was true what he had heard someone say—that no one moves from Manglerud. Or to Manglerud.

There were obviously very few secrets there, because all three remembered Mikael Bellman. Partly because he had been a bastard of a policeman at Stovner. But mostly because he had made a beeline for Julle's woman while Julle was serving a twelve-month sentence for an earlier drug conviction, which had been suspended but then was converted to jail time after someone had given him up for stealing gasoline. The woman was Ulla Swart, Manglerud's finest, and a year older than Bellman. When Julle's sentence was up and he strolled out of prison, having vowed to all and sundry that he was going to take care of Bellman, there had been two guys waiting in the garage where Julle kept his Kawasaki. They were wearing face masks and beat him black and blue with iron bars and promised there would be more where that came from if he touched either Bellman or Ulla. Rumor was that neither of the two had been Bellman. But one of them had been someone they called Beavis, Bellman's eternal lackey. It was the only card Roger Gjendem had when he called Truls "Beavis" Berntsen. All the more reason to pretend he had four aces.

"I just wanted to ask if there was any truth in the assertion that on instructions from Mikael Bellman you once beat up Stanislav Hesse, who was a deputy in the payroll department at the Stovner Police Station."

Thunderous silence at the other end.

Roger cleared his throat. "Well?"

"That's a damned lie."

"Which part?"

"I was never given any instructions by Mikael to do that. Everyone could see the fucking Pole was hitting on Bellman's wife. Could have been anyone taking matters into their own hands."

Roger Gjendem tended to believe the former, the part about the instructions. But not the latter, the part about "anyone." None of Bellman's other colleagues at Stovner that Roger had spoken to had anything directly bad to say about Bellman; however, it was evident that Bellman was not beloved, not a man for whom they would have answered a call to arms. Apart from one.

"Thank you—that was all," Roger Gjendem said.

Harry rummaged in his jacket pocket and put his phone to his ear.

"Yes?"

"Bjørn Holm here."

"I can see that."

"Christ. Didn't think you would have bothered to set up a contact list."

"I have. You should feel honored. You're one of the four names in it."

"What's the racket in the background? Where are you, actually?"

"Gamblers cheering because they think they're going to win. I'm at a horse race."

"What?"

"Bombay Garden."

"Isn't that a . . . Did they let **you** in?"

"I'm a member. What do you want?"

"Jesus, Harry, are you gambling on horses? Didn't you learn anything in Hong Kong?"

"Relax—I'm here checking up on Aslak Krongli. According to his office he was on police business in Oslo when both Charlotte and Borgny were killed. Not that unusual, actually, because it turns out he's quite often in Oslo. And I've just discovered the reason."

"Bombay Garden?"

"Yup. Aslak Krongli has a not-insubstantial gambling problem. Thing is, I've checked his credit card payments on the computer here. Time of payment and everything. Krongli has used his card a lot, and the times give him an alibi. Unfortunately."

"I see. And they've got the computer in the same room as the racecourse?"

"Eh? They're in the final stretch now—you'll have to talk louder!"

"They've . . . Forget it. I'm calling to say we've got semen off the ski pants that Adele Vetlesen was wearing at Håvass."

"What? You're kidding! That means—"

"We may soon have the DNA of the eighth guest. If it's his semen. And the only way we can be sure is by excluding the other men at Håvass."

"We need their DNA."

"Yes," said Bjørn Holm. "Elias Skog's fine, of course—we've got his DNA. Not so good with Tony Leike. We'd have found it at his house, no problem, but for that we need a warrant. And after what happened last time it's gonna be really tough."

"Leave it to me," Harry said. "We should also have Krongli's DNA profile. Even though he didn't kill either Charlotte or Borgny, he may have raped Adele."

"OK. How do we get it?"

"As a policeman he must have been at a crime scene at some point or other," Harry said. It was unnecessary to conclude his reasoning. Bjørn Holm knew where he was going with it. To avoid confusion and identity mistakes, fingerprints and DNA were routinely taken from all officers who had been present at a crime scene and had potentially contaminated it.

"I'll check the database."

"Well done, Bjørn."

"Wait—there's more. You asked us to investigate those nurse-uniform clothes, and we did. The pants had PSG on them. And I've checked. There's a disused PSG factory in Oslo, up in Nydalen. If it's empty and the eighth guest had sex with Adele there, we may still be able to find semen there."

"Mm. Knobbed in Nydalen and humped in Håvass. The eighth guest may just have fucked his escape route. PSG, you said. Is that the Kadok factory?"

"Yes, how . . . ?"

"Pal's father worked there."

"Repeat—there's a helluva racket now."

"They're crossing the finish line. See you."

Harry put the phone in his jacket pocket, swiveled around in his chair, so he didn't see the gloomy faces of the losers around the felt course, nor the croupier's smile. "Conglatulations again, Hally!"

Harry got up, donned his jacket and looked at the note the Vietnamese man was holding out for him. With the portrait of Edvard Munch. A thousand kroner.

"Mm, velly lucky," Harry said. "Put it on the green horse in the next race. I'll pick up the cash another day, Duc."

Lene Galtung was sitting in the living room staring at the double-glazed window, at the double-exposed reflection. Her iPod was playing Tracy Chapman. "Fast Car." She could listen to the song again and again, never got tired of it. It was about a poor girl wanting to flee from everything, just get in her lover's fast car and leave the life she had, working at the convenience store, being responsible for her drunken father, burn all the bridges. This could not have been further from Lene's own life; nevertheless, the song was about her. The Lene she could have been. The Lene she actually was. One of the two she saw in the double reflection. The ordinary one, the gray one. In all her years at school she had been scared stiff that the classroom door would open, someone would come in, point a finger at her and say, "We're on to you now—take off those fine clothes." Then they would toss her a few rags and say, "Now everyone can see who you really are, the illegitimate child." She had been sitting there, year in, year out, hiding, as quiet as a mouse, glancing at the door, just waiting. Listening to friends, listening for the telltale signs that would give her away. The embarrassment, the fear, the defense she put up seemed like arrogance to others. And she knew she overplayed her role as rich, successful, spoiled and carefree. She was not at all good-looking and radiant, like the other girls in her circle, the ones who could chirrup with a self-assured smile, "I don't have a clue," in the charming knowledge that whatever they didn't know couldn't possibly be important and that the world would never require any more from them than their beauty. So she had to pretend. That she was beautiful. Radiant. Superior to everything. But she was so tired of it. Had just wanted to sit in Tony's car and ask him to leave everything behind. Drive to a place where she could be the real Lene and not these two false personae who hated each other. As the song said, together, she and Tony could find that place.

The reflection in the glass moved. Lene recoiled when she realized it was not her face after all. She hadn't heard her come in. Lene straightened up and pulled out the earphones.

"Put the coffee tray there, Nanna."

The woman hesitated. "You should forget him, Lene."

"Stop it!"

"I'm just saying. He won't be a good man for you."

"Stop it—I told you!"

"Shh!" The woman smacked down the tray with a clatter on the table, and her turquoise eyes flashed. "You have to see common sense, Lene. We've all had to do that in this house when the situation demanded it. I'm just saying this as your—"

"As my what?" Lene snorted. "Look at you. What could you be to me?"

The woman ran her hands down the white apron, went to put one on Lene's cheek, but Lene waved it away. The woman sighed, and it sounded like a drop of water falling in a well. Then she turned and left. As the door closed behind her, the black phone next to Lene rang. She felt her heart leap. Since Tony had disappeared, her phone had been constantly switched on and always within arm's length. She grabbed it. "Lene Galtung."

"Harry Hole, Crime Squ—I mean, Kripos. I'm sorry to intrude, but I need to ask you for some help with a case. It's about Tony."

Lene could feel her voice careering out of control as she replied. "Has . . . has something happened?"

"We're looking for someone we suspect died from a fall in the mountains around Ustaoset."

She felt herself going dizzy; the floor was rising and the ceiling falling.

"We haven't located the body yet. It's been snowing and the search area is vast and extremely rugged. Can you hear me?"

"Y—yes, I can."

The policeman's voice, a touch hoarse, continued. "When the body has been recovered, we'll try to get it identified as soon as possible. But there may be extensive burns. Therefore, we require DNA now from anyone who might conceivably be the deceased person. And while Tony is a missing person . . ."

Lene's heart felt as if it were coming up her throat, ready to leap out of her mouth. The voice on the other end droned on.

"That is why I was wondering if you could help one of our forensics officers find DNA material in Tony's home."

"S-such as what?"

"A hair from a brush, saliva on a toothbrush—they know what they need. The important thing is that you, as his fiancée, give us permission and come to his house with a key."

"Of c-course."

"Thank you very much indeed. I'll send an officer to Holmenveien right away."

Lene hung up. Felt the tears coming. Put her iPod earphones back in.

Caught Tracy Chapman singing about taking a fast car and keeping on driving. Then the song finished. She pressed repeat.

65

Kadok

Nydalen embodied the deindustrialization of Oslo. The factory buildings that had not been demolished—and had not given way to gleaming, elegant designer glass-and-steel office buildings—had been converted into TV studios, restaurants and large, open-plan redbrick affairs with exposed ventilation and plumbing.

The latter were often rented by advertising firms who wanted to show that they thought in untraditional ways, that creativity flourished just as well in cheap industrial rooms as in the expensive and centrally located head offices of their well-established competitors. But the premises in Nydalen now cost at least as much, because all advertising agencies basically think in traditional patterns. That is, they follow the fashion and drive the prices upward for whatever is the fashion.

The owners of the disused Kadok factory site had, however, not participated in this bonanza. When the factory had finally closed fourteen years ago, after several annual deficits and the dumping of PSG in China, the founder's heirs went for one another's throats. And while they were arguing about who should have what, the factory, isolated behind the fences west of the Akerselva River, fell into decay. Shrubs and deciduous trees were allowed to grow wild and eventually masked the factory from its surroundings.

Bearing all this in mind, Harry thought the large padlock on the gate seemed strangely new. "Cut it," he told the officer beside him.

The jaws of the enormous bolt cutter went through the metal as if it were butter, and the lock was snipped as quickly as it had taken Harry to get a blue chit. The prosecutor at Kripos had sounded as if he had more important things to do than issue search warrants, and Harry had barely finished talking before he had the signed paperwork in his hand. And he had thought to himself that they could do with a couple of stressed-out, negligent prosecutors at Crime Squad as well.

The low afternoon sun flashed on the jagged glass of smashed windows high on the brick walls. It was a desolate place, typical of disused factories, where everything you see has been constructed for hectic, efficient activity, yet there is no one around. Where the echo of iron on iron, of workers shouting, cursing and laughing over the drone of the machines still reverberates silently between the walls, and the wind blows through the soot-darkened, broken windows, making the spiders' webs and the dead shells of insects quiver.

There was no lock on the door into the factory hall. The five men walked through a rectangular area with churchlike acoustics, which gave the impression of an evacuation rather than closure; work tools were still laid out, a pallet loaded with white buckets labeled PSG TYPE 3 stood ready to be driven away, a blue coat hung over the back of a chair.

They stopped when they reached the center of the hall. In one corner there was a kind of kiosk, shaped like a lighthouse and raised a few feet off the ground. Foreman's office, Harry thought. Around the walls ran a gallery, which at one end led into a mezzanine floor with its own rooms. Harry guessed they were the lunch room and administrative offices.

"Where should we begin?" Harry asked.

"The same place as always," Bjørn Holm said, casting around. "Top left-hand corner."

"What are we looking for?"

"A table, a bench with blue PSG on it. The stains on the trousers were rubbed in slightly below the back pockets, so she must have been sitting on something—in other words, she wasn't lying flat."

"If you begin down here, this officer and I will go upstairs with the bolt cutters," Harry said.

"Oh?"

"To open doors for you forensics boys. We promise not to spray semen anywhere."

"Very droll. Don't—"

"Touch anything."

Harry and the officer, whom he called "Officer" for the simple reason that he had forgotten his name two seconds after hearing it, stomped up a winding staircase, making the iron steps sing. The doors they met were open, and inside, as Harry had envisaged, there were offices from which the furniture had been removed. A cloakroom with rows of iron lockers. A large communal shower. But no blue stains.

"What do you think that is?" Harry asked, standing in the lunch room. He pointed to a narrow padlocked door at the back.

"Pantry," the officer said, already on his way out.

"Wait!"

Harry went to the door. Scratched a nail on the apparently rusty lock. It was genuine rust. He turned it around, looked at the cylinder. No rust.

"Cut it," Harry said.

The officer did as he was bidden. Then Harry opened the door.

The officer smacked his lips.

"Just a secret door," Harry said.

Behind it was neither a pantry nor a room, but another door. Fitted with what looked like a solid lock.

The officer dropped the bolt cutter.

Harry scanned the area and found what he was looking for. A large red fire extinguisher, fairly conspicuous, hanging from the middle of the wall in the lunch room. Hadn't Øystein mentioned something about that once? The materials they made where his father worked were so flammable that they were instructed to smoke by the river. Into which the cigarette ends were to be thrown afterward.

He lifted the extinguisher off the wall and carried it to the door. Stepped back a few strides, then ran forward, aimed and smashed the metal cylinder into the door like a battering ram.

The door split around the lock, but still clung to the frame.

Harry repeated the attack. Splinters flew all around.

"What the hell's going on?" he heard Bjørn call from the factory floor.

At the third attempt the door gave with a despairing scream and swung open. They stared into a pitch-black void.

"Can I borrow your flashlight?" Harry asked the officer, putting down the fire extinguisher and wiping off the sweat. "Thanks. Wait here."

Harry stepped into the room. There was a smell of ammonia. He shone the light along the walls. The room—which he estimated was nine square feet—had no windows. The beam swept across a black folding chair, a desk with a lamp and a Dell computer screen. The keyboard was relatively unworn. The desk was tidy and made of bare wood, no blue stains. In the wastepaper basket there were strips of paper, as though someone had been cutting out pictures. And, sure enough, a **Dagbladet** with the front page cut up. Harry read the headline over the missing picture and knew they had come to the right place. They had arrived. This was it.

DIED IN AVALANCHE

Harry instinctively shone the flashlight upward, onto the wall above the desk, past some blue stains. And there they were.

All of them.

Marit Olsen, Charlotte Lolles, Borgny Stem-Myhre, Adele Vetlesen, Elias Skog, Jussi Kolkka. And Tony Leike.

Harry concentrated on breathing from his diaphragm. On absorbing the information piecemeal. The pictures had been cut out of newspapers or were print-outs, probably from news pages on the Internet. Apart from the picture of Adele. His heart felt like a bass drum, dull thuds as it tried to send more blood to his brain. The picture was on photographic paper and so grainy that Harry assumed it must have been taken with a telephoto lens and then blown up. It showed a car window, Adele's profile in the front seat, from which the plastic cover did not seem to have been removed, and there was something protruding from her neck. A large knife with a shiny yellow handle. Harry forced his eyes to look further. Underneath the pictures hung a line of letters, also printed off a computer. Harry skimmed the introduction to one of them.

IT IS SO SIMPLE. I KNOW WHO YOU KILLED.
YOU DON'T KNOW WHO I AM, BUT YOU KNOW
WHAT I WANT.
MONEY. IF YOU DON'T PAY UP, THE COPS WILL
BE AROUND. SIMPLE, EH?

The text continued, but his eye was caught by the end of the letter. No name, no sign-off. The police officer was standing in the doorway. Harry heard his hand fumbling along the wall as he muttered: "Must be a light switch here somewhere."

Harry shone the light at the blue ceiling, onto four fluorescent tubes.

"There must be," Harry said, illuminating the wall above several blue stains, before the cone of light found a sheet pinned to the right of the pictures. A tiny alarm bell had begun to go off in his brain. The sheet was torn at the side and covered in hand-drawn lines and columns. But there were different hand-writing styles.

"Here it is," the officer said.

For some reason, Harry suddenly thought about the work lamp. And the blue ceiling. And the smell of ammonia. And realized at that instant that the alarm in his head had nothing to do with the paper.

"Don't . . ." Harry started.

But too late.

The explosion was not technically an explosion but—as it would appear in the report the fire chief would sign the following day—an explosionlike fire triggered by an electric spark from cables connected to a canister of ammonia gas that, in turn, ignited the PSG painted over the whole ceiling and splattered on the walls.

Harry gasped as the oxygen in the room was drawn into the flames, and he felt an immense heat bear down on his head. He automatically fell to his knees and ran his hands through his hair to see if it was alight. When he looked up again, flames were coming off the walls. He wanted to breathe in, but managed to stop the reflex. Got to his feet. The door was only six feet away, but he had to have . . . he stretched for the sheet of paper. For the missing page from the Håvass guest book.

"Move away!" The officer appeared in the doorway with the fire extinguisher under his arm and the hose in his hand. As though in slow motion, Harry saw it squirt out. Saw the golden-brown jet released from the hose splash against the wall. Brown that should have been white, liquid that should have been powder. And already, before he looked into the jaws of the flames that rose on two legs and roared at him from where the liquid landed, before he smelled the sweet sting of gasoline in his nostrils, before he saw the flames follow the jet of gasoline toward the officer standing in the doorway, with the handle still depressed, in shock, Harry knew why the extinguisher had been hanging from the middle of the lunch-room wall, on display, impossible to miss, red and new, screaming out to be used.

Harry's shoulder hit the policeman at waist height, folding him over the rampaging inspector and knocking him backward with Harry on top.

They sent a couple of chairs flying as they skidded under the table. The officer, gasping for air, gesticulated and pointed while opening and closing his mouth like a fish. Harry turned. Wrapped in flames, the red extinguisher rumbled and rolled toward them. The hose was spitting melted rubber. Harry shot up, dragging the officer after him, pulled him to the door, as a stopwatch ticked timelessly in his head. He shoved the swaying officer out of the room, onto the gallery, thrust him down to the floor alongside him as it came, what the fire chief in his report would describe as an explosion, which blew out all the windows and set fire to the entire lunch room.

The clipping room is burning. It's on the news. You have to serve and protect, Harry Hole, not demolish and destroy. You will have to pay compensation. If not, I will take something from you that you hold dear. In a matter of seconds. You have no idea how easy it will be.

66

After the Fire

The evening darkness had descended over Nydalen. Harry stood with a blanket over his shoulders and a large paper cup in his hand as he and Bjørn Holm watched the smoke divers running in and out with the last PSG buckets that would ever leave the Kadok factory.

"So he'd pinned up the pictures of the murder victims?" Bjørn Holm said.

"Yep," Harry said. "Except for the prostitute in Leipzig, Juliana Verni."

"What about the page? Are you sure it was from the Håvass guest book?"

"Yes. I saw the guest book when I was in the cabin and the pages were identical."

"And so you were standing a couple of feet from the name of the eighth guest, but you didn't see it?"

Harry shrugged. "Perhaps I need reading glasses. Things happened fucking quickly in there, Bjørn. And my interest in the page waned a bit when the officer started spraying gasoline."

"'Course. I didn't mean—"

"There were some letters on the wall. From what I could see they were blackmail letters. Maybe someone had already discovered him."

A fireman came toward them. His clothes creaked and groaned as he walked.

"Kripos, aren't you?" The man's voice resonated in a way that matched the helmet and boots. And he had body language that said boss.

Harry hesitated, but confirmed with a nod; no reason to complicate matters.

"What actually happened in there?"

"That's what I'm hoping you boys will eventually be able to tell us," Harry said. "But in general terms I think we can say that whoever found himself a rent-free office in there had a clear plan for dealing with uninvited guests."

"Oh?"

"I should have known as soon as I saw the fluorescent tubes on the ceiling. If they'd been working, the tenant wouldn't have needed a desk lamp. The switch was connected to something else, some kind of ignition device."

"You think so? Well, we'll get some experts in tomorrow morning."

"What does it look like inside?" Holm asked. "The room where it started."

The fireman scrutinized Holm. "PSG on the walls and ceiling, son. What do you **think** it looks like?"

Harry was tired. Tired of being on the receiving end, tired of being afraid, tired of always being too late. But right now most tired of grown men who never wearied of playing cock of the walk. Harry spoke in a low voice, so low that the fireman had to lean in to hear.

"Unless you're seriously interested in what my forensics officer thinks about the room you've just sent umpteen smoke divers into, I suggest you spit out what you know in concise but exhaustive terms. You know there was a guy sitting there planning six or seven murders. Which he carried out. And we're **very** interested to know if we can expect to find clues that might help us to stop this very, very bad man. Can you be concise like that?"

The fireman straightened. Coughed. "PSG is extremely—"

"Listen. We're asking you for the consequences, not the cause."

The fireman's face had gone a color that was not solely due to the heat from the burning PSG. "Burned out. Totally burned out. Papers, furniture, computer, everything."

"Thank you, boss," Harry said.

The two policemen watched the fireman's back as he left.

"My forensics officer?" Holm repeated, making a face as if he had swallowed something nasty.

"Had to sound like a bit of a boss, too."

"Good to outsmart someone when you've just been outsmarted yourself, isn't it?"

Harry nodded and pulled the blanket around him more tightly. "He said burned out, didn't he?"

"Burned out. How does that feel?"

Harry stared miserably at the smoke still seeping out of the factory windows into the fire company's searchlights.

"Like being knobbed in Nydalen," he answered, draining the rest of his cold coffee.

Harry drove away from Nydalen, but got no farther than the red light on Uelandsgate before Bjørn Holm rang again.

"Forensics has done tests on the semen on Adele's ski pants, and we've got a DNA profile."

"Already?" Harry exclaimed.

"Partial profile. But enough for them to state with ninety-three percent certainty that we have a match."

Harry sat up straight in the seat.

Match. What a wonderful word. Perhaps the day wasn't a waste, after all.

"Out with it!" Harry said.

"You've got to learn to savor dramatic pauses," Holm said.

Harry groaned.

"OK, OK. They found the matching DNA profile with hair from Tony Leike's hairbrush."

Harry stared into the distance.

Tony Leike had raped Adele Vetlesen at the cabin.

Harry hadn't seen it coming. Tony Leike? He couldn't make it compute. Violent criminal, yes, but to rape a woman who'd come to a cabin with another man? Elias Skog said he'd seen him holding her mouth and pulling her into the outhouse. Perhaps it wasn't a rape when it came down to it?

And then—all of a sudden—the pieces fell into place.

Harry saw it, crystal clear.

It wasn't a rape. And there it was: the motive.

The cars behind hooted. The light had turned green.

67

Prince Charming

It was a quarter to eight, and the day hadn't yet adjusted for color and contrast. The countryside was a grainy black-and-white version of itself in the gray morning light as Harry parked beside the only other car by Lake Lysern and ambled down to the jetty. County Officer Skai was standing at the edge with a fishing rod in his hand and a cigarette in the corner of his mouth. Wisps of mist hung in the air like cotton wool around the reeds that poked up from the black, oil-smooth water.

"Hole," said Skai without turning. "Up early."

"Your wife said you were here."

"Every morning from seven to eight. Only chance I have to think before the hustle and bustle starts."

"What have you caught?"

"Nothing. But there are pike in the reeds."

"Sounds familiar. 'Fraid the hustle and bustle starts a little earlier today. I've come about Tony Leike."

"Tony, yes. His granddad's farm was in Rustad, east of Lake Lyseren."

"So you remember him well?"

"This is a small place, Hole. My father and old Leike were friends, and Tony was here every summer."

"What memories do you have of him?"

"Erm, funny guy. Lots of people liked him. Especially the women. He was palsy with the girls, a sort of Elvis type. And managed to surround himself with a lot of mystery. Rumor was he had grown up alone with his unhappy, alcoholic mother until one day she sent him packing because the man she was with didn't like the boy. But women around here liked him a lot. And he them. That occasionally got him into some trouble."

"Like when he cozied up to your daughter?"

Skai flinched, as if he had gotten a bite.

"Your wife," Harry said. "I asked her about Tony, and she told me. It was your daughter Tony and a local boy were fighting over that time."

The policeman shook his head. "They weren't fighting—it was butchery, pure and simple. Poor Ole, he'd gotten it into his head that he and Mia were a couple because he'd fallen in love with her and was allowed to drive Mia and her friend to a dance. He wasn't a fighter, Ole—he was more the bookish kind. But he went after Tony. Who laid him out flat, drew a knife and . . . It was pretty nasty—we're not used to that sort of thing here."

"What did he do?"

"He cut off half his tongue. Put it in his pocket and left. We arrested Tony half an hour later at his grandfather's, told him the tongue was needed in surgery. Tony said he'd fed it to the crows."

"What I wanted to ask was whether you had ever suspected Tony of rape. Then or at any other time."

Skai spun around.

"Let me put it this way, Hole. Mia was never the same happy-go-lucky girl again. She still wanted the headcase, of course, but that's the way girls are at that age. And Ole moved away. Every time the poor kid opened his mouth around here it was a reminder for him and others of the dreadful humiliation. So, yes, I would say that Tony Leike is the violent type. But, no, I don't think he raped anyone. If so, he would have raped Mia, if I can put it like that."

"She—?"

"They were in the woods behind the dance hall. She didn't let Tony have his way. And he accepted that."

"You're sure? Sorry I have to ask, but it's—"

The hook leapt out of the water toward them. It glinted in the first horizontal rays of the sun.

"That's fine, Hole. I'm police, too, and I know what you're working on. Mia's a decent girl and doesn't lie. Not even on the witness stand. You can have the report if you want the details. I would just prefer it if Mia didn't have to go through all of this again."

"That won't be necessary," Harry said. "Thank you."

Harry had informed the detectives assembled in the Odin conference room that the person he had seen under the snowmobile—who had still not been found, despite the increased police effort—had Tony Leike's arthritic fingers. And then recounted his theory. He leaned back and waited for reactions.

The Pelican peered over her glasses at Harry, but seemed to be addressing the whole morning gathering.

"What do you mean you think Adele was willing? She was screaming for help, for goodness sake!"

"That was what Elias Skog thought at a later point," Harry said. "His first impression was that he was watching two people having consensual sex."

"But a woman who takes a man with her to a cabin doesn't have sex with a casual interloper in the middle of the night! Do you really have to be a woman to understand that?" she hissed, and with her new, sensationally unbecoming dreadlocks, she reminded Harry of a furious Medusa.

The response came from Harry's neighbor. "Do you really think gender automatically affords you superior knowledge of the sexual preferences of half of the earth's population?" Ærdal paused and studied the freshly cleaned nail on his little finger. "Hasn't it already been made clear that Adele Vetlesen changed partners at the drop of a hat? She agreed to have sex with a man she hardly knew at a disused factory in the middle of the night, didn't she?"

Ærdal lowered his hand, started work on the ring finger and mumbled so low that only Harry heard it. "Anyway, I've fucked more women than you, you scrawny bird."

"Women fell easily for Tony and vice versa," Harry said. "Tony arrived at the cabin late, Adele's boyfriend was annoyed about something and had gone to bed. He and Adele were able to flirt undisturbed. He was having trouble on the home front, and she had started to lose interest in the man she was there with. Adele and Tony were attracted to each other, but there were people everywhere in the cabin. So later that night they sneaked out and met by the outhouse. They kissed, groped, he stood behind her, pulled down his pants and was now so excited that there was what they call in the Sexual Offenses Unit 'pre-ejaculatory fluid' on the tip of his penis, which went over her ski pants before he could pull them down, and they had intercourse. She was so loud in her ecstasy that she awoke Elias Skog, who watched them from the window. And

I believe they woke her boyfriend up as well and that he saw them from his room. I don't think she could have cared less. Tony, on the other hand, tried to stifle her cries."

"If **she** couldn't have cared less, why would **he**?" the Pelican burst out. "After all, it's women who are stigmatized by this kind of looseness while men's status is only enhanced. Among other men, mind you!"

"Tony Leike had at least two good motives for stifling her cries," Harry said. "First of all, you would hardly wish to broadcast extracurricular sex if you're a fiancé plastered across the tabloids, and especially if your future father-in-law's money is about to rescue your investments in the Congo. Second, Tony Leike is an experienced mountaineer who knows the area well."

"What the heck does that have to do with the case?"

A chuckle was heard, and everyone turned to the head of the table, where Mikael Bellman was sitting.

"Avalanche," he said with a laugh. "Tony Leike was frightened Adele's howls would set off an avalanche."

"Tony must have known that many avalanches are triggered by humans," Harry said.

Guffaws of laughter spread around the table. Even the Pelican had to allow herself a smile.

"But what makes you think Adele's boyfriend saw them?" she asked. "And that Adele didn't care? Perhaps she was so enthralled that she forgot herself."

"Because," said Harry, leaning back in the chair, "Adele has done this before. She once texted her boyfriend a picture of herself being screwed by another man. A heartless message that would leave no one in any doubt. Her friends said she didn't get together with this boyfriend again after the trip to Håvass."

"Interesting," Bellman said. "But where does it take us?"

"To the motive," Harry said. "For the first time in this case we have a possible 'why.' "

"So we're moving away from the theory of a crazy serial killer?" Ærdal asked.

"The Snowman also had a motive," said Beate Lønn, who had just walked in and taken a seat at the end of the table. "Insane, but definitely a motive."

"This is simpler," Harry said. "Good old-fashioned jealousy. Motive for two out of three murders in this country. And in most other countries. In this sense, we humans are quite predictable."

"It may explain the murders of Adele Vetlesen and Tony Leike," said the Pelican, "but what about the others?"

"They had to be eliminated," Harry said. "They were all potential witnesses to the events at the cabin and could have told the police, and provided us with the motive we lacked. And maybe even worse: They had been witness to his total humiliation—he had been cheated on in public. For an unstable person that would be motive enough on its own."

Bellman clapped his hands. "I hope we have some answers soon. I've spoken to Krongli on the phone and he says the weather in the search area has improved, so now they can send in the dogs and use helicopters. Any reason you didn't mention why you suspected the body of being Tony Leike before, Harry?"

Harry shrugged. "I had assumed we would reach the body much more quickly, so I saw no reason to speculate aloud. After all, arthritis is not that unusual."

Bellman rested his gaze on Harry for a second before addressing the rest. "We have a suspect, folks. Anyone want to christen him?"

"The Eighth Guest," said Ærdal.

"Prince Charming," declared the Pelican.

For a few moments there was total silence, as though something had come up that required time to digest before they went on.

"Now, I'm no strategist," Beate Lønn began, in the secure knowledge that everyone in the room knew that Beate Lønn never commented on anything she hadn't researched thoroughly first, "but isn't there something here that makes you sit up and wonder? Leike had an alibi for the times of the murders, but what about all these leads pointing to him? What about the call from his home phone to Elias Skog? What about the murder weapon that was acquired in the Congo? Furthermore from an area where Leike had financial interests. Chance?"

"No," Harry said. "From day one Prince Charming has guided us toward Tony Leike. It was Prince Charming who paid Juliana Verni to go to the Congo because he knew that any clue pointing to the Congo would point to Tony Leike. And as far as his phone call to Elias Skog is concerned, today I checked something we should have checked long ago, but that we typically let go when we are getting close to a result. Because we resist any weakening of our evidence. Around the time the call went out from Leike's house to Skog there were three calls made from Leike's direct line in the Aker Brygge office building. Leike can't have been in two places at the same time. I'd bet two hundred kroner he was in Aker Brygge. Any takers?"

Silent but wide-eyed faces.

"Do you mean that Prince Charming called Elias Skog from Leike's house?" said the Pelican. "How—"

"When Leike came to Police HQ he told me there had been a break-in through the cellar door a few days earlier. That matches the time of the phone call to Skog. Prince Charming took a bike to disguise it as a standard burglary, innocent enough for us to make a note of it, but no more than that. Leike knows we don't do anything about that kind of break-in, so he didn't even report it. And with that Prince Charming had planted some irrefutable evidence against Leike."

"What a snake!" the Pelican erupted.

"I buy the explanation of how," Beate Lønn said. "But why? Why finger Tony Leike?"

"Because he knew that sooner or later we would link the murders with the Håvass cabin," Harry said. "And that would limit the number of suspects in such a way that everyone who had been there that night would have the spotlight on them. There were two reasons he tore out the page from the guest book. Number one, he had the names of those who were there, so that he could find them and kill them at his leisure, while we didn't and were therefore unable to stop him. Number two, and more important, he could keep his own name hidden."

"Logical," Ærdal said. "And to make quite sure we didn't go after him, he had to supply us with an apparent guilty party. Tony Leike."

"And that's why he had to wait until the end to kill Tony Leike," said one of the detectives, a man with an abundant Fridtjof Nansen mustache and whose surname was all Harry could recall.

His neighbor, a young man with bright, shiny skin and eyes, neither of whose names Harry could remember, interjected: "But unfortunately for him, Tony had an alibi for the times of the deaths. And since Tony's role as a scapegoat was redundant now, it was finally time to kill enemy **número uno.**"

The temperature in the room had risen, and the pale, tentative winter sun seemed to be brightening the proceedings. They were making progress; the knot had finally loosened. Harry could see that Bellman was sitting farther forward in his chair.

"That's all well and good," Beate Lønn said, and while Harry was waiting for the "but," he guessed what she was going to ask, knew she was going to play devil's advocate because she knew he had the answers. "But why has Prince Charming made this so unnecessarily complicated?"

"Because humans **are** complicated," Harry said, and could hear an echo of something he had heard and forgotten. "We want to do things that are complex, that mesh, where we control our fates and can feel like rulers of our own universes. The room that burned down at the Kadok factory—do you know what it reminded me of most? A control room. The headquarters. And it's not certain he even planned to take Leike's life. Perhaps he just wanted him arrested and convicted."

The silence was so pervasive that they could hear a bird twittering outside.

"Why?" asked the Pelican. "If he could have killed him? Or tortured him?"

"Because pain and death are not the worst that can befall mankind," Harry said, again hearing the echo. "Humiliation is. That was what he wanted for Leike. The humiliation of having everything you possess taken from you. The fall, the shame."

He saw a tiny smile playing on Beate Lønn's lips, saw her give a nod of acknowledgment.

"But," he continued, "as has been indicated, Tony had—unluckily for our killer—an alibi. And so Tony got away with the subsidiary punishment. Which was a slow and decidedly brutal death."

In the ensuing silence Harry sensed something flutter past. The smell of roasted meat. Then the room seemed to draw breath all at once.

"So what do we do now?" asked the Pelican.

Harry looked up. The twittering bird on the branch outside the window was a chaffinch. A migratory bird that had arrived too soon. That gave people hopes of spring, but that froze to death on the first frosty night.

Damned if I know, Harry thought. **Damned if I know.**

68

Pike

It was a long Kripos meeting that morning.

Bjørn Holm reported back on the forensic investigations at Kadok. No semen was found, nor any other physical evidence of the perpetrator. The room he had used was indeed completely burned out, and the computer had been reduced to a lump of metal, leaving no chance of recovering any data.

"He's probably been online using those unsecured networks in the area. Nydalen's full of them."

"He must have left some electronic trails," Ærdal said, but it sounded more like a refrain he had heard than something he could expatiate on beyond "must have" speculation.

"Of course, we could apply to access some of the hundreds of networks up there and search for whatever it is we don't know," Holm said. "But I have no idea how many weeks it could take. Or whether we would find anything."

"Leave it to me," Harry said. He had already gotten up and was on his way to the door while keying in a number. "I know someone."

He left the door ajar, and while he was waiting for an answer he heard one of the detectives say that no one they had spoken to had seen anyone come or go at Kadok, but that was not so surprising since it was hidden behind trees and bushes and, anyway, it was so dark now, in the winter months.

Harry got an answer. "Katrine Bratt's secretary."

"Hello?"

"Frøken Bratt is at lunch right now."

"Sorry, Katrine, but eating will have to wait. Listen . . ."

Katrine listened as Harry explained what he wanted.

"Prince Charming had pictures on the wall that had probably been printed off Internet news sites. With the search engine you could get onto the networks in the area, check the server logs and find out who has been on the news pages that covered the murders. Loads of people must have been—"

"Not as much as he was," Katrine said. "I'll just ask for a list sorted according to the number of downloads."

"Mm. You've learned this quickly."

"It's in the name. Katrine Bratt. **Bratt,** steep. Steep learning curve. Get it?"

Harry went back to the others.

They were playing the message that Harry had received from Leike's cell phone. It had been sent to NTNU, the technical university in Trondheim, for voice analysis. They had achieved useful results with sound recordings of bank robberies—in fact, better than with CCTV, since the voice—even if you try to distort it—is very difficult to disguise. But Bjørn Holm had been told that a bad recording of an indeterminate sound, coughing or laughter, was worthless and could not be used to make a voice profile.

"Damn," said Bellman, banging the table with his hand. "With a voice profile, a foothold, we could have started eliminating possible suspects from the case."

"Which possible suspects?" mumbled Ærdal.

"The base station signal tells us that whoever used Leike's phone was near the center of Ustaoset when he called," Holm said. "The signal faded right afterward—the operators' network has coverage only around the center of Ustaoset. But the fact that the signal faded strengthens the theory that it was Prince Charming who had the phone."

"Why's that?"

"Even when the phone's not being used the base station will pick up signals every other hour. The fact that it didn't receive any signals shows that the phone, before or after the call, was in the deserted mountain region around Ustaoset. Where perhaps it was carried during the avalanche and torture and so on."

No reaction. Harry knew that the euphoria from earlier had evaporated. He went to his chair.

"There's one possible way we could get a foothold, as Bellman suggested," he said softly, knowing that he no longer had to work to gain attention. "Cast your minds back to Leike's house and the break-in. Let's assume our killer broke into Leike's place to call Elias Skog from there. And let's assume that our white-clad crime scene officers were doing such a thorough job, as it appeared when I arrived and inadvertently . . . bumped into Holm . . ." Bjørn Holm tilted his head and sent Harry a spare-me-the-jokes look. "Shouldn't we already have fingerprints from Holmenveien that might well be . . . Prince Charming's?"

The sun lit up the room again. The others exchanged glances. Ashamed, almost. So simple. So obvious. And none of them had thought of it . . .

"It's been a long meeting with lots of new information," Bellman said. "Our brains are clearly beginning to get a little sluggish. But what do you think about this, Holm?"

Bjørn Holm slapped his forehead. "'Course we've got all the fingerprints. We did the investigation thinking Leike was the killer and his house a possible crime scene. We were hoping to find fingerprints that would match some of the victims'."

"Do you have many that were not identified?" Bellman asked.

"That's the point," said Bjørn Holm, smiling. "Leike had two Polish women who did the cleaning once a week. They'd been there six days before and done a thorough job. So we found prints only for Leike himself, Lene Galtung, the two Polish women and an unknown person whose prints definitely did not match those of the victims. We stopped looking for matches after Leike came up with his alibi and was released. But I don't remember off the top of my head where we found the unknown prints."

"But I do," Beate Lønn said. "I was given the report with sketches and photographs. The prints from X-One's left hand were found on top of the pompous and very ugly desk. Like so." She stood up and leaned on her left hand. "If I'm not much mistaken, it's where the landline is. Like so." She used her right hand to make the international sign for a telephone, thumb to her ear and little finger to her mouth.

"Ladies and gentlemen," Bellman said with a broad smile and a sweeping arm gesture, "I'll be damned if we don't have a genuine lead. Carry on searching for a match to X-One, Holm. But **promise** me it isn't the husband of one of the Polish women who joined them to make a few free calls home, all right?"

On the way out, the Pelican sidled up to Harry. She tossed one of her new dreads. "You might be better than I thought, Harry. But when you advance your theories, it wouldn't hurt to intersperse the occasional 'I think' here and there." She smiled and nudged him in the hip.

Harry appreciated the smile; the nudge in the hip, on the other hand . . . His phone vibrated in his pocket. He took it out. Not Rikshospital.

"He calls himself Nashville," said Katrine Bratt.

"Like the American town?"

"Yep. He's been on the websites of all the big newspapers, read the whole caboodle about the murders. The bad news is that's all I've got for you. Nashville's only been active on the Net for a couple of months, you see, and he's searched exclusively for things related to the murders. It almost seems as if Nashville has been waiting to be investigated."

"Sounds like our man, all right," Harry said.

"Well," Katrine said, "you'll have to search for men with cowboy hats."

"What?"

"Nashville. Mecca of country music and all that."

Pause.

"Hello? Harry?"

"I'm here. Right. Thanks, Katrine."

"Kisses?"

"All over."

"No, thank you."

They hung up.

Harry had been allocated an office with a view of Bryn and was observing some of the more unlovely details of the area when there was a knock at the door.

Beate Lønn was standing in the doorway.

"So, how does it feel to be in bed with the enemy?"

Harry shrugged. "The enemy's name is Prince Charming."

"Good. Just wanted to say we've run the finger-prints on the desk against the database and he's not on it."

"I didn't expect him to be."

"How's your dad?"

"Days away."

"Sorry to hear that."

"Thank you."

They looked at each other. And suddenly it struck

Harry that this was a face he would see at the funeral. A small pale face he had seen at other funerals, tear-stained, with large tragic eyes. A face as if made for funerals.

"What are you thinking about?" she asked.

"I know only one killer who has murdered in this way," Harry said, turning back to the view.

"He reminds you of the Snowman, doesn't he?"

Harry nodded slowly.

She sighed. "I promised I wouldn't tell you, but Rakel called."

Harry stared at the apartment buildings in Helsfyr.

"She asked about you. I said you were fine. Did I do the right thing, Harry?"

Harry took a deep breath. "Sure."

Beate remained in the doorway for a while. Then she left.

How is she? How is Oleg? Where are they? What do they do when night falls, who looks after them, who keeps watch? Harry rested his head on his arms and covered his ears with his hands.

Only one person knows how Prince Charming thinks.

The afternoon gloom descended without warning. The Captain, the overenthusiastic Hotel Bristol receptionist, called to say someone had called to ask if Iska Peller, the Australian lady in **Aftenposten,** was staying there. Harry said it was probably a journalist, but the Captain thought even the lowest press vermin knew the rules of the game; they had to introduce themselves by name and state where they worked. Harry thanked him and was about to ask him to call back if he heard any more, until he considered what this invitation would involve. Bellman called to say there was a press conference; if Harry felt like taking part, then . . .

Harry declined and could hear Bellman's relief.

Harry drummed on the desk. Lifted the receiver to phone Kaja, but cradled it again.

Raised it again and called some downtown hotels. None of them could recall being asked questions about anyone called Iska Peller.

Harry looked at his watch. He felt like a drink. He felt like going into Bellman's office, asking what the hell he had done with his opium, raising his fist and watching him cower . . .

Only one person knows.

Harry got up, kicked the chair, grabbed his wool coat and strode out.

He drove to town and parked in a glaringly illegal spot outside the Norwegian Theater. Crossed the street and went to the hotel reception desk.

The Captain had acquired his nickname while he was working as a doorman at the same hotel. The reason was probably a combination of the gaudy red uniform and the fact that he was continually commenting on, and issuing commands to, everyone and everything around him. Furthermore, he saw himself as the point person for anything of importance that happened downtown, the man with his finger on the city's pulse, the man who **knew.** The Informant with a capital **I,** an inestimable part of the police force's machinery that kept Oslo safe.

"Right at the very back of my brain, I can hear a rather special voice," the Captain said, tasting his own words with an appreciative smack. Harry caught the rolling eyes of the man standing next to the Captain behind the reception desk.

"Sort of gay," the Captain concluded.

"Do you mean high-pitched?" Harry asked, thinking of something Adele's friends had mentioned. Adele had said it was a turn-off the way her boyfriend spoke, like her gay flat mate.

"No, more like this." The Captain crooked his hands, fluttered his eyelashes and peformed a parody of a loud-mouthed queen. "I'm just sooo cross with you, Søren!"

His colleague, who, sure enough, was wearing a name tag inscribed SØREN, giggled.

Harry thanked him, and again it was on the tip of his tongue to ask the Captain to call him should anything else occur to him. He went outside. Lit a cigarette and looked up at the hotel sign. There was something . . . At that moment he spotted the Traffic Department car parked behind his and the overalled warden jotting down his registration number.

Harry crossed the street and held up his ID card. "I'm on police business."

"Makes no difference. No parking is no parking," Overalls said without pausing in his writing. "Send in a complaint."

"Well," Harry said, "you know we also have the authority to dish out parking fines if we want to?"

The man poked up his head and grinned. "If you think I'm going to let you write your own fine, you're wrong, pal."

"I was thinking more of **that** car." Harry pointed.

"That's mine and the Traffic—"

"No parking is no parking."

Overalls sent him a grouchy look.

Harry shrugged. "Send in a complaint. Pal."

Overalls slammed his notepad shut, spun on his heel and walked back to his car.

As Harry drove up Universitetsgata, his phone rang. It was Gunnar Hagen. Harry could hear the quiver of excitement in the usually controlled voice of the Crime Squad boss.

"Come here right away, Harry."

"What's happened?"

"Just come. The culvert."

Harry heard the voices and saw the flashes going off long before he had reached the end of the concrete corridor. Gunnar Hagen and Bjørn Holm were standing by the door to his old office. A woman from Krimteknisk was brushing the door and door handle for fingerprints while a Holm look-alike was taking pictures of half a boot print in the corner.

"The print's old," Harry said. "It was here before we moved in. What's going on?"

The look-alike gave a questioning look to Holm, who nodded that would be enough.

"One of the prison wardens discovered this on the floor by the door," Hagen said, holding up an evidence bag containing a brown envelope. Through the transparent bag Harry read his name. Printed on an address label stuck to the envelope.

"The prison warden figured it had been lying here for a couple of days, max. People don't go through this culvert every day, of course."

"We're measuring the moisture in the paper," Bjørn said. "We've put a similar envelope here and are waiting to see how long it takes to reach the same level of moisture. Then we work backward."

"There you go. Shades of **CSI**," Harry said.

"Not that the timing will help us," Hagen said. "There are no surveillance cameras where I assume he must have been. Which, of course, is fairly straightforward. Into a busy reception area, in the elevator, down here, no locked doors before you go up into the prison."

"No, why should we lock up here?" Harry said. "Anyone object to me having a smoke?"

No one answered, but looks were eloquent enough. Harry shrugged.

"I suppose at some point someone is going to tell me what was in the envelope," he said.

Bjørn Holm held up another evidence bag.

It was difficult to see the contents in the poor lighting, so Harry stepped closer.

"Oh, shit," he said and recoiled half a step.

"The middle finger," Hagen said.

"The finger looks as if it might have been broken first," Bjørn said. "Clean, smooth cut, no ragged skin. Chop. An ax. Or a large knife."

From the culvert came the resonant sound of rapid strides approaching.

Harry stared. The finger was white, drained of blood, but the tip was a bluish black.

"What's that? Have you taken fingerprints already?"

"Yes," Bjørn said. "And if we're lucky the answer is on its way."

"My guess is right hand," Harry said.

"You're correct. Well observed," Hagen said.

"Did the envelope contain anything else?"

"No. Now you know as much as we do."

"Maybe," Harry said, fidgeting with the cigarette packet. "But I know something else about the finger."

"We thought about that, too," Hagen said, exchanging glances with Bjørn Holm. The sound of clomping steps rose. "The middle finger of the right hand. It's the same finger the Snowman took off you."

"I've got something here," the female forensics officer interrupted.

The others turned to her.

She was squatting down holding an object between her thumb and first finger. It was grayish black. "Doesn't it look like the tiny stones we found at the Borgny crime scene?"

Harry went closer. "Yup. Lava."

The runner was a young man with a police ID card

hanging from the breast pocket of his shirt. He stopped in front of Bjørn Holm, placed his hands on his knees and gasped for breath.

"Well, Kim Erik?" Holm said.

"We found a match," the young man panted.

"Let me guess," Harry said, poking a cigarette between his lips.

The others turned their attention to him.

"Tony Leike."

Kim Erik looked genuinely disappointed: "H-how . . . ?"

"I thought I saw his right hand protruding from under the snowmobile, and it wasn't missing any fingers. So it must have been the left." Harry nodded toward the evidence bag. "The finger isn't broken, it's just distorted. Good old-fashioned arthritis. Hereditary but not contagious."

69

Looped Writing

The woman who opened the door of the terraced house in Hovseter was as broad-shouldered as a wrestler and as tall as Harry. She gazed at him and waited patiently, as if in the habit of giving people the necessary seconds to state their business.

"Yes?"

Harry recognized Frida Larsen's voice from the telephone. Which had made him visualize a slender, petite woman.

"Harry Hole," he said. "I found your address through the phone number. Is Felix in?"

"Out playing chess," she intoned flatly. A standard response, it seemed. "Email him."

"I would like to talk to him."

"What about?" She filled the doorway in a manner that prevented prying. And not only because of her size.

"We found a fragment of lava down at the police station. I was wondering if it was from the same volcano as the previous sample we sent him."

Harry stood two steps below her, holding the little stone. But she didn't budge from the threshold.

"Impossible to see," she said. "Email Felix." She made a move to close the door.

"I suppose lava is lava, eh?" Harry said.

She hesitated. Harry waited. He knew from experience that experts can never resist correcting laymen.

"Each volcano has its own unique lava composition," she said. "But it also varies from eruption to eruption. You have to analyze the stone. The iron-ore content can tell you a lot." Her face was expressionless, her eyes uninterested.

"What I would really like," Harry said, "is to inquire about these people who travel around the world studying volcanoes. There can't be that many of them, so I was wondering if Felix had an overview of the Norwegian contingent."

"There are more of us than you imagine," she said.

"So you're one of them?"

She shrugged.

"What's the last volcano you two were on?"

"Ol Doinyo Lengai in Tanzania. And we weren't on it, but nearby. It was erupting. Natrocarbonatite magma. The lava that emerges is black, but it reacts with air and after a few hours it's completely white. Like snow."

Her voice and face were suddenly alive.

"Why doesn't he want to speak?" Harry asked. "Is your brother mute?"

Her face went rigid again. The voice was flat and dead. "Email."

The door was slammed so hard Harry got dust in his eyes.

Kaja parked on Maridalsveien, jumped over the guardrail and trod carefully down the steep slope to the woods where the Kadok factory was situated. She switched on her flashlight and tramped through the shrubs, brushed away bare branches that wanted to thrust themselves into her face. The growth was dense, shadows leapt around like silent wolves and even when she stopped, listened and watched, shadows of trees fell upon trees, so that you didn't know what was what, like in a labyrinth of mirrors. But she wasn't frightened. It was an oddity that she who was so frightened of closed doors was not frightened of the dark. She listened to the roar of the river. Had she heard anything? A sound that ought not to be there? She went on. Ducked under a wind-blown tree trunk and stopped again. But the other sounds stopped the second she stopped. Kaja took a deep breath and finished her line of thought: as if someone who didn't want to be seen was following her.

She turned and shone the light behind her. Was no longer so sure about not being scared of the dark. Some branches swayed in the light, but they must be the ones she had disturbed, mustn't they?

She faced forward again.

And screamed when her flashlight lit up a deathly pale face with enlarged eyes. She dropped the flashlight and backed away, but the figure followed her with a grunting noise reminiscent of laughter. In the dark she could make out the figure bending down and standing up, then the next moment the blinding light from her flashlight was shining in her face.

She held her breath.

The grunted laughter stopped.

"Here," rasped a man's voice and the light jumped. "Here?"

"Your flashlight," the voice said.

Kaja took it and shone the light to the side of him. So that she could see him without blinding him. He had blond hair and a prognathous jaw.

"Who are you?" she asked.

"Truls Berntsen. I work with Mikael."

She had heard of Truls Berntsen, of course. The shadow. Beavis—wasn't that what Mikael called him?

"I'm—"

"Kaja Solness."

"Right, how do you . . . ?" She swallowed, refor-mulated the question. "What are you doing here?"

"Same as you," he answered with a single-toned rasp.

"Right. And what am I doing here?"

He laughed his grunt-laugh. But didn't reply. Stood right in front of her with his arms hanging down and away from his sides. One eyelid twitched as if an insect were trapped beneath it.

Kaja sighed. "If you're doing the same as me, you're here to keep an eye on the factory," she said. "In case he reappears."

"Yes, in case he reappears," said the Beavis type without taking his eyes off her.

"It's not so unlikely, is it?" she said. "He may not know it's burned down."

"My father worked there," Beavis said. "He used to say he made PSG, coughed PSG and became PSG."

"Are there a lot of Kripos people in the area? Did Mikael give you orders to come here?"

"You don't meet him anymore, do you? You meet Harry Hole."

Kaja felt a chill in her stomach. How on earth did this man know that? Had Mikael really told people about them?

"You weren't at Håvass," she said to change the topic.

"Wasn't I?" Grunted laughter. "I suppose I was free. Time off. Jussi was there."

"Yes," she said quietly. "He was there."

A gust of wind swept in, and she twisted her head to prevent a branch from scratching her face. Had he been following her or had he been here before she arrived?

When she turned to ask him, he wasn't there. She shone her flashlight between the trees. He was gone.

It was two in the morning when she parked on the street and went through the gate and up the steps to the yellow house. She pressed the button over the painted ceramic tile bearing the words FAM. HOLE in ornate looped writing.

After ringing for the third time she heard a low cough and turned to see Harry returning a service revolver to the lining of his trousers. He must have crept around the corner of the house without making any noise.

"What's up?" she asked, terrified.

"Just being extra careful. You should have phoned and said you were coming."

"Sh-shouldn't I have come?"

Harry went up the steps past her and unlocked the door. She followed him in, put her arms around him from behind, clung to his back and kicked the door shut with her heel. He freed himself, turned, was about to say something, but she stopped him with a kiss. A greedy kiss that demanded reciprocity. She put her cold hands up his shirt, felt from the glowing hot skin that he had come straight from bed, removed the revolver from his trousers and banged it down on the hall table.

"I want you," she whispered, bit his ear and pushed her hand down his trousers. His dick was warm and soft.

"Kaja . . ."

"Can I have you?"

She thought she could discern a slight hesitation, a certain reluctance. She wrapped her other hand around his neck, looked into his eyes. "Please . . ."

He smiled. Then his muscles relaxed. And he kissed her. Cautiously. More cautiously than she wanted. She groaned with frustration, undid his trouser buttons. Held his dick firmly without moving her hand, felt it grow.

"Fuck you," he sighed and lifted her. Carried her up the stairs. Kicked open the bedroom door and laid her on the bed. On his mother's side. She tilted back her head, closed her eyes, felt her clothes being removed, quickly, efficiently. Felt the heat radiating from his skin the moment he lowered himself onto her and forced her legs apart. Yes, she thought. Fuck me.

She lay with her cheek and ear against his chest, listening to his heartbeat.

"What were you thinking," she whispered, "when you were lying there knowing you were going to die?"

"That I was going to live," Harry said.

"Just that?"

"Just that."

"Not that you were going to . . . meet those you loved?"

"No."

"I did. It was strange. I was so frightened that something special was going to pieces. And then the horror passed and instead I was filled with peace. I just slept. And then you came. And woke me up. Rescued me."

Harry passed her his cigarette and she took a drag, then laughed gently.

"You're a hero, Harry. The type they give medals to. Who would have thought that of you, eh?"

Harry shook his head. "Believe me, sweetheart, I was thinking only of myself. I didn't spare you a thought until I reached the fireplace."

"Maybe not, but when you got there you still had very little air. By digging me out you knew we would use up the air twice as quickly."

"What can I say? I'm a generous guy."

She slapped his chest with a laugh. "A hero!"

Harry inhaled hard. "Or perhaps it was survival instinct outmaneuvering conscience."

"What do you mean?"

"The person I found first was so strong he almost managed to keep the pole. So I guessed it had to be Kolkka and that he was alive. I knew it was a question of seconds and minutes, but instead of digging him out, I prodded the snow to find you. You were quite still. I thought you were dead."

"So?"

"So maybe I was thinking deep down that if I dug out the dead one first the one who was alive might die in the meantime. In that way I could have all the air to myself. It's hard to know what governs your actions."

She went quiet. Outside, the snarl of a motorbike rose and fell. A motorbike in March. And today she had seen a migratory bird. Everything was out of balance.

"Do you always brood so much?" she asked.

"No. Maybe. I don't know."

She wriggled closer to him. "What are you brooding about now?"

"How he can know what he knows."

She sighed. "Our killer?"

"And why he's playing with me. Why he sends me a bit of Tony Leike. How he thinks."

"And how are you going to find out?"

He stubbed out the cigarette on the bedside table. Took a deep breath and released it in a long hiss. "That's the point. I can think of only one way. I have to talk to him."

"Him? Prince Charming?"

"Someone **like** him."

The dream came on the threshold of sleep. He was staring up at a nail. It was sticking out of a man's head. But there was something familiar about the face tonight. A familiar portrait, one he had seen so many times. Seen recently. The foreign object in Harry's mouth exploded and he twitched. He was asleep.

70

Blind Spot

Harry walked along the hospital corridor with a prison guard dressed in civilian clothing. Two strides in front was the doctor. She had informed Harry of his condition, prepared him for what he should expect.

They came to a door and the guard unlocked it. Inside, the corridor continued for a few yards. There were three doors in the wall to the left. A uniformed prison guard stood in front of one of them.

"Is he awake?" asked the doctor while the guard searched Harry. The officer nodded, put all the contents of Harry's pockets on the table, unlocked the door and stepped aside.

The doctor signaled that Harry should wait a moment and entered with the guard. She came back out immediately.

"Fifteen minutes, maximum," she said. "He's doing better, but he's weak."

Harry nodded. Took a deep breath. And stepped inside.

He stopped by the door and heard it close behind him. The curtains were drawn, and the room was dark, apart from a lamp by the bed. The light fell on a figure sitting semi-upright against a pillow, head bowed and long hair hanging down on each side.

"Come closer, Harry." The voice had changed; it sounded like the lament of unoiled door hinges. But Harry recognized it, and his blood ran cold.

He approached the bed and sat on the chair that had been provided. The man raised his head. And Harry stopped breathing.

He looked as if someone had poured hot wax over his face. Which had stiffened into a mask that was too tight, pulling the forehead and the chin back and turning the mouth into a small, lipless gap in a lumpy landscape of bony tissue. The laughter was two short blasts of air.

"Don't you recognize me, Harry?"

"I recognize the eyes," Harry said. "That'll do. It's you."

"Anything new from . . ." The small carplike mouth seemed to be forming a smile. "Our Rakel?"

Harry had prepared himself for this, braced himself the way a boxer braces himself for pain. Nonetheless, the sound of her name in his mouth made him clench his fists.

"You agreed to talk to me about a man. A man we think is like you."

"Like me? Better-looking, I trust." Again two short blasts. "It's bizarre, Harry. I've never been a vain man; I thought the pain would be the worst aspect of this illness. But do you know what? It's the deterioration. It's seeing yourself in the mirror, seeing the monster emerge. They still let me go to the bathroom alone, but I avoid the mirrors. I was a good-looking man, you know."

"Have you read the things I sent you?"

"I skimmed them. Dr. Dyregod's of the opinion I shouldn't wear myself out. Infections. Inflammations. Fever. She's genuinely concerned about my health, Harry. Quite astonishing when you consider what I've done, eh? Personally I'm more interested in dying. That's precisely where I envy those I . . . But you put a stop to that, didn't you, Harry?"

"Death would have been too kind a punishment."

Something seemed to ignite in the sick man's eyes and appeared as a cold white light from the slits in his face.

"At least I have a name and a place in the annals of history. People will read about the Snowman. Someone will inherit the mantle and act out my ideas in life. What do you have, Harry? Nothing. Quite the contrary—you've lost the little you had."

"True," Harry said. "You won."

"Do you miss your middle finger?"

"Well, I'm missing it right now." Harry raised his head and met the other's gaze. Held it. Then the small carp mouth opened. The laughter sounded like a gun with a silencer.

"At least you haven't lost your sense of humor, Harry. You know I'm going to demand something in return, don't you?"

"No pain, no gain. But go ahead."

The man twisted with some difficulty to the bedside table, lifted the glass of water standing there and put it to his mouth. Harry stared at the hand holding the glass. It resembled a white bird's claw. After finishing, the man carefully put the glass back and spoke. The lament was fainter now, like a radio on low batteries.

"I believe there is something in the prison manual about high suicide risks. At any rate, they watch me like hawks. They searched you before you came in, didn't they? Afraid you would bring me a knife or something similar. But I don't want to see any further deterioration, Harry. It's enough now, don't you think?"

"No," Harry said. "I don't think so. Talk about something else."

"You could have lied and said yes."

"Would you prefer that?"

The man waved a hand dismissively. "I'd like to see Rakel."

Harry raised an eyebrow. "Why's that?"

"I'd just like to say something to her."

"What?"

"That is a matter between her and me."

The chair scraped as Harry stood up. "It won't happen."

"Wait. Take a seat."

Harry took a seat.

The man looked down and tugged at the bedcover. "Don't misunderstand me. I have no regrets about the others. They were whores. But Rakel was different. She was . . . different. I just wanted to say that."

Harry studied him, dumbfounded.

"So what do you think?" the Snowman said. "Say yes. Lie if you have to."

"Yes," Harry lied.

"You're a bad liar, Harry. I want to talk to her before I help you."

"Out of the question."

"Why should I trust you?"

"Because you have no choice. Because thieves trust thieves when they have to."

"Do they?"

Harry forced a thin smile. "When I bought opium in Hong Kong, for a while we used a handicapped bathroom in the Landmark shopping mall, Des Voeux Road. I went in first, put a baby's bottle in the toilet tank in the cubicle on the far right. Went for a walk, looked at fake watches, returned and my bottle was still there. Always with the right quantity of opium in it. Blind faith."

"You said you used the bathroom 'for a while.' "

Harry shrugged. "One day the bottle disappeared. Perhaps the dealer cheated me, perhaps someone had seen us and made off with the money or the goods. There are no guarantees."

The Snowman eyed Harry thoughtfully.

Harry walked down the corridor with the doctor. The guard went first.

"That didn't take long," she said.

"He kept it brief," Harry said.

Harry strolled through the reception area, out to the parking lot, unlocked his car. Watched his hand tremble as he put the key in the ignition. The back of his shirt was drenched with sweat as he leaned against the seat.

He definitely kept it brief.

"Let's assume he's like me, Harry. After all, that assumption is vital if I am to be able to help you. Motive first. Hatred. A red-hot, burning hatred. This is the stuff of survival; it's the magma inside that keeps him warm. And, just like magma, hatred is a precondition of life, so that everything doesn't freeze to ice. At the same time the pressure from the internal heat will inevitably lead to an eruption, the destructive element released. And the longer it goes without an eruption, the more violent it will be. Now the eruption is in full flow, and it is violent. Which tells me you will have to search way back in time for the cause. Because it is not the actions committed out of hatred, but the cause of the hatred that will solve this riddle for you. The actions will make no sense without the cause. Hatred takes time to build up, but the cause is simple. Something happened. It's all about this one thing that happened. Find out what it is and you've got him."

Of all the metaphors, what had made him use a volcano? Harry drove down the steep, winding road from Bærum Hospital.

"Eight murders. He's the king now, at the top. He's built a universe in which everything appears to obey him. He's the puppet master, and he's playing with all of you. And especially with you, Harry. It's hard to see why you should have been the one— perhaps it's a matter of chance. Gradually, though, as he controls his puppets, he will look for more thrills. He will talk to the puppets, be close to them, enjoy his triumphs where he can enjoy them most, together with those over whom he triumphs. But he's well disguised. He doesn't stand out like a puppet master; he may even seem subservient, someone who is easily led, someone who is underestimated, someone you would never imagine could direct such a complex drama."

Harry was heading for downtown on the E18. There was a traffic jam. He shifted into the bus lane. He was a policeman, for Christ's sake. And this was urgent, urgent, urgent. His mouth was dry; the dogs were in full cry.

"He's close to you, Harry, of that I'm pretty certain; he simply can't let go. But he's closed in on you from a blind spot. Stolen into your life in some way and inspired trust at a time when you had your attention focused elsewhere. Or when you were weak. He's at home where he is. A neighbor, a friend, a colleague. Or someone who's simply there, right behind another person who is clearer to you, a shadow you don't even think about, other than as an appendix to this first person. Think about those who have crossed your field of vision. Because he has been there. You know his face already. He may not have exchanged many words with you, but if he's like me, he hasn't been able to restrain himself, Harry. **He's cozied up to you.**"

Harry parked outside the Savoy and went to the bar.

"What can I get you?"

Harry let his eyes wander along the bottles on the glass shelves behind the barman.

Beefeater, Johnnie Walker, Bristol Cream, Absolut, Jim Beam.

He was searching for a man with a burning hatred. Someone who didn't let his emotions stray. Someone with an armored heart.

His wandering eyes came to a halt. And jumped back. His mouth fell open. It was like a divine flash. And everything, **everything** was in that flash.

The voice came from a distance.

"Sir? Excuse me, sir?"

"Yes."

"Made a decision?"

Harry nodded slowly.

"Yes," he said. "Yes, I've made a decision."

71

Bliss

Gunnar Hagen was rolling a pencil between his forefingers and observing Harry, who for once was sitting—and not lying—in the chair in front of his desk.

"Technically, for the time being, you are employed by Kripos and therefore part of Bellman's team," the

Crime Squad boss said. "Ergo, an arrest by you would be a home win for Bellman."

"And if I—all this is still perfectly hypothetical— informed you and left the arrest to someone at Crime Squad, say, Kaja Solness or Magnus Skarre?"

"I would be forced to refuse such a generous offer even from you, Harry. As I said, I am bound by agreements."

"Mm. Bellman's still got a hold on you?"

Hagen sighed. "If I were to try something like taking an arrest off Bellman in Norway's biggest murder case, the Ministry of Justice would want to know everything right away. If I were to defy them and bring you back here to investigate this case, that would be regarded as disobeying orders. And it would hit the whole unit. Sorry, Harry, but I can't."

Harry mused, staring into middle distance. "OK, boss." He jumped up from the chair and strode to the door.

"Wait!"

Harry waited.

"Why are you asking me about this now, Harry? Has something happened that I ought to know about?"

Harry shook his head. "Just testing a few hypotheses, boss. That's our job, isn't it?"

Harry spent the hours until three o'clock making phone calls. The last one was to Bjørn Holm, who agreed to drive without a second thought.

"I haven't told you where or why," Harry said.

"No need," said Bjørn and continued, stressing every word. "I-trust-you."

There was a pause.

"Guess I deserved that," Harry said.

"Yes," said Bjørn.

"I have a feeling I apologized, but did I?"

"No."

"I didn't? OK. Mm . . . mm . . . mm. Christ, this is hard. Mm . . . mm . . ."

"Sounds like you've got a slow starter there, buddy boy," Bjørn said, but Harry could hear he was smiling.

"Sorry," Harry said. "I hope I have some fingerprints for you to check before we leave. If they don't match, you won't have to drive, if you get my drift."

"Why so secretive?"

"Because you trust me."

It was half past three when Harry knocked on the door of the small office at Rikshospital.

Sigurd Altman opened.

"Hi. Could you take a look at these?"

He passed the nurse a small pile of photographs.

"They're sticky," Altman said.

"They've come straight from the darkroom."

"Hm. A severed finger. What's that about?"

"I suspect the owner has been given a hefty dose of ketanome. I was wondering if you, as an anesthesia expert, can say whether we will be able to find any traces of the drug in the finger."

"Yes, no doubt—it circulates through the whole body with the blood."

Altman flicked through the photographs. "The finger looks pretty drained of blood, but in theory one drop is enough."

"Then the next question is whether you can assist us with an arrest tonight?"

"Me? Haven't you got pathologists who—"

"You know more than they do about this. And I need someone I can trust."

Altman shrugged, looked at his watch and passed the photographs back. "I'm off duty in two hours, so . . ."

"Great. We'll pick you up. You're going to be part of Norwegian crime history, Altman."

The nurse gave a wan smile.

Mikael Bellman called as Harry was on his way to Krimteknisk.

"Where've you been, Harry? Missed you at the morning meeting."

"Around and about."

"Around what?"

"Our wonderful city," Harry said, dropping an envelope on the bench in front of Kim Erik Lokker and pointing to his own fingertips to show him he wanted the contents checked for prints.

"I get nervous when you're not even on the radar for a whole day, Harry."

"Don't you trust me, Mi-ka-el? Afraid I'll end up on the drink?"

The other end went quiet.

"You report to me, and I would like to be kept informed, that's all."

"Reporting in to say there's nothing to report, boss."

Harry hung up and went in to see Bjørn. Beate was already waiting in his office.

"What did you want to tell us?" she asked.

"A real cops-and-robbers story," Harry said, taking a seat.

He was halfway through his narrative when Lokker stuck his head in the door.

"I've found these," he said, holding up a fingerprint transparency.

"Thanks," said Bjørn, sitting by the computer and taking the transparency. He put it on his scanner, brought up the file of the prints they had found on Holmenveien and started the matching program.

Harry was aware it would take only a couple of seconds, but he closed his eyes, felt his heart throbbing even though he knew—he knew. The Snowman knew. And had told Harry the little he had needed, formulated the words, made the sound wave that would trigger the avalanche.

This was how it had to be.

It should take only a couple of seconds.

His heart was thumping.

Bjørn Holm cleared his throat. But said nothing.

"Bjørn," Harry said, still with his eyes pinched shut.

"Yes, Harry."

"Is this one of those dramatic pauses you want me to savor?"

"Yes."

"Is it over now, you asshole?"

"Yes. And we have a match."

Harry opened his eyes. Sunlight. Flooding into the room, filling it so that they could veritably swim out on it. Bliss. Fucking bliss.

The three of them stood up at the same time. Staring at one another with open mouths that formed mute roars of delight. Then they embraced one another in a clumsy group hug, with Bjørn on the outside and little Beate squashed flat. They continued with muffled shouts and cautious high-fives, and Bjørn Holm concluded with what Harry considered above and beyond any normal demands of a Hank Williams fan, a flawless moonwalk.

72

Boy

The two men stood on a little grassy knoll—except that there was no grass—between the Manglerud church and the highway.

"We used to call it an earth hookah or an earth bong," said the man in the leather biker jacket, tossing long, thin strands of hair to the side. "In the summer we lay here smoking all the stuff we had. Fifty yards from the Manglerud Police Station." He smirked.

"There was me, Ulla, TV, his woman, plus a few others. Those were the days."

The man's eyes glazed over as Roger Gjendem took notes.

It had not been easy to find Julle, but in the end Roger had tracked him down to a bikers' club in Alnabru, where it turned out he ate, slept and lived his life as a free man; he moved no farther afield than the supermarket, to buy snuff and bread. Gjendem had seen it before, how prison made people dependent on familiar surroundings, routine, security. Though, strangely enough, Julle had agreed quite willingly to talk about the past. The operative word had been **Bellman.**

"Ulla was my woman and it was so fucking good because everyone around Manglerud was in love with Ulla." Julle nodded as if agreeing with himself. "But no one was so insanely jealous as him."

"Mikael Bellman?"

Julle shook his head. "The other one. The shadow. Beavis."

"What happened?"

Julle opened his palms. Roger had noticed the scabs. A jailbird migrating between dope in prison and dope outside. "Mikael Bellman snitched on me over some gasoline I stole; I already had a suspended sentence for hash, and so had to do time. I heard rumors that Bellman and Ulla had been seen together. Anyhow, when I got out and went to pick her up, the Beavis guy was waiting for me. Almost killed me. Said Ulla belonged to him. And Mikael.

Not to me, at any rate. And if I ever showed my face near . . ." Julle ran his forefinger across his lean neck with its gray stubble. "Pretty insane. And fucking scary. No one in the fucking gang believed me when I told them the Beavis guy had been so close to doing me in. The slavering idiot just trotted after Bellman."

"You mentioned something about quantities of heroin," Roger said. When he interviewed people in drug cases he always made sure he used precise terminology that could not be misunderstood, since the slang expressions changed quickly and meant different things in different places. For example, **smack** might mean cocaine in Hovseter, heroin in Hellerud and anything that got you high in Abildsø.

"Me, Ulla, TV and his woman were on a bike tour in Europe the summer I went to the slammer. We took a pound of boy with us from Copenhagen. Bikers like me and TV were checked at every single border crossing, but we sent the girls over separately. Jesus, they looked good, wearing summer dresses, with blue eyes and half a pound up their cunts. We sold most to a dealer down in Tveita."

"You're very open," Roger said while taking notes, putting brackets around "cunts" for later rewording and adding "boy" to a long list of synonyms for heroin.

"Time's lapsed, so they can't arrest anyone for it now. The point is that the dealer in Tveita was arrested. And was offered a reduced sentence if he snitched on the suppliers. Which, of course, he did, the scumbag."

"How do you know?"

"Ha! The guy told me a few years later, when we were doing time together in Ullersmo. He'd given the names and addresses of all fucking four of us, including Ulla. All that was missing was our national identity numbers. We were so fucking lucky that the case was shelved."

Roger took feverish notes.

"And guess who had the case at the Stovner cop shop? Guess who questioned the guy? Who, in all probability, recommended the case should be dropped, thrown out, shelved? Who saved Ulla's skin?"

"I'd like you to say, Julle."

"Very happy to. It was the cunt thief himself. Mikael Bellman."

"One last question," Roger said, knowing he had arrived at a critical point. Could the story be proved? Could the source be checked? "Do you have the name of the dealer? I mean, he's not risking anything and his name won't be mentioned anyway."

"Would I snitch on him, you mean?" Julle laughed out loud. "You bet your ass I will."

He spelled the name, and Roger turned a page and wrote it in capital letters while noticing that his jaw was broadening. Into a smile. He controlled himself and put on a straight face. But he knew the taste was going to be there for a long time: the sweet taste of a scoop.

"Thank you for your help," Roger said.

"Thank **you**," said Julle. "Just make sure you crush that Bellman—then we're even."

"Er, by the way, out of curiosity, why do you think the dealer told you he had informed on you?"

"Because he was frightened."

"Frightened? Why?"

"Because he knew too much. He wanted others to know the story in case the cop carried out his threat."

"Bellman **threatened** the informer?"

"Not Bellman. His shadow. He said if the guy so much as mentioned Ulla's name again he would put something in him that would shut him up. Forever."

73

Arrest

Bjørn Holm's Volvo Amazon turned in to Rikshospital, opposite the tram stop. Sigurd Altman stood waiting with his hands in his duffel-coat pockets. Harry beckoned to him from the backseat. Sigurd and Bjørn said hello, and they drove on to Ringveien, where they continued eastward toward the Sinsen intersection.

Harry leaned forward between the seats.

"It was like one of the chemistry experiments we did at school. In fact, you have all the ingredients you need to get a reaction, but you don't have the catalyst, the external component, the spark that's necessary to trigger it. I had the information—all I needed was something to help me assemble it in the correct fashion. My catalyst was a sick man, a murderer known as the Snowman. And a bottle on a bar shelf. All right if I have a smoke?"

Silence.

"I see. Well . . ."

They drove through the tunnel at Bryn, up toward the Ryen intersection and Manglerud.

Truls Berntsen stood on the old undeveloped site, looking up the slope toward Bellman's house.

How peculiar it was that he who had so often eaten dinner, played and slept there when they were growing up had not been there a single time since Mikael and Ulla took over the house.

The reason was obvious: He had not been invited.

He sometimes stood where he was now, in the afternoon dusk, looking up at the house to catch a glimpse of her. Her, the unattainable one no one could have. No one except him, the prince, Mikael. Now and then he wondered whether Mikael knew. Knew and that was why they didn't invite him. Or was she the one who knew? And made it clear to Mikael, without saying as much, that this Beavis he had grown up with was not someone they needed to associate with privately. At least not now that his career had finally taken off, and it was more important to move in the right circles, meet the right people, send out the right signals. It wasn't tactically astute to surround yourself with ghosts from a past that contained things best forgotten.

Oh, he knew that. He just didn't know why she

couldn't understand it: that he would never hurt her. The opposite. Had he not protected her and Mikael all these years? Yes, he had. He kept watch, was there for them, cleaned up. Ministered to their happiness. Such was his love.

The windows up there this evening were lit. Were they having a party? Were they eating and laughing, drinking wines the Manglerud liquor stores had never stocked, and speaking in the new way? Was she smiling and were her eyes sparkling, eyes that were so beautiful it hurt when they looked at you? Would she see more in him if he acquired money, became rich? Was that a possibility? Something so simple?

He stood for a while at the bottom of the explosion-riddled building site. Then he lumbered home.

Bjørn Holm's Amazon tilted majestically around the Ryen roundabout.

A sign showed the exit for Manglerud.

"Where are we going?" Sigurd Altman asked, leaning against the door.

"We're going where the Snowman said we should go," Harry said. "Way back in time."

They passed the exit.

"Here," Harry said, and Bjørn bore right.

"The E-Six?"

"Yep, we're going east. To Lyseren. Know these parts, Sigurd?"

"Well enough, but—"

"This is where the story starts," Harry said. "Many

years ago, outside a dance hall. Tony Leike, the man who owned the finger I showed you photos of before, is standing at the edge of the woods, kissing Mia, County Officer Skai's daughter. Ole, who's in love with Mia, goes out to look for Mia and bumps into them. Devastated and angry, Ole throws himself on the interloper, the charmer Tony. But now another side of Tony reveals itself. Gone is the smiling, charming flirt everyone likes. To be replaced by a beast. And like all animals that feel threatened, he attacks, with a fury and brutality that numb Ole, Mia and subsequent onlookers. The blood mist has descended; he takes out a knife and cuts off half of Ole's tongue before he is dragged away. And even though Ole is innocent in this matter, he is the one who is afflicted by shame. The shame of his unrequited love being exhibited in front of others, humiliation in rural Norway's ritual mating duel and his stunted speech as eternal evidence of his defeat. So he flees. Flees. Are you with me so far?"

Altman nodded.

"Many years pass. Ole has established himself somewhere new, has a job where he is well liked and respected for his abilities. He has friends—not many, but enough; all that counts is that they don't know his past. What's missing in his life is a woman. He has met some, via dating websites, personal ads, on the odd occasion at a restaurant. But they soon evaporate. Not because of his tongue, but because he carries the defeat with him like a knapsack full of shit. Because of an ingrained self-denigrating way of speaking, an anticipation of rejection and a suspicion of women who behave as if they actually **do** want him. The usual stuff. The stench of defeat that everyone flees. Then one day something happens. He meets a woman who has done the rounds. She even lets him live out his sexual fantasies; they have sex in a disused factory. He invites her on a ski trip in the mountains, as a first sign he means business. Her name is Adele Vetlesen, and she joins him with some reluctance."

Bjørn Holm turned off by Grønmo, where the smoke from incinerated garbage rose into the air.

"They have a great ski trip in the mountains. Maybe. Or maybe Adele is bored; she's a restless soul. They go to a cabin in Håvass, where there are already five people; Marit Olsen, Elias Skog, Borgny Stem-Myhre, Charlotte Lolles and a sick Iska Peller, who is sleeping off her fever in a room alone. After dinner they light the fire and someone opens a bottle of red wine while others go to bed. Like Charlotte Lolles. And Ole, who is lying in a sleeping bag in the bedroom waiting for his Adele. But Adele would rather be up. Perhaps at last she has begun to notice the stench. Then something happens. One last person arrives late at night. The walls are thin and Ole hears a new man's voice from the sitting room. He stiffens. It's the voice from his worst nightmare, from his sweetest dreams of revenge. But it can't be him; it **can't** be. Ole listens. The voice talks to Marit Olsen. For a while. Then it talks to Adele. He hears her laughing. But gradually they lower their voices. He hears the others go to bed in adjoining rooms. But not Adele. And not this man with the familiar voice. Then he hears nothing. Until the sounds outside reach his ears. He creeps over to the window, looks out, sees them, sees her eager face, recognizes her moans of pleasure. And he knows the impossible is happening; history is repeating itself. For he recognizes the man standing behind Adele, who is taking her. It's him. It's Tony Leike."

Bjørn Holm turned up the heat. Harry pushed himself back in the seat.

"When the others get up the following morning, Tony has left. Ole acts as if nothing has happened. Because he is stronger now; many years of hatred have hardened him. He knows the others have seen Adele and Tony; they have seen his humiliation, just like before. But he is calm. He knows what he is going to do. He might have been longing for it, this last nudge, the free fall. A couple of days later he has a plan ready. He returns to the Håvass cabin, maybe gets a lift there on a snowmobile, and tears out the page in the guest book detailing their names. For this time it won't be he who flees the witnesses in shame; they are the ones who are going to suffer. And Adele. But the person who will suffer most is Tony. He will have to carry all the shame Ole has carried; his name will be dragged through the mud; his life will be destroyed; he will be smitten by the same unjust God who allows tongues of the lovelorn to be severed."

Sigurd Altman rolled down the window and a soft whistling sound filled the car.

"The first thing Ole has to do is find himself a

room, a headquarters where he can work undisturbed and without fear of being discovered. And what could be more natural than the disused factory where he experienced the happiest night of his life? There he starts gathering information about his victims and planning in detail. Of course, he has to kill Adele Vetlesen first, as she was the only person at Håvass to know his full identity. Names that may have been exchanged up there would have been forgotten soon enough, and no copy of the guest book page existed. Sure about the cigarette, boys?"

No answer. Harry sighed.

"So he arranges to meet her again. He picks her up in a car. The inside of which he has covered with plastic. They drive to an undisturbed spot, probably the Kadok factory. There he takes out a large knife with a yellow handle. He forces her to write a postcard he dictates and to address it to her flat mate in Drammen. Afterward he kills her. Bjørn?"

Bjørn Holm coughed and shifted down a gear. "The autopsy shows he punctured her carotid artery."

"He gets out of the car. Takes a picture of her sitting in the passenger seat with a knife in the neck. The photograph: confirmation of revenge, of triumph. It's the first photo that goes on his office wall in the Kadok factory."

An oncoming car swerved out of its lane, but went back in and hooted its horn as it passed.

"Perhaps it was easy to kill her. Perhaps not. Nevertheless, he knows she is the most critical victim.

They hadn't met very often, but he can't know for sure how much she has told her friends about him. He only knows that if she is found dead and her death can be linked to him, a dumped lover will be the police's main suspect. **If** she is found. If, on the other hand, she apparently disappears, for example, during a trip to Africa, he is safe.

"So Ole sinks her body in a place he knows well, where the water is deep and, what's more, where people keep well away. The place with the jilted bride in the window. The ropery by Lake Lyseren. Then he travels to Leipzig and pays the prostitute, Juliana Verni, to take the postcard Adele wrote with her to Rwanda, to stay at a hotel under Adele's name and send the card to Norway. Furthermore, she has to bring Ole something back from the Congo. A murder weapon. A Leopold's apple. The special weapon is not plucked out of the air, of course; it has to have some connection with the Congo and prompt the police to become suspicious about the Congo traveler Tony Leike. Ole pays Juliana on her return to Leipzig. And perhaps it is there, standing over the trembling Juliana, in tears as she opens her mouth to receive the apple, that he begins to experience the joy, the ecstasy, of sadism, an almost sexual pleasure he has developed and nourished for years with his lonely daydreams of revenge. Afterward he dumps her in the river, but the body surfaces and is found."

Harry took a deep breath. The road had become narrower, and the forest had slunk in, was dense on both sides now.

"In the course of the next weeks, he kills Borgny Stem-Myhre and Charlotte Lolles. Unlike with Adele and Juliana, he doesn't try to hide their bodies—quite the contrary. Nevertheless, the police investigation does not lead them to Tony Leike, as Ole has hoped. So he has to continue killing, continue to leave a trail, to push them. He kills Marit Olsen, the MP, exhibits her in the Frogner pool. Now the police have to see the connection between the women, have to find the man with the Leopold's apple. But it doesn't happen. And he knows he will have to intervene, give a helping hand, take a risk. He watches Tony's house on Holmenveien until he sees him leave. Then he breaks in through the cellar, goes up to the living room and calls the next victim, Elias Skog, from Tony's phone on the desk. On the way out he steals a bike to make the break-in appear normal. Leaving fingerprints upstairs in the living room doesn't bother Ole; everyone knows the police don't investigate run-of-the-mill burglaries. Then he goes to Stavanger. At this point his sadism is in full bloom. He kills Elias by gluing him to the bathtub and leaving the tap running. Hey, gas station! Anyone hungry?"

Bjørn Holm didn't even slow down.

"OK. Then something does happen. Ole receives a letter. It's from a blackmailer. He writes that he knows Ole has killed and he wants money. Otherwise the police will be around. Ole's first thought is that it must be someone who knows he was at Håvass, so it must be one of the two survivors: Iska Peller or Tony

Leike. He excludes Iska Peller right away. She's Australian, went back and, anyway, is hardly likely to write in Norwegian. Tony Leike—what irony! They never met at the cabin, but Adele may of course have mentioned Ole's name while they were flirting. Or Tony may have seen Ole's name in the guest book. At any rate, Tony must have guessed the connection, since the murders appeared in the newspapers. The blackmail attempt squares pretty well with what the financial press is writing about Tony being desperately in need of funds for his Congo project. Ole makes a decision. Even though he would have preferred that Tony live with the shame, he has to turn to the second option before things spiral out of control. Tony has to die. He tails Tony. Follows him onto the train, which goes where Tony always goes—Ustaoset. Follows his snowmobile tracks, which lead to a locked Tourist Association cabin situated among cliffs and crevices. And that's where Ole finds him. And Tony recognizes the ghost, the boy from the dance hall, the boy whose tongue he cut off. And realizes what's in store for him. Ole takes his revenge. He tortures Tony. Burns him. Maybe to make him reveal possible partners in the blackmail venture. Maybe for his own enjoyment."

Altman rolled the window back up, hard.

"Cold," he said.

"While this is going on, he hears on the news that Iska Peller is in the cabin at Håvass. Ole senses that the final solution may be at hand, but smells a trap. He remembers the snowdrift above the cabin that locals said was dangerous. He makes a decision. Perhaps he takes Tony with him as a guide, heads for the Håvass cabin, starts the avalanche with dynamite. Then he drives the snowmobile back, unloads Tony— dead or alive—off the precipice and sends the snowmobile after him. If somehow the body is ever found, it will look like an accident. A man who has burned himself and is on his way to find help, perhaps."

The countryside opened up. They passed a lake with the moon reflected in it.

"Ole triumphs; he's won. He's tricked everyone, pulled the wool over their eyes. And he's started to enjoy the game, the feeling of being in power, of having everyone follow his directions. So the master, who has bound eight individual fates into one big drama, decides to leave us with a parting gesture. To leave me with a parting gesture."

A cluster of houses, a gas station and a shopping center. They took the left exit off a roundabout.

"Ole cuts off the middle finger of Tony's right hand. And he has Leike's phone. It's the one he used when he called me from the center of Ustaoset. My number is unlisted, but Tony Leike has it on his cell phone. Ole doesn't leave a message. Perhaps it is just playful whimsy."

"Or to confuse us," Bjørn Holm said.

"Or to show us his superiority," Harry said. "Like when he quite literally gives us the finger by leaving Tony's middle finger outside my door, inside Police HQ, right under our very noses. Because he can do that. He's Prince Charming, he's recovered from the shame, he's retaliated, avenged himself on all those who mocked him and on their understudies. The witnesses. The whore. And the lech. Then something unforeseen happens. The hideaway at Kadok is found. In fact, the police still don't have any evidence to lead them straight to Ole, but they're beginning to get dangerously close. So Ole goes to his boss and says that finally he'll take his vacation and accumulated personal time. He'll be away for a good while. His plane leaves the day after tomorrow, by the way."

"Nine-fifteen to Bangkok, via Stockholm," Bjørn Holm said.

"OK—lots of the details in this story are assumptions, but we're getting close. Here we are."

Bjørn turned off the road and onto the gravel in front of the large red-timber building. Stopped and switched off the ignition.

There was no light in any of the windows, but advertisements hung on the ground-floor walls, showing that a corner of the building had once been a grocery store. At the other end of the square, fifty yards in front of them and beneath a streetlight, stood a green Jeep Cherokee.

It was still. Sound-still, time-still, wind-still. From the top of the window on the driver's side of the Cherokee, cigarette smoke rose into the light.

"This is the place where it all began," Harry said. "The dance hall."

"Who's that?" Altman asked, nodding toward the Cherokee.

"Don't you recognize him?" Harry took out a packet of cigarettes, placed one between his lips, unlit, and stared hungrily at the tobacco smoke. "You might be deceived by the street lamp, of course. Most of the older street lamps cast a yellow light, making a blue car seem green."

"I've seen the film," Altman said. "**In the Valley of Elah.**"

"Mm. Good film. Almost Altman class."

"Almost."

"Sigurd Altman class."

Sigurd didn't answer.

"So," Harry said. "Are you happy? Was it the masterpiece you had envisaged, Sigurd? Or can I call you Ole Sigurd?"

74

Bristol Cream

"I prefer Sigurd."

"Pity it's not as easy to change first names as surnames," Harry said, leaning forward between the seats again. "When you told me you'd changed the usual -sen surname, I didn't think that the S in Ole S. Hansen might stand for Sigurd. But did it help, Sigurd? Did the new name make you into someone different from the person who lost everything in the gravel on this very spot?"

Sigurd shrugged. "We flee as far as we can. I suppose the new name took me part of the way."

"Mm. I've checked out a number of things today. When you moved to Oslo you started nursing studies. Why not medicine? After all, you had top grades from school."

"I wanted to avoid having to speak in public," Sigurd said with an ironic smile. "I assumed as a nurse I would be exempt."

"I called a speech therapist today, and he told me it depends which muscles are damaged. In theory, even with half a tongue you can train yourself to speak almost perfectly again."

"The s's are tricky without the tip of a tongue. Was that what gave me away?"

Harry rolled down the window and lit his cigarette. Inhaled so hard the paper crackled and rustled.

"That was one of the things. But we went off on the wrong track for a while. The speech therapist told me that people have a tendency to associate lisping with male homosexuality. In English it's called a 'gay lisp' and does not constitute lisping in a speech-therapy sense; it's just a different way of articulating the letter s. Gay men can switch lisping on and off; they use it as a sort of code. And the code works. The speech therapist told me an American university had done some linguistic research to see whether it was possible to deduce sexual tendencies in people by listening only to recorded speech. The results were fairly accurate; however, it transpired that the perception of a gay lisp was so strong that it overrode other language signals that were characteristic of straight men. When the receptionist at Hotel Bristol said that the man asking after Iska Peller spoke in an effeminate way, he was a victim of stereotypical thinking. It was only when he acted out how the person had spoken that I realized he had allowed himself to be duped by the lisp."

"There must have been a little more than that."

"Yes, indeed. Bristol. It's a suburb in Sydney, Australia. I can see you've figured out the connection now."

"Hang on," Bjørn said. "I haven't."

Harry blew smoke out of the window. "The Snowman told me. The killer wanted to be close. He had crossed my field of vision, he had cozied up to me. So when a bottle of Bristol Cream crossed my field of vision, it clicked at long last. I remembered seeing the same name, and telling someone something. Someone who had cozied up to me. And then I realized that what I had said had been misunderstood. I gave Iska Peller's place of residence as Bristol. By which the person inferred I meant Hotel Bristol, in Oslo. I said that to you, Sigurd. At the hospital, right after the avalanche."

"You have a good memory."

"For some things. When suspicion first fell on you, other things became quite obvious. Like you saying that one has to work in anesthesia to get hold of ketanome in Norway. Like a friend of mine saying that we often desire those things we see every day, which would suggest that whoever has sexual fantasies about women dressed in a nurse's outfit may work at a hospital. Like the screen name on the computer at the Kadok factory being Nashville, the name of a film directed by—"

"Robert Altman in 1975," Sigurd said. "A much-underrated masterpiece."

"And the chair at the hideaway at Kadok being, it goes without saying, a director's chair. For the master director, Sigurd Altman."

Sigurd didn't react.

"But still I didn't know what your motive was," Harry continued. "The Snowman told me that the killer was driven by hatred. And the hatred was engendered by one single event, one that lay back in the mists of time. Perhaps I already had a hunch. The tongue. The lisping. I got a friend from Bergen to do a little digging on Sigurd Altman. It took her about thirty seconds to discover your change of name on the national register and to connect it with the old name mentioned in Tony Leike's conviction for assault."

A cigarette was flicked out of the Cherokee window, leaving a trail of sparks.

"So there was just the question of the timeline left," Harry said. "We checked the duty roster at Rikshospital. That seems to give you an alibi for two of the murders. You were working when Marit Olsen and Borgny Stem-Myhre were killed. But both murders were committed in Oslo, and no one at the hospital can remember with certainty having seen you at the times in question. And since you travel between departments no one would have missed you if they hadn't seen you for a couple of hours. Correct me if I'm wrong, but I think you'll tell me you spend most of your free time alone. And indoors."

Sigurd Altman shrugged. "Probably."

"So there we are," Harry said with a clap of his hands.

"Just a minute," Altman said. "The story you've told is pure fiction. You don't have a scrap of evidence."

"Oh, I forgot to say: You remember the photos I showed you earlier today? The ones I asked you to flick through and you said were sticky?"

"What about them?"

"You get great fingerprints from them. Yours matched the ones we found on the desk at Leike's place."

Sigurd Altman's expression changed slowly as the realization sank in. "You only showed them to me . . . so that I would hold them?" Altman stared at Harry for a few seconds, as if turned to stone. Then he put his face in his hands. And a sound emerged from behind his fingers. Laughter.

"You considered almost every angle," Harry said. "Why didn't you think it prudent to find yourself a respectable alibi?"

"It didn't occur to me that I needed one." Altman took his hands away. "You would have seen through everything anyway, Harry, wouldn't you?"

The eyes behind the glasses were moist, but not devastated. Resigned. Harry had experienced this before. The relief at being caught. Being able to unburden yourself at last.

"Probably," Harry said. "I mean, officially, I didn't see through any of this. The man sitting in the vehicle over there did. He's the one who will arrest you."

Sigurd removed his glasses and dried his tears of laughter. "So you were lying when you said you needed me to tell you about ketanome?"

"Yes, but I wasn't lying when I said your name would go down in Norwegian crime history."

Harry nodded to Bjørn, who flashed his lights.

A man jumped out of the Cherokee in front of them.

"An old acquaintance of yours," Harry said. "At least his daughter was."

The man ambled over, slightly bow-legged, hitched up his trousers by the belt. Like an old policeman.

"One last thing I was wondering," Harry said. "The Snowman said you would steal up on me, unnoticed, while I was vulnerable, maybe. How did that come about?"

Sigurd put his glasses back on. "All patients admitted have to give the name of their next of kin. Your father must have given your name, because in the cafeteria one of the nurses mentioned that the father of the man who had caught the Snowman, Harry Hole himself, was on her ward. I took it for granted that someone with your reputation would be given the case. At that time I was actually working on other wards, but I asked the ward manager if I could use your father for an anesthesia paper I was writing, said he fit my test group exactly. I thought that if I could get to know you via your father then I would find out how the case was going."

"You could be **close,** you mean. Feel the pulse of the case and have your superiority confirmed."

"When you finally made an appearance, I had to take care not to ask you direct questions about the investigation." Sigurd Altman took a deep breath. "I didn't want to arouse suspicion. I had to be patient, wait until I had built up trust."

"And you succeeded."

Sigurd nodded slowly. "Thank you—I like to believe I inspire trust. By the way, I called my office at the Kadok factory the 'clipping room.' When you broke in I lost my mind. It was my home. I was so furious I was on the verge of disconnecting your father from the respirator, Harry. But I didn't. I would like you to know that."

Harry didn't respond.

"One more thing." Sigurd said. "How did you find out about the locked Tourist Association cabin?"

Harry shrugged. "By chance. A colleague and I had to stay the night. It seemed as if someone had just been there. And something was stuck to the wood stove. Bits of flesh, I guessed. It was a while before I connected it with the arm sticking out from under the snowmobile. It looked like an overdone sausage. The county officer went to the cabin, poked at the flesh and sent the pieces for DNA testing. We'll have the results in a few days. Tony kept personal possessions there. I found a family photo in a drawer, for instance. Tony as a boy. You didn't clean up after yourself properly, Sigurd."

The policeman had stopped by the driver's window, and Bjørn rolled it down. He stooped, looked past Bjørn and at Sigurd Altman.

"Hi, Ole," Skai said. "I am hereby arresting you for the murder of a whole load of people whose names I should have studied up on, but we'll take things one step at a time. Before I come around and open the door, I would like you to place both hands on the dashboard so that I can see them. I'm going to handcuff you, and you will have to accompany me to a nice, freshly spruced-up cell. The wife has made meatballs with mashed rutabaga. Seem to remember you like that. That sound all right, Ole?"

Part Eight

75

Perspiration

"What the fuck's this supposed to mean?"

It was seven o'clock, the Kripos building was stirring into life and in the doorway to Harry's office stood a fuming Mikael Bellman with a briefcase in one hand and a copy of **Aftenposten** in the other.

"If you're thinking about **Aftenposten**—"

"I'm thinking about this, yes!" Bellman smacked the newspaper down on the desk in front of him.

The headlines covered half the front page: PRINCE CHARMING ARRESTED LAST NIGHT. The press had gotten hold of the sobriquet **Prince Charming** the same day they had christened him in the Odin conference room. "Arrested last night" was not quite accurate, of course; it was more early evening, but Skai had not had time to send out the press release until midnight, after the TV stations' last news programs and before the newspapers' deadlines. It had been brief and did not specify the time or circumstances, only that Prince Charming, after intense investigation by local police, had been arrested outside the old dance hall in Ytre Enebakk.

"What's this supposed to mean?" Bellman repeated.

"I presume it means the police have one of Norway's most notorious killers under lock and key," Harry said, trying to release the high-backed chair.

"The police?" hissed Bellman. "The local police in"—he had to consult the newspaper—"Ytre Enebakk?"

"I don't suppose it matters who clears up the case so long as it's cleared up, does it?" said Harry, groping for the lever beside the seat. "How do these things work?"

Bellman shut the door. "Listen here, Hole."

"No 'Harry' anymore?"

"Shut your mouth and listen carefully. I know what's gone on here. You've been talking to Hagen and were told you couldn't hand over the arrest to him and Crime Squad; it was too risky. So, since you couldn't go for a home win, you went for a draw. You bequeathed the honor and the points to a police bumpkin who couldn't tell you one end of a murder investigation from the other."

"Me, boss?" Harry said, giving him a blue-eyed, aggrieved look. "One of the bodies was found in his district, so it's natural enough that he followed up on a local level. Then he picked up on this background story about Tony Leike. Damn fine police work, if you ask me."

The white patches on Bellman's forehead seemed to be turning all the colors of the rainbow.

"Do you know how this will be construed by the Ministry of Justice? They have put the investigation in my hands; I keep at it week after week, no result. Then along comes this fucking inbred and after a couple of days cuts us off on the inside lane."

"Mm." Harry yanked at the lever and the seat

tipped back violently. "Doesn't sound too good when you put it like that, boss."

Bellman placed his palms on the desk, leaned forward and snarled, sending small white spit balls in Harry's direction. "I hope it doesn't sound too good, Hole. This afternoon a lump of opium found in your house is going to the lab to be identified. Your goose is cooked, Hole!"

"And afterward, boss?" Harry bobbed up and down as he wrestled with the lever.

Bellman frowned. "What the hell do you mean?"

"What are you going to say to the press and the Ministry of Justice? When they see the date of the search warrant you used, issued in your name? And ask how it can be that the day after you find opium at a policeman's house, you give the selfsame officer a prominent position in your own investigative unit? Some might claim that if Kripos is governed like that, it's no wonder a country cop with one cell and a wife who cooks is better at finding killers."

Bellman's jaw dropped and he kept blinking.

"There!" Harry leaned against the seat back, now locked into position, with a contented smile on his face. And screwed up his eyes to meet the rush of air after the door was slammed.

The sun had slipped over the edge of the mountain as Krongli stopped the snowmobile, got off and went over to Roy Stille, who was standing beside a ski pole stuck deep in the snow.

"Well?"

"I think we've found it," Stille said. "This has to be the stick that Hole fellow marked the site with."

The soon-to-be-retired policeman had never had any ambitions to rise up the career ladder, but the thick white hair, the intent gaze and the calm voice were such that when he spoke, people concluded he was the superior officer, and not Krongli.

"Oh?" Krongli said.

He accompanied Stille to the edge of the precipice. Stille pointed. And there, down in the scree, he saw the snowmobile. He adjusted the binoculars. Focused on the bare, burned arm sticking out. Mumbled half aloud: "Oh, shit. At last. Or both."

The breakfast customers had begun to leave Stopp Pressen when Bent Nordbø heard a cough, looked up from **The New York Times**, removed his glasses, squinted and mustered the closest he would ever get to a smile.

"Gunnar."

"Bent."

The greeting, saying each other's name, was something they had from the lodge and always reminded Gunnar Hagen of ants meeting and exchanging smells. The Crime Squad boss sat down, but did not remove his coat. "You said on the phone you'd found something."

"One of my journalists has dug this up." Nordbø pushed a brown envelope across the table. "Looks like Mikael Bellman protected his wife in a drug case. It's old, so from a legal point of view they're untouchable, but in the press . . ."

"They're always touchable," Hagen said, taking the envelope.

"I believe you may safely regard Mikael Bellman as neutralized."

"At least a balance of terror can be achieved. He has things on me, too. Besides, I may not even need this—he's just been humiliated by an officer from Ytre Enebakk."

"I read that. And the Ministry of Justice has read it, too—isn't that so?"

"Up there, they read papers and keep their ears to the ground. But thank you, anyway."

"My pleasure—we help each other."

"Who knows—I may need this one day." Gunnar Hagen put the envelope inside his coat.

He didn't receive a response, as Bent Nordbø had already resumed his reading of an article about a young black American senator by the name of Barack Obama, who, the writer maintained in all seriousness, could one day become the president of the United States.

When Krongli was down, he called up to the others that he had arrived, and he untied the rope.

The snowmobile was an Arctic Cat and lay with its runners in the air. He dragged himself the ten feet to the wreck and instinctively became conscious of where he was placing his feet and hands. As if he were at a crime scene. He crouched down. An arm was protruding from under the snowmobile. He touched the vehicle. It was swaying on two rocks. He took a deep breath and tipped the snowmobile on its side.

The dead body lay on its back. Krongli's first thought was that it was **likely** a man. The head and face had been crushed between the vehicle and the rocks, and the result looked like the remains of a crab party. He didn't need to feel the smashed body to know it was like jelly, like a piece of tender meat with the bones removed, or that the torso had been squashed flat, hips and knees pulverized. Krongli would hardly have been able to identify the body, had it not been for the red flannel shirt. And the single, rotten, brown-stained tooth left in the lower jaw.

76

Redefinition

"What did you say?" Harry exclaimed, pressing the phone harder to his ear as if the mistake were there.

"I said the body under the snowmobile is not Tony Leike," Krongli said.

"Who, then?"

"Odd Utmo. A local recluse and guide. He always

wears the same red flannel shirt. And it's his snow-mobile. But it was the teeth that decided it. One single rotten stump of a tooth. God knows what happened to the rest of his teeth and the braces."

Utmo. Braces. Harry remembered Kaja telling him about the guide who had driven her to Håvass.

"His fingers, though," Harry said. "Aren't they distorted?"

"Sure. Utmo had terrible problems with arthritis, poor fella. It was Bellman who asked me to inform you directly. Wasn't quite what you hoped for, eh, Hole?"

Harry pushed the chair from the desk. "At least not quite what I was expecting. Could it have been an accident, Krongli?"

But he knew the answer before it came. There had been moonlight the whole evening and night; even without headlamps the ravine would have been impossible to miss. Especially for a local guide. Especially when he was driving so slowly that he landed only ten feet from a perpendicular drop of more than two hundred feet.

"Forget it, Krongli. Tell me about the burns."

The other end went silent for a bit before the answer came.

"Arms and back. The skin on the arms was cracked and you can see the red flesh beneath. Parts of the back are charred. And a brand has been scorched in between the shoulder blades . . ."

Harry closed his eyes. Saw the pattern on the wood-burning stove in the cabin. The smoking fragments of flesh.

"Looks like a stag. Anything else, Hole? We have to start moving—"

"No, that's it, Krongli. Thanks."

Harry hung up. Sat for a while deliberating. Not Tony Leike. Of course that changed the details, but not the bigger picture. Utmo was probably a victim of Altman's avenging crusade, someone who had found himself in the way of something or other. They had Tony Leike's finger, but where was the rest of his body? A thought struck Harry. If he was dead. In theory, Tony could be locked up somewhere. A place only Sigurd Altman knew about.

Harry tapped in Skai's number.

"He refuses to say a single word to anyone," Skai said, masticating something or other. "Apart from his lawyer."

"Who is?"

"Johan Krohn. Do you know him? Looks like a boy and—"

"I know Johan Krohn very well."

Harry called Krohn's office. Krohn sounded half welcoming and half dismissive, the way a professional defense lawyer should when a prosecuting authority calls. He listened to Harry. Then he answered.

"I'm afraid not. Unless you have concrete evidence that can establish beyond doubt that my client is keeping someone locked up or otherwise exposing someone to danger by not revealing their whereabouts, I cannot allow you to speak to Altman at this juncture, Hole. These are serious allegations you're making against him, and I don't need to tell you that it is my job to protect his interests as far as I am able."

"Agreed," Harry said. "You didn't need to tell me."

They hung up.

Harry looked out of the window at the downtown area. The chair was good—no doubt about that. But his eyes found the familiar glass building in Grønland.

Then he dialed another number.

Katrine Bratt was as happy as a lark, and twittered like one, too.

"I'm going to be discharged in a couple of days," she said.

"I thought you were there of your own free will."

"Yes I am, but I have to be formally discharged. I'm looking forward to it. They've offered me a desk job at the station when my sick leave runs out."

"Good."

"Anything special you want?"

Harry explained.

"So you'll have to find Tony Leike without Altman's help?"

"Yup."

"Any ideas where I can start?"

"Just one. Right after Tony disappeared we checked that he hadn't stayed anywhere around Ustaoset. Thing is, I've checked recent years a little more closely, and he's almost never registered at accommodations anywhere in Ustaoset—once or twice a Tourist Association cabin, that's all. And that's weird because he's been up there a lot."

"Perhaps the other times he was freeloading at the cabins, not registering or paying."

"He's not the type," Harry said. "I wonder if Tony has a cabin or something up there no one knows anything about."

"OK. Anything else?"

"No. Yes—see what you can find out about Odd Utmo's activities over the last few days."

"Are you still single, Harry?"

"What sort of a fucking question's that?"

"You sound less single."

"Do I?"

"You do. But it suits you."

"Does it?"

"Since you ask, no."

Aslak Krongli straightened his stiff back and looked up the scree.

It was one of the men in the search party who had called, and he was shouting again now, obviously excited. "Over here!"

Aslak uttered a low curse. The crime scene officers had finished, and the snowmobile and Odd Utmo had been hoisted to the top. It was complicated and time-consuming work, since the only possible access to the scree was by rope, and even that was hard enough.

During the lunch break one man had told them something a maid at the hotel had whispered into his ear in confidence: There had been bloodstains on the sheets in the room occupied by Rasmus Olsen, the husband of the dead woman MP, when he checked out. At first, she had thought it was menstrual blood, but then she had heard that Rasmus Olsen had been on his own and his wife had been at the Håvass cabin.

Krongli had answered that he must have had a local girl in his room or met his wife the morning she arrived in Ustaoset and they had made up in bed. The man had mumbled that it was not certain it was menstrual blood.

"Over here!"

What a hassle. Aslak Krongli wanted to go home. Dinner, coffee, sleep. Put this whole shitty case behind him. The money he had owed in Oslo was paid, and he would never go there again. Never go back down into the quagmire. It was a promise he would keep this time.

They had used a dog to be sure they found all the bits of Utmo in the snow, and it was the dog that had leapt up the scree and stood barking a hundred yards farther along. A hundred steep yards. Aslak assessed the climb.

"Is it important?" he shouted and set off a symphony of echoes.

He received an answer, and ten minutes later he was staring at what the dog had dug up from the snow. It was wedged in between the rocks so tightly that it must have been impossible to spot from the top.

"Jesus," Aslak said. "Who could that be?"

"Not Tony Leike, anyway," said the dog handler. "Here in the cold scree it would be a long time before the skeleton was picked that clean. Several years."

"Seventeen years." It was Roy Stille. The officer had followed them and was panting.

"She's been here seventeen years," Roy said, crouching down.

"She?" Aslak queried.

The officer pointed to the hips on the skeleton. "Women have a larger pelvis. We never did find her when she disappeared. That's Karen Utmo."

Krongli heard something he had never heard before in Roy Stille's voice. A quiver. The quiver of a man emotionally upset. Grief-stricken. But his granite face was as smooth as always, closed.

"Well, I never—so it was true, then," said the dog handler. "She killed herself out of anguish for her boy."

"Hardly," Krongli said. The other two looked at him. He had stuck his little finger in a delicate round aperture in the forehead of the skull.

"Is that a bullet hole?" the dog handler asked.

"Yep," said Stille, feeling the back of the skull. "And there's no exit wound, so I reckon we'll find the bullet in the skull."

"And should we bet that the bullet will match Utmo's rifle?" said Krongli.

"Well, I never," the dog handler repeated. "Do you mean he shot his wife? How is that possible? To kill a person you've loved? Because you think she and your son . . . it's like entering hell."

"Seventeen years," Stille said, getting up with a groan. "Seven years left before the murder was deemed too old. That must be what they call irony. You wait and wait, afraid of being found out. The years pass and then, when you're approaching freedom—bang!—you're killed yourself and end up in the same scree."

Krongli closed his eyes and thought, **Yes, it is possible to kill a person you have loved. Easily possible. But, no, you're never free. Never.** He would never come here again.

Johan Krohn enjoyed the limelight. You don't become the country's most popular defense counsel without enjoying it. And when he had agreed to defend Sigurd Altman, Prince Charming, without a second's hesitation, he knew there was going to be more limelight than he had hitherto experienced in his remarkable career. He had already reached his goal of beating his father as the youngest lawyer ever to appear before the Supreme Court. As a defense counsel in his twenties he was already being proclaimed the new star, the wonder boy. But that might have gone to his head a bit; he had not been used to so much attention at school. Then he had been the irritating top pupil who always waved his hand too eagerly in the classroom, who always tried a bit too hard socially and yet was always the last to know where the Saturday-night party was—if he knew about it at all. But now young female assistants and clerks might giggle and blush when he complimented them or suggested a dinner after work. And invitations rained down, to give talks, participate in debates on radio or TV and even go to the odd premiere his wife valued so highly. Such events may have occupied too much of his attention over recent years. At any rate, he had detected a downward trend in the number of legal triumphs, big media cases and new clients. Not so many that it had begun to affect his reputation, but enough for him to be aware that he needed the Sigurd Altman case. Needed something high-profile to put him back where he belonged: at the top.

That was why Johan Krohn sat listening quietly to the lean man with the round glasses. Listening while Sigurd Altman told a story that was not only the least likely story Krohn had ever heard but also a story he believed. Johan Krohn could already see himself in the courtroom, the sparkling rhetorician, the agitator, the manipulator, who nonetheless never lost sight of legal justice, a delight for both layman and judge. He was therefore disappointed at first when Sigurd Altman revealed his plans. However, after reminding himself of his father's repeated admonition that the lawyer was there for the client, and not vice versa, he accepted the case. For Johan Krohn was not really a bad person.

And when Krohn left Oslo District Prison, where Sigurd Altman had been transferred, he saw new potential in the assignment, which in its way, despite everything, was extraordinary. The first thing he did when he got back to his office was contact Mikael Bellman. They had met only once before—at a murder trial, of course—but Johan Krohn had immediately known where he was with Bellman. A hawk recognizes a hawk. So he appreciated how Bellman was feeling after the day's headlines about the county officer's arrest.

"Bellman."

"Johan Krohn. Nice to talk to you again."

"Good afternoon, Krohn." The voice sounded formal, but not unfriendly.

"Is it? I imagine you feel you've been overtaken down the final stretch."

Short pause. "What's this about, Krohn?" Teeth clenched. Angry.

Johan Krohn knew he was on to a winner.

Harry and Sis sat by their father's bed at Rikshospital. On the bedside table and on two other tables in the room there were vases of flowers that had appeared from nowhere in the last few days. Harry had done the rounds and read the cards. One of them had been addressed to "My dear, dear Olav," and was signed "Your Lise." Harry had never heard of any Lise, much less considered the notion that there may have been any women in his father's life other than his mother. The remaining cards were from colleagues and neighbors. It must have reached their ears that the end was nigh. And despite knowing that Olav would not be able to read the cards, they had sent these sweet-smelling flowers to compensate for the fact that they had not taken the time to visit him. Harry saw the flowers surrounding the bed as vultures hovering around a dying man. Heavy, hanging heads on thin stalk necks. Red and yellow beaks.

"You're not allowed to have your cell on here, Harry!" Sis whispered severely.

Harry took out his phone and read the display. "Sorry, Sis. Important."

Katrine Bratt got straight to the point. "Leike has undoubtedly been in Ustaoset and the surrounding district a fair bit," she said. "In recent years he's bought the odd train ticket on the Net, paid for fuel with a credit card at the gas station in Geilo. The same with provisions, mostly in Ustaoset. The only thing to stand out is a bill for building materials, also in Geilo."

"Building materials?"

"Yep. I went onto the lists of invoices. Boards, nails, tools, steel cables, Leca blocks, cement. Over thirty thousand kroners' worth. But it's four years old."

"Are you thinking what I'm thinking?"

"He's been building himself a little annex or something up there?"

"He didn't have a registered cabin to build an annex onto—we've checked. But you don't stock up with provisions if you're going to live in a hotel or a Tourist Association cabin. I reckon Tony built himself an illegal getaway in the national park, just as he told me he dreamed about. Well hidden from view, of course. A place where he could be very, very undisturbed. But where?" Harry realized he had gotten up and was pacing to and fro in the room.

"Well, you tell me," said Katrine Bratt.

"Wait! What time of the year did he buy this?"

"Let me see . . . The sixth of July, it says on the printout."

"If the cabin has to be hidden it must be somewhere off the beaten track. A desolate area without roads. Did you say steel cables?"

"Yes. And I can guess why. When Bergensians built cabins in the most wind-blown parts of Ustaoset in the sixties, they generally used steel cables to anchor them."

"So Leike's cabin would be somewhere wind-blown and desolate, and he has to transport thirty thousand kroners' worth of building materials there. Weighing at least a couple of tons. How do you do that in the summer, when there's no snow, so you can't use a snowmobile?"

"Horse? Jeep?"

"Over rivers, marshland, up mountains? Keep going."

"I have no idea."

"But I do. I've seen a picture of it. OK, bye."

"Wait."

"Yes?"

"You asked me to look into Utmo's activities during the final days of his life. There's not very much on him in the electronic world, but he did make some calls. One of the last ones he made was to Aslak Krongli. Just got voice mail, looks like. The very last conversation on his phone was with SAS. I went through their ticketing system. He booked a plane ticket to Copenhagen."

"Mm. He doesn't seem the type to travel much."

"That's for sure. A passport was issued to him, but he isn't registered in a single ticketing system. And we're talking many years here."

"So a man who has barely left his home district suddenly wants to go to Copenhagen. When would he have traveled, by the way?"

"Yesterday."

"OK. Thanks."

Harry hung up, grabbed his coat, turned in the doorway. Looked at her. The attractive woman who was his sister. Was about to ask if she was coping on her own, without him. But managed to stop himself asking such an idiotic question. When had she not coped without him?

"Take care," he said.

Jens Rath was in the reception area of the shared office. Inside his jacket and shirt, his back was drenched with perspiration. Because the police were paying him a visit. He had had a skirmish with the Fraud Squad a few years ago, but the case had been dropped. Nevertheless, he still broke out into a sweat whenever he saw a police car. And now Jens Rath could feel his pores opening big-time. He was a small man and looked up at the officer who had just risen to his feet. And continued to rise. Until he towered more than a foot above Jens and gave him a cursory, firm handshake.

"Harry Hole, Crime Sq—Kripos. We've come about Tony Leike."

"Anything new?"

"Shall we sit down, Rath?"

They took a seat in a pair of Le Corbusier chairs,

and Rath signaled discreetly to Wenche in reception that she **shouldn't** serve them coffee, which was standard policy when investors came visiting.

"I want you to show us where his cabin is," the policeman said.

"Cabin?"

"I saw you cancel the coffee, Rath, and that's fine—like you, I don't have much time. I also know that your Fraud Squad case has been dropped, but it would take me one phone call to reopen it. They may not find anything this time, either, but I promise you that the documentation they will demand you make available . . ."

Rath closed his eyes. "Oh my God . . ."

". . . will keep you busy for longer than it took to build a cabin for your colleague, pal and bedfellow Tony Leike. OK?"

Jens Rath's sole talent was that he could calculate worthwhile risks faster and more efficiently than anyone else. Accordingly, it took him approximately one second to respond to the calculation with which he had just been presented.

"Fine."

"We're leaving at nine tomorrow morning."

"How . . . ?"

"The same way you transported the materials. Helicopter." The policeman stood up.

"Just one question. Tony's always been very concerned that no one should know about this cabin—I don't even think Lene, his fiancée, knows about it—so how—"

"An invoice for building materials from Geilo, plus the photo of you three in work gear sitting on a pile of timber in front of a helicopter."

Quick nod of the head from Jens Rath. "'Course. **The** photo."

"Who took it, by the way?"

"The pilot. Before we left from Geilo. And it was Andreas's idea to send it with the press release when we opened the office. He thought dressing in work clothes was cooler than in suits and ties. And Tony agreed because he figured it looked as if we **owned** the helicopter. Anyway, the financial papers use the photo all the time."

"Why didn't you and Andreas mention the cabin when Tony was reported missing?"

Jens Rath shrugged. "Don't get me wrong—we're just as anxious as you for Tony to return pronto. We've got a project in the Congo that will go belly-up unless he can find ten million readies. But whenever Tony goes AWOL it's always because he wants to. He can look after himself. Don't forget he was a merce-nary. I would guess that right now Tony is sitting somewhere with a shot of the hard stuff, some exotic wildcat of a woman on his arm and grinning because he's come up with a solution."

"Mm," Harry said. "I assume the feline chomped off his middle finger, then. Fornebu Airport, nine tomorrow."

Jens Rath stood watching the policeman. The sweat was pouring off him; he was being washed away.

When Harry returned to Rikshospital Sis was still sitting there. She was leafing through a magazine and eating an apple. He surveyed the kettle of vultures. There were more flowers.

"You look worn out, Harry," she said. "You should go home."

Harry chuckled. "You can go. You've been sitting here on your own for long enough."

"I haven't been on my own," she said with a mischievous smile. "Guess who was here."

Harry sighed. "I'm sorry, Sis—I do enough guessing as it is in my job."

"Øystein!"

"Øystein Eikeland?"

"Yes! He brought a bar of milk chocolate with him. Not for Daddy, but for me. Sorry—there's none left." She laughed so much her eyes shrank into her cheeks.

When she got up to go for a walk, Harry checked his phone. Two missed calls from Kaja. He pushed the chair into the wall and leaned back.

77

Fingerprint

At ten minutes past ten the helicopter landed on a ridge west of the Hallingskarvet mountains. By eleven they had located the cabin.

It was so well hidden from view that even if they had known more or less where it was, they would have struggled to find it without Jens Rath's help. The cabin was built on rock high up to the east, the leeward side of the mountain, too high to be affected by avalanches. The stones had been carried there from surrounding areas and cemented in against two enormous rocks forming the side and rear walls. There were no conspicuous right angles. The windows resembled gun slits and were set so deep into the wall that the sun did not reflect off them.

"That's what I call a decent cabin," Bjørn Holm said, unstrapping skis and immediately sinking up to his knees in the snow.

Harry told Jens that they no longer needed his services, and that he should go back to the helicopter and wait there with the pilot.

The snow was not so deep by the front door.

"Someone dug here not that long ago," Harry said.

The door had a plate and a simple padlock, which ceded to Bjørn's crowbar without much protest.

Before opening it, they removed their mittens and put latex gloves on their hands and blue plastic bags over their ski boots. Then they entered.

"Wow," Bjørn said under his breath.

The whole cabin consisted of one single room of around fifteen by ten feet and was reminiscent of an old-fashioned captain's berth, with porthole-like windows and compact, space-saving solutions. The floor, walls and ceiling were made of coarse, untreated boards that had been given a couple of coats of white paint to exploit the little light that was let in. The short wall to the right was taken up by a plain countertop with a sink and a cupboard underneath. Plus a divan that obviously doubled as a bed. In the middle of the room there was a table with a single spindle-back chair spattered with paint. In front of one window stood a well-used writing desk with initials and snatches of songs carved into the wood. To the left, on the long wall where the rear rock was revealed, there was a black wood stove. To make maximal use of the heat, the flue was diverted around the rock to the right, then rose vertically. The wood basket was filled with birch and newspapers to get the fire started. On the walls hung maps of the local area, but there was also one of Africa.

Bjørn looked out of the window above the desk.

"And that's what I call a decent view. Jeez, you can see half of Norway from here."

"Let's get cracking," Harry said. "The pilot's given us two hours. There're clouds coming in from the coast."

As usual, Mikael Bellman had gotten up at six and jogged himself into consciousness on the treadmill in the cellar. He had been dreaming about Kaja again. She had been riding on the back of a motorbike with her arms around a man who was all helmet and visor. She had smiled so happily, showing her pointed teeth, and waved as they rode away. But hadn't they stolen the bike? Wasn't it his? He didn't know for sure, as her hair, which was fluttering in the wind, was so long it covered the license plate.

After running, Mikael had taken a shower and gone upstairs for breakfast.

He had steeled himself before opening the morning paper that Ulla—also, as usual—had placed next to his plate.

Lacking a photograph of Sigurd Altman, alias Prince Charming, they had printed one of County Officer Skai. He was standing outside the police station with his arms crossed, wearing a green cap with a long peak, like a fucking bear hunter. The headline: PRINCE CHARMING ARRESTED? And beside it, above the photograph of a smashed yellow snowmobile, another body found in Ustaoset.

Bellman had scanned the text for the word Kripos or—worst of all—his name. Nothing on the front page. Good.

He had opened the pages referred to, and there it was, photo and all:

The head of Kripos, Mikael Bellman, has said in a brief comment that he does not wish to make a statement until Prince Charming has been questioned. Nor has he anything in particular to say about the arrest of the suspect by Ytre Enebakk police.

"In general, I can say that all police work is teamwork. In Kripos we do not attach too much importance to individuals who receive the hero's garlands."

He shouldn't have said the last part. It was lies, would be perceived as lies and stank from some distance of a sore loser.

But it didn't matter. For if what Johan Krohn, the defense counsel, had told him on the phone was true, Bellman had a golden opportunity to fix everything. Well, more than that. To receive the garlands himself. He acknowledged that the price Krohn would demand was high, but also that it wouldn't be he who had to pay. But the fucking bear hunter. And Harry Hole and Crime Squad.

A prison guard held the door to the visitors' room open and Mikael Bellman let Johan Krohn go first. Krohn had insisted that since this was a conversation, not a formal interview, it should take place, as far as was possible, on neutral ground. Since it was inconceivable that Prince Charming would be allowed out of Oslo District Prison, Krohn and Bellman agreed on a visitors' room, one used for private meetings between inmates and family. No cameras, no microphones, just an ordinary windowless room; half-hearted attempts had been made to cheer the place up with a crocheted cloth on the table and a Norwegian tapestry, a bellpull, on the wall. Sweethearts and spouses were granted permission to meet here, and the springs on the semen-stained sofa were so worn that Bellman could see Krohn sink into the material as he took a seat.

Sigurd Altman was sitting on a chair at one end of the table. Bellman sat at the other end so that he and Altman were at almost exactly the same height. Altman's face was lean, his eyes deep-set, the mouth pronounced with protruding teeth, all of which reminded Bellman of photos of emaciated Jews in Auschwitz. And the monster in **Alien**.

"Conversations like this don't proceed by the book," Bellman said. "I therefore have to insist that no one take notes and anything we say not go beyond these walls."

"At the same time we have to have a guarantee that the conditions for a confession are honored on the prosecutor's side," Krohn said.

"You have my word," Bellman said.

"For which I humbly thank you. What else have you got?"

"What else?" Bellman gave a thin smile. "What else would you like? A signed written agreement?" Arrogant fucking prick of a counsel.

"Preferably," Krohn said, passing a sheet of paper across the table.

Bellman stared at the paper. He skimmed over it, his eyes jumping from sentence to sentence.

"Won't be shown to anyone, of course, if it doesn't have to be," Krohn said. "And the document will be returned when the conditions have been met. And this"—he passed a pen to Bellman—"is an S. T. Dupont, the best fountain pen you can find."

Bellman took the pen and placed it on the table beside him.

"If the story's good enough, I'll sign," he said.

"If this is supposed to be a crime scene, the person concerned tidied up after himself pretty well."

Bjørn Holm put his hands on his hips and surveyed the room. They had searched high and low and in drawers and cupboards, shone a flashlight everywhere for blood and taken fingerprints. He had put his laptop on the desk, connected it to a fingerprint scanner the size of a matchbox, similar to those used at some airports now for passenger identification. So far all the prints had matched one person in the case: Tony Leike.

"Keep going," Harry said, on his knees under the sink, dismantling the plastic pipes. "It's here somewhere."

"What is?"

"I don't know. Something or other."

"If we keep going, we'll certainly need some heat."

"Fire her up, then."

Bjørn Holm crouched down by the wood stove, opened the door and began to tear up and twist the newspaper from the wood basket.

"What did you offer Skai to get him to join your little game? He risks a great deal if the truth comes out."

"He's not risking anything," Harry said. "He hasn't said an untrue word. Look at his statements. It's the media that have jumped to the wrong conclusions. And there are no police instructions stipulating who can and who cannot arrest a suspect. I didn't need to offer anything for his help. He said he disliked me less than he disliked Bellman, and that was justification enough."

"That was all?"

"Hm. He told me about his daughter, Mia. Things haven't gone so well for her. In such cases parents always look for a cause, something concrete they can point to. And Skai figures it was the night outside the dance hall that marked Mia for life. Local gossip is that Mia and Ole had been going out and it wasn't just innocent kissing in the woods when Ole found Mia and Tony. In Skai's eyes Ole and Tony carry the blame for the daughter's problems."

Bjørn shook his head. "Victims, victims, wherever you turn."

Harry had come over to Bjørn, holding out his hand. In the palm lay pieces of what looked like wire cut from a fence. "This was under the drainpipe. Any idea what it is?"

Bjørn took the pieces of wire and studied them.

"Hey," Harry burst out. "What's that?"

"What's what?"

"The newspaper. Look—that's the press conference where we launched the Iska Peller ruse."

Bjørn Holm looked at the photo of Bellman, which had been uncovered when he had torn off the page in front. "Well, I'll be . . ."

"The newspaper's only a few days old. Someone's been here recently."

"Well, I'll be."

"There might be prints on the front pa—" Harry looked in the wood stove, where the first pages were just going up in flames.

"Sorry," said Bjørn. "But I can check the other pages."

"OK. Actually, I was wondering about the wood."

"Oh?"

"There isn't a tree for a three-mile radius. You check the papers and I'll take a walk around."

Mikael Bellman studied Sigurd Altman. He didn't like his cold eyes. Didn't like the bony body, the teeth pressing against the inside of his lips, the staccato movements or the clumsy lisp. But he didn't need to like Sigurd Altman to see him as his redeemer and benefactor. For every word Altman said, Bellman was a step nearer his triumph.

"I assume you've read Harry Hole's report presenting the course of events," Altman said.

"You mean Skai's report?" Bellman said. "Skai's presentation?"

Altman let slip a wry smile. "As you prefer. The story Harry told was astonishingly accurate, anyway. The problem with it is that it contains only one concrete piece of evidence. My fingerprints at Leike's. Well, let's say I was there. I was paying him a visit. And we talked about the good old days."

Bellman shrugged. "And you think a jury will fall for that?"

"I like to think I can inspire trust. But"—Altman's lips stretched and revealed his gums—"now I won't ever have to face a jury, will I."

Harry found the woodpile beneath a rock jutting out from the mountainside. It was covered by a green tarpaulin. An ax stood bowed in a chopping block, beside it a knife. Harry looked around and kicked the snow. Not much of interest here. His boot brushed something. An empty white plastic bag. He bent down. On it was a contents label. Thirty feet of gauze. What was that doing here?

Harry angled his head and examined the chopping block for a few moments. Looked at the black blade in the wood. At the knife. At the handle. Yellow, smooth. What was a knife doing on a chopping block? Could be several reasons, of course, yet . . .

He laid his right hand on the block in such a way that the remaining stump of his middle finger pointed upward and the other fingers were pressed down beside it.

Harry freed the knife cautiously with two fingers

at the top of the handle. The blade was as sharp as a razor. With traces of the material he was always seeing in his profession. Then he ran through the deep snow like a long-legged elk.

Bjørn looked up from the computer as Harry burst in. "Just more Tony Leike," he sighed.

"There's blood on the blade," Harry said, out of breath. "Check the handle for prints."

Bjørn held the knife with care. Sprinkled black powder on the smooth, varnished yellow wood and blew gently.

"There's only one set of prints here; however, they are tasty," he said. "Maybe there are epithelial cells here, too."

"Yes!" Harry said.

"What's the deal?"

"Whoever left the fingerprint cut off Leike's finger."

"Oh? What makes you—"

"There's blood on the chopping block. And he had gauze ready to bandage the wound. And I think I've seen that knife before. On a grainy photo of Adele Vetlesen."

Bjørn Holm whistled softly, pressed the transparency against the handle so that the powder stuck. Then he put the transparency on the scanner.

"Sigurd Altman, you might have a good lawyer to explain away the prints on Leike's desk," Harry whispered while Bjørn pressed the search button and they both followed the blue line that moved in fits and starts toward the right of the bar. "But not the print on this knife."

Ready . . .
Found one match.
Bjørn Holm pressed SHOW.
Harry stared at the name that came up.
"Still think the print belongs to the person who cut off Tony's finger?" Bjørn Holm asked.

78

The Deal

"After I saw Adele and Tony fucking like dogs by the outhouse, everything came back to me. Everything I had succeeded in burying. Everything the psychologist said I had put behind me. It was like an animal that had been chained up, but it had been fed, it had grown and was stronger than ever. And now it was free. Harry was absolutely right. I planned to avenge myself on Tony by humiliating him, just as he had me."

Sigurd Altman looked down at his hands and smiled.

"However, from there on Harry was wrong. I didn't plan Adele's murder. I just wanted to humiliate Tony in public. Particularly in front of those he hoped would become his in-laws, the dairy cow Galtung, who was going to finance that Congo adventure of his. Why would someone like Tony bother to marry a field mouse like Lene Galtung otherwise?"

"True enough." Mikael Bellman smiled to show he was on Altman's side.

"So I wrote a letter to Tony pretending to be Adele. I wrote that he had gotten me pregnant and I wanted the child. However, as a future single mother I would have to provide for it, and therefore I wanted silence money. Four hundred thousand, first time around. He was to show up with the money at midnight two days later, in the parking lot behind the Lefdal electrical appliances store in Sandvika. Then I sent Adele a letter, pretending to be Tony, and asked if we could meet at the same time and place for a date. I knew the setting would be to Adele's taste, and I assumed they hadn't exchanged names and phone numbers, if you know what I mean. The deception wouldn't be discovered until it was too late, until I had what I wanted. At eleven I was in position, sitting in my car with a camera ready. The plan was to take photos of the rendezvous however it ended up, a fight or fucking, and to send the whole thing to Anders Galtung with the story. That was all."

Sigurd looked at Bellman and repeated: "That was all."

Bellman nodded, and Sigurd Altman continued. "Tony arrived early. He parked, got out and looked around. Then he disappeared into the shadows under the trees by the river. I hid behind the steering wheel. Adele came. I rolled down the window to catch what happened. She stood there waiting, looking around, checking her watch. I saw Tony right behind her, so close it was unbelievable she couldn't hear him. I saw him pull out a large Sami knife and close his arm around her neck. She wriggled and kicked as he carried her to his car. When the door fell open I saw that he had plastic over the seats. I didn't hear what Tony said to her, but I picked up my camera and zoomed in. Saw him pressing a pen into her hand, obviously dictating what she was to write on a postcard."

"The postcard from Kigali," Bellman said. "He had planned everything in advance. She was going to disappear."

"I took pictures, not thinking about anything else. Until I saw him suddenly raise his hand and drive the knife into her neck. I couldn't believe my own eyes. Blood spurted out, spraying the windshield."

The two men were unaware that Krohn was gasping for air.

"He waited awhile, leaving the knife in her neck, as though he wanted to drain her of blood first. Then he lifted her up, carried her out to the rear of his car and dumped her in the trunk. As he was about to get back in the car, he stopped and seemed to sniff the air. He was standing under the light of a street lamp, and that was when I saw it: the same widened eyes, the same grin on his lips that he'd had when he pinned me down outside the dance hall and forced the knife in my mouth. Long after Tony had driven off with Adele, I was still in my car, numb with horror, unable to move. I knew I couldn't send a letter telling all to

Anders Galtung now. Or to anyone else. Because I had just become an accessory to murder."

Sigurd took a tiny, restrained sip of water from the glass in front of him and glanced at Johan Krohn, who nodded in return.

Bellman cleared his throat. "Technically speaking, you were not an accessory to murder. The worst charge would have been blackmail or deception. You could have stopped there. It would have been very unpleasant for you, but you could have gone to the police. You even had photographs proving your story."

"Nevertheless, I would have been charged and found guilty. They would have maintained that I, better than anyone else, knew Tony reacted with violence when put under pressure, and that I had started the whole business—it was premeditated."

"Hadn't you considered that this might happen?" Bellman asked, ignoring the admonitory glare from Krohn.

Sigurd Altman smiled. "Isn't it odd how often our own deliberations are the hardest to interpret? Or remember? I honestly don't recall what I anticipated would happen."

Because you don't want to, Bellman thought, nodding and **mm**-ing as if in gratitude to Altman for giving him new insights into the human soul.

"I deliberated for several weeks," Altman said. "Then I went back to the Håvass cabin and tore out the page in the guest book with all the names and addresses. And I wrote another letter to Tony, in which I said that I knew what he had done, and I knew why.

I had seen him fuck Adele at the cabin in Håvass. And I wanted money. Signed it Borgny Stem-Myhre. Five days later I read in the papers that she had been killed in a cellar. It should have stopped there. The police should have investigated the case and found Tony. That's what they should have done. Arrested him."

Sigurd Altman had raised his voice and Bellman could swear he saw tears welling up in the eyes behind the round glasses.

"But you didn't even have a lead; you were completely confused. So I had to keep feeding him more victims, threatening him with new names from the Håvass list. I cut out pictures of the victims from the papers and hung them on the wall of the clipping room in the Kadok factory with copies of letters I had sent in the victims' names. As soon as Tony killed one person, another letter arrived insisting they had sent the previous ones and now they knew he had two, three and four lives on his conscience. And that the price for their silence had risen accordingly." Altman leaned forward; his voice sounded anguished. "I did it to give you a chance to catch him. A killer makes mistakes, doesn't he? The more murders there are, the greater the chance he will be arrested."

"And the better he becomes at what he's doing," Bellman said. "Remember that Tony Leike was no novice at violence. You aren't a mercenary in Africa for as long as he was without having blood on your hands. As you yourself have."

"Blood on my hands?" Altman shrieked, in a sudden burst of anger. "I broke into Tony's house and called Elias Skog so you would find the trail at Telenor. It's you who have blood on your hands! Whores like Adele and Mia, murderers like Tony. If not—"

"Stop now, Sigurd." Johan Krohn had gotten to his feet. "Let's take a break."

Altman closed his eyes, raised his hands and shook his head. "I'm OK, I'm OK. Let's get this over and done with."

Johan Krohn eyed his client, glanced at Bellman and sat down.

Altman took a deep, tremulous breath. Then he continued. "After the third murder or so, Tony knew, of course, that the next letter was not necessarily from the person it purported to be from. Nonetheless, he went on killing them, in increasingly violent ways. It was as if he wanted to frighten me, make me pull back, to show that he could kill everyone and everything and in the end would kill me, too."

"Or he wanted to get rid of potential witnesses who had seen him and Adele," Bellman said. "He knew there had been seven other people at Håvass; he just didn't have the means to establish who they were."

Altman laughed. "Imagine! I swear, he even went up to the cabin to look at the guest book. Only to find the stub of a torn-out sheet. Tony Pony!"

"What about your motive for continuing?"

"What do you mean?" Altman asked, on the alert now.

"You could have given the police an anonymous tip-off much earlier in the case. Perhaps you wanted to get rid of all the witnesses as well?"

Altman tilted his head, so that his ear almost touched his shoulder. "As I said, it's difficult to keep tabs on all the reasons for doing what you do. Your subconscious is controlled by your survival instinct and is therefore often more rational than conscious thought. Perhaps my subconscious realized it would also be safer for me if Tony eliminated all the witnesses. Then no one would be able to say I was there, or suddenly recognize me one day on the street. But we will never get an answer to that, will we?"

The wood stove crackled and spat.

"But why on earth would Tony Leike chop off his own finger?" Bjørn Holm asked.

He had settled down on the sofa while Harry went through the first-aid kit he had found in the back of a kitchen drawer. It contained several rolls of bandages. And an astringent ointment that made blood coagulate faster. The date on the tube showed it was only two months old.

"Altman forced him," Harry said, rotating a tiny unlabeled brown bottle in his hand. "Leike had to be humiliated."

"You don't sound as if you believe that yourself."

"I damn well do believe it," Harry said, unscrewing the lid and sniffing the contents.

"Oh? There's not a single fingerprint here that isn't

Leike's, not a hair that isn't Leike's raven-black hair, not a shoe print that isn't size eleven and a half, Leike's. Sigurd Altman is ash blond and wears size eight and a half, Harry."

"He did a good job of cleaning up afterward. Remind me to have this analyzed." Harry slipped the brown bottle into his jacket pocket.

"A good job of cleaning up? In what probably isn't even a crime scene? The same man who didn't care about leaving big fat fingerprints on Leike's desk on Holmenveien? Who you said yourself didn't clean up very well at the cabin where he killed Utmo? I don't think so, Harry. And you don't, either."

"Fuck!" Harry shouted. "Fuck, fuck, fuck." He rested his forehead on his hands and stared at the table.

Bjørn Holm held one of the small pieces of wire from under the drainpipe in the air and scraped off the gold coating with his fingernail. "By the way, I think I know what this is."

"Oh?" Harry said, without lifting his head.

"Iron, chrome, nickel and titanium."

"What?"

"I had braces when I was a kid. The wires had to be bent and clipped on."

Harry suddenly looked up and stared at the map of Africa. He studied the countries that slotted into one another like jigsaw pieces. Except Madagascar, which was separate, like a piece that didn't fit.

"At the dentist's—"

"Shh!" Harry said, holding up a hand. Now he had it. Something had just clicked into place. All that could be heard was the wood stove and the gusting wind, which was closer outside now. Two jigsaw pieces that had been far apart, each on its own side of the puzzle. A maternal grandfather by Lake Lyseren. Father of his mother. And the photograph in the drawer at the cabin. The family photograph. The picture didn't belong to Tony Leike, but to Odd Utmo. Arthritis. What was it that Tony had told him? Not contagious, but hereditary. The boy with the large, bared teeth. And the man with the hard, pinched mouth, as if he were hiding a dark secret. Hiding his rotten teeth and braces.

The stone. The dark stone he had found on the bathroom floor in the cabin. He put his hand in his pocket. It was still there. He tossed it over to Bjørn.

"Tell me," he said with a gulp. "I came across this. Think it could be a tooth?"

Bjørn held it up to the light. Scraped it with his nail. "Could be."

"Let's get back," Harry said, feeling the hairs on his neck prickle. "Now. It wasn't fucking Altman who killed them."

"Oh?"

"It was Tony Leike."

"You must have read in the papers that Tony Leike was released after being arrested," Bellman said. "He had a wonderful little thing called an alibi. He could prove he was somewhere else when Borgny and Charlotte died."

"I know nothing about that," Sigurd Altman said, crossing his arms. "I know only that I saw him stick a knife into Adele's neck. And that the letters I sent caused the ostensible senders to be murdered right afterward."

"You're aware that that at least makes you an accessory to murder, aren't you?"

Johan Krohn coughed. "And you're aware, aren't you, that you made a deal that will serve up the real killer on a silver platter, for you and Kripos? All your internal problems will be solved, Bellman. You'll get all the credit, and you have a witness who will say in court that he saw Tony Leike kill Adele Vetlesen. What happened beyond that remains between you and me."

"And your client goes free?"

"That's the deal."

"What about if Leike kept the letters and they turn up at the trial?" Bellman said. "Then we have a problem."

"That's precisely why I have a feeling they won't turn up." Krohn smiled. "Or will they?"

"What about the photographs you took of Adele and Tony?"

"Went up in the blaze at Kadok," Altman said. "That bastard Hole."

Mikael Bellman nodded slowly. Then he lifted his pen. S. T. Dupont. Lead and steel. It was heavy. Once he had set it to paper, though, it was as if the signature wrote itself.

. . .

"Thanks," Harry said. "Over and out."

He received a rasping sound by way of answer and then it was still, with only the helicopter engine's monotonous noise outside his headset. Harry bent the microphone and looked out.

Too late.

He had just finished talking over the radio to the tower at Gardermoen Airport. For security reasons they had access to most information, including passenger lists. And could confirm that Odd Utmo had traveled on his pre-booked ticket to Copenhagen two days ago.

The countryside moved slowly beneath them.

Harry visualized him standing there with the passport of the man he had tortured and killed. The agent behind the counter routinely reading to see if the passport matched the name on the list and thinking—if he looked at the photo at all—that those were some braces. Looked up and registered the same dental work on the probably artifically browned teeth in front of him, braces that Tony Leike must have had to bend and cut to fit on top of his own porcelain high-rises.

They flew into a rainstorm that exploded on the Plexiglas bubble, ran to the sides in quivering streaks of water and disappeared. Seconds later it was as if they had never been there.

The finger.

Tony Leike had cut off his finger and sent it to Harry as a final red herring, to demonstrate that Tony Leike had to be considered dead. He could be forgotten, written off, put aside. Was it chance that Leike had chosen the same finger as Harry's missing digit, that he had made himself like him?

But what about the alibi, his watertight alibi?

Harry had entertained the thought before, but had rejected it because cold-blooded murderers are rarities, deviants, perverted souls in the true sense of the word. But could there have been someone else? Could the answer be as simple as Tony Leike working together with a sidekick?

"Fuck!" said Harry, loud enough for the sound-sensitive microphone to transmit the last part of the syllable to the other three headsets in the helicopter. He caught Jens Rath's sidelong glance. Maybe Rath had been right, after all. Maybe Tony Leike was indeed sitting with a shot of the hard stuff, some exotic wildcat of a woman on his arm and grinning because he had come up with a solution.

79

Missed Calls

At a quarter past two the helicopter landed at Fornebu, the old airport twelve minutes' drive from downtown. When Harry and Bjørn went through the door of the Kripos building and Harry asked the receptionist why neither Bellman nor any of the senior detectives were answering their phones, he was told they were all in a meeting.

"Why the hell weren't we called?" mumbled Harry as he strode down the corridor with Bjørn jogging after him.

He pushed open the door without knocking. Seven heads turned toward them. The eighth, Mikael Bellman's, didn't need to turn, as he was sitting at the end of the long table facing the door, and he was the one on whom all the others had been focused.

"Stan and Ollie," Bellman chortled, and Harry gathered from the chuckling that they had been a subject of conversation in their absence. "Where have you been?"

"Well, while you were sitting here and playing Snow White and the Seven Dwarfs we've been to Tony Leike's cabin," Harry said, throwing himself down on a free chair at the opposite end of the table. "And we have some news. It isn't Altman. We've arrested the wrong man. It was Tony Leike."

Harry didn't know what reaction he had expected, but at any rate it hadn't been this: none at all.

The POB leaned back in his chair with a friendly and quizzical smile.

" 'We've' arrested the wrong man? To my recollection, Skai was the officer who took it upon himself to arrest Sigurd Altman. And, regarding news value, this is pretty scant. As for Tony Leike, perhaps we should be saying, 'Welcome back.' "

Harry's gaze jumped from Ærdal to the Pelican

and back to Bellman as his brain churned. And drew the only possible conclusion.

"Altman," Harry said. "Altman said it was Leike. He knew all the time."

"He not only knew," Bellman said. "Just as Leike triggered the avalanche in Håvass, Altman set this whole murder case in motion, without even realizing it. Skai arrested an innocent man, Harry."

"Innocent?" Harry shook his head. "I saw the pictures in the Kadok factory, Bellman. Altman is involved here—I just don't know how as yet."

"But we do," Bellman said. "So if you wouldn't mind leaving this to us . . ." Harry heard the word **adults** forming in Bellman's mouth, but it came out as: ". . . enlightened ones, you can join in when you're up to speed, Harry. All right? Bjørn, too? So let's move on. I was saying that we cannot exclude the possibility that Leike had a partner, someone who committed at least two of the murders, the two for which Leike has an alibi. We know that when both Borgny and Charlotte died Leike was at business meetings, with several witnesses present."

"A clever bastard," said Ærdal. "Leike knew, of course, that the police would find a link between all the murders. So if he found himself a cast-iron alibi for one or two of them, he would automatically be cleared of the others."

"Yes," said Bellman. "But who is the accomplice?"

Harry heard suggestions, comments and queries fluttering past him in the room.

"Tony Leike's motive for killing Adele Vetlesen was

hardly the demand for four hundred thousand," the Pelican said. "But rather the fear that if it came out that he had gotten some woman pregnant, Lene Galtung would end the relationship and he could kiss the Galtung millions for the Congo project goodbye. So the question we should be asking ourselves is, Who had identical interests?"

"The other investors in the Congo," said the smooth-faced detective. "What about his partners at the office?"

"It's make-or-break for Tony Leike with the Congo project," Bellman said. "But none of those other finance squirts would have killed two people to secure their ten percent share in a project. Those guys are used to winning and losing money. Besides, Leike had to collaborate with someone he could trust at both a personal and a professional level. Bear in mind that the murder weapon was the same for Borgny and Charlotte. What did you call it, Harry?"

"A Leopold's apple," Harry intoned, still befuddled.

"Louder, please."

"A Leopold's apple."

"Thank you. From Africa. Same place Leike had been a mercenary. It is therefore fair to assume that Leike used one of his former comrades, and I think we should start there."

"If he used a mercenary for murders number two and three, why not for all of them?" the Pelican asked. "Then he would have had an alibi all the way through."

"He would have gotten a per-capita discount,

too," the Nansen mustache said. "The mercenary can't get any more than life imprisonment anyway."

"There may be angles we are unaware of," Bellman said. "Banal reasons, like not having enough time or Leike not having the money. Or the most usual reason in crime cases: It just happened like that."

Nods of agreement around the table; even the Pelican seemed content with the answer.

"Any other questions? No? Then I would like to use this opportunity to thank Harry Hole, who has been with us thus far. As we no longer have any use for his expertise, he will return to Crime Squad immediately. It was stimulating to experience another view of how to work on murders, Harry. You might not have solved this case, but who knows? There may be some interesting Crime Squad cases waiting for you down there in Grønland, if not murders. So thank you again. I have a press conference now, folks."

Harry looked at Bellman. He could not help but admire him. The way you admire a cockroach that you flush down the toilet and comes creeping back. Again and again. And in the end it inherits the world.

At Olav's bedside in Rikshospital, seconds, minutes and hours passed in a slow, undulating swell of monotony. A nurse came and went, Sis came and went. Flowers moved imperceptibly closer.

Harry had seen how many relatives could not bear to wait for the last breath of their loved ones, how in the end they prayed, begged for death to come and liberate them. Them, meaning themselves. But for Harry it was the opposite. He had never felt closer to his father than now, here, in this wordless room, where all was breathing and the next heartbeat. For seeing Olav Hole there was like seeing himself, in the peace-filled existence between life and nothingness.

The detectives at Kripos had seen and understood a lot. But not the evident link. Which made the entirety so much clearer. The link between the Leike farm and Ustaoset. Between the rumors and the ghost of a missing boy from the Utmo farm and a man who called the wasteland "my terrain." Between Tony Leike and the boy in the photograph, with his ugly father and beautiful mother.

Now and then Harry glanced at his cell phone and saw a missed call. Hagen. Øystein. Kaja. Kaja again. He would have to answer her calls soon. He called her.

"Can I come to your place tonight?" she asked.

80

The Rhythm

The rain beat down on the boards of the jetty.

Harry walked up behind the man standing at the edge, who was facing the other way.

"Morning, Skai."

"Morning, Hole," the officer said without turning. The tip of the fishing rod was bent toward the line that disappeared in the reeds on the opposite bank.

"Caught something?"

"Nope," Skai said. "Snarled on the fucking reeds."

"Sorry to hear that. Read the papers today?"

"They don't arrive before late morning in the sticks."

Harry knew that was not true, but nodded anyway.

"But I suppose they've written that I'm a village idiot," Skai said. "They had to get townsfolk in from Kripos to sort it out."

"As I said, I'm sorry."

Skai shrugged. "I've got no complaints. You gave it to me straight; I knew what I was doing. And it was a little bit fun, too. Not much happens out here, you know."

"Mm. They don't write much about you—they're mostly interested in Tony Leike being the killer, after all. Bellman is much-quoted."

"He certainly is."

"Soon they'll work out who Tony's father is as well."

Skai turned and looked at Harry.

"I should have thought of it before, and especially after we talked about the changing of names."

"Now I don't follow you, Hole."

"You were even the person who told me, Skai. Tony lived with his grandfather at the Leike farm. Mother's father. Tony had taken his mother's name."

"Nothing unusual in that."

"Maybe not. But in this case there was a good reason for it. Tony was hiding at his grandfather's. His mother sent him there."

"What makes you think that?"

"A colleague," Harry said, and for a second he seemed to have the night's scent of her in his nostrils again. "She told me something the Ustaoset officer had told her. About the Utmo family. About a father and a son who hated each other so intensely that it threatened to culminate in murder."

"Murder?"

"I've checked Odd Utmo's record. He was, like his son, known for his rages. As a young man he went to prison for eight years for committing a murder out of jealousy. After that, he moved into the wastelands. He married Karen Leike, and they had a son. The son reached his teens and was already good-looking, tall and a charmer. Two men and a woman in almost total isolation. A man who had a conviction for killing in a jealous rage. It looks like Karen tried to prevent a tragedy by sending her son away in secret and leaving one of his shoes in an area where there had just been a big avalanche."

"News to me, Hole."

Harry nodded slowly. "I'm afraid she managed only to postpone the tragedy. Her body has just been found at the bottom of a precipice with a bullet through the head. Not far away her husband and murderer was crushed beneath a snowmobile. He'd been tortured, had most of the skin on his back and arms burned off and his teeth ripped out. Guess who did it?"

"Oh, my God . . ."

Harry put a cigarette between his lips.

"How did you trace the link?" Skai asked.

"The similarity, the genes." He lit the cigarette. "Father and son. You can try to run, but it will always be there, like a curse. I think Odd Utmo realized the Håvass murders meant he would be hunted, too, and that it was the ghost of his own deceased son who was after him. So he fled from the farm up to this Tourist Association cabin that was safely hidden between precipices. He took a family photo with him, the family he had himself destroyed. Imagine, a frightened, maybe remorseful killer, alone with his thoughts."

"He had already been given his punishment."

"I found the photo. Tony was lucky—he took after his mother in looks. It was hard to see anything of the adult Tony in the photograph of the boy. But he already had the big white teeth. While his father hid his. That's where they were different."

"I thought you said it was the similarity that gave them away?"

Harry nodded. "They had the same disease."

"They were killers."

Harry shook his head. "Disease, as in physical ailment, Skai. I meant they both had arthritis. The family relationship was confirmed this morning. The DNA analysis of the flesh on the wood stove and Tony Leike's hair prove they are father and son."

Skai nodded.

"Well," Harry said. "I came by to thank you for your help and to bemoan the outcome. Bjørn Holm sends his regards to your wife and says she makes the best meatballs and mashed rutabaga he's ever tasted."

Flicker of a smile from Skai. "Most people think that. Even Tony liked them."

"Oh?"

Skai shrugged and pulled a knife from the sheath on his belt.

"I told you Mia was stuck on the boy, didn't I? It was soon after he had knifed Ole. She brought him home for lunch one day when she knew I wouldn't be there. The wife said nothing when they showed up, though there was a humdinger when I got to hear about it, of course. But you know what girls are like at that age and in love. I tried to explain that Tony was violent, fool that I was. I should have known the worse I made her boyfriend out to be, the more determined she would become to hang on to him. Then it's two together against the rest of the world, kind of. Well, you've seen it yourself with women who start writing letters to convicted murderers."

Harry nodded.

"Mia would have left home, followed him to the end of the world—there was no moderation in anything," Skai said, cutting the fishing line and reeling in.

Harry followed the retreat of the slack line. "Mm. End of the world."

"Yep."

"I see."

Skai stopped winding and looked at Harry. "No," he said with conviction.

"No what?"

"No to what you're thinking."

"Which is?"

"That Mia and Tony met again later. He broke up with her; since then they have never met. Her life has continued without him. She has nothing to do with this case, got it? You have my word. She is putting her life together again, so please don't . . ."

Harry nodded and took the cigarette, which had been extinguished by the rain, from his mouth.

"I'm not on the case anymore," he said. "But your word would have been good enough anyway."

As Harry drove from the parking lot he looked in the mirror and watched Skai packing up his fishing gear.

Rikshospital. He was in the rhythm now. Time was not chopped up by events; it flowed in an even stream. He had thought of asking for a mattress. That would be a bit like Chungking Mansions.

81

The Cones of Light

Three days passed. He was alive. Everyone was alive.

No one knew where Tony Leike was; the trail of the fake Odd Utmo ended in Copenhagen. A photograph of Lene Galtung with a shawl over her head and large sunglasses in the best Greta Garbo style was splashed across one newspaper. The headline was: NO COMMENT. And now no one had seen her for two days after she had gone into hiding, apparently at her father's house in London. The photograph of Tony in work clothes in front of the helicopter had been in several newspapers. It was captioned PRINCE CHARMING'S VANISHING ACT in one. He had now been dubbed Prince Charming; people had taken to it, and anyway, it suited Leike better than Altman. Strangely enough, no one in the press had managed to link Tony Leike with the Utmo farm yet. The mother and later Tony had obviously covered their tracks well.

Mikael Bellman had daily press conferences. On a TV talk show he demonstrated his pedagogic skills and flashed his winsome smile, explaining how the case had been cracked. His version of the story—that went without saying. And made it seem like an oversight that the killer had not been arrested; the important thing, first off, was that Tony "Prince Charming" Leike had been unmasked, rendered ineffective, sidelined.

The dark descended a few minutes later every evening. Everyone was waiting for spring or frost, one of the two, but neither came.

The cones of light swept across the ceiling.

Harry lay on his side, staring at the smoke from his cigarette, curling up toward the ceiling in intricate and ever-unpredictable patterns.

"You're so quiet," Kaja said, snuggling up to his back.

"I'll be here until the funeral," he said. "Then I'm off."

He took another drag. She didn't answer. Then, to his surprise, he felt something warm and wet on his shoulder blade. He put the cigarette on the edge of the ashtray and turned to her. "Are you crying?"

"Trying not to." She laughed with a sniffle. "I don't know what's gotten into me."

"Do you want a cigarette?"

She shook her head and dried the tears. "Mikael called today, wanting to meet."

"Mm."

She laid her head against his chest. "Don't you want to know what I answered?"

"Only if you want to tell me."

"I said no. Then he said I would regret that. He said you would drag me down. That it wasn't the first time you had done that to someone."

"Well, he's right."

She lifted her head. "But that doesn't matter—don't you understand? I want to be wherever you are." Tears began to roll again. "And if it's down, I want to be there, too."

"But there'll be nothing," Harry said. "Not even me. I'll have gone. You saw me at Chungking. It would be like right after the avalanche. The same cabin, but alone and abandoned."

"But you found me and got me out. I can do the same for you."

"What about if I don't want to get out? You don't have any more dying fathers to entice me with."

"But you love me, Harry. I know you love me. That's a good enough reason, isn't it? **I'm** a good enough reason."

Harry caressed her hair, her cheeks, caught her tears with his fingers, carried them to his mouth and kissed them.

"Yes," he said with a sad smile. "You are reason enough."

She took his hand, kissed it where he had kissed it.

"No," she whispered. "Don't say it. Don't say that's why you're going. So that you don't drag me down. I'll follow you to the end of the world—you see?"

He pulled her in to him. And at once felt something slacken, like a muscle that had been held in quivering tension for a long time without his realizing it. He let go, gave up, let himself fall. And the pain that had been there melted away, became something warm following the bloodstream around his body, softening it, giving it peace. The feeling of free fall was so liberating that he felt his throat thicken. And knew part of him had wanted it, this, also up there in the snowy mist above the scree.

"To the end of the world," she whispered, already breathing faster.

The cones of light swept across the ceiling, again and again.

82

Red

Harry was sitting by his father's bedside. It was still dark when a nurse came in with a cup of coffee, asked him whether he had had any breakfast and dropped a glossy magazine in his lap.

"You have to think about something else, you know," she said, angling her head and giving the impression she was about to stroke his cheek.

Harry dutifully flicked through the magazine while she tended to his father. But he couldn't distract himself with the celebrity press, either. Old photographs of Lene Galtung leaving premieres, gala lunches in her new Porsche. MISSING TONY was the headline, and the assertion was underpinned by comments not from Lene herself, but from celebrity friends. There were pictures outside the gates of a house in London, but no one had seen Lene there. At least no one had recognized her. There was a grainy photograph taken from a distance of a red-haired woman in front of Credit Suisse in Zurich, which the magazine claimed was of Lene Galtung, because they were able to quote Lene's hairstylist, who Harry assumed had been paid a sizable sum to say, "She asked me to curl her hair and dye it brick red." Tony was referred to as a "suspect" in what was portrayed as an average society scandal rather than one of the country's worst murder cases.

Harry got up, went into the corridor and called Katrine Bratt. It still wasn't even seven o'clock, but she was up. She was leaving today. Starting at the Bergen Police Station over the weekend.

He hoped she would take it easy at first. Although it was difficult to imagine Katrine Bratt taking anything easy.

"Last job," he said.

"And after that?" she asked.

"Then I'm off."

"No one will miss you."

". . . more than I will."

"There was a full stop at the end, dear."

"It's about Credit Suisse in Zurich. I'd like to know if Lene Galtung has an account there. She's supposed to have been given a whopping pre-inheritance. Swiss banks are tricky. Probably take some time."

"Fine—I'm getting the hang of this now."

"Good. And there's a woman whose movements I want you to check."

"Lene Galtung?"

"No."

"No? What's the name of the beast?"

Harry spelled it for her.

At a quarter past eight Harry pulled up outside the fairy-tale compound on Voksenkollen. There were a couple of cars parked, and through the raindrops

Harry could make out the tired faces and the long telephoto lenses of paparazzi. They seemed to have been camping there the whole night. Harry rang the bell by the gate and went in.

The woman with the turquoise eyes was standing by the door, waiting.

"Lene's not here," she said.

"Where is she?"

"Somewhere they won't find her," she said, motioning to the cars outside the gate. "And your people promised me you would leave her alone after the last interview. Three hours, it lasted."

"I know," Harry lied. "But it was you I wanted to talk to."

"Me?"

"May I come in?"

He followed her into the kitchen. She gestured to a chair, turned her back on him and filled a cup from a coffee machine on the countertop.

"What's the story?"

"Which story?"

"The one about you being Lene's mother."

The coffee cup hit the floor and smashed into a thousand pieces. She clutched the countertop, and he could see her back heaving. Harry hesitated for a moment, but then took a deep breath and said what he'd made up his mind to say.

"We've done a DNA test."

She whirled around, furious. "How? You haven't . . ." She came to an abrupt halt.

Harry's gaze met her turquoise eyes. She had fallen

for the bluff. He was aware of a vague sense of discomfort. Which could have been caused by shame. It melted away, nonetheless.

"Get out!" she hissed.

"Out to them?" Harry asked, nodding toward the paparazzi. "I'm finishing my police career, planning to travel. I could do with a little capital. If a hairstylist can be paid twenty thousand kroner for saying which hair color Lene requested, how much do you think I'd get for telling them who her real mother is?"

The woman took a step forward, raising a hand in anger, but then her tears flowed, the burning light in her eyes extinguished and she sank into a kitchen chair, impotent. Harry cursed himself, knowing he had been unnecessarily brutal. But time was not on his side for any finely attuned stratagems.

"I apologize," he said. "But I'm trying to save your daughter. And to do that I require assistance. Do you understand?"

He placed a hand upon hers, but she pulled it away.

"He's a killer," Harry said. "But she couldn't care less, could she? She'll do it anyway."

"Do what?" The woman sniffled.

"Follow him to the end of the world."

She didn't answer, just shook her head, weeping silent tears.

Harry waited. Stood up, poured himself a cup of coffee, tore a sheet off the paper-towel roll, put it on the table in front of her, sat down and waited. Took a sip. Waited.

"I said she shouldn't do what I did," she said. "She shouldn't love a man because he . . . because he made her feel **beautiful.** More beautiful than she is. You think it's a blessing when it happens, but it's a curse."

Harry waited.

"When you've seen yourself become beautiful in his eyes once, it's like . . . like being bewitched. And so you are. Again and again, because you think you'll be allowed to see it one more time."

Harry waited.

"I spent my early years on the move. We traveled around; I wasn't able to go to school. When I was eight the child-welfare people came for me. At sixteen I began to clean at the shipping company owned by Galtung. Anders was engaged when he got me pregnant. He wasn't the one with the money; she was. He had gambled in the stock market, but the prices for tankers fell and he had no choice. He sent me packing. But she found out. And it was she who decided I would keep the child, that I would be retained as a housecleaner, that my little girl would be raised as the daughter of the house. She couldn't have any children herself, so they took Lene from me. They asked what kind of upbringing I could offer her. Me, a single mother, uneducated, no family around me—did I really wish to deprive my daughter of the chance of a good life? I was so young and afraid, I thought they were right, that this was for the best."

"No one knew about it?"

She took the paper towel and wiped her nose. "It's strange how easy it is to deceive people when they want to be deceived. And if they are not deceived, they don't let it show. That didn't matter much to me. I had only been a womb to produce an heir for the Galtungs—so what?"

"Was that it?"

She shrugged. "No. After all, I had Lene. Nursed her, fed her, changed her diapers, slept by her. Taught her to speak, brought her up. But we all knew it was short-term. One day I would have to let go."

"Did you?"

She gave a bitter laugh. "**Can** a mother ever let go? A daughter can let go. Lene despises me for what I've done. For what I am. But look at her. Now she's doing the same."

"Following the wrong man to the end of the world?"

She shrugged again.

"Do you know where she is?"

"No. Only that she's left to be with him."

Harry took another swig of coffee. "I know where the end of the world is," he said.

She didn't answer.

"I can go and try to bring her back for you."

"She doesn't want to be brought back."

"I can try. With your help." Harry pulled out a piece of paper and placed it in front of her. "What do you say?"

She read. Then she looked up. The makeup had run from her turquoise eyes down her hollow cheeks.

"Swear to me that you'll bring my girl back safe and sound, Hole. Swear. Do that and I'll agree."

Harry studied her.

"I swear," he said.

Outside again, with a cigarette lit, he thought about what she had said. **Can a mother ever let go?** About Odd Utmo, who had taken a photograph of his son with him. **But a daughter can let go.** Can she? He blew out the cigarette smoke. Could **he** let go?

Gunnar Hagen was standing beside the vegetable counter at his favorite Pakistani grocer's shop. He stared at his inspector in utter disbelief. "You want to go back to the Congo? To find Lene Galtung? And that has nothing to do with the murder investigation?"

"Same as last time," Harry said, lifting a vegetable he didn't recognize. "We're after a missing person."

"Lene Galtung has not been reported missing by anyone except the gutter press, as far as I know."

"She has now." Harry took a sheet from his coat pocket and showed Hagen the signature. "By her biological mother."

"I see. And how am I going to explain to the Ministry of Justice that we should launch this search in the Congo?"

"We have a lead."

"Which is?"

"I read in **Se og Hør** that Lene Galtung asked to have her hair dyed brick red. I don't even know if that's a color we use in Norway; that's probably why I remembered it."

"Remembered what?"

"That it was the hair color given in the passport belonging to Juliana Verni from Leipzig. At the time I asked Günther to check if there was a stamp from Kigali in her passport. But the police didn't find it. The passport was gone, and I'm convinced Tony Leike took it."

"The passport? And?"

"Now Lene Galtung has it."

Hagen put some pak choi in his shopping basket while slowly shaking his head. "You're basing a trip to the Congo on something you read in a gossip rag?"

"I'm basing it on what I—or I should say Katrine Bratt—found out about what Juliana Verni has been doing recently."

Hagen started to make a move toward the man at the cash register. "Verni's dead, Harry."

"Do dead people catch flights? Turns out Juliana Verni—or let's say a woman with curly brick-red hair—has bought a plane ticket from Zurich to the end of the world."

"The end of the world?"

"Goma, the Congo. Early tomorrow."

"Then they will arrest her when they discover she has a passport belonging to a person who has been dead for nearly three months."

"I checked with ICAO. They say it can take up to a year before the passport number of a deceased person is crossed off the books. Which means someone may have traveled to the Congo on Odd Utmo's passport, too. However, we have no cooperation agreement with the Congo. And it's hardly an insurmountable problem buying your way out of prison."

Hagen let the cashier tote up his purchases while he massaged his temples in an attempt to preempt the inevitable headache. "So go and find her in Zurich. Send the Swiss police to the airport."

"We've got her under surveillance. Lene Galtung will lead us to Tony Leike, boss."

"She'll lead us to perdition, Harry." Hagen paid, took his items and marched out of the shop into rainy, wind-blown Grønlandsleiret, where people rushed past with upturned collars and downcast faces.

"You don't understand. Bratt managed to find out that two days ago Lene Galtung emptied her account in Zurich. Two million euros. Not a staggering sum and definitely not enough to finance a whole mining project. But enough to bridge a critical phase."

"Idle speculation."

"What the hell else is she going to do with two million euros in cash? Come on, boss—this is the only chance we'll get." Harry stepped up his pace to stay even with Hagen. "In the Congo you don't find people who don't want to be found. The fucking country is as big as Western Europe and consists largely of forest no white man has ever seen. Go for it now. Leike will haunt your dreams, boss."

"I don't have nightmares like you do, Harry."

"Have you told the next of kin how well you sleep at night, boss?"

Gunnar Hagen came to an abrupt halt.

"Sorry, boss," Harry said. "That was below the belt."

"It was. And actually I don't know why you're hassling me for my permission. You've never considered it important before."

"Thought it would be nice for you to have the feeling you're the man in charge, boss."

Hagen fired a warning shot across Harry's bow. Harry shrugged. "Let me do this, boss. Afterward you can give me the boot for refusing to obey orders. I'll take all the flak—it's OK by me."

"Is it OK?"

"I'm going to resign after this, anyway."

Hagen eyed Harry. "Fine," he said. "Go." Then he set off again.

Harry caught up with him. "Fine?"

"Yes. Actually it was fine from the very beginning."

"Oh? Why didn't you say so before then?"

"Thought it would be nice to have the feeling I was the man in charge."

Part Nine

83

The End of the World

She dreamed she was standing before a closed door and heard a cold, lone bird's cry from the forest, and it sounded so peculiar because the sun was shining and it was hot. She opened the door . . .

She woke up with her head on Harry's shoulder and dried saliva in the corners of her mouth. The captain's voice announced they were about to land in Goma.

She looked out of the window. A gray stripe in the east presaged the arrival of a new day. It had been twelve hours since they had left Oslo. In a few hours the Zurich flight with Juliana Verni on the passenger list would land.

"I'm wondering why Hagen thought it was all right to shadow Lene like this," Harry said.

"He probably valued your cogent arguments." Kaja yawned.

"Mm. He seemed a bit too relaxed. I figure he's got something up his sleeve. There's some guarantee he's got that they won't nail him to the wall for this."

"He might have something on someone in the Ministry of Justice," Kaja said.

"Mm. Or on Bellman. Perhaps he knows you and Bellman were having a relationship?"

"Doubt it," Kaja said, peering into the dark. "There are hardly any lights here."

"Looks like a power cut," Harry said. "The airport must have its own generator."

"Light over there," she said, pointing to a red shimmer north of the town. "What's that?"

"Nyiragongo," Harry said. "It's the lava lighting up the sky."

"Is that right?" she said, pressing her nose against the window.

Harry drank his glass of water. "Shall we go through the plan one more time?"

She nodded and straightened her seat back.

"You stay in the arrivals hall and keep an eye on the landing times. Make sure everything is going to plan. In the meantime I'll go shopping. It's only fifteen minutes to downtown, so I'll be back in plenty of time before Lene's plane lands. You watch, see if anyone is there to collect her, and stay on her tail. Since Lene knows my face I'll be outside in a taxi waiting for you. And should anything untoward happen, you call me at once. OK?"

"OK. And you're sure she'll stop over in Goma?"

"I'm not sure of anything at all. There are only two hotels in Goma that are still functional, and according to Katrine there's nothing booked in either Verni's name or Galtung's. But the guerrillas control the roads to the west and north, and the closest town south is an eight-mile drive."

"Do you really believe the only reason Tony has brought Lene here is to milk her for money?"

"According to Jens Rath, the project is at a critical stage. Can you see any other reason?"

Kaja shrugged. "What if even a killer is capable of loving someone so much that he simply wants to be with her? Is that so inconceivable?"

Harry nodded. As if to say, "Yes, you have a point," or, "Yes, it is inconceivable."

There was a humming and a clicking, like a camera in slow motion, as the wheels were lowered.

Kaja stared out of the window.

"And I don't like the shopping, Harry. Why the weapons?"

"Leike is violent."

"And I don't like traveling as an undercover cop. I know we can't smuggle our own weapons into the Congo, but couldn't we have asked the Congolese police for assistance with the arrest?"

"As I said, we have no extradition agreement. And it's not improbable that a financier like Leike has local police in his pay who would have warned him."

"Conspiracy theory."

"Yep. And simple mathematics. A policeman's wage in the Congo is not enough to feed a family. Relax—Van Boorst has a wonderful little hardware store and he's professional enough to keep his mouth shut."

The wheels emitted a scream as they hit the landing strip.

Kaja squinted out of the window. "Why are there so many soldiers here?"

"UN flying in reinforcements. The guerrillas have advanced in the last few days."

"What guerrillas?"

"Hutu guerrillas, Tutsi guerrillas, Mai Mai guerrillas. Who knows?"

"Harry?"

"Yes."

"Let's get this job done quickly and go home."

He nodded.

It had already grown lighter when Harry walked along the line of taxi drivers outside. He exchanged a few words with each and every one until he found someone who could speak good English. Excellent English, in fact. He was a small man with alert eyes, gray hair and thick blood vessels above the temples and sides of his high, shiny forehead. His English was definitely original, a kind of stilted Oxford variant with a broad Congolese accent. Harry explained to him that he would hire him for the whole day. They quickly agreed on a price and exchanged handshakes, a third of the agreed sum in dollars, and names, Harry and Dr. Duigame.

"In English literature," the man elucidated, openly counting the money. "But as we're going to be together the whole day you can call me Saul."

He opened the rear door of a dented Hyundai. Harry indicated where Saul was to drive, to the road by the burned-down church.

"Sounds like you've been here before," Saul said, steering the car along a regular stretch of pavement, which, as soon as it met the main traffic artery, became a moonscape of craters and cracks.

"Once."

"Then you should be careful." He smiled. "Hemingway wrote that once you have opened your soul to Africa you won't want to be anywhere else."

"Hemingway wrote that?" Harry asked with some skepticism.

"Yes, he did, but Hemingway wrote that sort of romantic shit all the time. Shot lions when he was drunk and pissed that sweet whiskey urine on their corpses. The truth is that no one comes back to the Congo if they don't have to."

"I had to," Harry said. "Listen, I tried to get hold of the driver I had last time when I was here, Joe from Refugee Aid. But there's no response from his number."

"Joe's gone," Saul said.

"Gone?"

"He took his family with him, stole a car and drove to Uganda. Goma's under siege. They'll kill everyone. I'm going soon, too. Joe had a good car—maybe he'll make it."

Harry recognized the church spire towering over the ruins of what Nyiragongo had eaten. He held on tight as the Hyundai rolled past the potholes. There were nasty scrapes and bumps to the chassis a couple of times.

"Wait here," Harry said. "I'll walk the rest of the way. Back soon."

Harry stepped out and inhaled gray dust and the smell of spices and rotten fish.

Then he started walking. An obviously drunk man tried to ram Harry with his shoulder, but missed and staggered into the road. Harry had a couple of choice words hurled after him and walked on. Not too fast, not too slow. Arriving at the only brick house in the square of shops, he went up to the door, banged hard and waited. Heard quick footsteps inside. Too quick to be Van Boorst's. The door was opened a fraction and half a black face and one eye appeared.

"Van Boorst at home?" Harry asked.

"No." The large gold teeth in the upper set glinted.

"I want to buy some handguns, miss. Can you help me?"

She shook her head. "Sorry. Good-bye."

Harry shoved his foot in the gap. "I pay well."

"No guns. Van Boorst not here."

"When will he be back, miss?"

"I not know. I not have time now."

"I'm looking for a man from Norway. Tony. Tall. Handsome. Have you seen him around?"

The girl shook her head.

"Will Van Boorst be coming home this evening? This is important, miss."

She looked at him. Sized him up. Her gaze lingered, from top to toe. And back. Her soft lips slid apart over her teeth. "You a rich man?"

Harry didn't answer. She blinked sleepily, and her matte-black eyes glistened. Then she smirked. "Thirty minutes. Come back then."

Harry returned to the taxi, sat in the front seat, told Saul to drive to the bank and called Kaja.

"I'm still sitting in the arrivals hall," she said. "No announcements to say anything except that the Zurich flight is on time."

"I'll check us into the hotel before I go back to Van Boorst and buy what we need."

The hotel lay to the east of downtown toward the Rwandan border. In front of reception was a parking lot coated with lava and wreathed with trees.

"They were planted after the last eruption," Saul said, as though reading Harry's thoughts. There were almost no trees in Goma. The double room was on the first floor of a low building by the lake and had a balcony overlooking the water. Harry smoked a cigarette, watching the morning sun glitter on the surface and glint off the oil rig far out. He checked his watch and went back to the parking lot.

Saul's state of mind seemed to have adapted to the sluggish traffic he was in: He drove slowly, talked slowly, moved his hands slowly. He parked outside the church walls, a good distance from Van Boorst's house. Switched off the engine, turned to Harry and asked politely but firmly for the second third of the sum.

"Don't you trust me?" Harry asked with a raised eyebrow.

"I trust your sincere desire to pay," Saul said. "But in Goma money is safer with me than with you, Mr. Harry. Shame but true."

Harry acknowledged the reasoning with a nod, flipped through the rest of the money and asked if Saul had something heavy and compact in the car, the size of a pistol, such as a flashlight. Saul pursed his lips and opened the glove compartment. Harry took out the flashlight, stuffed it in his inside pocket and looked at his watch. Twenty-five minutes had passed.

He strode down the street, his eyes fixed straight ahead. But sidelong glances registered men turning after him with appraising eyes. Appraising height and weight. The elasticity of his strides. The jacket hanging slightly askew and the bulky shape in the inside pocket. And dismissing the opportunity.

He went up to the door and knocked.

The same light steps.

The door opened. She glanced at him, then her gaze wandered past him, to the street.

"Quick, come in," she said, grabbing his arm and pulling him inside.

Harry stepped over the threshold and stood in the semi-gloom. All the curtains were drawn, apart from by the window over the bed, where he had seen her lying half naked the first time he was here.

"He not arrive yet," she said in her simple but effective English. "Soon come."

Harry nodded and looked at the bed. Tried to imagine her there, with the blanket over her hips. The light falling on her skin. But he couldn't. For there was something trying to catch his attention, something that was not right, missing, or was there and shouldn't have been.

"You come alone?" she asked, walking around him and sitting on the bed. Placing one hand on the mattress, allowing the shoulder strap of her dress to slip down.

Harry shifted his gaze to locate what was wrong. And found it. The colonial master and exploiter King Leopold.

"Yes," he said automatically, without quite knowing why yet. "Alone."

The picture of King Leopold that had been hanging on the wall was gone. The next thought followed hard on its heels. Van Boorst wasn't coming. He was gone, too.

Harry took half a step toward her. She tilted her head slightly, moistening her full red-black lips. And he was close enough to see now, to see what had replaced the painting of the Belgian king. The nail the picture had been hanging from impaled a bank-note. The face that made the note distinctive was sensitive and sported a well-tended mustache. Edvard Munch.

Harry realized what was going to happen, was about to turn, but something also told him it was far too late; he was positioned exactly as planned in the stage directions.

He sensed more than saw the movement behind him and didn't feel the precise jab in his neck, only the breath against his temple. His neck froze to ice and the paralysis spread down his back and up to his scalp. His legs buckled beneath him as the drug reached his brain and consciousness faded. His last thought before darkness enveloped him was how amazingly fast ketanome worked.

84

Reunion

Kaja bit her lower lip. Something was wrong.

She called Harry's number again.

And got his voice mail yet again.

For several hours, she had been sitting in the arrivals hall—which, as far as that went, was also the departures hall—and the plastic chair rubbed against all the parts of the body with which it came into contact.

She heard the whoosh of a plane. Immediately afterward the only monitor present, a bulky box hanging from two rusty wires in the ceiling, showed that Flight KJ337 from Zurich had landed.

She scanned the gathering of people every second minute and established that none of them was Tony Leike.

She phoned again, but cut the connection when she realized she was doing this for the sake of doing something, but it wasn't action—it was inertia.

The sliding doors to baggage claim opened and the first passengers with hand luggage came through. Kaja stood up and went to the wall beside the sliding doors so that she could see the names on the plastic signs and the scraps of paper the taxi drivers were holding up for the arriving travelers. No Juliana Verni and no Lene Galtung.

She went back to her lookout post by the chair. Sat on her palms, could feel they were damp with sweat. What should she do? She pulled down her sunglasses and stared at the sliding doors.

Seconds passed. Nothing happened.

Lene Galtung was almost concealed behind a pair of violet sunglasses and a large black man walking in front of her. Her hair was red and curly, and she was wearing a denim jacket, khaki trousers and solid hiking boots. She was dragging a wheeled bag tailor-made to the maximum measurements allowed for hand luggage. She had no handbag, but a small, shiny metal case.

Nothing happened. Everything happened. In parallel and at the same time, the past and the present; and in a strange way Kaja knew the opportunity was finally there. The opportunity she had been waiting for. The chance to do the right thing.

Kaja didn't look straight at Lene Galtung, just made sure she was to the left of her field of vision. Stood up calmly after she had passed, took her bag and began to follow her. Into the blinding sunlight. Still no one had addressed Lene, and judging from her quick, determined steps, Kaja assumed she had been schooled down to the last detail about what she was to do. She walked past taxis, crossed the road and got into the backseat of a dark-blue Range Rover. The door was held open for her by a black man in a suit. Slamming it after her, he then walked around to the driver's seat. Kaja slipped into the backseat of the first taxi in the line, leaned forward between the seats, reflected quickly, but concluded that basically there was no other way of formulating it. "Follow that car."

She met the driver's eyes and arched eyebrows in the rearview mirror. Pointed to the car in front of them, and the driver gave a nod of comprehension, but still kept the car in neutral.

"Double pay," Kaja said.

The driver jerked his head and let go of the clutch.

Kaja called Harry. Still no answer.

They crawled their way west along the main thoroughfare. The streets were full of trucks, carts and cars with suitcases tied to the roofs. On each side, people were walking with huge piles of clothes and possessions balanced on their heads. In some places the traffic had come to a complete standstill. The driver had obviously gotten the point, and he was keeping at least one car between them and Lene Galtung's Range Rover.

"Where are they all going?" Kaja asked.

The driver smiled and shook his head to signify that he didn't understand. Kaja repeated the question in French with no luck. In the end she pointed to the people shuffling past their car with an interrogative expression.

"Re-fu-gee," the driver said. "Go away. Bad people come."

Kaja mouthed an "Aha."

Kaja texted Harry. Trying to stave off panic.

In the middle of Goma the road forked. The Range Rover swung left. Farther on it took another left and rolled down toward the lake. They had come to a very different part of town, with large detached houses behind high fences and surrounded by well-tended lawns with trees to offer shade and keep out prying eyes.

"Old," the driver said. "The Bel-gium. Co-lo-nist."

There was no traffic in the residential area and Kaja signaled that they should hang back farther, even though she doubted Lene Galtung had any experience detecting tails. When the Range Rover stopped three hundred feet ahead, Kaja motioned to the driver to stop, too.

An iron gate was opened by a man in a gray uniform, the car drove in and the gate was closed again.

Lene Galtung could hear her heart pounding. It hadn't beaten like this since the telephone had rung and she had heard his voice. He had told her he was in Africa. And said she should come. That he needed her. That only she could help him. Save the fine project that was not only his, but would become hers, too. So that he could have work. Men needed work. A future. A secure life, somewhere children could grow up.

The chauffeur opened the door for her, and Lene Galtung stepped out. The sun was not as strong as she had feared. The house that stood before her was magnificent. Solid, built at leisure. Brick by brick. Old money. The way they would do it themselves. When she and Tony had met he had been so intrigued by her family tree. The Galtungs were a Norwegian aristocratic family, one of the very few that had not been imported, a fact Tony repeated again and again. Perhaps that was why she had decided to postpone telling him that she was like him: of normal, modest origins, a gray rock in the scree, a social climber.

But now they would create their own nobility, they would shine in the scree. They would build.

The driver went ahead of her, up the brick steps to the door, where an armed man in camouflage opened it for them. A genuine crystal chandelier hung from the ceiling in the entrance hall. Lene's hand squeezed the sweaty handle of the metal case containing the money. Her heart felt as if it would explode in her chest. Was her hair all right? Could you see the effects of the lack of sleep and the long journey? Someone was coming down the broad staircase from the first floor. No, it was a black woman, probably one of the servants. Lene gave her a friendly but not an exaggeratedly welcoming smile. Saw the glint of gold teeth when the woman acknowledged her with a cool, almost impudent smile and left through the door behind her.

There he was.

He stood on the landing on the first floor and looked down at them.

He was tall, dark and draped in a dressing gown. She could see the attractive thick scar gleam white against his tanned chest. Then he smiled. She heard her breathing quicken. The smile. It illuminated his face, her heart, held more light than any crystal chandelier could.

He strolled down the stairs.

She put her case on the floor and flew toward him. He opened his arms and received her. And then she was with him. She recognized his smell, stronger than ever. Mixed with another strong, spicy aroma. It had to come from the dressing gown, for now she saw that the elegant silk garment was too short in the arms and not at all new. It wasn't until she felt him freeing himself that she realized she had been cling-ing to him, and she let go abruptly.

"Darling, you're crying." He laughed, stroking her cheek with a finger.

"Am I?" She laughed, too, drying under her eyes and hoping her makeup hadn't run.

"I have a surprise for you," he said, taking her hand. "Come with me."

"But . . ." she said, turning to see that the metal case had already been removed.

They went upstairs and in through a door to a large, bright bedroom. Long, gossamer curtains swayed gently in the breeze from the terrace door.

"Were you asleep?" she asked, gesturing to the unmade four-poster bed.

"No." He smiled. "Sit here and close your eyes."

"But . . ."

"Just do as I say, Lene."

She thought she could hear a suggestion of annoy-ance in his voice and hastened to do what he said.

"They'll soon be arriving with Champagne, and then I want to ask you something. But first I'm going to tell you a story. Are you ready?"

"Yes," she said, and knew. Knew this was the moment. The one she had been waiting for. The moment she would remember for the rest of her life.

"The story I am going to tell you is about me. You see, there are a few things you ought to know about me before you answer my question."

"I understand." It was as if the Champagne bubbles were already coursing through her veins, and she had to concentrate in order not to giggle.

"I've told you I grew up with my grandfather, that my parents were dead. What I omitted to say was that I lived with them until I was fifteen."

"I knew it!" she exclaimed. Her eyes flew open.

Tony cocked an eyebrow. A delicately shaped, oh-so-beautiful eyebrow, she thought.

"I've always known you had a secret, Tony," she said, laughing. "But I also have a secret. I want us to know everything about each other, everything!"

Tony assumed a lopsided smile. "So let me continue without any more interruptions, my sweet Lene. My mother was deeply religious and met my father in a chapel. He had just been released after serving time for murdering someone in a fit of jealous rage, and while in prison he had found Jesus. For my mother this was something straight out of the Bible, a repentant sinner, a man she could help to find redemption and eternal life while she did penance for her own sins. That was how she explained to me her decision to marry the bastard."

"What—"

"Shh! My father repented for the murder by labeling everything that was not in praise of God a sin. I was not allowed to do any of the things other children did. If I contradicted him I got a taste of the belt. He tried to provoke me, say that the sun went around the earth, as it said in the Bible. If I protested, he beat me. When I was twelve I was in the outhouse with my mother. We used to do that. When I came out he hit me with a spade because he thought it was a sin, that I was too old to go to the bathroom with my mother. He marked me for life."

Lene gulped as Tony lifted a distorted, arthritic finger and ran it along the top part of the scar on his chest. And then she noticed his missing finger.

"Tony! What happ—"

"Shh! The last time my father beat me I was fifteen, and he used the belt for twenty-three minutes without a break. One thousand, three hundred and eighty seconds. I counted them. He hit me every four seconds, like a machine. Kept hitting me, his rage steadily increasing because I refused to cry. In the end his arm was so tired that he had to give up. Three hundred and forty-eight lashes. That night I waited until I heard his snoring, sneaked into their bedroom and poured a drop of acid into his eye. He screamed and screamed while I held him and whispered in his ear that if he touched me again I would kill him. And I felt him stiffen in my arms, I knew he knew I was stronger than he was. And he knew I had it in me."

"Had what in you, Tony?"

"Him. The killer."

Lene's heart stopped pumping. It was not true.

Couldn't be true. He had told her it wasn't him, they were mistaken.

"After that day we watched each other like hawks. And Mom knew it was either him or me. One day she came to me and said he had been to Geilo to buy ammunition for the rifle. I had to get away, and she had decided with my grandfather what had to be done. He was a widower and lived by Lake Lyseren. He knew he would have to keep me hidden; otherwise the old man would come after me. So I left. Mom made it look as if I had been killed in an avalanche. My father shunned society, so it was always Mom who did anything that required contact with people. He thought she had reported me missing, but in reality she had informed only one person what she had done and why. She and Officer Roy Stille, they . . . well, they knew each other very well. Stille was wise enough to know that the police could do little to protect me against Dad and vice versa, so he helped to cover our traces. I was fine at Grand-dad's. Until the message came that Mom had disappeared in the mountains."

Lene put out her hand. "Poor, poor Tony."

"I said: close your eyes!"

She winced at the snarl in his voice, retracted her hand and squeezed her eyes shut.

"I couldn't go to the service, my grandfather said. Nobody should find out I was alive. When he returned he told me word for word what the priest had said about her in his speech. Three sentences. Three sentences about the world's strongest, most beautiful woman. The last was, 'Karen trod lightly on this earth.' The rest was about Jesus and forgiveness of sins. Three sentences and forgiveness of sins she had never committed." Lene could hear Tony breathing heavily now.

"Trod lightly. The bastard priest stood there in the pulpit and said she had left no prints. Vanished as she had lived, without leaving a trace. On to the next verse in the Bible. Granddad told me this straight, no beating about the bush, and do you know what, Lene? It was the most important day in my life. Do you understand?"

"Er . . . no, Tony."

"I knew he was sitting there, the bastard who had killed her. And I swore I would take my revenge. I would show him. I would show them all. That was the day I decided that whatever happened I would not end up like him. Or her. Three lines. And neither I nor the bastard sitting there needed forgiveness for our sins. We would both burn. Rather that than share paradise with a god like this." He lowered his voice. "No one, no one was going to stand in my way. Do you understand me now?"

"Yes." Lene smiled. "And you've deserved it, Tony. Everything. You've worked so hard!"

"I'm glad you're so understanding, my sweet. Here comes the rest. Are you ready?"

"Yes," Lene said, clapping her hands. She would see, her too, sitting at home, envious, lonely and bitter, begrudging her own daughter the chance to experience love.

"I had it all in the palm of my hand," Tony said, and Lene felt his hand on her knee. "You, your father's money, the project here in Africa. I thought nothing could go wrong. Until I fucked that randy bitch at the cabin in Håvass. I couldn't even remember her name when I received a letter from her saying she was pregnant and wanted money. She was in the way, Lene. I was meticulous in my planning. Covered the car in plastic. Took a blank postcard of the Congo I had lying around, forced her to write a few lines explaining her disappearance. Then I plunged the knife into her neck. The sound of blood on plastic, Lene . . . it's something quite unique."

85

Edvard Munch

It was like someone had hammered an icicle into Lene's skull. Nevertheless she forced her eyes open again. "You . . . you . . . killed her? A woman you . . . slept with in the mountains?"

"My libido is stronger than yours, Lene. If you don't do what I ask, I get others to do it."

"But you . . . you wanted me to . . ." Tears strangled her vocal cords. "That's not natural!"

Tony chuckled. "She didn't mind, Lene. Juliana didn't, either. She was well paid for it, though."

"Juliana? What are you talking about, Tony? Tony?" Lene was groping like a blind person in the dark.

"A German whore from Leipzig I met regularly. She does anything for money. Did."

Lene felt the tears running down her cheeks. His voice was so calm; that was what made it all seem so unreal.

"Say . . . say it isn't true, Tony. Please stop now."

"Shh. I was sent another letter. You can perhaps imagine my shock when I saw that it contained a photo of Adele in my car with a knife in her neck. The letter was signed by someone called Borgny Stem-Myhre. She wrote that she wanted money—otherwise she would report me for the murder of Adele Vetlesen. Of course, I knew I would have to get rid of her. But I needed an alibi for the time of death in case the police started to link me with Borgny and the blackmail attempt. In fact, I had been thinking of sending Adele's little postcard from Africa the next time I was here, but then I happened on an even better idea. I contacted Juliana and sent her here to Goma. She traveled around using Adele's name, sent the card from Kigali, went to Van Boorst and bought an apple I had been thinking of serving up to Borgny. Juliana came back and we met in Leipzig. Where I let her have the first taste of the apple." Tony chuckled. "She thought it was a new sex toy, poor thing."

"You . . . you killed her, too?"

"Yes. And then Borgny. I followed her. She was unlocking the door to the apartment building where she lived when I went up to her with the knife. I took her down to the cellar in Nydalen, where I had everything prepared. Padlock. Apple. I gave her a shot of ketanome in the neck. Then I went to Skien, to an investors' meeting, where all my witnesses were waiting. The alibi. I knew that while we were raising a toast, Borgny would be doing the job herself. They all do in the end. Then I went back, went through the cellar, picked up my padlock, took the apple out of her mouth and went home. To you. We made love. You pretended to come. Do you remember?"

Lene shook her head, unable to speak.

"Close your eyes, I said."

She felt his fingers glide over her forehead and close her eyelids, like an undertaker would. Heard his voice drone on, as if to himself.

"He liked to hit me. I can understand that now. The feeling of power that lies in inflicting pain, seeing another person succumb to you, having thy will being done on earth as it is in heaven."

She could smell the scent on him, the scent of sex. Of a woman's sex. Then his voice was there again, close to her ear now. "As I killed them something began to happen. It was like their blood was watering a seed that had been there the whole time. I began to grasp what I had seen in my father's eyes that time. The recognition. For just as he saw himself in me, I began to see him when I looked at myself in the mirror. I liked the power. And the impotence. I liked the game, the risk, the simultaneous highs and lows. When you stand on top of the mountain with your head in a cloud and hear the choir of angels in paradise you also have to hear the hissing fires of hell beneath you for it to mean anything. That was what my father knew. And now I know it, too."

Lene saw red stains dancing on the insides of her eyelids.

"I didn't realize the extent of my hatred until a few years after I left home, when I was standing with a girl on the edge of the woods outside a dance hall. A boy attacked me. I saw jealousy burning in his eyes. I saw my father coming at me and my mother with the spade. I cut the boy's tongue out. They arrested me, and I was given a prison sentence. And there I discovered what it does to you. And why Dad never mentioned his spell in the clink. Not a word. I received a short sentence. Nevertheless I almost went mad inside. And while I was doing time I realized what I had to do. I had to have him put in prison for murdering my mother. Not kill him, but have him incarcerated, buried alive. First, though, I had to find the proof, the remains of my mother. So I built a cabin up in the mountains, far from civilization, to ensure there was no chance of anyone recognizing the boy who'd disappeared when he was fifteen. Every year I searched the plateau, acre by acre, began as soon as most of the snow had gone, preferably at night, when no one else was out and about, trawling precipices and avalanche areas. If I had to, I would stay the night in a Tourist Association cabin where people were only passing through. But some of the locals must have seen me anyway; at any rate, rumors began to circulate about the ghost of the Utmo boy." Tony chuckled. Lene opened her eyes, but Tony didn't notice; he was studying a cigarette holder he had just taken out of the pocket of the dressing gown. Lene hurriedly closed her eyes again.

"After Borgny's murder a letter came signed 'Charlotte,' who wrote that she had been behind the previous letter. I saw that I was caught in a game. It could have been another bluff or it could have been anyone who was in the Håvass cabin that night. So I went up to take a look at the guest book, but the page for that night had been torn out. So I killed Charlotte. And waited for the next letter. It came. I killed Marit. And then Elias. After that things went quiet. Then I read in the paper that they were asking people who had been to the Håvass cabin the same night as the murder victims to come forward. I knew, of course, that no one would guess I had been there, but also that if I came forward I might find out from the police who had been there. Find out who was after me. Who was left to kill. So I went straight to the person I assumed would know most. This detective, Harry Hole. I tried to pump him about the other guests. Fat lot of good that did. Instead, this Mikael Bellman came along and arrested me. Someone had used my phone to call Elias Skog, he told me. And then I saw the light. This wasn't about money; someone was trying to get me arrested. Imprisoned. Who could stand by and cold-bloodedly watch people being murdered and still persist . . . with this crusade against me? Who could hate me so much? Then the final letter arrived. This time he didn't reveal his identity, just wrote he had been to the Håvass cabin that night, as invisible as a ghost. Said I knew him all too well. And he was coming to get me. And then it clicked. At last he had found me. Dad."

Tony paused for breath.

"He had planned the same for me as I had planned for him. To be buried alive, incarcerated for life. But how had he managed it? I wondered if he had kept the Håvass cabin under surveillance. Is that how he knew I was alive? Had he been following me from a distance? After I got engaged to you, the celebrity gossip press started printing pictures of me, and perhaps even Dad occasionally flicked through those magazines. But he had to be working with someone. For example, he couldn't have gone to Oslo and broken into Elias's house; he couldn't have taken the photo of Adele with the knife in her neck. Or could he? I found out that he had fled the farm, the slippery bastard. What he didn't know was that I was now much more familiar with the area than he was, after searching for my mother for all those years. I found him at the Tourist Association cabin in Kjeften. I was as happy as a child. But it was an anticlimax."

Rustling of silk.

"I derived less pleasure from torturing him than I had hoped. He didn't even recognize me, the blind idiot. But it didn't matter. I wanted him to see me as he himself had never managed to be. A success. I wanted to humiliate him. Instead he saw me as himself. A killer." He sighed. "And I began to realize he hadn't been working with anyone. And he didn't have the ability to do all this alone—he was too fragile, too frightened and too cowardly. I started the avalanche at Håvass, almost in a panic. Because I knew now: There was someone else. An invisible, inaudible hunter standing in the dark somewhere with his breathing attuned to mine. I had to get away. Out of the country. Somewhere I couldn't be found. So here we are, my love. On the edge of a jungle the size of Western Europe."

Lene was trembling uncontrollably. "Why are you doing this, Tony? Why are you telling me . . . this?"

She felt his hand on her cheek. "Because you deserve it, my love. Because your name is Galtung and you will have a long eulogy when you die. Because I think it's right you should hear all about me before you give me your answer."

"Answer to what?"

"Whether you want to marry me."

Her brain was in a spin now. "Whether I want . . . want . . ."

"Open your eyes, Lene."

"But I . . ."

"Open them, I said."

She did as she was told.

"This is for you," he said.

Lene Galtung gasped.

"It's made of gold," Tony said. The sunlight gleamed on the golden-brown metal as it lay on a sheet of paper on the coffee table between them. "I want you to wear it."

"Wear it?"

"After you've signed our marriage contract, of course."

Lene blinked repeatedly. Tried to rouse herself from the nightmare. The hand with the distorted fingers moved across the table, covering hers. She looked down, looked at the pattern on the burgundy silk of his dressing gown.

"I know what you're thinking," he said. "That the money you've brought with you will only last a while, but marriage will give me certain inheritance rights when you die. You're wondering if I intend to take your life. Aren't you?"

"Are you?"

Tony chuckled and squeezed her hand. "Do you intend to stand in my way, Lene?"

She shook her head. All she wanted was to be there for someone. For him. As though in a trance, she took the pen he passed her. Guided it down to the paper. Her tears fell on her signature, causing the ink to blotch. He seized the document.

"That'll do nicely," he said, blowing on it and motioning toward the coffee table. "Now let's see you wearing it."

"What do you mean, Tony? It's not a ring."

"I mean I want you to open wide, Lene."

Harry blinked. A single lit bulb hung from the ceiling. He was supine on a mattress. He was naked. It was the same dream, except that he wasn't dreaming. Above him a nail stuck out of the wall, and on the nail was impaled the head of Edvard Munch. A Norwegian banknote. He yawned so hard it seemed his shattered jaw would tear, and yet the pressure continued, almost exploding his head. He wasn't dreaming. The ketanome had worn off and the pain allowed no further dreams. How long had he been lying here? How long till the pain drove him mad? He carefully twisted his head and scanned the room. He was still in Van Boorst's house and he was alone. He wasn't shackled; he could stand up if he wanted.

His gaze followed the wire attached to the handle of the front door and running through the room to the wall behind him. He carefully twisted his head the other way. The wire ran through the U bolt in the wall right behind his head. And from there to his mouth. Leopold's apple. He was tethered firmly in position. The door opened outward so that the first person to pull it would release the needles that would pierce his head from inside. And if he moved too much that would also release the needles.

Harry put his thumb and first finger on either side of his mouth. Felt the circular ridges. Tried in vain to get a finger underneath one of them. He had a coughing fit and everything went black as he struggled to breathe. He realized the ridges had caused the flesh around his pharynx to swell and he risked suffocation. The wire to the door handle. The severed finger. Was this chance, or did Tony Leike know about the Snowman? And was he intending to outdo him?

Harry kicked the wall and tensed his vocal cords, but the metal ball stifled the scream. He gave up.

Leaned against the wall, braced himself for the pain and forced his mouth shut. He had read somewhere that the human bite is not much weaker than that of the white shark. Yet his jaw muscles only just managed to press the ridges down before his mouth was forced back open. There seemed to be a pulse, a living iron heart in his mouth. He touched the wire hanging from the apple. His every instinct shrieked for him to pull it, to pull the apple out. But he had seen a demonstration of what would happen, had seen photos of crime scenes. If he had not seen . . .

And at that second Harry knew. Knew not only how he himself would die but also how the others had died. And why it had been done like that. He experienced an absurd desire to laugh. It was so devilishly simple. So devilishly simple that only a devil could have devised it.

Tony Leike's alibi. He hadn't had an accomplice. That is to say, the victims themselves had been his accomplices. When Borgny and Charlotte had come to after being drugged they hadn't a clue what it was they had in their mouths. Borgny had been locked in a cellar. Charlotte had been outside, but the wire from her mouth had led to the trunk of the wrecked car in front of her, and however much she struggled, scraped and pulled at the trunk lid, it was, and remained, locked. Neither of them had a chance in hell of escaping from where they were, and when the pain was too great they had taken the predictable route. They had pulled the wire. Had they anticipated what would happen? Had the pain made them give way to hope, the hope that pulling the wire would retract the circular ridges in the mysterious object? And while the women had slowly but surely gone through the agonies of doubt and conjecture before the inevitable act, Tony Leike was many miles away at a dinner or a lecture, secure in the knowledge that his victims would perform the final part of the job themselves. Giving him the best possible alibi for the time of the death. In the strictest sense, he hadn't even murdered them.

Harry twisted his head to see what radius of movement he had without tightening the steel wire.

He had to do something. Anything. He groaned, thought the wire seemed to tighten; he stopped breathing, stared at the door. Waited for it to open, for . . .

Nothing happened.

He tried to remember Van Boorst's demonstration of the apple, how long the ridges remained out if there was no resistance. If only he could open his mouth even wider, if only his jaws . . .

Harry closed his eyes. It struck him how strangely normal and obvious the idea seemed, how little resistance he felt. Quite the opposite—he felt relief. Relief at inflicting even more pain on himself, if necessary, risking his own life in an attempt to survive. It was logical, simple, the black void of doubt repressed by a bright, clear, insane idea. Harry turned around on his stomach with his head against the U bolt so that there was some slack in the wire. Then he cautiously got up onto his knees. Touched his jaw. Found the point.

The point where everything centered: the pain, the jaw joint, the knot, the jumble of nerves and muscles that only just held his jaw together after the incident in Hong Kong. He wouldn't be able to hit himself hard enough; there had to be body weight behind it. His first finger tested the nail. It protruded about two inches from the wall. A standard nail with a large, broad head. It would smash through everything that came in its path if there was enough force. Harry took aim, rested his jaw against the nail in rehearsal, stood up to calculate at what angle he would have to fall. How deep the nail would have to penetrate. And how deep it **must** not penetrate. Neck, nerves, paralysis. Did calculations. Not coldly and calmly. But he calculated, anyway. Forced himself. The nail head was not like the top of a T; it sloped down toward the shank, so it would not necessarily tear everything with it on its way out. Finally, he tried to identify anything he hadn't considered. Until he realized this was his brain trying to delay events.

Harry took a deep breath.

His body would not obey. It protested, resisted. Wouldn't lower his head.

"Idiot!" Harry strove to shout, but it turned into a whistle. He felt a hot tear trickle down his cheek.

Enough crying, he thought. **Time to die a little now.**

Then he brought his head down.

The nail received him with a deep sigh.

. . .

Kaja was fumbling for her cell phone. The Carpenters had just shouted a three-part "Stop!" And Karen Carpenter answered, "Oh, yes, wait a minute." The text alert.

Outside the car, night had fallen with sudden brutality. She had sent three messages to Harry. Told him what had happened and that she was parked up the road from the house Lene Galtung had entered, awaiting further instructions and a sign of life.

WELL DONE. COME AND PICK ME UP FROM THE STREET SOUTH OF THE CHURCH. EASY TO FIND—IT'S THE ONLY BRICK HOUSE. COME STRAIGHT IN—IT'S OPEN. HARRY.

It was in Norwegian. She passed on the address to the taxi driver, who nodded, yawned and switched on the engine.

Kaja texted back in Norwegian, "On my way," as they drove north along the illuminated streets. The volcano lit up the night sky like an incandescent lamp, obliterating the stars and lending everything a faint bloodred shimmer.

Fifteen minutes later they found themselves on a darkened bomb crater of a street. A couple of paraffin lamps hung outside a shop. Either there was another power cut or this neighborhood didn't have electricity.

The driver stopped and pointed. Van Boorst. Sure enough, there it was, a brick house. Kaja looked around. Farther up the street she saw two Range Rovers. Two bleating mopeds passed with wobbly lights. Heavy African disco came belting out of one door. Here and there she could see the glow of cigarettes and white eyes.

"Wait here," Kaja said, pushing her hair up into the peaked cap and ignoring the driver's warning cries when she opened the door and slipped out.

She walked quickly up to the house. She had no naïve preconceptions about the chances a white woman had in a town like Goma after nightfall, but right now darkness was her best friend.

She could make out the door with black lava boulders on either side, knew she had to hurry. She felt it coming; she would have to preempt it. She almost stumbled, rushed onward, breathing through an open mouth. Then she was there. She placed her fingers on the door handle. Although the temperature had sunk surprisingly fast after the sun had set, sweat was streaming down between her shoulder blades and her breasts. She forced herself to press the handle down. Listened. It was so eerily quiet. As quiet as the time when . . .

Tears thickened like a viscous cement mix in her throat.

"Come on," she whispered. "Not now."

She closed her eyes. Concentrated on breathing. Emptied her brain of any thoughts. She would manage this now. Her thoughts slowed. Delete, delete. That's the way. Just one tiny thought left, then she could open the door.

Harry woke with something yanking at the corner of his mouth. He opened his eyes. It was dark. He must have fainted. Then he became aware of the wire pulling at the ball that was still in his mouth. His heart started, accelerated, hammered away. He pushed his mouth up against the bolt, absolutely clear that none of this would help if someone opened the door.

A strip of light from outside struck the wall above him. The blood glistened. He guided his fingers into his mouth, placed them over the teeth in his lower jaw and pressed. The pain made everything go black for a second, but he felt his jaw give. It was dislocated! As he pressed his jaw down with one hand, he took the apple with the other and pulled.

He heard sounds outside the door. **Fuck, fuck, fuck!** He still couldn't get the apple past his teeth. He pressed his jaw down farther. The sound of bone and tissue crunching and tearing resonated as if it came from his ears. He might just be able to pull his jaw down so far on one side that he could get the apple out sideways, but there was a cheek in the way. He could see the door handle moving. There wasn't time. No time. Time stopped here.

That last tiny thought. The Norwegian text message. **Gaten. Kirken.** The street. The church. Harry didn't use those endings. **Gata. Kirka.** That's what he said. Kaja opened her eyes. What was it he had said on her veranda when they were talking about the title of the Fante book? He never texted. Because he didn't want to lose his soul, because he preferred not to leave any traces when he disappeared. She had never received a single text from him. Not until now. He would have called. This didn't stack up; this was not her brain finding excuses not to open the door. This was a trap.

Kaja gently let go of the door handle. She felt a warm current of air on her neck. As though someone were breathing on her. She canceled the "as though" and turned.

There were two of them. Their faces melded into the darkness.

"Looking for someone, lady?"

The feeling of déjà vu struck her before she had answered. "Wrong door, that's all."

At that moment she heard a car start up; she turned and saw the rear lights of her taxi swaying along the street.

"Don't worry, lady," the voice said. "We paid him."

She turned back and looked down. At the pistol pointing at her.

"Let's go."

Kaja considered the alternatives. Didn't take long. There weren't any.

She walked ahead of them toward the two Range Rovers. The rear door of one swung open as they approached. She got in. It smelled of spiced after-shave and new leather. The door slammed behind her. He smiled. His teeth were large and white, the voice gentle, cheerful.

"Hi, Kaja."

Tony Leike was wearing a yellow and gray combat uniform. Holding a red cell phone in his hand. Harry's.

"You were told to go straight in. What stopped you?"

She shrugged.

"Fascinating," he said, angling his head.

"What is?"

"You don't seem the slightest bit afraid."

"Why should I be?"

"Because you're going to die soon. Have you really not understood?"

Kaja's throat constricted. Even though part of her brain was screaming that this was an idle threat, that she was a police officer and he would never take the risk, it was unable to drown out the other part, the one that said Tony Leike was sitting in front of her and knew exactly what the situation was. She and Harry were two kamikaze clods a long way from home, without authorization, without backup, without a Plan B. Without a hope.

Leike pressed a button and the window slid down.

"Go and finish him off, then take him up there," he said to the two men, and the window slid back up.

"I think it would have added a touch of class if you had opened the door," Leike said. "I sort of think we owe Harry a poetic death. Now, though, we'll have to opt for a poetic farewell." He leaned forward and peered up at the sky. "Beautiful red color, isn't it?" She could see it in his face now. Heard it. And her voice—the one that told the truth—told her. She really was going to die.

86

Caliber

Kinzonzi pointed to Van Boorst's brick house and told Oudry to drive the Range Rover right to the door. Kinzonzi got out and waited for Oudry to pocket the car key and follow. The order was simple: Kill the white man and take him there. It aroused no emotion. No fear, no pleasure, not even tension. It was a job.

Kinzonzi was nineteen years old. He had been a soldier since he was eleven. The PDLA, the People's Democratic Liberation Army, had stormed his village. They had smashed his brother's head with the stock of a Kalashnikov and raped his two sisters while forcing his father to watch. Afterward the commander had said that if his father didn't perform intercourse with his younger sister in front of them, they would kill Kinzonzi and his elder sister. But before the commander had finished his sentence, Kinzonzi's father had impaled himself on one of their machetes. Their laughter had filled the air.

Before leaving, Kinzonzi had eaten the first decent meal he'd had for several months and was given a beret, which the commander said was his uniform. Two months later he had a Kalashnikov and had shot his first human, a mother in a village who refused to hand over her blankets to the PDLA. He had been twelve when he lined up with other soldiers to rape a young girl not far from where he had been recruited. When it was his turn it suddenly struck him that the girl could have been his sister; the age would have been right. But when he studied her face he saw that he could no longer remember their faces: Mom, Dad, his sisters. They were gone, erased from his memory.

Four months later, he and two comrades chopped the arms off the commander and watched him bleed to death, not out of revenge or hatred but because the CFF, the Congo Freedom Front, had promised to pay them better. For five years he had lived off what the CFF raids in the northern Kivu jungle brought in, but all the time they had had to watch out for other guerrillas, and the villages they came to had been so plundered by others over time that they could barely feed themselves. For a while the CFF had negotiated with the government army: disarmament for amnesty and employment. But discussions broke down over wages.

Hungry and desperate, the CFF attacked a mining company extracting coltan, even though they were aware that mining companies had better weapons and soldiers than they did. Kinzonzi had never had any illusions that he would live a long life or that he would die any other way than from fighting. So he hadn't even blinked when he found himself staring up the gun barrel of a white man speaking to him in a foreign language. Kinzonzi had just nodded for him to get it over with. Two months later the wounds were healed, and the mining company was his new employer.

The white man was Mr. Tony. Mr. Tony paid well but showed no mercy if he saw the slightest sign of disloyalty. Yes, he spoke to them and was the best boss Kinzonzi had ever had. And yet Kinzonzi would not have hesitated for a second to shoot him if it had been worth his while. But it wasn't.

"Hurry up," Kinzonzi said to Oudry, loading his pistol. He knew it could take time for the white policeman to die from the metal apple that would be activated in his mouth when they opened the door, so he would shoot him at once in order to get going to Nyiragongo, where Mr. Tony and the women were waiting.

A man who had been seated on a chair smoking outside the adjacent shop got up and was lost in the darkness, mumbling angrily.

Kinzonzi regarded the door handle. The first time he had been here was to pick up Van Boorst. It was also the first time he had seen the legendary Alma. At that time Van Boorst had been spending all his money on Singapore sling, protection and Alma, who was not exactly cheap to maintain. Then Van Boorst, in his desperation, committed the final mistake of his life: blackmailing Mr. Tony with threats of going to the police. The Belgian had seemed more resigned than surprised when they came, and had finished his drink. They had carved him up into suitably large pieces to feed to the paradoxically fat pigs outside the refugee camp. Mr. Tony had taken over Alma. Alma of the hips, gold tooth and the sleepy fuck-me look that could have given Kinzonzi another reason to put a bullet in Mr. Tony's head. If it had been worth his while.

Kinzonzi pressed the handle. And pulled the door hard. It swung open but was stopped halfway by a thin steel wire fastened to the inside of the door. The moment it tightened, there was a loud, clear click and the sound of metal on metal, like the sound of a bayonet thrust into an iron sheath. The door opened with a creak.

Kinzonzi stepped in, dragged Oudry after him and slammed the door. The bitter smell of vomit stung their nostrils.

"Switch on the light."

Oudry did as he was ordered.

Kinzonzi stared at the end of the room. On the wall, drenched in blood, a banknote hung from a bare nail, from which a red stream led down to the floor. On the bed, in a pool of yellow vomit, lay a blood-covered metal ball with long needles sticking out, like rays of a sun. But no white policeman.

The door. Kinzonzi whirled around with his gun at the ready.

No one there.

He dropped to his knees and looked under the bed. No one.

Oudry opened the door to the only closet in the room. Empty.

"He's fled," Oudry said to Kinzonzi, who was standing by the bed pressing a finger into the mattress.

"What is it?" Oudry asked, going closer.

"Blood." He took the flashlight from Oudry. Followed the trail of blood to where it stopped in the middle. A trapdoor with an iron ring. He advanced on the hatchway, ripped open the door and shone the light down into the darkness beneath. "Get your gun, Oudry."

His comrade went outside and returned with his AK-47.

"Cover me," said Kinzonzi, descending the ladder.

He reached the bottom and held the pistol and flashlight in a double grip as he swiveled around. The beam swept over cupboards and shelves along the wall. Continued over a free-standing unit in the middle of the floor with grotesque white masks on the shelves. One with rivets for eyebrows, a lifelike one with a red asymmetrical mouth going right up to the ear on one side, one with empty eyes and a spear tattooed on both cheeks. He shone the light on the shelves on the facing wall. And stopped suddenly. Kinzonzi went rigid. Weapons. Guns. Ammunition. The brain is a fantastic computer. In a fraction of a second it can register tons of data, crunch them and reason its way to the correct answer. So when Kinzonzi swung the light back onto the masks, it already had the right answer. The light fell on the white mask with the asymmetrical mouth. Displaying the molars. Glistening red. The same way the blood on the wall under the nail had glistened.

Kinzonzi had never had any illusions that he would live a long life. Or that he would die any other way than from fighting.

His brain told his fingers to squeeze the trigger of his pistol. The brain is a fantastic computer.

In one microsecond the finger squeezed, at the same time as his brain had already finished its reasoning. It had the answer. Knew what the outcome would be.

Harry had known there was only one solution. And there wasn't any time to waste. So he had smacked his head against the nail a little higher this time. He had hardly felt it when the nail perforated his cheek or when it struck the metal ball inside. Then he had lowered himself onto the bed, forced his head against the wall and pulled back with his full weight while trying to tense the muscles in his cheek. At first nothing happened. Then the nausea came. And the panic. If he threw up now, with the Leopold's apple in his mouth, he would suffocate. But it was unstoppable; he could already feel his stomach contracting to send up the first load through the esophagus. In desperation, Harry raised his head and hips. Then let himself fall hard. And felt the flesh of his cheek give, tear, rip open. Felt the blood stream into his mouth, down the trachea, activating the coughing reflex, felt the nail bang against his front teeth. Harry put his hand in his mouth, but the apple was slippery from all the blood; his fingers slithered on the metal. He inserted one hand behind the ball, pushed while pressing his jaw down with the other. Heard it scrape against his teeth. Then—in a huge surge—the vomit came.

Maybe that was what had forced the metal apple out. Harry lay with his head against the wall, looking at the shiny death-bringing invention, which now sat on the mattress, bathed in his sick.

Then he got up, naked and on shaky legs. He was free.

He staggered toward the front door, then remembered why he had gone to the house. At the third attempt he managed to open the trapdoor. He skidded in his own blood on the way down the steps and fell into the pitch black. Lying on the concrete floor and gasping for breath, he heard a vehicle pull up. He heard voices and doors slamming. Harry struggled to his feet, groped in the dark, took the steps in two strides, got a hand on the hatch and closed it as he heard the front door open and the savage click of the apple.

Harry moved back down the ladder with care until he sensed the cold concrete floor beneath his soles. Then he closed his eyes and strained his memory. Conjured up the image of his previous visit here. The shelves to the left. Kalashnikov. Glock. Smith & Wesson. The case with the Märklin rifle. Ammunition. In that order. He fumbled his way forward. Fingers strayed over a gun barrel. The smooth steel of a Glock. And, there, they recognized the shape of a Smith & Wesson, .38-caliber, the same as his service revolver. He took it with him and fumbled on toward the boxes of ammunition. Felt the wood on his fingertips. He heard angry voices and footsteps above. Just had to open the lid. Needed a little luck now. He stuffed his hand in and grabbed one of the cardboard packets. Ran his fingers over the contours of the cartridge. **Fuck—too big!** As he raised the lid of the next wooden box, the trapdoor opened. He grabbed at a packet, had to take a chance on it being the right caliber. At that moment light penetrated the cellar darkness, a circle, as from a spotlight, lit up the floor around the steps. It gave Harry enough light to read the label on the packet: 7.62 MILLIMETERS. **Fuck!** Harry looked on the shelf. There. The box next to it: .38-caliber. The light went from the floor and skittered across the ceiling. Harry saw the silhouette of a Kalashnikov in the opening and a man on his way down the steps.

The brain is a fantastic computer.

As Harry pulled open the lid of the box and took a cardboard packet, it had already done its calculations. It was too late.

87

Kalashnikov

"There wouldn't be a road here if we hadn't been running a mining business," Tony Leike said as the car bounced along the narrow, rough pavement. "Entrepreneurs like me are the only hope for people in countries like the Congo to get to their feet, to follow us, to become civilized. The alternative is to leave them to their own devices so that they can continue doing what they have always done: kill one another. Everyone on this continent is both a hunter and a victim. Don't forget that as you look into the imploring eyes of a starving African child. Give him a bit of food and those eyes will soon be looking at you again, from behind an automatic weapon. And then there is no mercy."

Kaja didn't answer. She stared at the red hair of the woman in the passenger seat. Lene Galtung had neither moved nor said anything, merely sat there with an erect back and retracted shoulders.

"Everything in Africa goes in cycles," Tony continued. "Rain and drought, night and day, eating and being eaten, living and dying. The course of nature is everything, nothing can be changed; swim with the flow, survive for as long as you can, take what's offered—that's all you can do. Because your forefathers' lives are your life, you cannot make a change, development is not possible. That's not African philosophy, just the experience of generations. And it is the **experience** that has to change. It is experience that changes mind-sets, not the other way around."

"And if it's your experience that white people exploit you?" Kaja said.

"The idea of exploitation has been sown by white men," Tony said. "But the term has proved to be a useful tool for African leaders who need to point to a common enemy to get their people behind them. Right from the dismantling of colonialist governments in the sixties, they have used white people's feelings of guilt to acquire power, so the real exploitation of the population could begin. The whites' guilt about colonizing Africa is pathetic. The real crime was to leave Africa to its own butchering and destructive ways. Believe me, Kaja, the Congolese never had it better than under the Belgians. The revolts had no foundation in popular will, but in individuals' greed for power. Tiny factions stormed the Belgians' houses here by Lake Kivu because the houses were so elegant they assumed they would find something there they desired. That was how it was, and that is how it is. That's why properties always have at least two gates, one at each end. One through which robbers can charge in and one through which inhabitants can flee."

"So that was how you left the house without me seeing you?"

Tony laughed. "Did you really think it was you tailing us? I've been keeping an eye on you ever since you both arrived. Goma is a small town with little money and a clear power structure. It was very naïve of you and Harry to come alone."

"Who's naïve?" Kaja said. "What do you think will happen when it comes out that two Norwegian police officers have disappeared in Goma?"

Tony hunched his shoulders. "Kidnapping is a relatively common occurrence in Goma. It wouldn't surprise me if the local police soon receive a letter from a freedom fighter demanding an exorbitant sum of money for you two. Plus the release of named prisoners who are known opponents of President Kabila's regime. Negotiations will continue for a few days, but lead nowhere, as of course the demands will be impossible to meet. And then you won't be seen again. Daily fare, Kaja."

Kaja tried to catch Lene Galtung's eye in the mirror, but she kept her gaze averted.

"What about her?" Kaja said. "Does she know you've killed all these people, Tony?"

"She does now," Tony said. "And she understands me. That's real love for you, Kaja. And that's why Lene and I are getting married this evening. You're invited." He laughed. "We're on our way to the church. I think it will be a very atmospheric ceremony when we swear eternal fidelity to each other, don't you, Lene?"

At that moment Lene bent forward in her seat, and Kaja saw the reason for her retracted shoulders: Her hands were held behind her back by a pair of pink handcuffs. Tony leaned over, grabbed Lene's shoulder and roughly pushed her back. Just then Lene twisted around to face them, and Kaja recoiled in horror. Lene Galtung was nearly unrecognizable. Her face was smeared with tears, one eye was swollen, and her mouth was forced open in such a way that her lips formed an O. Inside the O Kaja glimpsed gold metal. From the golden sphere hung a short red wire.

And the words Tony uttered were for Kaja an echo of another marriage proposal on the threshold of death, a burial in snow: Till death do us part.

. . .

Harry slipped behind the shelf of masks as the figure stepped down from the ladder, turned and flashed his light. There was nowhere to hide, just a countdown to when he would be seen. Harry closed his eyes so as not to be blinded, while opening the packet of cartridges with his left hand. Took four bullets; his fingers knew exactly what four bullets felt like. He swung the cylinder to the left with his right hand, let the by-now-reflexive movements take place, the way they had when he was sitting alone in Cabrini-Green and, out of sheer boredom, practicing quick-loading. But here he was not alone enough. Nor bored enough. His fingers trembled. He saw the red insides of his eyelids as the light fell on his face. He braced himself. But no shots were fired. The light moved. He wasn't dead, not yet. His fingers obeyed. They pushed bullets into four of the six empty chambers, relaxed, fast, one-handed. The cylinder fell into place. Harry opened his eyes as the light hit his face again. Blinded, he fired into the sun.

The light swung upward and over the ceiling, and was gone. The echo of the shots hung in the air while the flashlight rolled on its own axis, making a loud rumbling noise and shining a low beam around the walls like a lighthouse.

"Kinzonzi! Kinzonzi!"

The flashlight came to rest against the shelf. Harry rushed forward, grabbed it, rolled onto his back, holding the flashlight at arm's length, as far from his body as possible, braced his legs against the shelving unit and pushed off toward the ladder until he had the trapdoor directly above him. Then the bullets came, sounding like whiplashes, and he felt the spray of concrete dust against his arm and chest as they bored into the floor by the flashlight. Harry took aim and shot at the illuminated figure standing astride the hatchway. Three quick squeezes.

The Kalashnikov came first. It hit the floor beside Harry's head with a loud bang. Then came the man. Harry just managed to wriggle away before the body landed. No resistance. Meat. Dead weight.

It was quiet for a couple of seconds. Then Harry heard Kinzonzi—if that was his name—give a low groan. Harry got up, still with the flashlight at his side, saw a Glock lying on the floor near Kinzonzi and kicked it away. He grabbed the Kalashnikov.

Then he dragged the other man to the wall, as far from Kinzonzi as possible, and shone the light on him. Predictably enough, he had reacted as Harry had; blinded, he had shot into the sun. Harry's detective eyes automatically registered that the man's groin was soaked in blood; the bullet must have continued up into his stomach but was hardly likely to have killed him. A bleeding shoulder, so one bullet had probably entered his armpit. That explained why the Kalashnikov had come first. Harry crouched down. But that didn't explain why the man wasn't breathing.

He shone the light on his face. Why the **boy** wasn't breathing.

The bullet had gone in under his chin. From the angle he had fired the lead must have passed into his mouth, through his palate and up into the brain.

Harry inhaled. The boy couldn't have been much more than sixteen or seventeen. An altogether good-looking lad. Wasted beauty. Harry stood up, put the gun barrel to the dead man's head and shouted: "Where are they? Mr. Leike. Tony. Where?"

He waited a bit.

"What? Louder. I can't hear you. Where? Three seconds. One.

"Two . . ."

Harry pressed the trigger. The weapon must have been on full auto because it fired at least four times before he managed to release his finger. Harry closed his eyes when the salvo hit his face, and when he opened them again he saw that the boy's attractive features had disintegrated. Harry noticed hot, wet blood was running down his naked body.

Harry stepped over to Kinzonzi. Stood astride him, shone the flashlight on his face, pointed the gun to his forehead and repeated the question word for word.

"Where are they? Mr. Leike. Tony. Where? Three seconds . . ."

Kinzonzi opened his eyes. Harry saw the whites quiver. The terror of dying is a prerequisite for wanting to live. It had to be, at least here in Goma.

Kinzonzi answered, slowly and clearly.

88

The Church

Kinzonzi lay quite still. The tall white man had placed the flashlight on the floor so that it lit up the ceiling. Kinzonzi watched him put on Oudry's clothes. Watched him tear his T-shirt into strips and tie them around his chin and head so that the gaping jaw, the wound running from his mouth to his ear, was covered. Tightened it to stop the jaw from hanging on one side. Blood soaked through the cotton material as Kinzonzi looked on.

He had answered the few questions the man had asked. Where. How many. What weapons they had.

Now the white man went to the shelf, pulled out a black case, opened it and examined the contents.

Kinzonzi knew he was going to die. A young, violent death. But perhaps not now, not tonight. His stomach stung as though someone had poured acid on him. But it was OK.

The white man was holding Oudry's Kalashnikov. He moved toward Kinzonzi, stood over him with the light behind his back. A towering figure with his head wrapped in white cloth, the way they used to bind the chin for death before the deceased was buried. If Kinzonzi was going to be shot, it would happen now. The man dropped the torn strips of T-shirt he hadn't used on Kinzonzi.

"Help yourself."

Kinzonzi heard him groaning as he went up the ladder.

Kinzonzi closed his eyes. If he didn't wait too long, he could stop the worst bleeding before he fainted from blood loss. Get to his feet, crawl across the road, find people. And he might be lucky; they **might** not belong to the Goma vulture species. He might find Alma. He could make her his. Because she had no man now. And Kinzonzi no longer had an employer. He had seen what was in the case the tall white man had taken with him.

Harry stopped the Range Rover in front of the low church walls, radiator to radiator with the chunky Hyundai that was still standing there.

A cigarette glowed in the car.

Harry switched off the headlamps, rolled down the window and stuck his head out.

"Saul!"

Harry saw the cigarette glow move. The taxi driver came out.

"Harry. What happened? Your face . . ."

"Things didn't quite go as planned. I didn't imagine you'd still be here."

"Why not? You paid me for the whole day." Saul ran his hand over the hood of the Range Rover. "Nice car. Stolen?"

"Borrowed."

"Borrowed car. Borrowed clothes, too?"

"Yes."

"Red with blood. The previous owner's?"

"Let's leave your car here, Saul."

"Will I want this trip, Harry?"

"Probably not. Does it help if I say I'm one of the good guys?"

"Sorry, but in Goma we've forgotten what that means, Harry."

"Mm. Would a hundred dollars help, Saul?"

"Two hundred," Saul said.

Harry nodded.

". . . and fifty."

Harry got out and let Saul take the wheel.

"Are you sure that's where they are?" Saul asked as the car purred onto the road.

"Yes," Harry said from the backseat. "Someone once told me that it's the only place where people in Goma can get to heaven."

"I don't like the place," Saul said.

"Oh?" Harry said, opening the case beside him. The Märklin. The instructions for how to assemble the rifle were glued to the inside of the lid. Harry set to work.

"Evil spirits. Ba-Toye."

"You studied at Oxford—didn't you say?" Greased parts readily clicked into place.

"You don't know anything about the fire demon, I suppose."

"No, but I know these," Harry said, holding up

one of the cartridges from its own compartment in the Märklin case. "And I would back them against Ba-Toye."

The feeble yellow interior light made the gold-colored cartridge casing gleam. The lead bullet inside had a diameter of sixteen millimeters. The world's largest caliber. When he had been working on the report after the Redbreast investigation, a ballistics expert had told him the caliber of a Märklin was way beyond all sensible limits. Even for shooting elephants. It was better suited to felling trees.

Harry clicked the telescopic sights into place. "Put your foot down, Saul."

He laid the barrel over the top of the empty passenger seat and tested the trigger while keeping his eye some distance from the sights because of the bumpy ride. The sights needed adjusting, calibrating, fine-tuning. But there would be no chance to do that.

They had arrived. Kaja looked out of the car window. The scattered lights beneath them was Goma. Farther away, she saw the illuminated oil rig on Lake Kivu. The moon glittered in the greenish-black water. The last part of the road was no more than a dirt track winding around the top, and the car headlamps swept across the bare black moonscape. When they had reached the highest plateau, a flat disc of rock with a diameter of around a hundred yards, the driver had headed for the far end, through clouds of drifting white smoke tinted red by the Nyiragongo crater.

The driver switched off the ignition.

"May I ask you something?" Tony said. "Something I have given a lot of thought to over the last few weeks. How does it feel to know you're going to die? I don't mean how it feels to be afraid because you're in danger. I've experienced that several times myself. But to be absolutely certain that, here and now, your life will cease to exist. Are you capable . . . of communicating that?" Tony leaned forward a fraction to catch her eye. "Just take your time to find the right words."

Kaja held his gaze. She had expected to panic. But it just didn't come. Emotionally, she was like the stone in the terrain around them.

"I don't feel anything," she said.

"Come on," he said. "The others were so frightened that they couldn't even answer, could only babble. Charlotte Lolles was transfixed, as if in shock. Elias Skog couldn't keep his language clean. My father cried. Is it mere chaos or is there some reflection? Do you feel sorrow? Remorse? Or relief that you don't have to put up a fight anymore? Look at Lene, for example. She's given up and is going to her death like the meek lamb she is. How is it with you, Kaja? How much do you long to relinquish control?"

Kaja could see there was genuine curiosity in his eyes.

"Let me ask you instead how much you longed to **gain** control, Tony," she said, scouring her mouth for moisture. "When you killed one person after the other, under the guidance of an invisible person who turned out to be a boy whose tongue you had cut off. Can you tell me that?"

Tony looked into the middle distance and slowly shook his head, as if answering another question.

"I had no idea until reading on the Net that good old Skai had arrested someone from my village. Ole, no less. Who would have thought he had the guts?"

"The hatred, don't you mean?"

Tony took a pistol from his pocket. Checked his watch.

"Harry's late."

"He'll come."

Tony laughed. "But unfortunately for you minus a pulse. I liked Harry, by the way. Really. Fun to play with. I called him from Ustaoset—he had given me his number. Heard the voice mail say he would have no network coverage for a couple of days. That made me laugh. He was at the cabin in Håvass, of course, the sly fox." Tony rested the pistol in one palm while stroking the black steel with the other. "I could see it in him when we met at the police station. That he was like me."

"I doubt that."

"Oh, yes, he is. A driven man. A junkie. A man who does what he must to have what he wants, who walks over dead bodies, if need be. Isn't that right?"

Kaja didn't answer.

Tony checked his watch again. "I guess we'll have to start without him."

He'll come, Kaja thought. I'll have to play for time.

"So you ran away, didn't you?" she said. "With your father's passport and teeth?"

Tony looked at her.

She knew that he knew what she was doing. And also that he liked it. Telling her. How he had tricked them. They all did.

"Do you know what, Kaja? I wish my father were here to see me now. Here, on the top of my mountain. To see me and understand me. Before I killed him. The way that Lene understands that she must die. The way I hope you understand, too, Kaja."

She felt it now. The fear. More as a physical pain than a fit of panic that would cause her rational brain to implode. She saw clearly, heard clearly, reasoned clearly. Yes, clearer than ever before, she thought.

"You started killing to hide that you had been unfaithful," she said, her voice hoarser now. "To safeguard the Galtung millions. But what about the millions you have tricked Lene out of here—are they enough to save your project?"

"I don't know." Tony smiled, grasping the butt of the pistol. "We'll have to see. Out."

"Is it worth it, Tony? Is this really worth all these lives?"

Kaja gasped as the gun barrel was jabbed into her ribs. Tony's voice hissed in her ear.

"Look around you, Kaja. This is the cradle of humanity. See what a human life is worth. Some die and even more are born in one unending feverish race, around and around, and one life gives no more sense than any other. But the game makes sense. The passion, the fervor. The gambling addiction, as some idiots call it. It's everything. It's like Nyiragongo. It's all-consuming, all-destroying, but it is a prerequisite of all life. No passion, no meaning, no boiling lava within, and everything out here would be stone dead, frozen stiff. Passion, Kaja—do you have any? Or are you a dead volcano, a speck of human dust, summed up in three sentences in a eulogy?"

Kaja jerked away from the barrel, and Tony cackled with amusement.

"Are you ready for the wedding, Kaja? Ready to thaw?"

She smelled the stench of sulfur. The driver had opened the door, watched Kaja with indifference, pointed a short-barreled gun at her. Even here in the car, thirty feet from the edge of the crater, she could feel the overwhelming heat. She didn't move. The black man leaned in and grasped her arm. She let him pull her without offering any resistance, just made sure she was heavy enough for him to be off balance, so that when she suddenly bounded out he would be caught by surprise. The man was amazingly slight and probably a bit shorter than she was. She struck with her elbow. Knowing it was much more powerful than a fist. Knowing that the neck, the temple, the nose were good targets. The elbow hit something with a crunch, and the man fell and dropped his weapon. Kaja lifted her foot. She had learned that the most effective way to neutralize a person on the ground was to trample on the thigh. The combination of a full-bodied stamp from the top and the pressure from the ground underneath will immediately cause such widespread bleeding to the thigh muscles that the person will be rendered incapable of pursuit. The alternative is to stamp on the chest and neck with potentially fatal consequences. She had her eyes fixed on the exposed neck when the moonlight fell on the man's face. She hesitated for a fraction of a second. He couldn't have been older than Even.

Then she felt arms enclosing her from behind, her own arms forced into her sides and the air from her lungs expelled as she was lifted off the ground with her legs kicking helplessly. Close to her ear Tony's voice sounded cheerful. "Good, Kaja. Passion. You want to live. I'll make sure his wages are docked—I promise you."

The boy on the ground in front of her got to his feet and grabbed his weapon. The indifference was gone now; a white fury shone in his eyes.

Tony pressed her hands together behind her back and she felt thin plastic ties being tightened around her wrists.

"So," said Tony. "May I ask you to be Lene's maid of honor, Frøken Solness?"

And now—at last—it came. The panic. It emptied her brain of all else, rendered everything blank, clean, cruel. Easy. She screamed.

89

The Wedding

Kaja stood at the edge looking down. The scorching air rose, hit her face like a hot breeze. The poisonous smoke had already made her dizzy, but perhaps that was just the tremulous air blurring her vision, making the lava quiver, down there in the abyss, where it shone with tinges of yellow and red. A strand of hair fell into her face, but her hands were bound behind her back with the plastic ties. She stood shoulder to shoulder with Lene Galtung, who, Kaja assumed, must have been drugged from the way she stood staring in front of her like a sleepwalker. A white-clad, living corpse with only frost and wasteland within. A shop dummy dressed as a bride in the window of a ropery.

Tony was right behind them. She felt his hand on the small of her back.

"Do you take the man at your side and promise to love, honor and respect him for better, for worse, for richer, for poorer, in sickness or in health . . ." he whispered.

This wasn't out of cruelty, he had explained. It was just so practical. There wouldn't be a trace left of them. Barely a question. People in the Congo disappear every day.

"I hereby declare you married."

Kaja mumbled a prayer. She imagined it was a prayer. Until she heard the words: ". . . because it is impossible for me and the person I want to have to be together."

The words from Even's farewell note.

A car engine roared in a low gear with headlamps scanning the skies. The Range Rover appeared on the other side of the crater.

"And there are the others," Tony said. "Wave good-bye—there's good girls."

Harry didn't know what sight would greet him when they turned onto the plateau by the crater. Kinzonzi had said that, apart from the women, Mr. Tony had only his chauffeur with him. But that he and Mr. Tony were armed with automatic weapons.

Before they reached the top Harry had offered Saul the chance to be dropped off, but he had declined. "I have no family left, Harry. Maybe it is true that you are on the side of the angels. Anyway, you paid for the whole day."

They skidded to a halt.

The headlights pointed across the crater, to the clutch of three standing on the edge. Then they disappeared in a cloud, but Harry had seen them and already summed up the situation: one man with a short-barreled gun behind the three of them. One parked Range Rover. And no time. Then the cloud wafted past and Harry saw that Tony and the other man were shielding their eyes as they watched the car, as though expecting something.

"Switch off the engine," Harry said from the back-seat, resting the Märklin on the front seat. "But leave the lights on."

Saul did as instructed.

The man in camouflage knelt down with the gun to his shoulder and took aim.

"Flash the lights a couple of times," Harry said, putting his eye to the sights. "They're waiting for some signal or other."

Harry squeezed his left eye shut. Closed out half the world. Closed out the wan faces, the fact that Kaja was there, that Lene was there with bulging cheeks and shock-blackened eyes, that these seconds counted. Closed out the turquoise eyes examining him as he said the words: "I swear." Closed out the popping sound of a shot that told him they had sent the wrong signal, closed out the **clunk** as the bullet hit the car body, followed by another thud. Closed out everything that did not concern the light refraction on the windshield, the light refraction in the quivering heat above the crater, the bullet's probable deviation to the right, the same way the clouds of steam were drifting. He knew that now he was being sustained by one thing: adrenaline. Knew the effect of the natural stimulant would be short. It could wear off at any second. But as long as his heart was still supplying blood to the brain, it was the second he needed. For the brain is a fantastic computer.

Tony Leike's head was half hidden by Lene's, but it was a little higher.

Harry aimed at Kaja's pointed teeth. Moved to the gleaming ball between Lene's lips. Moved the sights up higher. No fine-tuning. Chance. Place your bets, last race.

A cloud of steam was coming from the left.

Soon they would be enshrouded in it, and as if he had been granted a second of visual clarity, Harry saw it: that when the cloud had passed no one would be standing there any longer. Harry pressed the trigger. Saw Kaja blink above the cross on the sights.

I swear.

He was doomed. At last.

The inside of the car felt as if it would explode with the sound; his shoulder as if it would be knocked out of joint. There was a small frost-white perforation in the windshield. The bloodred cloud covered everything on the other side of the crater. Harry took a deep, tremulous breath and waited.

90

Marlon Brando

Harry was lying on his back, floating. Floating away. Sinking into Lake Kivu while the blood, his and that of others, mingled with the lake's, became one, disappeared in the universe's great sleep, and the stars above him were extinguished in the cold, black water. Peace in the depths, silence, nothingness. Until he resurfaced in a bubble of methane gas, a night-blue corpse with Guinea worm–infected flesh that seethed and churned beneath the skin. And he had to get out of Lake Kivu to live. To wait.

Harry opened his eyes. He could see the hotel balcony above him. He rolled onto his side and swam the few yards to the shore. Rose from the water.

Soon dawn would break. Soon he would be sitting on the plane back to Oslo. Soon he would be in Gunnar Hagen's office telling him it was over. That they were gone, gone forever. That they had failed. So he, too, would try to be gone.

Trembling, Harry wrapped himself in the large white towel and walked toward the stairs up to his hotel room.

When the cloud passed, no one was standing by the edge of the crater.

Harry's sights had automatically sought the marksman. Found him, and he had been on the point of firing. But discovered he was looking at the man's back, heading for the car. Then the Range Rover had started up, passed them and gone.

He had moved the sights back to where he had seen Kaja, Tony and Lene. Adjusted the optics. Seen the footprints. Three sets.

Then he had thrown down the rifle, jumped out of

the car and run around the crater with his revolver held in front of him. Had run and prayed. Skidded onto his knees beside them. Already knowing he had lost before he focused.

Harry unlocked his hotel-room door. Went to the bathroom, removed the wet bandage around his head and applied a new one he had been given at the front desk. The temporary stitches held his cheek together; it was a different matter with his jaw. His bag was packed and ready by the bed. The clothes he would travel in hung over the chair. He took the cigarette pack out of his trouser pocket, went onto the balcony and sat down on one of the plastic chairs. The cold dulled the pain in his jaw and cheek. He looked out over the shimmering silver lake he would never see again as long as he lived.

She was dead. The lead bullet with a diameter of half an inch had pierced her right eye, taking with it the right half of her head, taking Tony Leike's large white front teeth through his skull, opening a crater at the back and spreading everything over three hundred square feet of volcanic rock.

Harry had vomited. Spat green mucus on them and staggered backward.

He flipped two cigarettes out of the packet. Put them between his lips and felt them bobbing up and down against his chattering teeth. The plane left in four hours. He had arranged to go to the airport with Saul. Harry was so exhausted he could hardly keep his eyes open, yet neither could nor wanted to sleep. The ghosts were refused admission for the first night.

"Marlon Brando," she said.

"What?" Harry replied, lighting the cigarettes and passing her one.

"The macho actor whose name I couldn't remember. He has the most feminine voice of them all. Woman's mouth, too. Have you noticed, by the way, that he lisps? It's not that audible, but it's there, like a kind of overtone the ear doesn't perceive as a sound, but the brain registers anyway."

"I know what you mean," Harry said, inhaling and observing her.

She had been sprayed with blood, tissue, bone fragments and brain matter. It had taken a long time to cut the plastic ties binding her wrists; his fingers had simply not obeyed him. When she was finally free she had gotten to her feet, while he lay on all fours.

And he had done nothing to stop her grabbing Tony's jacket collar and belt, and rolling the body off the edge into the crater. Harry had not heard a sound, only the whisper of the wind. He had watched her looking down into the volcano until she turned to him.

He nodded. She didn't need to explain. That was how it had to be done.

She had cast an inquiring glance at the body of Lene Galtung. Harry had weighed the practical versus the moral considerations. The diplomatic consequences versus a mother having a grave to visit. The truth versus a lie that might have made life more livable. Then he had gotten to his feet. Lifted Lene Galtung, almost collapsing under the weight of the slight, young woman. Stood on the edge of the abyss, closed his eyes, felt the longing, swayed for a second. And then let her go. Opened his eyes and watched her descent. She was already a dot. Then she was swallowed by the smoke.

"People disappear in the Congo every single day," Kaja had said on the drive back from the volcano with Saul, and Harry had sat in the backseat, holding her.

He knew it would be a short report. No traces. Vanished. They could be anywhere. And the answer to all the questions they would be asked would be this: People disappear in the Congo every single day. Even when she asked, the woman with the turquoise eyes. Because it would be simplest for them. No body, no internal inquiry, which was routine when officers had fired a shot. No embarrassing international incident. No dropping of the case, at least not at an official level, but the continued search for Leike would just be for appearances' sake. Lene Galtung would be reported missing. She hadn't had a plane ticket and the immigration authorities in the Congo hadn't registered her entry into the country. It was for the best, Hagen would say. For all parties. At any rate, those parties that counted.

And the woman with the turquoise eyes would nod. Accept what she was told. But she might know anyway, if she listened to what he didn't say. She could choose. Choose to hear him say her daughter was dead. That he had aimed between Lene's eyes instead of what he assumed would be accurate, a little farther to the right. But he had wanted to be sure the bullet didn't deviate so far to the right that he might shoot his colleague, the woman with whom he was working on this job. She could choose that or the lie that pushed sound waves up ahead, the ones that gave hope instead of a grave.

They changed planes in Kampala.

Sat in hard plastic chairs by the gate, watching planes coming and going, until Kaja fell asleep and her head slid down onto Harry's shoulder.

She was woken by something happening. She didn't know what, but something had changed. The room temperature. The rhythm of Harry's heartbeat. Or the lines in his drained, pale face. She saw his hand putting the phone back in his jacket pocket.

"Who was it?" she asked.

"Rikshospital," Harry said, his eyes going absent to her, slipping past her, disappearing out of the panoramic windows, to the horizon of the concrete runway and the dazzling light-blue sky.

"He's dead."

Part Ten

91

Parting

It rained at Olav Hole's funeral. The turnout was as Harry had expected: not as good as at Mom's funeral, but not embarrassingly sparse.

Afterward Harry and Sis stood outside the church receiving condolences from old relatives whose names they had never heard, old teaching colleagues they had never seen and old neighbors whose names they recognized, but not their faces. The only people whose turn to face the Grim Reaper was not imminent were Harry's police colleagues: Gunnar Hagen, Beate Lønn, Kaja Solness and Bjørn Holm. Øystein Eikeland definitely looked as if he were on the point of checking out, but excused himself by saying that he had been on a real bender the night before. And that Tresko, who couldn't come, sent his regards and condolences. Harry scanned the church for the two he had seen on the bench at the very back, but they had obviously left before the coffin was borne out.

Harry invited everyone for meatballs and beer at Schrøder's. The small gathering had a lot to say about the weather, but little about Olav Hole. Harry finished up his apple juice, explained he had a prior arrangement, thanked everyone for coming and left.

He hailed a taxi and gave the driver an address in Holmenkollen.

There was still some snow on the lawns at these heights.

As they drove up to the black timber house, Harry's heart was beating hard. And, even harder, standing in front of the familiar door, after ringing and hearing the approach of footsteps. Familiar steps, too.

She looked as she always had. As she always would. The dark hair, the gentleness in her brown eyes, the slim neck. Fuck her. She was so beautiful it hurt.

"Harry," she said.

"Rakel."

"Your face. I saw it in church. What happened?"

"Nothing. They say it will heal fine," he lied.

"Come in and I'll make some coffee."

Harry shook his head. "I have a taxi waiting down on the road. Is Oleg here?"

"In his room. Do you want to see him?"

"Another day. How long are you staying?"

"Three days. Maybe four. Or five. We'll see."

"Can I see you both soon? Would that be OK?"

She nodded. "I don't know if I did the right thing."

Harry smiled. "Well, who knows what that is?"

"In church, I mean. We left before we . . . got in the way. You had other things to think about. Anyway, we went for Olav's sake. You know that he and Oleg . . . well, they got along. Two reserved personalities. You can take nothing for granted."

Harry nodded.

"Oleg talks about you a lot, Harry. You mean more

to him than you ever realized." She looked down. "More than I ever realized, too, perhaps."

Harry cleared his throat. "So everything here is unchanged since . . . ?"

Rakel nodded quickly so he was spared from having to complete the impossible sentence. Since the Snowman had tried to kill them in this very house.

Harry gazed at her. He had only wanted to see her, hear her voice. Feel her eyes on him. He hadn't wanted to ask her. He cleared his throat again. "There's something I have to ask you."

"What's that?"

"Can we go into the kitchen for a minute?"

They went in. He sat at the table opposite her. Explained slowly and at some length. She listened without interrupting.

"He wants you to visit him at the hospital. He wants to ask you for forgiveness."

"Why should I agree?"

"You have to answer that one for yourself, Rakel. But he doesn't have much time left."

"I've read you can live for a long time with that disease."

"He doesn't have much time left," Harry repeated. "Think about it. You don't need to answer now."

He waited. Saw her blink. Saw her eyes fill, heard the almost noiseless crying. She gasped for breath.

"What would you do, Harry?"

"I would say no. But then I'm a pretty bad human being."

Her laughter mixed with the tears. And Harry

wondered how much it was possible to miss a sound, a certain oscillation of the air. How long you could yearn for a certain laugh.

"I need to be going now," he said.

"Why?"

"I have three meetings left."

"Left? Before what?"

"I'll call you tomorrow."

Harry got up. He had heard music from the first floor. Slayer. Slipknot.

After getting into the taxi and giving the next address, he thought about her question. Before what? Before he wanted to have everything finished. To be free. Maybe.

It was a short drive.

"This one might take a little longer," he said.

He breathed in, opened the gate and went to the door of the fairy-tale house.

He thought he could see the turquoise eyes following him from the kitchen window.

92

Free Fall

Mikael Bellman stood inside the entrance of Oslo District Prison watching Sigurd Altman and a prison guard saunter toward the counter.

"Checking out?" the officer behind the counter asked.

"Yes," said Altman, handing over a form.

"Anything from the minibar?"

The second officer chuckled at what was undoubtedly standard at releases.

Personal effects were unlocked from a cupboard and returned with a broad smile. "Hope your stay met expectations, Herr Altman, and that we see you again soon."

Bellman held the door open for Altman. They walked down the stairs together.

"The press are outside," Bellman said. "So let's go through the culvert. Krohn's waiting for you in a car at the rear of Police HQ."

"Master of bluffs," Altman said with a barbed smile.

Bellman didn't ask what he was alluding to. He had other questions. The final ones. And a thousand feet within which to have them an-swered. The lock buzzed, and he pushed open the door to the culvert. "Now that the deal is done I thought you might be able to tell me a couple of things."

"Shoot, Bellman."

"Like why you didn't correct Harry as soon as you realized he was going to arrest you?"

Altman shrugged. "I considered the misunderstanding a priceless treat. I understood entirely, of course. What was not understandable was that the arrest would take place in Ytre Enebakk. Why there? And when there's something you don't understand, it's best to keep your trap shut. So I did, until the blinding light, until I saw the whole picture."

"And what did the whole picture tell you?"

"That I was in a seesaw situation."

"What do you mean by that?"

"I knew about the conflict between Kripos and Crime Squad. And I saw that it gave me an option. Being in a seesaw situation means that you're in a position to apply weight to one side or the other."

"But why didn't you try the same deal with Harry that you did with me?"

"In a seesaw situation you always turn to the losing party. That's the party that is more desperate, more willing to pay for what you have to offer. It's a simple gambling theory."

"Why were you so sure that Harry wasn't on the losing side?"

"I wasn't sure, but there was another factor. I had begun to get to know Harry. He's not like you, Bellman, a man of compromises. He couldn't care less about personal prestige; he only wants to catch the bad boys. All the bad boys. He would have seen things in the following way: If Tony was the main actor, I was the director. And therefore I should not get off lightly. I figured that a career man like you would see things differently. And Johan Krohn agreed with me. You would see the personal gain in being the person who caught the murderer. You knew that people were anxious to know who did it, who physically performed the killing, not who did the thinking. If a film flops, it's great for a director to have Tom Cruise in the main role because he's the one people will slaughter. Audiences and the press like to have things simple, and my crime is indirect, complicated. A court of law would undoubtedly have handed down a life sentence, but this case isn't about courts of law, but about politics. If the press and the people are happy, the Ministry of Justice is happy, so everyone can go home more or less happy. Getting away with a slap on the wrist, maybe a suspended sentence, is a cheap price to pay."

"Not for everyone," Bellman said.

Altman laughed. The echo drowned out his footsteps. "Take some advice from someone who knows. Let it go. Don't let it eat you up. Injustice is like the weather. If you can't live with it, move. Injustice is not part of the system's machinery. It is the machinery."

"I'm not talking about me, Altman. I can live with it."

"And I'm not talking about you, either, Bellman. I'm talking about the person who can't live with it."

Bellman nodded. For his part, he certainly could live with the situation. There had been telephone calls from the ministry. Not from the minister himself, of course, but the feedback could be interpreted in only one way. That they were happy. That this would have positive consequences, both for Kripos and for him personally.

They went up the stairs and into the daylight.

Johan Krohn stepped out of his blue Audi and extended a hand to Sigurd Altman as they crossed the road.

Bellman watched the released man and his counsel until the Audi disappeared around the bend, en route to Tøyen.

"Don't you say hi when you come to see us, Bellman?"

Bellman turned. It was Gunnar Hagen. He was on the sidewalk across the road, no jacket, arms folded.

Bellman went over, and they shook hands.

"Anyone spreading gossip about me?" Bellman asked.

"Here at Crime Squad everything is brought to light," Hagen said with a broad smile, shivering and rubbing his hands for warmth. "By the way, I have a meeting with the Ministry of Justice at the end of next month."

"Oh, yes," Bellman said, unconcerned. He knew very well what the meeting would be about. Restructuring. Downsizing. Transfer of responsibility for murder cases. What he didn't know was what Hagen meant with his allusion to everything coming to light.

"But you know all about the meeting, don't you," Hagen said. "We've both been requested to forward a recommendation for the future organization of murder investigations. The deadline's approaching."

"I hardly think they'll lay much weight on our one-sided presentations," Bellman said, looking at Hagen and trying to interpret where he was going. "I suppose we just have to give our opinions, in the name of tolerance."

"Unless we both believe that the present structure is

preferable to all the investigations being placed under one roof," Hagen said through chattering teeth.

Bellman chortled. "You're not wearing enough clothes, Hagen."

"You could be right. But I also know what I would think about a new murder unit being led by a policeman who had used his position to let his future wife go free after she had been smuggling drugs. Even though witnesses had pointed her out."

Bellman stopped breathing. Felt his grip slacken. Felt gravity taking hold of him, his hair rising, his stomach falling. This was the nightmare he had been having. Nerve-jangling in sleep, brutal in reality: the fall without any rope. The solo climber's fall.

"Looks like you're feeling the cold, too, Bellman."

"Fuck you, Hagen."

"Me?"

"What do you want?"

"Want? Long-term, I want the force to be spared yet another public scandal calling into doubt the integrity of the regular policeman. As far as restructuring is concerned . . ." Hagen's head receded between his shoulders and he stamped his feet on the ground. "The Ministry of Justice might want murder investigation resources all in the same pot, irrespective of the leadership question. If I were to be asked to lead such a unit I would, of course, consider the offer. But, in general, I think things are functioning well as they are. By and large, murderers receive their punishment, don't they? So if my counterpart in this matter shares that view, I will be prepared to continue with investigations both in Bryn and here at Police HQ. What do you think, Bellman?"

Mikael Bellman felt the jerk as the rope caught him after all. Felt the harness tighten, felt himself being torn into two, felt his back unable to cope with the strain and breaking, the mixture of pain and paralysis. He dangled, helpless and dizzy, somewhere between heaven and earth. But he was alive.

"Let me think about it, Hagen."

"Think away. But don't take too much time. Deadline, you know. We have to coordinate."

Bellman watched Hagen's back as he loped to the entrance of Police HQ. Then turned and stared over the rooftops of Grønland. Studied the town. His town.

93

The Answer

Harry was standing in the middle of the living-room floor, looking around, when the phone rang.

"It's Rakel. What are you doing?"

"Examining what's left," he said. "After a person dies."

"And?"

"There's a lot. And yet not much. Sis has said what

she wants, and tomorrow some guy's coming to buy up the goods and chattels. He intimated he would pay fifty thousand to buy everything, lock, stock and barrel. And he'll clean up after himself. That's . . . er . . ." Harry couldn't find the word.

"I know," she said. "It was like that for me when my father died. His things, which had been so important, so irreplaceable, seemed to lose their meaning. It was as if he alone was the one who had given them value."

"Or perhaps it's those of us left realizing we have to clean up. To burn. To start afresh." Harry went into the kitchen. Looked at the photograph hanging under the kitchen cupboard. A photo from Sofies Gate. Oleg and Rakel.

"I hope you said good-bye properly," Rakel said. "Saying good-bye is important. Especially for those left behind."

"I don't know," Harry said. "We never properly said hello, he and I. I let him down."

"How was that?"

"He asked me to dispatch him. I refused."

The line went quiet. Harry listened to the background noise. Airport noises.

Then her voice was back. "Do you think you should have helped him on his way?"

"Yes," Harry said. "I do. I think so now."

"Don't think about it. It's too late."

"Is it?"

"Yes, Harry. It's too late."

The line went quiet again. Harry could hear a

nasal voice announcing boarding for a flight to Amsterdam.

"So you didn't want to meet him?"

"I can't do it, Harry. I suppose I'm a bad human being, too."

"We'll have to try to do better next time, then."

He could hear her smiling. "Can we do that?"

"It's never too late to try. Say hello to Oleg from me."

"Harry . . ."

"Yes?"

"Nothing."

Harry stood looking out of the kitchen window after she had hung up.

Then he went upstairs and started to pack.

The doctor was waiting for Harry when he came out of the bathroom. They continued down the last stretch of the corridor toward the prison guard.

"His condition is stable," she said. "We might transfer him back to prison. What's the purpose of this visit?"

"I want to thank him for helping us to clear up a case. And to get back to him about a wish he had expressed."

Harry took off his jacket, gave it to the guard and held out his arms while he was searched.

"Five minutes. No more. OK?"

Harry nodded.

"I'll come in with you," said the prison guard, who

was unable to take his eyes off Harry's disfigured cheek.

Harry arched an eyebrow.

"Rules for civilian visits," the officer said. "It has come to our attention that you've resigned from the force."

Harry shrugged.

The man had gotten out of bed and was sitting on a chair by the window.

"We found him," Harry said, pulling a chair close. The prison guard stood by the door, but was within hearing distance. "Thanks for your help."

"I kept my part of the bargain," the man said. "What about yours?"

"Rakel didn't want to come."

The man's face didn't move a muscle; he just shrank as if hit by an ice-cold gust of wind.

"We found a bottle of medicine in the first-aid kit at Prince Charming's cabin. I had a drop of the contents analyzed yesterday. Ketanome. Same as he used on his victims. Do you know the drug? Fatal in large doses."

"Why are you telling me this?"

"I was given some of it myself recently. In a way, I liked it. But then I like all kinds of drugs. Only you know that, don't you? I told you what I did in the bathroom at the Landmark in Hong Kong."

The Snowman eyed Harry. Glanced cautiously at the prison guard and then back at Harry.

"Oh, yes," he said in a monotone. "In the cubicle at the end on . . ."

"The right," Harry said. "Well, as I said, thanks. Don't look in the mirror."

"Same applies to you," the man said and offered him a bony white hand.

When Harry was shown out at the end of the corridor, he turned and caught a glimpse of the Snowman tottering toward them with the guard. Before going into the bathroom.

94

Glass Noodles

"Hi, Hole." Kaja smiled up at him.

She was sitting in the bar, on a low stool, on her hands. Her gaze was intense, her lips bloodred, her cheeks glowing. It struck him that he had not seen her wearing makeup before. And it was not true what he had once believed, in his naïveté, that a woman cannot be made more beautiful with cosmetics. She was wearing a plain black dress. A short gold necklace with white pearls rested against her collarbone, and when she breathed it reflected soft light.

"Been waiting long?" Harry asked.

"No," she said, getting up before he had a chance to sit down, pulling him over, laying her head on his shoulder and holding him like that. "I'm just a little cold."

She didn't care about other people in the bar watching her; she didn't let go, instead stuffing both hands under his suit jacket, stroking his shirted back up and down to get them warm. Harry heard a discreet cough, looked up and received a friendly nod from a man with body language that said head waiter.

"Our table is ready," she said.

"Table? I thought we were only having a drink."

"We have to celebrate the end of the case, don't we? I ordered the food beforehand. Something very special."

They were shown to a table by the window in the fully occupied restaurant. A waiter lit the candles, poured apple cider into the glasses, put the bottle back in the ice bucket and left.

She raised her glass. "**Skål.**"

"To what?"

"To Crime Squad continuing as before. To you and me catching bad men. To being here now. Together."

They drank. Harry set his glass down on the cloth. Moved it. The base had left a wet mark. "Kaja . . ."

"I've got something for you, Harry. Tell me what your greatest wish is right now."

"Listen, Kaja . . ."

"What?" she said, breathless, and leaned forward, eager to hear.

"I told you I would be on my travels again. I'm leaving tomorrow."

"Tomorrow?" She laughed, and the smile faded as the waiter unfolded their napkins and spread them, heavy and white, over their laps. "Where to?"

"Away."

Kaja stared down at the table without saying a word. Harry wanted to put his hand on hers. But refrained.

"So I wasn't enough?" she whispered. "We weren't enough?"

Harry waited until he could catch her eye. "No," he said. "We weren't enough. Not enough for you, not enough for me."

"What do you know about what's enough?" Her voice was thick with tears.

"Quite a lot," Harry said.

Kaja breathed heavily, tried to control her voice. "Is it Rakel?"

"Yes. It was always Rakel."

"But you said yourself she didn't want you."

"She doesn't want me the way I am now. So I have to repair myself. I have to be well again. Do you understand?"

"No, I don't understand." Two tiny tears clung to the lashes under her eyes, wavering. "You **are** well. The scars are just—"

"You know very well it's not **those** scars I'm talking about."

"Will I ever see you again?" she asked, trapping one of the tears with a fingernail.

She grasped his hand, squeezed it so tight the knuckles went white. Harry looked at her. Then she let go.

"I won't bring you back another time," she said.

"I know."

"You won't cope."

"Probably not." He smiled. "But then who does?"

She tilted her head. Then she smiled with those small pointed teeth of hers.

"I do," she said.

Harry remained in his chair until he heard the soft slam of a car door in the darkness and the diesel engine starting up. He looked down at the cloth and was about to get up when a soup plate came into view and he heard the head waiter's voice announce: "Special order, at the lady's instructions, flown over from Hong Kong. Li Yuan's glass noodles."

Harry stared down at the plate. She is still sitting in her chair, he thought. The restaurant is a soap bubble and now it is taking off, hovering over the town and is gone. The kitchen never runs out and we never land.

He got up and made a move to leave. But changed his mind. Sat down again. Lifted the chopsticks.

95

The Allies

Harry left the dance restaurant that was no longer a dance restaurant, went down the hill to the seamen's school that was no longer a seamen's school. Continued to the bunkers that had defended against the country's invaders. Beneath him were the fjord and the town, hidden by mist. Cars crept forward carefully with yellow cats' eyes. A tram emerged from the mist like a ghost gnashing its teeth.

A car stopped in front of him, and Harry jumped into the front seat. Katie Melua oozed through the speakers with her honey-dripping agony, and Harry desperately searched for the off switch on the radio.

"Jesus Christ, what you look like!" Øystein said, horrified. "The surgeon must have definitely failed the sewing course. But at least you'll save a few kroner on the Halloween mask. Don't laugh or your mug'll tear again."

"I promise."

"By the way," Øystein said, "it's my birthday today."

"Oh, fuck. Here's a smoke, from me to you. Free."

"That's exactly what I wanted."

"Mm. Any bigger presents you'd like?"

"Like what?"

"World peace."

"The day you wake up to world peace, you don't wake up, Harry. Because they've dropped the big one."

"OK. No private wishes?"

"Not a lot. New conscience, maybe."

"New conscience?"

"The old one's not so good. Nice suit you've got. Thought you had only the one."

"It's Dad's."

"Jesus, you must have shrunk."

"Yes," Harry said, straightening his tie. "I have shrunk."

"How's Ekeberg Restaurant?"

Harry closed his eyes. "Fine."

"Do you remember the leaky shack we sneaked into that time? How old were we? Sixteen?"

"Seventeen."

"Didn't you dance with the Killer Queen there once?"

"Possibly."

"Frightening to think that the MILF of your youth has ended up in an old people's home."

"MILF?"

Øystein sighed. "Look it up."

"Mm. Øystein?"

"Yes."

"Why did you and I become pals?"

"Because we grew up together, I suppose."

"Is that all? A demographic coincidence? No spiritual fellowship?"

"Not that I've noticed. As far as I know, we've only ever had one thing in common."

What's that?"

"No one else wanted to be pals with us."

They wound their way through the next stretch of road in silence.

"Apart from Tresko," Harry said.

Øystein snorted. "Who stank so much of toe-fart no one else could bear sitting next to him."

"Yes," Harry said. "We were good at that."

"We nailed that one," Øystein said. "But, Christ, how he stank."

They laughed together. Gentle, lighthearted. Sad.

Øystein had parked the car on the brown grass with the doors open. Harry clambered up onto the top of the bunker and sat on the edge with his legs dangling. From the speakers inside the car doors Springsteen sang about blood brothers one stormy night and the vow that had to be kept.

Øystein passed Harry the bottle of Jim Beam. A lone siren from the town rose and fell until it lost power and died. The poison stung Harry's throat and stomach, and he threw up. The second swig went better. The third was fine.

Max Weinberg sounded as if he were trying to destroy the drumhead.

"It often strikes me how I **ought** to wish I had more regrets," Øystein said. "But I don't give a shit. I think I just accepted from my first waking second that I was an asshole. What about you?"

Harry ruminated. "I have loads of regrets. But perhaps that's because I carry around such high notions of myself. In fact, I imagine I could have chosen differently."

"But you fucking couldn't."

"Not at that time. But next time, Øystein. Next time."

"Has it ever happened, Harry? Ever in the fucking history of mankind?"

"Just because nothing has happened doesn't mean that it can't happen. I don't know that this bottle is going to fall if I drop it. Fuck, which philosopher was it again? Hobbes? Hume? Heidegger? One of the headcases beginning with **H**."

"Answer me."

Harry shrugged. "I think it's possible to learn. The problem is that we learn so damned **slowly**, so that by the time you've realized something, it's too late. For example, someone you love might ask you for a favor, an act of love. Like helping him to die. Which you say no to because you haven't learned, you haven't had the insight. When you do finally see the light, it's too late." Harry took another swig. "So instead you perform the act of love for someone else. Perhaps for someone you hate, even."

Øystein accepted the bottle. "Got no idea what you're blabbering on about, but it sounds fucked up."

"Not necessarily. It's never too late for good actions."

"Don't you mean it's always too late?"

"No! I always thought we hate too much for it to be possible for us to obey other impulses. But my father had a different opinion. He said hatred and love are the same currency. Everything starts with love, and hatred is the reverse side of the coin."

"Amen."

"But that must mean you can go the other way, from hatred to love. Hatred must be a good starting point for learning, for changing, for doing things differently next time."

"Now you're so optimistic I'm considering puking, Harry."

The organ came in the refrain, a whine, cutting through like a circular saw.

Øystein leaned his head to the side while flicking ash. And Harry was almost moved to tears. Simply because he saw the years that had become their lives, that had become them, in the way his friend flicked ash as he had always done, leaning to the side as if the cigarette were too heavy, his head angled as if he liked the world better from a slanted perspective, the ash on the floor of the smokers' shed at school, down an empty beer bottle at a party they had gate-crashed, on the cold, rough concrete of a bunker.

"Anyway, you're beginning to get old, Harry."

"Why do you say that?"

"When men start quoting their fathers, they're old. The race has been run."

And then Harry found it. The answer to her question about what he most wanted right now. He wanted an armored heart.

Epilogue

Bluish-black clouds swept over Hong Kong's Island's highest point, Victoria Peak, but it had finally stopped raining, after dripping constantly since the beginning of September. The sun poked through, and a huge rainbow formed a bridge between Hong Kong Island and Kowloon. Harry closed his eyes and let the sun warm his face. The spell of good weather had come just in time for the horse-racing season, due to open in Happy Valley later that evening.

Harry heard the buzz of Japanese voices approach and then pass the bench on which he was sitting. They were coming from the funicular railway, which since 1888 had attracted tourists and locals up here to the fresh air above the town. Harry opened his eyes again and flicked through the racing program.

He had contacted Herman Kluit as soon as he'd arrived in Hong Kong. Kluit had offered Harry a job as a debt collector—that is, he had to trace people who were trying to flee their debts. In this way, Kluit would not have to sell the debt with a substantial discount to the triad, or think about the brutal recovery methods they employed.

It would have been stretching things to say Harry enjoyed the job, but it paid well and was simple. He didn't have to recover the money, just locate the debtors. However, it turned out that his appearance—six feet four and a grinning scar from mouth to ear—was often enough for them to settle their accounts on the spot. And he very rarely had to resort to using a search engine on a server in Germany.

The trick, nevertheless, was to keep off dope and alcohol, which he had succeeded in doing thus far. There were two letters waiting for him at the reception desk today. How they had found him he had no idea. Only that Kaja must have been involved. One letter bore the logo of the Oslo Police District on the envelope, and Harry guessed Gunnar Hagen. With the other he didn't need to guess—he immediately recognized Oleg's upright and still-childish hand-writing. Harry had put both letters in his jacket pocket without making a decision on when or indeed whether he would read them.

Harry folded the racing program and put it down beside him on the bench. He peered across to the Chinese mainland, where the yellow smog was becoming thicker by the year. But up here, at the top of the mountain, the air still felt almost fresh. He looked down on Happy Valley. On the cemeteries, west of the Wong Nai Chong Road, where there were separate sections for Protestants, Catholics, Muslims and Hindus. He could see the racecourse, where he knew jockeys and horses were already on the turf being tested before the evening's races. Soon the spectators would be pouring in: those with hope, those without, the lucky and the unlucky. Those who went to have their dreams fulfilled and those who went purely to dream. The losers who took uncalculated risks and those who took calculated risks, but lost anyway. They had been here before, and they all came back, even the ghosts from the cemeteries down there, the several hundred who died in the great fire at Happy Valley Racecourse in 1918. For tonight it was definitely their turn to beat the odds, to conquer chance, to stuff their pockets full of crisp Hong Kong dollars, to get away with murder. A couple of hours from now they would have entered the gates, read the racing program, filled the coupons with the day's doubles, quinielas, exactas, triples, superfectas—whatever their gambling god was called. They would have lined up by the bookies, holding their stakes at the ready. Most of them would have died a little every time the tape was crossed, but redemption was only fifteen minutes away, when the starting gates opened for the next race. Unless you were a bridge jumper, of course, someone who risked all his assets on one horse in a race. But no one complains. Everyone knows the odds.

But you have those who know the odds, and then you have those who know the outcome. At a racecourse in South Africa they recently found pipes under the starting gates. The pipes contained compressed air and mini-darts with tranquilizers that could be fired into the horses' stomachs by pressing a remote control.

Katrine Bratt had informed him that Sigurd Altman was booked into a hotel in Shanghai. It was barely an hour's flight away.

Harry cast a final glance at the front page of the program.

Those who know the outcome.

"It's just a game." Herman Kluit used to say that. Perhaps because he used to win.

Harry looked at his watch, got to his feet and started to walk to the tram. He had been tipped off about a promising horse in the third race.